THE NIGHT STALKER

About the author

Born in Brazil of Italian origin, Chris Carter studied psychology and criminal behaviour at the University of Michigan. As a member of the Michigan State District Attorney's Criminal Psychology team, he interviewed and studied many criminals, including serial and multiple homicide offenders with life imprisonment convictions.

Having departed for Los Angeles in the early 1990s, Chris spent ten years as a guitarist for numerous rock bands before leaving the music business to write full-time. He now lives in London and is the *Sunday Times* bestselling author of *The Executioner* and *The Crucifix Killer.*

Visit www.chriscarterbooks.com

Also by Chris Carter

The Crucifix Killer
The Executioner

CHRIS CARTER

THE NIGHT STALKER

SIMON &
SCHUSTER

London · New York · Sydney · Toronto · New Delhi

A CBS COMPANY

First published in Great Britain by Simon & Schuster UK Ltd, 2011
A CBS Company
First published in paperback in 2012

3 5 7 9 10 8 6 4 2

Simon & Schuster UK Ltd
1st Floor
222 Gray's Inn Road
London WC1X 8HB

www.simonandschuster.co.uk

Simon & Schuster Australia
Sydney

Simon & Schuster India
New Delhi

A CIP catalogue record for this book
is available from the British Library

Paperback B ISBN 978-0-85720-297-0
Paperback A ISBN 978-0-85720-298-7

Typeset by Hewer Text UK Ltd, Edinburgh
Printed and bound by CPI Group (UK) Ltd, Croydon, CR0 4YY

This novel is dedicated to my family and to Coral Chambers, for being there for me when I most needed someone.

Acknowledgements

I am tremendously grateful to several people without whom this novel would never have been possible.

My agent, Darley Anderson, who is not only the best agent an author could ever hope for, but also a true friend. Camilla Wray, my literary guardian angel, whose comments, suggestions, knowledge and friendship I could never do without. Everyone at the Darley Anderson Literary Agency for striving tirelessly to promote my work anywhere and everywhere possible.

Maxine Hitchcock, my fantastic editor at Simon & Schuster, for being so amazing at what she does. My publishers, Ian Chapman and Suzanne Baboneau, for their tremendous support and belief. Everyone at Simon & Schuster for working their socks off on every aspect of the publishing process.

Samantha Johnson for lending a sympathetic ear to so many of my terrible ideas.

My love and most sincere thanks go to Coral Chambers, for keeping me from breaking.

One

Doctor Jonathan Winston pulled the surgical mask over his mouth and nose and checked the clock on the wall of autopsy room number four on the underground floor of the Los Angeles County Department of Coroner. 6:12 p.m.

The body on the stainless steel table a few feet in front of him was of an unidentified white female in her late twenties, early thirties. Her shoulder-length black hair was wet, its tips plastered to the metal table. Under the brightness of the surgical light, her pale skin looked rubbery, almost unhuman. It hadn't been possible to identify the presumed cause of death at the location where the body was found. There was no blood, no bullet or knife wounds, no lumps or abrasions to her head or torso and no hematomas around her neck to indicate she'd been strangled. Her body was clear of traumas, except for the fact that her mouth and vagina had been stitched shut by whoever had killed her. The thread used was bulky and heavy – the stitches untidy and careless.

'Are we ready?' Doctor Winston said to Sean Hannay, the young forensic assistant in the room.

Hannay's eyes were glued to the woman's face and her sealed lips. For some reason he felt more nervous than usual.

'Sean, are we OK?'

'Umm, yes, Doctor, sorry.' His eyes finally met Doctor Winston's and he nodded. 'We're all set here.' He positioned himself to the right of the table while the doctor activated the digital recording device on the counter closest to him.

Doctor Winston stated the date and time, the names of those present, and the autopsy file number. The body had already been measured and weighed, so he proceeded to dictate the victim's physical characteristics. Before making any incisions, Doctor Winston meticulously studied the body, looking for any marks that could help identify the victim. As his eyes rested on the stitches applied to the victim's lower body, he paused and squinted.

'Wait a second,' he whispered, stepping closer and carefully moving the victim's legs apart. 'Please pass me the flashlight, Sean.' He extended his hand towards the forensic assistant without taking his eyes off the victim. Concern crept into his gaze.

'Something wrong?' Hannay asked, handing Doctor Winston a small metal flashlight.

'Maybe.' He directed its beam towards something that had caught his eye.

Hannay shifted his weight from foot to foot.

'The stitches aren't medical suture,' Doctor Winston said for the benefit of the audio record. 'They're amateurish and imprecise. Like a teenager sewing a patch onto an old pair of ripped jeans.' He moved closer still. 'The stitches are also too spread apart, the gaps between them are too wide, and . . .' he paused, cocking his head, '. . . no way.'

Hannay felt his whole body shiver. 'What?' He stepped forward.

Doctor Winston drew a deep breath and slowly looked up at Hannay. 'I think the killer left something inside her.'

'What?'

Doctor Winston concentrated on the flashlight beam for a few more seconds until he was sure. 'The light is being reflected off something inside her.'

Hannay bent down, following the doctor's gaze. It took him only a second to see it. 'Shit, the light *is* reflecting off something. What is it?'

'I don't know, but whatever it is it's large enough to show through the stitches.'

The doctor straightened up and grabbed a metal pointer from the instrument tray.

'Sean, hold the light for me; like this.' He handed the flashlight to the young assistant and showed him exactly where he wanted him to focus the beam.

The doctor bent over and inserted the tip of the metal pointer between two of the stitches, guiding it towards the object inside the victim.

Hannay kept the flashlight steady.

'It's something metallic,' Winston announced, using the pointer as a probe, 'but I still can't say for certain what it could be. Pass me the stitch-cutting scissors and the forceps, will you?'

It didn't take him long to slice through the stitches. As he cut through each one, Doctor Winston used the forceps to pinch and pull the thick black thread from the victim's skin, placing it into a small plastic evidence collection container.

'Was she raped?' Hannay asked.

'There are cuts and bruises around her groin that are consistent with forced penetration,' Doctor Winston confirmed, 'but they could've been caused by the object that's been inserted into her. I'll take some swabs and send them up to the lab together with the thread samples.' He placed the scissors and the forceps on the used instrument tray. 'Let's find out what the killer has left us, shall we?'

Hannay tensed as Doctor Winston inserted his right hand into the victim. 'Well, I was right, it's not a small object.'

A few silent, uneasy seconds went by.

'And it's oddly shaped too,' the doctor announced. 'Sort of squared with something strange attached to its top.' He finally managed to grab hold of it. As he pulled it out, an attachment at the top clicked.

Hannay stepped forward to gain a better look.

'Metal, relatively heavy, looks handmade . . .' Doctor Winston said, staring at the object in his hand. 'But I'm still not sure what . . .' He paused and felt his heart hammer inside his chest as his eyes widened in realization. 'Oh my God . . .'

Two

It took Detective Robert Hunter of the Los Angeles Robbery Homicide Division (RHD) over an hour to drive from the Hollywood Courthouse to the disused butcher's shop in East LA. He was paged over four hours ago, but the trial in which he was testifying had run a lot later than he'd expected.

Hunter was part of an exclusive elite; an elite that most LAPD detectives would give their right arm *not* to become part of. The Homicide Special Section (HSS) of the RHD was created to deal solely with serial, high-profile and homicide cases requiring extensive investigative time and expertize. Inside the HSS, Hunter had an even more specialized task. Due to his criminal behavior psychology background, he was assigned to cases where overwhelming brutality had been used by the perpetrator. The department tagged such cases as UV, *ultra-violent*.

The butcher's shop was the last in a parade of closed-down businesses. The whole neighborhood seemed to have been neglected. Hunter parked his old Buick next to a white forensic crime lab van. As he stepped out of the car, he allowed his eyes to study the outside of the buildings for a while. All the windows had been covered by solid metal shutters. There was so much graffiti on the outside walls Hunter couldn't tell what color the buildings had originally been.

He approached the officer guarding the entrance, flashed his badge and stooped under the yellow crime-scene tape. The officer nodded but remained silent, his stare distant.

Hunter pushed the door open and stepped inside.

The foul smell that hit him knocked him back and made him gag – a combination of putrid meat, stale sweat, vomit and urine that burned his nostrils and stung at his eyes. He paused for a moment before pulling the collar of his shirt up and over his nose and mouth as an improvised mask.

'These work better,' Carlos Garcia said, coming out of the back room and handing Hunter a surgical nose mask. He was wearing one himself.

Garcia was tall and slim with longish dark hair and light blue eyes. His boyish good looks were spoiled only by a slight lump on his nose, where it had been broken. Unlike all the other RHD detectives, Garcia had worked very hard to be assigned to the HSS. He'd been Hunter's partner for almost three years now.

'The smell gets worse once you enter the back room.' Garcia nodded towards the door he'd just come out of. 'How was the trial?'

'Late,' Hunter replied as he fitted the mask over his face. 'What have we got?'

Garcia tilted his head to one side. 'Some messed up stuff. White female victim, somewhere in her late twenties, early thirties. She was found on the stainless steel butcher's work-top in there.' He pointed to the room behind him.

'Cause of death?'

Garcia shook his head. 'We'll have to wait for the autopsy. Nothing apparent. But here comes the kick. Her lips and her vagina were *stitched* shut.'

'What?'

Garcia nodded. 'That's right. A very sick job. I've never seen anything like it.'

Hunter's eyes darted towards the door behind his partner.

'The body's gone,' Garcia offered before Hunter's next question. 'Doctor Winston was the Forensics lead here tonight. He wanted you to see the body and the scene in the exact way in which it was found, but he couldn't wait any longer. The heat in there was accelerating things.'

'When was the body taken away?' Hunter mechanically checked his watch.

'About two hours ago. Knowing the doc, he's probably halfway through the autopsy already. He knows you hate sitting in on those, so there'd be no point in waiting. By the time we finish looking around this place, I'm sure he'll have some answers for us.'

Hunter's cell phone rang in his pocket. He grabbed it and pulled his surgical mask down, letting it hang loosely around his neck. 'Detective Hunter.'

He listened for a few seconds. 'What?' His eyes shot towards Garcia, who saw Hunter's entire demeanor change in an instant.

Three

Garcia made the trip from East LA to the Los Angeles County Department of Coroner in North Mission Road in record time.

Their confusion doubled as they approached the entrance to the coroners' parking lot. It was blocked off by four police vehicles and two fire engines. More police cars were inside the lot. Several uniformed officers were moving around chaotically, shouting orders at each other and over the radio.

The media had descended upon the scene like ravenous wolves. Local TV and newspaper vans were everywhere. Reporters, cameramen and photographers were doing their best to get as close as they could. But a tight perimeter had already been established around the main building, and it was being strictly enforced by the LAPD.

'What the hell is going on here?' Hunter whispered under his breath as Garcia pulled up by the entrance.

'You'll have to move along, sir,' a young policeman said, coming up to Garcia's window and frantically gesturing for him to drive on. 'You can't—'

He stopped as soon as he saw Garcia's badge. 'I'm sorry, Detective; I'll clear a path right away.' He turned to face the other two officers who were standing next to their vehicles. 'C'mon guys, make way.'

Less than thirty seconds later, Garcia was parking his Honda Civic just in front of the stairway that led up to the main building.

Hunter stepped out of the car and looked around. A small group of people, most of them in white coats, were huddled together at the far end of the parking lot. Hunter recognized them as lab technicians and coroner staff.

'What happened here?' he asked a fireman who had just come off the radio.

'You'll have to ask the chief in charge for more details. All I can tell you is that there was a fire somewhere inside.' He pointed to the old hospital-turned-morgue.

Hunter frowned. 'Fire?'

Certain arson cases were also investigated by the HSS, but they were rarely considered UV. Hunter had never been assigned as the lead detective in any of them.

'Robert, over here.'

Hunter turned and saw Doctor Carolyn Hove coming down the steps to greet them. She'd always looked a great deal younger than her forty-six years. But not today. Her usually perfectly styled chestnut hair was disheveled, her expression solemn and defeated. If the Los Angeles County Coroner had ranks, Doctor Hove would be second in command, just under Doctor Winston.

'What in the world is going on, Doc?' Hunter asked.

'Absolute hell . . .'

Four

Hunter, Garcia and Doctor Hove climbed up the steps together and entered the main building via its large double doors. Several more police officers and firemen were lingering around in the entry foyer. Doctor Hove guided both detectives past the reception counter, down another set of stairs and onto the underground floor. Even though they could all hear the extraction fans working at full power, a sickening smell of chemicals and burned flesh hung in the air. Both detectives cringed and reflexively cupped their hands over their noses.

Garcia felt his stomach churn.

Right at the end of the corridor, a section of the floor directly in front of autopsy room four was drenched in water. Its door was open but it seemed to have been dislodged off its hinges.

The fire chief in charge was giving instructions to one of his men when he saw the group approaching.

'Chief,' Doctor Hove said, 'these are Detectives Robert Hunter and Carlos Garcia of the RHD.'

No handshakes, only polite nods.

'What happened here?' Hunter asked, craning his neck to try to see inside the room. 'And where's Doctor Winston?'

Doctor Hove didn't reply.

The chief took off his helmet and wiped his forehead with a gloved hand. 'Some sort of explosion.'

Hunter frowned. 'Explosion?'

'That's right. The room has been checked and there are no hidden fires. In fact, the fire itself looked to have been minimal. The sprinklers put it out even before we got here. At the moment we don't know what caused the blast, we'll have to wait for the fire investigator's report.' He looked at Doctor Hove. 'I was told that this is the largest of all the autopsy suites, and it doubles as a lab, is that right?'

'Yes, that's correct,' she confirmed.

'Are any volatile chemicals – maybe gas canisters – stored in there?'

Doctor Hove closed her eyes for a moment and let out a heavy breath. 'Sometimes.'

The chief nodded. 'Maybe there was a leak, but as I said, we'll have to wait for the investigator's report. It's a sturdy building with solid foundations. As it's a basement room, the walls down here are much thicker than the ones throughout the rest of the building, and that helped contain the blow. Though it was a powerful enough blast to cause a lot of internal damage, it wasn't powerful enough to compromise the structure. For now, there isn't much more I can tell you.' The chief took off his gloves and rubbed his eyes. 'It's very messy in there, Doctor, in a *very* bad way.' He paused as if unsure of what else to say. 'I'm really sorry.' His words were coated with grief. He nodded solemnly at the rest of the group and made his way back upstairs.

They all stood in silence at the entrance to what used to be autopsy room four, their eyes taking in the destruction. At the far end of the room tables, trays, cabinets and trolleys were bent out of shape and turned over everywhere, showered in debris and bits of skin and flesh. Part of the ceiling and the back wall were damaged and covered in blood.

'When did this happen?' Garcia asked.

'An hour, maybe an hour and fifteen minutes ago. I was in a meeting in the second building. There was a muffled bang and the fire alarms went berserk.'

What was bothering Hunter was the amount of washed-up blood and the number of black impermeable covers he could see scattered around the room, covering bodies or body parts. The cooler body storage facility was located on the wall opposite where the blast occurred. None of the fridges looked damaged.

'How many bodies were out of the coolers in here, Doc?' Hunter asked tentatively.

Doctor Hove knew Hunter had already caught on. She lifted her right hand, showing only the index finger.

Hunter let out a laden breath. 'An autopsy was taking place.' It was a statement rather than a question and he felt a shiver grab hold of his spine. 'Doctor Winston's autopsy?'

'Shit!' Garcia ran a hand over his face. 'No way.'

Doctor Hove looked away, but not fast enough to hide the tears that were forming in her eyes.

Hunter's gaze stayed on her for a couple of seconds before returning to what was left of the room. His throat went dry, and a choking sadness surrounded his heart. He'd known Doctor Jonathan Winston for over fifteen years. He'd been the Los Angeles Chief Medical Examiner for as long as Hunter could remember. He was a workaholic and brilliant at his job. He always tried his best to conduct most of the autopsies on murder victims whose death circumstances had been deemed out of the ordinary. But most of all, to Hunter, Doctor Winston was like family.

The best of friends. Someone on whom he'd counted on numerous times. Someone who he respected and admired like few others. Someone he'd sincerely miss.

'Two people were present.' Doctor Hove's voice faltered for an instant. 'Doctor Winston and Sean Hannay, a 21-year-old forensic assistant.'

Hunter closed his eyes. There was nothing he could say.

'I called as soon as I found out,' Doctor Hove said.

Garcia's expression was one of pure shock. He'd seen many dead bodies in his career, several of them grotesquely disfigured by a sadistic killer. But he'd never personally known any of the victims. And despite meeting Doctor Winston for the first time only three years ago, they'd quickly become friends.

'How about the kid?' Hunter finally asked. And for the first time, Garcia heard Hunter's voice quiver.

Doctor Hove shook her head. 'I'm sorry. Sean Hannay was finishing his third year of pathology at UCLA. His ambition was to become a forensic scientist. I was the one who approved his internship only six months ago.' Her eyes glistened. 'He wasn't even supposed to be in this room. He was just helping out.' The doctor paused and considered her next words carefully. 'I asked him to do so. It was supposed to be me assisting Jonathan.'

Hunter noticed that the doctor's hands were shaking.

'It was a special circumstances death,' she continued. 'Jonathan always asks me to assist on those. And I would've, but I got held up in my meeting and asked Sean to take over for me as a favor.' Her eyes filled with horror. 'He wasn't the one who was supposed to have died here today – I was.'

Five

Hunter understood what was going through Doctor Hove's mind. In the immediate aftermath of the blast, her self-preservation instinct had kicked in and she had felt relief. She'd had a lucky escape. But now reason and guilt were settling in and her mind was punishing her in the worst possible way. *If my meeting hadn't run late, Sean Hannay would still be alive.*

'None of this is your fault, Doc,' Hunter tried to reassure her, but he knew that words would have little effect. Before accepting anything, they all needed to understand what had happened in that room.

Hunter took a step up to the autopsy room door as his mind tried to process the scene in front of him. Right now, nothing was making sense. Suddenly, something caught his eye and he squinted for a second before turning to face Doctor Hove.

'Are autopsies ever videotaped?' he asked, pointing to something on the floor that resembled a camera tripod leg.

Doctor Hove shook her head. 'Very rarely, and the request has to be approved either by me or . . .' her eyes moved from Hunter to the inside of the room, '. . . the chief medical examiner.'

'Doctor Winston himself.'

A single, hesitant nod from Doctor Hove.

'Do you think he might've chosen to record this autopsy?'

Doctor Hove considered it for a moment and her face flared with hope. 'There's a chance. If he considered the case intriguing enough.'

'Well, even if he did,' Garcia cut in, 'how would that help us? The camera was certainly blown to shit like most of the room. Just look at it.'

'Not necessarily,' the doctor said slowly.

All eyes went back to her.

'Do you know something we don't?' Hunter asked.

'Autopsy room four is sometimes used as a lecture room,' the doctor explained. 'It's the only examination suite we have equipped with a video camera connection hub. It links directly to our mainframe computer. That means that the images are simultaneously stored into our mainframe hard drive. To videotape a lecture or an examination, all a doctor has to do is set up a digital camera, hook it to the hub and they're good to go.'

'Can we find out if Doctor Winston did that?'

'Follow me.'

Doctor Hove moved purposefully back to the same stairway they'd come down and went up to the ground floor. They passed the reception area before continuing through a set of metal double doors and into a long and empty hallway. Three-quarters of the way down, they turned right. A single wooden door with a small frosted glass window stood at the end of the corridor. Doctor Hove's office. She unlocked it, pushed the door open, and led them inside.

Doctor Hove went straight to her desk and logged onto her computer. Both detectives gathered behind her.

'Only mine and Doctor Winston's login has administrator's

rights access to the video directory on the mainframe computer. Let's see if we got anything.'

It took Doctor Hove only a few clicks to get to the video directory where all recordings were stored. Inside the main folder there were three subdirectories – New, Lectures and Autopsies. The doctor expanded the directory named *new* to find only one .mpg file. The timestamp on it indicated that it had been created an hour ago.

'Bingo. Jonathan did record the autopsy.' Doctor Hove paused and anxiously looked at Hunter. He noticed that she had fractionally pulled her hand away from the mouse.

'It's OK, Doc; you don't have to watch this. We can take it from here.'

Doctor Hove hesitated for a second. 'Yes I do.' She double-clicked the file. The screen flickered and the computer launched its default video player application. Hunter and Garcia moved closer.

The pictures weren't of great quality, but clearly showed a white female body on an autopsy table. The image had been filmed from above and at an angle, and was partially zoomed in so that the table occupied most of the screen. On the right, two other people in white lab coats could be seen from mid-torso down.

'Can you zoom out?' Garcia asked.

'The image was recorded this way,' Hunter replied, shaking his head. 'We're not controlling a camera here. This is just playback.'

On the screen, one of the two people to the right of the table moved towards the body's head and bent down to examine it. Doctor Winston's face suddenly appeared in the shot.

'There's no sound?' Garcia asked as he watched Doctor Winston's lips move in silence. 'How come there's no sound?'

'The microphones on the cameras we use to video examinations aren't of great quality,' the doctor explained. 'We usually don't even turn them on.'

'I thought pathologists had a habit of dictating every step of their examinations.'

'And we do,' she confirmed. 'Onto our own personal recording devices. We take them into the examination rooms with us. Whatever Jonathan was using, is now mangled up with everything else in that room.'

'Great.'

'*Eyes – hazel, skin is well cared for, earlobes look like they've never been pierced* . . .' Hunter said before the video showed Doctor Winston turning away from the camera. 'Damn! I can't see his mouth any more.'

'You can lip-read?' The question came from Doctor Hove, but her surprised look was mirrored on Garcia's face.

Hunter didn't reply. He kept his attention on the screen.

'Where in the world did you learn to do that?' Garcia asked.

'Books,' Hunter lied. Right now, the last thing he wanted to do was talk about his past.

They watched in silence for the next few seconds.

'Jonathan is performing a regular external examination of the body,' Doctor Hove confirmed. 'All the victim's physical characteristics are listed, including first impressions of their wounds, if any. He'd also be looking for any physical marks that could help identify the victim – she was brought in as a Jane Doe.'

On the screen, Doctor Winston paused and an intrigued look passed across his face. They all watched as his assistant handed him a small flashlight. Bending over, he focused the light directly on the stitches applied to the victim's lower body, moving the light up and down and from side to side. He seemed baffled by something.

'What is he doing?' Garcia instinctively tipped his head to one side, trying to get a better view.

The video played on and they all watched as Doctor Winston used a metallic pointer to probe through the stitches and into the victim's body. The doctor's lips moved and they all looked at Hunter.

'*It's something metallic,*' Hunter translated, '*but I still can't say for certain what it could be. Pass me the stitch-cutting scissors and the forceps, will you?*'

'There was something inside her?' Doctor Hove frowned.

On the screen, Doctor Winston turned away from the camera again and proceeded to use a pair of scissors to slice through the stitches. Hunter noticed there were five in total. The doctor inserted his right hand into the victim.

Moments later, Doctor Winston managed to retrieve an object. When he turned, only its edge flashed past the camera.

'What was that?' Garcia asked. 'What was left inside the victim? Did anyone see?'

'Not sure,' Hunter replied. 'Let's wait, he might turn and face the camera again.'

But he never did.

Within seconds there was a blast and the whole image was substituted by static. The words – *Room 4. Signal fail* – flashed across the center of the screen.

Six

Absolute silence filled the room for several seconds. Doctor Hove was the first to speak.

'A bomb? Someone put a bomb inside a murder victim? What the hell . . . ?'

There was no reply. Hunter took over at the computer and was already clicking away, rewinding the images. He pressed play again, and the video resumed from just a couple of moments before Doctor Winston pulled his hand from inside the victim's body, gripping the unidentified metallic object. All eyes reverted back to the screen.

'I can't make it out exactly,' Garcia said. 'It moves past the camera too fast. Can you slow it down?'

'It doesn't matter what it looks like,' Doctor Hove said almost catatonically. 'It was a bomb. Who the hell puts a bomb inside a victim, and why?' She took a step back and massaged her temples. 'Terrorist?'

Hunter shook his head. 'The location of the attack alone defeats the very essence of terrorism. Terrorists want to cause as much damage as possible with as much loss of life as possible. I hate to state the obvious, Doc, but this is a morgue, not a shopping mall. And the blast wasn't even powerful enough to destroy a whole medium-sized room.'

'Besides,' Garcia said, with no sarcasm in his voice, 'most bodies in here are already dead.'

'So why would someone place a bomb inside a dead body? It doesn't make any sense.'

Hunter held the doctor's gaze. 'I can't tell you the answer to that question right now.' He paused for a moment. 'We need to stay focused here. I'm assuming that no one else has seen this footage?'

Doctor Hove nodded.

'We need to keep it this way for now,' Hunter said. 'If news gets out that a killer has placed a bomb inside a victim, the press will turn this into a carnival. We'll spend more time giving pointless interviews and answering stupid questions than investigating anything. And we can't afford to lose any more time. Despite our emotions on this, what we have here is someone who is crazy enough to kill a young woman, place an explosive device inside her body and stitch it shut. Consequently, he also took the life of two other innocent people.'

New tears started to form in Doctor Hove's eyes. But she had worked with Hunter in many cases over the years and there was no one in law enforcement she trusted more than him. She nodded slowly and for the first time Hunter saw anger in her face.

'Just promise me you'll catch this sonofabitch.'

Before leaving the coroners building, Hunter and Garcia stopped by the Forensics lab and picked up all the available information the team had collected so far. Most of the lab test results would take at least a couple of days. Since Hunter had never got a chance to see the body as it was found at the crime scene, the reports, notes and photographs were all he had to go on at the moment.

He already knew that the body had been found eight hours ago in the back room of the disused butcher's shop in East LA. An anonymous phone call had tipped off the police. Hunter would get a copy of the recording later.

On their way back to East LA, Hunter slowly flipped through all the information in the forensic file. The crime-scene pictures showed that the victim had been left naked, lying on her back on a dirty metal counter. Her legs were together and stretched out but not tied. One of her arms was hanging off the side of the counter, the other rested on her chest. Her eyes were left open, and Hunter had seen the expression in them many times before – pure fear.

One of the pictures showed a close-up of her mouth. Her lips had been stitched shut with thick black, thorn-like thread. Blood had seeped through the needle punctures and ran down her chin and neck, indicating that she was still alive when it was done. Another close-up showed that the same thing had been done to her lower body. Her groin and inner thighs were also smeared with blood that had seeped through the puncture wounds. There was some swelling around the stitches – another indication that she had died hours after being violated by needle and thread. By the time she died, the wounds had already started to go septic. But that wouldn't have caused her death.

Hunter checked the location photographs. The butcher's shop was a dirty mess. Its floor was covered in crack pipes, old syringes, used condoms, and rat droppings. The walls were plastered with graffiti. Forensics had found so many different fingerprints it looked like a party had taken place in that back room. The truth was: right now only an autopsy examination could shed light onto the case.

Seven

Everyone had already left by the time Garcia dropped Hunter back to his car. Crime-scene tape still marked the perimeter around the butcher's shop. A sole uniformed cop guarded the entrance.

Garcia knew Hunter would take his time, looking at every possible detail inside the shop.

'I'm gonna head back and see what I can do with the crime-scene photos and the Missing Persons database. As you said, our priority is in identifying who she was.'

Hunter nodded and stepped out of the car.

The foul smell seemed to have intensified threefold as Hunter flashed his badge at the officer and entered the shop for the second time that evening.

As the door shut behind him, Hunter was left in pitch-black darkness. He clicked his flashlight on and felt a surge of adrenalin rush through his body. Every step was accompanied by the crunching of glass or the squelching sound of something moist under his feet. He moved on past the old meat display counter and approached the door at the back. As he got closer, Hunter heard the buzzing of flies.

This new room was spacious and linked the front of the store to the small freezer-room at the back. Hunter paused by the door, struggling with the putrid stench. His stomach was begging him to leave, threatening to erupt at any moment and causing him to gag and cough violently a few times. His surgical mask was having little effect.

He slowly allowed the beam of his flashlight to move around the room. Two oversized metal sinks sat against the far wall. To their right was an empty floor-to-ceiling storage module. Rats moved freely on its shelves.

Hunter screwed up his face.

'There had to be rats,' he cursed under his breath. He hated rats.

In an instant his mind took him back to when he was eight years old.

On his way back from school, two older kids stopped him and took his Batman lunchbox from him. The lunchbox had been a birthday present from his mother a year earlier, just months before cancer robbed him of her. It was his most prized possession.

After taunting Hunter for a while by throwing the lunchbox back and forth to each other, the two bullies kicked it down an open manhole.

'Go get it, deaf boy.'

Hunter's mother's death was devastating for him and his father, and coping with its aftermath proved particularly difficult. For several weeks, as her disease progressed, Hunter sat alone in his room, listening to her desperate cries, feeling her pain as if it was his own. When she finally passed away, Hunter started experiencing severe loss of hearing. It was his body's psychosomatic way of shutting off the grief. His temporary deafness made Hunter an even easier target to the bullies. To escape being cast aside even more, he'd learned to lip-read by himself. Within two years, with the same ease that it had gone away, his hearing came back.

'You better go get it, deaf boy,' the bigger of the two bullies repeated.

Hunter didn't even hesitate, hurrying down the metal ladder as if his life depended on it. That was exactly what the bullies wanted him to do. They pushed the lid back over the manhole and walked away, laughing.

Hunter found the lunchbox down at the bottom and made his way back up the ladder, but no matter how hard he tried, he just didn't have the physical strength to push the lid aside. Instead of panicking, he went back down to the sewage passageways. If he couldn't get out the same way he went in, he'd simply have to find another way out.

In semi-darkness, clenching his lunchbox tight to his chest, he started down the tunnel. He'd traveled only about fifty yards through filthy, stinking sewage water when he felt something drop from the ceiling onto his back and tug at his shirt. Reflexively, he reached for it, grabbed it and threw it as far away from him as he could. As it hit the water behind him, it squeaked, and Hunter finally saw what it was.

A rat as big as his lunchbox.

Hunter held his breath and slowly turned to face the wall to his right. It was alive with rats of every shape and size.

He started shivering.

Very carefully, he turned around and faced the wall to his left. Even more rats. And he could swear all their eyes were locked on him.

Hunter didn't think, he simply ran as fast as he could, splashing water high in the air with every step. A hundred and fifty yards ahead he came to a metal ladder that led him to another manhole. Again, the lid would not budge. He returned to the passageway and carried on running. Another two hundred yards, another manhole, and Hunter finally hit a little luck. At the top, the lid was half on, half off. With his skinny body, he had no problem squeezing through the gap.

Hunter still had the Batman lunchbox his mother had given him. And ever since then, rats had made him very uneasy.

Now, Hunter pushed the memory away, bringing his attention back to the butcher's shop back room. The only other piece of furniture in it was the stainless steel counter where the victim's naked body had been laid out. It was positioned about six feet from the open freezer-room door on the back wall. Hunter studied the counter from a distance for a long while. There was something odd about it. It was way too high off the ground. When he checked the floor, he found that bricks had been placed under each of its four legs, elevating the counter another foot to foot and a half.

Just like the crime-scene photos showed, the floor was littered with dirty rags, used condoms and discarded syringes. Hunter moved inside, taking short steps, carefully checking the floor before each one. The temperature in the room seemed to be at least five degrees higher than outside, and he felt sweat trickling down the small of his back. As he approached the stainless steel counter, the buzzing noise coming from the flies got louder.

Despite the flies, the nauseating smell and the melting heat, Hunter took his time. He knew the Forensics team had done the best job they could, but crime scenes could offer a lot more than simple physical evidence. And Hunter had a gift when it came to understanding them.

He carefully circled the metal counter for the fifth time. The main question swimming around in his mind was whether the victim had died in that room, or whether the butcher's shop had been nothing more than a simple dumping ground.

Hunter decided to take the victim's place.

He hopped onto the metal counter before lying down in the exact position the victim had been found and switching off his flashlight. He kept absolutely still, allowing the sounds, the smell, the heat, and the darkness of the room to envelop him. His shirt was clinging to his body, wet with sweat. From the photographs, he remembered the look in her eyes, the horror expression frozen on her face.

He switched on his flashlight but remained in the same position, his eyes taking in the graffiti that adorned the entire ceiling.

A moment later, something caught his eye. He squinted and sat up. His gaze locked onto the ceiling directly above the metal counter. The realization came in three seconds flat and his eyes widened.

'Oh Jesus!'

Eight

Katia Kudrov stepped out of her bathtub and wrapped a fluffy white towel around her shoulder-length black hair. Scented candles illuminated her luxurious bathroom in the penthouse of an exclusive apartment block in West Hollywood. The candles helped her relax. And tonight she wanted nothing more than to unwind.

Katia had just finished her first American tour as the principal violinist concertmistress with the Los Angeles Philharmonic. Sixty-five concerts in as many cities in seventy days. The tour had been a tremendous success, but the grueling schedule had left her exhausted. She was looking forward to a well-deserved break.

Music found its way into Katia's life at a very early age, when she was only four. She remembered vividly sitting on her grandfather's lap while he tried to rock her to sleep to the sound of Tchaikovsky's *Violin Concerto in D Major*. Instead of falling asleep, she fell in love with the sounds she heard. The next day, her grandfather gave Katia her first violin. But Katia wasn't a natural, far from it. For years her parents endured the agonizing and ear-piercing noises of her long practice sessions. But she was dedicated, determined and hard-working, and eventually she began playing music that could make the angels smile. After a long spell in

Europe, she had come back to LA thirteen months ago after being offered the concertmistress seat with the Los Angeles Philharmonic.

Katia stepped out of the bathroom, paused in front of the full-length mirror in her bedroom, and studied her reflection. Her features were nearly perfect – large brown eyes, a small nose, high cheekbones and full lips that framed a faultless smile. At thirty, she still had the body of a high-school cheerleader. She checked her profile, sucking her stomach in for several seconds before deciding that she'd gained a small potbelly. Probably from all the junk food she ate at the many cocktail parties she'd had to attend during the tour. Katia shook her head in disapproval.

'Back on the diet and in the gym from tomorrow,' she whispered to herself, reaching for her pink bathrobe.

The cordless phone on her bedside table rang and she looked at it dubiously. Not many people had her home number.

'Hello,' she finally answered after the fifth ring, and could swear she heard a second click on the line, as if someone had picked up the extension in her study, living room or kitchen.

'How's my favorite superstar?'

Katia smiled. 'Hi Dad.'

'Hi there, baby. So how was the tour?'

'Fantastic, but extremely exhausting.'

'I bet. I read the reviews. Everyone loves you.'

Katia smiled. 'I'm so looking forward to two weeks of no rehearsals, no concerts, and certainly no parties.' She made her way out of her bedroom and onto the mezzanine that overlooked her spacious living room.

'But you have some time for your old man, right?'

'I always have time for you when I'm not touring, Dad. You're the one who's always so busy, remember?' she challenged.

He chuckled. 'OK, OK, don't rub it in. I'll tell you what. I can tell you're tired by your voice, how about you have an early night and we catch up over lunch tomorrow?'

Katia hesitated. 'What are we talking about here, Dad? One of your quick "I gotta go, let's grab a sandwich" deals, or a proper sit-down, three-course, no-cells-allowed lunch?'

Leonid Kudrov was one of the most famous film producers in the USA. His lunch engagements usually never lasted more than thirty minutes, which Katia knew well.

There was a small pause and this time Katia was sure she heard a click on the line. 'Dad, are you still there?'

'I'm here, baby. And I'll take option number two, please.'

'I mean it, Dad. If we're having a proper lunch, there'll be no phone calls, and you're not rushing away after half an hour.'

'No cells, I promise. I'll clear my afternoon schedule. And you can pick the restaurant.'

Katia's smile was more animated this time. 'OK. How about we meet at Mastro's Steak House in Beverly Hills at one o'clock?'

'Great choice,' her father agreed. 'I'll make the reservation.'

'And you won't be late, will you, Dad?'

'Of course not, honey. You're my superstar, remember? Look, I gotta go. An important call just came in.'

Katia shook her head. 'What a surprise.'

'Have a good sleep, darling. I'll see you tomorrow.'

'See you tomorrow, Dad.' She rang off and placed the receiver in her bathrobe pocket.

Taking the stairs down to the living room, Katia made

her way into the kitchen. She felt like having a glass of wine, something to relax her even more. She selected a bottle of Sancerre from the fridge. As she fumbled inside one of the worktop drawers for the corkscrew, the phone in her pocket rang again.

'Hello?'

'How's my favorite superstar?'

Katia frowned.

Nine

'Oh please, tell me you're not cancelling on me already, Dad?' Katia wasn't impressed.

'Dad?'

Katia suddenly realized that the voice at the other end of the line wasn't her father's. 'Who is this?'

'Not your daddy.'

'Phillip, is that you?'

Phillip Stein was the new conductor for the Los Angeles Philharmonic, and Katia's latest affair. They'd been seeing each other for four months, but three days before the end of the tour they'd gotten into a heated argument. Phillip had fallen head over heels for Katia, and wanted her to move in with him. Katia liked Phillip and she had enjoyed their affair, but certainly not with the same intensity as he did. She wasn't ready for that type of commitment, not now. She had hinted at the idea that maybe they should take a few days off from seeing each other – just to see how things panned out. Phillip hadn't taken the suggestion well, throwing a tantrum and conducting the worst concerto of his career that night. They hadn't spoken since.

'Phillip? Who's Phillip? Is that your boyfriend?' the voice asked.

Katia shivered.

‘Who is this?’ she asked again, firmer this time.

Silence.

An uncomfortable sensation made the hairs on the back of Katia’s neck stand on end. ‘Look, I think you dialed the wrong number.’

‘I don’t think so.’ The man chuckled. ‘I’ve been dialing this number every day for the past two months.’

Katia breathed out, relieved. ‘See, now I’m sure you’ve got the wrong number. I’ve been away for a little while. I actually just got back.’

There was a pause.

‘It’s no big deal, it happens,’ Katia said kindly. ‘Look, I’m gonna put the phone down so you can redial.’

‘Don’t put the phone down,’ the man said calmly. ‘I haven’t dialed the wrong number. Have you checked your answering machine yet, Katia?’

The only phone in Katia’s apartment with an answering machine was the one at the far end of the worktop in the kitchen. She covered the mouthpiece with her hand and quickly made her way towards it. She hadn’t noticed the blinking red light until then. Sixty messages.

Katia gasped. ‘Who are you? How did you get this number?’

Another chuckle. ‘I’m . . .’ there was a click on the line again, ‘. . . a fan, I guess.’

‘A fan?’

‘A fan with resources. The kind of resources that make information very easy to come by.’

‘Information?’

‘I know you are a fantastic musician. You love your Lorenzo Guadagnini violin more than anything in this world. You live in a penthouse apartment in West Hollywood. You’re allergic to peanuts. Your favorite composer is Tchaikovsky and you love driving that torch red, convertible Mustang of yours.' He paused. 'And you're having lunch with your father tomorrow at one o'clock at Mastro's Steak House in Beverly Hills. Your favorite color is pink, just like the bathrobe you're wearing now, and you were just about to open a bottle of white wine.'

Katia froze.

'So how dedicated a fan am I, Katia?'

Instinctively, Katia's eyes shot towards her kitchen window, but she knew she was too high up for anyone in one of the neighboring buildings to be able to spy on her.

'Oh, I'm not peeping on you through the window,' the man said with a sneer.

The light in the kitchen went out and the next voice Katia heard didn't come from her phone.

'I'm standing right behind you.'

Ten

On any given night Hunter's insomnia would rob him of at least four hours of sleep. Last night, it had kept him awake for almost six.

It was after cancer took his mother from him when he was just seven years old that his sleeping problems started. Alone in his room, missing her, he would lie awake at night, too sad to fall asleep, too scared to close his eyes, too proud to cry. Hunter grew up as an only child in an underprivileged neighborhood of South Los Angeles. His father made the decision never to remarry, and even with two jobs, he struggled to cope with the demands of raising a child on his own.

To banish the bad dreams, Hunter kept his mind occupied in a different way – he read ferociously, devouring books as if they empowered him.

Hunter had always been different. Even as a child, his brain seemed to work through problems faster than anyone else's. At the age of twelve, after a battery of exams and tests suggested by the principal of his school in Compton, he was accepted into the Mirman School for the Gifted on Mulholland Drive as an eighth-grader.

But even a special school's curriculum wasn't enough to slow his progress down.

By the age of fifteen, Hunter had glided through Mirman,

condensing four years of high school into two, and amazing all of his teachers. With recommendations from everyone, he was accepted as a 'special circumstances' student at Stanford on its Psychology School Program.

In college, his advancement was just as impressive, and Hunter received his PhD in Criminal Behavior Analysis and Biopsychology at the age of twenty-three. And that was when his world was shattered for a second time. His father, who at the time was working as a security guard for a branch of the Bank of America in downtown Los Angeles, was shot dead during a robbery gone wrong. Hunter's nightmares and insomnia came back then – even more forcefully, and they hadn't left him since.

Hunter stood by the window in his living room, staring at a distant nothing. His eyes felt gritty and the headache that had started at the rear of his skull was quickly spreading. No matter how hard he tried, he simply couldn't shake the images of the woman's face from his mind. Her eyes open in horror, her lips swollen and sealed together. Did she wake up alone in that butcher's shop and try to scream? Was that why the thread had dug so deep into the flesh around her lips? Did she claw at her mouth in desperate panic? Was she awake when the killer placed a bomb inside her before sewing her shut? The questions were coming at him like tidal waves.

Hunter blinked and the woman's face was substituted by Doctor Winston's and the video images they'd retrieved from the morgue – his eyes wide in shock as he finally understood what he was holding in his hand, as he finally realized that death had caught up with him, and there was nothing he could do. Hunter closed his eyes. His friend was gone, and he had no clue why.

A distant police siren brought Hunter out of his daze and he shivered with anger. What he saw on the ceiling of the butcher's shop last night changed everything. The bomb was meant for no one else but the woman who was left there. Doctor Winston, his friend, someone he considered family, had died for no reason – a tragic mistake.

Hunter felt a pain start in his right forearm. Only then did he realize he'd been clutching his fist so tight blood couldn't find its way to his arm. He swore to himself that whatever happened, he'd make this killer pay for what he'd done.

Eleven

Due to the sensitivity of Hunter's investigation, the entire operation was moved from the third to the fifth floor of Parker Center, LAPD's Robbery Homicide Division HQ in North Los Angeles Street. The new room was spacious enough for two detectives, but with only a small window on the south wall it felt claustrophobic. When Hunter arrived, Garcia was studying the crime-scene photographs that had been placed on a large magnetic board to the right of Hunter's desk.

'We're a little stuck when it comes to identifying her,' Garcia said as Hunter fired up his computer. 'The crime-scene team got several close-up shots of the stitches to her lips, but only one shot that shows her entire face.' He pointed to the top photograph on the board. 'And as you can see, it isn't a great one.'

The photo had been taken at an angle and the left side of the victim's face was partially obscured. 'Apart from the video, we've got no pictures from the autopsy room,' Garcia continued. 'This is all we have to work with. If she was local to where she was found, we can't really go around asking people and showing them a photograph of someone with her lips stitched shut. It'll creep the hell out of everybody. And someone would no doubt talk to the media.' He stepped back from the board.

'Missing Persons?' Hunter asked.

'I got in touch with them last night, but because this is the only photo we have, and the stitches and swelling to her lips are so prominent, the face-recognition software they use won't work. If they run this picture against their database and she happens to be in there, they'll never get a match. We needed a better picture.'

'Sketch artists?'

Garcia nodded, checking his watch. 'They aren't in yet, neither are the computer guys. But you know they can perform miracles with airbrushing and retouching, so there's hope. The problem is, it can take a while.'

'We don't have a while,' Hunter replied.

Garcia scratched his chin. 'I know, Robert, but without an autopsy report, a DNA profile, or the knowledge of any specific physical marks that could help us identify her, we're stuck.'

'We've gotta start somewhere, and right now the only place we can start is with the Missing Persons files and those pictures,' Hunter said, clicking away on his computer. 'The two of us will have to go through them manually until we get something from the composite drawing team.'

'The two of us? Manually? Are you serious? Do you know how many people get reported missing in LA every week?'

Hunter nodded. 'On average eight hundred, but we can narrow the search down using what we already know – Caucasian woman, brunette, hazel eyes, age between twenty-seven and thirty-three. Judging by the length of the counter and the position the body was left, I'd say she was somewhere between five five and five eight. Let's start the search with women who have been missing for anywhere up to two weeks. If we get nothing, we'll go back further.'

'I'll get right on it.'

'How about her fingerprints?'

Garcia quickly shook his head. 'I've checked with Forensics. They've been running them against the National Automated Fingerprint ID System since last night. So far no matches. She doesn't seem to be in the system.'

Hunter had a feeling she wouldn't be.

Garcia poured himself some coffee from the machine on the counter. 'Any clues from the butcher's shop?'

Hunter had emailed himself the photo of the ceiling he'd taken with his cell phone last night. When the file downloaded, he hit the print button.

'Yes, this.' He showed Garcia the printout.

'Graffiti?' Garcia asked after studying the photograph for a moment.

Hunter nodded. 'I took this picture while lying on the counter in the same position the victim was found.'

Garcia raised an eyebrow. 'You lay on that?' He pointed to the photograph of the dirty metal counter on the pictures board, but didn't wait for a reply. 'What exactly am I looking at here?'

'Blended with the graffiti colors, Carlos. Look for the different lettering.'

A moment later Garcia saw it and his whole body tensed. 'Well, I'll be dipped in shit.'

Hidden amongst the colors and shapes, a line of small spray-painted black letters seemed out of place. It read: IT'S INSIDE YOU.

Twelve

Before Garcia could ask anything further, Captain Blake entered the room without knocking.

Barbara Blake had taken over the Los Angeles Robbery Homicide Division's leadership after the retirement of its long-standing captain, William Bolter, two years earlier. Her name had been put forward for captaincy by Bolter himself, upsetting a long list of candidates. She was an intriguing woman – elegant, attractive, with long black hair and mysterious dark eyes that never gave anything away. Despite reservations by some at the division, she had quickly gained a reputation for being a no-nonsense, iron-fist captain. She wasn't easily intimidated, took shit from no one, and she didn't mind upsetting high-powered politicians or government officials if it meant sticking to what she believed was right. In just a few months she had earned the trust and respect of every detective under her command.

Captain Blake and Doctor Winston's friendship went back a long way – over twenty years. The news of his death had hit her like a sucker punch to the gut, and she wanted answers.

As she stepped into the room, she instantly picked up on the tension coming from Garcia. Her eyebrows rose. 'What happened? Have we got something already?'

Garcia handed her the printout. 'From the butcher's shop.'

Just like Garcia, she didn't see it at first. 'What the hell am I looking at?'

Garcia pointed at the letters.

The captain's eyes shot in Hunter's direction. 'This was on the wall in the shop?'

'On the ceiling. Directly above where the victim was left.'

'But the ceiling is covered in graffiti. Why do you think these words have anything to do with our victim?'

'Two reasons. One, that's not graffiti like the rest of the ceiling, that's a handwritten message. Two, the paint was more vivid than the rest of the graffiti, too fresh.'

The captain's eyes returned to the printout.

Hunter paused and all of a sudden started searching his desk.

'What are you looking for?' the captain asked.

'The DVD with the video file we got from the morgue yesterday. I want to check something.' He found it and popped it into his computer's disk drive.

Garcia and Captain Blake joined Hunter by his desk.

As the video started playing, Hunter fast-forwarded it to the scene where Doctor Winston retrieved the bomb from inside the stitched victim. The player application in Hunter's computer didn't have a frame-by-frame function. He had to keep on clicking the play/pause button to slowly advance it to the exact spot he wanted. He watched a small segment a couple of times before turning to face Garcia and the captain.

'His back is towards the camera, so we have to guess the correct moment,' Hunter said, 'but look at Doctor Winston's arm movement right here.'

All eyes were glued to the screen.

Hunter rewound and played the sequence twice over.

'There's a small jerk.' Garcia nodded. 'As if his hand came unstuck.'

'Exactly,' Hunter agreed. 'Do you have a stopwatch?'

Garcia pulled his sleeve up to reveal his wristwatch. 'Sure.'

'Time it. Ready? Go.' Hunter clicked the play button. Exactly ten seconds later, the screen was filled with static.

'A ten-second delay trigger mechanism?' the captain said, looking at Hunter. 'Like a grenade?'

'Something like that.'

'Most grenades' trigger mechanisms have to be manually activated,' Garcia said. 'Who activated that one?'

Hunter rubbed his face. 'That's the question that's been knocking around in my head. Whoever placed the bomb inside the victim couldn't be sure of the exact moment of extraction. That means that the bomb couldn't have been on a timer or have been remotely activated.'

Garcia nodded.

'So what if in this case the trigger was held in place not by a pin like most grenades, but by the confined space where the bomb was placed?' Hunter suggested. 'A spring trigger of some sort, held tight by the victim's own body.'

Garcia and Captain Blake exchanged glances as they considered it for a moment.

'So extracting the bomb from the victim would've released the trigger,' Garcia said, scratching his forehead. 'It's possible – and very creative.'

'Fantastic,' the captain said, pinching the bridge of her nose. 'To the killer this is all just a game.' She showed Hunter the printout again. 'He even told us it was inside her.'

Hunter shook his head. 'The killer wasn't informing us, Captain.'

'Sorry?'

'The killer was informing the *victim*.'

Thirteen

Captain Blake leaned against the edge of Garcia's desk and folded her arms. 'You've lost me, Robert.'

'Have a look at that printout again, Captain,' Hunter said. 'The killer wrote "It's inside *you*" not "It's inside *her*". He wasn't communicating with us.'

'Why would the killer try to communicate with a dead body?'

'Because she wasn't dead when he left her.'

The captain ran a finger over her right eyebrow and pulled a face. 'You lost me even more now.'

Hunter walked up to the pictures board. 'There were several things that were bothering me about the crime-scene photos. That's why I wanted to have a look at the butcher's shop again myself.' He pointed to one of the pictures. 'Look at the position the body was found in, the arms in particular. One is hanging down from the side of the counter and the other is resting awkwardly on her chest. The fingers on her right hand are spread apart and half bent, as if she was trying to dig at something. I don't think the killer left her in this particular position.'

'The body might've been interfered with, Robert,' the captain countered. 'It was an anonymous phone call that gave us the body's location, remember?'

Hunter nodded. 'Yes, and I listened to the 911 recording. It's a girl's voice. Not older than sixteen or seventeen, and she sounded hysterical. The reason why she didn't wanna give us her name is probably because she was going into that room to shoot up.'

'OK, so the girl didn't touch the body,' the captain said, accepting his theory. 'But maybe you're reading too much into this message. Maybe the killer didn't put a great deal of thought into it. So he wrote *you* instead of *her*, no big deal.'

It was Garcia's turn to disagree. 'That would suggest that the writing on the ceiling was a spur-of-the-moment thing, Captain.' He rubbed the lump on his nose. 'We're talking about someone who put together his own explosive device and probably engineered the trigger mechanism himself. He then placed it all inside the victim in some way that it wouldn't be triggered until found and extracted. All of that while she was still alive.' He shook his head and faced the pictures board. 'Whatever this killer did, Captain, nothing was on the spur of the moment. He thought it all through. And that's what makes him so dangerous.'

Fourteen

Captain Blake let out a frustrated breath and started pacing the room. Her high heels clicked against the wooden floor.

'It doesn't make any sense. If the victim was still alive when she was left in that butcher's shop, and the message on the ceiling was meant for her, how come she was dead when we found her? Who killed her, the rats?' She pulled a photograph from the board and studied it for a moment. 'Independently of whatever happened to the victim, the fact still remains that someone placed a bomb inside her and stitched her shut. The only way of getting that bomb out was to cut through the stitches and pull it out.' She paused and allowed her eyes to move from one detective to the other. 'Don't tell me you think the killer expected the victim to do that by herself?'

No one replied.

Hunter massaged the back of his neck, and for a moment allowed his fingers to rub the rough scar on his nape.

The captain turned towards him. 'I know you, Robert. If you think the message was left for the victim instead of us, you must have a theory on this. I'm all ears.'

'I don't have a proper theory yet, Captain, just too many ifs.'

'You've gotta have something brewing in that brain of

yours,' the captain pushed. 'Indulge me, because right now I hate what I'm hearing.'

Hunter took a deep breath. 'Maybe the bomb's how the killer wanted her to die.'

Captain Blake's eyes narrowed. 'You think the bomb was supposed to blow up inside her, while she was still alive?'

Hunter tilted his head to one side, musing over the possibility.

Captain Blake sat down in Hunter's chair. 'You're going to have to develop on that, Robert. If this killer thought everything through so thoroughly as Garcia has suggested, and if the bomb was supposed to blow up inside the victim as you're suggesting, why didn't it? What happened? Did the killer make a mistake? How would the trigger mechanism be activated while the bomb was *inside* her? And if he didn't kill her, how the hell did she die?'

'As I said, too many ifs, Captain,' Hunter replied calmly. 'And at the moment I don't have the answers. With everything that's happened, we don't have much to go on. I don't know if the killer made a mistake or not. I don't know why the bomb didn't blow up inside her, or how it was supposed to be activated in the first place. Without the autopsy report we'll probably never know the real cause of death. What we do know is that it's nothing apparent. She wasn't shot, stabbed, or strangled. I also don't believe she was poisoned.' He paused. 'But there's a possibility she suffocated.'

Captain Blake threw Hunter a perplexed look. 'How's that?'

Hunter pointed to an enlarged picture of the victim's face. 'Suffocation causes the blood vessels around the eyes and behind the delicate skin on the cheeks to burst. See here.' He indicated on the photo. 'This sort of old-person's-skin look is a consequence of burst blood vessels. There's a good chance she suffocated. I confirmed it with Doctor Hove. But again, without an autopsy we'll never be certain.'

'So you're saying that you think she might've suffocated by herself, after the killer left her there?'

Hunter nodded.

'On what? The foul smell of the place?'

Hunter shrugged. 'Her own vomit . . . her tongue . . . Who knows? Maybe the victim had a bad heart. But just imagine if she was still alive when she was left in that butcher's shop – unconscious, but still alive. She wakes up, naked, frightened, in pain, and with parts of her body stitched shut. That'd certainly be enough to trigger a severe panic attack in most people.'

Captain Blake massaged her closed eyelids, considering Hunter's suggestion. She knew that a panic attack could easily cause someone to vomit, gag or hyperventilate. With the victim's mouth sewn tightly shut, she'd have no way of drawing in breath and increasing the flow of oxygen to her lungs. That would've made the victim's panic turn into mindless desperation. If she'd puked, the vomit had nowhere to go. Choking and asphyxiating would've been just a breath away. And then . . . certain death.

Fifteen

The results of the chemical tests done on the spray paint used on the ceiling of the butcher's shop came in by 2:00 p.m. and threw up nothing special. The paint came from a can of Montana Tarblack – probably the most popular brand of spray paint in the USA. Every graffiti artist in the country used it. The handwriting analyses confirmed what Hunter already suspected – the killer had used his non-writing hand to spray the words onto the ceiling. Simple, but effective. Hunter had requested that the whole room be dusted again, and this time they should include the ceiling. Every print found was to be run through the National Automated Fingerprint ID System.

Hunter leaned back in his chair, closed his eyes and gently ran the tip of his finger up and down the bridge of his nose. His brain kept trying to make sense of such a senseless act.

If there had been no bomb, if the victim had been found simply stitched shut, Hunter would have a steadier psychological path to follow. The stitches to the mouth on their own would have suggested the possibility of a retaliation kill – a lesson being taught. The victim might have said something she shouldn't have – about the wrong person, to the wrong person, or both. The act could have been performed as a way to symbolize shutting her up.

The stitches to her mouth and lower body together would have upped the stakes to a possible sexual or love betrayal and revenge. *If you can't keep your mouth and legs shut, I'll shut them for you.* That would've clearly placed a deceived husband, boyfriend or lover right at the top of their list of persons of interest. And that possibility was still pretty much alive in Hunter's mind. But he still had the bomb to deal with. Why place a *bomb* inside the victim? Experience also told him that the overwhelming majority of what were considered crimes of passion were spur-of-the-moment acts, generated by irrational anger and an almost total loss of control. Very rarely did it come in the form of a planned, calculated and brutal vengeance act.

One possibility that kept nagging Hunter was that there could have been more than one perpetrator, more specifically, a gang. Crimes like this one weren't beyond the scope of certain gangs in Los Angeles. Some were notorious for their violence and their bad-ass, don't-fuck-with-us attitude. Sending a warning to other gangs in the form of brutal beatings and murders happened more often than the mayor of Los Angeles would care to admit. These gangs also had a direct link to gun trafficking. Getting hold of a ready-made bomb, a grenade, or materials to make their own wouldn't have been a problem. The victim could've belonged to some gang leader. Some of them liked to think of their women as possessions. If she'd betrayed him, especially if she did it with a rival gang member, this could have been their way of blowing her off.

And then there was the possibility that the stitches carried no symbolism whatsoever. As Captain Blake had suggested, they could simply be dealing with an extremely sadistic killer, someone who enjoyed hurting people for the sheer pleasure of it. And Hunter knew that if that were the case, more victims would follow.

'The Missing Persons files we requested should be with us in the next forty-five minutes or so,' Garcia said, coming off the phone and dragging Hunter away from his thoughts.

'Great. You can start going over them if I'm not here.' Hunter reached for his jacket. There was only one person he knew in LA who'd have knowledge of guns, explosives, trigger mechanisms and gangs. It was time to call in some favors.

Sixteen

D-King was probably the best-known dealer in Hollywood and Northwest Los Angeles. Though he was known as a dealer, no one was ever able to prove it, least of all the District Attorney's office. They'd been trying to nail him to anything substantial without success for the past eight years.

D-King was young, intelligent, a fierce businessman, and very dangerous to anyone who was stupid enough to ever cross him. Allegedly, he dealt not only in drugs, but prostitution, stolen goods, weapons . . . the list went on and on. He also had a string of legitimate businesses – nightclubs, bars, restaurants, even a gym. The IRS couldn't touch him either.

Hunter and D-King's paths had crossed for the first time three years ago, during the notorious Crucifix Killer investigation. An unprecedented chain of events forced them into a standoff, and into reaching a decision that despite them being on different sides of the law, made them respect each other.

Hunter pulled D-King's address from the police computer. Where else but Malibu Beach, where the super-famous and the super-rich called home.

As he brought his car to a stop by the enormous double iron gates fitted with security cameras, Hunter had to admit he was impressed. The two-story building was majestic: an ivy-covered, double bow-front brick construction with square granite piers every twenty feet.

Before Hunter had a chance to reach for the intercom button, a strong male voice called out.

'May I help you?'

'Yes, I'm here to see your boss.'

'And you are?'

'Tell D-King it's Robert Hunter.'

The intercom clicked off and a minute later the iron gates parted.

The driveway was flanked by millimeter-perfect trimmed hedges. Hunter parked his rusted Buick Lesabre next to a pearly white Lamborghini Gallardo, just in front of a six-car garage. He climbed up the steps to the main house, and as he reached the top, the door was opened by a six-foot-three, two-hundred-and-seventy-pound muscle-bound black man. The man frowned at Hunter's car.

'It's an American classic,' Hunter retorted.

Not even a ghost of a smile from the muscleman.

'Please, follow me.'

The interior of the house was just as impressive as the outside. Twelve-feet-high ceilings, designer furniture and walls covered with oil paintings – some of them Dutch, a few of them French, all of them valuable.

As Hunter crossed the Italian-marbled floor in the living area, he noticed a jaw-droppingly beautiful black woman in a bright yellow bikini sitting among overstuffed cushions. She lifted her eyes from the glossy magazine in her hands and gave Hunter a warm smile. He politely nodded back and smiled internally. *Even rock stars and sports superstars don't have it this good.*

The muscleman guided Hunter through a pair of sliding

glass doors and out to the backyard and pool area. Four young and attractive topless women were by the edge of the pool, giggling and splashing water at each other. Three other musclemen in suits were strategically positioned around the yard. D-King was sitting at one of four artfully weathered teak tables at the poolside, under a white umbrella. His blue silk shirt was unbuttoned, revealing a muscular torso adorned with chains and diamonds. The blonde woman sitting with him was also topless. A single white gold loop ring pierced her left nipple.

'Detective Robert Hunter?' D-King said with a smile but without getting up. 'Yo, wuz up, dawg? Now that's a motherfucking surprise. How long has it been, three years?' He indicated the chair opposite his.

Hunter took it. 'Something like that.' He nodded at the blonde woman, who replied with a wink.

'Can I offer you something, Detective?' D-King said, tilting his head towards his blonde friend. 'Lisa here can mix you the most amazing cocktail.'

Hunter's eyes stole a peek at Lisa, who smiled naughtily. 'Anything you like.'

Hunter shook his head. 'I'm fine for now, thanks.'

'OK,' D-King cut in, 'so now that I know you're not here for the company or the drinks, what can I do for you, Detective?'

Hunter's eyes subtly moved to Lisa and then back to D-King. He got the hint.

'Lisa, why don't you go play with the other girls?' He didn't phrase it as a request. She undid the sarong around her waist and stood up. Only then Hunter realized that she was fully naked. Not a hint of embarrassment crossed her face as she paused in front of him for a long moment. Her body was as close to perfection as Hunter had ever seen. Lisa slowly turned and walked away, her hips swinging as if she were on a catwalk. The tattoo on her lower back read – *I know you're looking.*

'That's right, baby, dance it up,' D-King called out before turning to Hunter. 'Admit it, Detective,' he teased, 'I know how to live, don't I? Hugh Heffner and Larry Flynt have got shit on me. *Playboy* and *Hustler* can kiss my black ass all the way to Mississippi. My girls are hotter.'

'What do you know about homemade explosive devices?'

The smile vanished from D-King's lips. 'I know they go bang.'

Hunter kept a poker face.

'Officially, notta thing.'

'And unofficially?'

D-King scratched the small scar above his left eyebrow with his pinky while scrutinizing Hunter. 'If you're here unofficially, why don't you have a drink?'

'I'm not thirsty.'

They regarded each other for a few more seconds.

'First time we met you bullshitted for a while before coming clean. I hope we're past that crap. What's this really about, Detective?'

Hunter leaned forward and placed a close-up photograph of the victim's face on the table in front of him, rotating it around to face D-King.

'Oh, hell no, dawg.' He cringed and moved back. 'Last time you showed me a picture of a dead woman, all fucking hell broke loose.'

'Do you know who she is?'

'And that's exactly the question that started it all.' His eyes moved back to the picture, and involuntarily D-King rubbed his lips with the tips of his fingers. 'Oh damn. That's some nasty shiiit. Some motherfucker stitched her mouth shut?'

'Do you know who she is?' Hunter asked again.

'She ain't none of my girls if that's what you're asking,' he replied after a brief pause.

'Could she have been on the game?'

'Not looking like that.' Instantly D-King's hands came up in surrender. 'Sorry, bad joke. Anybody could be on the game these days. She looks to have been attractive enough. I don't think I've ever seen her before though.' He tried to read Hunter's expressionless face and failed. 'The problem is that nowadays a lot of girls are trying to go it alone, creating websites and all, doing their own thang, you know what I'm saying? It's hard to be sure. But if she was a top working girl in the Hollywood area, I'd know.'

The other four women who were playing by the edge of the pool decided to join Lisa, who was now sitting on a floating chair sipping a colorful drink.

D-King's eyes moved down to the picture again. 'This is too fucking nasty, man. And knowing the kind of shit you get involved with, I'm sure whoever did this did it while she was still alive, right?'

'Could this have been done by a gang?' Hunter asked. 'Or a pimp?'

D-King's face clouded over. Helping the police was never part of his agenda. 'I wouldn't know,' he replied coldly.

'C'mon, D-King, look at her.' Hunter tapped the photograph on the table, but kept a steady voice. He was aware all three musclemen around the yard had their eyes on him. 'Her mouth wasn't the only part of her body that was stitched shut. Whoever did this did a real nasty job on her. And you were right. It was done while she was still alive.'

D-King shifted in his seat. Violence against women had a way of lighting a fuse inside him. His mother had been beaten to death by his own drunken father while he was locked in the closet. He was ten. D-King never forgot her screams and pleas for mercy. He had never forgotten the sound of her bones breaking as his father repeatedly hit her, over and over again. He heard those sounds almost every night in his dreams.

D-King sat back and looked at his fingernails, flicking the end of each one with his thumb. 'You mean could this be some sort of trademark retaliation?' He shrugged. 'Who knows? Possibly. If she belonged to a homeboy and she either stole from him or decided to fuck around, I wouldn't be surprised. Some people don't look kindly at being fucked with. Examples have to be made, do you feel me? This could even be considered mild by some standards.' He paused and looked at the picture again. 'But if this is payback for her being somebody's woman and getting dirty somewhere else, you can expect to get another body – the motherfucker she was doing it with. This kind of revenge comes in twos, Detective.' He pushed the photo back towards Hunter. 'What does this have to do with homemade explosive devices?'

'More than it looks.'

D-King chuckled. 'You never give anything away, do you?' He had a sip of the dark green colored drink in front of him. 'Actually, if last time we saw each other is anything to go by, I don't really fucking wanna know what this is all about.' He regarded Hunter like a poker player about to bet his whole stash before tapping the picture with his index finger. 'But this is fucking offensive, man, and I owe you one anyway. Let me look into it and I'll get back to you.'

Seventeen

Garcia turned on the fan and stood in front of it for a minute before going back to his desk. He couldn't even imagine how hot that room would be during summer.

He'd been going over the crime-scene pictures in his computer, enhancing and scrutinizing them, looking for anything they could use to point them in the right direction as to the victim's identity. So far, nothing. No tattoos or surgery scars. The moles and freckles he could see on her arms, stomach, neck and cleavage were too common and not prominent enough to really be classed as identifying marks. As far as he could tell, she was a natural brunette and her breasts were her own.

Her arms showed no signs of needle marks and her frame wasn't skinny and wasted. If she was a junkie, she certainly didn't look like one. Despite the small patches on her cheeks that carried that old-person's-skin look Hunter had mentioned, the victim couldn't have been any older than thirty-three, at a stretch. If the old saying that the eyes are the windows to the soul was true, then her soul was scared beyond belief when she died.

Garcia leaned forward, placed his elbows on his desk and rubbed his eyes with the heels of his hands. He reached for his coffee cup, but it had long gone cold. Before he could pour himself a new one, a clicking sound announcing the arrival of a new email came from his computer. The Missing Persons files he'd requested. They'd promised to send them over in forty-five minutes. That had been two hours ago.

Garcia read the email and let out a high-pitched whistle. Fifty-two brunette Caucasian women with hazel eyes, aged between twenty-seven and thirty-three, and somewhere between five five and five eight in height had been reported missing in the past two weeks. He unzipped the attachment containing all the files and started printing them out, first the photographs, then their personal information sheets.

He poured himself a new cup of coffee and gathered all the printouts into one pile. The photos would have been brought into the Missing Persons Unit by the person who reported them as missing. Even though Missing Persons would have asked for a recent picture, Garcia knew that some of those photographs could be over a year old, sometimes more. He'd have to allow for subtle changes in appearance such as hair length and style, and fullness of the face due to weight loss or gain.

The main problem Garcia faced was that he had only the close-up photo of the victim, the one from the crime scene, to compare them to. The swelling on the victim's lips together with the thick black threaded stitches forcing them tightly together deformed the bottom half of her face. Matching any of the photographs sent from Missing Persons to that one would be a long and laborious task.

An hour later Garcia had reduced the possible matches from fifty-two to twelve, but his eyes were getting tired, and the more he looked at the pictures, the fewer distinguishing features he saw.

He spread the twelve printouts out on his desk, creating

three lines of four with their respective information sheets next to them. The photos were all of reasonable quality. There were six face portraits, passport-style; three where the subject had been cropped from a group picture; one showed a wet-haired brunette sitting on a jet ski; another smiling brunette was by the pool; and the last picture showed a woman at a dinner table holding a glass of champagne.

Garcia was about to start the whole process again when Hunter walked through the door and saw him hunched over his desk, staring intensely at the group of neatly arranged photographs.

'Are those from Missing Persons?' Hunter asked.

Garcia nodded.

'Anything?'

'Well, I started with fifty-two possibilities and have been comparing them to our crime-scene photos for over an hour now. The swelling on our victim's face makes things a lot harder. I'm now down to these,' he nodded at the twelve photos on his desk, 'but my eyes are starting to play tricks on me. I'm not sure what I'm supposed to look for any more.'

Hunter stood in front of Garcia's desk and allowed his eyes to jump from photo to photo, spending several seconds on each one. A moment later his gaze settled on the facial close-up of the unidentified victim. He moved them all nearer together, making a new photo group before reaching for a blank sheet of paper.

'Every face can be looked at in several ways,' Hunter said, placing the sheet of paper over the first photo at the top of the group, covering two-thirds of it. 'That's how composite sketches are created. Individual characteristics added together one by one.'

Garcia moved closer.

'The shape of the head and ears, the shape of the eyebrows, eyes and nose, the mouth, the jaw line, the chin . . .' As he mentioned each facial feature, Hunter used the paper sheet to cover all the other ones. 'We can very crudely use the same principle here.'

A few minutes later they had discarded another eight photographs.

'I'd say our victim could be any of these four,' Hunter said finally. 'They share all the same physical features – oval face, small nose, almond-shaped eyes, arched eyebrows, prominent cheekbones . . . the same as our victim.'

Garcia agreed with a nod.

Hunter checked the personal fact sheets Garcia had stapled to the back of each picture. They'd all been reported missing over a week ago. Their home and work addresses were scattered all over town. At first glance there seemed to be no other similarities between the four women other than their looks.

Hunter glanced at his watch. 'We've gotta check them all out today.'

Garcia reached for his jacket. 'I'm ready.'

Hunter handed him two of the photographs. 'You take those and I'll take these two.'

Garcia nodded.

'Call me if you get lucky.'

Eighteen

Whitney Myers drove through the tall iron gates of the sumptuous mansion in Beverly Hills just forty-five minutes after she had received the call. She parked her yellow Corvette C6 at the far end of the wide cobblestone courtyard, took off her dark glasses, and placed them on her head like an arc to hold her shiny, long black hair back. She grabbed her briefcase from the passenger's seat, checked her watch and smiled to herself. Considering LA's afternoon traffic and the fact that she had been in Long Beach when she got the call, forty-five minutes was lightning fast.

She was greeted at the steps that led up to the mansion's main entrance by Andy McKee, a short, overweight, brilliant attorney-at-law.

'Whitney,' he said, using a white handkerchief to wipe the sweat from his forehead. 'Thank you for coming so quickly.'

'Not a problem,' she smiled as she shook his hand. 'Whose house is this? It's gorgeous.'

'You'll meet him inside.' He looked at her appraisingly and the sweat returned to his forehead.

Whitney Myers was thirty-six years old with dark eyes, a small nose, high cheekbones, full lips and a strong jaw. Her smile could be considered a weapon with the power of turning steady legs into gelatinous goo. Many strong and eloquent men had babbled incoherently and giggled like kids after she hit them with it. She looked like a model on a day off, even more beautiful because she wasn't trying.

Myers started her career as a police officer at the age of twenty-one. She worked harder than anyone in her bureau to move through the ranks and make detective as quickly as she could. Her intelligence, quick thinking and strong character also helped push her forward, and by the age of twenty-seven she finally received her detective's shield.

Her captain was quick to recognize that Myers had a gift when it came to persuasion. She was calm, articulate, attentive and extremely convincing when putting her point across. She was also good with people. After six months on an intensive and specialized course with the FBI, Myers became one of the chief negotiators for the West and Valley bureaus of the LAPD and the Missing Persons Unit.

But her career as a detective with Los Angeles' finest came to an abrupt end three years ago, after her efforts to negotiate a suicidal jumper off the roof of an eighteen-story-high skyscraper in Culver City went terribly wrong.

The aftermath of what happened that day put Myers' entire life under severe scrutiny. An investigation was launched into her conduct, and Internal Affairs came down on her like a heavy downpour. After several weeks, the IA investigation was inconclusive and no charges were brought against her, but her days with the LAPD were over. She'd been running her own missing persons investigation agency since then.

Myers followed McKee through the house, past a double staircase and down a hallway lined with pictures of famous movie stars. The hallway ended in the living room. The room was so imposing it took Myers a few seconds to notice a six-foot-two, broad-shouldered man standing at an arched window. In his right hand he held an almost empty glass of Scotch. Despite being in his mid-fifties, Myers could see he had a boyish charm about him.

'Whitney, let me introduce you to Leonid Kudrov,' McKee said.

Leonid put his glass down and shook Myers' hand. His grip was tense and the expression on his face was the same she'd seen in every face that had ever hired her – desperation.

Nineteen

Myers declined the offer of a drink and listened attentively to Kudrov's account of events, taking notes every other sentence.

'Have you called the police?' she asked while Leonid refilled his glass.

'Yes, they took my details but they barely listened to what I was saying. Gave me some bullshit about elapsed time, independent adult, or something like that, and kept putting me on hold. That's when I called Andy and he called you.'

Myers nodded. 'Because your daughter is thirty years old and you couldn't substantiate your reason for believing she's gone missing, it's normal practice to wait at least twenty-four hours before she can be officially considered a missing person.' Her voice was naturally confident, the kind that inspired trust.

'Twenty-four hours? She could be dead in twenty-four hours. That's bullshit.'

'Sometimes it's even more, depending on the evidence given.'

'I tried telling him that,' McKee added, wiping his forehead again.

'She's an adult, Mr. Kudrov,' Myers explained. 'An adult who has simply failed to turn up for a lunch appointment.'

Kudrov glared at Myers and then at McKee. 'Has she heard a fucking word I said?'

'Yes,' Myers replied, crossing her legs and flipping through her notes. 'She was thirty minutes late for your lunch. You called her several times. She never answered and never returned any of your messages. You panicked and went to her apartment. Once there you found a towel on the kitchen floor, but nothing else seemed out of place except for a bottle of white wine that should've been in the fridge. Her car keys were on a tray upstairs. You found her priceless violin in her practice room, but you said that it should've been in the safe. From what you could tell there was no sign of any sort of struggle or a break-in, and the place didn't seem to have been burgled. The building's concierge said that no one had visited her that night.' She calmly closed her notebook.

'Isn't that enough?'

'Let me explain how the police would think, how they are trained to think. There are way more Missing Persons cases than there are detectives working them. The number one rule is to prioritize, only allocate resources when there's no doubt the person in question has really gone missing. If she were a minor, an amber alert would've been issued all across the country. But as an independent adult who's only been unreachable for less than twenty-four hours, protocol dictates the police go through a checklist first.'

'A checklist? You're shitting me.'

A quick headshake. 'I shit you not.'

'Such as?'

Myers leaned forward. 'Is this an adult who: one – may be in need of assistance? Two – may be the victim of a crime or foul play? Three – may be in need of medical attention? Four

– has no pattern of running away or disappearing? Five – may be the victim of parental abduction? And six – is mentally or physically impaired?' Myers placed her sunglasses on the coffee table next to her. 'From that list, only having no pattern of running away or disappearing checked out. The police's initial thoughts would be – because Miss Kudrov is a sane, independent, financially sufficient and unattached adult woman, she could've simply decided she needed a break from everything. There's no one she really needs to give account of her actions to. She doesn't have a nine-to-five job, and she isn't married. You said she just got back from a long tour with the Los Angeles Philharmonic.'

Kudrov nodded.

'It must be very stressful. She could've jumped on a plane and gone to the Bahamas. She could've met someone in a bar last night and decided to spend a few undisturbed days with that person somewhere else.'

Leonid ran a hand though his cropped hair. 'Well, she didn't. I know Katia. If she had to cancel an appointment with me or anyone else, she would've called. It's just the way she is. She doesn't let people down, least of all me. We have a great relationship. If she had decided that she needed a break, she would've at least let me know where she was going.'

'How about her mother? Am I right in assuming you and she aren't together any more?'

'Her mother passed away several years ago.'

Myers kept her eyes on Leonid. 'I'm sorry to hear that.'

'Katia didn't just decide to take a trip somewhere. I'm telling you, something is wrong.'

He started pacing the room. Emotions were starting to fly high.

'Mr. Kudrov, please—'

'Stop calling me Mr. Kudrov,' he cut her short. 'I'm not your teacher. Call me Leo.'

'OK, Leo. I'm not doubting you. I'm just explaining why the police acted the way they did. If Katia hasn't showed up in twenty-four hours, they'll be all over this case like ugly on a moose. They'll use every resource available to find her. But you better be prepared, because with your celebrity status, the circus will come next.'

Leonid squinted at McKee before moving his stare back to Myers. 'Circus?'

'When I said that the LAPD will use every resource available, I meant that. Including you and your status. They'll want you to make your own appeal to the public, to personalize the case. Maybe even hold a conference here at your house. They'll broadcast Katia's photo on TV and in the newspapers, and they'll prefer a family picture instead of a lone shot – it's more . . . *touching*. The picture will be copied and plastered all over LA, maybe even the whole of California. Search parties will form. They'll ask for clothes for the dog search teams. They'll want hairs and other samples for DNA tests. The media will camp outside your gates.' Myers paused for breath. 'As I said, it will turn into a circus, but the LAPD Missing Persons Unit is very good at what they do.' She hesitated for effect. 'Leo, given your status and social class, we have to consider the possibility that your daughter was kidnapped for ransom. No one has attempted to contact you?'

Leonid shook his head. 'I've been in the house all day and have left specific instructions at my office to divert any unidentified caller to my home line. No calls.'

Myers nodded.

'Something is wrong. I can feel it.' Leonid pinned Myers down with a desperate stare. 'I don't want this splattered all over the news unless it's really necessary. Andy told me you are the best at what you do. Better than the LAPD Missing Persons. Can *you* find her?' He made it sound less of a question and more like a plea.

Myers gave McKee a look that said, *I'm flattered.*

He returned a shy smile.

'I will do my best.' Myers nodded, her voice confident.

'So do it.'

'Do you have a recent picture of your daughter?'

Kudrov was already prepared and handed Myers a colored eight-by-twelve-inch photograph of Katia.

Myers' eyes grazed the picture. 'I'll also need the keys to her apartment, the names and phone numbers of everyone you can think of who she could've contacted. And I need it all by yesterday.'

Twenty

Hunter called both contacts on the two Missing Persons personal fact sheets he had with him. Mr. Giles Carlsen, a hair salon manager from Brentwood, had contacted the police ten days ago to report Cathy Greene, his roommate, as missing. On the phone, Carlsen told Hunter that Miss Greene had finally turned up the morning before. She'd been away with a new male friend she'd met in her dance class.

The second contact, Mr. Roy Mitchell, had contacted the police twelve days ago. His 29-year-old daughter, Laura, had simply disappeared. Mr. Mitchell asked Hunter to meet him at his home in Fremont Place in an hour.

Hancock Park is one of the most affluent and desirable areas in all of Southern California. In sharp contrast to most Los Angeles neighborhoods, houses in Hancock Park are set well back from the street, most power and telephone lines are buried, and fences are strongly discouraged. As Hunter turned into Fremont Place, it became obvious that invasion of privacy wasn't one of the area's main concerns.

The house's half-moon-shaped driveway was paved in cobble block and merged into a parking area large enough for two buses. At the center of it stood a massive stone fountain. The sun was just reaching the horizon, and the sky behind the terracotta brick two-story house was being painted in 'photo moment' fiery red streaks. Hunter parked his car and climbed out.

The front door was answered by a woman in her mid-fifties. She was a picture of elegance, with longish hair neatly tied in a ponytail, a magnetic smile, and skin most women half her age would kill for. She introduced herself as Denise Mitchell and showed Hunter into a study rich with art, antiques, and leather-bound books. Standing before a tall mahogany sideboard crowded with photographs was a stocky man, a donut shy of being fat. He was at least half a foot shorter than Hunter with a full head of disheveled gray hair and a matching moustache.

'You must be the detective I spoke to on the phone,' he said offering his hand. 'I'm Roy Mitchell.'

His handshake was as practiced as his smile, strong enough to show strength of character but soft enough not to intimidate. Hunter showed him his credentials and Roy Mitchell tensed.

'Oh God.'

His whisper wasn't quiet enough to escape his wife's ears. 'What's wrong?' she asked, moving closer, her eyes pleading for information.

'Can you give us a moment, honey,' Roy replied, trying in vain to conceal his concern.

'No, I'm not giving you a moment,' Denise said, her stare now fixed on Hunter. 'I want to know what happened. What information do you have on my daughter?'

'Denise, please.'

'I'm not going anywhere, Roy.' Her eyes never left Hunter. 'Did you find my daughter? Is she OK?'

Roy Mitchell looked away.

'What's going on, Roy? What got you so spooked?'

No reply.

'Somebody talk to me.' Her voice faltered.

'I'm not with the Missing Persons Unit, Mrs. Mitchell,' Hunter finally offered, showing her his credentials once again. This time she looked at them a lot more attentively than she had at the door.

'Oh my God, you're from Homicide?' She cupped her hands over her nose and mouth as tears filled her eyes.

'There's a chance that I'm in the wrong house,' Hunter said in a steady but comforting voice.

'What?' Denise's hands started shaking.

'Maybe we should all have a seat.' Hunter indicated the leather Chesterfield sofa by a six-foot-tall Victorian lampshade.

The Mitchells took the sofa and Hunter one of the two armchairs facing it.

'At the moment we're trying to identify someone who shares several physical characteristics with your daughter,' Hunter explained. 'Laura's name is one of four which have come up as a possible match.'

'As a possible match to a homicide victim?' Roy asked, placing a hand on his wife's knee.

'Unfortunately, yes.'

Denise started crying.

Roy took a deep breath. 'I gave the other detective a very recent picture of Laura, do you have it?'

Hunter nodded.

'And still you can't be sure if this victim of yours is Laura?' Denise asked, her mascara starting to run down her face. 'How come?'

Roy clamped his eyes shut for an instant and a single tear rolled to the tip of his nose. Hunter could see he'd already picked up on the possibility of the victim being unrecognizable. 'So you're here to ask us for a blood sample for a DNA test?' he said.

It was obvious that Roy Mitchell was a lot more clued up on police procedures than most people. Since the introduction of DNA testing, in a situation such as the one Hunter was facing, it was a lot more practical for the police to collect samples and match them to the victim first. That way they could later approach only the identified family, instead of putting several innocent ones through the panic and the traumatic experience of looking at a photograph of a gruesomely disfigured victim.

Hunter shook his head. 'Sadly, a DNA test won't help us.'

For a moment it was as if there wasn't enough air in the room for all three of them. 'Do you have a picture of the victim?' Roy finally asked.

Hunter nodded and flipped through several sheets of paper inside the folder he'd brought with him. 'Mrs. Mitchell,' he said, catching Denise's eyes, 'this woman might not be your daughter. There's no reason for you to look at this picture right now.'

Denise stared at Hunter with glassy eyes. 'I'm not going anywhere.'

'Honey, please.' Roy tried again.

She didn't even look at him.

Hunter waited, but the determination in her eyes was almost palpable. He placed the close-up of the victim on the coffee table in front of them.

It took Denise Mitchell just a fraction of a second to recognize her. 'Oh my God!' Her shivering hands shot to her mouth. 'What have they done to my baby?'

All of a sudden the room they were in looked different

– darker, smaller, the air denser. Hunter sat in silence for several minutes while Roy Mitchell tried to console his wife. Her tears weren't hysterical; they were simply full of pain – and rage. In different circumstances Hunter would have left, giving the Mitchells some time to grieve before coming back the next morning with a list of questions, but this wasn't like any other case, this killer wasn't like any other killer. Right now Hunter didn't have a choice. Laura's parents were his best, and at the moment, only source of information on Laura. And he needed information like he needed air.

Denise Mitchell grabbed a tissue from the box on the side table and wiped her tears away before finally standing up. She approached a small desk next to the window where several photo frames were arranged, most of them containing pictures of Laura at different stages of her life.

Roy didn't follow, instead slumping himself deeper into the sofa, as if he could somehow escape the moment. He made no attempt to wipe away his tears.

Denise turned to face Hunter, and she looked like a complete different woman from the one who'd greeted him at the door minutes earlier. Her eyes were horribly sad.

'How much did my daughter suffer, Detective?' Her voice was low and hoarse, her words coated in pain.

Their eyes locked for a long moment and Hunter saw a mixture of grief and anger burning deep inside her.

'The truth is that we don't know,' he finally replied.

With a trembling hand Denise brushed a strand of loose hair behind her right ear. 'Do you know why, Detective? Why would someone do something like that to anyone? Why would someone do it to my Laura? She was the sweetest girl you could ever meet.'

Hunter held her gaze firmly. 'I'm not gonna pretend I understand what sort of pain both of you are going through, Mrs. Mitchell. I'm also not gonna pretend this is easy. We're after the answers to those same questions and at the moment I can't tell you much because we don't have much. I'm here because I need your help to catch who did this. You knew Laura better than anyone.'

Denise's eyes never left Hunter's face, and he knew what her next question would be even before the words left her lips.

'Was she . . .' her voice croaked as she fought the tears catching in her throat yet again, '. . . raped?'

Roy Mitchell finally looked up. His stare went from his wife to Hunter.

There were very few things in life Hunter hated more than having to hide the truth from grieving parents, but without an autopsy on Laura's body, the best he could do was tell Denise and Roy that again he didn't know. As a psychologist, he knew that the uncertainty of never knowing the answer to such a question would torture them for the rest of their lives, putting their marriage, even their sanity, in jeopardy.

'No, Laura wasn't raped,' Hunter said with unflinching eyes and without an ounce of hesitation. Certain lies were worth telling.

Twenty-One

The uncomfortable moment stretched until Denise broke eye contact with Hunter, returning her stare to the photographs on the desk. She picked up a small silver frame.

'Laura was always talented, you know? Always very artistic.' She walked over and handed Hunter the frame. The photograph showed a little girl of about eight surrounded by crayons and tiny pots of watercolor paint. She looked so happy and her smile was so contagious, Hunter couldn't help but smile back, for a second forgetting that that little girl was gone and in the most horrifying manner possible.

'In school, every year without fail, she was awarded an honors certificate in arts,' Denise said proudly.

Hunter listened.

A sad grin threatened to part Denise's lips but she held it back. 'She only started painting professionally late on, but she'd always loved it. It was her refuge from all things bad. Every time she got hurt, she went back to the brushes. It was what cured her when she was a child.'

'Cured her?' Hunter's expression tightened and his gaze bounced between Denise and Roy.

'One day when Laura was eight, for no apparent reason, she had some sort of seizure,' Denise explained. 'She couldn't move or breathe properly, her eyes disappeared into her head and she almost choked to death. It petrified us.'

Roy nodded and then took over. 'We took her to four different doctors. Experts, they said.' He shook his head as if irritated. 'But none of them could diagnose what had happened. In fact, they didn't have a clue.'

'Did it happen again?'

'Yes, a few more times.' Denise again. 'She went through every possible examination, including CAT scans. They found nothing. No one knew what was wrong. No one could tell us what was triggering her seizures. About a week after her last episode, Laura picked up a brush for the first time. And that was it. The seizures never came back.' Denise touched the edge of her right eye with the tip of her fingers, trying to stop the new tear that had just formed from rolling down her cheek. 'No matter what anyone says, I know her painting is what made them stop. It's what made her well again.'

'You said her seizures made her choke?'

Denise nodded. 'It terrified us every time. She couldn't breathe. Her skin changed color.' She paused and looked away. 'She could've died so many times.'

'And the seizures simply stopped all together?'

'Yes,' Roy continued. 'Right after she started painting.'

Hunter got up and handed the frame back to Denise. 'Was Laura in a relationship?'

Denise let out a deep sigh. 'Laura didn't really get deeply involved with anyone. Another of her self-defense mechanisms.' She walked over to the bar by the large bookcase. 'If you read any of the articles about her and how she got her career started, you'll read about her pain of being cheated on by her fiancé. She found him in bed with another woman.

It destroyed her inside.' Denise poured herself a double dose of whiskey from a decanter and dropped two ice cubes in it. 'Would you like one?' She raised her glass.

Hunter's biggest passion was single malt Scotch whiskey, but unlike most, he knew how to appreciate its flavor and quality instead of simply getting drunk on it.

'No, thank you.'

'Roy?' She faced her husband.

He shook his head.

Denise shrugged, took a small sip and closed her eyes as the liquid traveled down her throat.

'To drown her pain, Laura went straight back to painting. Something that she hadn't done for several years. By chance, a gallery curator saw one of her canvases, and that was how her new career started. But not before she suffered a great deal.'

'From a broken heart?' Hunter said.

Denise nodded and looked away. 'Patrick was the one who insisted they moved in together after only four months,' she continued. 'He told Laura he couldn't stand being away from her, that he loved her more than anything. He was one of those who had a way with words. A charmer who usually got what he wanted. I'm sure you know the type. And Laura believed him. She fell desperately in love with him and his seductive charm.'

'You said his name is Patrick?'

Denise nodded. 'Patrick Barlett.'

Hunter wrote the name down in his notebook.

'Laura used to work in a bank. Patrick was a big investor. That's how they met. She found out about his affair because that day she felt unwell just after lunch,' Denise recalled. 'Something she'd eaten. Her boss told her to take the rest of the day off and she went home. Patrick was in their bed with his slut secretary or PA or something.' She shook her head. 'For someone who was supposed to be intelligent, you'd thought that he would've at least gone to a motel.' She chuckled nervously. 'So much for loving Laura more than anything, huh? That was only three months after they'd moved in together. Since then, relationships became a thing of the past for Laura. She had flings, affairs, but nothing serious.'

'Any recent ones?'

'No one Laura thought was worth mentioning.'

'So after Laura split from Patrick, was that it between them?'

'For her, yes.'

'And for him?'

'Ha!' Denise said with contempt. 'He never let go. He tried apologizing with flowers and gifts and phone calls and whatever else he could think of, but Laura didn't wanna know any more.'

'How long did he carry on all that for?'

'He never stopped.'

Hunter's eyebrows arched in surprise.

'He visited her exhibition last month and begged her to have him back yet again. She obviously told him where to go.'

'So he's been after her, asking for forgiveness and trying to get her back for . . . ?'

'Four years,' Roy confirmed. 'Patrick is not the sort of man who takes no for an answer. He's the sort of man who gets what he wants, no matter the price.'

Twenty-Two

The word *obsession* flashed at the back of Hunter's mind. Four years was more than enough time for most people to take the hint and move on. Denise told him how possessive and jealous Patrick used to be of Laura, and though during the time they were together he'd never been violent towards her, he did have a problem with his temper.

'Do you know if anyone other than you had an extra set of keys to Laura's apartment?'

Denise had another sip of her drink and thought about it for a minute before looking at Roy.

'Not that we know of,' he said.

'Laura never mentioned if she'd given the keys to anyone else?'

A firm shake of the head from Denise. 'Laura never allowed anyone to go into her apartment or her studio. Her work was very private to her. Even though she was successful, she never did it for the money. She painted for herself. It was a way of expressing what was going on inside her. She didn't even like exhibiting that much, and that's what most artists live for. As far as I know, she never took any dates back to her apartment. And she never, never got emotionally involved.'

'How about any close friends?'

'I was her closest friend.' A slight quiver came into her voice.

'Anyone other than family?'

'Painters are very lonely people, Detective. They spend most of their time by themselves, working on a piece. She had acquaintances, but no one she could really call a close friend.'

'She didn't keep in touch with any of her old school, university or work friends?'

Denise shrugged. 'Maybe, by phone or the odd drink, but I couldn't tell you who.' She paused. 'The only other person I can think of is Calvin Lange, the curator of the Daniel Rossdale Art Gallery. The person who kick-started her career. He was very fond of her, and she of him. They talked on the phone and met quite frequently.'

Roy nodded his agreement.

Hunter noted Calvin Lange's name down and his eyes returned to the photo frames on the wooden desk. 'Being a successful artist consequently means having fans, I suppose.'

Denise nodded proudly. 'Her work was admired and loved by many.'

'Did Laura ever mention any . . .' he searched for the right words, ' . . . *insistent* fans?'

'You mean . . . like a stalker?' Her voice faltered for an instant.

Hunter nodded.

Denise finished the rest of her whiskey in one gulp. 'I never thought of it, but she did mention something a few months ago.'

Hunter put down the picture frame he was holding and took a step in Denise's direction. 'What exactly did she tell you?'

Denise's gaze moved to a neutral point on the white Nepalese rug in the center of the room as her memory struggled to remember. 'Just that she'd started receiving some emails from someone who said he was in love with her work.'

'Did she ever show you any of these emails?'

'No.'

Hunter looked at Roy questioningly, who shook his head.

'Did she tell you what they said?'

Denise shook her head. 'Laura played it down, saying that it was just a fan being flattering of her work. But I did get the feeling that something about it had spooked her.'

Hunter wrote again in his notebook.

Denise moved closer, stopping at an arm's reach from Hunter. She looked into his eyes. 'How good are you and your team, Detective?'

Hunter frowned as if he hadn't understood the question.

'I wanna know if you can catch the sonofabitch who hurt my daughter and took her from me.' The grief in her voice was gone, substituted by undeniable anger. 'Don't tell me you're gonna do the best you can. The police are always doing the best they can, and their best is rarely good enough. I know you're gonna do your best, Detective. What I want you to do is look me in the eyes and tell me your best *will* be good enough. Tell me you'll catch this sonofabitch. And tell me you *will* make this sack of shit pay.'

Twenty-Three

Whitney Myers used the little gadget Leonid Kudrov had given her to activate the gates to the underground garage in Katia's apartment block. As she drove in, she immediately spotted Katia's torch red V6 convertible Mustang parked in one of the two spaces reserved for her penthouse apartment. Myers took the empty spot next to it, got out and placed her right palm on the Mustang's hood. Stone cold. Through the window, she checked its interior. All seemed fine. The car alarm light was blinking on the dashboard, indicating that it was active. Myers paused and allowed her eyes to roam the whole of the garage. The place was well lit, but there were many dark spots and corners where someone could hide. She noticed only one security camera, on the ceiling, facing the garage's entrance door.

Myers retrieved a pair of latex gloves from the box in the back seat of her car and rode the elevator up to the penthouse. There, she used the keys Leonid Kudrov had given her to gain access to Katia's apartment. No alarm. No signs of forced entry.

She softly closed the door behind her and paused for an instant. The living room was immense and decorated with a lot of style. Myers took her time looking around. Nothing seemed out of place. No signs of a fight or struggle.

She made her way to the spiral stairwell in the corner and moved up to the top floor. On the mezzanine landing, she found Katia's car keys in a tray on a tall chest of drawers crowded with family photographs.

Myers moved on down the corridor and entered Katia's bedroom. The walls were painted in pink and white, and there were enough stuffed toys on the perfectly made king-size bed to keep a crèche occupied for weeks. Myers checked the pillows on it. No smell. No one had slept in that bed last night.

Katia's two suitcases lay on the end of the bed seat. They were both open, but it looked like she hadn't had time to unpack them. The bedroom's balcony door was locked from the inside. Again, no signs of forced entry.

Myers moved on to the walk-in closet. Katia's collection of dresses, shoes and purses took her breath away.

'Wow.' She ran her hand down the front of a Giambattista Valli dress. 'A dream wardrobe,' she whispered. 'Katia had taste.'

In the en-suite bathroom, she noticed a hair towel was missing from the rail.

Myers moved out of the bedroom and into the next room along – Katia's practice den. The room was spacious but simple. A stereo system on a wooden sideboard, a couple of music stands, a mini fridge on the corner and a comfortable armchair pushed up against a wall. Katia's violin case was on a small coffee table by the door. Her priceless Lorenzo Guadagnini was lying inside it.

Leonid had told her that Katia was obsessed with her Guadagnini violin. If it weren't by her side, it'd be in her safe behind the large painting of Tchaikovsky on the wall, no exceptions.

Myers found the painting and checked the safe. Locked. Despite her previous confidence that Katia had just skipped town for a few days, she was getting a very bad feeling about this.

Myers returned downstairs and walked into the kitchen. It was as big as most studio apartments in Los Angeles. Black marble worktops and floors, polished steel appliances and enough pots and pans hanging from a center island that could give any small restaurant a run for their money.

The first thing Myers noticed was the missing hair towel from the en-suite bathroom upstairs. It was lying on the floor a few steps away from the fridge. She picked it up and brought it to her nose – a sweet, fruity smell that matched the bottle of designer hair conditioner in Katia's bathroom.

Myers looked around. There was a bottle of white wine on the breakfast table. No glasses were out. No corkscrew either. But what really caught her attention was the blinking red light on the answerphone at the far end of the worktop. She walked over and looked at the screen.

Sixty messages.

'I guess Katia is a popular woman.'

Myers pressed play.

'You have sixty new messages,' announced the prerecorded woman's voice. 'Message one.'

Absolute silence.

Myers frowned.

At the end of it there was a beep, and the machine moved on to the next message.

Silence.

And the next.

Silence.

And the next.

Silence.

'What the hell?' Myers took a seat on the barstool next to her. Her eyes settled on the large clock hanging from the wall above the door.

The messages kept on playing, not a whisper in any of them. After maybe the fifteenth or twentieth message, Myers picked up on something that made her skin crawl.

'No fucking way.' She pressed the stop button and then rewound the messages back to the very first one. She started from the beginning again. Her eyes returned to the clock above the door, and this time she let them play all the way to the fifty-ninth message. Silence in every single one of them, but the pattern she found told her that that silence had its own chilling meaning.

'I'll be goddamned.'

The last message started playing, and suddenly the silence was substituted by a long stretch of static, catching Myers by surprise and making her jump.

'Jesus . . .' She brought a hand up to her thumping heart. 'What the hell was that?' She rewound it, leaned closer to the machine, and played the message again.

Static noise blasted through the tiny answerphone speaker.

Myers moved even closer.

And what she heard, half-hidden by the static sound, sent a cold shiver down her entire body.

Twenty-Four

From the car, even before leaving the Mitchells' driveway, Hunter called the Office of Operations and asked them to gather all the information they could on Patrick Barlett, Laura's ex-fiancé. He'd just become a priority person of interest in the investigation.

Hunter disconnected and speed-dialed Garcia's number. He gave him the lowdown on everything he'd found out from the Mitchells and they met half an hour later at the entrance to an old warehouse turned apartment block in Lakewood, minutes away from Long Beach.

Hunter looked subdued but Garcia didn't have to ask. He knew that breaking the news to parents that their daughter had been the victim of a monstrous killer was already hard enough. But to have to tell them that they couldn't even give her a proper burial because the body had been blown to pieces was really the stuff of nightmares.

They rode the elevator up to the top floor in silence.

Laura Mitchell's apartment was an astonishing two thousand square feet loft conversion. The living area was simple but stylish with black leather furniture and sumptuous rugs. The kitchen was to the right of the entrance door and the sleeping area to the left – both modern, spacious and decorated with taste. But the bulk of the apartment was taken by her art studio.

Set at the far end and surrounded by large windows, including two skylights, it was filled with canvases of all sizes. The largest one was at least twelve foot by six.

'Wow, I always loved loft conversions,' Garcia said looking around. 'I could fit four of my apartment in here.' He paused and checked the door. 'No forced entry. You said that her parents told you that they last heard from her two and a half weeks ago?'

Hunter nodded. 'Laura and her mother were close. They called or met each other almost every other day. The last time they talked was on the 2nd of this month. A Wednesday. That was just a couple of days after the last night of Laura's latest exhibition in a gallery in West Hollywood. Her mother tried to contact her again on the 5th, and that's when alarm bells started ringing.'

'In between the 2nd and the 5th?' Garcia said, his eyes narrowing. 'That's around two weeks ago.'

Hunter drew a deep breath and his expression hardened. 'And if she was taken by the killer . . .' He didn't complete his thought, allowing the gravity of his suggestion to simply hang in the air.

'Shit!' Garcia said in realization. 'She was killed yesterday. If the same person who killed her also kidnapped her, it means he kept her hostage for two weeks.'

Hunter walked towards the sleeping area.

'Have Missing Persons been through here?'

'Yes, Detective Alex Peterson, from the West Bureau was in charge of the investigation,' Hunter confirmed, opening the drawer on the bedside table – a sleeping eye mask, two cherry-flavored Chapsticks, a small pen flashlight and a packet of Tic

Tacs. 'I've already got in touch with him and explained that the case has now escalated to a homicide investigation. He said he didn't have much, but he'll send us everything he's got. He found her laptop on the sofa in the living area. They've processed it but got only her fingerprints.'

'How about the files in the hard drive?'

Hunter tilted his head to one side. 'It's password protected. The computer is with the Information Technology Division, but there was no urgent request until I talked to them a few minutes ago, so nothing yet.'

They checked her wardrobe – several dresses, a few of them designer, jeans, T-shirts, blouses, jackets and a substantial collection of shoes and handbags. In the kitchen Hunter checked the fridge, the cupboards, and the trash can. Nothing out of the ordinary. They moved to the living area and Hunter spent a few minutes looking through the photos and the book titles on the shelf unit next to the sofa before making his way into the studio.

Laura Mitchell was a lyrical abstractionist painter, and her work consisted mostly of collections of colors and shapes loosely applied to canvases. The studio floor was littered by a rainbow of paint splashes – almost a work of modern art in itself. Tens of finished paintings were organized against the west wall. Spread around the main working space were three canvas stands, two of them covered by once-white sheets. The third one, occupying a center position, held a thirty-six-by-twenty-four-inch semi-completed painting. Hunter studied it for a few moments before lifting the sheets from the other two stands. Both paintings also appeared unfinished.

Garcia took his time looking through some of the completed canvases resting against the wall.

'I never understood modern art, you know.'

'What do you mean?' Hunter asked.

'Look at this painting.' He stepped out of the way so Hunter could take a look. It was another thirty-six-by-twenty-four-inch canvas displaying pastel green and orange colors surrounded by vibrant red and a touch of blue and yellow. To Garcia the colors seemed to have no co-ordination.

'What about it?'

'Well, this is named "Lost men in a forest of giant trees".'

Hunter raised an eyebrow.

'Exactly. I see no men, there is no forest and nothing on it resembles a tree.' He shook his head. 'Go figure.'

Hunter smiled and walked over to the large window on the left of the studio. Locked from the inside. He looked around the studio again before frowning and returning to the bedroom where he rechecked Laura's wardrobe.

'Did you find something?' Garcia asked while he watched Hunter move purposefully into the bathroom.

'Not yet.' He searched through the dirty laundry basket.

'What are you looking for?'

'Her painting clothes.'

'What?'

'In her living room you'll find three photos of Laura taken while she was working. In all three she's wearing the same old greenish shirt and track pants, both covered in paint splashes.' He checked behind the door. 'And an old pair of tennis shoes. Have you seen them anywhere?'

Instinctively Garcia looked around. 'No.' Confusion started to settle in. 'Why do you need her clothes?'

'I don't, I'm just trying to establish that they are missing.' Hunter returned to the studio and motioned towards the easel holding the uncovered and unfinished painting. 'It looks like Laura was last working on this canvas. Now check this out.' He indicated a paint palette thick with crusts of different dried colors. It was casually lying on a wooden unit next to the stand. To its right was a jar containing four different-sized brushes. The water in the jar was muddy with oil paint residue. Resting on the palette, and now sticking to it as if glued, was another brush. Its tip was dry, hard and caked in bright yellow paint. 'Now look around her studio,' Hunter continued. 'She seemed to have been pretty organized. But even if she wasn't, painters don't just simply leave the brush they're working with laying around thick with paint to dry out. It would be just as easy for her to drop it into the cleaning jar.'

Garcia thought for a moment. 'Something caught her attention while she was working, maybe a sound, a knock on the door . . .' he said, following Hunter's line of thought. 'She put the brush down to go check it out.'

'And the probable reason why we can't find her working clothes and shoes is because she was wearing them when she was abducted.'

Hunter paused next to several finished canvases arranged against the back wall. Something about the long one on the far right called his attention. It displayed an astonishing gradient variation moving from yellow at one end to red at the other. He took a few steps back and tilted his head sideways. The canvas was leaning tall against the wall at a sixty-five-degree angle, but it was supposed to be looked at horizontally, not vertically. From a distance, the color combination became almost hypnotic. Laura certainly had talent and an astounding understanding of colors, but that wasn't what had caught Hunter's eye.

He approached the painting, crouched down next to it, and studied the floor around the canvas for a moment before looking behind it.

'Now *this* is interesting.'

Twenty-Five

Whitney Myers got to her office in Long Beach to find Frank Cohen, her assistant and expert researcher, flipping through computer printouts. He looked up when Myers closed the door behind her.

'Hey there,' he said, pushing his glasses up his long and pointy nose. 'Any luck?' He knew Myers had spent most of the day going over Katia's penthouse apartment in West Hollywood.

'A few clues.' She dumped her bag on the chair behind her glass-top desk and reached for the jug of freshly brewed coffee that perfumed the entire office. 'Whoever abducted Katia . . .' she poured herself a cup and stirred in a teaspoon of brown sugar, '. . . did it from inside her apartment.'

Cohen leaned forward.

'Just as her father said, I found the towel in the kitchen. The smell on it was very faint, but it matched the hair conditioner in her bathroom upstairs. Both of her suitcases were at the end of her bed.'

'Suitcases?' Cohen frowned.

Myers walked to the large window that overlooked West Ocean Boulevard. 'Katia Kudrov had just returned from her tour with the Los Angeles Philharmonic. She had been away for two months,' she explained. 'She didn't even have time to unpack.'

'Did you find her purse, cell phone?'

Myers shook her head. 'Only her car keys, as her father had said.'

'Any signs of forced entry?'

'None. All locks intact. Doors, windows, balcony.'

'Struggle?'

'None, unless you count a towel on the kitchen floor and a bottle of white wine sitting out of the fridge as one.'

Cohen twisted his lips from side to side. 'Was she in a relationship?'

'Not with anyone who'd be waiting for her in her apartment if that's what you're thinking. Katia had started seeing the Philharmonic's new conductor, a guy called Phillip Stein. Apparently he was just a fling, though, nothing serious.'

'Did he feel the same?'

'Oh, he fell for her. Her father said it's always just a fling with her. Katia doesn't do heavy relationships. Music is her real love.'

Cohen pulled a face. 'Deep.'

'Katia and this Phillip guy were on the same tour together, and before you ask, there were no signs that he'd been home with her that night. She broke everything off a few days ago, just before their last concert.'

'I bet he didn't like that at all.'

'Not one bit.'

'So where is he now? Better yet, where was he on the night they got back to LA?'

'In Munich.'

'Munich, Germany?'

A quick nod. 'He was *that* upset. Never came back with the Philharmonic after their last concert. Flew directly to Germany. That's where his family is from. He couldn't have done it. No matter how much motive he had.'

Cohen paused and tapped the top of his pen against his teeth. 'Aren't those flashy apartment blocks in West Hollywood packed with security – CCTV cameras and all? If someone took this Katia woman from her apartment, it must've been picked up somewhere.'

'You would've thought so, wouldn't you? You're right, there's a camera inside the elevator, two at reception, one on the penthouse landing and one in the underground car park. Conveniently, there was a power surge that blew the fuse box on the night Katia returned from her tour. All the cameras were down for a few hours. We've got no footage.'

'Nothing at all?'

'Nothing. Her father never thought to ask the building's concierge about cameras. That's why he never mentioned anything when we met.'

Cohen pulled a face.

'I know. This thing screams professional kidnapping, doesn't it?'

'Has anyone got in touch with the family yet? Ransom request?'

Myers shook her head and returned to her desk. 'Nothing, and that's what gets me. Everything so far points to a professional job. Professionals are always after money. Katia and her family are rich enough for the ransom to be in the millions. She's been gone for over forty-eight hours and nothing, no communication of any sort.'

Cohen tapped the pen against his teeth again. He'd been working with Myers for long enough to know that in a professional kidnapping, communications between the kidnappers and the ransom party were usually established quickly, if possible, before the party had a chance to involve the authorities. If the abductor wasn't after money, then

Cohen knew they weren't dealing with a kidnapper, they were dealing with a predator.

'But this gets worse,' Myers said, sitting back in her chair. 'Our kidnapper likes to play.'

Cohen stopped with the pen tapping. 'What do you mean?'

'There was an answerphone in her kitchen.'

'Yes, and . . . ?'

Myers allowed the suspense to stretch. 'The machine was full to capacity. There were sixty new messages.'

Cohen's left eye twitched. 'Sixty?'

Myers nodded. 'I listened to every single one of them.' She paused and took a sip of her coffee. 'Not a word, zip, absolute silence, not even heavy breathing.'

'They were *all* blank?'

'It sounded that way. I thought there was something wrong with the phone or the machine, until I got to the last message.'

'And . . . ?' Cohen's eager eyes widened.

'Have a listen yourself.' Myers searched her handbag for her digital voice recorder and tossed it over to Cohen.

He quickly placed it in front of him on his desk, readjusted his glasses on his nose and pressed play. Several silent seconds went by. Then a low-pitched white noise oozed out of the tiny speaker. It lasted a few seconds.

'Static?'

'That's what it sounds like at first, doesn't it?' Myers replied. 'But listen again – like you mean it this time.'

Cohen reached for the voice recorder, rewound it, brought it close to his right ear, and listened carefully to it one more time – very attentively this time.

His blood ran cold.

'What the fuck?'

Covered up by the static-like sound there was something else, something that sounded like a whisper. Cohen listened to it a couple more times. There was no denying it; the undecipherable murmur was definitely there.

'Is somebody saying something or just trying to catch his breath?'

'Not a clue.' Myers shrugged. 'I did exactly what you just did. Listened to it over and over again. I'm still none the wiser. But I'll tell you something. If the intention of whoever left that message was to scare Katia, that would've done it. It sounds like a poltergeist ready to come through the phone. It freaked the hell out of me.'

'You think this could be the abductor's voice?'

'Either that or someone with a very sick sense of humor.'

'I'll get this to Gus at the studio.' Cohen jiggled the voice recorder in his hand. 'If we transfer this into his voice analyzing program, we could clean it up and slow it down. I'm sure we'll decipher whatever it is that he's saying. If he *is* saying something, that is.'

'Great, do it.'

'Does her father know about this?' Cohen knew that Myers was in constant contact with Leonid Kudrov, but with nothing of significance to report back, it was fast getting frustrating.

'Not yet. I'll wait and see if Gus can make something out of it before giving Mr. Kudrov another call.' Myers ran her hand through her hair. 'Now are you ready for the next twist?'

Cohen's eyes shot in Myers direction. 'There's more?'

'When I was listening to the messages, for no specific reason, I kept looking at the clock in Katia's kitchen.'

'OK.'

'Suddenly, I realized that there was a common factor that linked all of those messages.'

'What factor?'

'A time signature.'

'A what?'

'I know it sounds crazy, but I went over every message twice. It took me a while.' She moved to the front of her desk and leaned back against its edge. 'They're all twelve seconds long.'

Cohen's eyes narrowed. 'Twelve seconds? All sixty of them?'

'Precisely. Not a second more, not a second less. Even the last message with the noise and the creepy murmur – twelve seconds exactly.'

'And that's not a fault with the machine?'

'Nope.'

'Did anyone set the message recording time to only twelve seconds?'

Myers looked at Cohen inquisitively. 'I didn't even know you could do that.'

'I'm not sure you can, but I'm just trying to cover all angles.'

'Even if that's possible, who'd set a message recording time to only twelve seconds?'

Cohen had to agree. 'OK,' he said as his stare returned to the voice recorder. 'Now that's officially messed up, and I'm officially intrigued. There's gotta be a meaning to it. No fucking way the twelve seconds thing is a coincidence.'

'No fucking way,' Myers agreed. 'Now we're just going to have to find out what it means.'

Twenty-Six

'What?' Garcia asked, facing Hunter and moving towards the canvas. 'What have you found?'

'We need to get the Forensics guys in here, now.' He paused and looked up at his partner. 'Someone was hiding behind this canvas.'

Garcia crouched down next to Hunter.

'Look at this.' Hunter pointed to the floor just behind the canvas base. 'Can you see the dust marks?'

Garcia squinted as he moved his face so close to the floor it looked like he was about to kiss it. Moments later he saw it.

Since it had been placed there, regular house dust had settled on the floor around the canvas edge. Garcia saw a long, dragging dust mark.

'The canvas was moved forward,' he finally admitted.

'Enough for a person to get behind it,' Hunter noted.

Garcia bit his bottom lip. 'Laura could've moved it forward herself.'

'She could've, but check this out.' Hunter pointed to a spot further behind the canvas, closer to the wall.

Garcia squinted again. 'What am I supposed to be looking at?'

Hunter reached for his pen flashlight. 'Look again.' He handed it to Garcia.

Garcia directed the light beam to the spot Hunter had indicated. This time it didn't take him long to see it.

'I'll be damned.'

Just a few inches from the wall, he identified the faint outline of foot imprints left in the dust. Clear indications that someone had been standing there.

'Look at it one more time,' Hunter said. 'See anything that strikes you as odd?'

Garcia returned his attention to the imprints. 'Nope, but you obviously have, Robert. What am I missing?'

'The amount of variation on the imprints.'

Garcia looked for a third time. 'There's barely any.'

'Exactly. Isn't that strange?'

It finally clicked. When standing in a confined space for even a small amount of time, it was natural for anyone to fidget and shift his or her weight from foot to foot, to try to move into a more comfortable position every time the old one becomes uncomfortable. That shifting should, in theory, leave behind several different onionskin imprints. There were none. And that could only mean two things – either the killer didn't wait long, or – and the thing that really bothered Hunter – the killer was preternaturally patient and disciplined.

Hunter's cell phone rang in his pocket.

'Detective Hunter.'

'Detective, it's Pam from Operations,' said the voice at the end of the line. 'I've emailed you all the information we managed to get on Patrick Barlett. At the moment he's out of town.'

'Out of town?'

'He's been away at a conference in Dallas since Tuesday evening. He's flying back tomorrow – mid-afternoon. Everything checked out.'

'OK, thanks, Pam.'

Hunter disconnected and returned his attention to the space behind the large canvas and the faint foot imprints. A strong and fast perpetrator could have covered the distance between there and where Laura would have been standing in a flash, too fast for her to react. But Hunter didn't believe her attacker had surprised her in that way. If he had, there would have been some sort of a struggle, and there were no such signs anywhere. If someone had crept up behind her and sedated her in some way, Laura would have no doubt dropped her paint palette and brush, not placed it on the unit next to the stand. The surrounding floor area where Laura would have stood while working on her canvas was covered in small speckles and splashes of paint, not blotches and smudges caused by a palette hitting the ground.

'Pass me the flashlight, Carlos.'

Garcia handed it to him and Hunter moved its beam to a point on the brick directly behind the large canvas.

'Something else?' Garcia asked.

'Not sure yet, but brick walls are notorious for pulling fibers out of fabrics if you lean against them.' Hunter kept inching the beam up. When he got to a point about six feet from the floor, he paused and moved forward, stopping just millimeters from the wall, careful not to disrupt the dust. 'I think we might have something.'

He reached for his phone and dialed the number for the Forensics team.

Twenty-Seven

West Hollywood is famous for its nightlife, celebrity culture and diverse atmosphere. Themed bars, chic restaurants, futuristic and exotic nightclubs, art galleries, designer boutiques, sports centers, and the most varied selection of live music venues will keep you entertained from sunset to sunset. Informally referred to as 'WeHo' by most Angelinos, the word is that if you can't get your kicks in West Hollywood, then you're probably already dead.

It was just past 6:00 p.m. when Hunter and Garcia got to the Daniel Rossdale Art Gallery in Wilshire Boulevard. The building was small, but stylish. Smoked glass together with concrete-and-metal frames were used to create a pyramid-style structure that could be considered a sculpture on its own.

Calvin Lange, the gallery's curator and Laura Mitchell's closest friend, had agreed to a meeting. Laura's last exhibition had been at his gallery.

Hunter and Garcia were shown to Calvin Lange's office by an attractive and elegantly dressed assistant.

Lange was sitting behind his desk, but stood up as both detectives entered the room. He was a wiry, sandy-haired, smiling man in his early-thirties.

'Gentlemen,' he said as he firmly shook their hands.

'You said over the phone that this was about Laura Mitchell?' He indicated the two leather chairs in front of his desk and waited for both detectives to have a seat. 'Have there been any problems with any of her paintings purchased from this gallery?' He paused and quickly studied both detectives' expressions. Then he remembered Laura's mother's phone call to him two weeks ago. 'Is she OK?'

Hunter filled him in.

Calvin Lange's eyes flicked from Hunter to Garcia and then back to Hunter. His lips parted but no words came out. For an instant he looked like a little kid who'd just been told Santa Claus was a con. Still in shocked silence, he approached the minibar built into the tall wooden unit on the north wall, and with a trembling hand reached for a glass. 'Can I offer you a drink?' His voice quivered.

'We're fine,' Hunter said, taking in all his movements.

Lange poured himself a large glass of Cognac and quickly took a mouthful. That seemed to bring some of the color back to his face.

'I was told by Mrs. Mitchell that you were probably Laura's closest friend outside the family,' Hunter said.

'Maybe . . .' Lange shook his head as if disoriented. 'I'm not sure. Laura was a very private person, but we got on well. She was . . . fantastic: funny, talented, intelligent, beautiful . . .'

'She exhibited in this gallery not so long ago, is that right?' Garcia asked.

Lange told them that Laura's exhibition had run from the 1st to the 28th February and it'd been a tremendous success – very well attended, and all of the twenty-three pieces she'd exhibited had been sold. Laura had only been present for about two hours on the opening and closing nights, and Lange said she hadn't seemed at all upset, worried or anxious at either of them.

'Was that the last time you saw her?' Hunter asked.

'Yes.'

'And did you use to keep in contact regularly? Phone calls, texts, that sort of thing?'

Lange moved his head from side to side. 'Not that regularly. We usually chatted on the phone two maybe three times a month. It really depended on how busy we both were. Sometimes we did lunch, dinner or drinks together, but again, nothing regular.'

'Mrs. Mitchell also told me that her ex-fiancé was here on her closing night,' Hunter said.

Lange's eyes shot in Hunter's direction.

'Do you remember seeing him talking to Laura at all?'

Lange took another sip of his Cognac and Hunter noticed his hands had started shaking again.

'Yes, I'd forgotten all about that. He'd had a little too much to drink. He really upset her that night,' Lange recalled. 'They were by the staircase at the back of the gallery, away from the main floor and the crowd. I was looking for her because I wanted to introduce her to an important buyer from Switzerland. When I finally found her, I went over and that's when I noticed she looked unhappy. As I joined them, he walked away angrily.'

'Did she tell you what happened?'

'No, she didn't want to talk about it. She went straight into the ladies' room and came out again about ten minutes later, but before doing so, she asked me to get him out of here, before he made a scene with the guests.'

'A scene?' Hunter questioned. 'Did she tell you why?'

Lange shook his head. 'But I sensed it was because he was jealous.'

Garcia craned his neck. 'Jealous of whom? Did Laura have a date with her that night?'

'No, but I saw her talking to someone earlier that night. And I know they swapped phone numbers because she told me.'

'Could you describe him?' Garcia asked.

Lange bit his lower lip and looked at a distant nothing as if considering something. 'I can do better than that. I think I might have a picture of him.'

Twenty-Eight

Calvin Lange lifted his right index finger at both detectives, asking them for a minute, and reached for the phone on his desk.

'Nat, we still have the photos from Laura Mitchell's exhibition, right? . . . Great, can you bring your laptop into my office, please . . . Yeah, now is good.' Lange put the phone down and explained that they always photographed and sometimes videoed their exhibitions, especially the artists' nights. The photos were used for brochures, advertisement campaigns and their own website.

'How about your CCTV footage?' Hunter asked. He'd noticed six cameras in total on their way up to Lange's office.

Lange gave him an embarrassed headshake. 'We recycle hard drive space every two weeks.'

There was a soft knock on the door and the same assistant who had guided Hunter and Garcia into Lange's office earlier stepped into the room carrying a white laptop.

'You've met Nat,' Lange said, motioning her to his desk.

'Not properly,' she replied with the same smile she'd given them earlier. Her eyes stayed on Hunter.

'Natalie Foster is my assistant,' Lange explained, 'but she's a great photographer and very good with computers. She's also our webmaster.'

Natalie shook both detectives' hands. 'Please, call me Nat.'

'These are detectives from the Homicide Division,' Lange told her.

Natalie's smile quickly slipped from her face. 'Homicide?'

Hunter explained the reason for their visit and Natalie's entire body tensed. Her eyes searched for Lange's and Hunter could tell her mind had flooded with questions.

'We need to take a look at the photographs from Laura's exhibition, Nat,' Lange said.

It took a few seconds for his words to register. 'Umm . . . yes, of course.' She placed the laptop on Lange's desk and fired it up. As the computer booted, an anxious silence hovered over the room. Natalie typed in a password and scrolled a trembling finger across the laptop's mouse pad as she searched for the pictures directory.

Hunter grabbed a small bottle of water from the drinks cabinet. 'Here, have some of this, it'll help.' He poured some into a glass with ice and brought it over to her.

'Thank you.' She forced a smile before taking two large sips and returning her attention to the computer.

A few more mouse clicks later and Natalie set the picture display to full screen.

'OK, here they are.'

The first picture was a wide shot of the main gallery floor on the opening night of Laura Mitchell's exhibition. It looked full to capacity.

'How many people were here that night?' Hunter asked.

'About a hundred and fifty.' Lange looked at Natalie for confirmation. She nodded. 'And there were a few more outside waiting to get in.'

'Entry wasn't by invitation only?' Garcia asked.

'Not always, it depends on the artist,' Lange replied. 'Most, especially the more famous and egocentric ones, like to make their launch nights invitation- and RSVP-only.'

'But not Laura.'

'Not Laura,' Lange confirmed. 'She wasn't like most artists who think they're God's gift. She insisted her exhibitions were open to everyone and anyone. Even on artists' nights.'

Most of the photographs were of Laura smiling and chatting to people. She was usually surrounded by a group of four or five. A few of the photographs showed her posing in front of a canvas or with a fan. She certainly was a very attractive woman. Hunter could hardly make the connection with the crime-scene photos he'd seen.

'Wait,' Lange said, stepping closer. His eyes squinted as he studied the photograph that had just appeared on the screen. 'I think that's him – the guy who swapped numbers with Laura.' He pointed to someone standing at the back of the frame. He was tall with short dark hair and was dressed in a dark suit, but his face was partially obscured by a waiter carrying a tray of drinks. Natalie used the zoom feature at the bottom of the screen to enlarge it, but it didn't make the man's face any clearer. He looked to be around the same age as Laura Mitchell.

'Have any of you seen him before?' Hunter asked.

Lange shook his head, but Natalie looked uncertain. 'I think I have, at one of our previous exhibitions.'

'Are you sure? Can you remember which one?'

She took a moment. 'I can't remember which exhibition it was, but he looks familiar.'

'Are you sure you saw him here in the gallery? Not in a coffee shop, restaurant, nightclub . . . ?'

Natalie searched her memory again. 'No, I think it was here at the gallery.'

'OK, if you see him again, or you remember which exhibition, you call me, all right? If he comes in, don't try to talk to him, just call me.'

Natalie nodded and moved on with the pictures.

'Stop,' Lange said again a few pictures later. This time he indicated another tall, well-built man standing just a couple of paces behind Laura. He was looking at her as if she was the only person in the room. 'That's her ex-fiancé. I think his name is . . .'

'Patrick Barlett,' Hunter confirmed, once again enlarging the picture. 'We'll need a copy of all these files.'

'Sure,' Natalie said. 'I can burn them onto a CD for you before you leave.'

Just a few pictures from the end of the archive, Lange told Natalie to stop again. There he was. The tall, mysterious, phone-swapping stranger. He was standing right next to Laura. But this time he was looking straight at the camera.

Twenty-Nine

Small but very well equipped, Gustavo Suarez's studio was set in the basement of a single-story house in Jefferson Park, South Los Angeles.

Gus had been an audio engineer for twenty-seven years, and with a perfect-pitch ear it took a single note from any instrument for him to immediately place it on a music scale. But his understanding of sounds went much beyond musical notes. He was fascinated by their vibrations and modulations, what created them and how they could be altered by location and the environment. Because of his knowledge, gifted ear and experience, Gus had been called upon by the LAPD on several occasions where some sort of sound, noise or audio recording played a critical part in an ongoing investigation.

Whitney Myers had met Gus for the first time through the FBI, while training to be a negotiator. Their paths crossed again soon after, when she became a detective for the LAPD. As a private investigator, Myers had required Gus' expertize on only two other occasions.

Gus was forty-seven years old, with a shaved head and more tattoos than a Hell's Angel. But despite the intimidating look, he was as docile as a puppy. He opened the door to Frank Cohen and was instantly disappointed.

'Where's Whitney?' he asked, looking past Cohen's shoulders.

'Sorry, Gus, it's only me. She's tied up.'

'Damn, man. I got my best shirt on.' He ran his hands down the front of his freshly ironed dark blue shirt. 'Even splashed on some cologne and all.'

'Splashed?' Cohen took a step back and covered his nose. 'You smell like you bathed in the stuff. What the hell is it, Old Spice?'

Gus frowned. 'I *like* Old Spice.'

'Yeah, no shit. More than most by the smell of it.'

Gus disregarded his comment and guided him down to the basement and into his studio.

'So how can I help you guys this time? Whitney didn't tell me much over the phone.' He took a seat in his engineer's chair and wheeled himself closer to his sound desk.

Cohen handed him Myers' digital recorder. 'We got this from an answering machine.'

Gus brought the device closer to his right ear and pressed play. As the strange sound came through, he reached for the bowl of Skittles next to the recording console. Gus had a thing for Skittles, they helped him relax and concentrate.

'We think there's a voice, or a whisper, or something hidden in the middle of all that static,' Cohen offered.

Gus swirled a bunch of Skittles from his right cheek to his left one. 'It's not hidden, it's just there,' he announced, playing the recording from the beginning again. 'Definitely someone's voice.' He got up, walked over to a cabinet and retrieved a thin cable that looked like iPod headphones. 'Let me hook this thing up so we can have a better listen.'

Through the studio speakers, the sound was louder, the out-of-breath whisper more evident, but not clearer.

'Is he using a device to conceal his voice?' Cohen asked, stepping closer.

Gus shook his head. 'It doesn't sound like it. This is pure static. Interference caused by another radio wave electronic device or a bad signal. Whoever made the call was probably standing next to something, or on a spot affected by a signal dip. I'd say the static noise was unintentional.'

'Can you clean it up?'

'Of course.' Gus smiled smugly and turned on the computer monitor to his left. As the recording played again, audio lines vibrated animatedly on the screen. Gus had another handful of Skittles while watching them attentively.

'OK, let's tweak this baby a little.' He clicked a few buttons and slid some faders on the digital equalizer inside the application on his screen. The static noise was reduced by at least 90 per cent. The out-of-breath whisper now came through much clearer. Gus reached for a pair of professional headphones and listened to the whole thing again. 'OK, now *this* was deliberate.'

'What was?' Cohen craned his neck in Gus' direction.

'The forced whisper. Whoever's voice this is, it isn't naturally hoarse and whispering soft. And *that* is clever.'

'In what way?'

'Every human voice travels along certain frequencies that are part of one's personal identity, as identifiable as fingerprints or the retina. They have certain high, low and medium tones that don't vary, even if you try to disguise your voice by naturally altering it in any way, like a falsetto or baritone or whatever. With the right equipment, we can still identify those tones and match them to someone's voice.'

'You have that equipment, right?'

Gus looked offended. 'Of course I've got that equipment.

Look around. I've got whatever you need for voice identification.'

'So what's the problem?'

Gus leaned back in his chair and let out a long sigh. 'I'll show you. Place the tips of your fingers just below your Adam's apple.'

'What?'

'Like this.' Gus placed the tips of two of his fingers on his throat.

Cohen pulled a face.

'Just do it.'

Reluctantly Cohen copied Gus' movement.

'Now, say something, anything, but try to disguise it in some way . . . high, low, gravel, child's voice, it doesn't matter. When you do, you'll feel your vocal cords vibrate. Trust me.'

Cohen looked at Gus with a you've-gotta-be-kidding-me face.

'Go on.'

He finally conceded and, putting on an extremely high-pitched voice, recited the opening three lines of *Othello*.

'Wow, profound. I never took you for a Shakespeare fan,' Gus said, suppressing a smile. 'Did you feel them vibrate?'

Cohen nodded.

'When we have any sort of vocal cord vibration, then we have those distinct frequencies I told you about. Now, do the same thing but go for a *very* soft whisper instead.'

Cohen repeated the same three lines in the most delicate whisper he could muster. His eyes narrowed as he looked back at Gus. 'No vibration.'

'Exactly,' Gus confirmed. 'That's because the sounds aren't being formed by your vocal cords, but by a combination of the air being exhaled from your lungs, and your mouth and tongue movements.'

'Like whistling?'

'Like whistling. No vibration, no identifiable frequencies.'

'Smart motherfucker.'

'That's what I said.'

'So this is the best we can do? We still don't know what he's saying.'

Gus smiled cynically. 'You don't pay me the big bucks just to give you back a tape with undecipherable whispering, do you? What I mean is that because he forced his own voice into a slow, dragging whisper, we won't be able to clean it or alter it back to its original pitch. So even if you have a suspect, it will be very hard to get a voice match from this. And I'm pretty sure he knew that.'

'But you'll be able to alter it enough so we can understand what he's saying, right?'

A confident smile came back from Gus. 'Watch my magic.' He went back to the digital equalizer, twisted a few more buttons and slid some more faders before loading a pitch shifter onto a separate screen. He placed a small section of the audio recording into a constant loop and worked on it for a few minutes. 'Oh, hello,' he said, frowning.

'What? What?'

Gus automatically reached for the Skittles. 'We've got something else. Some sort of faint hissing noise right in the background.'

'Hissing?'

'Yeah, something like a frying pan or maybe rain against a distant window.' He listened to it again. His eyes went back to one of his monitors and he pulled a face. 'Its frequency is very similar to the static noise. And that messes things up a little.'

'Can't you do something with all this?' Cohen nodded at all the equipment in the studio.

'Is today stupid-question day? Of course I can, but to properly identify it I'll have to run it against my library of sounds.' Gus started clicking away on his computer. 'All that can take a while.'

Cohen checked his watch and let out a deflated breath.

'Relax, that won't affect me cleaning up the whispering voice. That'll take me no time at all.' Gus went back to his buttons and faders. A minute later he seemed satisfied. 'I think I got it.' He pressed play and rolled his chair away from the mixing desk.

The same whispering voice Cohen and Myers had tried so hard to decipher poured out of the loudspeakers, as clear as daylight.

Cohen's jaw dropped as he looked at Gus.

'Motherfucker.'

Thirty

The first thing Hunter did when he and Garcia got back to Parker Center was get a copy of all the photographs taken at Laura Mitchell's exhibition to Brian Doyle, the IT Unit supervisor at ITD. Hunter knew that potentially every single person in those pictures was a suspect, but his immediate interest was in identifying the stranger who'd swapped phone numbers with Laura. The photograph Hunter had flagged showed a clear enough image of the stranger's face to allow Doyle to blow it up and run it against the unified police database.

'That laptop you called about earlier,' Doyle said as he transferred all of the pictures to his hard drive, 'the one that was sent to us by Missing Persons about two weeks ago, belonging to . . .' He started searching his messy desk.

'Laura Mitchell,' Hunter confirmed. 'That's her in those pictures.'

'Oh, OK. Anyway, we bypassed her password.'

'What? Already?'

'We're fantastic, what can I say?' Doyle smiled and Hunter pulled a face. 'We ran a simple algorithm application against it. Her password was just a combination of the first few letters of her family name and her date of birth. Now, you said you needed to have a look at her emails?'

'That's right. Her mother said she'd received a few fan emails that'd scared her.'

'Well, that won't be easy, I'm afraid. The email application on her computer was never used,' Doyle explained, 'which means she didn't download emails, she simply read them online. We checked the computer registry, and at least there she was smart. She never said "yes" when the operating system asked her if she wanted the computer to remember her password every time she logged onto her email online. Her Internet history was also automatically deleted every ten days.'

'Her email password ain't the same as her computer's?'

A quick headshake.

'How about this algorithm application you ran on her PC?'

'It won't work online. Internet security against email account attacks has gotten a lot tougher over the years. All the major email service providers lock you out for several hours, sometimes indefinitely if you try a certain number of incorrect passwords.' Doyle shook his head again. 'Also, if she didn't keep these emails in her account, I mean, if she deleted them after she read them, which is probable since you said they scared her, then the chances of retrieving the full message is basically zero. Unless you find the email provider where the message originated from, the best you gonna get are fragments. And you'll have to go straight to her provider – Autonet. We can't do shit from here. You know what that means, right? Warrants and court orders and what have you. Plus, you can be searching for days, weeks . . . who knows . . . and still get zip.'

Hunter ran a hand over his face.

'I have people going over the rest of the files on her hard drive now. I'll let you know if we come across anything.'

Thirty-One

Whitney Myers stood still, staring at the computer screen and the audio lines as they vibrated like electrified worms. Cohen had just loaded the digital recording Gus had given him onto his computer. The once jumbled whisper she'd retrieved from Katia Kudrov's answering machine was now as clear as daylight.

'YOU TAKE MY BREATH AWAY . . .' Pause. 'WELCOME HOME, KATIA. I'VE BEEN WAITING FOR YOU. I GUESS IT'S FINALLY TIME WE MET.'

The recording was on an endless loop, playing through Cohen's loudspeakers. After the fifth time, Myers finally tore her eyes away from the screen and hit the Esc key.

'Gus said this is actually his voice, there's no electronic device disguising it?'

Cohen nodded. 'But he was clever. He used his own whisper to alter it. If he's ever caught, we'll never get a voice match. At least not with this recording.'

Myers stepped back from Cohen's desk, lightly running two fingertips against her top lip. She always did that when she was thinking. She knew she had to play the recording to Leonid Kudrov when she met him at his house in two hours' time. She had no doubt it would drive terror into an already petrified heart.

'Do you still have my Dictaphone with all the sixty messages?' she asked, returning to her desk and flipping through her notebook.

'Yep, right here.'

'OK, play the last message again.' She paused. 'Actually, just *after* the last message. What I'm interested in is the electronic answering machine voice announcing the time the message was left.'

'Eight forty-two in the evening,' Cohen replied automatically.

Myers' eyebrows rose.

'I listened to it so many times it's ctched on my brain,' he explained.

'You're sure?'

'Positive.'

Myers' eyes returned to her notebook. 'According to Katia's father, he called his daughter from his cell phone at eight fifty-three that night. The call lasted four minutes and twelve seconds.'

'She answered that call, didn't she?'

Myers nodded.

'But eleven minutes earlier the answering machine picked it up. Was she out?'

Myers flipped a page. 'Nope, the building's concierge said that she arrived at around eight o'clock. He took her suitcases up to the penthouse for her.' Myers' fingers returned to her upper lip for an instant. 'Of course. The towel on the kitchen floor. Katia must've been in the shower.' She quickly checked her notes again. 'Shit! Remember I told you we have no CCTV footage from the cameras in her building because there was a power surge that blew the fuse box.'

'Yep.'

'Well, the cameras went down just before eight.'

Cohen cleared his throat as he leaned forward. 'And we already know there's no fucking way that was a coincidence.'

'That means the kidnapper knew *exactly* the time she'd be arriving home.' Myers paused and fought back an uneasy feeling. 'He was already waiting for her inside her apartment when she got there. That's why he says welcome home. He *knew* she was home.'

Cohen's whole expression changed. 'So he made that last call from *inside* her apartment?'

'It looks that way.'

'Why? Why make the call if he was already there?'

'I'm not sure. Fear factor? Sadism? It doesn't matter.'

Cohen felt every hair on his body stand on end. 'Oh my God.'

'What?'

'The background hissing noise that Gus picked up in the recording. At the studio he told me that it sounded like rain hitting a window far away, or maybe even a strong shower somewhere.' Cohen's eyes moved to Myers'. 'The kidnapper was inside her bedroom when he made that call. He was watching her shower.'

Thirty-Two

The next morning Captain Blake was already waiting for Hunter in his office by the time he walked in at 7:51 a.m.

'Carlos told me you identified the victim.'

Hunter nodded. 'Her name is Laura Mitchell.' He handed the captain a two-sheet report.

She scanned it and paused. 'The killer stalked her from inside her own apartment?' Her stare quickly bounced between both detectives.

'That's what it looks like, Captain,' Hunter confirmed.

'How did he get in? Any signs of forced entry?'

He quickly shook his head.

'She could've let the killer inside herself,' Garcia offered.

The captain nodded. 'Which means that the killer could've used a false identity to sneak into the building and ring her doorbell, or maybe he was known to her, or he posed as a collector or buyer and made an appointment or something. But still, why hide behind a painting? It makes no sense.'

'Exactly,' Hunter agreed. 'And that's why I don't think Laura opened the door to the killer and invited him in, but the possibility that he was known to her is real.'

Captain Blake thought for a moment. 'The perpetrator could've had his own set of keys.'

Hunter nodded. 'Either that or he's a master locksmith.'

'Did she have a boyfriend, a lover?'

'We're talking to her ex-fiancé later today. His flight from Dallas lands at 2:45 p.m.'

'How long has he been away?'

Hunter rubbed his forehead. 'Since Tuesday evening.'

'Well, that takes him off the suspects list, doesn't it?'

'I wouldn't say that just now, Captain.'

Captain Blake faced Hunter. 'Well, let's see, he's been out of LA since Tuesday evening. Our victim's body was found two days ago – Wednesday afternoon, remember? No exact time of death, but the crime-scene forensic report said that it wouldn't have been more than three to six hours prior to the discovery of the body. That means that he wasn't in Los Angeles when she died, Robert.'

'Yes,' Hunter agreed, 'but we also have no proof that our killer *actually killed her*, remember, Captain? He could've dumped her in that butcher's shop – alive – hours before she died. Even the night before, giving the ex-fiancé an almost perfect alibi. We need more information before we start discarding suspects at this point.'

'OK, I can go with that,' the captain agreed. 'How about this other guy Carlos told me about? The one who tried to pick Laura up on the last night of her exhibition?'

Hunter searched his desk for a copy of the picture of the stranger she was referring to and handed it to her. The captain stared at it for a few seconds.

'We've been running this picture against the unified police database since yesterday. No matches yet. We've also got a team of uniformed officers going around every art gallery, exhibition hall, museum, art school, cafe, anywhere and everywhere where exhibitions take place. The chaperone at the Daniel Rossdale Art Gallery said she was certain she'd seen him before at a previous exhibition. Which means this guy is probably genuinely into art. Hopefully someone, somewhere will recognize him.'

'The door to door of Laura's apartment building gave us nothing,' Garcia said. 'Two to three weeks is a hell of a long time for any of the neighbors to remember hearing anything out of the ordinary, or seeing anyone suspicious.'

'Have Forensics found anything else in her apartment?'

Hunter poured himself a glass of water. 'They recovered several black fibers from a brick wall. No results yet, but a possible clue.'

'Which is?'

'A few of the fibers came from a point about six foot from the floor.'

'Any hairs?' Captain Blake asked.

'None.'

'So whoever was there was wearing a hat or a ski mask or something,' she concluded.

'The assumption is that while hiding, the attacker flattened his back against the brick wall,' Hunter said. 'If we're right and the fibers came from some sort of head garment, he should be between six foot and six four.'

'And if they haven't?'

'Then the fibers could've come from a sweater and we're looking for a seven-foot giant.'

'At least he'll be easy to spot,' Garcia joked.

'No sign of a struggle?' the captain asked without a hint of a smile.

'None.'

She turned and stared at the crime-scene photographs pinned to the pictures board. No matter how often she looked at them, they made her wince every time. Violence in this city seemed to get worse with each passing year.

'Talk to me, Robert, 'cause I'm really starting to dislike this whole thing. It's been two days since we found Laura's body. Two days since this scumbag blew a bomb inside a morgue and killed two other people, one of them being one of my best friends, and we've got shit so far. Why was she kept hostage for so long before being murdered? Has the Mitchell family received any sort of ransom requests or demands?'

Hunter shook his head. 'No. And if we're right, whoever this killer is, he's not after a ransom. Murder/kidnappings are rarely about money.'

Captain Blake felt a chill start at the base of her neck. 'You think he kept her for sexual pleasure?'

'It's possible. But with no autopsy report we'll never know if Laura Mitchell was raped or not.'

Captain Blake let out a heartfelt sigh.

'There's always a reason why a kidnapper would keep a hostage without demanding money for the victim's return,' Hunter offered. 'The two most common are revenge or an obsession with the victim, where the aggressor just can't let go. Nine times out of ten it starts out as some sort of platonic love . . . to the power of a thousand.' Hunter paused and allowed his eyes to rest on the portrait photograph of Laura Mitchell. 'And almost undoubtedly that obsession is, or becomes, sexual.'

The captain shifted her weight from one foot to another.

'But something here isn't matching,' Hunter continued.

'What do you mean?'

'One thing we do know for sure from the crime-scene pictures is that the killer didn't torture Laura.'

The captain's brow furrowed.

'Torture, degradation and sadistic sexual abuse are a big part of most murder/kidnappings,' Hunter explained. 'When the reason behind the kidnapping isn't money, if and when the victim is found, there are usually clear indications of physical torture and abuse.' He walked up to the pictures board. 'Before identifying her, Garcia and I went through these pictures with a fine-toothed comb and a magnifying glass trying to identify any physical marks that could point us in the right direction.' He shook his head. 'Not a scratch. Laura had no bruises other than the ones caused by the stitches and her own nails.'

'If whoever kidnapped her was after revenge,' Garcia said, 'he would've tortured her, Captain. If he were obsessed with her, there's a good chance he would've raped her. In both cases, her body should've shown bruises.'

'Once the aggressor starts using violence to get what he wants . . .' Hunter continued, '. . . then we're into a very fast downward spiral. His dominance over her, the false sense of power it gives him, will hook him like a drug. The violence will escalate, the rapes will become more aggressive until . . .' He let the sentence hang in the air.

'But that's not what we have here.' Garcia took over. 'We've got the kidnapping, the keeping of the victim and the murder, but not the violence.'

Captain Blake almost choked on Garcia's words. '*Not* the violence?' She glanced at the pictures board and then back at both detectives. 'He placed a bomb inside her and stitched her shut – while she was still alive. What the hell do *you* consider violent?'

'That's precisely the problem, Captain,' Hunter cut in. 'The violence only came at the end, with the murder. And we all agree it was gruesomely sadistic. But the lack of any bruising on Laura's body indicates that the killer wasn't violent towards her while she was held captive. There was no escalation. It went from zero violence to monstrous in one quick step.'

'And that tells us what?'

Hunter held her stare. 'That we're dealing with an extremely unstable, explosive individual. When he loses his temper, someone loses their life.'

Thirty-Three

Patrick Barlett was one of the top financial advisors in the whole of California. He ran his own company from the fortieth floor of the famous 777 Tower.

Barlett's company reception office was decorated to impress. Hunter thought he no doubt subscribed to the theory that money attracts money.

There were two receptionists standing behind a semicircular steel and green-glass reception counter. Their synchronized smiles greeted Hunter and Garcia as they approached the counter. Hunter flashed his credentials, but was careful to keep his thumb over the word *homicide*. The receptionists' smiles lost some of their sparkle. Two minutes later, Hunter and Garcia were shown into Patrick Barlett's office.

If his company's reception was impressive, Barlett's office was majestic. The entire west wall was one huge floor-to-ceiling window, offering the sort of panoramic views of Los Angeles few had ever seen. The floors were pristine bare oak boards. The walls were painted white with just a hint of blue. The entire office was full of sharp edges and gleaming surfaces.

Barlett greeted both detectives with an overpowering handshake.

'Please, come in,' he said in a smooth, deep voice. 'I'm

sorry for the mess, I just got in. I came straight from the airport.'

Barlett was thirty-one years old, as tall as Garcia but with a strong, quarterback frame, tanned skin and a full head of brown hair. His eyes were dark, nearly black. His facial bone structure was as attractive as any Hollywood superstar.

As Hunter explained the reason for their visit, he saw something change inside Barlett's eyes, as if something precious had been smashed to pieces.

Barlett sat behind his imposing desk unable to speak for a minute. His stare stayed on Hunter for several seconds before switching to a small picture frame on his desk. The photo showed three couples at what looked like a gala dinner. Patrick and Laura were sitting side by side. They looked happy. They looked in love.

'There's got to be some sort of mistake.' The smoothness in his voice had given way to an anguished quiver.

Hunter shook his head. 'Unfortunately, no.'

'There must've been. Who identified the body?'

'Mr. Barlett,' Hunter's voice sounded firmer this time, 'there's no mistake.'

Patrick's eyes returned to the photo frame for an instant before breaking away and finding refuge in the panoramic view. His hands moved from his desk to his lap, like a kid trying to hide the fact that they were shaking.

'When did you last see Miss Mitchell, Mr. Barlett?' Garcia asked.

Silence.

'Mr. Barlett?'

His gaze moved back to both detectives. 'Huh? Please call me Patrick.'

'When did you last see Miss Mitchell, Patrick?' Garcia repeated, a fraction slower this time.

'Weeks ago, on the last night of her exhibition at . . .' he searched the air for the name but didn't find it, '. . . in West Hollywood somewhere.'

'The Daniel Rossdale Gallery?' Hunter helped him.

'Yes, that's the one.'

'Were you invited?' Garcia again.

'It wasn't an invitational exhibition.'

'I mean, did Miss Mitchell know you were going? Did she ask you to go?'

Barlett's entire demeanor changed into something a lot harder.

'Am I being accused here?' He didn't wait for a reply. 'This is absolutely ridiculous. If you think I'd ever be capable of hurting Laura, then you guys are probably the worst detectives this town has ever seen. Either that, or you didn't bother doing a background check on us. We have history together. I love Laura. I'd take my own life before I hurt her.'

Hunter noticed that Barlett didn't even mention the fact that he wasn't in town when Laura's body was found.

'Did you try contacting her again after the exhibition? Apparently you didn't part on very good terms that night.'

'What?' Patrick glared at Garcia. 'That's bullshit. You need to get your facts right, Detective. I drank a little too much that night and I acted like a jerk, I admit it. But that was all. Nothing more. And yes, I tried calling her the next day to apologize, but all I got was her answering service.'

'Did you leave a message?'

'Yes.'

'Did she call you back?'

Barlett gave Garcia a nervous chuckle. 'No, she never does. I'm used to it.'

'Why do you say you acted like a jerk?' Garcia again. 'What happened?'

Barlett paused, trying to decide if he should say any more. 'Since it's obvious you have me as a suspect, I think we should adjourn this conversation until I have my lawyer present.'

'We're not accusing you of anything, Patrick,' Garcia countered. 'We're just clearing up a few points.'

'Well, it looks and sounds like an interrogation to me. So, if it's all the same to you, I really think I should have my lawyer present.' He reached for the phone on his desk.

Garcia leaned back in his chair and ran a hand over his stubbled chin.

'That's your prerogative, Patrick,' Hunter took over, 'but that won't help anyone. It will certainly waste time, though. Time we could spend hunting Laura's killer.'

Patrick paused mid-dial and stared at Hunter.

'I understand this line of enquiry might seem upsetting to you, but at the moment everyone is a suspect and we wouldn't be doing our job if we didn't come knocking at your door. Laura's final exhibition night seems to be the last time anyone saw Miss Mitchell alive. You were seen arguing with her that night.' Hunter leaned forward. 'You're an intelligent man, so think about it. Given your well-documented outbursts, your history with Laura Mitchell, and the fact that you've been trying to get her back for the past four years without success, does it come as a surprise to you that we're here? What would you do if you were us?'

'I would never hurt Laura,' Barlett repeated.

'Fine, but this ain't the way to prove it. No matter what

you do, lawyer or no lawyer, you'll still have to answer our questions. We'll just get a warrant and drag this thing out for a lot longer.' Hunter emphatically allowed his eyes to focus on the photo on the desk. Barlett followed his stare. 'Whoever killed Laura, the woman you loved so much, is still out there. Do you really think that fighting us and wasting time is such a good call?'

Barlett's eyes didn't leave the photograph.

Hunter and Garcia waited.

'I was jealous, I admit it,' he finally said as his eyes became glassy. 'That guy was shadowing Laura everywhere she went like a hungry dog. Staring at her all the time as if she were naked or something. Then I saw them talking. Laura was a very private person, not the flirty type, so of course I was jealous. But there was something different about that guy.'

'Different how?' Hunter asked.

'I don't know. The look in his eyes when he stared at her. As I said, he was shadowing her. Just a few steps away from wherever she was, but he wasn't there for her art.'

'How do you know that?'

'Because not once did he look at any of the paintings. While everyone else was walking around, admiring the exhibition, his eyes were on her . . . *only* on her. As if Laura *was* the exhibition.'

'Don't you think that your opinion of this man could've been distorted by the fact that you were jealous of him?' Garcia suggested.

Barlett shook his head. 'I was jealous of him, all right, especially after I saw him chatting to Laura and the way she was smiling at him, but that's not the reason he caught my attention. I spotted the way he was staring at her way before they talked. I'm telling you, he wasn't there for the exhibition. He was there for her.'

'And you told Laura that?' Garcia asked.

'Yes, but she wouldn't listen. She got angry. She thought I was jealous. But I was just trying to protect her.'

Hunter retrieved a snapshot from a folder he'd brought with him. It was one of the photos they'd got from the Daniel Rossdale Gallery. The one showing the tall, dark-haired stranger who had swapped phone numbers with Laura. He was standing next to her, staring at the camera. Hunter placed the photo on the desk in front of Patrick. 'Is this the person you're referring to?'

Patrick moved closer. His eyebrows contracted. 'Yes, that's him.'

'And you'd never seen him before?'

'Not before that night, no.'

Hunter's phone rang in his pocket.

'Detective Hunter,' he answered and listened for a long moment. His eyes lit up as he faced Garcia.

'You're kidding me.'

Thirty-Four

'So, where exactly are we going?' Garcia asked, easing his car out of the parking spot.

'Norwalk,' Hunter said, punching the address he was given over the phone into the GPS system.

One of the officers they had visiting art galleries with a snapshot of the man who'd swapped phone numbers with Laura Mitchell on the final night of her exhibition had hit gold. The owner of an exclusive gallery in Manhattan Beach had recognized the person in the photo. Nine months ago he'd purchased a canvas by Laura Mitchell from the gallery during one of their exhibitions.

Most art galleries will ask their clients to allow the purchased piece to remain on display until that particular show is over. The Manhattan Beach Gallery always insisted on taking down a name and contact number for its clients.

The man's name was James Smith.

Norwalk is a mostly middle-class neighborhood located seventeen miles southeast of downtown Los Angeles. It took Hunter and Garcia fifty-five minutes to get from South Figueroa Street to the address they were given on the poorer side of Norwalk.

The address led them to an old, gray concrete monstrosity. A six-story-high public housing unit with dirty windows which was in desperate need of a coat of paint. Garcia parked his car across the road from the building's entrance. A group of five guys who were bouncing a basketball around just a few yards away stopped all activity. Ten eyes were glued to Hunter and Garcia.

'*¿Que passa* five-o?' the tallest and fittest one of the group called as both detectives crossed the street. He had no shirt on and his muscles glistened with sweat. Most of his torso, arms and neck were covered in tattoos. Hunter recognized some of them as prison branding. '*¿Qué quieres aquí, puercos?*' He let go of the ball and folded his arms defiantly. The other four grouped up behind him like a defensive line-up.

'*No somos policías*,' Hunter said, flashing his gym membership card. He knew the group was way too far away to be able to see it properly. 'I'm from the City of Los Angeles Housing Authority.' He flicked his head towards Garcia. 'He's from Pensions and Welfare.'

The whole group's hard-ass demeanor evaporated in an instant.

'Oh man, I gotta go,' the one with glasses said, checking his watch. 'I've got a job interview in an hour.'

'Yeah, me too,' the skinny, shaven-headed one said.

They all nodded and mumbled in Spanish as the group broke away, all five of them reaching for their cell phones.

Garcia couldn't hide his smile.

The entrance lobby was in as much need of attention as the rest of the building. Dirty walls, water stains on the ceilings, and the stale smell of cigarettes greeted Hunter and Garcia as they came through its metal and wired-glass doors.

'Which floor?' Garcia asked.

'Fourth.'

Garcia reached for the elevator call button.

'You gotta be kidding, right?' Hunter chuckled. 'Have you noticed the state of this place? That's a risk too far.' He gestured towards the stairs. 'Safer to use those.' They took the steps two at a time.

The fourth floor corridor was long, narrow, badly lit and it smelled of old fried onions and piss. They passed a semi-open door where a baby was crying somewhere inside. The TV in the living room was on, showing some sort of court-room program.

'Not really the sort of place you'd expect an art lover to live,' Garcia commented.

Apartment 418 was two doors from the end of the corridor. Hunter knocked and waited fifteen seconds.

No reply.

He knocked again and moved his ear to the door. Ten seconds later he heard someone approaching from inside. The door unlocked with a loud clang and then was pulled back a fraction, just the length of the security chain. The lights inside the apartment were off. All he could see was a pair of eyes looking out from about a foot away from the door. The sweet smell of jasmine seeped through from inside.

'Mr. Smith?' Hunter asked. 'James Smith?'

Silence.

Hunter subtly placed the tip of his boot against the bottom of the door and lifted his badge. 'We were wondering if we could ask you a few questions?'

Two more seconds of silence. Suddenly, in a desperate reaction, the door was pushed forward with a jerk, but Hunter's foot stopped it from slamming shut.

'James . . . ? What the hell?' Hunter called.

The tension on the door relaxed as Smith let go of it.

They heard the hustle of foot scuffing inside the apartment, moving deeper within, and away from them. Hunter looked at Garcia quizzically for a split second. They both realized it at the same time.

'Fire escape . . .'

Thirty-Five

Hunter pointed to the far end of the hall. 'Back alley . . . go . . . now.'

Garcia spun around on the balls of his feet and took off down the corridor like a locomotive. Hunter pushed the apartment's door open but it halted at the security chain. He slammed his left shoulder hard against it. Once was all it took. The chain came undone from the doorframe, wooden splinters flying through the air. Hunter saw and heard the door at the end of the apartment's hallway slam shut. He dashed towards it but didn't get there in time. A step away from it he heard the lock turn. Mechanically he tried the handle. Nothing.

'Smith, c'mon . . .' He shoved his shoulder against the door. It didn't budge. He tried again, harder this time. Solid as stone. He took two steps back and sent his boot straight onto the door handle. Once, twice, three times. The door rattled a little but that was all. He knew it was pointless carrying on. The door probably had surface-mounted deadbolt locks on the other side. Hunter could shoot the hinges off, but that would be overkill, and way too hard to justify in a report.

'Smith, c'mon, open up.'

Chances were he was already halfway down the fire ladder.

'Fuck!'

Hunter backtracked down the corridor to the next room along on the right, which was on the same side as the room James had locked himself in. The door was shut but not locked. He pushed it open and stepped inside. The room was in almost complete darkness. Hunter didn't look for a light switch – no time – and dashed towards the window on the far wall, almost tripping over something on the floor. Just like the room James had gone into, the window faced the building's back alley. There were no curtains, but the glass had been sprayed with black paint. It was an old-style window. Two panels. The bottom one had slots for fingers at the bottom. No locks, just a single rotating latch. Hunter undid it and pushed the bottom panel up. Stuck.

'Shit.'

With his fingers in the slots he shook the window so vigorously the entire frame rattled. He tried again. The panel slid up a couple of inches, enough for him to get his hands under the frame. Much better grip. With one big push, the panel creaked and slid all the way up. Hunter craned forward and looked out. James was rushing down the last rungs of the metal fire escape ladder.

'Goddamnit.'

Smith didn't look back. He jumped from the ladder and hit the ground running. He was fast and agile.

Hunter searched the alley for Garcia. He saw Smith zigzag between a few large trash cans and then dive through an open door about twenty yards ahead.

Garcia finally appeared, coming from the alley's entrance on the right, sprinting like an Olympic champion.

'The Chinese restaurant's back door,' Hunter called from

the window. 'Past those trash cans on the right. He got in through the kitchen.'

Garcia hesitated for a beat, considering if he should run back the way he came in and try to cut James off at the front of the shops. Going back and around would take too long. By the time he got there James would be gone. He carried on forward, sidestepping the trash cans and disappearing through the same door James had done seconds earlier.

Hunter turned around and hurried back out of the room. If he was fast and lucky enough, he could cut Smith off at the top of the street. He'd taken only two steps away from the window when his cyes caught a glimpse of something on the walls.

The light that now poured in through the open window had erased the darkness.

What he saw made him stop dead.

Thirty-Six

Garcia rushed through the back door of the Chinese restaurant and found himself inside a crowded kitchen. Lunchtime was in full swing. Three chefs were standing by a large ten-burner cooker where several woks were sizzling away. One of the woks seemed to have caught on fire and flames were shooting up from its bowl at least a foot and a half high. Two sous chefs were by a long metal workstation covered with freshly cut vegetables along with three waitresses. One of them had her back flat against the wall next to the double swinging doors that led to the restaurant's dining room, as if she'd just been pushed out of the way. On the floor directly in front of her was an overturned metal tray. Several bowls of noodles and soup were scattered on the ground. All eight of them were yelling loudly in Mandarin. Garcia didn't have to understand them to know that they weren't yelling at each other, or about the spilled food. It was a nervous reaction.

Garcia figured from their reaction that he was about ten to fifteen seconds behind Smith.

All eyes were on Garcia as he came through the alley door. Everyone took a step back. A fraction of a second later they were all yelling and gesticulating at him. Garcia didn't even miss a step. As he skipped over the dishes on the floor and burst through the swinging doors, he could understand only one word – *asshole*.

The shocked expression from the kitchen staff was mirrored on the faces of every customer in the main dining room. Some had turned to look at this new crazy man who'd blasted out of the kitchen, and some were still staring at the restaurant's front door, where the previous one had just exited.

Garcia ran through the restaurant, expertly avoiding the manager and a waitress on the way.

Outside, the street was full of people coming and going in both directions. Garcia looked left, then right. No one was running. No one looked surprised. There was no commotion. Garcia took two steps forward, lifted himself onto the tips of his toes and looked both ways again. He cursed under his breath as he realized that he didn't even know what Smith was wearing. Only his eyes had been visible when he opened the door to his apartment. From the exhibition picture, he knew what Smith looked like, but not from the back. Any tall male walking away from him could be Smith.

Garcia searched the street for Hunter. He was certain that while he followed Smith in through the restaurant, Hunter would be trying to cut him off at the top end of the street, but he was nowhere in sight.

'Shit, Robert, where are you?'

He approached a group of three guys standing just a few yards away. 'Did any of you see a tall guy come running out of that restaurant just a few seconds ago?'

They all looked at him, then at the restaurant's door, then back at him.

'Sure,' the short stocky one said, and they all nodded at each other at the same time. 'He went . . . that way.' One of them pointed left, the other one right, and the stocky guy pointed at his crotch. All three burst out laughing. 'Get the fuck outta here, cop. We ain't seen shiiit.'

Garcia didn't have time to argue. He took a step back and checked up and down the street once again.

No Hunter.

No Smith.

Garcia had to hand it to him. Smith was smart. He knew no one had gotten a good look at him. He could be wearing a suit or a hooded jacket. As soon as he hit the street in front of the restaurant, instead of carrying on running and sticking out like a sore thumb, he slowed down to a walking pace. Just another guy strolling along a street full of shops. He'd look as suspicious as everyone else.

Garcia took his cell out of his pocket and called Hunter. 'Where are you? Did you get him?' His eyes were still roaming up and down the street.

'No, I'm still at the apartment.'

'What? Why? I thought you'd try to cut him off.'

'I take it you don't have him either.'

'No. He was clever. He mixed in with the crowd. And I don't have a clue what sort of clothes he was wearing.'

'I'll call and put an APB out on him right now.'

'Why are you still at his apartment?'

A short pause.

'Robert?'

'You've gotta come see this room.'

Thirty-Seven

Garcia stood motionless by the door to the small square room. The window was now fully open, allowing daylight in. The weak light bulb at the center of the ceiling was also on. A musty smell of old paper and dust lingered in the air, the kind of smell you'd get inside a basement storage room of a bookshop, or a newspaper archive. Hunter was standing next to a large wooden table piled high with magazines, journals, printouts and newspapers. Piles and piles of them were stacked all around the floor, overcrowding the room – Smith was either some sort of collector, or one of those people who was scared of throwing anything away.

Garcia's eyes crawled around the room, trying to take everything in. Every inch of every wall was taken by some sort of drawing, article, clipping, sketch or photograph. They came from newspapers, magazines, websites, journals, and many of them had been drawn, written or taken by Smith himself. There were literally hundreds of images and articles. Garcia stepped inside and his eyes moved to the ceiling. The bizarre collage continued there as well. Every available space was covered.

'Jesus . . .' Something tightened low in Garcia's gut. He recognized the woman in all the pictures and sketches straight away. There was no mistake. Laura Mitchell. A love heart had been drawn around several of the photographs with a thick red marker pen. Like kids do with pictures of their idols.

'What the fuck is this place?' Garcia whispered.

Hunter turned and looked around the room again as if he was seeing it for the first time.

'A sanctuary of some sort? His own private archive? Maybe a research room? Who knows?' A shrug. 'This guy seems to have collected everything that was ever published about Laura. Judging by the discoloration of some of the pictures and newspaper articles, some of these are quite old.' His gaze flickered to the piles of paper everywhere.

Garcia turned his attention to the magazines and newspaper stacks. 'Is she in every one of these?'

'I haven't checked them all. But if I had to have a guess, I'd say yes.' Hunter pulled a newspaper from the bottom of one of the stacks. It was a copy of the *San Diego Union-Tribune*.

Garcia's left eyebrow lifted a fraction. 'San Diego?' He noticed the date. 'That paper is three years old.'

Hunter started flipping through the newspaper. 'The problem is: none of the newspapers, magazines or journals are folded or opened onto a particular page or article. I've checked a few already. I assume he kept them because of something on the entertainment section.' He folded the paper and showed it to Garcia. 'But as you can see, there are no marks. Nothing is circled, underlined or highlighted.'

'Anything about Laura?'

Hunter scanned the page.

Most of the articles were music-related – gig and album reviews. He flipped the paper over and carried on. At the bottom corner of the page he saw a review for an art exhibition and nodded. 'She was exhibiting in San Diego back then.'

Garcia craned his neck. There were no pictures. He randomly pulled another newspaper from the bottom of another pile. He came up with a copy of the *Sacramento Bee*. 'This one is from a year and a half ago.' He quickly found the entertainment section and scanned through another exhibition review. 'He's been stalking her for years,' he said, looking around the room one more time. 'He knew everything there was to know about her. Collected everything there was to collect. Talk about being patient. He waited years for the right moment to make his move. Laura never had a chance.'

Thirty-Eight

Hunter and Captain Blake had to pull all the stops to get an overworked and understaffed Forensics division to send two evidence technicians to a non-crime scene so fast. First impressions showed no indications that anyone else other than James had been inside that apartment. There was no hidden cell or prison room. If Smith was their killer, he'd kept Laura Mitchell captive in a secret location somewhere else. And that secret location was probably where he was heading to right now. The difference this time was that he now knew the police were onto him, and that would certainly influence his actions. He'd be edgy, maybe even in a panic. And a killer in a panic was catastrophic. Hunter knew that only too well from harsh experience.

They needed to catch him fast. Before he left Norwalk. Before he disappeared.

They didn't.

Hunter had immediately arranged for James Smith's snapshot to be emailed from Parker Center to Norwalk's LA Sheriff's Department Station. Available black-and-white units were dispatched to search the streets almost immediately. Officers on foot patrol and inside Norwalk's Metrolink

Station were also sent Smith's picture via SMS text. Airports, train and bus stations were put on high alert. But six hours after Hunter and Garcia had knocked on Smith's door, he still hadn't been sighted.

Both evidence techs had been going over the apartment for the past three and a half hours. They'd need confirmation from the lab, but their best guess, based on what they'd seen, was that all the fingerprints they'd found so far seemed to have come from only one person – James Smith.

Key points inside Smith's bedroom and both bathrooms were sprayed with Luminol but no blood was detected. They also ran a UV light test on all the bed linen and on the fabric sofa and rug in the living room. No evidence of semen stains either.

Hunter and Garcia kept out of the way, staying in the collage room. There was enough in there to keep a platoon occupied for a week. Initially, Hunter wasn't worried about sieving through everything. All the information on those pages seemed to pertain to Laura Mitchell, not James Smith. What he was looking for was some sort of personal diary, or journal, or notebook. Anything that could give them a clue to where Smith might have gone or who he was.

They found nothing. No documents, no passport, no driver's license. Not even any utility bills.

'Anything that could give us any sort of lead, guys?' Hunter asked one of the techs some time later.

'Yeah, my guess is you're looking for a cleaning freak,' he said, bending down and sliding his index finger across the top of the skirting board before showing the result to Hunter. 'Nothing, no dust. My wife is pretty tight on her housecleaning, but even she doesn't dust the skirting boards every time she cleans. The only place with any dust is that freaky room you guys have been in. There's a cupboard in the kitchen packed solid with cleaning materials. Enough bleach to fill a Jacuzzi. This guy is either obsessed with cleaning, or he was expecting us.'

The door to door of the building also produced no information of interest. Most residents said they'd never even seen the person who lived in apartment 418. The ones who did never talked to him. The next-door neighbor, a small, fragile man in his sixties with glasses as thick as bulletproof glass, said Smith always said hi to him whenever they bumped into each other on the corridor. He said Smith was always very polite. That sometimes Smith went out dressed in a suit. No one else in that building ever wore a suit. The old man also said that the walls in the building weren't very thick. He could often hear Smith cleaning, vacuuming, scrubbing and moving around. He did that a lot.

The Forensics agents took shoes and underwear from Smith's wardrobe, and a razor blade, a comb, a toothbrush and a deodorant spray can from his bathroom. They didn't want to take any chances where a DNA signature was concerned.

Night had darkened the sky when Hunter received a call from Operations.

'Detective Hunter? It's Pam from Operations.'

'What have you got for me, Pam?'

'Well, next time you decide to go after someone, please can you pick a person with a more unique name. James is the most common first name in the United States. Smith is the most common last name in the United States. Put them together and we have approximately three and a half million males in the USA called James Smith.'

'Great.'

'In the LA area alone there are about five hundred of them. But the interesting thing is: none are registered to the Norwalk address you gave me.'

Thirty-Nine

Her eyelids flickered in rapid succession but she failed to open them. Her consciousness was returning to her like waves breaking over a beach. But each time her mind hinted at clearing, an undertow of blackness would pull her back into nothing.

The only thing she seemed to be certain of at that moment was the smell. Something like mothballs and strong disinfectant all rolled up into one. It felt as if the vile odor had traveled in through her nose, down her throat and into her stomach, burning everything in its way. Her guts felt like writhing snakes trying to climb out of her body.

Her eyes flickered again, this time for a little longer, and with great effort she managed to force them open. The light around her was dim and weak, but it still burned at her retinas like lightning bolts. Gradually, she began taking in her surroundings. She was lying on her back on some hard and uncomfortable surface, inside a hot and humid place. Old and rusty metal pipes ran across the ceiling in all directions, disappearing as they reached the mold-infested cinder block walls.

She tried lifting her head, but the movement sent waves of nausea rippling through her stomach.

Slowly, the numbness that controlled her body started to subside, and as it did, it was substituted by agonizing pain.

Her lips felt as if they were being ripped from her face by several pairs of pliers at the same time. Her jaw hurt as if it had been broken. She tried opening her mouth, but the pain that rose from the effort almost sent her back into unconsciousness. Tears started streaming down her face as she urged her brain to work and tell her what to do. She tried moving her arms – surprisingly, no pain. More surprisingly, they weren't restrained.

Shivering, she brought her hands to her face and touched her lips with the tips of her fingers. The shivering turned into uncontrollable convulsions of fear as she realized why she couldn't move them.

Her mouth had been stitched shut.

Desperation took over.

Robotically and without any sense of reality, her trembling fingers tapped the stitches on her lips like a mad pianist. Her wailing and frantic muffled screams echoed throughout the room, but there was no one there to hear them. The thread used on her mouth dug deeper into her skin as she tried to move her lips again. She tasted blood.

Suddenly, as if a switch had been flicked on inside her head, she became aware of a much more intense and terrifying pain. It was coming from between her legs. It shot through her body with such ferocity it felt like evil had just climbed inside her.

Instinctively, her hands moved towards the source of the pain, and as they touched her body and the other stitches, she felt her strength leaving her.

Panic erupted inside her, and her body's defense mechanism inundated her bloodstream with adrenalin, numbing the pain just enough for her to be able to move. Guided now by pure survival instinct, she forced herself to sit up.

Sound disappeared, time slowed, and the world turned black and white in front of her eyes. Only then did she realize she was naked and had been lying on some sort of stainless steel table. Strangely, the tabletop seemed higher off the ground than one would expect. At least another foot or so.

She looked down at her bare feet, and all of a sudden it dawned on her. Her legs were also unrestrained. Frantically her terrified eyes searched the room – large, square with a concrete floor and a metal door directly in front of her. The door didn't seem to be locked. The walls were lined with empty wooden shelves.

Without wasting any more time or caring if this was a cruel trap or not, she jumped to the floor. The impact as her feet hit the ground sent a shudder up her spine. A millisecond later, the most unimaginable pain exploded inside her. Her legs lost all their strength and she fell to her knees, shivering. She looked down and all she saw was blood.

Forty

It was now three full days after Laura Mitchell's body had been found and not much had materialized. James Smith, or whoever he really was, had simply vanished. The Forensics agents were right: all the fingerprints found in the apartment did come from a single person. They'd been running them against the National Automated Fingerprints ID System for several hours. So far no matches. It didn't look like James Smith had ever been in the system.

The DNA result would still be at least another day or so. Whoever James Smith was, he was smart.

Choosing the most common American male name automatically hid him under layers upon layers of other people. Even if Hunter asked Operations to narrow the LA's James Smith list down by filtering on age and approximate height, it'd still be too long. Besides, it was obvious that James Smith wasn't his real name.

The apartment in Norwalk had been rented and paid in cash, a year in advance. Hunter talked to the landlord, a Mr. Richards. He was a retired shop owner and lived in Palmdale. He told Hunter that he'd only seen James Smith twice – first when he initially rented the property two years ago, and then again twelve months later when he renewed his lease agreement and paid the next full year in advance, plus extras – more than enough to cover all utility bills. So that was the reason they found no bills in the apartment.

Mr. Richards told Hunter that in the two years Mr. Smith had been renting his apartment, he'd been a great tenant, the best he'd ever had.

'He never causes any trouble,' Mr. Richards told Hunter. 'He's also never requested anything else, unlike most of my previous tenants. They were always calling and asking me for a new fridge, or stove, or mattress, or electric shower, or whatever. They were always complaining that there was something wrong with the apartment, but not James. He never complained.'

'Did you check any documentation when Mr. Smith rented your apartment?' Hunter asked. 'You know, background checks, references or anything like that?'

Mr. Richards shook his head. 'There was no need. He paid cash and the full year in advance, which means he could never default on a payment.'

Hunter was more than aware that Los Angeles was definitely the city for if you've got the cash, you get the goods, no questions asked.

'Did Mr. Smith ever tell you what he did for a living?'

Another shake of the head from Richards.

The snapshot Hunter had of James Smith was quickly released to the press. The picture was by no means perfect. His face was at least 30 per cent obscured, but it was the best they had. With a little luck, someone out there would know who he was. A dedicated phone line was created to receive calls. So far they'd got a mountain of dead ends and people claiming to be James Smith himself, challenging the police to come and get them.

They'd also found the painting Smith had purchased nine months ago along with several DVDs in his apartment. All of them homemade. All of them of Laura Mitchell. Apparently, all of them shot by Smith himself. Hours and hours of footage of Laura at exhibitions, dinner parties, arriving at and leaving her art studio, walking into her gym, browsing in shopping malls, and so on. There were no time-stamps on any of the footage, but judging by her different hairstyles and slight differences in weight, they had been shot over a period of years. They could be seen as surveillance in preparation for an abduction, or plain obsessive stalking. Hunter didn't want to jump to any conclusions until he had more evidence.

'OK,' Captain Blake said, putting the ten-page report she was reading down on her desk. 'What's confusing me is . . . if this James Smith is our killer, and he's obviously been collecting intel on Laura Mitchell for a few years, how come he only decided to strike now?'

'That's not unusual, Captain,' Hunter said, walking over to the window in the captain's office. 'Very few people have the mental strength to become a killer overnight. The vast majority of serial killers, or people who have shown tendency to becoming one, have fantasized about their actions for months, years, sometimes decades. For most, the fantasy alone is enough to satisfy them. Some will go as far as doing all the preparation, the research, the stalking, the surveillance, collecting intel, maybe even capturing the victim, but bottle out right at the last minute. Maybe it took James all these years to gather the courage to finally act out his fantasy.'

'And we know our killer doesn't mind waiting,' Garcia said.

The phone on Captain Blake's desk rang. She answered it on the third bell.

'What?' she barked.

As she listened her eyes darted towards Hunter.

'Shit! Seal the entire place and keep everyone else away from that building, do you hear me? And I mean *everyone*. We're on our way.'

Forty-One

The abandoned preschool was located in Glassell Park, Northeast Los Angeles. Cracked walls, broken windows, subsiding floors, cobwebs, and crumbling wooden doorframes was all that was left of the once bustling single-story building. Instead of cartoon characters, gang graffiti now decorated the walls both outside and inside. Several police vehicles and a forensic crime-scene van took over the parking lot to the right of the school. The press had parked all over the place. Reporters and photographers, together with an ever growing crowd of onlookers were being held back at the twenty-five-yard perimeter line created by yellow crime-scene tape and numerous officers.

Hunter, Garcia and Captain Blake got out of the car, sidestepped the crowd and quickly stooped under the tape, approaching the two police officers standing by the main building's entrance. They were both silent.

'Sorry, sir, but I got orders from high up not to let anyone in there for now,' the most senior of the two officers said, acknowledging both detectives' badges.

'I gave that order,' Captain Blake replied firmly, displaying her credentials.

Both officers immediately stood to attention.

'Captain,' a short, overweight male reporter with thick

glasses and a terribly disguised bald patch called from the pack. 'What's going on? Who is the victim? Why are you here? Care to give the people of Los Angeles some information?' His questions ignited an onslaught of frantic shouts from everyone.

All Los Angeles crime beat reporters knew that LAPD captains didn't usually attend crime scenes, no matter what division or bureau they were from. When they did, there was always a reason. And it was never good news. When the captain of the LAPD Robbery Homicide Division turned up at a crime scene, something was definitely wrong.

Captain Blake ignored the questions and returned her attention to the officer. 'Were you first response?'

He nodded but avoided her eyes.

'C'mon, Captain, give us something. Why are you here? What's going on in there?' The bald reporter insisted.

Captain Blake still paid no attention. 'Who else other than Forensics has seen the body?'

'Only me and my partner, ma'am, Officer Gutierrez.' He tilted his head in the direction of the building behind him. 'He's inside, guarding the entrance to the basement.'

'No one else?' she pressed.

'No one else, ma'am. We got a call from dispatch earlier to come down here and investigate a 911 call – someone claiming to have found a body. We radioed Homicide and Forensics as soon as we walked into that room. We got our orders back almost immediately – not to let anyone else in. Forensics are the only ones we've allowed through.'

'The body is in the basement?' Hunter asked.

'Yes, at the end of the corridor turn left and you'll be in the old kitchen. At the back of it you'll see a few steps that'll take you down to a storage room. The body is in there.' His next words came out no louder than a whisper. 'What in God's earth . . . ?'

Minutes later, Hunter, Garcia and Captain Blake found Officer Gutierrez at the back of the old kitchen, guarding the steps to the storage room just like his partner had said. His youthful face couldn't hide the shock of what he'd seen down in that room.

The cement staircase going down to the basement was worn out, narrow and steep, illuminated by a single light bulb that hung from the water-infiltrated ceiling above the landing at the top. With each step they took, the smell of disinfectant grew stronger. Brilliant forensic light seeped through the rusty metal door at the bottom. As they approached it, Hunter felt his blood rush and warm his skin as if he'd just stepped out into the baking sun. He opened the door, and all he saw was blood.

Forty-Two

Doctor Hove was standing by the far wall talking to her lead Forensics agent, Mike Brindle. They were both wearing white Tyvek coveralls. A stainless steel table occupied the center of the large room. The concrete floor was covered in sticky, coagulated blood. Not splashes and sprinkles, but thick, vampiric pools of it. A few small and delicate bloody handprints traced a short trajectory from the table to the ghostly pale, naked body of a brunette woman lying on her back just a few steps from the door. Her arms had been carefully placed by her side, her legs stretched out.

'Jesus Christ,' Captain Blake murmured, bringing a hand to her mouth as she felt her stomach churn.

The woman's lips had been stitched shut, and though her torso and legs were caked in blood, the black, thorn-like stitches to her lower body were clearly visible.

Doctor Hove approached them in silence and Hunter shot her a questioning look.

The doctor nodded in confirmation. 'Judging by what we have in this room, I'd say it's the same killer,' she said in a hushed voice.

Hunter and Garcia did their best to avoid stepping into the pools of blood and approached the body on the floor. Captain Blake stayed by the door. Hunter crouched down and examined what he could of the woman without touching her. Garcia did the same but his eyes kept returning to her once attractive face, as if something was bothering him. A few seconds later he frowned at Hunter. 'Jesus, she's a carbon copy of Laura Mitchell. They could've been sisters.'

Hunter nodded. He'd noticed the uncanny resemblance from the door.

Captain Blake pinched the bridge of her nose, closed her eyes and took a deep breath. She knew exactly what that meant.

Hunter turned to Doctor Hove. 'Is this how you found the body?'

'No,' Mike Brindle replied, stepping closer. 'We photographed everything and then turned her over. Her body was facing down; right cheek against the floor, facing left towards the wall. Her left arm was extended as if she was reaching for something. Her position gave us the impression that she was probably crawling towards the door, but lacked the strength to get there.'

Hunter's eyes wandered the room again, taking in more of the scene. 'The handprints?'

'They're hers,' Brindle confirmed. 'The few bloody sneaker shoeprints you saw on the floor outside and on the steps going up haven't been confirmed yet. But judging by the runaway smear pattern in some of them, I'd say they belong to the scared teenager who dialed 911 – anonymously, he left no name and no address.' He paused and his stare returned to the woman on the floor. 'Rigor mortis started not long ago, but the heat and humidity in this room could have delayed it for up to five hours, maybe a little more.'

'So she definitely died today?' the captain asked.

Brindle nodded.

Garcia's attention went from the body to the large distribution of blood on the floor. 'She's got no wounds I can see other than her stitches. Where did all this blood come from?'

Doctor Hove and Mike Brindle exchanged an uneasy glance. 'I'll have proper confirmation with the autopsy,' the doctor replied, 'but right now, all this indicates some sort of internal hemorrhage.'

Captain Blake's eyes widened.

'All this blood . . .' the doctor shook her head as if she was struggling to find the right words, ' . . . dripped out of her through the stitches.'

'Holy shit.' Garcia rubbed his face with his right hand.

'She's also got tiny abrasions on both of her hands and knees,' Doctor Hove continued. 'We think she came off that table and collapsed to the ground. Maybe because she was dizzy or in tremendous pain, but she was still alive. The abrasions were probably caused by the fall and her crawling towards the door. Her prints are on that table, so we concluded that she was left there by the killer, but there isn't a speck of blood on it. She didn't start bleeding until she was on the ground.'

'And then there's this,' Brindle said, walking over to where Captain Blake was standing. 'Excuse me, Captain.'

She frowned and took a step to her right.

Brindle pointed to the wall directly behind where the captain was standing. Only then did they see the set of small spray-painted black letters – IT'S INSIDE YOU.

Forty-Three

Captain Blake's lips parted in disbelief. They were exactly the same words Hunter had found spray-painted on the ceiling in the butcher's shop where Laura Mitchell's body had been found. Her stare refocused onto the body on the floor for a moment before moving back to Doctor Hove.

'OK, I thought what we had here was just suspicion and conjecture. I was obviously wrong. But if you knew this was the same killer, given that he placed a bomb inside his first victim that took the lives of two other people inside one of your autopsy rooms . . .' she pointed to the letters on the wall, ' . . . and again he's telling us he did the same here, what the hell are we doing in this room? Where's the bomb squad? And why did you risk turning the body over?'

'Because whatever it was the killer placed inside her this time,' Hunter replied, gently rubbing between his eyebrows, 'it's already gone off inside her.'

'Judging by where she bled from,' the doctor added, 'that's exactly what we think. As we said, it all points to an internal hemorrhage, but not one we've ever seen before.'

'What do you mean?' Captain Blake asked.

'Internal hemorrhages usually occur from traumatic injuries, blood vessel rupture or certain specific diseases, carcinoma being one of them. But the blood accumulates inside the body, hence the term *internal*. And the amount is just a fraction of what you see here. This woman bled as if she had been mutilated. Whatever it was that caused it, it was inside her.'

No one said anything for a moment.

'There was nothing else in this room other than what you can see,' Brindle took over. 'The body, those old shelves on the walls and that stainless steel table.' He gestured towards it. 'There are no chains, no ropes or any sort of restraints anywhere. A closer look at the victim's wrists and ankles shows no abrasions or marks. She wasn't tied down. She also couldn't have been locked in here because there's no lock on that door.' He shook his head as he considered it. 'The truth is: we can't find anything that suggests why she wasn't allowed to just walk out of here. So far there are no indications that anyone else was in here with her when she died. It looks like the killer simply dumped her on that table and left. And as we said, she wasn't bleeding then. But the killer somehow knew she would never get out of this room alive.'

Hunter had already noticed that the table in the room had been raised higher off the ground than normal. 'Does this look strange to anyone?' He pointed to the wooden blocks under each of the four table legs.

Everyone frowned.

'The first victim, Laura Mitchell,' he continued, 'was left on a stainless steel counter inside a butcher's shop in East LA. That counter had also been raised higher off the ground by bricks. First I thought that maybe the old butcher there had been some sort of a giant, but no, I checked. He was five foot eight.'

'So you think the killer did this deliberately?' the captain asked. 'Why?'

'I'm not sure yet.'

They all paused as they heard heavy footsteps coming down the stairs. A couple of seconds later a crime lab agent also dressed in white Tyvek coveralls pulled the door open. He brought with him a large, black plastic flight case.

'It's OK, Tom,' Brindle said, reaching for the case. 'I know how to set it up.'

The agent left the case with Brindle and exited the room.

'This is why we had to turn her body over,' Doctor Hove explained as Brindle undid the locks to the case and started unpacking its contents. 'That's a portable tactical X-ray unit. It's mainly used for the investigation of small- to medium-sized objects like parcels, boxes and luggage. The picture it produces is not of the same quality as you'd get from a proper hospital X-ray machine, but it'll serve our purposes here. We're pretty confident that whatever was placed inside her has, as Robert said, gone off, and that's what killed her. But we all know what this killer is capable of.' She looked at Captain Blake. 'I don't wanna move her before I have an idea of what we're dealing with.'

They all watched as Brindle set up the equipment. 'Since we don't have a tripod,' he said, 'can somebody hold the camera over her?'

'I'll do it,' Garcia said, returning to the body and once again carefully avoiding the pools of blood. He took the small digital camera from Brindle.

'Just keep it directed at her stomach. Two to three feet away will do,' Brindle explained before approaching the laptop he'd set up on top of the black plastic flight case. 'That's all there is to it. The camera connects wirelessly to the computer and produces an X-ray image. You can press the on button now, Carlos.'

He did, and all eyes reverted to the laptop screen as the image materialized.

Brindle and Doctor Hove's eyes widened in amazement and confusion, and they both craned their necks a little closer.

Hunter squinted, trying to understand what he was looking at.

Captain Blake's jaw dropped and her mouth went instantly dry, but she was the only one who managed to ask the question in everyone's mind.

'In the name of God, what . . . the *hell* . . . is that . . . inside her . . . ?'

Forty-Four

Hunter knew that with everything his brain was trying to process, sleep just wouldn't come. And he'd have to wait until morning for any sort of answer. Forensics were still processing the basement room in the old preschool, though he didn't hold out any great hopes about what they'd find. Doctor Hove would expedite the body's autopsy, but that'd only be at first light.

He collected some files from his office before making his way back to his place and then onto Jay's Rock Bar, a joint just two blocks away from his apartment. It was one of his favorite drinking spots. Great Scotch, fantastic rock music and friendly staff. He ordered a double dose of Glenturett 1997 with a single cube of ice and sat at a small table towards the back.

Hunter sipped his drink slowly for a minute, allowing its strong flavor to take over his palate. In front of him, spread out on the table, were all the photographs they'd received from Missing Persons. He scanned through them carefully, and despite the disfigurement to the new victim's face caused by the rough stitches, he knew she wasn't among them.

He needed to search the MPU database again, go back four, maybe five weeks, but as before, with the stitches and swelling, the face recognition software wouldn't work.

Doing it manually again would take too long. Hunter would have to wait until the end of the autopsy and use the new face close-ups once the stitches have been removed from the victim's mouth.

He finished his drink and debated if he should have another one. His eyes rested on the wall closest to him and all its paintings and decorations. He observed them for a moment. That's when a new thought entered his mind.

'It can't be . . .' he whispered as he shook his head.

Hunter gathered all his files together and rushed back to his apartment.

Sitting at the table in his living room, he fired up his computer and accessed the MPU database. He knew the criteria he used for the new search would reduce the output result considerably. He wasn't expecting any more than three, maybe five matches.

He was wrong.

Seconds later the screen flickered and the displayed table showed that his search had produced a single match. Hunter double-clicked it and waited for the file to upload.

As the new photograph materialized on his screen, Hunter let out a heavy breath.

Forty-Five

Special autopsy room one was located down a different corridor, separate from all the other chambers. It was usually used for postmortem examinations of bodies that could still pose some sort of contamination threat – highly contagious viral diseases, exposure to radioactive materials and so on. The room, with its own cold storage facility and separate database system, was sometimes used during high-profile serial killer cases, like the Crucifix Killer investigation a few years ago – a security precaution to better contain sensitive information.

The image they got from the portable tactical X-ray unit in the basement of the disused preschool in Glassell Park didn't reveal much, but whatever it was that the killer had placed inside his second victim, it sure as hell wasn't a bomb, Doctor Hove had no doubt of that. The picture showed a solid, triangular shape with a rounded base. Something that resembled a large but very thin slice of pizza. She'd never seen anything like it, and the only way she could find out any more about it was by extracting it from the body.

Doctor Hove had had almost no sleep, and turned up at the LACDC even before the crack of dawn. She just wanted to get on with things. At that time in the morning she had to perform the autopsy of the new victim on her own, no assistant. It would take longer than usual.

It was just past 7:00 a.m. when Doctor Hove called Hunter's cell.

During the short trip from Hunter's apartment to the morgue, he heard a report of shots fired in Boyle Heights and another of an armed robbery in progress in Silver Lake through the police radio. He drove past three light-flashing, siren-wailing police cars and two ambulances. The day had barely started. How could such an incredible city be so saturated with insanity?

The main coroners building at the LACDC was an intriguing piece of architecture with hints of Renaissance styling. Terracotta bricks and light gray lintels gave it an Oxford college look. Its business hours were the same as any city office – Monday to Friday, 8:00 a.m. to 5:00 p.m. Except under special request, no autopsies were ever carried out in the evenings or weekends. This was certainly one of those.

Hunter had called Garcia from the car and he wasn't surprised to find him already waiting in the empty parking lot.

'You got here quick,' Hunter said, stepping out of his old Buick.

'I got no sleep. I was waiting for this call.'

Hunter looked at him suspiciously. 'How about Anna?'

Garcia bobbed his head to one side. 'She got no sleep either. She insisted on staying up with me. She said that at least we could spend a few hours together since we haven't had much time for each other lately. But you know how perceptive she is. She's already picked up that the case we're working on isn't just a regular one. She never says anything, but you can see the worry in her face.'

Hunter nodded understandingly. He was very fond of

Anna. She was the unseen strength behind his partner. Most cops' wives would never understand or stick by their husbands like Anna did. Divorce numbers amongst the police in Los Angeles were around 70 per cent. But Hunter could never see that happening to Anna and Garcia. They were made for each other.

On the other hand, Hunter himself had never been married. The few relationships he'd had over the years had never really worked out. They'd always start well. But the pressures and commitments imposed by his job had a way of taking their toll on most love stories.

Hunter paused and turned as he heard the sound of another car entering the lot.

Captain Blake parked her silver metallic Dodge Challenger next to Garcia's Honda Civic.

'I wanna see this for myself,' she explained as she closed the door and pressed a button on her key. The car's head-lights flicked twice followed by a muffled click. 'I want to get a better idea of who the hell we're dealing with here. What kind of freak has claimed the lives of four people in my city so far.'

A silent and haggard-looking Doctor Hove let them into the building. With most of its lights turned off, and without the hustle and bustle of people, orderlies, and pathologists moving around, the place looked and felt like a horror movie mausoleum. The cold, antiseptic odor that was all too familiar to them seemed stronger this early in the morn-ing. The underlying smell of death and decomposition followed their every step, scratching the inside of their nostrils. Garcia fought the shiver that threatened to run up his spine as they walked past the empty reception area and turned into a desolate hallway. No matter how many times he and Hunter had walked those corridors, he'd never get used to the empty feeling that took over him every time.

'There's no point in explaining it until you see it for yourselves,' Doctor Hove said, punching the code into the metal keypad by the door to the special autopsy room. 'And if you thought the bomb left inside the first victim was crazy, wait until you see this.'

Forty-Six

The room was large and bright, lit by two rows of florescent lights that ran the length of the ceiling. Two steel tables dominated the main floor space, one fixed, one wheeled.

They stepped through the door and were immediately hit by a blast of cold air and an immense feeling of sadness that seemed to chill their bones. The brunette woman's body was lying uncovered on the fixed table. The stitches to her mouth and body had been removed, now substituted by new ones that outlined the Y incision. In a strange way she looked peaceful. The immeasurable suffering that was etched on her face just a few hours ago seemed to have vanished, as if she was grateful to someone for removing those terrible stitches from her body.

They all put on latex gloves and approached the table in silence. Doctor Hove buttoned up her white lab coat and moved around to the other side of the body.

Hunter stared at the woman's face for a long time. There was little doubt in his mind.

'I think her name is Kelly Jensen,' he said quietly, retrieving a black-and-white printout from the folder he'd brought with him and handing it to the doctor.

Captain Blake and Garcia craned their necks across the table. Doctor Hove had a good look at it before holding it close to the woman's face. Without the stitches to her lips, and washed of all that blood, the resemblance was undeniable.

The doctor nodded in agreement. 'On looks alone I'd say you're right, Robert.'

'Her file says that when she was a teenager she tripped and fell through a glass window in school,' Hunter continued, reading from a file sheet. 'Two large shards pierced the back of her left shoulder leaving a V-shaped scar. Her right elbow was also cut and she should have a semicircular scar just below the joint.'

Doctor Hove lifted her right arm and they all bent over to take a look at her elbow. An old and faint semicircular scar marked the skin a couple of centimeters below the joint. Very quickly they all repositioned themselves around the head of the table. The doctor didn't have to lift her upper body far, just a few inches was all that was needed. On the back of her left shoulder, scar tissue marked by the evidence of old stitches formed a sideways V-shape.

'I don't think there's much doubt now, is everyone agreed?' Doctor Hove lowered the victim body back down.

'Who is she?' the captain asked.

'The information I have at the moment isn't much, just what was passed to Missing Persons. Thirty years old from Great Falls in Montana. She was reported missing twenty-one days ago.' Hunter paused to clear his throat. 'Now here comes the punch. The person who reported her as missing was her agent.'

'Agent?' Garcia asked.

Hunter nodded. 'Kelly Jensen was a painter.'

Forty-Seven

Everyone held their breaths. Captain Blake was the first to slash the silence.

'How old was the first victim?'

'Laura Mitchell was thirty,' Garcia replied.

'And when did she go missing?'

Garcia looked at Hunter.

'She was reported missing fifteen days ago,' he replied.

Captain Blake closed her eyes for an instant. 'Fantastic,' she said, 'so we're dealing with some psycho killer who's after pretty, brunette, 30-year-old painters, and has a hard-on for stitching their bodies shut?'

Hunter didn't reply.

'Are there any more brunette 30-year-old painters who are missing?'

'I searched all the way back to ten weeks, Captain, Laura Mitchell and Kelly Jensen were the only two.'

The captain's gaze returned to the body on the table. 'Well, that's something I guess.' She turned to face Hunter and Garcia. 'We'll talk about this back at PC. What do we have here, Doc?' she asked Doctor Hove.

The doctor stepped a little closer to the autopsy table.

'Well, just like the first victim, the stitches the killer applied to his second one were amateurish, to say the least.'

The doctor pointed to Kelly Jensen's mouth. 'Actually, they were more like knots than anything else. Ten in total, five to each body part.'

'Same as the first one,' Hunter confirmed.

Doctor Hove nodded.

'So you're saying we shouldn't be looking for anyone with medical knowledge?' the captain asked.

'If he has any, he didn't show it here. The thread used is also very thick. What in medical suture we call a number six or seven. Thread sizes are identified by the United States Pharmacopeia,' she explained. 'Seven is the thickest. In comparison, a size four thread is roughly the diameter of a tennis racquet string. The thread used here will be going to the lab for proper analysis today, but there's no doubt he used some sort of nylon.' Doctor Hove turned and retrieved a folder from behind her. 'Her organs were healthy, but dehydrated. They also showed symptoms of mild malnutrition.'

The captain shifted on her feet. 'The killer starved her?'

'Possibly, but not for long. The symptoms are consistent with one, maybe two days of starvation at the most. She was deprived of food and water either on the day or the day before she died.' She lifted her right hand in a wait gesture. 'Before any of you raise this point, the stitches to her mouth were brand new, probably inflicted just hours before she died. That wasn't the reason why she'd had no food or water.'

'Any guesses?' Captain Blake asked as her eyebrows arched.

Doctor Hove tucked her dark hair behind her ears. 'There could be any number of reasons. Some sort of ritual on the killer's part, the victim herself refusing to eat as an act of defiance or because she felt sick, or angry, or anything . . .' She shrugged almost imperceptibly.

'Did you find any sort of marks at all on her body, Doc?' Hunter took over.

The doctor's face morphed as if Hunter had asked the million-dollar question.

'Now here is where it starts to get interesting.' She took a step to her right and allowed her eyes to refocus on Kelly Jensen's ghostly white face. 'I couldn't find a single scratch on her.'

Captain Blake looked puzzled. 'Nothing?'

'Nothing,' Doctor Hove confirmed. 'As we said earlier, her wrists and ankles are totally free from marks and abrasions. We know she wasn't restrained to that table in the kitchen basement of the preschool. But I can't find anything that suggests she was restrained *at all* during the time she was held captive either.' The doctor paused. 'My examination of the inside of her mouth and the skin around it also showed no evidence that she was gagged.'

'Which means the killer wasn't concerned with the victim making any sort of noise,' Garcia noted.

Doctor Hove nodded. 'She was either drugged up to her eyeballs, or locked inside a very secure and soundproofed room, or both. Toxicology results will take a few days.'

'Needle marks?' Hunter asked.

'Not even a little nick. Except for the tiny scrapes to her palms and knees, which I'm pretty sure she got when she fell to the floor, she doesn't have a scratch on her. Take away the stitches, and there's not a shred of evidence the killer ever touched her.'

Everyone went silent for a moment.

Hunter thought back to how long he'd spent going over

every inch of the crime-scene pictures of Laura Mitchell. Just like Kelly Jensen, she didn't have a scrape on her.

Hunter's attention shifted to Kelly's hands and his brow furrowed. Every one of her nails had been filed, witch-style. As pointy and as sharp as possible.

'Did you find anything under her nails, Doc? Why are they so . . . claw-like?'

'Good spot, Robert,' the doctor agreed. 'And the answer is – I'm not sure why. But I did find something under them, yes – some sort of dark copper-colored dust. It could be clay or brick dust, maybe even dry dirt. Again, we'll need to wait for the lab results to be sure.'

Hunter bent down and examined Jensen's hands more closely.

'I'll put an urgent tag with anything related to this case that gets sent to the lab,' the doctor reassured them. 'Hopefully we'll start getting results in a day or two. But unfortunately, due to the severity of her internal injuries and the amount of blood that was discharged, we won't be able to establish with any certainty if she was raped or not. If there was any trace of it, it's been washed away by her own blood.'

The entire room seemed to tense with those words.

Doctor Hove walked over to the metal counter and retrieved something from a plastic tray. 'Now this is the cause of it all, and it's as grotesque as it's ingenious,' she said, returning to the autopsy table. The strange metallic object she was holding was about eight inches long, a quarter-inch wide and two inches deep. At first glance it looked like several long and narrow slices of metal stacked up on top of each other like a deck of cards.

There were curious looks all round.

'This is what the killer placed inside her,' the doctor said, her voice a touch sadder than before.

The curious looks turned into confused frowns.

'What?' Captain Blake spoke first. 'I don't know what that is, Doc, but it sure as hell isn't what we saw through that X-ray machine of yours.'

'Not in this state, no,' the doctor agreed.

'And what in God's creation does that mean?'

Doctor Hove moved back to the other side of the autopsy table, putting some distance between herself and the other three.

'What this is, is a weapon like I've never seen before. Here we have a stack of twelve quarter-inch-wide razor blades held together by a very strong and potent spring mechanism. These blades are laser sharp. And when I say laser sharp, I mean a Samurai sword cuts like a baseball bat when compared to these.'

Hunter rubbed his eyes and shifted uncomfortably.

'I don't get it,' Garcia said, shaking his head. 'As the captain said, that isn't what we saw. So what did you mean when you said not in this state, Doc?'

'You obviously remember what we saw inside her body when we used the X-ray machine, right?' Doctor Hove clarified. 'Big, triangular shape with a rounded base? Something like a large protractor?' She didn't wait for a reply. 'OK, how do you suppose the killer managed to get that inside her? You'll have to agree that its rounded base was way too wide for it to be simply inserted into her body.'

Hunter let out a deep, heavy breath, his eyes back on the object in the doctor's hands. 'Some sort of spreading knife.'

Captain Blake's attention swung to Hunter. 'Some sort of what?'

'That's exactly it,' the doctor confirmed, showing everyone the long and thin metal object again. 'In this closed format, the killer would've had no problems inserting this thing into her before sewing her shut.'

The shiver Garcia had fought off as he entered the building returned, and this time he was powerless against it.

'Once inside,' the doctor continued, 'this happened.' She held the object by one of its tips using only her thumb and index finger. With her other hand's forefinger she clicked an almost invisible button at the top of it.

WHACK.

Forty-Eight

Caught completely by surprise, everyone jumped back.

'Shit!' Captain Blake let out in a high-pitched voice, bringing a hand to her mouth.

'Holy crap, what the fuck?' Garcia's hands shot up towards his face in a protective reflex.

In a fraction of a second, with a loud metallic thwack, the blades on the object in Doctor Hove's hands had snapped open exactly like a Chinese hand fan. Every shocked eye in the room was on it, and though their mouths were half-open, not a word was uttered. Doctor Hove carefully placed the object down on Kelly's stomach, its narrower tip just touching her pubic bone.

'This is about the position this thing was found inside her,' she finally said, her voice quieter, her tone darker than before. 'As you can see, the area it covers is almost the entire width of her abdomen.'

Captain Blake let go of the breath she had been holding for the past minute.

'As I said,' the doctor moved on, 'these blades are laser sharp on both edges. The springs that were used to smack them open are small but very powerful. Able to generate several pounds of pressure. Probably the equivalent to someone hatching down with a meat cleaver. This thing sliced through everything in its path.'

She indicated a large female body organ diagram on the wall behind her.

'Her urethra, bladder, cervix, uterus, ovary, vaginal cavity, everything in her reproductive system was mutilated instantly. The blades also managed to rip through muscle, her appendix and part of her large intestine. Her pelvic bone was chipped. There was no way she could've survived this. The internal hemorrhage she suffered was . . . unthinkable, but death wouldn't have been instantaneous. The pain she went through is something that even Satan would've had trouble imagining.'

Hunter ran a hand over his mouth. 'How long?'

'How long did she suffer for?' The doctor shrugged. 'Depends on how strong she was. A matter of minutes, probably. But to her I'm sure it felt like days.'

All eyes returned to the object the doctor had placed on Kelly's stomach.

'So how does this thing work again?' Captain Blake asked.

'Simple,' the doctor said, picking it up. 'The blades are way too sharp for anyone to touch them, so moving them back to their starting position could pose a problem, but there's a retracting mechanism built into it.' She indicated a round screw just a couple of centimeters from the object's base – the side that held one of the ends of the blades together. Using a screwdriver she retrieved from a glass-fronted cabinet, Doctor Hove began to turn it slowly. As she did, the blades started retracting behind each other, closing the fan-like knife. Less than a minute later they were all stacked up like a deck of cards just like before.

'The trigger is this button,' the doctor indicated it with her finger, 'very similar to the ones you see in click pens.'

They all moved closer to have a better look.

'So if this thing went off inside her, who clicked it on?' the captain asked.

'Well, I said the trigger is very similar to a clicking pen mechanism, but not identical. The difference is that this one is much more sensitive. I also said this was an ingenious piece of work. Check this out.' She stepped back, holding the strange knife just as she had moments earlier. This time, instead of clicking the trigger with her finger, she simply jerked it down about four inches, as if shaking a cocktail shaker, but only once.

WHACK. The knife fanned out with a metallic thud once again.

'It activates itself,' the doctor said. 'All it needs is a little bump.'

Hunter's mind went into overdrive. 'Fuck! The table . . . and the counter . . . that's why . . . the impact.'

Captain Blake gave him a slight headshake, still not with him.

'Do you think a clicking trigger mechanism just like that one could've been used to activate the bomb that was placed inside Laura Mitchell?' Hunter faced the doctor.

She thought about it for a second and her face transformed as realization dawned. 'It could've been easily adapted, yes. It's such a sensitive mechanism that Doctor Winston could've activated it by mistake as he pulled the bomb out of the victim without even noticing it.'

'How tall was she?' Hunter asked, nodding at Kelly Jensen's body.

'Five six,' the doctor replied.

Hunter turned to Captain Blake. 'The table inside the old preschool, and the butcher's counter in East LA had both been raised off the ground about a foot by wooden blocks or bricks. Neither of the victims was very tall. Laura Mitchell was five seven. The killer was making sure that his victims wouldn't just climb down from where they were once they woke up. They had to *jump* down. Like a kid out of a bunk bed.'

'Oh God!' Doctor Hove's eyes returned to the knife. 'The impact as their feet hit the ground would've jerked the object inside them.'

'Enough to activate the trigger mechanism?' Captain Blake asked.

'Easily,' Doctor Hove replied. A moment later she brought a hand to her mouth as she realized what it all meant. 'Jesus! The killer wanted to make them kill themselves without them knowing it.'

Forty-Nine

'OK,' Captain Blake said closing the door to Hunter and Garcia's office just minutes after getting back to Parker Center. 'What the hell is going on? I can almost get my head around a psycho being obsessed with painters. Both of them brunettes. Both of them somewhere in their thirties. Both of them attractive. In this city, that kind of obsession is *normal crazy*. But this thing about placing something inside the victims . . . something as absurd as a bomb, or as . . .' she shook her head as words escaped her ' . . . fucked up as a fan-out knife, and then stitching their bodies shut, that's completely dancing-around-the-room-naked-smothered-in-peanut-butter crazy.' She looked at Hunter. 'But this isn't what we're dealing with here, is it? This guy isn't insane. He's not hearing the devil's voice in his head or drinking his own piss, is he?'

Hunter shook his head slowly. 'I don't think so.'

'An obsessed stalker going after his idols, then?'

Hunter tilted his head from side to side. 'First impressions . . . maybe, but if you look closely at the evidence, it goes against the possibility of an obsessed fan being behind these murders.'

'How so? What evidence are you talking about?'

'The lack of bruising.'

Captain Blake's brow furrowed so hard, her eyebrows almost met.

'Two victims,' Hunter indicated with his fingers. 'Both kidnapped and held hostage for around two weeks. You remember what Doctor Hove said, right? That if we take away the savagery of the stitches and the way in which they died, they were both untouched. Not a scratch. The killer didn't lay a finger on them while they were in captivity.'

'OK,' the captain agreed. 'And how does that relate to the obsessed fan theory?'

'Obsessed fans spend a lot of time creating fantasies in their heads about their idols, Captain,' Hunter explained. 'That's why they become obsessed in the first place. Most of these fantasies are sexual, some are violent, but none is about kidnapping their idols so they could chat for weeks over hot milk and donuts. If this guy were a fan obsessed enough to kidnap, chances are he wouldn't be able to resist acting out at least one of his fantasies. Especially if he was prepared to kill them anyway. And if he did that, there would've been some sort of bruising somewhere on their bodies.'

Captain Blake looked pensive. They'd never be able to obtain confirmation that either of the victims had been raped. But Hunter was right; the lack of bruising on both of their bodies suggested that wasn't what this killer was after. An obsessed fan was starting to sound improbable.

'So who the hell could be capable of something like this?' she asked. 'A split personality job?'

'Again, possible, but with what we have so far it's hard to say.'

'Why?' she challenged. 'You said so yourself, the killer went from passive to absurdly violent in one quick step.

Isn't that an indication of extreme mood swings? A drastic change in personality?'

Hunter nodded. 'Yes, but the way he carries out his violence contradicts the theory.'

'How's that?'

'The time and preparation behind both murders was too extensive.'

'Slow down, big brain, I ain't following you,' she countered.

Hunter continued. 'Mood swings and extreme personality changes have to be triggered, usually by a very strong emotion – like rage, or love, or jealousy. They don't simply occur out of the blue. The new mood, or personality, takes over and stays for a while, but as soon as that rage, or whatever emotion it was that triggered it is gone, so is the personality. The person goes straight back to his or her normal self.' He snapped his fingers. 'Like waking up from a trance. How long do you think this trance can last, Captain?'

She started to catch on. 'Not long enough.'

'Not long enough,' Hunter agreed. 'The killer crafted a bomb and that knife from hell himself, not to mention the unique self-activating trigger mechanism. He also took time preparing the location where the victims were left, and then calmly sewed their body parts shut. All that takes a lot of time. Both preparing and executing it.'

'And that would mean that the killer would've had to have been in an altered state of mind for days, maybe weeks,' Garcia added. 'Highly unlikely.'

Hunter nodded. 'And then there's also the current accepted opinion of modern psychology that Multiple Personality Syndrome doesn't really exist. It's a therapist-induced disorder perpetuated by a never-ending barrage of TV talk shows, novels and ill-conceived Hollywood movies.'

'What?'

'Basically, modern psychology believes that Multiple Personality Syndrome is complete bullshit.'

Captain Blake leaned against Hunter's desk and undid both buttons on her suit jacket. 'So we're dealing with someone who knows exactly what he's doing?'

'I'd say so, yes.'

'His creativity is proof of that,' Garcia added.

Hunter nodded. 'He's also patient and self-disciplined, a rare virtue nowadays, even in the calmest of individuals. Add that to the level of craftsmanship he's showed so far, and it wouldn't surprise me if he were a watchmaker or even an artist himself. Maybe some sort of sculptor or something.'

The captain's eyes widened. 'Like a *failed* sculptor? Someone who was never as successful as his victims? You think this could be payback?'

Hunter shifted his weight to his left foot. 'No. I don't think this is born out of revenge.'

'How can you be sure? Envy is a powerful emotion.'

'If the killer is a failed artist after revenge because he never made it big, he wouldn't target other artists. It'd make no sense. They wouldn't be the reason he never made it.'

Garcia bit his bottom lip and bobbed his head in agreement. 'The revenge would've been against agents, or gallery curators, or art critics and journalists, or all of the above. People who can make or break an artist's career, not fellow artists.'

Hunter nodded. 'Also Laura Mitchell and Kelly Jensen's resemblance to each other isn't just a coincidence, Captain.

His victims mean more to him than just a vehicle for revenge.'

'The killer also used the same MO, but inserted a different killing device into each of his victims,' Garcia added. 'I don't think that was random. I think there's a meaning behind it.'

'What?' Captain Blake asked. A speck of irritation crept into her tone as she crossed to the window. 'What kind of relation could a bomb and a knife that didn't even exist on this earth until a few days ago have with two painters?'

No one replied. The silence that followed held a different meaning for each of them.

'So this new victim fucks up our lead on the James Smith guy, right?' the captain blurted. 'Everything we found in his apartment was about Laura Mitchell, not Kelly Jensen.'

'Maybe not,' Garcia argued. He started fidgeting with a paper clip.

'And how's that?'

'Maybe he's got another room somewhere else. Another apartment maybe,' Garcia offered.

'What?' Captain Blake glared at him.

'Maybe he's that smart, Captain. He knows that with two victims, if he gets caught and only one of the rooms is found, he has a good chance of walking.' He placed the paper clip, now bent out of shape, down on his desk. 'As we already know, he adopted the name James Smith because he knew if anything happened, his name alone would hide him under a mist of people.' He showed the captain his right index finger. 'He pays his rent up front.' Now the middle finger. 'He pays his bills up front. If he *is* our guy, we know for sure he's got at least one more place somewhere else: the place where he keeps his victims, 'cause we know he didn't keep them in that apartment. If that's the case, he could easily have another rented apartment somewhere else. Maybe under a complete different name. That's why we can't find him.'

Captain Blake leaned against the windowsill. 'It's an unlikely possibility.'

Garcia cracked his knuckles. 'It's also unlikely that anyone would create his own bomb, his own crazy knife, his own trigger mechanism and place it inside a victim before stitching her body shut.' He paused for effect. 'C'mon, Captain, the evidence says this guy is everything but predictable. He's smart, very slick and very patient. Would it really surprise you if he *did* have another collage room somewhere else? It gives him deniability.'

'Garcia is right, Captain,' Hunter said, sitting at the edge of his desk. 'We can't discard James Smith simply because the room we found didn't have anything about Kelly Jensen.'

'And has he been sighted anywhere yet? Have the phone lines produced any useful tips?'

'Not yet.'

'That's just great, isn't it?' She pointed to the street outside. 'Over four million people in this city and no one seems to know who this James Smith really is. The guy has simply vanished.' She crossed to the door and opened it. 'We're chasing a fucking ghost.'

Fifty

When Hunter got back to his office, he found an email from Mike Brindle in Forensics – the lab results from the fibers found on the wall behind the large canvas in Laura Mitchell's apartment were in. They had been right in their assumption. The fibers had come from a common wool skullcap. That meant that whoever had hid behind that canvas was somewhere between six foot and six four.

The results for the faint footprints were also in, but because they were set on house dust, and therefore smudged, they weren't 100 per cent accurate. The conclusion was that they'd probably come from size eleven or twelve shoes, which was consistent with the height theory. The interesting fact was that they had found no sole marks. No trademark imprints, or grooves, or anything. A completely flat sole. Mike Brindle's take on it was that whoever had waited in Laura's apartment had used some sort of shoe cover. Probably handmade. Probably soft rubber or even synthetic foam. That would have no doubt also muffled the perpetrator's footsteps.

After analyzing the entire studio floor for any more size eleven or twelve foot imprints, Brindle arrived at the same conclusion as Hunter and Garcia had. After hiding behind the large canvas resting against the back wall, Laura

Mitchell's attacker had somehow diverted her attention and very quickly gotten to her with a strong sedative, probably an intravenous one.

'I've got the personal info on Kelly Jensen from research,' Garcia said as he walked through the door, carrying a green plastic folder.

'What do we have?' Hunter asked looking up from his computer.

Garcia took a seat behind his desk and flipped open the folder. 'OK, Kelly Jensen, born in Great Falls, Montana, thirty years ago. Her parents haven't been notified yet.'

Hunter nodded.

Garcia continued. 'She started painting in high school . . . At the age of twenty, against her parents' wishes, she relocated here to Los Angeles . . . She spent several years struggling and being rejected by every agent and art gallery in the business . . . blah, blah, blah, your typical LA story, except she was a painter, not an actress.'

'How did she get noticed?' Hunter asked.

'She used to sell her work on the oceanfront – a street stall. Got noticed by none other than Julie Glenn, New York's top art critic. A week later, Kelly got an art agent, a guy called Lucas Laurent. He was the one who reported her as missing.' He paused and stretched his arms high above his head. 'Kelly's career took off quickly after that. Julie Glenn wrote a piece about her in the *New York Times*, and within a month, the canvases Kelly couldn't give away at the beach were selling for thousands.'

Hunter checked his watch before grabbing his jacket. 'OK, let's go.'

'Where?'

'To see the person who reported her missing.'

Fifty-One

The traffic was like a religious procession and it took Garcia almost two hours to cover the twenty-three miles between Parker Center and Long Beach.

Lucas Laurent, Kelly Jensen's agent, had his office on the fifth floor of number 246 East Broadway Street.

Laurent was in his thirties, with olive skin, dark brown eyes and neatly cut hair that was starting to gray. The wrinkles that already surrounded his lips came from heavy smoking, Hunter guessed. His navy blue suit was well fitting, but his tie was a masterpiece of bad taste. A Picasso-style monstrosity of chunky color pieces that only someone with enormous amounts of confidence could wear. And confidence Laurent certainly had – the quiet kind that came with wealth and success.

He stood up from behind his twin pedestal desk and greeted Hunter and Garcia by the door. His handshake was as firm as a businessman's ready to close a large deal.

'Joan told me you're detectives with the LAPD?' he said as he eyed Hunter. 'I hope you're not actually artists and this was just a trick to get you into my office without an appointment.' He smiled and deep crinkles appeared at the edges of his eyes. 'But if it was, it certainly shows you've both got creativity and ambition.'

'Unfortunately, we're the real thing,' Hunter said, showing Laurent his credentials. The agent's smile faded fast. Only then did he remember he'd reported Kelly as missing a couple of weeks ago.

Hunter told him only what he needed to know and watched as the color vanished from his face. Laurent slumped back in his chair, his eyes catatonically looking through Hunter.

'But that's just ludicrous . . . murdered? By whom? And why? Kelly was an artist, not a drug dealer.'

'That's what we're trying to find out.'

'But she had an exhibition scheduled in Paris in less than two months' time . . . it could have made us close to a million.'

Hunter and Garcia exchanged a quick, concerned glance. *Strange time to be thinking about money.*

Laurent ruffled inside his desk's top drawer for a pack of cigarettes. 'I don't usually smoke in my office,' he explained, 'but I really need this. Do you mind?'

Both detectives shrugged.

Laurent brought a cigarette to his lips, lit it up with a shaking hand and took a drag as if his life depended on it.

Hunter and Garcia sat in the two salmon-colored armchairs in front of Laurent's desk and began asking him about his relationship with Kelly and his knowledge of her personal life. From Laurent's answers, just like from his comment about making millions a moment ago, they quickly gathered that Laurent's relationship with Kelly had been 99 per cent business.

'Did you have a set of keys to her apartment?' Garcia asked.

'God, no.' Laurent had one last drag of his cigarette,

walked over to the window and stubbed it out on the ledge before flicking the butt onto the street below. 'Kelly didn't like having people in her apartment or her studio. She wouldn't even allow me to see any of her pieces until they were completely finished, and even then I almost had to beg her to show them to me. Artists are very self-centered and eccentric people.'

'Her apartment is in Santa Monica and her art studio in Culver City, is that right?' Garcia asked.

Laurent nodded nervously.

'Am I right in thinking you and Miss Jensen attended some social engagements together? Dinners . . . receptions . . . exhibitions . . . awards, things like that?'

'Yes, quite a few over the three years I've been representing her.'

'Have you ever met anyone she was seeing? Has she ever taken a date to any of these engagements?'

'Kelly?' He laughed tensely. 'I couldn't think of anything that'd be farther from her thoughts than a relationship. She was stunning. She had men throwing themselves at her, but she just didn't wanna know.'

'Really?' Hunter said. 'Is there a reason why?'

Laurent shrugged. 'I never asked, but I know she was really hurt by someone she was in love with a few years ago. The kind of hurt that never goes away. The kind of hurt that makes you wary of every relationship you have from that day on. You know what I mean?'

'Do you know if she had casual relationships?' Garcia asked.

Another shrug. 'Probably, as I said, she was stunning; but I never met anyone she was dating. She never mentioned anyone either.'

'Did she ever mention anything about emails? Something that'd scared or upset her lately?' Hunter took over.

Laurent frowned, taking a few seconds to remember. 'Nothing in particular. I'm not sure about any of them being scary or upsetting, but I'm sure she got a few strange ones from infatuated fans. It happens more than you think. I just tell all my artists to disregard them.'

'Disregard them?'

'Fans come with fame, Detective; it's a package deal that you can't opt out of. And unfortunately some of them are just plain weird, but they usually mean no harm. All the artists I represent get them every now and then.' His eyes moved back to the pack of cigarettes on his desk and he quickly debated if he should have another one. He started fidgeting with a black-and-gold Mont Blanc pen instead. 'I've been Kelly's agent for three years, and in that time I've never seen her unhappy, or worried. She always had a smile on her face, as if it were tattooed to her lips. I really can't remember ever seeing Kelly unhappy.'

'When did you last speak to Miss Jensen?' Garcia asked.

'We were supposed to meet up for lunch on the . . .' he flipped open a leather-bound diary on his desk and quickly leafed through it, ' . . . the 25th February, to discuss Kelly's upcoming exhibition in Paris. Kelly had been very excited about that particular trip for months, but she never turned up for the meeting, and she never called to cancel either. When I tried getting hold of her, all I got was her answering service. Two days later I gave up trying and contacted the police.'

'Was she involved with drugs, gambling, anything of the bad sort you know of?' Garcia asked this time.

Laurent's eyes widened for an instant. 'God, no. At least

not that I know of. She barely drank. Kelly was your typical good girl.'

'Financial difficulties?'

'Not with the kinda money she was making. Every one of her paintings sells for thousands. Probably more now.'

Hunter wondered if he threw a hundred bucks out the window, would Laurent jump after it?

Before leaving, Hunter paused by the door to the office and turned to face Laurent again. 'Do you know if Miss Jensen was friends with another LA painter – Laura Mitchell?'

Laurent looked at him curiously before shaking his head. 'Laura Mitchell? I'm not sure. Their styles are very different.'

Hunter turned to look back at him curiously.

'Believe it or not,' Laurent clarified, 'many painters are funny in that way. Some won't mix with different style artists.' He pouted reflexively. 'Some won't mix with other artists at all. Why do you ask?'

'Just wondering.' Hunter handed Laurent a card. 'If you think of anything else, please don't—'

'Wait!' Laurent cut him short. 'Laura Mitchell and Kelly *did* meet. It was a few years ago. I'd forgotten all about that. Right at the start of Kelly's career. I had just started representing her. She was interviewed for a cable TV documentary. Something about the new wave of American artists from the West Coast, or something along those lines. Several artists took part in it. I think it was all filmed at the . . .' his eyes moved to a blank spot on the wall ' . . . Getty Museum or maybe at the Moca, I can't be sure. But I'm in no doubt Laura Mitchell was one of the artists who was there that day.'

Fifty-Two

Night had already darkened the sky by the time Hunter and Garcia got back to Parker Center. They both felt exhausted.

'Go home, Carlos,' Hunter said rubbing his eyes. 'Spend the night with Anna. Take her out for dinner or a movie or something. There ain't much we can do now but review information, and our brains are both too fried to process anything at this time.'

Garcia knew Hunter was right. And Anna would really appreciate having her husband for an entire night. He reached for his jacket.

'Aren't you coming?' he asked as Hunter turned his computer on.

'Five minutes,' Hunter replied with a nod. 'Just gonna check something on the net.'

It took Hunter a lot longer than he expected to find any references to the documentary Kelly Jensen's agent had mentioned. It was a low budget production by the Arts and Entertainment cable TV Channel called *Canvas Beauty, The Upcoming Talents from the West Coast*. It had only aired once, three years ago. He called the A & E TV network office in LA, but at that time of night, there was no one there who could assist him. He'd have to contact them again in the morning.

Hunter didn't go straight home after he left his office. His mind was too full of thoughts for him to try to brave the solitude of his apartment.

If the killer was really forcing his victims to kill themselves by impact-activating a trigger mechanism, then they were right about Laura Mitchell, the first victim. She wasn't supposed to have died on that butcher's counter. She was supposed to have jumped down from it. The bomb was supposed to have gone off inside her. But the trigger was never activated. She died from suffocation. Her mother had told Hunter about the choking seizures Laura used to suffer when young. Possibly some psychological condition that had ceased to manifest itself after she started painting. Hunter knew that such conditions could easily be shocked back to life by a traumatic experience, like severe panic. The kind of panic she would have experienced in that dark back room, alone, with her mouth and body stitched shut.

Hunter drove around aimlessly for a while before ending up at the oceanfront on Santa Monica Beach.

He liked watching the sea at night. The sound of waves breaking against the sand together with the quietness calmed him. It reminded him of his parents and of when he was a little kid.

His father used to work seventy-hour weeks, jumping between two awfully paid jobs. His mother would take any work that came her way – cleaning, ironing, washing, anything. Hunter couldn't remember a weekend when his father wasn't working, and even then they struggled to pay all their bills. But Hunter's parents never complained. They simply played the cards they were dealt. And no matter how bad a hand they got, they always did it with a smile on their faces.

Every Sunday, after Hunter's father got home from work, they used to go down to the beach. Most times they got there as everyone else was packing up and getting ready to leave. Sometimes the sun had already set. But Hunter didn't mind. In fact, he preferred it. It was like the whole beach belonged to him and his parents. After Hunter's mother passed away, his father never stopped taking him to the beach on Sundays. Sometimes, Hunter would catch his father wiping away tears as he watched the waves break.

There were tourists everywhere, especially down Third Street Promenade and in the many beach bars that lined the oceanfront. A boy sped past him in rollerblades, quickly followed by a younger girl, clearly struggling with her technique.

'Slow down, Tim,' she called after the boy pleadingly. He didn't even look back.

Hunter sat on the sand for a while, watching the waves and breathing in the sea breeze. He spotted a group of night surfers in the distance. Five in total, two of them female. They seemed to be having a great time. A boy was practicing his soccer juggling skills close to the water. He was good, Hunter had to admit. A couple holding hands walked past in silence and both nodded a cordial hello at Hunter, who returned the gesture. He watched them walk away, and for a moment he lost himself in a memory. Something few people ever knew about him – he'd been in love once, long ago.

Unconsciously his lips spread into a melancholic smile. As the memory developed, the smile faded and an empty pit took hold of his stomach. A lonely tear threatened to form at the corner of his eye. But the memory was interrupted by his cell phone ringing in his pocket. The display window read – unknown number.

'Detective Hunter.'

'*Wassup, dawg*?' D-King said in his chilled-out lilt. Loud hip-hop music was playing in the background.

'Not much,' Hunter replied.

D-King wasn't one for beating around the bush. 'Sorry, dawg, there's no word on the street, you know what I'm saying. The Chicanos, the Jamaicans, the Russians, the Chinese, the Italians, whoever . . . no one knows anything about no girl getting a stitch job. She wasn't a gang hit, at least not a known gang.'

'Yeah, I figured that out since we last talked.'

'Did you find out who she was?'

'Yeah.'

D-King waited, but Hunter didn't follow up.

'Let me guess, she wasn't a working girl.'

'That's right.'

'I told you, dawg. I would've known if she was.' There was a hesitant pause. 'Listen, I gotta go, but I'll keep asking around. If I hear anything, I'll give you a holler.'

He disconnected, brushed his hands against each other, clearing off the sand before grabbing his jacket and walking back to his car. The throng of people around the bars was starting to die down, and for a moment Hunter considered going inside. He could do with a shot of single malt . . . or five. Maybe *that* would completely clear his mind.

A woman sitting at one of the many outside tables laughed loudly, catching Hunter's attention. She was attractive with short brunette hair and a magnificent smile. Their eyes met for a brief instant and he remembered that Kelly Jensen's apartment was in Santa Monica. Her art studio wasn't far either. Culver City was practically the next neighborhood.

The file Hunter had got from Missing Persons said that the investigating officer had visited both locations without any major breakthroughs. The suspicion was that Kelly had been abducted from her home address as she parked her car and made her way into her apartment building. There were no witnesses and no CCTV camera footage.

Hunter checked his watch. He and Garcia had planned on checking out both places tomorrow, but what the hell. He was already there, and there was no way he'd be getting any sleep anytime soon.

Fifty-Three

Kelly Jensen's apartment was on the second floor of a luxurious building on the exclusive San Vicente Boulevard, a stone's throw away from the west end of Santa Monica Beach.

Hunter parked his car just outside her apartment block and observed the traffic for a while. Cars came and went every ten to fifteen seconds. As he got out and closed the door behind him, he recognized Kelly's car as described in the information sheet he'd received from Missing Persons – a candy white 1989 anniversary Pontiac Trans-Am T-top in pristine condition. It was parked just a few spaces from where he had pulled up. Hunter put on a pair of latex gloves before mechanically looking up at the surrounding buildings. There were several lights on. He approached Kelly's car and cupped his hands over the driver's window. Its interior looked to be spotlessly clean.

Hunter already had the keys to Kelly's apartment. They had been sent to Parker Center together with the MPU case files, and those were in the back seat of his car. He let himself into the building and made his way up to the second floor. After fumbling for the right key, he unlocked the door to Kelly's apartment, stepped inside and paused by the entrance for a moment before trying the light switch. Nothing.

'Great.' He flicked on his flashlight.

Her living room was spacious and nicely decorated. Hunter took his time looking around. The tidiness was almost compulsive, except for the dust that had accumulated since Kelly had gone missing. Every object seemed to have its place.

There were a few photo frames on a long glass sideboard against one of the walls – most of the photos were of her and her parents.

The kitchen was open plan, on the west side of the living room. No lights worked there either. Hunter opened the fridge and was immediately slapped across the face by a gust of warm, putrid air.

'Damn!' He jumped back, slamming the door shut. The power must've been off for a few days now. He exited the kitchen and moved further into the apartment.

The bedroom was enormous, probably bigger than Hunter's entire one-bedroom flat. In the en-suite bathroom he found a large collection of make-up items and several bottles of face, hand and body creams. Her bed was perfectly made. On her dresser Hunter found another portrait of her parents, some necklaces and bracelets, and a collection of fragrances. The drawers were overflowing with lingerie and summer clothes.

Hunter returned his attention to Kelly's parents' portrait. She looked a lot more like her mother than her father. Hunter couldn't help but think about the pain they were about to go through when the sheriff in Great Falls knocked on their door. It was the worst news any parent could ever receive. He'd been the bearer of such news more times than he cared to remember.

As he placed the frame back on the dresser, his flashlight beam reflected on the silver frame and his body tensed. The frame worked like a mirror, and he caught a glimpse of a dark figure standing right behind him.

Fifty-Four

Click.

Hunter heard the muffled sound of a semi-automatic pistol being cocked inches away from the back of his head. But before the person standing there had a chance to say or do anything, he spun on the balls of his feet and swung his arm around with purpose. The flashlight caught the intruder's pistol-holding arm with a loud thud.

Gun and flashlight flew across the room, smashing against the wardrobe door and falling to the floor. The flashlight ended up under the bed, facing the wall, its deflected beam now just strong enough to keep the room from slipping into total darkness.

Hunter's left hand was already at his shoulder holster. He'd managed to wrap his fingers around the handle of his gun when the intruder delivered a well-placed kick to his abdomen, catching Hunter right at the pit of his stomach. Air left him like a ripped balloon and he stumbled backwards, gasping for oxygen. Hunter knew another kick would quickly follow. This time it came in the form of a side sweep to the right side of his body, around the same height as the first one, but Hunter was ready for it. He blocked it with the outside of his forearm and unleashed a devastating blow with his left fist, catching the intruder square in the chest. Hunter used his momentum to step forward and sent in a follow-up punch to the face. It was blocked with martial-art precision. Hunter didn't miss a step, another left punch to the side of the torso – blocked. Right punch to the chest – blocked. Left elbow to the face – blocked.

What the fuck? Hunter thought. Can this guy see in the dark or what?

A new, higher and more powerful jump kick came from the intruder. Hunter saw it late, but even so, his rapid reaction allowed him to swerve most of his head out of the way. The tip of the intruder's boot grazed Hunter's right eyebrow, nicking it. Hunter used his swerving motion to gain speed and pirouetted his body around three hundred and sixty degrees. The movement took only a split second, and at the end of it Hunter delivered a new punch with his left fist straight to the intruder's ribcage. But some last-minute intuition told him to take some of the power off the strike. Even so, this time there was no blocking. The intruder doubled over and stumbled back. In a blink of an eye Hunter reversed his movement, spinning his body in the opposite direction. As he faced his attacker again, he was holding his gun with his right arm fully extended. The barrel of his weapon just inches away from his attacker's face.

'Move and you'll be having dinner with Elvis.'

'Fuck, that was a fast draw.'

Hunter frowned. It was a woman's voice.

'Who the fuck are you?' she asked.

'Me?' Hunter cocked his gun. 'Who the fuck are you?'

'I asked first.'

'Well, I have a gun.'

'Yeah? So did I.'

'Well, guess what? I still have mine, and it's pointing right at your face.'

A split-second pause.

'OK, point taken.' She lifted her hands but didn't say a word.

'I'll ask again, in case you forgot – who the hell are you?'

'My name is Whitney Myers.' Her voice was calm.

Hunter waited but Myers offered nothing else. 'And . . . ? Is your name supposed to mean anything to me . . . ?'

'I'm a private missing persons investigator. If you allow me to move I can show you my credentials.'

'Your hands are going nowhere for now, buttercup.'

He looked at her suspiciously. Even through the weak light coming from under the bed, Hunter could tell Myers was wearing dark trousers and shirt, flat-soled shoes, a small pouch belt around her waist and a black skullcap.

'You dress more like a burglar than a PI.'

'Well, you don't dress like a cop either,' she stabbed back.

'How do you know I'm a cop?'

She tilted her head in the direction of the wardrobe. 'Standard issue LAPD flashlight.' A short pause. 'Unlike your gun. Nothing standard about that. HK USP tactical pistol. A Navy Seals favorite. You're obviously part of some special section, or a pretty big gun fanatic. I'm guessing both.'

Hunter's gun was still aimed dead at her eyes. 'If you knew I was a cop, why the hell did you attack me like that?'

'You never gave me a chance to say a word. I was about to politely ask you to turn around slowly when suddenly you turned into Captain America on crack. I was just defending myself.'

Hunter considered it. 'If you're a PI, who hired you?'

'You know I can't tell you that. It's privileged information.'

Hunter's gaze moved to his gun and then back to Myers. 'Under the circumstances, I don't think you've got much of a choice.'

'You and I both know you're not gonna shoot me.'

Hunter chuckled. 'I wouldn't be so confident if I were you. All I need is a reason.'

Myers didn't reply.

'Plus I can arrest you for breaking and entering. You know how it goes. You'll have to drag a lawyer down to the station, then you'll be properly interrogated . . . yada, yada, yada . . . and we'll find out anyway. So you'd better tell me something, or this is about to become a *very* long night for you.' Hunter could feel thin lines of blood running down the right side of his face from the cut just above his eyebrow. He stood perfectly still.

Myers fixed Hunter down with a solid stare. She could see the resolve in his eyes. He wasn't about to let her go easy. But Myers also wasn't about to tell Hunter the truth about Katia and Leonid Kudrov. She wasn't prepared to tell him her secrets, or that – out of habit and as a way of keeping her updated with who her potential clients could be – Myers was sent a daily list of names, including photographs, of new additions to the Missing Persons Unit database. The list was compiled and filtered by her LAPD informer, Carl O'Connor.

O'Connor wasn't a detective with the MPU. Pure and simple, he was a computer geek, an old friend, and the database administrator for the Valley Bureau of the LAPD. His unlimited access to essential information where missing persons were concerned had given Myers the advantage she needed in many cases. When she received Kelly

Jensen's photograph, Myers immediately saw the resemblance to Katia Kudrov, and that was why she was at Kelly Jensen's apartment in that specific moment. She was looking for clues.

There was no way she was telling Hunter all that. But Myers knew she had to tell him something. She improvised as fast as she could.

'OK. The person I'm working for is an ex-boyfriend,' she lied with the steadiest of faces.

Hunter frowned. 'Name?'

Myers smiled. 'You know I can't give you his name. Not without his consent or a court order. You have neither.'

'And he went to you instead of the Missing Persons Unit?'

'What can I say? Some people just don't trust the LAPD.'

Myers relaxed her right arm.

'Hey, hey, hey,' Hunter called with a lilt in his voice. 'Easy there, pumpkin. What are you doing?'

She brought her hand to the side of her body, rubbing it while taking a deep breath. 'I think you've broken a couple of my ribs.'

Hunter didn't move. 'No I haven't. And at least you're not bleeding.'

Myers glanced at the cut above Hunter's eyebrow. 'I've never seen anyone move that fast. I had you right in my sights. You were supposed to be knocked out cold.'

'Lucky for me I got out of the way, then,' Hunter said, gently stretching his neck. 'How did you get in here? There were no signs of forced entry.'

Myers gave Hunter a charming smile. This was getting complicated. She stood her ground.

'I'm doing all the talking here, and you still haven't told me your name or shown me any police ID yet. Hell, I'm not even sure for a fact that you *are* LAPD. I know you're not MPU. So who are you?'

'How do you know I'm not with the Missing Persons Unit?'

Her face went dead serious. ''Cause I used to be part of them.'

Fifty-Five

Hunter kept his gaze on Myers for several seconds. She held his stare with identical determination.

'OK,' Hunter finally said, 'let's see that PI license you were talking about. But very slowly.'

'Let's see that police badge you were talking about,' Myers challenged.

Hunter pulled open the left side of his leather jacket. His badge was clipped onto his belt.

Myers acknowledged it with a nod, unzipped her pouch belt and handed Hunter a black leather wallet.

He scrutinized her identity card before returning his attention to Myers. Dark eyes, small nose, high cheekbones, full lips, perfect skin, and an athlete's body.

Hunter finally holstered his weapon before picking up his flashlight together with Myers' gun – a Sig Sauer P226 X-5 semi-auto pistol.

'Being a PI must pay well,' he said, releasing the magazine and checking for a chambered round before handing the empty pistol back to Myers. 'This is a two and a half grand gun.' He slipped the magazine into his pocket.

'Why? Are you looking for a new job? I could certainly use a guy like you. Good benefits and health insurance.'

Hunter took a paper tissue from a dispenser on the

dresser and cleared some of the blood from his face. 'Yeah? Well, I couldn't use a boss like you.'

Myers smiled. 'Oh, you're quick with the comebacks too? I guess the chicks dig that.'

Hunter ignored her comment.

'Are you gonna tell me who you are now, or shall I just call you Mr. Detective?' she asked, folding her arms.

'My name is Robert Hunter.' He handed her wallet back to her. 'I'm a detective with the LAPD.'

'Which section?' She nodded at his badge. 'As I said, I know you're not Missing Persons.'

Hunter placed the flashlight on the dresser. 'Homicide Special.'

Myers eyes widened. She knew exactly what that meant. For a beat she seemed lost for words. 'When?' she asked.

'When what?'

'Don't play dumb. You don't look the type, and I'm through fucking around. Do you know when Jensen died?'

Hunter studied Myers' face and saw a hint of desperation there. He mechanically checked his watch before conceding. 'Yesterday.'

'Was her body found yesterday or did she die yesterday?'

'Both. She'd been dead for only a few hours when we found her.'

'Whoever took her kept her for almost three weeks before killing her?'

Hunter didn't reply. He didn't need to. Myers knew exactly the implications of such an act by a kidnapper/murderer.

'How was she murdered?' she asked.

Silence.

'Oh c'mon, I'm not asking for any major investigation secrets. I know the protocol and I know what you can and cannot disclose. If not from you, how long do you think it'll take me to find that information out? A couple of phone calls, maybe. I've still got contacts and connections in the force.'

Hunter still said nothing.

'Fine. I'll find out my way then.'

'The killer used a knife.'

Myers ran the tips of her fingers against her upper lip.

'How many victims?'

Hunter looked back at her curiously.

She continued. 'How many victims have you got so far? If you're Homicide Special it means this guy has either killed before or Kelly Jensen was killed in a particularly horrific way . . . or both. And if I had to take a guess I'd say both.'

Hunter remained silent.

'You're looking for a serial killer, aren't you?'

'For someone who used to be a cop, you sure jump to conclusions very quickly.'

Myers' eyes moved away from Hunter.

'OK, it's your turn to share,' he said. 'Who's this ex-boyfriend you're working for?'

Myers didn't want to embroil herself further in her lie. 'You want information from me now?' Her eyebrows arched.

'Are we back playing games again, sweetheart?' Hunter challenged. 'I thought you said you were through fucking around.'

Myers glared at him again.

'Kelly Jensen is dead. Murdered in a way your nightmares

couldn't produce. Your Missing Persons case is over. That's all you need to know.'

'Client/investigator confidentiality privileges don't end once the case is over. You know that.'

'The ex-boyfriend could be a suspect.'

A second of hesitation.

'He isn't,' Myers said confidently. 'Or do you think I didn't have him thoroughly checked out before taking the case. And you said that Kelly was killed yesterday. He's been out of the country for five days.'

'If you're so sure of his innocence, why not give me his name and let me check him out too.'

A long, uncomfortable moment played out between them before Myers put out her right arm, the palm of her hand facing up. Her eyes staring straight into Hunter's. 'Can I have my ammunitions clip back?'

Hunter knew she was asking for a trust gesture. A give in order to receive kind of thing. He slowly retrieved the magazine from his pocket and placed it in her hand. Myers didn't load it into her gun. Instead, she just stared at it for a long moment. Her lie was snowballing into something she knew she wouldn't be able to control. She needed to get out of there before she made a mistake.

'You know I can't give you his name. If I do I'll never get another client again. But I can hand you everything I have on the case. Maybe you can find something there.'

Hunter saw her right eye twitch ever so slightly.

Myers looked down and checked her watch. 'Give me a few hours to gather everything together and you can have whatever I have.'

Hunter continued to observe her.

'I know where to find you.'

Hunter watched Myers leave the room before reaching into his pocket. He looked down at the Private Investigator's ID he'd slipped out of her leather wallet.

'And I know where to find you,' he whispered to himself.

Fifty-Six

Kelly Jensen's art studio was a refurbished mechanic's garage behind a row of shops in Culver City. The street was narrow and hidden away from the main roads, at the top of a small hill. To the right of her studio was a small parking lot, where all the shop owners kept their vehicles during the day. At that time at night it was completely empty. The only light came from a lamppost on the corner, its bulb old and yellowing. Hunter looked around for security cameras. Nothing.

The studio was spacious and well organized. There were shelves and drawers for every different paint color, type of brush, palette, and canvas sizes. All finished paintings were placed on a large wooden rack that occupied the entirety of the north wall. There was only one canvas stand, positioned just a few feet from the large window that faced west. Kelly liked watching the sunset while working, Hunter guessed. A paint-splattered cloth covered the painting on the stand. Unlike Laura Mitchell, Kelly seemed to only work on one canvas at a time.

Hunter lifted the stained cloth and checked the painting underneath it. Dark, shadowy skies against a placid lake that surrounded the ruins of an old building on top of a steep sloping hill. Hunter stepped back to get a better view.

Kelly was a realist painter, and the effect she achieved

with that particular canvas was so vivid it was like standing at the shore, looking out into the horizon. But she'd done something Hunter had never seen before. It was as though the whole scenery was seen through a smoky glass. Everything had a sad, gray tint to it, as if the weather was about to close in on you with a vengeance. The painting looked so real it made Hunter feel cold. He pulled the collar of his jacket tighter against his neck.

Kelly's ample working space was uncluttered. The only furniture around the place were the shelves and drawer units against the walls, the storing rack, and an old, beat-up armchair several feet away from the window, facing the canvas stand. There were no six-foot canvases, partitions, or anything else for that matter. No place for anyone to hide behind. There was an improvised kitchen area in one corner, and a small bathroom in the opposite one. Hunter checked everywhere. There was no way the killer could've waited and then sneaked up on Kelly in there without her noticing it.

Hunter walked back up to the window and stared out into the night. Because her studio was at the top of a hill, the view was unobstructed and quite astonishing. No wonder Kelly used to paint facing that view. He checked the locks. All quite new and very secure. The small parking lot was to the far left, but only part of it was visible from the window.

Suddenly, just a couple of feet from where he was, something moved outside the window with incredible agility.

'Shit!' Hunter jumped back, his hand going for his gun.

The black cat ran the length of the window ledge in just a split second. Hunter stood motionless, both arms extended, his grip tight around his pistol handle, his pulse racing.

'Goddamn it! Not twice in one night,' he finally breathed out. How could he not have noticed the cat? He moved closer and looked again. The lack of any light outside made the window work almost as a two-way mirror. At night, a person dressed all in black could have observed Kelly without being noticed. Hunter unlocked the window, pushed it open and welcomed the cool breeze that kissed his face. He leaned forward and looked out, first right then left, in the direction of the parking lot. That's when he noticed something at the far wall blink at him.

Fifty-Seven

The shrieking scream that came from her TV made Jessica Black wake with a start. She'd fallen asleep on the sofa and hadn't even noticed the old, black-and-white B-movie horror film that had started.

She rubbed her gritty eyes, pulled herself up into a sitting position, and looked around her living room for Mark, her boyfriend. He was nowhere to be seen.

The woman on the screen screamed again and Jessica groggily reached for the remote control that had fallen between her legs, and switched the set off. The scented candle she'd lit earlier had burned halfway through, and the entire room now carried the sweet smell of apples and cinnamon. Jessica watched the flame burn for a minute. Her Wechter acoustic guitar was resting by the side of the sofa next to her. Still watching the flame, she ran her hand across the strings and allowed her memories to catch up with her.

Jessica had got her first acoustic guitar on her tenth birthday. Her father had bought it for her as a present in a garage sale. It was an old and scratched plank of wood with rusty strings that sounded more like a dying dog than a musical instrument. But even at that age, Jessica understood her father had spent money he couldn't afford just to make her happy. And happy she was.

Her fascination with the instrument had started two years earlier. Just like every afternoon before she had gotten sick, her mother had taken Jessica to the park close to where they lived. That day there was an old black man playing guitar just yards away from the bench her mother liked to sit on. That day, instead of running around with the other kids, Jessica sat on the grass in front of the old man and watched him play all afternoon, mesmerized by the sounds he could get out of only six strings.

The old man never returned to the park, but Jessica never forgot him. A week later her mother fell ill with something no one could diagnose. Her disease advanced quickly, eating away at her from the inside and transforming her from a smiling, vital woman into an unrecognizable bag of skin and bones. Jessica's father faded along with his wife. As the disease progressed, so did his depression. His pay as a supermarket clerk was barely enough to keep them going, and when he lost his job two months after his wife had gotten ill, their financial situation collapsed.

Jessica's mother died the day after doctors finally found out she had developed a rare carcinoid tumor.

Jessica's last happy memory of her mother was that day in the park, both of them listening to the old guitar man.

Jessica took to the guitar as if that memory lived in every note she plucked. She had no money for lessons, magazines or music books, but she spent every possible second with her beloved instrument. Soon she'd developed her own unique style of tapping and fingerpicking the strings, exploring every sound the instrument could give her. She could play the guitar like no one had ever heard. At the age of nineteen she was offered a record deal by a small independent record company based in South Los Angeles. Through them she'd released six albums and done countless tours over the years. Jessica became well known and well respected in the jazz music scene, but her music wasn't mainstream enough to be played by the most popular radio stations.

Three years ago, the manager of her record company decided to go back to basics and record a few videos of Jessica playing by herself before uploading them onto YouTube. He was betting on her beauty as well as her talent.

Jessica was stunning in a simple way. Five foot six with a dancer's lithe body, straight shoulder-length black hair, magnetic dark brown eyes, full lips and flawless skin. She attracted looks anywhere she went.

The gamble paid off, but even he hadn't expected it to take off as it did. Through word of mouth and social networking, Jessica's YouTube videos went stratospheric. Over one million worldwide hits in the first month alone, placing her name on YouTube's front page as the most watched clip. Today, as many of Jessica's albums were sold and downloaded as those of mainstream, world-famous pop bands.

Jessica's attention returned to her living room. A single, empty dinner plate and a half-drunk bottle of red wine sat on the small glass table in front of her. Seeing that made her remember that she'd eaten alone, and reality finally caught up with her. Mark wasn't in. And he wouldn't be coming back anytime soon.

Jessica and Mark had met at the Catalina Jazz Club on Sunset Boulevard two years ago, after one of her gigs. That night she had been sitting at the bar, surrounded by fans and a few music reporters when she'd noticed someone hanging out by the stage. He was tall, with broad shoulders and a strong physique. His long midnight-black hair was tied back Viking-style. But his good looks weren't what caught Jessica's attention. It was the intriguing way he was studying her guitar.

She'd excused herself from the crowd and approached him, wondering what was so interesting about her instrument. They'd chatted for a while and she found out that Mark was also a guitarist. He'd been classically trained, but instead of following that route he'd formed his own hard rock band. They were called Dust, and they'd just signed their first record deal a few days before.

The chat turned into dinner somewhere along Sunset Strip. Mark was funny, intelligent and charming. Several more dates followed and eight months later they'd rented a large warehouse loft conversion in Burbank together.

With the help of the Internet and the music video channels, Dust's first album became a worldwide sensation. Their second had just been mixed down and it was scheduled for release in a month's time. Their grueling touring schedule was about to begin again. As a pre-tour warm-up they were doing a series of eight secret gigs in smaller venues all around California. The first one was tonight in Fortuna. Mark and the band had left that morning.

Jessica crossed her legs under her and checked her watch – 1:18 a.m. She'd fallen asleep in an awkward position and the left side of her neck had gone stiff. She sat there for a while longer, nursing the pain and dreading the loneliness of her bed. But spending the night in the living room would probably make her miss him even more. She had one last sip of her wine and blew out the scented candle before heading to bed.

Jessica wasn't the best of sleepers, and sometimes she would toss and turn for a long while before finally falling into a light sleep. Tonight though, with the help of the wine, she started dozing almost immediately.

Click, click.

She blinked a few times before opening her eyes. Had she really heard something or was that her mind playing tricks on her? The bedroom curtains weren't drawn, and the full moon just outside her window was enough to keep total darkness out. Jessica allowed her eyes to roam the room slowly – nothing. She lay still, listening attentively but the sound didn't repeat itself. A minute later she started drifting back into sleep.

Click, click.

Her eyes shot open this time. There was no doubt in her mind. She'd heard something. And it was coming from inside her apartment. Jessica sat up in bed and brushed her fingers against the touch lamp on her bedside table. Her eyes narrowed slightly. Had she left a tap on somewhere? But if that was it, why wasn't the sound constant?

Click, click.

She held her breath and her pulse surged in her neck. There it was again. It was coming from just outside her bedroom door. It sounded like a shoe heel lightly clicking against the corridor's wooden floor.

'Mark?' she called and instantly felt silly for doing so. He wouldn't be back for several weeks.

Jessica hesitated for an instant, debating what to do. But what else could she do? Stay in bed worrying for the whole night? It was probably nothing but she had to go check it out. Slowly, she slid out of bed. She was wearing nothing but a tiny pair of shorts and the thinnest of sleeveless shirts.

She stepped outside her room and switched on the hallway lights. Nothing. She waited a moment. No sound. She grabbed Mark's old baseball bat from the storage closet before proceeding cautiously down the corridor. An uncomfortable shiver ran through her as her bare feet touched the cold tiles of the bathroom floor. All the faucets were securely off. There were no drips. She walked back and checked the living room, the kitchen, Mark's games room and her practice den. The entire apartment was absolutely still, except for the tick-tock that came from the clock in the kitchen. She rechecked the windows – all closed – doors – all locked.

Jessica shook her head and chuckled as her eyes focused on the baseball bat in her hands.

'Yeah, I'm a real home-run hitter, me.' She paused. 'But just in case, I'm keeping you by the bed.'

Back in her room, Jessica looked around one more time before resting the baseball bat against her bedside table and getting back into bed. She switched off the lamp and snuggled under the covers once again. As her eyes closed, every hair on her body stood on end. Some hidden instinct inside her exploded into life. Some sort of danger sensor. And the only thing she could sense was that she wasn't alone in that room. Someone else was there with her. That's when she heard it. Not a clicking sound coming from outside, but a hoarse whispering voice coming from the only place she didn't check.

'You forgot to look under your bed.'

Fifty-Eight

Hunter had spent the rest of the night on the computer discovering who Whitney Myers really was.

In the morning, after a strong cup of black coffee, he made his way back to Culver City and Kelly Jensen's studio. The blinking red light he'd seen last night from her window was a wireless CCTV camera, hidden away in an alcove in the wall. The camera was pointing straight at the small parking lot. There were no computers in Kelly's studio, so the camera couldn't have belonged to her.

At 6:00 a.m. only one of the shops that shared the car parking lot with Kelly's studio was open – Mr. Wang's convenience store. Hunter's luck was in; the wireless camera belonged to the elderly bird-like Chinese man.

Mr. Wang's wrinkled face and observant eyes only hinted at how much he'd lived, what he'd seen and the tremendous knowledge he'd accumulated over so many years.

He told Hunter that he'd asked his son, Fang Li, to install the camera at the back after his old Ford pickup truck was broken into one too many times.

Hunter asked him how far back he kept the recordings.

'Year,' Mr. Wang replied with a wide smile that seemed to never fade.

Hunter's face lit up in surprise. 'You have recordings going back a year?'

'Yes. Every minute.' His voice was like a whisper, but the words came out quickly, as if he was about to run out of time for what he wanted to say. His pronunciation was perfect, indicating that he'd been in America for many years, but the sentences were staccato. 'Fang Li too smart. Good with computers. He make program that box files. Twelve months – files delete automatic. Don't need do nothing.'

Hunter bobbed his head. 'Clever. Can I have a look at them?'

Mr. Wang's eyes narrowed to such a thin line, Hunter thought he'd closed them. 'You wanna see in store's computer?'

A quick nod. 'Yes. I'd like to see the footage from a few weeks ago.'

Mr. Wang bowed and his smile spread even wider. 'OK, no problem, but me no good. Need talk to Fang Li. He not here. I call.' Mr. Wang reached for the phone behind the counter. He spoke Mandarin. The conversation didn't last longer than a few seconds. 'Fang Li coming,' he said, putting the phone down. 'Be here very fast. Not live far.' He consulted his watch. 'Not go to work yet. Too early.'

Hunter asked Mr. Wang about Kelly Jensen. He said that she came into the shop almost every day when she was around, but sometimes she'd disappear for weeks. He liked Kelly very much. He said she was very polite, always happy and very beautiful.

'In my country, whole village be asking her to marry.'

Hunter smiled and looked around the shop while he waited. He bought a cup of microwavable coffee and a packet of teriyaki-flavored beef jerky. A few minutes later Fang Li arrived. He was in his late twenties, with longish black hair that shined like in a shampoo commercial. His features were striking, a replica of what his father must have looked like when he was younger, but much taller and well built. He quickly spoke to his father before turning and offering his hand to Hunter.

'I'm Fang Li, but everybody calls me Li.'

Hunter introduced himself and told him the purpose of his visit.

'OK, come with me and I'll show you.' Li guided Hunter through a back door that led into a large, well-organized storage room. The entire place carried a sweet and pleasant smell, a combination of exotic spices, condiments, soaps, fruit and unburned incense. At the far end of it, up a set of wooden stairs was the shop's office. Hundreds of Chinese calendars hung from the walls – Hunter had never seen so many. It was like they used them as wallpaper. Apart from the calendars there were several old, metal filing cabinets, a wooden shelf rack, a water cooler and a large desk with a computer monitor on it. Chinese characters danced across the screen.

Li chuckled as he read them.

'What does that mean?' Hunter asked.

'Be yourself. There's no one better suited for the job.'

Hunter smiled. 'Very true.'

'My father likes this kinda thing. Proverbs and all, you know. But he prefers to create his own, so I programed a little screen saver for him. It reads from a list of his own wise sayings.'

'So is that what you do? Computer programing?'

'Pretty much.'

'Your father said that you could store as much as a whole year's worth of footage.'

'That's right. My father's pretty much obsessed with organization.' He pointed out the window at the storage room. 'Nothing's ever out of place with him.'

Hunter nodded.

'He's also big on security. We've got five cameras filming twenty-four hours a day. One picking up the front door, one facing the parking lot out back, and three inside the shop. There's no way we could archive that much data without having a ridiculous amount of hard drive space or compressing the hell out of the footage. So I created a small program that automatically compresses the files that are over three days old and then archives them into external high-capacity hard drives.' Li rolled his chair back and pointed at four small black boxes under the desk. 'At the end of twelve months, those files auto-delete to create more space.' He paused and faced Hunter. 'So what do you need, Detective?'

Hunter wrote something down on a piece of paper and placed it on the desk in front of Li. 'I need a copy of all the footage you have between those dates.'

Li looked at the paper. 'An entire week's worth? From all five cameras?'

'Maybe, but let's start with the footage from the one in the parking lot.'

Li coughed. 'That's one hundred and sixty-eight hours of footage. Even compressed that'll take . . .' his eyes narrowed and his lips moved without a sound for a second, '. . . around thirty DVDs. Maybe a few more. When do you need them for?'

'Yesterday.'

Li's face paled. He checked his watch. 'Even if I had a

professional multi-DVD copier, which I don't, it'd still take most of the day.'

Hunter thought about it for a beat. 'Wait a second. You said that older files are stored in those external hard drives, right?' He pointed at the black boxes. 'Will the files from those dates be in one of them?'

Li quickly picked up on what Hunter was suggesting and his lips spread into a smile. 'They will be, yes. Very good idea. You could take the whole hard drive. There's nothing in them but archived CCTV footage. Nothing that my father would need, anyway. You can link the drive to any computer, easy. It will save you tons of time, but you'll still have to uncompress the files on your side.'

'We can do that.'

Li nodded. 'Let me show you how to find them.'

Fifty-Nine

Hunter made it back to Parker Center in less than half an hour and went straight into the Information Technology Division. Brian Doyle was at his desk, speed-reading through a pile of papers. He was wearing the same clothes as yesterday. His eyes were bloodshot and his face unshaven. An empty pizza box was by the edge of the desk and the coffee percolator in the corner was practically empty.

'Have you been here all night?' Hunter asked.

Doyle looked up but said nothing. His stare went straight through Hunter.

'Are you OK?'

Doyle's eyes finally focused. 'Umm? Yeah, sorry, I'm fine.' He placed the sheet he was reading on the desk. 'Just understaffed and overworked. Everyone always needs everything ASAP. I've got cases piling up everywhere. And this afternoon there's this huge sting operation going on.' He leaned back in his chair and studied Hunter for a second. 'What the hell happened to your face?' He pointed at the cut above his eyebrow.

Hunter shook his head. 'Walked into a door.'

'Of course you did. Just hope the door isn't gonna sue the department.'

'She won't.'

'*She*? A *woman* did that to you?'

'Long story.'

'I bet.' He cleared a space at the edge of his desk and leaned against it. 'OK, Robert, for you to be here, it's gotta be something urgent.'

Hunter nodded. 'But I only need about three minutes of your time, Jack. Then I'm out of here.'

'Is this about the psycho who killed Doctor Winston with that bomb?'

An almost imperceptible nod. Hunter felt his chest tighten around his heart as he remembered he'd never see his old friend again.

'He was a good man. I met him a couple of times.' Doyle checked his watch. 'What do you need?'

Hunter handed him the high-capacity hard drive and waited while Doyle hooked it up to his PC. Unsurprisingly, all the directories in the hard drive were perfectly organized – first by camera location and then by date.

'Can these files be uncompressed in bulk?' Hunter asked.

'Not simultaneously. They're massive. It'd be too processor intensive and it'd crash any machine, but . . .' Doyle lifted his index finger, 'you could line them up inside an application. As soon as one file finishes uncompressing, it'll automatically move to the next one in the list. That way you don't even have to be there. Just leave it working and come back when it's all done.'

'That'll work for me.'

Doyle smiled. 'Please tell me you don't need all of these files. There're hundreds of them. This will take days.'

'No.' Hunter shook his head. 'Just a handful of them – to start with.'

'OK, in that case I'll tell you the easiest thing to do.

Because this is an external drive, I can link it up to an empty laptop instead of clogging up the machine in your office. That way you can work on your machine if you need to and just leave the laptop on the side, as it does its thing. Give me five minutes and I'll have it all set up for you.'

Sixty

The phone on Hunter's desk rang almost the second he entered his office. It was Doctor Hove.

'Robert, I'm about to send you some lab results on Jensen. I got my team to fast-track whatever they could.'

'Thanks, Doc. What do we have?' He gestured for Garcia, who'd just come in, to grab his phone and listen in.

'OK, as we expected, the victim was sedated. We found traces of a drug called Estazolam in her blood. It's a sleeping agent.'

'Usually prescribed for short-term treatment of insomnia, right?' Hunter confirmed.

Doctor Hove had forgotten that Hunter knew more about insomnia than most doctors.

'That's right. Now, given its relatively high concentration, we figured that's what the killer used to sedate her on the day she died. Before dumping her in that basement. He didn't overdo it, though. He used just enough to knock her out for a couple of hours or so.'

Hunter leaned back in his chair.

'But the interesting thing is: we also found faint traces of another drug. Something called Mexitil. It's an anti-arrhythmic drug.'

'Anti- what?' Garcia blurted.

'A common drug used to treat a heart condition called ventricular arrhythmia.'

Hunter started leafing through sheets of paper on his desk.

'If you're looking for her medical records, Robert, don't bother,' the doctor said, recognizing the sound of pages turning. 'Her heart was as strong as a racing horse's. She didn't have the condition.'

Hunter stopped and thought for a split second. 'What are the side effects of this Mexitil, Doc?'

'Very good, Robert. Mexitil is pharmacologically similar to Lidocaine, which as you know is a local anesthetic. Its major side effect is light drowsiness and confusion. But if taken by someone who doesn't suffer from ventricular arrhythmia, that light drowsiness can become moderate to severe. And you don't even need high doses of the drug to cause it. But that's about all it does. It won't knock you out. It won't even make you doze off.'

Hunter considered it. It made sense. That was probably why neither of the victims had any restraint marks. If the killer kept them in a constant state of confusion and drowsiness, he didn't need to immobilize them.

'Would there be any other reason why the killer chose to use Mexitil?' Hunter asked. 'If he just wanted them high, he could've used a number of drugs.'

'It's an easy drug to obtain on the Internet.'

'So are most drugs nowadays, Doc,' Garcia countered.

'True.' There was a short pause. 'There's always the chance that he's familiar with the drug. He might suffer from the condition himself.'

Hunter was already clicking away on his computer, searching the Internet for more information about the drug.

'Could you check your database, Doc? Go back five . . . no, ten years. Look for any case where Mexitil was found in a murder victim's blood?'

'No problem.' This time the sound of pages turning came from Doctor Hove's side. 'I've also got a result on the dark copper-colored dust retrieved from under the victim's fingernails. It's brick dust.'

Hunter's eyebrows arched.

'We might be able to identify exactly what kind of brick it is. I'll let you know if we can.' The doctor coughed to clear her throat. 'At first I thought that maybe she tried to claw her way out of wherever she was kept. Somewhere with a brick wall. But as you well know, if that had been the case, she'd certainly have cracked and broken nails . . . maybe even missing ones. None were even chipped. They were filed down into claws, remember? Maybe the killer has a bizarre fetish for pointy fingernails.'

Hunter's eyes quickly moved from his computer to the pictures board. 'Nothing else was found under her nails?'

'Yes, bits of her own skin,' the doctor confirmed. 'She scraped at her mouth, her groin and the stitches before dying.'

'Only *her* skin?'

'That's right.'

Hunter nodded to himself. 'OK, Doc. Call me if anything else comes up.' He put the phone down and stared at his own fingernails for a moment. 'A weapon,' he whispered.

'A what?' Garcia asked, rolling his chair away from his desk.

'A weapon. That's why her fingernails were so claw-like.' Hunter stood up and approached the pictures board. 'Look at the crime-scene pictures of our first victim.' He pointed to the ones of Laura Mitchell's hands. There was nothing strange about her fingernails.

'No filing,' Garcia agreed.

'Having pointy fingernails didn't come from the killer, as the doctor suggested. Kelly used a brick wall to sharpen them herself. I think she wanted to attack her captor. In an empty cell, it was the only weapon she could think of.'

Garcia pinched his bottom lip. 'But nothing else was found under her nails except brick dust and her own skin. So she never got the chance to use them.'

'That's right.' Hunter had returned to his desk and was flipping through his notebook. 'The doctor said that Kelly's organs showed mild symptoms of dehydration and malnutrition, right? I think she starved herself.'

Garcia frowned.

'Mexitil. Kelly had no needle marks on her, remember?'

'He was feeding it to her through her food.'

Hunter leaned against his desk. 'Most probably, and she figured out the food was drugged.'

'So she stopped eating to get rid of the dizziness.' Garcia picked up Hunter's train of thought. 'But wouldn't that make her too weak to fight back?'

'It would if she'd gone without food for a few days, but that wasn't the case.'

'One day only. That's what Doctor Hove said, right?'

Hunter nodded. 'Mexitil isn't a proper sedative. Kelly would've only needed to be off it for a few hours.'

'Enough to get rid of the dizziness, but not enough to take all of her strength away. But how would she know that?'

'She didn't. She gambled.'

'So she filed her nails into the only weapon she could think of.' Garcia ran a hand through his hair while exhaling. 'She wanted out of there. She was trying to do something herself because she knew she was running out of time, and she'd run out of hope. She got tired of waiting for us to save her.'

Hunter's cell phone started ringing.

'Detective Hunter,' he said, bringing the clamshell phone to his ear.

'Detective, this is Tracy from the Special Operations switchboard. I'm managing the information line on the suspect you're looking for, James Smith.'

'Yes?'

'I've got someone on the line who claims to be him.'

Hunter pulled a face. 'Yeah, well, we've had about fifty of those so far. Just take his—'

'Detective,' Tracy interrupted, 'I think you should take this call.'

Sixty-One

Hunter snapped his fingers at his partner to get his attention. He didn't have to; Garcia had already noticed the change in Hunter's expression.

'Start a trace?' Hunter said to Tracy.

'We're all set here, Detective.'

Hunter nodded to himself. 'OK, put him through.'

There was a click on the line followed by a second of static.

Hunter waited.

So did the person on the other end of the line.

'This is Detective Robert Hunter.' Hunter eventually broke the silence. He was in no mood for games.

'Why are you after me?' The sentence was delivered in a calm, unrushed tone. The voice was like a muffled whisper, as if his phone's mouthpiece had been wrapped in several layers of cloth.

'James Smith?'

There was a short pause. 'Why are you after me?' he repeated in the same cool tone.

'You know why we're after you.' Hunter's calm voice matched Smith's. 'That's why you ran, isn't it?'

'The newspapers all across town have my picture in them. They say the police want to speak to me in relation to an ongoing investigation, but no other details are given. So I want you to tell me: why are you after me? How am I related to any ongoing investigation?'

'Why don't you come in, James? We can sit down and talk. I'll tell you anything you wanna know.'

A bitter chuckle. 'I'm afraid I can't do that just now, Detective.'

'Right now that's your best option. What else can you do? You can't run or hide forever. As you said, your photograph is all over the papers. And it's going to stay there. Sooner or later someone will recognize you – on the streets, in a shop, driving around. You know you're not invisible. Come in and let's talk.'

'The picture in the papers is crap and you know it – grainy, out of focus and partially obscured. It's a desperate attempt. I had trouble recognizing myself. The newspapers won't carry on publishing that picture forever, 'specially if you get no results from it. In a week's time I could dance naked on Sunset Strip and no one would recognize me.'

Hunter didn't reply. He knew it was only too true.

'So I'm gonna ask you one more time, Detective. Why are you after me? And how am I related to a major ongoing investigation?'

'If you don't know why we're after you, how do you know we're running a *major* investigation? None of the papers mentions it.'

'I'm not that stupid, Detective. If the LAPD got the papers to publish a snapshot of every person they'd like to talk to, there wouldn't be enough paper in California for all the pictures. The few that do get published are always related to a major investigation. Something big is going on, and somehow you think I'm involved.'

Smith was right, Hunter thought, he wasn't stupid.

'So you're telling me that you figured all that out by yourself, but you have no idea why we came to your door?'

'That's exactly what I'm telling you.'

Something in Smith's tone intrigued Hunter. 'So why don't you come in, and we can clear everything up?'

'Goodbye, Detective.'

'Wait.' Hunter stopped Smith before he was able to disconnect. 'Do you know which section of the LAPD I'm with?'

Garcia looked at his partner and frowned.

Smith hesitated for a second.

'Fraud?'

Garcia's brow creased even further.

The pause that followed stretched for several seconds.

'No, I'm not with the fraud squad.'

Silence.

'James? You still there?'

'Which section?'

Hunter noticed a different tension in Smith's voice.

'Homicide.'

'*Homicide*? Look, I don't like going through switchboards. Give me a number where I can contact you directly.' The tension in his voice had morphed into anxiety.

'Why don't you give me your number?'

'If you wanna play games, suit yourself. Goodbye, Detective.'

'OK.' Hunter stopped him again. 'We'll play it your way.' He gave Smith his number and the line went dead. Hunter quickly pressed a button on his cell phone and got the Special Operations switchboard again. 'Tracy, are you there?'

'I'm here, Detective.'

'Tell me you've got something.'

'Sorry, Detective, whoever this guy is, he really ain't stupid. He's using a pre-paid cell phone. Either a very cheap one with no GPS chip, or he knows how to deactivate them.'

Hunter knew the logic of how GPS chip phones worked. They emitted a locator beacon every fifteen or so seconds, similar to the ones used by airplanes. GPS satellites could then very quickly pin the phone location down to the nearest fifteen to twenty feet. It was obvious James Smith knew that too.

'How about triangulation?' Hunter asked.

'As I said before, this guy ain't dumb, Detective. He was on the move during the call. And I mean he was moving fast. The phone was immediately switched off once he disconnected.'

'Shit!' Hunter ran a hand through his hair. He knew that triangulation is the most accurate method of locating a cell phone that doesn't send out a position signal. A live cell phone is in continual relay with surrounding cell phone towers to ensure they get the best signal available. Triangulation works by identifying the three towers receiving the strongest signal from the phone and drawing their coverage radius. At the point where the three orbits intersect, that's where the phone is located. Its accuracy depends on how close together the three signal receiving towers are. In a city like Los Angeles, where there are simply hundreds and hundreds of cell phone towers, the accuracy can be almost as precise as with a GPS chip. And that's where the being on the move problem comes from. In Los Angeles, cell phone towers are relatively close together. The process of triangulating can take as long as ten to fifteen minutes. If during that process the cell phone in question moves out of range of one of the three triangulating towers and into the range of a new one, the whole process fails and it has to start again from the beginning. If James Smith was calling from a moving car or even a bus, his signal would be constantly jumping from tower to tower in the space of minutes. Triangulation would be virtually impossible. Tracy was right. James Smith was no first-timer.

'OK, Tracy, here's what I want you to do . . .'

Sixty-Two

It was one of those Los Angeles spring mornings that made people happy to be alive. Crisp blue skies, gentle winds, and temperatures not higher than twenty-two degrees Celsius. People just couldn't help but smile. It was on days like these that every detective in the force wished the LAPD issued unmarked convertibles. In the absence of those, Garcia's Honda Civic would do. At least it had air conditioning, something that Hunter's ancient Buick didn't.

On their way to Century City and the A & E TV network studios, Garcia came level with a scarlet red convertible BMW with its top down. A short-haired brunette with her eyebrows plucked to the thinnest of lines had her head resting on the driver's shoulder. He was a brawny man with a bullet head polished to shine, wearing a gym vest that looked two sizes too small for his frame. Hunter observed them for a minute. The woman seemed completely loved up. She brushed her fingers through her hair casually, and for an instant she reminded him of Anna, Garcia's wife.

'Would you ever hurt Anna?' Hunter asked, suddenly turning to face Garcia.

The question was so surprising and out of character that Garcia had to do a double take and almost swerved. '*What?*'

'Would you ever physically hurt Anna?'

'That's what I thought I heard you say. What the hell, Robert? Is that question for real?'

A few seconds went by. If Hunter was joking, he wasn't giving anything away.

'I guess that means *no*, then,' Hunter said.

'It means *hell no*. Why would I ever hurt Anna? Physically or any other way?'

Garcia had met Anna Preston in high school. She was a sweet girl with an unusual beauty. Garcia fell in love almost immediately. It took him ten months to gather the courage to ask her out though. They started dating during their sophomore year and Garcia proposed straight after their graduation. Hunter didn't know of a couple whose love for and dedication to each other matched theirs.

'No matter what happened, no matter what she did,' Hunter pressed, 'you wouldn't hurt her, in any way?'

The confusion stamped across Garcia's face intensified. 'Have you lost your mind? Listen to me. No matter what she does, no matter what shc says, no matter what anything – I would *never* hurt Anna. She's everything to me. Without her, I don't exist. Now what in the world are you trying to say, Robert?'

'Why?' Hunter's voice sounded even. '*Why* wouldn't you ever hurt her? No matter what she did . . . or said . . . or anything . . .'

Garcia had been Hunter's partner for almost four years, since he had joined the RHD. He knew Hunter wasn't a conventional detective. He could figure things out faster than anyone Garcia had ever met. Most of the time, no one even understood how he did it until he explained, and then it all seemed so simple. Hunter listened a lot more than he spoke. When he did speak, not everything he said made sense at first, but in the end, everything always slotted into place like a jigsaw puzzle. But sometimes Garcia had to admit Hunter seemed to inhabit a different dimension to everyone on this planet. This was one of those times.

'Because I love her.' Unconsciously, Garcia's words came out coated in tenderness. 'More than anyone or anything in this world.'

'Exactly.' A smile stretched across Hunter's lips. 'And, I think, so does our killer.'

Sixty-Three

The traffic began to unclog, but Garcia was still anesthetized by Hunter's words. Anxious drivers started sounding their horns behind them. The more impatient ones were already shouting abuse out of their windows. Garcia disregarded them and edged forward slowly in his own time. His attention was still on Hunter.

'Please tell me there's sense behind the madness. What are you saying, Robert? That the killer is in love with my wife?'

'No, not with Anna,' Hunter replied. 'But what if the killer thinks he's in love with all his victims.'

Garcia's eyes narrowed as he thought about it. 'What, *both* of them?'

'Yes.'

'At the same time?'

'Yes.'

'And we're not talking obsessed fan love?'

'No.'

His eyes narrowed further. 'If he's really in love with them, why would he kill them in such a brutal way?'

'I didn't say he *was* in love with them,' Hunter clarified. 'I said he *thinks* he's in love with them. But what he's really in love with is their image. Who they represent, not who they are.'

Silence.

Realization came seconds later.

'Sonofabitch! Both of the victims remind him of someone else,' Garcia finally caught on. 'Someone he loved. That's why they look so alike.'

Hunter nodded. 'It's not them he wants. It's who they remind him of.' He watched the convertible BMW pull away. 'The lack of bruising prior to the stitching on both victims has been bothering me from the start. I kept thinking: since he doesn't kidnap them for ransom, there's gotta be a reason why he keeps them instead of killing them straight away, but more importantly, there's gotta be a reason why he never touches them until the last minute. It didn't make any sense. No matter which path I followed, I couldn't see how there'd be no bruising. If the killer was keeping these women to satisfy his sexual needs, there'd be bruising . . . For revenge, there'd be bruising . . . Generalized hate against women, or even brunette painters induced by some past trauma, there'd be bruising . . . If he were an obsessed fan, there'd be bruising . . . Sadistic paranoia, there'd be bruising . . . Pure homicidal mania, there'd be bruising . . . Nothing fitted.'

Garcia raised his eyebrows.

'I heard it first a few days ago, when we were interviewing Patrick Barlett, but I guess it just got filed away in my subconscious.'

'Patrick Barlett?' Garcia frowned. 'Laura Mitchell's ex-fiancé?'

Hunter nodded as he watched the traffic flow. A black woman driving a white Peugeot to their right was shaking her head and gesticulating while apparently singing along to something. She noticed Hunter looking at her and smiled, embarrassed. He smiled back before continuing.

'Patrick said that he'd never hurt Laura, no matter what. He loved her too much.'

'Yeah, I remember that.'

'Unfortunately, that day I was more worried about observing Patrick's reactions than anything else. It just escaped me. But it happens more often than you think. It's a spin-off of the combination of two conditions known as *transference* and *projection*.'

Garcia frowned.

'Some husbands look for prostitutes that remind them of their own wives,' Hunter explained. 'Some people look for girlfriends or boyfriends that look like an old high-school sweetheart or a teacher, or even their own mothers or fathers.'

Garcia thought back to a childhood school friend who, in fourth grade, had fallen in love with his history teacher. When he was old enough to date, every girlfriend he had was the spitting image of that teacher, including the one he'd gone on to marry years later.

'Anyway,' Hunter moved on, 'it wasn't until a moment ago that the idea of resembling someone paired up with transference and projection came into my head.'

'Shit!' Garcia let out a slow breath through clenched teeth, the confusion finally starting to clear in his mind. 'When he looks at the women he's abducted, his mind sees someone else, because he *wants* them to be someone else. Someone he was *truly* in love with. Someone he would never hurt, no matter what. That's why there's no bruising.'

A quick nod from Hunter. 'That's the projection side.'

'But wait a second.' Garcia shook his head. 'He still kills them . . . very brutally. Doesn't that go against this theory?'

'No, it strengthens it. The stronger the transference and projection, the easier it is for the killer to be disappointed.

They might have the same looks as the person he wants them to be, but they won't act, or talk, or do anything else in the same way. No matter how much he wants it, they'll never be who he wished they were.'

Garcia thought about it for a beat. 'And as soon as he realizes that, why keep them, right?'

'That's right. But he still can't bring himself to kill them directly. That's why they're still alive when he leaves them. That's why he's not even there when they are supposed to die. He can't bear to see them go. And that's why he created the self-activating trigger mechanism.'

'So he doesn't have to be there.'

'Exactly,' Hunter agreed.

Garcia remained thoughtful. 'So this true love of his, is she dead?'

'Most probably,' Hunter admitted. 'And that might be why he cracked. His mind just can't let go of her.'

Garcia puffed his cheeks out before letting them deflate slowly. 'Do you think she died in the same way his victims died, stitched up? Do you think he killed her as well?'

Hunter stared out the window at a cloudless, baby blue sky, and wished his thoughts were just as clear. 'There's only one way we can find out.'

He reached for his phone.

Sixty-Four

The Los Angeles branch of the A & E TV network was located in Century City. It occupied fifteen offices on the ninth floor of building two of the famous Twin Century Plaza Towers. It was no coincidence that the buildings resembled the twin towers that were destroyed in 2001 during the terrorist attack in Manhattan's World Trade Center. They'd been designed by the same architect.

The red-haired woman behind the reception counter at the A & E TV network entry lobby was what you'd call striking rather than pretty.

She smiled politely as Hunter and Garcia approached the counter before lifting her index finger to signal that she'd only be a moment.

Seconds later she touched her earpiece and a blinking blue light went off.

'How can I help you, gentlemen?' Her gaze bounced between both detectives and settled on Hunter. Her smile gained an extra twinkle. He explained that they needed to talk to someone about an old documentary their studio had produced. The receptionist glanced at their badges and her demeanor changed. A quick internal call and two minutes later they were being shown into an office at the end of a long corridor. The placard on the door read Bryan Coleman – Director of Production.

The man sitting behind the desk smiled as Hunter and Garcia appeared at his door. He too had a hands-free earpiece on. The blue light was blinking. He motioned both detectives inside, stood up and moved to the front of his desk. He was at least two inches taller than Hunter, with close-cropped dark hair and piercing brown eyes set closely together behind horn-rimmed glasses.

Hunter closed the door behind him and waited. The two chairs in front of Coleman's desk were occupied by boxes. Both detectives stood.

'We need to get that redelivered today . . .' Coleman said into the hands-free while nodding at Hunter and Garcia. He listened for only half a second before cutting off whomever he was speaking to. 'Listen, if we don't get it redelivered today, we're gonna get our account transferred to a different company, do you get me?' Another pause. 'Yeah, this afternoon is fine, before three o'clock even better . . . I'll be waiting.' He removed the hands-free from his right ear and threw it on his desk.

'I'm sorry about the mess,' Coleman said, shaking both detectives' hands before clearing the boxes off the two seats. 'We're expanding. We were supposed to be moving premises, but a few months ago the company across the hall from us went bust.' He shrugged indifferently. 'Recession, you know? So we decided to take their offices instead. It's easier, but no less stressful.' He pointed to the phone on his desk. 'Delivery companies are slick little bastards. If you let them, they'll walk all over you.'

Hunter and Garcia nodded politely.

'So?' Coleman clapped his hands together. 'What can I do for you?'

'We're looking for a documentary about West Coast

artists that was produced by your network,' Hunter said, taking a seat.

'Do you know the name of this documentary?'

Hunter checked his notebook. 'Yes, it's called *Canvas Beauty, The Upcoming Talents from the West Coast.*'

Coleman cocked his head back. '*Canvas Beauty*?' he said with a surprised chuckle. 'Wow. That was three maybe four years ago.'

'Three,' Hunter confirmed.

'I was in the production team for that. Very low budget stuff.' Coleman took off his glasses and started polishing them with a piece of cloth. 'That documentary was a fluke. A promotional trick. You sure that's the one you want?'

Hunter rested his left elbow on the arm of his chair and his chin on his knuckles. 'What do you mean, a fluke?'

'The only reason it was shot in the first place was because of our regional director at the time,' Coleman explained. 'His daughter was an artist, a painter. She'd been trying to break into the scene for some time without much success. So suddenly a new documentary script found its way to the top of our schedule. You know the drill – include a few truly talented upcoming artists, heavily feature his daughter in the middle of it all and hope for the best.'

'Did it work?'

Coleman nodded hesitantly. 'I guess it did its job. She got noticed and I think she's doing OK with her art. That regional director left us a couple of years ago, so I wouldn't really know.'

'What's her name?' Garcia asked. 'The regional director's daughter?'

'Ummm . . .' Coleman started fidgeting with a ballpoint pen.

'Martina,' he remembered. 'That's it, Martina Greene. May I ask why you're interested in that particular documentary?'

'We just wanna have a look at it and find out which other artists were featured,' Hunter replied. 'Were they filmed individually? I mean, on different locations, on different days?'

Another chuckle from Coleman. 'Nope. As I said, it was *really* low budget. Even our director wouldn't be able to justify spending real money on it. So we crammed the whole thing into one day's shooting. We got all the artists together one afternoon at the . . .' he looked away for a second as if struggling to recall, '. . . Moca Museum in South Grand Avenue.'

'Were they all women?'

Coleman frowned and thought about it for an instant. 'On that particular documentary, yes.'

'And do you know if it was aired again? Maybe recently?'

'I can check, but I wouldn't think so. As I said, it wasn't a very good piece of work.' He pulled himself closer to his computer and typed something into his keyboard.

When the result came back a few seconds later, he repositioned his computer monitor so Hunter and Garcia could have a look. 'Nope, aired once two weeks after it was produced and that was it.'

'Do you have any more recent documentaries or interviews in the same vein as that one?' Garcia asked. 'I mean, featuring Los Angeles female painters?'

A look of interest came over Coleman's face. 'Anyone in particular?'

'If you could just show us whatever you have, we'd be very grateful,' Hunter was quick to answer. He didn't want Coleman's curiosity piqued further.

Too late. Once a reporter, always a reporter.

Coleman twitched in his chair before returning to his computer. 'When you say "more recent", how recent do you mean?'

'A year, maybe two.'

This time the search took a little longer.

'OK, in the past two years we've produced three programs on painters,' Coleman said, 'but they weren't exclusively on Los Angeles or Californian artists.'

Garcia frowned. 'That's it, three programs in two years?'

'Very few people are interested in the art of painting, or in the life of modern painters,' Coleman explained, sitting back in his chair. 'We live in a capitalist world where money rules, Detective, and to us viewing numbers is what translates into money – advertising time. If we air a documentary on hip-hop, rap, or whatever trendy new singer is storming the charts, our viewing numbers hit the roof. We air one on painters or any less popular branch of the arts, that number drops to less than a third, even during prime time. Get the picture?'

'Could we get copies of all three,' Hunter said, 'together with the *Canvas Beauty* one?'

'Of course.'

'We'll also need a copy of the work log for the *Canvas Beauty* documentary. Names of everyone who worked on it – cameraman, make-up artists, production and editing team . . . everyone.'

'No problem. I'll put you in touch with Tom, our archives guy. He'll get you whatever you need.'

As Hunter closed the door behind him, Coleman reached for the phone and dialed the private number of a very good friend of his: Donald Robbins, the lead crime reporter at the *LA Times*.

Sixty-Five

The CCTV files from Mr. Wang's convenience store had finished uncompressing. He wasn't sure what he was hoping to find from the footage, but the Missing Persons investigator's assumption that Kelly Jensen had been abducted from Santa Monica, either while parking her car, or walking from it to her apartment building didn't sit right. Even in the dead of night, San Vicente Boulevard was way too busy. Cars drove by every ten seconds or so. Someone could look out the window at any time. It was just too risky. A risk that her killer could've easily avoided by taking Kelly from her much quieter studio in Culver City. And the small parking lot at the back provided a perfect location for an abduction. It was secluded and badly lit. If Hunter were the one planning to kidnap Kelly, that's where he'd have done it from.

Hunter checked his watch. It was late. Before leaving the office, he quickly read through the email he'd received from Jenkins, a good friend from the Records and Identification Division. It contained all the information he'd requested about Whitney Myers and her time with the force, but Hunter had found it hard to concentrate. The punishing headache that had been pounding his brain for the past two hours was threatening to intensify. He needed food. But the cupboards and the fridge back in his place hadn't seen supplies in days. Besides, the only thing he knew how to cook well was popcorn, and he'd already had his share of it this month. He decided to go for something a little healthier. He printed out the contents of the attachment to Jenkins' email, grabbed the laptop and headed for his car.

Uncle Kelome's, a small Hawaiian restaurant in Baldwin Hills, served the best Aloha-style shrimp in the whole of Los Angeles. Hunter loved the food and the relaxed atmosphere. And right now there was nothing that he needed more than to relax, even if only for a few minutes while having his favorite, Volcano Shrimp Platter. The fact that their bar also kept a respectful stock of single malt Scotch was a welcome bonus.

Hunter placed his order at the counter and took a table at the far end of the dining room, hidden away from the often noisy bar. He sat down and buried his head in his hands. His headache was so intense it felt like his brain was about to burst inside his head.

A waitress brought him his drink and placed it on the table in front of him.

'Thank you,' he said without looking up.

'Not a problem, but if you'd like those files I promised you, I'm gonna need my ID back.'

Hunter lifted his head too quickly, and for a fraction of a second his vision was filled with blurry dots. His eyes quickly refocused on Whitney Myers' face.

She smiled.

Hunter didn't.

'Can I sit down?' she asked, already pulling out the chair opposite him.

Despite himself, Hunter appraised Myers. She looked different tonight. Her hair was loose, falling over her shoulders. She was wearing a dark blue pencil skirt suit. The top button on her blazer was undone, showing a silk white blouse underneath. Her make-up was so light it was almost invisible, but it skillfully accentuated her features. Hunter noticed that the group of guys sitting at the table to his right had all turned to look at her; two of them were almost drooling. Hunter's eyes moved from Myers to the glass in front of him and then back to her.

'Balvenie, 12-year-old single malt,' she announced before touching her glass against his. She was drinking the same. 'It's always a pleasure finding someone else who appreciates a proper drink.'

Hunter placed his hands on the table but didn't say anything.

'Wow, you look shattered,' she continued. 'And I'm sorry about that.' She gestured towards the cut above his eyebrow before placing a palm on the left side of her torso. 'You were right, my ribs aren't broken, but they're bruised to shit.'

Still silence from Hunter, but it didn't seem to bother her.

'I must admit, your file is quite a read. A child prodigy. Really?' She pulled a face. 'Attended the prestigious Mirman School for the Super Brainy on a scholarship, and cruised through their entire curriculum in two years. After that, Stanford, also on a scholarship. Received your PhD in Criminal Behavior Analysis and Biopsychology at the age of twenty-three? That's impressive.'

Not a word from Hunter. Myers carried on.

'Made detective in record time and was immediately asked to join the RHD . . . now that really *is* impressive. You must've kissed a lot of ass or impressed the hell out of some important people.'

Still nothing from Hunter.

'Now a detective with the infamous HSS, and you're affectionately called the one-man zombie squad by most of your department.' She smiled. 'Cute nickname. Did you come up with that yourself?'

She continued, unfazed by his lack of response.

'Your specialty is ultra-violent crime, and you hold an impressive arrest record. Your book is still mandatory reading at the FBI National Center for the Analysis of Violent Crimes. Have I left anything out?'

Hunter had never written a book, but one of his university professors was so impressed with his thesis paper on Criminal Conduct that he forwarded it to his friend at the FBI academy in Virginia, who passed it on to the academy director. A few weeks later a young Robert Hunter was invited to Quantico to talk to a class of experienced officers and instructors. The one-day talk became a week-long seminar, and at the end of it the director asked Hunter's permission to use his thesis as required reading material for all field officers. Now no one graduates from Quantico without reading it.

'So you read my life story,' Hunter finally said. 'It must've been a pretty boring few minutes.'

'On the contrary. I thought it was very colorful.' Myers smiled again. 'Though there's a strange gap. For a couple of years it seems you just disappeared off the face of the earth. Not a scrap of information on you anywhere. And my research team is the best there is.'

Hunter said nothing.

'I have to ask you this: why the hell did you become a cop? With a résumé like that you could be with the FBI, NSA, CIA, take your pick.'

'Do you have an obsession with getting me a new job?'

She smiled.

The waitress brought Hunter his shrimp platter. As she walked away, Hunter's eyes moved from his glass to Myers. 'I ordered orange juice.'

'I know,' she replied casually. 'But you would've ordered Scotch anyway. I was just saving you some time.' She paused. 'You must be hungry. Look at the size of that platter.'

'Would you like some?'

She shook her head. 'I'm fine, thanks. Knock yourself out.'

Hunter dipped a jumbo shrimp into the pot of hot sauce and took a bite.

Myers waited a few seconds. 'If you're as good as your file says you are, then you've also checked me out, and by now you will know I lied.'

Hunter nodded. 'There's no ex-boyfriend.'

Myers studied Hunter's face for a moment. 'But you already knew that yesterday, right?'

He nodded again.

'If you knew I was lying, why didn't you take me in?'

'No point. You used to be a cop. You knew there was really nothing we could do to force you to tell us who your client really is. If you didn't want to co-operate, we would've just wasted a lot of time. And time is something I don't have. Call it a little professional courtesy.'

Myers smiled. 'Bullshit. You thought you could find out whom I was working for on your own. But it wasn't quite so easy, was it?'

They regarded each other for a moment.

'The reason I was in Kelly Jensen's apartment last night was because I wanted to follow a hunch,' Myers finally admitted, taking a sip of her drink.

'And that hunch was . . . ?'

'That Kelly's disappearance and the disappearance of the woman I'm looking for were connected.'

Hunter put his fork down.

'I didn't find anything in her apartment to confirm that hunch. She wasn't taken from there. But there are other similarities that are hard to ignore.'

'What other similarities?'

'How many victims?' Myers countered. 'How many victims have you got so far? And I'm seriously not fucking around this time. If you wanna know what I know, you've gotta talk to me.'

Hunter sat back and used a paper napkin to wipe his mouth. 'Kelly Jensen was the second victim.'

Myers nodded and placed a photograph of an attractive brunette on the table. 'Was this the first victim?' She held her breath.

Hunter's eyes moved to the picture. On looks, the woman in it could've been Laura or Kelly's sister. He shook his head. 'No, that's not her . . . Who is this?'

Myers breathed out. 'She's not on any Missing Persons list,' she continued. 'Her father tried to report her as missing but MP ran her through their regular six-point checklist. She met only one condition, so they weren't immediately prepared to allocate time to her.'

'Who is she?' Hunter repeated.

Myers sat back. 'Her name is Katia Kudrov. She's the principal violinist concertmistress with the Los Angeles Philharmonic.'

'A musician?'

'That's right.' Myers paused. 'The first victim, was her name Laura Mitchell?'

Hunter sat back in his chair. It was obvious that Myers had done her homework where missing persons were concerned.

Myers waited.

'Yes, Laura Mitchell was the first victim we found.'

The tips of Myers' fingers moved straight to her upper lip. 'She was also a painter. This killer is after artists.'

'Wait up, it's too soon to get to that conclusion. And *artist* is too vast a field. If we're gonna go down that path then we'd have to include dancers, actresses, sculptors, magicians, jugglers . . . the list goes on and on. So far, he's kidnapped and killed two painters, and that's all we have to go on. The fact that Katia's profession falls into the *vast* category of being an artist is a simple coincidence at this point.' Hunter tapped the picture on the table. 'When did she go missing?'

'Four days ago. Laura went missing about a week after Kelly, right?'

'You're good with names and dates.'

'Yes, I'm *very* good with names and dates. So we have no specific time signature between kidnapping and murder?'

'*We*?'

Myers glared at Hunter. 'Katia Kudrov is still my *private* case. At the moment she's a missing person, not a homicide victim. I spent most of today checking Katia's background against Kelly's.' She placed a folder on the table. 'Other than being the same age and sharing some physical characteristics, they've got absolutely nothing else in common. No substantial link.'

Hunter went silent again.

Myers leaned forward. 'Trust me, Robert, the last thing I wanna do is work with the LAPD. But the only way we'll be able to get a better idea if your psycho has really kidnapped Katia without wasting precious time is if we share what we know.' She tapped the folder she'd just placed on the table. 'And the optimum word here is *share*. So if I tell you what I know, you tell me what you know. And don't even think about giving me the classified information excuse bullshit. I'm not a reporter. I have as much to lose as you do if any of the information about this case leaks. We want the same thing here – to catch this fucker. Your victims are already dead. Katia may still be alive. Do you really wanna waste time?'

After reading the file on Whitney Myers that Jenkins had sent him, Hunter wasn't surprised that she wasn't prepared to give him any information on her investigation for free.

For a long while they simply stared at each other in silence. Myers was trying hard to read Hunter's expression. But she certainly wasn't expecting his next question.

'Did *you* kill them?'

Sixty-Six

The uncomfortable silence stretched between them. Neither Hunter nor Myers moved. Neither of them broke eye contact. But Myers' stare lost all its warmth.

Hunter had read all the information Jenkins had sent him on Myers' last ever case with the LAPD.

Myers had been called to try and resolve a situation that had developed in a tower block in Culver City a few years ago. A 10-year-old boy had managed to gain access to the roof of an apartment block and was sitting on the ledge, eighteen floors off the ground. The boy, who everyone knew by the name of Billy, wasn't responding to anyone, and understandably, no one wanted to approach him. His parents had died in a car crash when he was only five, and since then he'd been living with his aunt and uncle, who'd become his legal guardians. They'd gone out for the afternoon and left Billy alone in the apartment.

Billy had no history of mental illness, but the few neighbors who knew him said that he was always very sad, never smiled, and never played with any of the other kids.

Myers saw no other way other than to break protocol and go up to the roof without waiting for the proper backup team.

The report Hunter had read had said that Myers had

spent only ten minutes trying to talk Billy down when he simply got up and jumped.

Myers was so distraught that she'd had to take time off work, but she'd refused to see the police shrink. Two days after the incident, Billy's uncle and aunt jumped from the same spot Billy did. Their wrists were tied together by a zip-tie handcuff. A suicide pact from two grief-stricken guardians would've been the conclusion, if not for the fact that three neighbors had seen a woman who fitted Myers' description leaving the building minutes after Angela and Peter hit the ground.

'Peter and Angela Fairfax,' Hunter clarified.

'Yes, I know who you're referring to.' Her tone was firm.

'Did you push them off that roof?'

'What the fuck does that have to do with this?'

Hunter finally had a sip of his whiskey. 'You just asked me to share information from an ongoing investigation with someone I only just met. You used to be a cop, so you know that's against protocol. But I don't mind breaking it, if it means I'll get a step closer to catching this guy. The problem is: the file I read on you says there's a big chance that you handcuffed two innocent people together and then threw them off the top of an eighteen-story-high building. If you're a real loose cannon, then this conversation ends here.' He retrieved Myers' private investigator's ID from his pocket and placed it on the table in front of her. She didn't reach for it. Her gaze could've burned a hole in Hunter's face.

'What do you think?'

Hunter's left eyebrow lifted slightly.

'The file *I* read says that you're a good judge of character. So, I wanna know: do you think I could've pushed two innocent people off a rooftop?'

'I'm not here to judge you. But I wanna hear the truth – from you, not from a file written by an Internal Affairs investigator and some police shrink.'

'And I wanna hear your opinion.' Her voice was defiant. 'Do you think I pushed two innocent people off a building?'

Myers' credentials before the rooftop incident were impeccable. She'd worked very hard to make detective and she took pride in being one. She was good at it, one of the best. Her track record proved it. Even after leaving the force and becoming a private investigator, her success rate was impressive. Hunter knew that people like her didn't just flip, didn't just lose their mind out of the blue. He considered her a moment longer and then leaned forward.

'I think you allowed yourself to get personally involved with that case,' Hunter said in a steady voice. 'But you were an experienced detective, so it must've been something that rocked you pretty badly. My guess is that you suspected something really bad was happening in that family. To Billy in particular. But you didn't have enough evidence to substantiate it. I think that maybe you went back to try and get an explanation from Billy's guardians, but things went badly wrong.'

No reaction from Myers.

'If I'm right . . . then I would've probably done the same thing.'

Myers sipped her drink slowly, her eyes still on Hunter's face. She placed the glass back down on the table. Hunter held her stare without flinching.

'She jumped,' Myers said calmly. 'Angela Fairfax jumped.'

Hunter waited.

'That day I was the first to reply to a potential jumper,' she began. 'I made it there in two minutes flat, and started breaking protocol straight away. I had no choice. I just didn't have the time to wait for backup. My intelligence on the boy was almost none. When I got to the rooftop, I found this kid sitting with his legs dangling from the edge of the building. He was just sitting there with his teddy bear, drawing onto a pad of paper. Billy was tiny. He looked so fragile . . . so scared. And that's why I couldn't wait for backup. A strong gust of wind and he would've taken off like a kite.'

She tucked a strand of loose hair behind her left ear.

'He was crying,' she continued. 'I asked him what he was doing sitting on the edge of that building. He said he was drawing.' She had another sip of her drink, a long one. 'I told him that wasn't a very safe place to sit and draw. Do you know what he said?'

Hunter said nothing.

'He said that it was safer than being in his apartment when his uncle was home. He said that he missed his mom and dad so much. That it was unfair that they had to die in a car crash and not him. That they didn't hurt him like his uncle Peter did.'

Hunter felt something catch in his throat.

'I could see the boy was hurting,' Myers proceeded, 'but my priority was to get him away from that ledge. I kept on talking to him, all the while taking small steps forward, getting closer and closer in case I needed to reach for him. I asked him what he was drawing. He ripped the sheet of paper from the pad and showed it to me.' For the first time her eyes moved away from Hunter's face to a blank spot on the tabletop. 'The drawing was of his bedroom. Very simple, sketched using lines and stickman figures with skewed faces. There was a bed with a little stickboy in it.' Myers paused and swallowed dry. 'A bigger stickman was lying on top of him.'

Hunter listened.

'And here comes the sucker punch from hell: standing right next to the bed was a stickwoman.'

'His aunt knew.' It wasn't a question.

Myers nodded and her eyes became glassy. 'They were his guardians. They were supposed to protect him. Instead, they were raping his soul.' She finished her whiskey in one gulp. 'Right there and then I promised him that if he came with me, if he got off that ledge, his uncle would never hurt him again. He didn't believe me. He asked me to cross my heart and hope to die. So I did.' A heartfelt pause. 'That was all that was needed. He said he believed me then because I was a police officer, and police officers weren't supposed to lie, they were supposed to help people. Billy got up and turned towards me. I offered him my hand and he extended his tiny little arm to take it. That's when he slipped.'

'So he never jumped as the report said?'

Myers shook her head.

Neither of them spoke for a few moments.

The waitress returned to the table and frowned as she saw Hunter's uneaten platter. 'Something wrong with the food?'

'What?' Hunter shook his head. 'Oh no, no. It's fantastic. I haven't finished it yet. Just give me a few more minutes.'

'I'll have one more of these.' Myers pointed to her empty glass. 'Balvenie, 12-year-old.'

The waitress nodded and went on her way.

'I lunged towards him,' Myers continued. 'My fingers brushed his tiny hand. But I just couldn't grip it. He was so fragile that his body almost disintegrated when he hit the ground.'

Hunter ran his hand through his hair.

'It took me two days to build up the courage to go back to Billy's building.' She paused to find her words. 'Actually, I think what built up inside me wasn't courage – it was pure hate. I didn't want a confession. I wanted to teach them a lesson. I wanted them to feel at least a fraction of the fear Billy felt.' Her voice was suddenly coated with anger. 'He was a 10-year-old boy, so hurt and so scared that he'd rather jump off the top of a building than go back to the family that was supposed to love him. You're a psychologist. You know that 10-year-old boys aren't supposed to commit suicide. They shouldn't even understand the concept.'

The waitress returned with Myers' drink and placed it on the table.

'I got to their apartment and confronted them. Angela started crying, but Peter was as cold as ice. He couldn't have cared less. Something took over me right there and then. So I forced them to cuff themselves to each other, and took them to the rooftop. To the same spot Billy had fallen from. And that's when it happened.'

Hunter leaned forward but said nothing, allowing Myers to continue at her own pace.

'Angela started crying uncontrollably, but not because she was scared. The guilt inside her just exploded and she let everything out. She said that she was so ashamed of herself, but she had been terrified of what Peter would do to her and Billy if she told anyone. Peter also used to rape and beat her up too. She said that she thought about taking Billy and running away, but she had nowhere to go. She had no money, no friends and her family didn't care for her. That's when Peter lost it up there. He told her to shut the fuck up and slapped her across the face. I almost shot him for that.'

Myers paused for another sip.

'But Angela beat me to it. The slap didn't faze her. She said she was tired of being afraid. She was tired of being helpless against him, but not any more. She looked at me and her eyes burned with determination. She said, "Thank you for finally giving me the chance to do something. I'm so sorry about Billy." Then, without any warning, she threw herself off the rooftop. Still cuffed to Peter.'

Hunter was studying Myers, searching for signs of dissembling – rapid facial movements, fluttering of the eyes. She displayed only a sorrowful calm.

'Angela was a heavy-built woman. Peter was tall and skinny. He wasn't expecting it. Her weight pulled at him like a crane, but he managed to hold her for a few seconds. Long enough for his frightened eyes to look at me. Long enough for him to ask for my help.' A pause. 'I just turned and walked away.'

They sat in silence for a while as Hunter digested the story.

'So what do you have to say? Do you think I'm lying?' Myers finally asked.

That was why Myers had never recounted those events to anyone investigating her case years ago. Hunter knew no Internal Affairs investigator would have believed her. On the contrary, they'd crucify her for seeking revenge.

'As I said,' Hunter said, 'I would've done the same thing.'

Sixty-Seven

Hunter and Myers talked for over an hour more. They shared information. She told him how the evidence she'd collected suggested that Katia Kudrov had been taken from inside her apartment in West Hollywood. She told him about the sixty messages on Katia's answer machine, and how they were all exactly twelve seconds long. She told him about the sound analyses on the last message, the deciphering of the hoarse whispering voice – 'YOU TAKE MY BREATH AWAY . . . WELCOME HOME, KATIA. I'VE BEEN WAITING FOR YOU. I GUESS IT'S FINALLY TIME WE MET.' – and why they believed the kidnapper had made the last call from inside her bedroom, probably while watching her shower.

Myers handed Hunter a copy of all the recordings, including the deciphered last one, together with several files. Her research was as good as she had said it was.

Hunter kept his side of the bargain, but he told Myers only what she really needed to know. He told her about the stitches to the victims' mouths, but not to their lower bodies. He never mentioned that the killer left any devices inside his victims. He also didn't say anything about the bomb, the spray-painted messages. He said the killer had used a knife and simply left it at that.

Hunter finally finished his shrimp platter before leaving Uncle Kelome's. His headache wasn't gone, but it was now bearable. Hunter contacted Operations and asked them to get started straight away on a file on Katia Kudrov.

Back in his apartment, he sat in his living room, nursing a new glass of single malt. He didn't even bother with the lights. Darkness suited him just fine. His brain kept going over everything Myers had told him. There was no concrete evidence that the same person who'd taken Laura Mitchell and Kelly Jensen had also abducted Katia Kudrov, but Hunter's mind had already started finding links in the method of their disappearance.

Katia had been abducted from inside her own apartment. That was consistent with the way in which Laura Mitchell, the first victim, had been kidnapped. Despite his suspicions, Hunter had yet to find out from where Kelly Jensen had been taken.

The phone messages left on Katia Kudrov's answering machine also bothered him. The fact that they were all twelve seconds long was evidence enough that they'd been left by the same person. One message a day, over sixty days. That again implied that they were dealing with someone patient and self-disciplined. A person who didn't mind waiting. It was almost like a game he played with his victims. But why twelve seconds? It wouldn't have been a random choice, he was sure.

Hunter played through the copy of the recordings Myers had given him. He heard the kidnapper's hoarse whisper, first as a mass of static sound, then as the deciphered voice. He rewound it and played it again. Over and over.

Hunter sat back in his beaten-up black leather sofa and rested his head against the backrest. He needed to watch the CCTV footage from Kelly's studio parking lot, but he was exhausted. His eyelids were starting to feel heavy. And when sleep came Hunter's way, he always grabbed it with both hands.

He fell asleep right there in his living room. Five consecutive and dreamless hours, something that very rarely happened. When he woke up, he had a stiff neck, and the taste in his mouth was as if he had eaten from a garbage can, but he felt rested and his headache was mercifully gone. He had a long shower, allowing the warmth and strong jet of water to massage his neck muscles. He shaved with an old razorblade that seemed to rip the hairs from his face instead of cutting them. He cursed. He had to go the grocery store sometime soon.

After making himself a strong cup of black coffee, Hunter returned to his living room and to the laptop he'd brought home with him.

Mr. Wang's hidden parking lot camera was set to record twenty-four hours a day, but Hunter had a feeling he'd only need to watch the night footage. This killer didn't strike him as someone who'd risk hanging around an abduction scene in the middle of the day, in plain view of everyone. If Kelly Jensen had really been taken from her studio location, chances were, it would've been done at night.

Because the parking lot was secluded and mainly used by shop owners, the movement of cars and people was minimal. Anything out of the ordinary would stand out. There was no need for Hunter to watch every minute of the fifty-six hours of night footage he had. After a quick test, he found out that he could speed up playback to six times its original playing speed and still be able to spot anything suspicious. That meant it would take him just over an hour to go through a whole eight hours. Hunter checked his watch – 6:22 a.m. He had enough time to skim through the first recorded night before making his way to Parker Center.

He didn't need to watch it for long.

The timestamp at the bottom right-hand corner of the screen read 8:36 p.m. when an old Ford Fiesta entered the parking lot and stopped directly behind Kelly's Trans-Am. Hunter sat up and slowed the footage down to normal playing speed. A few seconds later someone stepped out of the car – male, tall, well built. He leaned against the driver's door and nervously looked around the lot as if checking if anyone else was around. He looked uncomfortable as he lit up a cigarette. Hunter paused the picture and enhanced it by zooming in, but the quality he got from the laptop's imaging application wasn't great – too pixilated and grainy – so he couldn't properly make the man's face. He was sure the LAPD computer guys would be able to clean it up. Hunter pressed play again. Thirty seconds later, the passenger's door opened and a leggy blonde stepped out. She moved around to where the nervous male was standing, kneeled down in front of him, undid his belt, pulled down his trousers and took him in her mouth.

Hunter smiled and rubbed his chin. Just a couple of thrill seekers. He sped up the footage again. The couple moved from oral to full-blown sex – over the hood and against the driver's door. They were there for thirty-eight minutes.

Hunter moved on. At 9:49 p.m. Mr. Wang jumped into his pickup truck and left, leaving only Kelly's car in the parking lot. At 10:26 p.m. Hunter slowed the footage down once again.

'What the hell?'

He leaned closer to the screen and watched the events that unfolded in the next minute as his jaw dropped.

'Sonofabitch.'

Sixty-Eight

In complete darkness she sat shivering, curled up into a tight ball. She felt lightheaded, nauseous and every muscle in her body ached with feverish intensity. Her throat scratched as if she'd swallowed a ball of barbed wire.

She had no real idea of how long she'd been locked up in that cell. She guessed a few days. There was no way she could be sure. The room had no windows and the weak light bulb inside the metal mesh box on the ceiling only came on for a few minutes at a time. The intervals were uneven. Sometimes four, sometimes fivc times a day. But the light always came on just before she was given food. It was like training a lab rat.

She was given four meals a day, slid to her on a plastic tray through a special hatch at the bottom of the cell's heavy wooden door. The cell was small, ten paces long by eight wide, with bare brick walls, concrete floors, a metal-framed bed and a bucket on the corner, which was emptied once a day.

She moved her head and felt the room spin around again. The dizziness seemed to never go away. She wasn't even sure if she was awake or asleep. It felt as if she was caught somewhere between the two states. The only thing she was sure of was that she was scared – really scared.

He watched her bring her hands to her face and wipe away the tears that never seemed to stop. He wondered how much more scared she'd be if he made a noise. If he made her realize that she wasn't really alone. If she knew he was right there, hiding in the darkness, just three paces from her. How would she react if he extended his hand and touched her skin, her hair? How terrified would she be if he whispered something in her ear?

He smiled as he watched her shiver one more time. Maybe it was time she found out.

Sixty-Nine

Between pausing and fast-forwarding, Hunter spent another half an hour studying the CCTV camera footage from Kelly Jensen's studio parking lot. There were three main sections that interested him. The first was timestamped between 10:26 and 10:31 p.m. The second from 11:07 to 11:09 p.m. And the last one from 11:11 to 11:14 p.m.

The drive from Hunter's apartment in Huntingdon Park to Parker Center took him twenty-five minutes. He went straight into the IT Division, but at that time in the morning there was no one there except a new eager-to-impress recruit to the team. He was wearing a freshly ironed white shirt and a conservative gray tie. His matching suit jacket was resting on the back of his chair. No one in IT ever wore a shirt and tie, never mind a suit.

The young recruit told Hunter that Brian Doyle would probably come in late. He'd gone out celebrating the night before. The long-standing investigation he'd been personally involved in had finally come to an end. They'd successfully apprehended a serial pedophile after a sting operation that had lasted the whole day.

'The guy they caught . . .' the recruit told Hunter, 'he's married with two kids – one is ten, the other is twelve years old. Those are exactly the ages of the kids he used to groom online.' He shook his head as if the entire world had lost its logic. 'Is there anything I can help you with, Detective?' the recruit asked, jerking his head towards the laptop under Hunter's arm.

'What's your name, kid?'

'Garry, sir.' He offered his hand. 'Garry Cameron.'

Hunter shook it. 'I'm Robert, and if you call me *sir* one more time, I'll arrest you for defamation.'

Cameron smiled and nodded.

'I'm afraid I need to talk to Jack, Garry. I need him to run a few pieces of video footage through one of his super applications.'

Cameron's smile widened. 'Well, that's my field of expertize – video and audio analyses. That's the main reason I was transferred here.'

Hunter let out a surprised chuckle. 'I'll be damned. So I guess you're just the man I need.' He placed the laptop on Cameron's desk and they both waited in silence while it booted up. Hunter brought up the video player application and queued up the pre-selected segments. 'This is the original footage, taken from a private CCTV camera,' he explained before pressing play.

Cameron put on his computer glasses and leaned forward. The footage started off with an empty parking lot, except for a candy white Trans-Am T-top with dark tinted rear windows. The picture quality wasn't good, made worse by the lack of lighting.

'Nice car,' Cameron noted.

They watched for only a few seconds before a mysterious male figure approached the lot on foot from the right. He was tall, somewhere between six two and six four with a strong, football player's physique. He was wearing dark clothing; shoes, trousers, gloves, skullcap and a jacket with its collar pulled up. The problem was: Mr. Wang's camera was on the east side of the lot, facing west, and so was the stranger. So far he could only be seen from the back. He stopped by the driver's door to the Trans-Am, reached inside his jacket and retrieved a long, flat piece of metal that resembled a school ruler. Like a professional car thief, the man slid the stick of metal down through the window slot and into the car door. In one quick movement he yanked it up. He tried the handle and the door opened as if he'd used a key.

'You don't look like a CATS, Detective,' Cameron said, referring to the Commercial Auto Theft Section of the LAPD without diverting his attention from the screen.

'I'm not.'

On the screen, the man bent down, put his hand inside the car and popped the hood.

Cameron frowned.

The man quickly rechecked the lot's entrance – no one was coming. Without ever facing east he moved to the front of the car and lifted the hood before bending over the engine and reaching for something in the main block. There was no way they could see exactly what he was doing, but whatever it was, it only took him three seconds. He closed the hood and returned to the driver's side. One more look around before opening the door and disappearing inside and into the back seat.

'Strange,' Cameron commented. 'What's this about?'

'You'll see.'

The video application jumped straight to the next section Hunter had queued up. Cameron checked the timestamp clock at the bottom right-hand corner of the screen and noticed that the footage had jumped forward thirty-six minutes.

'I take it that our mysterious man is still inside the car?' Cameron asked.

'Never moved.'

They carried on watching. This time a slender brunette appeared, coming in from the same direction the man did earlier – Kelly Jensen. Her hair was tied back in a ponytail. She was wearing blue jeans, flat shoes and a faded brown leather jacket.

'Oh shit,' Cameron murmured, already guessing what was about to happen.

Kelly approached the car and searched her handbag for her car keys. Oblivious to the fact that someone was already inside waiting for her, she opened the door and got into the driver's seat. The darkness, the position of the car, and the angle in which Mr. Wang's camera was set, made it impossible for Hunter and Cameron to see through the windscreen. Zooming in on the picture didn't help either.

Cameron pulled his glasses from his face and rubbed his eyes.

Nothing happened for the next two minutes. When the timestamp at the bottom of the screen read 11:11 p.m. the passenger's door opened and the man stepped out of the car. He paused and looked around slowly, checking he was still alone. Satisfied, he made his way to the other side, opened the driver's door and retrieved the keys from the ignition before opening the trunk. As if lifting nothing heavier than a shopping bag, he picked Kelly up with both arms. She was knocked out cold, but it was easy to tell she was still alive.

The man carefully placed her in the trunk and stood still for a long while, looking down at her as if admiring her. He finally returned to the front of the car, opened the hood and tweaked something in the engine block again. Moments later he got into the driver's seat and took off.

'Shit,' Cameron said, looking at Hunter, his complexion paler than minutes ago. 'What do you need me to do?'

'I've looked at this footage several times,' Hunter said. 'That guy doesn't face the camera once, but he looks around a few times, checking his ground.'

Cameron nodded. 'Yeah, I noticed that.'

'OK, so I was wondering – if we slowed this thing down completely, and then moved it frame by frame, we might be lucky enough to get at least a partial face shot in there somewhere.'

'It's possible,' Cameron said, checking his watch. 'I can start working on it right away. I'll have to transfer the footage to my computer and then analyze it again using professional software, but it shouldn't take me more than an hour, two at the most.'

Hunter placed a card on the desk. 'Call me the moment you get anything.'

As he turned to leave, Cameron stopped him.

'Detective, is there a chance she's still alive?'

Hunter didn't say anything. He didn't have to.

Seventy

'Sonofabitch!'

Garcia exclaimed as he watched a copy of the footage Hunter had left with Cameron in ITD. The timestamp on the screen showed that Kelly Jensen had been taken on the 24th February. Their suspicion was that Laura Mitchell, the first victim, had been abducted between the 2nd and the 5th of March.

'So he abducts Kelly first, but murders her second,' Garcia said.

Hunter nodded.

'Why?'

'If we're right about the killer projecting the image of the person he wanted them to be onto his victims, then it's just a matter of time before they do or say something that'd break that spell. Something that'd make him see them for who they really are.'

'Laura broke the spell first.'

'It looks that way, yes.'

Garcia returned his attention to the footage Hunter had retrieved from Mr. Wang's shop. 'Do we have a facial shot?'

'No yet, but ITD are working on it.'

Garcia's eyes returned to his computer screen and the footage. 'You were right when you said that we were dealing with someone who is patient.'

'Not only patient,' Hunter replied. 'He's calm, collected and confident. He staked out Kelly's studio location for several nights no doubt, before making his move. And when he did, he was precise. No time wasted, no struggle, no chance for her to react. This guy is different, Carlos. He takes his victims from places where they are supposed to feel safe; their homes . . . their work studios . . . their cars . . .'

Garcia nodded. 'Judging from that footage, what would you say he is . . . ? Six two, six three . . . ? Weighs around two hundred pounds . . . ?'

'That sounds about right. And that is consistent with the perpetrator's height theory from the skullcap fibers retrieved from the brick wall in Laura's studio. I've called Forensics and told them to pick Kelly's Trans-Am up from Santa Monica and go through every inch of that cockpit and boot.'

Garcia watched the footage one more time in silence.

Hunter had also gotten in touch with the bureaus' Traffic Divisions. The killer had driven Kelly's car out of her studio parking lot and onto Los Angeles' streets, and there were thousands of traffic and CCTV cameras spread across town. Kelly's Trans-Am was an easy car to spot, so the killer would've wanted to swap vehicles as soon as possible. He probably had a van waiting and ready to go someplace close, but he was clever, he didn't just dump her car and leave. A classic Trans-Am abandoned on a side street somewhere would've raised too many eyebrows. It would've alerted the police to start looking for Kelly almost immediately. The killer also knew not to return her car to the studio's parking lot. From his surveillance, he would've known that Kelly never left it there overnight. He wouldn't want to risk one of the shop owners noticing it and calling the cops. Instead, he'd driven it back to Santa Monica and parked it in the same spot she always did – right in front of her apartment block. Rule one of being a criminal: raise as little suspicion as possible. This guy seemed to have written that rule.

Hunter was hoping that a traffic camera somewhere had picked up some of that journey. It was a long shot, but right now, any shot was worth taking.

'Anything from Operations on any stitched victims? Anything anywhere in the country?' Garcia asked.

Hunter had asked the Office of Operations to start a nationwide search – any deaths where a brunette female victim had been found with stitches to her mouth, sexual organ, or both. If the killer was really transferring his feelings and projecting the image of the person he once loved onto his victims, there was a good chance that that person had died in a similar way.

'Nothing so far.'

'How far back are we searching?'

'Twenty-five years.'

'Really? That long ago?'

Hunter leaned against his desk. 'We might as well cover all angles.'

'What do you mean?'

'What if we're right about the love theory, but the person the victims remind our killer of isn't an ex-wife, or girlfriend, or even someone he's been infatuated with all his life. What if it's someone else? Someone he also loved. Someone he'd never hurt no matter what?'

Garcia thought about it for a brief moment. 'His mother?'

Hunter nodded. 'It's a possibility. Either his mother or a guardian – like an aunt, an older sister or cousin or something.' Hunter paused and reached for a folder on his desk. 'Have you ever heard of Katia Kudrov?'

Garcia frowned and shook his head at the same time. 'Who's she?'

Hunter pulled a portrait out of an envelope.

Garcia's heart skipped a beat. 'Holy shit. She's almost the spitting image of Laura and Kelly. Who the hell *is* she?'

Hunter took his time telling Garcia everything that had happened since he met Whitney Myers.

'This is a copy of Whitney's investigation file. She's covered every angle. She even has her own forensic specialist.'

'And . . . ?' Garcia started flipping through the pages.

'Nothing substantial. The fingerprints found belonged to Katia herself, her father or the person she was seeing at the time.'

Garcia's eyebrows arched.

'He's not a suspect. He wasn't even in the country at the time of the abduction. It's all there, have a look through later.'

'So her father never filed a Missing Persons report?'

Hunter shook his head. 'Not officially. That's why she wasn't in any of the lists MP sent us. Last night was the first I ever heard of her.'

'Do you think our killer has her?'

'I'm not sure. Sometimes I think my mind is chasing ghosts.'

'What kinda ghosts?'

Hunter shrugged and started picking at the scab that had formed on the cut above his eyebrow.

'I think there are several similarities in the way Katia, Laura and Kelly were abducted. But then again, there are only so many ways a person *can* be abducted. That's why I'm worried about wasting time and chasing a connection that might not even be there. As Whitney said, officially Katia Kudrov isn't even a Missing Persons case, she was never reported.' He picked at the scab too hard and a tiny blob of blood started to form. Hunter wiped it away with the heel of his hand. 'Our research team is already looking into the background of Laura and Kelly, searching for any more connections other than looks and profession. I've asked them to include Katia in that search.'

Hunter's cell phone rang and he fumbled for it in his jacket pocket. 'Detective Hunter.'

'Detective, it's Garry Cameron from ITD.'

'Garry . . . tell me you got something.' His eyes darted towards Garcia expectantly.

'Sorry, Detective, no facial image whatsoever,' Garry sounded defeated. 'I went through every single frame of the footage you gave me, enhancing them every way I could. The guy never gets himself into a revealing angle.' A quick pause. 'In a couple of frames there's a flash of skin but that's all. All I can tell you other that what you've already seen is that he's Caucasian. I'm really sorry, Detective.'

Hunter disconnected and closed his eyes. He needed some sort of break in this investigation. Four people were dead. James Smith was still missing after that bizarre phone call, and if Katia Kudrov had been taken by the same person who took Laura and Kelly, she was running out of time fast.

Seventy-One

Like a contagious disease, Hunter's bad luck seemed to spread throughout every aspect of the investigation. The documentaries he and Garcia got from the A & E TV network revealed nothing. Bryan Coleman was right about the *Canvas Beauty* production: it looked low budget right from the starting credits. Laura Mitchell and Kelly Jensen did appear in it, but for no longer than a few minutes each. They mainly spoke about how living in the West Coast had influenced the way in which they painted.

As Coleman had said, the majority of the piece concentrated on Martina Greene, the daughter of the old A & E TV regional director. The whole thing played more like an advertisement than anything else. Besides Martina, Laura and Kelly, only two other female painters appeared in the documentary – one of them, just like Martina, was naturally blonde. The other one was much older – in her fifties. Hunter checked with both of them, neither had seen nor spoken to Laura or Kelly since. Neither of them recognized James Smith from the picture Hunter showed them either.

Hunter's team was checking the background of every single person whose name was on the *Canvas Beauty* documentary credits list. So far, everyone had checked out, but the list was long.

The other three documentaries Hunter and Garcia had obtained from the A & E TV network featured several painters from all over the country – none of them brunette females in their thirties.

Doctor Hove's lab had confirmed that the dust retrieved from under Kelly Jensen's nails had come from a mixture of mortar and red clay, consistent with common wall bricks. That meant that she could've been kept absolutely anywhere, from a self-built underground bunker to an inside room or an outside garage.

Hunter's traffic camera gamble didn't pay off either. The closest road camera to Kelly Jensen's art studio was a mile away. Her Trans-Am was never spotted on the night she was taken. The South Bureau Traffic Operations' captain had explained that most of the inner-city cameras were only infraction activated – like going through a red light or breaking the speed limit. They didn't film twenty-four hours a day. The ones that did were strategically positioned on main roads, avenues and interstates. Their principal function was to alert Traffic Divisions about congestion hotspots and accidents.

Early the morning after Kelly's disappearance, a camera in Santa Monica picked up her car as it traveled down San Vicente Boulevard going west, in the direction of her apartment building. But the cameras don't monitor the whole of the boulevard. The vehicle was lost as it approached the final stretch that led to the beachfront.

As Hunter had requested, Forensics had picked up the car from Santa Monica and gone over every inch of its interior and boot. The hairs found matched to Kelly Jensen. The few dark fibers retrieved from the driver's seat matched the ones found on the wall behind the large canvas in Laura

Mitchell's apartment. They came from the same skullcap. There were no fingerprints.

It was close to midnight, and for the first time since the beginning of spring the sky had clouded over. Menacing rain clouds and strong winds were closing in from the north, bringing with them the unmistakable smell of wet grass and turf. Hunter was sitting in his living room, reading through reports from his research team into Laura, Kelly and Katia's professional and personal lives. Their backgrounds were totally different from each other. Other than physically having the same overall look and being an artist by profession, the team hadn't found any other links between the three women.

Laura had come from a success-story family. Her father, Roy Mitchell, started his life slum-poor. Having run away from violent and abusive parents when young, most of the food Roy ate in his early years came from trash cans in the back alleys of hotels and restaurants. He was only fourteen when he started selling discarded secondhand books he bought from hotel staff. By the age of eighteen he'd opened his first bookstore, and from there business prospered. His autobiography – *Back Alley Books* – topped the US non-fiction book chart for twelve weeks, and spent a further thirty-three in the top twenty-five. He married the young lawyer who helped him set up his book business, Denise, at the age of twenty. Laura was the younger of their two children.

Kelly, on the other hand, had had a pretty unadventurous life. Born into a small, church-going family in Montana, she was destined to become just another Treasure State housewife, tending to her husband, kids and garden. Her arts schoolteacher recognized her talent when it came to painting, and for years kept on telling her that she shouldn't walk away from her gift.

Katia came from the richest of all three families, but she never took anything for granted. She became a violinist of her own accord, and no matter how much money her family had, talent and dedication can't be bought. Everything she'd achieved, she did it through her own hard work.

Hunter put the report down and stretched his arms high above his head. From his small bar, he poured another double dose of single malt. He needed something comforting and rich on the palate this time. His eyes rested on the bottle of Balblair 1997 and his mind was made. He dropped a single cube of ice in his glass and heard it crack as the dense, honey-colored liquid hit it. He brought the glass to his nose and breathed in the sweet, vanilla oak vapors for a moment. He took a small sip, allowing the alcohol to reach every corner of his mouth before swallowing it. If heaven had a taste, this would be pretty close to it.

Hunter stared out his window at a city that he had never really understood, and that was getting crazier and crazier by the day. How could anyone understand the madness that went around in this town?

A thin sheet of rain had started falling. Hunter's gaze dropped to the files and photographs scattered on his coffee table. Laura and Kelly stared back at him with terrified pleading eyes, their ragdoll smiles grotesquely outlined by rough stitches and black thread.

Knock, knock.

Hunter frowned as his eyes first shot towards his front

room door and then quickly to his watch. Way too late for visitors. Besides, he couldn't even remember the last time someone knocked on his door.

Knock, knock, knock. A lot more urgent this time.

Seventy-Two

Hunter put down his glass, grabbed his gun from his holster, which was hanging from the back of a chair, and approached his front door. There was no peephole. Hunter hated them: they provided any assailant with a very easy kill shot. Just wait until the lens darkens and put a bullet through it. Training and instinct told him to stay to the right of the doorframe, out of reach of the door swing. That would avoid him being slammed in the face if anyone kicked the door in as he unlocked it. It would also put Hunter out of the direct blast path of a powerful weapon, should anyone be waiting to blow a hole through the door.

He undid the main lock and pulled the door back, letting it rest, fractionally open, on the security chain. From the outside, only part of his face was visible through the gap.

'Expecting the bad guys?' Whitney Myers asked with an amused grin.

She was wearing a cropped, black leather biker's jacket with an AC/DC T-shirt underneath. Her blue jeans were faded and torn at her left knee, a look that was perfectly complemented by her silver-tip cowboy boots. Hunter looked her up and down. He was not amused.

'Are you gonna invite me in or shoot me with that gun you're holding behind your back?'

Hunter closed the door, undid the security chain and pulled it back open again. He was also wearing faded jeans – though his weren't torn – but not much else.

It was Myers' turn to look him up and down. 'Well, somebody is a gym bunny.' Her eyes paused at the tight muscles of his abdomen before slowly moving up to his chest, making sure she grabbed a good look of his biceps, and then finally back to his face.

'Did you get lost on your way to a rock gig or something?' He stood on the doorway, his gun still in his right hand. 'What in the world are you doing here . . . and at this time of night?'

As her gaze moved past Hunter and into his apartment, Myers' expression changed. 'I'm sorry . . . are you . . . with someone?'

Hunter allowed the embarrassing moment to stretch for a couple of seconds before shaking his head.

'No.'

He stepped back and fully opened the door, giving her a silent invitation.

Hunter's front room was oddly shaped, with furniture that looked to have belonged to the Salvation Army. There were four mismatched chairs around a square, wooden table that he used as his computer desk. A laptop, together with a printer and a small table lamp were crammed onto it. A few feet away from the far wall was a beaten-up black sofa. The coffee table in front it was overflowing with pictures and police reports. Across the room Myers saw a glass bar with an impressive collection of single malt Scotch.

'I can see you're not a man who cares for extravagant decoration.'

Hunter gathered the pictures and papers from the coffee

table into a pile and moved them out of the way. He reached for a white T-shirt that was on the back of one of the chairs and put it on.

Myers looked away, hiding her disappointment. She approached the dark wood sideboard to the right of the glass bar where a few lonely picture frames were arranged. Two of the photographs were black and white and looked to be old. Both were of the same smiling couple. Hunter looked like his father, but he had his mother's understanding eyes, Myers noted. Most of the other photographs showed Hunter and another man, heavier and about two inches taller. From Myers' research she knew he was Hunter's old RHD partner, Scott Wilson, who'd died in a boat accident a few years ago. Two other photographs showed Hunter receiving commendations from the Mayor of Los Angeles and the Governor of California. The last picture, the one hiding right at the back was of a younger-looking Hunter dressed in a graduation gown and holding a university diploma. He looked like he'd just conquered the world. His father was proudly standing by his side. His smile could've brightened a dark day.

With his arms folded, Hunter stood by the window, waiting.

Myers' eyes moved from the pictures to the glass bar and the neatly arranged bottles. 'Do you mind if I have a drink?'

'If you promise to tell me why you're here, sure, go right ahead.'

She poured herself a double dose of Balblair 1997 and dropped a single cube of ice in it.

Hunter's face remained impartial but he was impressed. 'Good choice.'

Myers had a sip of her drink. 'Do you have a CD player?'

Hunter's eyes narrowed. 'Why? Are you suddenly in the mood for some *Back in Black*?'

She smiled and her gaze moved momentarily down to her shirt. 'That *is* my favorite AC/DC album, but we can listen to it later if you like. Right now, you've gotta listen to this.' Myers pulled a CD case from her handbag. ''Cause you won't believe me if I'd told you.'

Seventy-Three

The rain was coming down a little harder now, drumming against the window just behind Hunter. The wind had also picked up.

'Give me a sec,' he said before disappearing down a small corridor. Moments later he returned with a portable stereo system.

'I found this on the Internet, almost by chance,' Myers said as Hunter cleared the table, placed the stereo on it and plugged it in.

'What is it?'

'An interview.'

Hunter paused and looked up. 'With Katia?'

Myers nodded and handed him the CD. 'It was first aired by KUSC Radio. It's a dedicated classical music FM station.'

Hunter nodded. 'Yeah, I know it. It's run by the University of Southern California.'

Myers pulled a face. 'I didn't know you were into classical music.'

'I'm not, but I read a lot.'

Myers moved on.

'The entire interview is about an hour long with a few classical pieces thrown in so the whole thing isn't just talk. In the first half, Katia is talking to the radio DJ, answering questions he puts to her. In the second half, she's answering questions that were phoned or emailed in by listeners.' She tilted her head to one side. 'I'm not that cruel, so I'm not gonna make you listen to the whole thing. I've copied only the important bits.'

Hunter slotted the CD in, pressed play, and adjusted the volume.

'Welcome back. This is KUSC Radio, the best in classical music in Los Angeles and California.' The DJ's voice sounded exactly like what most people would expect the voice of a classical music station DJ to sound like – velvety and soothing. 'We're back with our special guest this afternoon, someone most of you will need no introduction to. The Los Angeles Philharmonic concertmistress, Katia Kudrov.'

A small section of a violin solo faded in for several seconds and then out again.

'OK, just before the break we talked about your early beginnings and how much you struggled to dominate your instrument, but now we're moving onto something a little more personal – love and romance. Is that OK?'

There was a small pause, as if Katia was considering something.

'Yeah, sure, as long as you don't make me blush.' Her voice was delicate but not fragile. There was confidence in her tone.

'I promise I won't. OK, you describe yourself as a hopeless romantic. Why?'

A timid chuckle. ''Cause I am, really. And here comes the first blush. My favorite movie is *Pretty Woman*.' Giggles.

'Yeah, I'd say that's reason enough to blush,' the DJ laughed.

'I'm like a little girl when it comes to love. I know this

might sound naïve, but I'd love for that kind of fairy tale to exist.'

'The "true love" fairy tale?'

'Yes. The magical make-you-float-on-air kind of love. Sparks flying the first time you set eyes on someone and you just know you were made for each other.'

'Have you ever been that much in love?'

Another chuckle. 'No, not yet. But there's no rush, and I have my music. That really does make me float on air.'

'I'd say your music makes us all float on air.'

'Thank you.' A short pause. 'And now I'm really blushing.'

'So, judging by your comment about sparks flying the first time you set eyes on someone means you believe in love at first sight?'

'Absolutely.'

'And what would someone have to say or do to grab your attention?'

'Nothing.'

'Nothing?'

'Nothing. I believe that love is a lot more than words, or looks. It's something that hits you and then just takes over, without any warning. I believe that when you meet the person you're supposed to spend the rest of your life with—'

'The proverbial "soul mate"?' the DJ interrupted.

'Yes, your soul mate. I think that when we meet that person, we just know. Even from a silent moment. Even if he doesn't say a word at first.'

'OK, I guess I can see what you mean, but he can't be silent forever. He'll have to say something eventually. So what would that have to be? How would he grab your attention?'

'He wouldn't have to do or say anything in particular, but let me tell you my favorite romantic story.'

'OK.'

'As a teenager, my grandmother's first ever job was as a flower girl in a street market in Perm in the old Soviet Union. My grandfather worked in a tailor shop, just a few streets from the market. Her first day at work was the very first time he saw her, and just like that, he fell madly in love. My grandfather was an attractive man, but he was also very, very shy. It took him sixty days to gather up the courage to finally say something to her.'

'Sixty?' the DJ commented.

'Every morning on his way to work he walked past her stall. Every morning he'd promise himself that'd be the day he'd speak to her. And every morning when he saw her, he'd become too nervous. Instead of speaking to her, he'd just walk on in silence.'

'OK, so what happened?'

'What my grandfather didn't know was that my grandmother had also fallen in love with him from the first day she saw him. Every day she watched him walk past the flower stall, and every day she hoped that he'd stop and ask her out. So one morning, he gathered all the courage he could muster, walked up to my grandmother, looked her in the eye and managed to whisper five little words: "You take my breath away."'

Myers reached over and pressed the pause button.

Hunter's memory flashed back to the deciphered answering machine recording Myers had given him a few days ago. The very first words Katia's kidnapper had said had been exactly those – YOU TAKE MY BREATH AWAY . . .

By the way Myers looked at Hunter, he knew that there was more to come.

Seventy-Four

'Fifty-nine days walking past the flower stall in silence,' Myers said, her stare fixed on Hunter. 'Fifty-nine silent messages left on Katia's answering machine. And I'm sure you remember the first five words on the sixtieth message.'

Hunter nodded but said nothing.

'Now this next part of the interview comes after a couple of commercial breaks. The DJ is asking Katia questions that were phoned or emailed in by listeners.' She pressed the pause button again and the interview resumed. It started with animated laughter.

'OK,' the DJ said, 'I've got another question here from one of our callers. This is going back to you being a hopeless romantic, and about you finding your knight in shining armor.'

'OK . . .' Katia sounded hesitant.

'The question is: you said that you believe that love is a lot more than words, or looks. You also said that you believe that when you meet the right person, your "soul mate", you'll just know. Even from a silent moment, like your grandparents. What I'd like to know is how long is that moment? How much silence do you need before you know?'

'Umm.'

Laughter from the DJ. 'That's not a bad question. So how

long is that moment? How quickly do you think you'll be able to know if you've met the right person?'

There was a pause as Katia thought about it. 'Twelve seconds,' she finally replied.

Hunter's stare met Myers but neither said a word.

'Twelve seconds?' the DJ asked. 'That's a strange number. Why twelve?'

'Well, I'd probably know in ten seconds flat, but I'd give it another two seconds just to be absolutely sure.' Katia and the DJ both laughed.

'That's a very good answer,' the DJ agreed.

Myers reached over and pressed the stop button. 'Before you ask,' she said, 'I checked, the station has no record of who called in with that question.'

'Remind me when that was aired again?'

'Eight months ago, but this recording was passed on to other radio stations.' She retrieved a notebook from her bag. 'KCSN in Northridge, KQSC and KDB in Santa Barbara, KDSC in Thousand Oaks and even KTMV, which is a smooth jazz station. It's been aired all over the court. I got this from KUSC's website. Anyone can listen to it online, or download it. Even if the kidnapper wasn't the one who called in with the question, he could've heard the interview and got his idea from there.' She had another sip of her Scotch. 'You and I know that those twelve seconds of silence in every message weren't just coincidence.'

Hunter said nothing.

'You know what this means, don't you?' There was excitement in Myers' voice. 'Katia's abduction is about *love*, not hate. Whoever took her is desperately *in love* with her. So that pretty much discards the possibility of your sadistic killer being the one who kidnapped her.'

Hunter remained silent. His expression gave nothing away.

'Katia had been seeing the new conductor for the Los Angeles Philharmonic, Phillip Stein, for the past four months. He was, and still is, completely obsessed with her. But she broke it all off just a few days before the tour ended. He didn't take the break well at all.'

'But he couldn't have done it. He flew straight to Munich after their last concert in Chicago. I read your report.'

'And you double-checked that just to be sure, didn't you?'

Hunter nodded. 'Any other lovers, ex-boyfriends . . . ?'

'Her previous boyfriend lives in France, where she was before coming back to the US. If she had any other lovers, she kept them well hidden. But I don't think her kidnapper was a lover.' She paused for a moment. 'I think we're dealing with an obsessed fan. Somebody who is so in love with her his whole reality is distorted. That's why he took what she said in that interview so tremendously out of context. His wants to give her her fairy-tale love story.'

Myers almost jumped out of her skin when Hunter's phone vibrated against the tabletop, announcing a new incoming call. The caller ID read *Restricted call.*

He didn't even have to answer it to know that his night was about to get a whole lot darker.

Seventy-Five

Rain was still falling by the time Hunter got to Cypress Park, Northeast Los Angeles. He hadn't said anything after he disconnected from the call. He hadn't said a word during it either. He'd just listened. But Myers knew from the defeated way he closed his eyes for just a second – they had another victim.

Cypress Park was one of the first suburbs of Los Angeles. Developed just outside the downtown area at the beginning of the twentieth century, it had been created as a working-class neighborhood, whose main attraction was its proximity to the railroad yards. That's where the victim's body had been found, inside one of the abandoned buildings along the tracks.

The old railroad yards still occupied a vast area, but great parts of it were now just wastelands. One of these wastelands was located directly behind Rio de Los Angeles State Park. Half a mile north from there, still inside this desolated area and sandwiched between the train tracks and the LA River was an old maintenance depot. On a rainy, moonless night, the flashing police lights could be seen from quite a distance.

Forensics were already there.

Hunter parked next to Garcia's car. A young policeman, wearing a standard issue LAPD raincoat and holding what could only be described as a kid's size umbrella, came up to his door. Hunter pulled his collar up and tighter around his neck, refused the umbrella, and started walking up to the brick building. His hands were tucked deep inside his pockets. His eyes were low, searching the ground, doing his best to avoid stepping into any puddles.

'Detective Hunter?' a man called from the perimeter.

Hunter recognized Donald Robbins' voice – the pain-in-the-ass *LA Times* reporter. He'd covered every case Hunter had been involved in. They were old friends without ever being friends.

'Is this victim related to the case you're already investigating? Perhaps a painter as well?'

Hunter didn't lose stride or look up, but he wondered how the hell Robbins had found out about the victims being painters.

'C'mon, Robert. It's me. You're after another serial killer, aren't you? Is he an artist stalker?'

Still not even an acknowledgement from Hunter.

The outside of the brick building was a mess of graffiti and colors. Garcia, together with two police officers, was standing under an improvised canvas shelter by the entrance to the old depot. The metal door directly behind them had been graffitied with the silhouette of a long-haired pole dancer bending forward. Her spread legs created a perfect upside-down V shape.

Garcia had just zipped up his forensic Tyvek coveralls when he saw Hunter coming around the corner.

'You *have* noticed that it's raining, right?' Garcia said as Hunter reached the shelter.

'I like rain,' Hunter replied, using both hands to brush the water off his hair.

'Yeah, I can see that.' Garcia handed him a sealed plastic bag containing a white hooded coverall.

'Who called it in?' Hunter asked, ripping the bag open.

'Old homeless guy,' the officer closest to the door confirmed. He was short and stout with a bulldog-like face. 'He said that he sometimes sleeps here. Tonight, he wanted to get out of the rain.'

'Where's he now?'

The officer pointed to a police car twenty-five yards from where they were.

'Who talked to him?' Hunter looked at Garcia, who shook his head.

'I just got here.'

'Sergeant Travis,' the officer replied. 'He's with him now.'

Hunter nodded. 'Have any of you been inside?'

'Nope, we got here after Forensics. Our orders are to stay out here soaking our asses in this shitty rain and act like nightclub doormen to all of you big Homicide boys.'

Garcia frowned and looked at Hunter.

'I guess you were right at the end of your shift when you got this call, right?' Hunter said.

'Yeah, whatever.' The officer ran two fingers over his peach-fuzz moustache.

Hunter zipped up his coveralls. 'OK, Officer . . . ?'

'Donikowski.'

'OK, Officer Donikowski, I guess you can do your night-club doorman job now.' He nodded at the door.

Garcia smirked.

The first room was about fifteen feet wide by twenty deep. The walls were also covered in graffiti. Rain spat onto the floor through a windowless frame to the left of the door. Discarded food cans and wrappers were piled up in one corner, together with an old straw mattress. The floor was littered with all different sorts of debris. Hunter could see no blood anywhere.

The familiar, strong crime-scene forensic light was coming from the next room along, where hushed voices could be heard.

As they approached the door, Hunter picked up on a mixture of smells – mostly stale urine, mold and accumulated garbage. All of them the kind of odors you'd expect to find inside an old, derelict building, sometimes used by drifters. But there was a fourth, fainter smell. Not the kind of putrid stench you get when a body starts to rot, but something else. Something Hunter knew he'd smelled before. He paused and sniffed the air a couple of times. From the corner of his eye he noticed Garcia doing the same thing. He was the one who recognized it first. The last time Garcia smelled that same smell he'd thrown up within seconds. This time was no different.

Seventy-Six

The second room was smaller than the one Hunter and Garcia were in, but identical in shape and state of deterioration – graffitied walls, windowless frames, piles of garbage on the corners and all sorts of debris scattered around the floor. Doctor Hove and Mike Brindle were standing by a door on the far wall that led into a third chamber. The same portable tactical X-ray unit they'd used in the basement of the preschool in Glassell Park had been set up on the floor next to them. Three paces to the left of the unit, lying on her back, was the naked body of a Caucasian brunette female. Hunter could see the thick black thread used to stitch her mouth and lower body from across the room. There was very little blood surrounding the body.

'Where's Carlos?' Doctor Hove asked. 'I thought he was waiting for you outside.'

Hunter didn't reply, didn't move, didn't breathe. He just stood perfectly still, his eyes fixed on the brunette's face. Her skin had turned a light shade of purple, indicating blood pooling. Like the two previous victims, the lower part of her face had swollen, due to the stitches to her mouth. But even so, there was something familiar about her. Hunter felt his skin burn as adrenalin ran through him.

'Robert,' the doctor called again.

Hunter's eyes finally refocused on her.

'Are you OK?'

'I'm fine.'

'Where's Carlos? I thought he'd be with you.'

'I'm here,' Garcia said as he walked through the door behind Hunter. He looked a little paler than a moment ago. The strange, faint smell they'd picked up outside was more prominent in the room. Garcia brought his hand to his mouth and cringed as he fought to keep his stomach from erupting again.

Hunter approached the body in silence and crouched down next to it. Her face was starting to puff up. He didn't need to touch her to know that her body was now in full rigor mortis. She'd been dead for at least twelve hours. Her eyes were closed, but everything about her features looked familiar. The nose, the cheekbone structure, the shape of the chin. Hunter moved closer still and had a look at her hands and fingers. Most of her fingernails were broken or chipped. Despite the purpling of the skin, at first glance Hunter could see no severe hematomas. There were no cuts or abrasions either. The swelling to her body wasn't due to physical abuse.

Hunter moved around to the other side. She had a single-color tribal tattoo on her right shoulder.

Garcia was studying the body in silence from a standing position, his hand still covering his nose and mouth.

'Do you know who she is?' the doctor asked, noticing the way Hunter kept looking back at her face. 'Is she another painter from your list of missing persons?'

Garcia shook his head. 'I can't place her. I know the face is a little swollen, but I don't think she was on the lists.'

'She's not a painter,' Hunter said, standing back up again. 'She's a musician.'

Seventy-Seven

Garcia's eyes returned to her face and he frowned. He'd had a very good look at Katia Kudrov's photographs since Hunter told him about her. The woman on the floor didn't look like Katia.

'It's not Katia Kudrov,' Hunter said, reading what his partner was thinking.

Garcia frowned harder.

'You know her?' he asked.

'She looks familiar. I've seen her before, I'm just not sure where.'

'So how do you know she's a musician?' Brindle this time.

'She's got calluses on all the fingertips of her left hand, except her thumb, where the callus is on the first joint.'

Brindle looked hesitant.

'String instrument musicians get those,' Hunter explained. 'The fingertip ones from pressing down on the strings, and the thumb joint one from sliding their hands up and down the instrument's arm, like a violin, cello, guitar, bass, whatever.'

Doctor Hove nodded. 'One of my Forensics technicians is learning to play the guitar. He's always complaining his fingertips hurt like hell and keeps on picking off the loose skin.'

Hunter turned around and looked in the direction of the room he came in from. 'She was found in this room?'

Brindle nodded. 'At the exact location she is right now. Unlike the victim from Glassell Park, we didn't need to turn her over to use the X-ray machine. She was found on her back. There's no indication that anyone has touched the body either.'

Hunter looked around at the ceiling and walls for an instant. 'What's in that room?' He nodded towards the next chamber.

'Same as in here and the previous room,' Doctor Hove replied. 'More graffiti and garbage.'

Hunter moved closer and pulled the creaking door open. The forensic light was strong enough to illuminate most of the next chamber.

'There's no bed, or table, or counter, or anything? She was just left in here on the floor?'

'No,' Brindle clarified. His head tilted back a fraction and his eyes moved towards the ceiling. 'Upstairs.'

Hunter peeked inside the third room again. The staircase was to the left of the door, hugging the wall.

'I've got two agents up there working the scene,' Brindle continued. 'It looks like she was left on a wooden table.' He knew what Hunter would ask next and nodded before the question came. 'The table was lifted about a foot off the ground by wooden blocks, just like in Glassell Park.'

'The words . . . ?'

Brindle nodded again. '*It's inside you.* Painted onto the ceiling this time.'

Garcia had a quick look inside the next room. 'So she managed to get off the table, come all the way down those stairs, and out here before finally dying?'

'Before collapsing,' Doctor Hove said, grabbing both detectives' attention again. 'Death took a while to come, but not before tremendous suffering.'

'And she probably crawled her way down here,' Brindle took over. 'She must've been a very strong woman, physically and mentally. Her will to stay alive was nothing short of exceptional. The kind of pain she went through, most people wouldn't have been able to move at all, never mind make it all the way down here.'

Hunter's stare moved to the X-ray unit on the floor and the laptop screen. It seemed to be turned off.

Brindle and Doctor Hove followed his gaze. 'Given what we know and the fact that the MO and signatures are the same,' the doctor said, 'I'm sure the killer used the same trigger mechanism he used before, but this time it didn't trigger a fan-out knife or a bomb. Let me show you.'

Garcia cleared his throat uncomfortably while the doctor brought the laptop back to life.

'We'd just finished capturing this when you arrived,' Brindle explained.

As the image of the object left inside her body materialized on the screen, both detectives moved closer.

No one said a word.

Hunter and Garcia squinted at the same time, trying to make sense of what they were looking at.

'No way,' Hunter said. 'Is that what I think it is?'

Brindle and Doctor Hove nodded in unison. 'We think so.'

A couple more seconds and Garcia finally saw it, his eyes widening in disbelief.

Seventy-Eight

The digital clock on Hunter's microwave read 3:42 a.m. when he stepped back into his apartment and closed the door behind him. He wasted no time walking into every room and turning on all the lights. For now he just didn't want any more darkness. He was tired, but for the first time he welcomed insomnia. He wasn't sure he'd have the strength to deal with the nightmares he knew would come as soon as he closed his eyes.

After the body had been removed and taken to the morgue, Hunter and Garcia had spent a long time looking around the old depot, especially the room upstairs. It was a large chamber, which had probably been used as one of the main storage areas. Two of the walls were lined from floor to ceiling with long wooden shelves. A large carpenter's workbench occupied the center of the floor. As Brindle had said, it had been raised about a foot off the ground by wooden blocks. There was so much garbage and debris around the place, Forensics could take weeks analyzing it, and maybe months to process it all. The exact same words as before – IT'S INSIDE YOU – had been spray-painted onto the ceiling, just like in the butcher's shop. If there'd been any tire tracks on the soft ground outside, the rain did a good job of washing them away.

The homeless man who'd found the body was in his late sixties, frail and undernourished. He'd walked a long way, hoping to have a roof over his head for the night and escape the rain that he had smelled in the air an hour before it started. He never saw anyone around the old depot. Just the girl lying on the floor, naked, with her mouth stitched up like a ragdoll. He never touched her. He never even got close to her. And by the time Hunter talked to him, he still hadn't stopped shaking.

It had been exactly seven days since they had found the body of Laura Mitchell. Kelly Jensen's body was discovered three days after that, and now they had a new unidentified female victim. Counting Doctor Winston and the young Forensics assistant who died in the explosion in the autopsy room, they had five victims in one week. Hunter knew that while their investigation was moving at a snail's pace, the killer was sailing with the wind.

In the kitchen, Hunter poured himself a glass of water and drank it down in large gulps, as if trying to put out a fire somewhere inside him. He was sweating as if he'd just run five miles. He reached for his cell phone and dialed Whitney Myers' number before walking over to his living room window. The rain had only stopped ten minutes before. The sky was dark and dull. Not a single star.

'Hello . . .' Myers answered after a single ring.

'It's not her . . .' His voice was heavy. 'It's not Katia.'

'Are you sure?'

'Positive.'

An uneasy pause.

'Do you know who she is?' Myers pushed. 'Is she on the MP list?'

'No, she's not on the list. But she looks familiar.'

'Familiar? In what way?'

'I think I've seen her before. I just can't think where.'

'Police environment . . . ?'

'I don't think so.'

'Court of law . . . ? Witness . . . ? Victim . . . ?'

'No, somewhere else.'

'A bar . . . ?'

'I don't know.' Hunter ran his hand through his hair and let his fingertips rest at the back of his neck. Unconsciously they traced the contour of his ugly scar. 'I don't think I've ever met her or seen her on the streets or in a bar or anywhere like that. I think I've seen a picture of her. Maybe in a magazine or an advertisement . . .'

'She's that famous?'

'I don't know. I might be wrong. I'm wracking my brain here trying to remember, but I've got nothing, and I'm dead tired.'

Myers said nothing.

Hunter moved away from the window and started pacing his living room.

'If you get me a photo of her, maybe I can help,' Myers offered.

'No one will recognize her from the crime-scene photos. She's been dead for over twelve hours. The killer could've dumped her there yesterday, or even the day before. We were lucky that a homeless drifter wanted to use the place for shelter tonight, or else she could've been decomposing by the time we got to her.' Hunter paused by his bookcase, absentmindedly browsing through the titles. His eyes stopped as he reached the fifth book on the top shelf. 'Shit!'

'What? What happened?'

Hunter ran his hand over the spine of the book.

'I know where I've seen her before.'

Seventy-Nine

Hunter had to wait until 7:30 a.m. to find out for certain who the latest victim was. The central branch of the Los Angeles Public Library on West 5th Street could easily be called Hunter's home away from home, he spent so much time in there. Its opening time was 10:00 a.m., but he knew most of the staff, and he knew that one of them in particular, Maria Torres from Archives, was always there very early.

Hunter was right. He'd seen the victim's face before. He'd passed her picture many times as he walked through the Arts, Music and Recreation department on the library's second floor. One of her CDs, *Fingerwalking*, was featured on the middle shelf of the 'we recommend' display in the jazz guitar section. The display faced the main walkway. Its cover was a black-and-white close-up of her face.

From the library, Hunter made it to the LA morgue twenty minutes after Doctor Hove had called him saying she was done with the autopsy. Garcia was already there.

The doctor looked more than exhausted. No amount of make-up could disguise the black circles under her eyes, and they looked as if they'd sunken deeper into her skull. Her skin looked tired, with the pallor of someone who hadn't seen the sun in months. Her shoulders were hunched forward, as if she was having trouble carrying the invisible weight on them.

'I guess none of us had much sleep,' Garcia said, noticing Hunter's heavy-looking eyelids as he joined them by the entrance to the autopsy room. 'I tried you at home . . .'

Hunter nodded. 'I was in the library.'

Garcia pulled a face and checked his watch. 'Ran out of books at home?'

'I knew I'd seen the victim before,' Hunter said. 'Her name is Jessica Black.' He pulled a CD case from his pocket.

Garcia and Doctor Hove took turns looking at the cover.

'There's another picture inside,' Hunter said.

The doctor pulled the cover booklet out and flipped it open. Inside there was a full body picture of Jessica. She was standing with her back against a brick wall. Her guitar resting against it by her side. She had on a sleeveless black shirt, blue jeans and black cowboy boots. The tattoo on her right shoulder was clearly visible. Doctor Hove didn't need to check it again. She knew it was exactly the same tattoo the victim on her autopsy table had on her shoulder. She'd looked at it for long enough.

'I just found out about her fifteen minutes ago,' Hunter explained. 'I called Operations from the car and asked them to get me an address and whatever else they can on her. We'll check it after we leave here.' He nodded at Garcia who nodded back. 'Missing Persons don't have her,' he continued; 'she was never reported missing.'

Silence took over as they entered the autopsy room and paused by the examination table. All eyes settled on Jessica's face. The stitches had been removed from her lips, but the scars where they'd dug so deep into her skin remained.

There were scratch marks all around her mouth. Hunter could tell that Jessica herself had made them in blind panic, as she desperately clawed at the stitches with whatever was left of her nails. How much she'd suffered, no one could even begin to imagine.

'We were right,' the doctor broke the silence. Her voice was throaty. 'The killer burned her from the inside.'

Garcia shook off a shiver. 'How?'

'Using exactly what we thought he'd used. He inserted a signal flare inside her.'

Garcia closed his eyes and took a step back. Last night, it had been the faint smell of burned human flesh inside the old depot that had made him sick to his stomach. It was one of those smells you never forget. And Garcia had never forgotten it.

'Well, not exactly a signal flare,' the doctor corrected herself, 'but a variation of one.' She indicated the long counter behind her where a metal tube had been placed inside a metal tray. The tube was five inches long by half an inch in diameter. 'This is the aluminum tube that was placed inside her.'

Hunter moved closer to take a better look. The tube was sealed at one of its ends. No one said anything, so Doctor Hove moved on.

'Signal – or warning – flares are the most common type of flares out there. They're also quite easy to obtain. You'll find them in any boat at the marina or even in road safety kits, which can be easily purchased from pretty much anywhere. But they aren't the only type of flares you can get . . .' she paused and allowed her eyes to return to the aluminum tube inside the tray, '. . . or create yourself.'

'Heat flares,' Hunter said.

The doctor nodded. 'Precisely. Unlike signal flares, their main purpose isn't to burn bright and produce a warning signal. Their purpose is just to burn *hot*.' She picked up the tube. 'Essentially, a flare is just a container, a tube packed with chemicals that can produce a brilliant light or intense heat without an explosion. And that's exactly what the killer created and inserted into his victim.'

'How long did that burn for?' Hunter asked.

The doctor shrugged. 'Depends on what chemicals were used and how much of each. This is going up to the lab straight after here. But the killer wouldn't have needed much at all. Heat flares burn at ridiculously intense heat. Just a few seconds of direct contact would be enough to completely carbonize human flesh.' She paused and slowly rubbed her face. 'The damage that that fan-out knife caused to the second victim . . .' she shook her head, 'that's cotton candy compared to what we have here.'

Garcia drew a deep breath and shifted his weight from foot to foot.

Doctor Hove turned the tube over and showed them a small click button at its sealed-off base. 'Same sensitive impact-activated trigger mechanism. When her feet touched the ground, this thing clicked and produced a tiny spark. Enough to ignite the chemicals inside the tube. Similar to an oven lighter, really.'

'How can a fire ignite and keep on burning inside a human body?' Garcia asked. 'Doesn't it need oxygen?'

'The same way a flare ignites and burns underwater,' Hunter said. 'It uses an oxidizing agent, which directly feeds the fire with oxygen atoms. Underwater flares carry a higher oxidizer mixture, so even in an environment with no oxygen, the fire never dies.'

Garcia looked at Hunter as if he were from outer space.

Doctor Hove nodded again. 'The higher the oxidizer mixture, the stronger the initial deflagration.'

Hunter hadn't thought of that.

'And in English that is . . . ?' Garcia asked.

'When the initializing spark hits the chemicals, it produces an . . . impact, so to speak. That impact causes the whole thing to ignite at once, but not to explode. That uniform ignition is a deflagration – a combustion a few steps short of an explosion. Deflagration creates a bubble of super-heated gas. In this case, that bubble would've shot out the top of the flare canister like a bullet a millisecond before the fire. That bubble had to expand until it lost strength.' Doctor Hove closed the fingers of her right hand into a fist and then reopened them slowly, creating a bubble-growing illusion. 'It wouldn't have propagated much, probably only millimeters, but while it was expanding, whatever it touched, it completely vaporized it.'

Garcia felt his stomach start to churn again.

'The pain she must've suffered is . . . indescribable,' the doctor confirmed. 'Most fire victims die from smoke inhalation, not from the injuries sustained. Basically, their lungs collapse because they can't process the smoke and they suffocate – sometimes even before they feel any pain at all from their scorched flesh. But that's not the case here. There was no smoke. She felt every last pinprick of pain that came to her.' She placed the metal tube down and let go of a deep breath. 'As you know, the second victim was severely mutilated from inside. She suffered a lot, but that mutilation caused intense loss of blood. We all know that when a human being loses a certain amount of blood, the body simply shuts down, like going into hibernation or being anesthetized. The person starts to feel cold and tired, the pain disappears and they fall asleep before dying.' She ran her hand over her mouth. 'But not if you're burned. The blood loss is minimal. There's no hibernation or anesthetized effect. There's only grotesque pain.'

Eighty

Doctor Hove pointed to a clear plastic bag on the metal counter behind her. Its contents seemed to be a small gooey mass of soft tar.

'That's all that was left of her entire reproductive system. It's been scorched beyond any recognition by heat and fire. Even *I* couldn't tell what was what.'

Not a word from Hunter or Garcia. The doctor carried on.

'Her uterus, ovaries, and bladder exploded inside her abdominal cavity. Death came from a series of major organ failures, but that would've taken some time. During that time, she felt every ounce of pain her body could've taken. Until it could take no more.'

Garcia's eyes kept going back to the plastic bag with the blackened contents.

'Was she drugged?' Hunter asked.

'Without a doubt, but toxicology results will take a couple of days. My guess is that the killer used Estazolam again.'

'Any signs of malnutrition or dehydration?'

Doctor Hove shook her head. 'None. And just like the previous victim, I won't be able to tell if she was sexually assaulted or not.'

By the time Hunter and Garcia made it back to Parker

Center, their research team had compiled a three-page report on Jessica Black.

Born in South Los Angeles, she had turned thirty less than a month ago. The report went on to explain about her poor childhood, how she lost her mother when she was only nine, and about her fascination with acoustic guitars because of an old blues guitar man she saw in the park when she was a child. It also explained about her rise to fame once her videos were posted onto YouTube. Her concerts were sold out weeks in advance. She and her boyfriend, Mark Stratton, who was also a guitarist, but with a metal band called Dust, shared an apartment in Melrose.

Hunter tried the apartment phone number – no answer. He tried Mark's cell phone – straight to his voicemail. He didn't leave a message.

Hunter and Garcia made it to Melrose in forty-five minutes. Jessica and Mark's apartment was on the top floor of a private condo surrounded by a forest of California Bay trees in North Kings Road. The building's concierge, Scott, was a tall and reedy man in his late-twenties with a shaved head and a trendy goatee. He said that he hadn't seen Jessica for a few days. Five to be exact.

'How about Miss Black's partner?' Garcia asked.

'Mark? He's been away for . . . four days now,' Scott replied. 'His band, Dust, is just about to release their new album, so they hit the road for a bunch of pre-tour gigs before the real tour begins.'

'Do you know when he's supposed to be back?'

Scott shook his head. 'Not exactly, but it'll be a few weeks.'

Hunter's eyes roamed the building's entry lobby and settled on the security camera in the far-left corner.

'How many CCTV cameras are there in the building?' he asked.

'Four,' Scott said. 'One just outside the main entrance, that one here in the lobby.' He pointed to the camera Hunter had spotted. 'One on the entrance to the underground garage, and one inside the elevator.'

'And how long do you keep your CCTV footage?'

'For a month. Everything is stored into a hard drive.'

'We're gonna need copies of everything, going back to the day you last saw Miss Black.'

'Sure, that's not a prob . . .' Scott hesitated for an instant.

'Something wrong?'

'Well, four days ago we had a fuse box overload and all the cameras went down for a few hours in the middle of the night. And if I remember correctly, it happened on the day Mark left on tour.'

Hunter remembered what Myers had told him about the CCTV cameras in Katia Kudrov's apartment building in West Hollywood. They had all conveniently gone down the night she disappeared. A fuse box overload.

'We'll need copies of whatever you have.'

'Sure.'

'How about any visitors?' Garcia asked. 'Do you remember anyone calling in on or around the day you last saw Miss Black? Maybe delivering something, a workman checking something . . . Any reason to go up to their apartment?'

'Mark and Jessica didn't really have people over. They preferred to go out, which they did a lot. Anyway, every visitor, service or delivery has to go through the front desk and details are always taken down.' He checked the computer log. There was nothing.

'Did you notice anyone suspicious hanging around the

building on the days prior to Mark leaving on tour?' Garcia asked.

Scott laughed. 'Other than Mark and Jessica we have two up-and-coming Hollywood actresses, one rock singer, one rapper, one TV presenter and two radio DJs living here. There are always strange and eager people around just waiting to get a glimpse of their idols, or an autograph or photo.'

Hunter took down the name of the concierge on duty the night the cameras went down – Francisco Gonzales. He'd be on duty again later that evening.

As they got back to the car, Hunter tried Mark's cell phone again. Still voicemail. He needed to get in touch with Mark as soon as possible. He needed access to their apartment. He called Operations and asked them to get back to him with Dust's manager's name, office and cell phone number. While they were at it, he asked them to get Jessica's manager's details as well.

Hunter disconnected and ten seconds later his cell phone rang.

'Talk about fast response,' Garcia joked.

'Detective Hunter,' he said, bringing the phone to his ear. He listened for a moment. 'You're kidding me. When? . . . Where is he? . . . OK, we're on our way.'

'What's going on?' Garcia asked as soon as Hunter closed his phone.

'James Smith has been arrested.'

Eighty-One

James Smith was sitting alone inside interrogation room number two on the second floor of Parker Center. His hands were cuffed together, and he had them resting on the metal table in front of him. His fingers were picking at each other, anxiously. His eyes were fixed on the far wall, as if watching some invisible movie being played on a screen only he could see.

Hunter, Garcia and Captain Blake were regarding Smith from the other side of the two-way mirror in the adjacent observation room. Hunter paid particular attention to his eyes and facial movements.

'He's not our guy,' Hunter said in a steady voice. He kept his arms folded over his chest.

'What?' Captain Blake blurted out with annoyance. 'This is the first concrete lead we've managed to follow through since we found the first victim. Since Jonathan died in that autopsy room seven days ago for no reason. You haven't even spoken to him yet.'

'I don't have to. He's not our killer.'

'And you know that how?' Her hands moved to her hips. 'Or you gonna tell me that together with your lip-reading ability you're also psychic?'

'Do you know where he was arrested, Captain?'

She glanced at Garcia, who gave a tiny shrug.

'I haven't looked at the arrest report yet. Why?'

'Lakewood,' Hunter said. 'He was arrested in Lakewood.'

'OK, and . . . ?'

'Around the corner from Laura Mitchell's apartment.'

'Your point is . . . ?'

'He was arrested because I told Operations to send two teams of plain clothes officers to stake out her place.'

The captain frowned. 'When did you do that?'

'After I talked to him on the phone.'

'You knew he'd go back to her place?'

'I suspected he'd observe it.'

'Observe it? Why?'

'Because his mind refuses to believe something has happened to Laura Mitchell. He needed to check it out for himself.'

The captain's stare returned to Garcia for a moment before moving back to Hunter. 'You better start making sense, Robert. And right now is a good time.'

Hunter finally turned and faced Captain Blake. 'When we spoke on the phone, he thought I was a detective with the fraud squad.'

'Fraud squad? Why?'

'Because *that's* his crime, Captain – impersonating. We all know James Smith isn't his real name. Nevertheless, he's managed to obtain a driver's license, an ID card, a library card, maybe even a passport, all under a false identity. That can get him one to five years inside. But as he said on the phone to me, that's not enough to trigger a major investigation. That's why he couldn't understand why his photo had hit the papers. Why we were after him. When he found out I was with the Homicide Division, he hesitated for a moment, then there was a distinct change in his voice.'

'Like what?'

'Trepidation . . . fear, but not for himself, or of being caught.'

The captain looked lost.

'The reason why he hesitated was because at first he couldn't figure out why Homicide would be after him. But as we all know, he's far from stupid. He quickly realized that it must've been something linked to his obsession.'

'Laura Mitchell,' Garcia said, comprehending.

Hunter nodded. 'We know that they exchanged phone numbers at the exhibition. We checked Laura's cell phone records. Just a couple of days before the presumed time-frame of her disappearance, she received a call from a payphone in Bellflower.'

'That's the next neighborhood along from Norwalk,' the captain said. 'Smith's apartment is in Norwalk, right?'

Hunter and Garcia nodded.

'Only one call?'

'That's right. My guess is that they talked that day, maybe arranged to talk on the phone again later that week or even meet up somewhere. She didn't turn up or he got no reply on his next call. He kept on trying, still no answer. He got worried, maybe a little annoyed. When I mentioned Homicide on the phone to Smith, it took him just a few seconds to make the connection.'

'So he started staking out Laura Mitchell's place to try to spot her, get some sort of confirmation,' Garcia said.

'That's what I figured he'd do,' Hunter agreed.

'Well, for someone who isn't stupid, that's a pretty dumb thing to do, don't you think?' the captain shot out. 'You're gonna tell me that he didn't at least suspect her place would've been watched?'

'You saw the pictures of his collage room, right? He's been obsessed with Laura Mitchell for years. The kind of obsession that overrides rational thought, Captain – pure, undying love. Of course he knew it was dangerous. Of course he knew he could be caught. But he couldn't help it. He needed to find out. He needed to make sure she was OK.'

'Like an addiction?'

'Stronger than an addiction, Captain. It's a compulsion.' Hunter turned towards the officer in the room. 'Has he requested a lawyer yet?'

'Not yet. He said he wanted to talk to you.'

All eyes moved to Hunter.

His gaze returned to James Smith for a moment longer. 'OK, let's do it.'

Eighty-Two

James Smith's eyes darted towards Hunter as soon as he entered the interrogation room.

'I'm Detective Robert Hunter of the Homicide Special Section. We talked on the phone a couple of days ago.' Hunter placed a tray with a coffee pot and two mugs on the metal table. 'Coffee?'

'She was kidnapped and murdered?' Smith's voice was edgy and concerned. His eyes looked haunted.

'It's fresh.' Hunter poured two cups and slid one over towards Smith. 'And you really look like you could use some.'

Smith's eyes didn't leave Hunter's face. 'Laura was kidnapped and murdered?' He pleaded rather than asked this time.

Hunter pulled the chair across the table from Smith and sat down before sipping his coffee.

'They told me I was being arrested on suspicion of the kidnap and murder of Laura Mitchell.'

'Yes, she was kidnapped . . . and murdered,' Hunter said and paused for a second. 'Everyone in the station has their money on you. They think you did it.'

Smith closed his eyes for a fraction of a second and breathed out a heartfelt breath. 'When?'

Hunter regarded him.

'When was she murdered?' There was pain in his voice.

'A few days before we knocked on your door.' In contrast, Hunter's voice was calm and collected.

Smith kept his eyes on Hunter but his stare was distant. The kind of stare you get when your mind is somewhere far away.

'We know that you talked to Laura on the last night of her exhibition at the Daniel Rossdale Art Gallery. And we've seen the room inside your apartment.'

His focus returned to Smith's stare.

'I have the right to have an attorney present, don't I?'

'Of course you do, but I'm not here to interrogate you.'

Smith chuckled. 'Really? So what's this, a friendly chat? You're here to be my buddy, is that it?'

'Right now, you need all the friends you can get.'

'Friends won't help. You already said that everyone's money is on me. Your mind is already made up. You'll believe what you wanna believe no matter what.'

'Try me.' Hunter leaned forward.

Smith's focus moved to the two-way mirror and the tension intensified. 'Do you really think I'd be able to hurt Laura . . . in any way?' His gaze returned to Hunter. 'I love her in a way you'll never understand.'

Hunter allowed the moment to settle.

'The kind of love that strangles your heart and keeps you awake at night?' he countered. 'The kind of love that makes it hard for you to breathe when she's near, even if she never notices you? The kind of love that if you have to wait forever for just a simple touch, or a kiss, you will?'

Smith went silent.

'Yes, I know the kind of love you're talking about.'

Smith interlaced his fingers together so tight his knuckles started to lose their color.

'Is that how you loved her?' Something in Hunter's voice made Smith believe that maybe he understood.

'I knew Laura from the bank. Way before she became a famous painter.' Smith's tone was full of melancholy. He gave Hunter a sad headshake. 'But she didn't know me. She never noticed me. I don't think she even knew I existed. I spoke to her a couple of times back then, in the coffee room. She was always nice, don't get me wrong, but every time I talked to her, I had to reintroduce myself. I was never important or attractive enough for her to remember who I was.' His eyes filled with sadness. 'I wasn't even invited to her leaving party.'

Inside the observation room, Captain Blake turned to Garcia. 'We need a list of names and photographs of all bank employees from Laura Mitchell's section during her last six months there.'

Garcia was already on the phone. 'I'm on it.'

On the other side of the glass Smith relaxed the tight grip on his hands and blood returned to his knuckles. 'I stayed with the bank for another two years after she left. But I followed her career from the beginning. I read every article, attended every exhibition. I even started liking and appreciating art.' A sliver of confidence crept into his eyes. 'Then one day I looked in the mirror and decided that I wouldn't be weak any more. I decided that I *was* important and attractive enough for her to notice me, I just needed to polish off some rough edges.'

'So you created your new identity,' Hunter pressed.

'More than an identity. I created a whole new *person*. New diet, strict exercise program, new haircut, new hair color, colored contact lenses, new wardrobe, new attitude, new way of talking, new everything. I became someone she would notice. Someone she would talk to and flirt with. Someone she'd like to spend time with. I became James Smith.'

Hunter had to admire his determination.

'I went to every one of her exhibitions. But I still couldn't sum up the nerve to say hello to her again. I was scared she'd recognize me. That she'd see straight through me . . . that she'd laugh at me.'

Hunter knew exactly why. Changing a person's appearance is easy – it can be done in one afternoon or, in the case of changing a person's body shape, with the right diet and exercise program – a few months. Changing a person's personality is much harder, though – it requires work, determination, willpower and it can take years. Smith used to be a shy, low self-esteem, low-confidence, scared-of-rejection person, and though he looked completely different on the outside, he was yet to overcome all his personality glitches.

'She approached you that night, didn't she?' Hunter concluded.

Smith nodded. 'I was so surprised, I stuttered.' A glimpse of a smile graced his lips as he remembered.

'Did she give you her number?'

'Yes.'

'Did you call her?'

'Yes.'

'Do you remember when?' Hunter leaned forward and placed his elbows on the table.

'I remember the day, the time, and everything that was said.'

Hunter waited.

'It was the 4th March, at 4:30 p.m. I used a payphone and called her on her cell. She was on her way to her studio. We talked for a while and she asked me to call her back just before the weekend. She said that maybe we could go out for a drink or even dinner. She practically asked me out.' Smith's eyes moved from Hunter's face to the far wall for a long moment. When they moved back to Hunter, a liquid sheen had formed over them. 'You're a detective. Do you really think that after all I've done, after so many years trying to get her attention, trying to get her to notice me, to talk to me . . . when she finally does, I'd hurt her in any way?'

'Why did you run when we knocked on your door?'

'I panicked,' Smith replied with no hesitation. 'I knew that I had broken the law by living under a false identity. I know that I could be locked away for several years for it. Suddenly the police were at my door. I did what most people in my shoes would do, I didn't think, I just ran. Before I had time to consider, my picture was in every paper in town. I knew then that something was definitely not right. That's when I called you.'

Hunter remained silent. His stare locked on Smith's face. He'd said all that without flinching, without vacillating and without breaking eye contact with Hunter. If he was lying, Hunter decided, he was a master at it.

'*She* approached me that night,' Smith said again. '*She* smiled at me. *She* flirted with me. *She* gave me her number and asked me to call her. *She* wanted to have dinner with me . . . to go out on a date with me.' Smith faced the two-way mirror. 'I'd been dreaming about the day she'd finally noticed me for years. My dream had just come true. Why in the name of God would I hurt her?'

Eighty-Three

Hunter splashed some cold water over his face and stared at his tired reflection in the mirror. James Smith had requested an attorney. No matter what happened, without actual proof of any involvement between Smith and Laura Mitchell, the LAPD could only hold him without charge for a maximum of forty-eight hours. Captain Blake was already talking to the DA's office about charging Smith with fraud and impersonation. That way, they could keep him off the streets for longer, at least until they had more information on him, his story and his whereabouts on the nights of all three murders.

After leaving the interrogation room, Hunter had finally managed to get in touch with Mark Stratton, Jessica Black's boyfriend. Experience counted for nothing in these situations. There was no easy way to tell someone that their life had just been wrecked. That the person they loved the most had been taken away from them by a brutal killer. People dealt with loss and pain in their own way, but it was never easy.

Hunter didn't disclose every detail over the phone. He kept the information down to the bare minimum. Not surprisingly, Stratton thought the call was a prank at first, a very bad joke from one of his buddies. Many of them were notorious for their dark and distasteful sense of humor. Hunter knew denial is the most common initial shock reaction to sad news. When realization finally set in, Stratton broke down the way most people did. The same way Hunter had broken down years ago when a RHD detective knocked on his door to tell him his father had been shot in the chest by a bank robber.

Hunter splashed some more water on his face and wet his hair. The darkness inside him was lurking around again, murky and deep.

Stratton told Hunter that he'd be making his way back to LA as soon as possible – sometime today, and that he'd call Hunter as soon as he got back. Jessica Black's body still had to be positively identified.

Garcia was reading something on his computer screen when Hunter got back to his desk. 'Are you OK?' he asked. He understood exactly how difficult making those calls was.

Hunter nodded. 'I'm fine. Just needed to cool down, that's all.'

'Are you sure? You don't look fine.'

Hunter approached the pictures board and studied the photographs of all three victims again.

'Robert,' Garcia called, his voice just a few decibels louder.

Hunter turned and faced him. 'His interval between kidnapping and murdering his victims is shortening.'

'Yeah, I noticed that,' Garcia agreed. 'Kelly Jensen was the first to be kidnapped. She was killed almost three weeks later. Laura Mitchell was taken about a week after Kelly, but she was the first to die. We still don't know for sure, but it looks like Jessica Black went missing no longer than five days ago, and she turned up dead yesterday. It went from weeks to days. So either Jessica Black lost no time in breaking his spell, or he's simply losing patience.'

Hunter said nothing.

Garcia sat back in his chair and pinched his chin. 'I was just checking the results from your national search on brunette victims with any sort of stitching to their mouths, sexual organs or both.'

'And . . . ?'

'Not a goddamn thing. It seems like most of the files only date back fourteen to fifteen years. Beyond that, we've got almost nothing.'

Hunter thought about it for a moment. 'Damn.'

'What . . . ?'

'Police records only started to be properly digitized . . . what? Maybe ten, twelve years ago at a stretch?'

'Something like that.'

'The problem is that the amount of everyday cases is so huge, most police departments around the country don't have the budget or the personnel to deal with the backlog. Most cases older than maybe fifteen years are probably just sitting inside boxes, getting dusty, down in basement storage rooms. Database searches will *never* get to them.'

'Great. So even if we're right, but it happened over fifteen years ago, we'll never know?'

Hunter was already typing away on his computer. 'Police files and databases might not be properly backlogged yet, but . . .'

Garcia waited but nothing else was forthcoming. 'But what?'

'But newspaper ones certainly are. I was stupid, I should've thought of that at first and searched the national news archives as well as the police ones.'

Hunter and Garcia searched the net and specific newspaper databases for hours, scanning through any piece that flagged up according to their search criteria. Three and a half hours later Garcia started reading a 20-year-old local newspaper article and felt a shiver run down his spine.

'Robert,' he called, placing both elbows on his desk, clasping his hands together and squinting at his screen. 'I think I might have something here.'

Eighty-Four

Los Angeles was a trendy nightclub Mecca full of see-and-be-seen clubs, which made the existence of a local bar like the Alibi Room a blessing. It dated back to the days of smoke-filled interiors and drunken games of pool. The place was really just one room with some vintage carpet, a line of locals bellied up to the bar, a single pool table with iffy geometrics and dead rails, a decent jukebox packed with rock albums and the best dive bar attraction of all time: cheap booze.

Whitney Myers spotted Xavier Nunez as soon as she walked through the door. He was sitting at one of the few low oak tables next to a window to the left of the bar. Two bottles of beer and a basket of corn tortillas were on the table in front of him.

Nunez was an odd-looking man. In his mid-thirties, he had a shaved head, long pointy face, large dark eyes, bowl ears, small crooked nose, pitted skin and lips so thin they looked like they'd been drawn using a marker pen. The slogan on his shirt read – *Tell your tits to stop staring at me*.

Nunez was another of Myers' contacts, whom she paid very handsomely when she needed information. He worked for the Los Angeles County Department of Coroner.

'Nice shirt,' Myers said as she came to his table. 'Get loads of girls when you wear it, do you?'

Nunez took a swig of his beer and looked up at her. Nunez was about to comment on her remark, but Myers smiled at him, and all he could do was melt in his seat.

'So, what have you got for me?'

Nunez reached for the plastic folder on the seat next to him.

'These were really hard to get.' He spoke with a heavy Puerto Rican accent.

Myers had a seat across the table from him.

'That's why I pay you so well, Xavier.' She reached for the folder but he pulled it away from her.

'Yeah, but special circumstances cases are *really, really* hard to get, d'you know what I mean? Maybe I deserve a little extra for it.'

Myers paused and smiled again, but this time there was no warmth in it. 'Don't go there, honey. I can be very nice when you play the way the game should be played. You know that I pay you more than enough. But if you wanna play hardball, trust me . . .' she placed her hand on his and gave it a subtle but firm squeeze, '. . . I can become a real bitch. The kinda bitch you and your homies don't wanna fuck with. So are you sure you wanna roll like this?'

Something in her voice and her touch made Nunez' mouth go dry.

'Hey, I was just joking. I know you pay me enough. I was talking more like you know . . . you and me . . . dinner . . . sometime . . . maybe . . .'

The warmth came back to her smile. 'As attractive as you are, Xavier, I'm already taken,' she lied.

He tilted his head from side to side. 'I'd settle for meaningless sex.'

Myers finally took the folder from Xavier. 'How about you settle for what we agreed?' Her voice was menacing.

'OK, that will do too.'

Myers flipped open the folder. The first photograph was of Kelly Jensen's face. The stitches to her mouth hadn't been removed yet. She stared at it for several seconds. Though she'd been told about it by Hunter, seeing the photographs brought a new dimension to the evil of the crime.

Myers moved to the next picture and froze. They were of the second set of stitches to Kelly Jensen's body. Hunter had never told her about those. She had to take a deep breath before moving on. The next photo was a wide shot of Kelly Jensen's entire body. Myers studied it carefully.

'Where are the cuts?' she whispered to herself, but it didn't escape Xavier's ears.

'Cuts?' he said. 'There are none.'

'I was told the killer used a knife to kill her.'

'Apparently he did. But he didn't cut her on the outside.'

Myers looked questioningly.

'He inserted it into her.'

Myers' whole body turned into gooseflesh.

'And the knife is no knife I've ever seen. There's a picture of it in there.'

Myers quickly leafed through all the photos until she found it.

'Jesus Christ . . . What in the name of God . . . ?'

They were dealing with a monster here. She had to find Katia. And fast.

Eighty-Five

Hunter looked up from his computer screen. Garcia had his stare fixed on his PC monitor, his brow creased in a peculiar way.

'What have you got?'

A couple more seconds before Garcia finally looked up. 'A 20-year-old article.'

'About what?'

'A family murder/suicide. Husband found out that his wife was sleeping with someone else, lost his head, killed the someone else, his 10-year-old kid, his wife and then blew his head off with a shotgun.'

Hunter frowned. 'Yes, and . . . ?'

'Here's where it gets interesting. It says that the husband stitched parts of his wife's body shut before killing her.'

Hunter's eyes widened.

'But that's all. It gives no further details as to which body parts.'

'Did he shoot his wife?'

'Again, it doesn't say, and that's what's strange about it. It's a potentially big story, but the article is quite brief.'

'Where did this happen?' Hunter got up and approached Garcia's desk.

'Northern California, Healdsburg in Sonoma County.'

Hunter took control of Garcia's computer mouse and scrolled through the article. It was about five hundred words long. Garcia was right, it was too brief, mentioning what happened almost by passage. No specific details were given other than the ones involved. The victims had been Emily and Andrew Harper – mother and son, and Emily's lover, Nathan Gardner. Emily's husband, Ray Harper, had carried out all three executions before shooting himself in the couple's bedroom. There were two pictures. The larger of the two showed a two-story white-fronted house with an impeccable lawn, completely surrounded by yellow crime-scene tape. Three police vehicles were parked on the street. The second picture showed a couple of county sheriff deputies bringing a dark polyethylene body bag out of the front door. The expression on their faces told its own story.

'Is this the only article?' he asked. 'No follow-up?'

Garcia shook his head. 'Nope, I've already checked. Nothing on the Harper case prior or after that date. Which again, I find hard to believe.'

Hunter scrolled up and checked the name of the newspaper – the *Healdsburg Tribune*. He checked the name of the reporter who covered the story – Stephen Anderson. After a quick search, he had the address and phone number for the newspaper headquarters.

The phone rang for thirty seconds before someone answered it on the other side. The person sounded young. He told Hunter that he'd never heard of a reporter called Stephen Anderson, but then again, he'd only been with the paper for six months. He was with the newspaper's Sonoma University trainee program. After asking around, the kid returned to the phone and told Hunter that according to one of the most senior reporters, Mr. Anderson had retired nine years ago. He still lived in Healdsburg.

Hunter disconnected and got the operator for Sonoma County. Stephen Anderson's name wasn't listed. He clicked off again and called the Office of Operations. Less than five minutes later he had an address and phone number.

Eighty-Six

It was just past eight in the evening when Stephen Anderson answered his phone inside his home office on the outskirts of Healdsburg. Hunter quickly introduced himself.

'Los Angeles Police Department?' Anderson said, sounding worried. His voice was husky. Hunter could tell it came from years of smoking rather than natural charm. 'Are you sure you've got the right person, Detective?'

'I'm certain,' Hunter replied, motioning Garcia to listen in.

'And what will this be about?'

'An article you wrote twenty years ago flagged up on one of our searches. Unfortunately the article is quite brief. I was wondering if you wouldn't mind giving us a few more details on it.'

Even down the phone line, the silence that followed felt uncomfortable.

'Mr. Anderson, are you still with me?'

'Call me Stephen, and yes, I'm still here,' he said. 'Twenty years ago . . . That must be the Harper family murder tragedy.'

'That's right.'

A new brief silence. 'You said my article flagged up in an LAPD investigation search. I'm guessing, a homicide investigation?'

'That's correct.'

Hunter heard the sound of a lighter being flicked a couple of times.

'You have a victim over there that's been stitched up?'

This time the silence came from Hunter. Anderson was quick on the uptake. Hunter chose his next words carefully.

'It sounds like there could be similarities between the Harper case and one of our ongoing investigations, yes, but as I said, your article doesn't describe what happened in great detail.'

'And those similarities would be the stitching of the victim's body?'

'I didn't say that.'

'Oh, c'mon, Detective, I spent thirty-five years as a reporter. I know that the similarities you're referring to couldn't just be a jealousy-fueled family murder/suicide, or someone blowing his head off with a shotgun. You're an LA cop – the city where the freaks come out to play. You probably have crimes like those happening on your doorstep every week. From my article, the only unusual aspect about the Harpers incident is the mentioning of stitches.'

There was no doubt about it, Anderson was quick on the uptake. Hunter conceded.

'Yes, we have a case here where stitches have been applied to the victim's body.'

The silence returned to the line for a moment.

'Do you remember any more details?' Hunter pushed. 'Or is the reason why your article was so brief with no follow-ups was because that was all the information you ever had on the case?'

'Do you know anything about Sonoma County, Detective?'

'The biggest wine production county in California,' Hunter replied.

'That's correct.' Anderson coughed a couple of times to clear his throat. 'You see, Detective, Sonoma lives off its wine production county status in every possible aspect – not only by producing great wine. There are special events every month of the year all around the county which pull in the crowds. Agricultural festivals, holiday celebrations, street fairs, music carnivals and more. There's always something happening somewhere.'

Hunter could already see where Anderson was going with this.

'We can't compare to Los Angeles or Vegas, but we have our share of tourists. Publicizing something as horrific as what happened that day would've benefited no one. The *Tribune* wouldn't have sold any more copies than it did on a day-to-day basis either.' Anderson coughed again, a lot heavier this time. 'I didn't get to see the scene, but yes, I did find out the details. On that same day I was approached by Chief Cooper and Mayor Taylor. We talked for a long time, and it was decided that it would be in the town's best interests if the paper didn't sensationalize the story, and by that I mean I agreed to play it down. So between the police, the mayor and the paper, a very heavy lid was placed over the whole incident.'

'We really need to know those details, Stephen.'

The pause that followed felt laden.

'You're not gonna be breaking your promise to the police chief or the mayor,' Hunter insisted. 'None of what you tell me will go any further, but I do need to know those details. It could save lives.'

'It's been twenty years, I guess,' Anderson said after taking a long drag of his cigarette. 'Where would you like me to start?'

Eighty-Seven

'I knew the Harpers quite well,' Anderson began. 'You have to understand that Healdsburg isn't a big town, even today. Back then we didn't have more than maybe nine thousand people living here. Ray Harper was a shoemaker and his wife, Emily, was a teacher in the primary school. They'd been married for over fifteen years, and I guess, like in so many longstanding marriages, things weren't a bed of roses any more.'

Hunter was busy taking notes.

'Emily started sleeping with another schoolteacher, Nathan Gardner, which in a city this small, isn't a very smart idea, unless you think you're invisible.'

Hunter heard Anderson take another drag of his cigarette.

'Somehow Ray found out during that year's winter school break. Now Ray had always been a very calm person. I'd never known him to lose his head. Actually, I'd never known him to even raise his voice. He was just your regular, every-day, church-going, quiet kinda guy. And that's what was so out of character about what he did.'

Garcia looked like he was about to ask something but Hunter lifted his hand, stopping him. He didn't want to rush Anderson.

'Well, that day Ray completely lost control, as if he was possessed. He went over to Nathan's apartment and killed him first, before going back to his house and killing his kid, his wife, and then splattering his brains all over the walls with a double-barreled shotgun.'

Anderson coughed and Hunter waited as he heard the cigarette lighter being flicked on again.

'How did he kill them?'

'That was the reason why Chief Cooper and Mayor Taylor asked to talk to me that day. Because of the way Ray went about his killing business. Ted Bundy is a boy scout compared to what he did.' Anderson paused. 'In Nathan's apartment, Ray tied him down and used a meat cleaver to cut his . . . penis off.' A longer pause this time. 'That was it. Nothing else. Ray simply left him there to bleed to death. Now, you might ask – how come Nathan didn't scream his head off and alert the whole neighborhood. Well, the reason would be because Ray used a shoe needle and thread to stitch Nathan's mouth shut.'

Garcia's eyes flickered towards Hunter.

'Ray went from Nathan's apartment back to his house . . .' Anderson continued, '. . . killed his kid inside his truck, and then did the same thing he did to Nathan to his wife, Emily. He stitched her mouth shut too.'

Hunter had stopped writing.

'But it didn't end there.'

Hunter and Garcia waited.

'Ray took what he'd cut off Nathan with him, shoved it inside his wife, and stitched her shut as well.'

Garcia flinched but Hunter's face remained neutral. His blue eyes locked onto a blank page in his notebook.

'I still can't believe that Ray did what he did. Not the Ray Harper we knew. It just couldn't have been the same person. As I said, it was like he was possessed.'

A short pause, a new cigarette drag.

'After stitching his wife shut, Ray sat on the floor in front of her and blew his brains all over the room with his shotgun.'

'And you're sure those facts are correct?' Hunter asked. 'You said you never saw the crime scene for yourself.'

A nervous chuckle.

'Yes, I'm sure. I didn't see the crime scene, but I saw the pictures with my own eyes. Those images will be imprinted in my brain forever. Sometimes I still have nightmares about them. And the words . . .'

'Words?' Hunter cocked his head forward.

There was no response.

'Stephen?' Hunter called. 'Are you still there? What words?'

'Ray left his wife tied to their bed all stitched up. But before blowing his head off, he used blood to write something on the wall.'

'And what did he write?' Garcia asked.

'He wrote the words – *He's inside you*.'

Eighty-Eight

Hunter came off the phone with the Healdsburg Police Department after speaking to Anderson and went straight down to Captain Blake's office. He caught her as she was getting ready to go home for the day.

'I need to go up to Healdsburg first thing tomorrow morning,' he said, letting the door close behind him. 'I'll be away for one, maybe two days.'

'What?' She looked up from her computer screen. 'Healdsburg? Why the hell?'

Hunter ran her through everything he'd found out. Captain Blake listened to the whole story in absolute silence, her face immutable. When he was finished, she breathed out as if she'd been holding her breath for minutes.

'When did all that happen, again?'

'Twenty years ago.'

Her eyebrows lifted. 'Let me guess, because that case is older than fifteen years, the files aren't in the Unified California Police Database, nothing's been digitized, right?'

Hunter nodded. 'I've searched by date, town and victim names. There's nothing. The records will be in paper form in the Healdsburg PD storage archives.'

'Great. So other than the newspaper article and the reporter's story, what do we have?'

'I just got off the phone with Chief Suarez in Healdsburg. He wasn't the chief back then. He was transferred and relocated from Fair Oaks nine years ago, a year after the entire Healdsburg Police Department was moved to its new location. He hadn't even heard of the Harper case.'

Captain Blake paused and looked at Hunter sideways. 'Wait a second. Why are you going to Healdsburg? Homicide case files would've been filed with the Sonoma District Attorney's office, and that's in . . .'

'Santa Rosa,' Hunter confirmed. 'I've called them as well.' He pointed to his watch. 'After office hours. There was nobody there who I could talk to. But if the case files aren't in the California Police DB, it means that either the Sonoma DA's office don't have them, or they're piled up in some dusty room still waiting to be digitized. I'd like to have a look at the crime-scene pictures and the autopsy reports if I can get them, but the police and the DA case files won't help us much. They'll just describe what happened back then in a little more detail than Stephen did. It was a family murder/suicide, Captain. Open and shut case. No witness accounts, no investigation records, if there even was one. They had nothing to investigate. Wife sleeps with another man, husband gets jealous, loses control . . . the lover and the whole family pays the ultimate price. Case closed. We have replica cases up and down the country.'

Captain Blake sat back on her chair and rested her chin on her knuckles. 'And you wanna talk to someone who was involved in the case?'

Hunter nodded. 'The old chief of police retired seven years ago, but he still lives in Healdsburg. Somewhere near Lake Sonoma. I don't really wanna talk to him over the phone.'

The captain saw something shine in Hunter's eyes. 'OK, talk to me, Robert. What are you really after? Do you think our killer came from Healdsburg?'

Hunter finally had a seat on one of the wingback chairs in front of the captain's desk. 'I think our killer was there, Captain. I think he saw that crime scene.'

Captain Blake studied Hunter for a beat. 'A trauma?'

'Yes.'

'You mean . . . a shock trauma, induced by what he saw?'

'Yes.' Hunter ran a hand over his left arm and felt the bullet scar on his triceps. 'The similarities between what happened in Healdsburg twenty years ago and what we have happening here today are too strong to be coincidental.'

Captain Blake said nothing.

'The way Ray Harper killed his family . . . the way he killed his wife's lover . . . even big city, seasoned Homicide detectives would find such a crime scene hard to deal with, never mind a small town's police department whose idea of a tough crime is probably jaywalking.'

The captain started fidgeting with one of her earrings. 'But hold on. If the Healdsburg Police Department did their job properly, then not many people would've had access to that crime scene. Presumably officers and the sheriff's coroner, that's all.'

Hunter nodded. 'That's why I need to talk to the old chief of police, and hopefully find the crime-scene logbook. We need to establish the whereabouts of everyone who had access to it that day.'

The captain's eyes stayed on Hunter while her brain searched for answers. 'Could a similar kind of trauma occur just by looking at the crime-scene pictures?'

Hunter considered. 'It would depend on how mentally

vulnerable the person was at the time. But yes, deeply disturbing photographs can easily initiate something inside a person's mind.'

Captain Blake paused while she thought about it. 'But the kills aren't exactly the same as the one in Healdsburg. Our victims aren't tied down. The words he uses aren't exactly the same either.'

'That's not uncommon, Captain. A trauma can be like a large picture that's flashed in front of your eyes. Not everyone will remember every single detail perfectly. Adaptation is also a major consequence of crimes derived from early traumas. That's what he's doing.'

Captain Blake closed her eyes and shook her head slowly.

'There's one more thing, Captain,' Hunter said, standing up. 'Emily Harper, the woman that was stitched shut and killed in Healdsburg twenty years ago was a schoolteacher.'

'Yeah, I know, you told me that. And . . . ?'

Hunter paused by the door. 'She taught arts and music.'

Eighty-Nine

Hunter thought about driving to Healdsburg, but even with zero traffic it would've taken him at least seven hours to cover the four hundred and fifty miles. Spending over fifteen hours on the road was simply out of the question.

So Hunter caught the 6:30 a.m. nonstop flight from LA's LAX to Healdsburg municipal airport. The flight was on time, and by 8:10 a.m. Hunter was driving his rental Chrysler Sebring out of the relatively empty Hertz forecourt.

Even without a map or an in-car navigation system, it took Hunter no longer than fifteen minutes to get from the airport to the Healdsburg Police Department in Center Street.

Chief Suarez was in his late fifties, stocky, intimidating, with a presence that projected itself without him having to speak. He looked like a man who had spent way too much time in the same job. As he'd told Hunter over the phone, he'd never heard of the Harper case. It had happened eleven years before he was transferred to Healdsburg. But Chief Suarez was also a very thorough and inquisitive man, and overnight he researched what he could.

'One of the first people I met when I moved here was a guy named Ted Jenkins,' the chief told Hunter after showing him into his office. 'Coffee?' he gestured towards an aluminum thermal flask on his desk.

Hunter shook his head. 'I'm OK, Chief, thanks. I grabbed one as I was leaving the airport.'

Chief Suarez laughed. 'Yeah, and I bet it tasted like cat piss.'

Hunter conceded. 'Probably just a step above it.'

'No, no. You've gotta try this.' He grabbed a mug from a tray on top of the metal filing cabinet by the window and poured Hunter a cup. 'No one makes coffee like my Louise. She's got a gift. Like a family secret. How do you take it?'

Hunter had to admit that even from that distance, the coffee smelled incredible. 'Black is great.'

'I like you already. That's how coffee is *meant* to be drunk.' The chief handed Hunter the cup.

'You were telling me about Ted Jenkins,' he said before having a sip. 'Wow.' His eyes widened.

Chief Suarez smiled. 'Good, isn't it? I'll ask Louise to make you a flask before you leave.'

Hunter nodded his thanks.

'OK. Ted Jenkins. He's the editor for the *Healdsburg Tribune*. Back then he was just a reporter. I had a drink with him last night after I got off the phone with you. He certainly remembers what happened. A terrible case where a cheated husband lost his head and killed his wife, his kid, the wife's lover and then blew his own head off with a shotgun. Huge for a place like Healdsburg, but for an LA cop . . . ?' Chief Suarez leaned forward, placed both hands on his desk and interlaced his fingers. 'One of the reasons I made chief of police is because I'm a very curious man, Detective. And your phone call yesterday got my curiosity steaming.' He paused and took a sip of his coffee. 'I looked you up. Had a quick chat with your captain this morning too.'

Hunter said nothing.

The chief reached for his reading glasses and his eyes moved to a notepad on his desk. 'Los Angeles Police Department – Homicide Special Section. Your specialty – ultra-violent crimes. Now that's something us folks over here only see in movies.' His eyes returned to Hunter over his spectacles. 'Your captain told me you're the best there is. And that got my old brain thinking. Everyone knows Los Angeles is a crazy town, Detective. Gangs, drugs, drive-by shoot-outs, serial killers, mass murderers, killing sprees, and worse. Why would a murder case that happened twenty years ago in a small town like Healdsburg interest the Homicide Special Section in LA?'

Hunter sipped his coffee.

'So late last night I went down to our archives room to look for the case files. Turns out that anything older than ten years was stuck under piles and piles of junk inside unmarked cardboard boxes at the back of a smelly and cobweb-filled room. It took me and an officer nearly five hours to find them.' He tapped a very old-looking paper folder next to his desktop PC.

Hunter moved to the edge of his seat.

'Imagine my surprise when I saw the pictures and read the reports of what had *really* happened.' He handed the file to Hunter.

Hunter flipped it open and the first photograph he saw made his heart skip a beat.

Ninety

The woman was in her late twenties, early thirties. It was hard to tell from the photo because her face was swollen and battered, but even so, Hunter could see she'd been pretty, very pretty.

A large bruise covered the left side of her forehead, eye and cheekbone. Her shoulder-length black hair was wet and sticking to her face. Her large hazel eyes, that Hunter was sure had once dazzled many men, were wide open. Her terrifying fear was frozen in them like a snapshot. Just like Laura, Kelly and Jessica, her lips had been stitched tightly shut with thick black thread, but the stitches were neat and tidy, unlike those on the victims in Los Angeles. Blood had seeped through the needle punctures and run down to her chin and neck. She was alive when he stitched her up. A brownish substance had also accumulated between her lips and at the corners of her mouth – vomit. She had been sick and the discharge had had nowhere to go.

The second picture was a close-up of the words that had been written the wall – HE'S INSIDE YOU. Ray Harper had used blood to write them. The third picture showed the next set of stitches on her body. Her groin and inner thighs were also smeared with blood that had seeped through the puncture wounds. She'd been tied to the bed by her wrists and ankles in a spread-eagled position. But the bed had been tipped on its end and pushed up against a wall, placing the victim in a standing position and facing the inside of the room.

Hunter moved to the next picture – a male body lying on the floor directly in front of the bed and the female victim. His entire head and most of his neck were missing. A double-barreled shotgun was lying partly over his torso and partly in an enormous pool of blood. Both of his hands were resting on the gun's stock. From the destruction to his head, Hunter knew he'd discharged both rounds simultaneously, and that the barrel ends had been placed under his chin.

Hunter skipped the rest of the photos and skimmed over the report and the autopsy files. He finally found what he was looking for as he got to the last page inside the folder – the crime-scene log sheet. Eight different people had had direct access to the Harper crime scene that day – the county coroner, a county forensic investigator, the county sheriff together with two of his deputies, Chief Cooper and two other Healdsburg police officers.

'Are Officer Perez or Officer Kimble still with the police department?' he asked Chief Suarez.

The chief scratched a thin scar under his chin. 'Officer Perez retired four years ago. He lives just down the road from me. His son is with the fire department. Officer Kimble passed away a few years back. Pancreatic cancer won that battle.'

'I'm sorry to hear that.' Hunter's attention returned to the log sheet. 'Do you know any of these deputies from the County Sheriff's Office, Peter Edmunds or Joseph Hale?'

The chief nodded. 'Sure, but they aren't deputies any more. Peter Edmunds is Captain of Field Services and Operations and Joseph Hale is Assistant Sheriff of the Law

Enforcement Division. They both live in Santa Rosa. They're great guys.'

Hunter rubbed his eyes for an instant. The county coroner, the county forensic investigator, the county sheriff, and Healdsburg old chief of police, Chief Cooper, would all be over sixty-five years of age today. It wasn't impossible but there was very little chance any of them would've become a serial killer in their old age. That meant that everyone who had attended the crime scene was accounted for, unless someone hadn't been logged in. But if that was the case, Hunter had no way of finding out who else had seen the scene. Instinctively he flipped through the files and the pictures again and suddenly frowned. Something caught his eye. He returned to the photographs, this time studying every picture attentively. When he reached the last one, he flicked back to the files and scanned them again, all the way to the last page.

'Are these all the case files or is there another folder somewhere in your archives room?' he asked.

'That's it. Nothing else.'

'Are you sure?'

Chief Suarez arched his eyebrows. 'Yes I'm sure. I told you, it took us five hours to find those files. We've been through every single one of the old boxes, and believe me, there were quite a few of them. Why?'

Hunter closed the folder on his lap.

'Because there's something missing.'

Ninety-One

The drive to Chief Cooper's house took Hunter less than fifteen minutes.

He stepped out of the car, and as he closed the door behind him, a woman came out onto the house's porch. She was in her mid-sixties, slender but not skinny. She wore a simple blue dress and a pocketed apron. She had a long angular face framed by straight gray hair falling to her shoulders.

'Morning,' she said with a smile. Her voice was a little hoarse, as if she'd been fighting off a cold. 'You must be the detective from Los Angeles Tom mentioned.' Her blue eyes fixed on Hunter's face. They were as tender as her voice.

'Yes, ma'am,' Hunter said, approaching her. He produced his credentials and she scrutinized them like a seasoned pro.

'My name is Mary,' she offered, extending her hand. 'Tom's wife.'

'It's a pleasure to meet you, ma'am.'

They shook hands and Hunter was surprised by how much strength she packed in her tiny hand.

'Tom is down by the lake, fishing.' She shook her head in a mock-disapproving way. 'He's always fishing. Well . . .' she laughed, 'at least it gives him something to do. Or else he'd be hammering things in the house all day long.'

Hunter smiled back politely.

'Just follow that path over there all the way down the small hill,' she said, pointing to a narrow trail that seemed to lead deep into the woods to the right of the house. 'You can't miss him.' She paused and quickly assessed the sky. 'Do you have a raincoat in that car of yours?'

'I'm afraid I don't.'

Mary gave him a sweet smile. 'Wait just a minute, then.' She walked back into the house. A few seconds later she reappeared carrying a police-issue raincoat. 'Rain ain't far away, you better take this or you might catch a cold.' She handed him the coat. 'Tom's got enough coffee and cakes with him to feed the two of you for a day and a half.'

Hunter thanked her again and disappeared down the trail. It twisted left and right several times, getting steeper the deeper Hunter moved into the forest. It led down to a secluded spot by Lake Sonoma. He paused as he reached a rock and dirt landing at the bottom of the path. There was no one there. The lake was placid, still even. Hunter took a step back and listened for a moment. Something didn't seem right.

Suddenly he swung around, drawing his gun.

'Woah, easy.' The man standing about five feet from him with his hands up in the air was in his late-sixties, tall and lean. He had two tiny tuffs of white hair over his ears, black rimmed glasses pushed up all the way to the bridge of his nose, and a cotton white moustache that seemed way too thick for his thin face and lips. Despite his age, he still looked like he could handle himself in any sort of fight.

'You heard me coming up behind you?' His voice was commanding.

'Something like that,' Hunter replied, his gun still targeting the old man.

'Damn, I'm either losing my touch or you've got fantastic

hearing. And that was a fast draw if I've ever seen one.' He waited a few seconds. 'I'm Tom Cooper. You must be Detective Robert Hunter from the Los Angeles Robbery Homicide Division. Do you mind if I lower my hands?'

'Yeah, sorry about that.' Hunter flicked the safety into place and holstered his gun.

'You're not very light on your feet, though. I could hear you coming from halfway down the hill.'

Hunter looked down at his now dirt-covered boots. 'I wasn't expecting a stealth exercise.'

Chief Cooper smiled. 'Sorry, old habits die hard.' He offered his hand.

Hunter shook it firmly.

'I'm all set up over here.' He pointed to another trail that went around some trees and to the left. Hunter followed him into a second clearance where a fisherman's chair and a small weave basket packed with food were arranged by the water. 'Help yourself to some coffee and cake if you like. Do you fish?'

'I tried it once when I was a kid.' Hunter shook his head as he poured coffee from one of the two large thermal flasks into a cup. 'I wasn't any good at it.'

Chief Cooper laughed. 'No one is good at it if you only do it once. I've been doing it for years and I still have a lot to learn.' He reached for a thin fishing rod, grabbed a couple of live black lugworms from a container, and pushed their slimy bodies through the hook. 'I prefer live bait, it's . . .'

'Nicer for the fish,' Hunter finished. 'And since you don't keep them, might as well give them a nice treat in exchange for having their mouths hooked.' He had a sip of his coffee and nodded. It was just as good as the one he had back at the police station.

The chief studied Hunter curiously before looking at his setup. 'No fish net or containers to take my catch back up to the house.' He nodded. 'You're observant, but I guess you wouldn't be a detective if you weren't.' He swung his hook into the lake. 'OK, I know you didn't come all this way to learn about fishing or to shoot the breeze. You said on the phone that you needed to talk to me about the Harper case.'

Hunter nodded. 'Do you remember it well?'

Chief Cooper stared back at Hunter and his playful tone had vanished. 'You don't forget a crime scene like that, Detective. I don't care how experienced you are. I know you've been through the station first 'cause Chief Suarez just called me. You saw the pictures, right? Could anyone forget those images?'

Hunter said nothing.

'You didn't tell me much over the phone, but I guess you didn't have to. The way I see it, the only reason the LAPD RHD would be interested in a 20-year-old case from a small town is because you guys must have something down there that's pretty close to what happened here.'

Hunter stared at his reflection in the water for a moment. 'If I'm right, Chief, it's a lot closer than you think.'

Ninety-Two

Chief Cooper slotted his fishing rod into the appropriate hook next to his chair and turned to face Hunter.

'When I left LA this morning, my main concern was finding the log sheet for the Harper crime scene. There are only eight names on it.' He retrieved his notebook from his jacket pocket. 'Yours and two of your officers, Kimble and Perez. The Sonoma County sheriff at the time, Sheriff Hudson and two of his deputies, Edmunds and Hale. The county coroner at the time, Doctor Bennett and a forensic investigator, Gustavo Ortiz. Is that right?'

Chief Cooper didn't have to think about it. He nodded immediately.

'Can you remember if anyone else saw that scene, anyone at all? Someone who somehow wasn't logged onto the sheet?'

The chief shook his head firmly. 'No one else saw the scene. Not once we got there.' He poured himself some more coffee. 'The Harper house was only about a block away from the old police station. Tito, their neighbor at the time, called the station saying he heard a gunshot. Tito was, and still is, a pretty accomplished hunter. So when he said he heard a shotgun being fired, I knew it couldn't have been a mistake. I was at the station when he called. It took me less than a minute to get there. I was first at the scene.' He paused and looked away. 'I'd never seen anything like it. Not even in case studies. And to tell you the truth, I hope I never see anything like it again.'

The sky was getting menacingly dark and the wind had picked up a notch.

'A minute after I got to the house, Officers Kimble and Perez arrived. I knew straight away I had to get the County Sheriff's Office involved. Despite our restricted experience with homicides, we all knew the protocol. We immediately isolated the house. No one other than the three of us had access to the scene.'

'Until the sheriff and the coroner arrived,' Hunter added.

'That's right. As you said, Doctor Bennett, who is now retired, had an investigator with him, Gustavo Ortiz. He's now the chief coroner investigator for Santa Clara County. Sheriff Hudson had two deputies with him, Edmunds and Hale.'

Hunter nodded. 'Chief Suarez told me. Edmunds is a captain now and Hale is assistant sheriff. They both live in Santa Rosa.'

Chief Cooper confirmed this. 'No one else entered the house or saw the scene. I am sure because I was there until all the photographs were taken and the bodies removed.'

Thin rain started falling, but neither man moved.

'The Harpers had a son, right? Andrew,' Hunter said.

Chief Cooper nodded slowly.

'I've been through all the files down at the station. There's no photograph of the body, no autopsy report and no mention of what happened to him. It's like all the files on the kid are missing.'

The way Chief Cooper looked at Hunter made the hairs on the back of his neck stand on end.

'His files aren't missing. They aren't there because his body was never found.'

Ninety-Three

'What?' Hunter cleared the rain from his eyebrows and stared back at Chief Cooper. 'Never found? So how did you know he was murdered?'

The chief let out a deep sigh. His glasses were so heavy with rain Hunter could barely see his eyes. 'The truth is that we didn't know. But that was what the evidence told us.'

'What evidence?'

Chief Cooper finally pulled the nylon hood of his raincoat over his head and retreated a few steps back to the shelter of a large tree. Hunter followed him.

'The Harpers tragedy happened on a Sunday,' the chief explained. 'Every Sunday, without fail, for the six years previous to that day, Ray took his son fishing. Sometimes to Lake Sonoma, sometimes to Rio Nido, and sometimes to Russian River. They're all within driving distance. I went with them several times. Ray was a great fisherman, and his boy was starting to get pretty good at it too.

'Tito, the neighbor who called in "shots fired", saw Ray and his kid packing the truck a couple of hours before he heard the shot. The owner of the gas station a few blocks away from their house also confirmed seeing the kid in the passenger's seat of Ray's truck while Ray went into the store to buy some ice cream. Andrew never came back to the house with his father. When Forensics checked the truck, they found the kid's shirt and shoes. There was blood on the shirt, on the shoes, on the car's dashboard, and on the inside of the passenger's door. The kid's blood. The lab confirmed it.'

'Wasn't there an investigation into the boy's disappearance?'

'Yes, there was. But we found nothing other than what I just told you. We don't know where he took his son, Detective – Sonoma Lake, Rio Nido or Russian River. There are also acres and acres of forest surrounding Healdsburg and the rivers. He could've killed his son and buried or left him to the wolves somewhere in the forest. He could've weighted the kid's body down and dumped him in the lake or the river. Finding the body without knowing where he went that day was a pretty impossible task. Though we did try, we never found it.'

The chief took off his glasses and rubbed the bridge of his nose where the pads had left two sunken red marks.

'Ray was a good man, but he suffered from depression,' he continued. 'I think he found out about Emily's affair a few days earlier because there was thought put into what he did. It wasn't your typical loss of control murder, though it might've looked that way from all the mess and blood. We figured Ray found out that Emily saw her lover when she thought it was safe to do so. So he got his kid out of the house and killed him first, disposing of the body somewhere. He then went over to Nathan Gardner's apartment, disfigured him and left him there, bleeding to death, but not before stitching his mouth shut. After that, Ray returned to his house to confront his wife, and to complete his crazy killing plan.'

Chief Cooper paused and looked straight into Hunter's eyes.

'And I have no doubt that in Ray's plan, no one was coming out alive. *No one.*'

Ninety-Four

Garcia stood across the room from the unmade bed, staring at the mess of clothes and objects on the floor.

Mark Stratton, Jessica Black's boyfriend, had cut short his band's pre-tour and come back to LA in the early hours of the morning. Garcia accompanied him to the morgue so he could positively identify her body.

No matter how physically or mentally strong anyone is, seeing a loved one lying naked on a cold metal morgue's body-tray will cut through their defenses. Despite all the stitches having been removed, Jessica's face seemed to have frozen with an expression of terror and pain. Mark didn't have to ask if she'd suffered.

His legs gave away within seconds of him being in the room, but Garcia managed to grab him before he hit the floor.

Hunter had told Mark over the phone that there was a possibility that Jessica had been abducted from inside their own apartment. He explained that it was very important that the police and a forensic team had a look at it as soon as possible. It was also very important that he didn't disturb anything. It didn't quite work that way.

Since Mark had come off the phone to Hunter late yesterday, he hadn't stopped shaking. He had incessantly called his home number and Jessica's cell phone, leaving message after message. He just couldn't think straight. Emotions took over and he had lost it, destroying his hotel room in anger and frustration.

Without knowing what had happened, the rest of his band had to kick his door in and hold him down. It took the tour manager a couple of hours to get things organized, including a flight back to LA. By then Mark was tramp-drunk, and at the airport he wasn't allowed to board the plane.

'Aviation rules,' explained the young woman at the airline counter. 'He's way too inebriated to fly. I'm sorry.'

That had been the last daily flight back to Los Angeles. In the end, they had to hire a private plane to take him back.

After a cab dropped him by his private condo, Mark, still half-drunk, stumbled rather than walked through his front door. At that moment all hope of things not being disturbed inside his apartment was lost. He didn't stop calling Jessica's name for hours, walking from room to room, turning lights on and off as if she would suddenly magically appear. He opened her wardrobe and rummaged through her clothes. He emptied drawers and cupboards. He lay down on their bed, hugged her pillow and cried until he had no more tears left.

Mark was now sitting quietly in his kitchen, his eyes bloodshot and sore.

Garcia picked up a photo frame from the bedroom floor – Jessica and Mark holidaying somewhere sunny. They looked happy and in love.

He returned the frame to the dresser, turned to face the unmade bed once again and considered what to do. They couldn't cordon off Mark and Jessica's apartment because it wasn't an official crime scene. The chances of him getting a Forensics team dispatched to the apartment before confirming Jessica had been abducted from there were less than slim. The chances of that Forensics team finding any sort of clue in a scene that had been compromised and completely messed with were virtually none.

Garcia walked out of the room, down the long corridor and into the living room. On the stylish glass table that sat between the sofa and the wall-mounted TV set, he found several music magazines. The top one had Jessica on its cover. Out of pure curiosity he flipped it open and looked for the article. It was a two-page interview through which she talked about being a successful musician and her life in general, but one subheader caught his attention – *On Love*. Garcia allowed his eyes to skim through the section, but just a few lines in he paused. A chill ran down his spine as if he'd been suddenly hit by an arctic wind. He read the lines again just to be sure.

'No fucking way.' He grabbed the magazine and rushed back to his office.

Ninety-Five

Hunter left Chief Cooper's house by Lake Sonoma just before lunchtime, but he wasn't ready to fly back to LA just yet. His mind was batting thoughts back and forth and he needed to organize them before moving on. He remembered driving past the city library on the way to the chief's house. He decided to start there.

The building was a single-story structure that couldn't even be compared to some of LA's high-school libraries. Hunter parked in the adjacent lot, pulled the collar of his jacket tight against his neck and dashed to the entrance. The rain that had started earlier was still coming down.

The woman at the information desk lifted her eyes from her computer screen and smiled sympathetically as Hunter came through the door.

'I guess you forgot your umbrella, huh?'

Hunter brushed the water off his hair and sleeves before smiling back. 'I wasn't expecting the heavens to open.'

'Spring downpour. We're famous for those over here. It'll pass soon enough,' she offered with a renewed smile and a couple of paper tissues.

'Thanks.' He took them and dried his forehead and hands.

'I'm Rhonda, by the way.'

They shook hands.

'I'm Robert.'

Rhonda was in her mid-twenties with short, spiky, black-dyed hair. Her face was ghostly pale and her make-up was one step short from being full goth.

'So . . .' she said, fixing Hunter with her dark eyes. 'What brings you to Healdsburg's library? Actually, what brings you to Healdsburg at all?'

'Research.'

'Research? About Healdsburg's wineries?'

'No.' Hunter thought for a second. 'I guess I'm looking for an old school yearbook.'

'A yearbook? An old friend, huh? From which school?'

Hunter paused. 'How many schools are there in Healdsburg?'

Rhonda laughed. 'It doesn't look like you know much about this research of yours.'

Hunter agreed with a smile. 'The truth is: I'm just trying to find a picture of a kid who lived here many years ago.'

'A kid?' Her expression changed to concern and she took a step back from the counter.

'No, look, I'm a cop from Los Angeles,' Hunter said, producing his badge. 'Something that happened here twenty years ago has suddenly become of interest to us. I'm just trying to gather some information, that's all. A picture would help.'

Rhonda studied the badge and then Hunter's face. 'Twenty years ago?'

'That's right.'

She hesitated for a beat. 'So you must be talking about what happened to the Harpers. And if you're looking for a picture of a kid, you must be talking about Andrew Harper.'

'You knew him?'

She looked uncertain. 'Sort of. I was only five when it happened. But he used to come to our house sometimes.'

'Really? How come?'

'We lived in the same street. He was friends with my brother.'

'Does your brother still live here?'

'Yep. He's an accountant and runs his own practice in town. You probably drove past his office on your way here.'

'Do you think I could have a chat with him?'

Another hesitant moment.

'Whatever information he can give me might help a lot,' Hunter pushed.

Rhonda regarded Hunter for a second longer.

'I don't see why not.' She checked her watch. 'I'll tell you what. It's coming up to my lunch break. Why don't I take you there and introduce you to him?'

Ninety-Six

Rhonda said hello to Mrs. Collins at the reception desk in the anteroom of her brother's small accountancy practice and pointed to his office door.

'He's not with anyone, is he?'

Mrs. Collins smiled kindly as she shook her head.

'I think he was just getting ready to go out for lunch, dear. You can go right in, Rhonda.'

Rhonda knocked twice and pushed the door open before a reply.

Ricky was pretty much the opposite of his sister. Tall with neatly trimmed hair and a sportsman's physique, he was dressed conservatively in a light gray suit, baby blue shirt and a blue on red tie. The introductions were quick and to the point, and Ricky's smile dissipated once Rhonda told him why she'd brought Hunter to see him.

'I'm sorry, but I don't see how I can help,' he said to Hunter, looking a little rattled. 'I was ten when it happened and we weren't even here, remember?' He directed the question to Rhonda, who nodded. 'It happened during Christmas vacation and we had gone over to Grandma's house in Napa. We only heard about it when we got back.'

'I understand, and I don't want you to tell me about the incident. I know you know nothing about that. But if you could tell me a little about Andrew himself, that could help. Rhonda told me that you were friends?'

Ricky looked at his sister in a reprimanding way. 'I guess.' He shrugged. 'He . . . didn't have many friends.'

'Why was that?'

Another shrug. 'He was very quiet and shy. He much preferred spending time with his comic books than with people.'

'But you guys did spend some time together, right? Played games, that kinda stuff?'

'Yeah, sometimes, but not always. He was . . . different.'

Hunter's eyes narrowed a fraction. 'In what way?'

Ricky paused and checked his watch before crossing to the door to his office and sticking his head outside. 'Mrs. Collins, if anyone calls, I'm out for lunch.' He closed the door behind him. 'Why don't you have a seat?'

Hunter took one of the two chairs in front of Ricky's desk. Rhonda preferred to lean against the window frame.

'Andrew was . . . sad most of the time,' Ricky said, returning to his desk.

'Did he ever tell you why?'

'His parents argued a lot, and that really upset him. He was very close to his mother.'

'Not so close to his father?' Hunter asked.

'Yes, he was as well, but he talked about his mother more.'

Hunter's cell phone vibrated in his pocket and he subtly checked the display window – Whitney Myers. Hunter returned the phone to his pocket without answering it. He'd call her later.

'Kids always talk about their mothers,' Rhonda offered.

'No.' Ricky shook his head firmly. 'Not the way he did.

He talked about her as if she was a goddess. Like she couldn't do anything wrong.'

'Idolizing her?' Hunter asked.

'Yes. He put her on the pedestal. And when she was sad, he was *really* sad.' Ricky started fidgeting with a paper clip. 'I know that sometimes he used to watch his mom cry and that just ate away at him.' A nervous chuckle escaped Ricky's lips. 'He used to watch her a lot . . . in a weird way.'

Rhonda cocked her head. 'What does that mean?'

Ricky's eyes moved from her to Hunter, who kept his face steady.

'Andrew told me about this secret hiding place he had. And I know he used to spend a lot of time there.'

Hunter knew that a secret or special place wasn't uncommon amongst kids. Especially ones like Andrew – sad, quiet, with few friends – the bullied ones. It's usually just an isolated location where they can get away from everything and everyone that upsets them. A place where they feel safe. But if a child starts reverting to it more and more, it's usually because they feel the need to increase their isolation – from everyone and everything. And the consequences can be severe.

'That's not so bad,' Rhonda said. 'Me and my friends used to have a secret place when we were kids.'

'Not like Andrew's,' Ricky countered. 'At least I hope not. He took me there one day.' A muscle flexed on his jaw. 'He made me promise to never tell anyone.'

'And . . . ?' Rhonda asked.

Hunter waited.

Ricky's eyes moved away from both of them. 'I'd pretty much forgotten about that place.' His stare returned to Hunter. 'His secret place was this secluded bit in the attic in his house. Their attic was packed with boxes and boxes of junk and old furniture. There was so much stuff piled up that it created a wall, a partition of sorts, dividing the attic into two separate spaces. If you went up there via the stairs in the house, you could only see one of them. The other one was completely hidden behind this barricade of stuff. You couldn't even get to it, unless you started moving things. And you'd have to move a lot of things.'

'And this hidden space in the attic was Andrew's secret place?' Rhonda asked.

'That's right.'

'But you just said no one could get to it,' she challenged.

'Not through the house,' Ricky clarified. 'Andrew used to climb up the trellis on the outside wall and get in through this tiny round window on the roof.'

'The roof?'

'Yes. He was good at it too. He could climb that wall like a real-life Spiderman.'

'So what was so strange about his secret attic place?' Rhonda asked.

'It was directly above his parents' bedroom. He said that when they were in the room, he could hear everything.'

'Oh my God.' Rhonda pulled a face. 'You think he used to listen to them while they were doing it?'

'More than that. You remember his house, right?'

She nodded.

He turned towards Hunter. 'It was an old-style wooden house, with high ceilings. Andrew had scraped away at the gaps between some of the wooden planks in the attic's floor, at different locations. I know because he showed them to me. Through them he could see the entire bedroom. He used to spy on his parents.'

'No way,' Rhonda said with wide eyes. 'That's just nasty. What a pervert.' She cringed.

'But what freaked me out about the place,' Ricky continued, 'was that in this little corner I saw a few cotton balls and rags stained with blood.'

'Blood?' Hunter asked.

'Blood?' Rhonda repeated.

Ricky nodded. 'I asked him about it. He told me it was from a nosebleed.'

Hunter frowned.

'When Andrew was younger he'd got really ill with flu, and that somehow messed up the inside of his nose. I know that's true because it happened in school a few times. If he started sneezing or if he just blew his nose a little too hard, blood would go everywhere.'

Hunter sensed Ricky's uneasiness. 'But you didn't believe the bloody cotton balls and rags came from his nosebleed, did you?'

Ricky looked at his sister and then at the paper clip he'd been fidgeting with. It was all bent and out of shape. He lifted it up and showed it to Hunter. 'I saw some of these on the floor next to the cotton balls. They also had blood on them. Maybe he was picking at his nose with paper clips, who knows? As I said, he was stranger than most. I didn't know what was going on, but the whole place felt creepy. I told Andrew that I had to go home and got out of there as quick as I could.'

Hunter knew why the bloody cotton balls, rags and paper clips – Andrew was self-harming. He was substituting pain for pain, trying to take hold of his suffering. He couldn't control the emotional pain he went through every time his parents argued, so, to disconnect from that hurt, he created his own, by inflicting his own wounds. That way he could calmly watch himself bleed, detached from his own suffering and his underlying rage. It was a pain he could completely control, down to how deep the cut was, and how much he'd bleed.

Ricky paused and rubbed his face with both hands.

'Look, I know Andrew was a little weird, but most 10-year-old kids are in one way or another.' His eyes moved to Rhonda. 'Some of us still are.'

She flipped him her middle finger.

'But he was a nice kid,' Ricky continued. 'And if you ask me, I think that what his father did was a very cowardly act. Andrew never had a chance. He didn't deserve to die.'

Everyone went silent.

To Hunter, all the pieces were starting to fall into place.

Ninety-Seven

The room he was in was illuminated only by candles – twelve in total. Their flames flickered in an unsynchronized dance, bouncing shadows against the walls. He raised his eyes towards his naked body reflected in the large wall mirror. Bare feet on a cold cement floor, strong legs, broad shoulders, athletic body and icy cold eyes. He stared at his face for a long while, analyzing it carefully before twisting his body left, then right, checking his back.

He walked over to the table on the corner and picked up one of the many pre-paid cell phones on it, dialing a number he knew by heart.

It rang twice before it was answered by a calm but firm voice.

'Do you have the information I asked you for?' he asked, his eyes moving to the workstation in front of him.

'Yes, it wasn't a problem.'

He listened carefully.

The information was more surprising than upsetting, but his face displayed no signs of anxiety. He disconnected and ran his right hand over the large blood-coated needle and thread he'd left on the workstation.

He'd have to change his course of action, adapt, and he didn't like change. Deviating from well-laid plans meant increasing his risk, but right now, he wasn't sure it mattered any more.

He checked his watch. He knew exactly where she'd be in a few hours' time. The information had been so easy to come by it made him laugh.

He faced the mirror once again and stared deep into his own eyes.

It was time to do it again.

Ninety-Eight

'Shit!'

She checked her car's clock and cursed under her breath as she turned into her street in Toluca Lake, southeastern San Fernando Valley. She had no doubt she'd be late, and she hated being late.

The gala charity fundraising event was scheduled to start in seventy-five minutes' time. The drive from her house alone would take her at least half an hour. That gave her around forty-five minutes to have a shower, do her hair and make-up and get dressed. For a woman who took as much pride in her appearance as she did, that was almost impossible.

Her secretary had reminded her in plenty of time, as she'd asked her to, but an accident on Hollywood Freeway cost her an extra thirty-five minutes, and in an event where the Mayor of Los Angeles, the Governor of California and quite a few A-list celebrities were supposed to be attending, being late wasn't the best plan of action.

To save time, she decided that she'd have her hair up and tied back. She also had a pretty good idea of which dress and shoes she'd be wearing.

Her home was a large, two-story, cul-de-sac house by Toluca Lake itself. She knew the house was way too big for her alone, but she had fallen in love with it when she was first property searching.

She parked her Dodge Challenger on her paved driveway and her eyes involuntarily checked the dashboard clock again.

'Shit, shit.'

She'd been so concerned with the time and being late that she didn't even notice the white van parked on the street, almost directly in front of her house.

She stepped out of her car and fumbled inside her handbag for the key while walking to her front door. As she got to the porch, she heard a ruffling noise coming from the trimmed shrubs of her small front yard. She paused and frowned. A few seconds later the noise returned. It sounded like some sort of scratching.

'Oh, please don't tell me I've got rats,' she whispered to herself.

Suddenly she heard a sniffing cry and a tiny white puppy stuck its head through the bushes. It looked frightened and hungry.

'Oh my God.' She crouched down, put her handbag on the floor and extended a hand. 'Come here, little one. Don't be scared.' The puppy stepped further out of the bushes, sniffing at her hand.

'Oh, you poor thing. I bet you're hungry.' She patted its head, running a hand up and down its white fur. It was shivering. 'Would you like some milk?'

She did not hear him walk up behind her. In her crouched position it was easy for him to dominate her. His strong hands pushed her forward into the bushes where the white puppy had come from, while at the same time pressing a wet cloth over her mouth. She tried to react, dropping the puppy and desperately trying to reach behind her to grab hold of her assailant. But it was too late; he knew it, and so did she.

Within seconds, her world faded to black.

Ninety-Nine

Garcia went straight back to his desk in Parker Center and fired up his computer. He needed to search the Internet for online editions of art magazines and journals.

Two hours later he was starting to get a headache from squinting at the screen, and he still hadn't found what he was looking for. His gaze returned to the copy of the music magazine he'd taken from Jessica Black's apartment and a thought crept into his mind. He considered it for only a few seconds before grabbing his jacket and flying out the door once again.

Garcia wasn't as familiar with the central branch of the Los Angeles Public Library as Hunter was, but he knew they kept a microfilm and database archive on all their magazines and journals. He just hoped their Arts department was as accomplished as Hunter said it was.

Garcia found a free workstation, sat himself down and started searching through articles. He searched for any piece about either Laura Mitchell or Kelly Jensen, especially one-to-one interviews.

It took him just under two and a half hours to find the first one – an interview with Kelly Jensen for *Art Today* magazine. As he read the lines he'd been looking for, he felt a rush of blood inundate his veins.

'This is fucking crazy,' he said, pressing the print button. He collected his printout and returned to his seat. Laura Mitchell was now his next target.

An hour later he got to the end of the list of all the Laura Mitchell interviews he'd found in the system – nothing.

'Fuck!' he cursed under his breath. His eyes were getting tired and watery. He needed a break, a cup of coffee and an Advil.

Suddenly a crazy thought came into his head and he paused for a moment, considering the alternatives.

'Oh, what the hell,' he whispered as he decided that it was worth a shot.

Garcia wouldn't find a better collection of art magazines and articles on Laura Mitchell than the ones they'd uncovered inside the dark room in James Smith's apartment. Smith seemed to have collected everything that was ever published on her. He was still under custody, and his apartment was still seized by police as part of an ongoing investigation.

Garcia stood by the door to the dimly lit collage room, staring at the magazines and newspapers piled just about everywhere.

'Damn!' he whispered to himself. 'This is gonna take me forever.'

In fact, it took him two hours and three piles of magazines and journals. Laura Mitchell's last interview had been with *Contemporary Painters* magazine, eleven months ago. It was a small article – less than fifteen hundred words.

He almost choked when he read the lines.

'Sonofabitch.'

Every hair on his body stood on end. He knew that this kind of coincidence just didn't exist.

As he rushed out of the building, his cell phone rang in his pocket. He checked the display window before answering it.

'Robert, I was just about to call you. You're not gonna believe what I just found out—'

'Carlos, listen,' Hunter interrupted urgently, 'I think I know who we're after.'

'What? Really? Who?'

'I have no doubt he doesn't go by his real name any more, but his original name was Andrew Harper. I need you to get in touch with Operations and the research team immediately. We need everything and anything we can get on him.'

Garcia stopped walking and frowned at nothing. His memory searching for the name. 'Wait a second,' he remembered, 'isn't that the name of the kid Stephen told us about on the phone? The one who was murdered by his father?'

'Yep, that's him, and I don't know how he got away, but I don't think he was murdered that day.'

'Come again?'

'I think that somehow he survived. And I think he was in the house when it happened, Carlos.'

'What?'

'I'll tell you everything when I get back to LA. I'm at the airport now. I'll land at LAX in about two hours. But I think the kid was hiding in the house.'

'No way.'

'He watched his father violate his mother's body, stitch her shut, write a blood message on the wall and then kill her before blowing his own head off . . .'

Garcia stayed silent.

'I think the kid saw everything. And now he's repeating history.'

One Hundred

Clouds were gathering when Andrew Harper turned his van into State Highway 170, going north. From the back seat of the brown station wagon in front of him, a kid of about nine smiled and waved at him, an ice-cream cone in his hand. It wasn't as if Andrew ever needed reminders for his mind to take him back to that day, they were everywhere he looked, but at the sight of the kid and his ice cream, Andrew twitched like a cow shaking off flies as vivid images flooded his memory. In an instant, he was transported back to his father's truck that Sunday morning. His father had driven just a couple of blocks before stopping at that gas station.

'I have a surprise for you,' Ray Harper said, turning to face little Andrew who was sitting in the passenger's seat. His lips smiled but his eyes betrayed him. 'But first, let me go get you some ice cream.'

Andrew's eyes widened. 'Ice cream? Mom doesn't like me to have ice cream. She said that since my cold, ice cream isn't good for me, Dad.'

'I know she doesn't, but you like ice cream, don't you?'

Andrew nodded eagerly.

'One single scoop can't hurt. This is a special day, and if you like ice cream, you can have ice cream. What flavor?'

Andrew thought about it for a beat. 'Chocolate brownie,' he said, his happiness almost oozing through his pores.

A few minutes later Ray came back to the car with two cones. Andrew bit into his as if the whole thing would vanish in thin air if he didn't eat it immediately. Less than a minute later he had finished his cone and started licking his fingers.

Ray had just finished his ice cone when a single, powerful sneeze exploded out of Andrew, and with it came blood. Andrew didn't manage to cover his nose in time and blood splattered everywhere: dashboard, windshield, door, but mainly all over his shirt. The nosebleed that followed was short but intense, enough to drip onto his trousers and shoes. Ray instantly reached for Andrew, tipped his head back slightly and used the edge of Andrew's shirt to clear the smudges around his nose and mouth. The bleeding stopped within two minutes.

'OK,' Ray said with an apologetic frown. 'Maybe it wasn't such a good idea after all.'

Andrew smiled before looking down at his bloody shirt and cringing.

'It's OK, kiddo,' Ray said, putting a hand on the kid's head. 'I said I had a surprise for you, remember?' He reached behind his seat, and from under his coat he retrieved a gift-wrapped box. 'This is for you.'

Andrew's eyes lit up. 'But it's not my birthday and it's not Christmas yet, Dad.'

'This is a pre-Christmas present. You deserve it, son.' Sadness masked Ray's face for an instant. 'Go ahead, open it. I know you'll like it.'

Andrew ripped the paper from around the box as fast as

he could. He loved presents, though he never got many of them. His whole face morphed into one huge smile. The top item was a brand new T-shirt. On its front was a large Wolverine print, Andrew's favorite character from the X-Men Marvel comics.

'WOW!' was all he could say.

'Go ahead, check the next one,' Ray urged him.

Andrew could tell what it would be even before opening the box – a new pair of trainers, also covered in Wolverine and X-Men prints. Andrew looked at his father, half-shocked.

'But, Dad, these are really expensive.' He knew his family had been struggling with money lately.

Ray's eyes became glassy. 'You deserve a lot more, son.' He paused for an instant. 'I'm sorry I could never give you all that you deserve.' He kissed Andrew's forehead again. 'Why don't you try everything on? That way you can get rid of that dirty shirt.'

Andrew hesitated.

Ray knew how shy his son was. 'I'll go and get us a couple of sodas and you can get changed, OK?'

Andrew waited until his father had reentered the gas station's shop and quickly stripped off his bloody shirt and threw it in the back seat. The scar on his chest from last night stuck out from the other ones across his torso because it was so red and itchy. He rubbed it gently with the tips of his fingers. He'd learned never to use his fingernails in case the wounds started bleeding again. By the time Ray returned to the truck with a paper bag and two bottles of Mountain Dew, Andrew's favorite soda, he was dressed in his new shirt and trainers.

'They look great on you, kiddo,' Ray said, handing him a bottle.

Andrew smiled. 'I'll have to take the shoes off, Dad. They'll get dirty when we get to the lake.'

Something in Ray's eyes changed. His whole being was filled with grief and sorrow. 'I have to tell you something, son. We're not gonna go fishing today.'

The sadness was mirrored on Andrew's face. 'But Dad, Mom said that if I caught a big fish today, you wouldn't fight any more. She promised.'

Tears returned to Ray's eyes but he held them there. 'Oh, honey, we won't fight any more. Never again.' He placed a hand on the boy's nape. 'Not after today.'

Andrew's eyes glistened with happiness. 'Really? You promise, Dad?'

'I promise, kiddo, but I need you to do something for me.'

'OK.'

'I have something very important to do today, that's why we can't go fishing.'

'But it's Sunday, Dad. You don't work on Sundays.'

'What I have to do today isn't work. But it's something very, very important.' He paused for an instant. 'You told me once that you have a secret place, isn't that right?'

Andrew looked concerned.

'Do you still have it?'

The boy nodded shyly. 'Yes, but I can't tell you where it is, Dad. It's secret.'

'That's OK. I don't want you to tell me where it is.' He reached under his seat for something. 'What I need you to do is go to your secret place and stay there all day long. You can play with these.' Ray showed him three six-inch figurines – Wolverine, Professor X and Cyclops.

'Wow.' Andrew couldn't believe his eyes. It got better and better.

'What do you say? Do you like your presents?'

'Yes, Dad. Thank you very much.' He reached for the toys.

'It's all right, son, but can you do that for me? Can you go to your secret place and just stay there until tonight, playing with your new toys?'

Andrew slowly peeled his eyes from the figurines and refocused them on his father's anxious face. 'You won't fight with Mom again?'

Ray gave him a coy headshake. 'Never again,' he whispered.

'Promise?'

'I promise, son.'

Another animated smile. 'OK then.'

'Don't come out until tonight, you hear?'

'I won't, Dad. I promise.'

'Here.' Ray gave him the paper bag. 'There are chocolate bars – Butterfingers; I know they're your favorite – some Pringles, a cheese and ham sandwich and two more bottles of soda, so you don't get hungry or thirsty.'

Andrew took the bag and looked inside.

'Don't eat everything at once or else you'll be ill.'

'I won't.'

'OK then. Is your secret place close by? Can you walk there?'

'Yes, I can walk there, Dad. It's not far.'

Ray hugged his son again, this time for a very long time. 'I love you, Andrew. I'll always love you, son, no matter what. Please remember that, OK?'

'I love you too, Dad.' While his father battled with tears,

Andrew opened his door and skipped on down the road with his new shirt, trainers and toys. His father had promised never to fight with his mother again. It was the happiest day of his life.

One Hundred and One

Andrew turned on the radio, hoping that music would help push the memories away, but it was already too late. His mind was on a rollercoaster trip, and the memories and images just kept on coming.

He remembered that it had taken him only a few minutes to get back to his house after leaving his father at the gas station. He stuck the figurines in his coat pocket, jumped the fence and waited in the bushes that led to the backyard. He just wanted to make sure his mother wasn't out there. It was too cold for her to sit out back anyway. Dashing to the wall, he started climbing up the trellis as he did every day, this time being even more careful than usual not to dirty his new trainers. He squeezed through the small round window at the top and entered his secret place.

The first thing he did, as always, was to take off his shoes and slip into a thick pair of woolen socks. The attic floorboards were steady, and he'd identified the squeaky spots long ago, but he still had to be careful when moving around up there. Andrew had already developed a way of tiptoeing and sliding his feet across the floor that allowed him to move around in almost total silence.

Andrew placed the three figurines on top of a wooden crate in the corner and stared at them with smiling eyes. His gaze flicked over to a bag of cotton balls and a box of paper clips on the floor by the crate. He felt something warm start growing inside him. Something he hadn't felt in a long while. Suddenly he stuck his tongue out at the cotton balls and paper clips, mocking them. He wouldn't be needing them any more. His father had promised him that he'd never fight with his mother again. And his father always kept his promises. They would go back to being a happy family like they used to be. And that meant that he wouldn't have to initiate his own pain any more.

Andrew slotted himself in his favorite corner and grabbed a handful of comic books. He'd read them all, but he didn't mind.

He must've been sitting there, flipping through his magazines for almost two hours when he heard a noise inside his parents' room. Andrew put the comics down and looked through one of the many gaps he'd created in the floor. His mother had just walked into the room. She was wrapped in a fluffy yellow towel. Her hair was still wet and combed back. Andrew took his eye off the gap before his mother let go of her towel. He'd seen her naked before, but it had been by mistake. She'd been standing on a blind spot from any of Andrew's floor gaps. When she finally reappeared, she had nothing on. Andrew knew it was wrong to look at his mother or father naked. He'd seen them hiding under the covers, making strange noises. He knew that's what all the kids in school called *a fuck*, but from where he was standing, neither of them looked like they were enjoying it very much.

He went back to his comics, knowing that he had to be extra quiet now, but then he heard the door to his parents' room being slammed shut with tremendous violence. His eye returned to the gap and his breath froze for several seconds. His father was standing by the shut door, but his face was almost unrecognizable, covered in so much rage it frightened Andrew down to his soul. His father's hands, arms and shirt were soaked in blood. His mother was standing naked and paralyzed across the room from her husband.

'Oh my God. What happened? Where's Andrew?' she asked, panic stalking her voice.

'You don't have to concern yourself with Andrew, you lying whore,' Ray blasted in such an angry voice the room almost shook. 'You should concern yourself more with your fucking lover.'

Emily hesitated.

'I don't think you'll be fucking him any more.' From his pocket he took something out. To Andrew it looked like a very bloody piece of meat.

Emily let out a strangled cry. 'Oh my God, Ray. What have you done? What on God's earth have you done?' Her hands shot towards her open mouth in absolute terror.

'I made sure that Nathan, that pathetic excuse for a man, will never wreck another home again.' He smiled a satanic smile. 'I also made sure that he won't be able to say a word when he meets his maker. You could say that his lips are sealed.' He took two steps in Emily's direction.

She took one pace back and tried to cover her body with her hands.

'Why did you have to do it, Emily? Why did you have to destroy our family? Why did you have to betray my love this way? Why did you have to make me do these things?' Spit flew from Ray's mouth. He returned the bloody piece of meat to his pocket. 'Do you remember what we used to say to each other?' He didn't wait for a reply. 'We used to say – *You are the one, honey. You are the one I've been looking for all my life. You are my soul mate. We'll never be apart because you are the person I want to spend the rest of my life with.* Do you remember that?'

Silence.

'ANSWER ME.'

Ray's yell was so loud and full of rage, Andrew immediately wet himself up in the attic.

'Ye— yes.' Emily had started crying and shivering so violently she was almost hyperventilating.

'But I wasn't the one, was I? You lied to me, you deceitful bitch. You made me believe that what we had was sacred . . . special . . . everlasting. But it wasn't, was it? I wasn't enough for you.'

Emily's lips wouldn't move.

'Was he the one?' Ray asked. 'Was Nathan the one for you?' He moved a step closer. Emily's back was against the wall. She had nowhere else she could go. 'Did you love him?'

No reply.

'Did. You. Love. Him . . . ?' Something changed in Ray's entire demeanor, like someone else was taking over. Someone beyond evil.

Emily's voice was completely gone. Her vocal cords frozen by sheer fear. In a reflexive and thoughtless action, she nodded ever so slightly.

That was all Ray's rage needed to erupt.

'If that's what true love means to you, then you should have it. You should have it inside you forever. You and him, together as one – forever.' He moved towards her with such speed and purpose that not even an army of soldiers could have stopped him. His closed fist hit the side of her head with so much power she collapsed to the ground, unconscious.

Above them, Andrew was petrified, too scared to respond,

his voice had disappeared and his eyes had almost lost the ability to blink. His mind too young and naïve to cope with all the images. But he never moved. He never took his eye off the gap.

For the next hour Andrew watched the monster inside his father surface.

Ray dragged Emily's body to the bed and tied her down. He then grabbed a long piece of thick black thread and a needle, and proceeded to meticulously stitch her mouth shut. He retrieved whatever strange piece of bloody meat he had with him, spread Emily's legs apart and forced it into her before stitching her shut. Ray then used her blood to write something on the wall. The letters were big enough for Andrew to be able to read them – HE'S INSIDE YOU.

Ray tipped the bed on one end so his wife was in a standing position and pushed it against the far wall.

Tears streamed out of Andrew's eyes.

From the box on top of the wardrobe, Ray took his double-barreled shotgun, sat on the floor directly in front of Emily, crossed his legs, rested the shotgun on his knees and waited.

He didn't have to wait long. A few minutes later Emily opened her eyes. She tried to scream but the stitches on her lips kept most of the sound trapped inside her body. Her disbelieving eyes rested on her husband's face.

He smiled at her.

'Was this what you wanted, Emily?' His tone had changed – serene, understanding, as if he'd suddenly found eternal peace within himself. 'This is all your fault. And I hope you rot in hell for it.' Ray tilted his head back and placed the barrels of the shotgun under his chin. His finger tightened its grip on the trigger.

Emily convulsed in anticipation of what was about to happen, and in realization of what Ray had done. He'd lost his mind completely. She was certain he'd killed their son, her lover. The contents of her stomach catapulted into her mouth and were blocked by Ray's stitching. She panicked and started to choke. Oxygen couldn't find its way into her lungs.

With his head tilted back, Ray took a deep breath and pulled the trigger. And on that last fraction of a second just before the shotgun hammers were released, he saw them. Hidden between the wooden ceiling boards. He saw them because the light reflected on them and they blinked.

He saw his son's terrified eyes staring straight down at him.

One Hundred and Two

She woke up but didn't open her eyes. She knew she hadn't been unconscious for too long – five, ten minutes maximum. As the damp cloth was pressed against her nose and mouth back at her front door, she recognized the characteristic smell straight away – ether. She also realized that in her crouched position, ambushed by a surprised attack coming from behind her, and against an opponent that was certainly stronger than she was, fighting would have been pointless.

Instinct immediately kicked into action. As soon as she realized that her attacker was using an anesthetic to subdue her, she knew exactly what kind of reaction he'd be expecting from her. She played along, holding her breath for as long as she could and faking a struggle. Her initial mouthful of ether would no doubt knock her out, but not for too long. If she could act convincingly enough that she was fighting her attacker and gasping for air, he would believe that she'd taken in enough breaths to render her unconscious for a long while.

It worked.

Her assailant didn't hold the cloth to her nose for longer than twenty-five seconds, believing she was under.

Now, Captain Blake remained totally still and silent. She could hear the rattling of a car engine. She felt the hard floor under her vibrate and bump every so often. She opened her eyes very slightly to get a better idea of her environment. There was no doubt: she was lying down in the dark back cabin of a van, speeding somewhere. Her hands were tied behind her back, but her feet weren't restrained. That could give her a chance. Her cell phone and handbag were gone – no surprise there.

For now she knew there was nothing she could do but wait.

She had always been very in tune with her mind's clock. She figured they had driven for about an hour before they came to a complete stop. The van seemed to be moving at a reasonable speed for most of the journey, which meant that somehow they'd managed to avoid most of the stop-start traffic Los Angeles was so famous for. Wherever he'd taken her, she was pretty sure it was somewhere out of town.

She heard the driver's door open and then slam shut. He was coming for her. It was show time.

She quickly slid down towards the back door, getting as close to it as she could. She would only have one chance at this. She brought her knees close to her chest and waited. This time the element of surprise was on her side. She heard the doors being unlocked and prepared herself.

As the doors opened, she kicked out as hard as she could. Her feet thundered against her captor's chest. For the first time in her life she wished she had worn stiletto heels to work.

As she'd predicted, it caught her captor totally by surprise. It knocked the breath out of him and sent him tumbling backwards, straight to the ground.

She threw her body forward and pushed herself to the edge of the van's back cabin. Her legs were shaking so hard from fear and adrenalin she was unsure if she'd be able to stand up. As she fought to steady them and jumped out of the van, her eyes quickly scanned her surroundings. The van was parked in front of a large old building, but there was nothing else around except wasteland, unkempt vegetation and the narrow road they'd obviously taken to get there.

Her gaze dropped to the floor and fear rose in her throat like a tsunami. Her captor was gone.

'Fuck!'

Panic took over and she started running in the direction of the road, but she didn't have the proper shoes for it and her hands were still tied behind her back. All she managed was an awkward, wobbly dance for a few strides before her legs were hooked from under her with amazing force and precision. She hadn't even heard him come up behind her again.

She hit the ground hard with a thud, shoulder first, then head. Her vision blurred and all she could see was a figure towering over her.

'So, clever bitch wants to play rough, huh?' His voice was calm but very menacing. 'Well, check this out.'

His fingers closed into a fist.

'It's pain time, whore.'

One Hundred and Three

Whitney Myers checked her watch before answering her cell phone after the third ring.

'Whitney, I've got some information for you,' Leighton Morris said in his usual overexcited voice. Morris was another of Myers' LAPD contacts, who she called upon every now and then when she needed inside information.

'I'm listening.'

'That detective you asked me to keep an eye out for, Robert Hunter . . . ?'

'Yeah, what about him?'

'He boarded a plane early this morning.'

'A plane? Where to?'

'Healdsburg in Sonoma County.'

'Sonoma County? What the hell? Why?'

'That I don't know. But it's certainly something to do with the case he's investigating at the moment, which by the way, is very hush-hush.'

'He left this morning, you said?'

'That's right, and he just booked a return ticket for this afternoon.' There was a brief pause. 'Actually, he should be boarding pretty soon.'

Myers checked her watch again. 'Into LAX?'

'You got it.'

'Do you have the flight details?'

'Right here.'

'OK, text them to me.'

She disconnected and waited.

One Hundred and Four

There were no delays, and Hunter landed at LAX right on schedule. With no luggage to collect, he walked through the gates just minutes after touching down. Garcia was already there, waiting for him with a folder under his arm.

'Are you parked on a meter?' Hunter asked.

Garcia pulled a face. 'Are you crazy? This is official business. We've got perks.'

Hunter smiled. 'OK, let's grab a coffee and I'll run you through everything I got. Anything from Operations or the research team yet?'

'Not a scrap so far. I just checked with them.'

They found an isolated table towards the back of the Starbucks in Terminal One. Hunter proceeded to tell Garcia all he found out about the Harpers. He told him about Andrew's secret place in the attic and the peepholes. He told him about the self-harming and that he was sure that Andrew had somehow survived and witnessed everything that happened that day, twenty years ago. After that, Andrew had vanished.

'If his father was that brutal, how did Andrew survive?'

'I don't know exactly what happened that day. No one does except Andrew. But he's alive. And the pressure cooker in his head finally blew.'

'You mean something triggered it?'

Hunter nodded.

'And there were no pictures of him whatsoever?'

'I couldn't find any. It's a small town, small school. Back then the school's yearbook only featured high-school students. Andrew was in fifth grade when it happened.' He rubbed the scar on his nape. 'I think we were right about the killer using projection and transference together with a deep love for the person the victims remind him of.'

'His mother. The person he loved the most at that age. The person he'd never hurt, no matter what.'

'No matter what.'

'Oedipus complex?'

'I don't think he was in love with his mother in a romantic way, but he was a very shy kid with few friends. His parents were everything to him. In his mind, they could do no wrong.'

'Could his feelings have mutated into a combination of maternal and romantic love all rolled up into one?'

Hunter considered the theory. 'It's possible, why?'

'OK, it's my turn. Let me show you what I found out.' Garcia flipped open the folder he'd brought with him and took out the music magazine he'd found in Jessica Black's apartment. He quickly ran Hunter through what had happened with Mark Stratton, how he'd failed to control himself, and how he'd completely trashed a possible abduction scene. 'By chance I came across this magazine when I was in their apartment. There's an interview with Jessica Black in it. In a particular section, the interviewer asked her about love.'

'What about it?'

'He asked her what true love meant to her.' Garcia pushed

the magazine over to Hunter and pointed to some highlighted lines. 'That was her answer.'

Hunter's eyes went over the lines and he paused. His heart skipped several beats. He read them again.

'To me true love is something uncontrollable. Like a fire that burns really bright inside you and consumes everything around it.'

'A fire that burns bright inside you?' Garcia said, shaking his head. 'It didn't sound like a coincidence to me. So I went back to the office and searched the net . . . found nothing. I then remembered you told me how good the magazine archives were at the public library, so I took a trip downtown.'

'And . . . ?'

'I found this.' From the folder he retrieved a copy of the printout he had got from the library and pushed it over towards Hunter. 'An interview with Kelly Jensen for *Art Today* magazine. Another question about true love and how she viewed the subject.' He pointed to the highlighted lines. 'Check her answer out.'

Love hurts, and true love hurts even more. I must admit that I haven't been very lucky in that department. My last experience was very painful to me. It made me realize that love can be like a crazy knife that sits inside you, and at any moment it can simply flick open. And when it does it cuts you. It slices through everything inside you. It makes you bleed. And there's very little you can do about it.

'Shit,' Hunter whispered, running a hand through his hair.

'In the library I couldn't find any similar articles on Laura Mitchell. Then I had this crazy idea of going back to James Smith's apartment.'

'Best collection of magazines and articles you'll ever find on Laura.'

'Exactly,' Garcia agreed. 'It took me a few hours, but I found this.' He handed Hunter the copy of *Contemporary Painters*.

Another question about love. Hunter read the highlighted lines – *True love is the most incredible thing. Something you can't control. Something that explodes inside you like a bomb when you're least expecting it and you're totally consumed by it.*

'He's giving them love,' Garcia said. 'Not his love, but what they consider to be true love, according to what he'd read. According to their own words.'

Hunter agreed mutely. 'His mind is in a real mess. He's got no understanding of what love is. And I'm not surprised. To Andrew real love was what his parents had between them, but what he witnessed that night shattered that understanding into a million little pieces, and he's been trying to put them back together ever since.'

'OK, but why now?' Garcia asked. 'If the trauma occurred twenty years ago, why is he only acting now?'

'Traumas aren't straightforward, Carlos,' Hunter explained, 'no psychological wound is. Many traumas suffered by people at one stage or another in their lives will never manifest themselves into actions. A lot of the time not even the traumatized person knows what catalyzes it. It just suddenly explodes inside their heads and they have no control over themselves. In Andrew's case, just seeing Laura, Kelly or Jessica's picture on a magazine or newspaper could've done it.'

'Because they didn't just resemble his mother physically, but they were the same age she was when she died, and they were all artists.'

'Exactly.' Hunter's cell phone started ringing – the screen said *Restricted Call.*

'Detective Hunter,' he said, bringing the phone to his ear.

'Hello, Detective. How did you like my birth city?'

Hunter's surprised stare shot in Garcia's direction. 'Andrew . . . ?'

One Hundred and Five

Garcia's eyes widened in surprise. He thought he'd heard wrong, but the expression on Hunter's face left little doubt.

'Andrew Harper . . . ?' Hunter repeated, keeping his voice steady.

A chuckle came down the phone. 'No one has called me Andrew in twenty years.' The sentence was delivered in a calm tone. His voice like a muffled whisper. Hunter remembered the whispering voice he'd heard on the recording Myers had retrieved from Katia Kudrov's answering machine.

'Do you miss being called by your real name?' Hunter's tone matched Andrew's.

Silence.

'I know you were there, Andrew. I know you saw what happened that day in your house. But why did you run? Where did you go? Why didn't you allow people to help you?'

'Help me?' He laughed.

'No one could've coped with what you went through alone. You needed help then. You need help now.'

'Cope? How could anyone cope with watching his father transform into a monster right in front of his eyes? A father who only hours earlier had given me the best presents I'd ever got. A father who'd promised me that everything would be fine. That there'd be no more fights. A father who said that he loved my mother and me more than anything. What kind of love is that?'

Hunter didn't have an answer.

'I've researched you. You used to be a psychologist, didn't you? Do you think you could've helped me cope?'

'I would've done my best.'

'That's bullshit.'

'No, it isn't. Life isn't meant for us to go through it on our own. We all need help from time to time. No matter how strong or tough we think we are. A person alone just can't deal with certain life situations. Especially not when you're only ten years old.'

Silence.

'Andrew?'

'Stop calling me Andrew. You don't have the right to do that. No one does. Andrew died that night, twenty years ago.'

'OK. What name would you like me to call you?'

'You don't need to call me anything. But since you were so kind to fuck everything up. To go digging into something you had no right to, I have a surprise for you too. I take it that your phone has video-streaming capabilities, right?'

Hunter frowned.

'I'm sending you a short video I made earlier. I hope you enjoy it.'

The line went dead.

'What happened?' Garcia asked.

Hunter shook his head. 'He's sending me some sort of video.'

'A video? Of what?'

Hunter's phone beeped – *Incoming video request.*

'I guess we're just about to find out.'

One Hundred and Six

Hunter immediately pressed the yes button accepting the request. Garcia moved closer and craned his neck. Their eyes were glued to the small progress bar on Hunter's cell phone screen as it filled itself up very slowly. Time seemed to drag.

The phone finally beeped again – *Download complete. Watch it now?*

Hunter pressed yes again.

The picture was grainy, the quality substandard. It had obviously been recorded using a cheap cell phone camera, but there was no doubt who they were looking at.

'What the fuck?' Garcia moved even closer.

Tied to a metal chair in the center of an empty room was a woman. Her head was slumped forward, her dark hair falling over her face covering her features. But neither Hunter nor Garcia needed to see her face to know who she was.

'Am I going crazy?' Garcia asked, wide-eyed, the color draining from his face.

No words left Hunter's lips.

'How the fuck did he get Captain Blake?' Garcia's eyes were still cemented to the screen.

Still silence from Hunter.

The video played on.

Captain Blake slowly lifted her head and Hunter felt something close tight around his heart. She was bleeding from the nose and mouth and her left eye had almost swollen shut. She didn't look drugged, just in severe pain. The picture focused on her face for just a few more seconds before fading to black.

'This is crazy,' Garcia said, fidgeting like a kid.

Hunter's phone rang again. He answered it immediately.

'If you're wondering,' the whispering voice said, 'she's still alive. So I'd be very careful of your next move. 'Cause how long she stays that way depends on it. Back off.'

The line disconnected.

'What did he say?'

Hunter told him.

'Shit. This is so messed up. Why take the captain? And why send us a video? That's completely contrary to his MO. He hasn't done that with any of the previous victims.'

'Because Captain Blake isn't like any of the previous victims, Carlos. She doesn't remind him of his mother. He didn't take her for that reason. She's security . . . a bargaining tool.'

'What?'

'On the phone he said, "Be very careful of your next move. 'Cause how long she stays alive depends on it. Back off." He's using her as a guarantee.'

'Why?'

''Cause we're getting close, and he wasn't expecting it. We know who he is . . . or used to be. He knows it's just a matter of hours before we catch up with him.'

Garcia bit his bottom lip. 'He's panicking.'

'Yes. That's why the video. And when they panic and deviate from their original plan, they make mistakes.'

'We don't have time to wait for him to make a mistake, Robert. He's got the captain.'

'He's already made the mistake.'

'What? What mistake?'

Hunter pointed to his phone. 'He sent us a video. We need Internet access.'

'Internet?' Garcia frowned. 'Can we trace it?'

'I don't think so. He's not that stupid.'

'So why do we need the Internet?'

Hunter looked around and saw a thirty-something man sitting at a table in the corner. He was typing into his laptop.

'Excuse me, are you online?'

The man looked up, his gaze quickly jumping from Hunter to Garcia, who was right behind his partner. The man nodded skeptically. 'Yeah.'

'We need to borrow your computer very quickly,' Hunter said, having a seat and pulling the laptop towards him.

The man was about to say something when Garcia placed a hand on his shoulder, showing him his badge.

'Los Angeles Homicide Division, this is important.'

The man lifted both hands in the air in surrender and stood up.

'I'll be right over there.' He pointed to the corner. 'Take your time.'

'Why do you need the Internet all of a sudden?' Garcia asked, taking a seat next to Hunter.

'Give me a sec.' He was busy Googling something. A web page loaded and he scanned it as fast as he could.

'Fuck.'

Hunter grabbed his phone and watched the video again, frowning at it.

'Damn.'

He Googled something else. A new page loaded and he scanned it again. 'Oh shit,' he whispered, checking his watch. 'Let's go,' he said, standing up.

'Go where?'

'Santa Clarita.'

'What? Why?'

'Because I know where the captain is being held.'

One Hundred and Seven

Aided by Garcia's car's lights and siren, they were eating ground fast. They hooked onto Interstate 405 and Garcia hit the fast lane doing eighty-five miles an hour.

'OK, how do you know where the captain is being held?' Garcia asked.

Hunter played the video again and showed his partner. 'Because she told me.'

'Huh?'

'Pay attention to her lips.'

Garcia's attention diverted from the road for just a second, enough for him to notice the captain's lips moving ever so slightly.

'I'll be damned.'

'The captain knew there was only one reason Andrew was shooting this video. She knew we would watch it.'

'More to the point,' Garcia added, 'she knew *you* would watch it. So what did she say?'

'St Michael's Hospice.'

'What?'

'That's why I needed the Internet. I thought she'd said St Michael's *Hospital*. But there isn't one, there never was. So I watched the video again and realized she'd said *hospice*, not hospital. St Michael's Hospice in Santa Clarita closed down nine years ago, after a fire destroyed most of the building.' Hunter typed the address into Garcia's GPS navigational system. 'There it is.'

'Shit,' Garcia said. 'Out towards the hills. Completely isolated.'

Hunter nodded.

'So if we suspect that's where the captain is being held, why are we going there without a SWAT team?'

'Because Andrew said that how long the captain lived depended on our actions. He's somehow monitoring what we do.'

'How?'

'I don't know, Carlos. But he called me just minutes after I landed. I'd been away less than a day. How the hell did he know I'd gone to Healdsburg this morning?'

Garcia had no answer.

'SWAT teams are great, but they aren't exactly subtle. If Andrew gets a sniff that we might know where he is, he'll get to Captain Blake a lot faster than we or any SWAT team can get to him. And then it's game over.'

'So what are we gonna do?'

'Everything we can. We might be able to surprise him. He doesn't know that we know. The surprise factor is on our side. If we do this right, we can end this – now.'

Garcia stepped on the gas.

One Hundred and Eight

In Santa Clarita they drove up Sand Canyon Way in the direction of the hills and turned right into a small narrow road that ran another five hundred yards towards the entrance to the old St Michael's Hospice.

'We better come off-road somewhere around here and walk the rest of the way,' Hunter said as they got within two hundred yards of the entrance. 'I don't wanna alert him that we're coming.'

Garcia nodded and found a hidden place behind some tall trees to leave the car.

They quickly walked the rest of the way through the high vegetation and found a covered position about seventy-five yards from the derelict St Michael's Hospice building.

It was a two-story rectangular structure covering around one thousand square feet. Most of the outside shell had crumbled, the majority of the roof had caved into the top floor, and there were clues everywhere that a large fire had taken place some time ago. At certain spots they could see right through the building. Debris was scattered all around the grounds.

'Are you sure about this?' Garcia asked. 'There seems to be nothing here.'

Hunter pointed to the ground around what used to be the building's main entrance – a series of fresh tire tracks.

'Someone has been here recently.'

The tracks led away from the front of the building and disappeared around and towards the back – the only place where the walls seemed intact. Hunter and Garcia spent a few minutes observing from a distance, looking for surveillance cameras or any other signs of security or life. Nothing.

'Let's get closer,' Hunter said.

The tire tracks stopped by a large staircase and wheelchair ramp that led down into the building's underground floor. There were several footprints on the steps, going in both directions. They all seemed to belong to the same person.

'Whatever's happening here, it's down there.' Garcia nodded at the stairs.

Hunter pulled out his gun.

'Only one way to find out. Are you ready for this?'

Garcia grabbed his weapon. 'No, but let's do it anyway.'

One Hundred and Nine

Surprisingly, the double swing doors at the bottom of the staircase weren't locked. Hunter and Garcia pushed them open and stepped inside.

The first room was an old-style reception lobby. A battered semicircular counter was fixed to the wall on the left. Broken furniture was scattered around everywhere, covered in dust and old rags. Beyond the reception counter there was another set of swing doors.

'I don't like this one bit,' Garcia whispered. 'There's something just not right about this place.'

Hunter looked around slowly. He still could see no surveillance cameras or any other type of security against intruders. He nodded at Garcia and they both carefully approached the new set of doors.

Hunter tried the handles – unlocked. They moved through.

The doors led them into a wide corridor, stretching for about thirty-five feet. One single dim light bulb kept it from plunging into total darkness. From where they were standing they could see only one door, halfway down the corridor.

'OK, I'm not one to believe in vibes, or auras, or crap like that,' Garcia said, 'but there's definitely something fucked-up about this place. I can feel it in my soul.'

They kept moving stealthily forward until they reached the lonely door on their left. Again – unlocked. They moved inside.

The room was about twenty-five feet by twenty, and was kitted out like a carpenter's workshop. A large wooden drawing desk, a heavy-duty workstation counter, two old metal filing cabinets, wall-mounted shelves, and a paraphernalia of instruments and tools hanging from the walls and scattered around the room.

Hunter and Garcia stood still for a moment, taking everything in. When they finally approached the drawing desk, they froze.

'Holy shit,' Garcia whispered. His eyes settled on the building plans and the photographs on the desk. They showed one item only. An object they'd seen before. The fan-out knife that was retrieved from inside Kelly Jensen's body.

Across the room, Hunter recognized the items inside a small box on top of the workstation – the self-activating clicking mechanism. There were three of them, ready to be used. Next to them he found another box with two aluminum tubes. Hunter and Garcia didn't need to look at them closely to know exactly what they were – practice runs for the flare that was inserted into Jessica Black's body. This was his creative chamber of horrors, Hunter thought. His death factory.

'Look at this,' Garcia said, checking some of the other drawings on the desk. 'Plans for the bomb used on Laura Mitchell.'

An uneasy silence followed.

Garcia allowed his eyes to roam the room one more time. 'He can build almost any sort of torture and death instrument in here.'

Hunter's eyes were also rechecking the room – ceiling, corners, strategic places . . . Still he could see no surveillance of any kind.

'Here we are!' Garcia said, reaching for a sheet of paper he found stuck to the wall.

'What have you got?'

'Looks like the underground floor plan for this place.'

Hunter moved closer and studied the drawing. The corridor they were in led into a new, transversal hallway. That hallway went around in a large squared path. Four corridors, and according to the plans they were looking at, each corridor held two rooms. There was no other exit on the other side. The only way out was to come back to where they were and go up the stairs they'd come down from.

Garcia felt his blood run cold. 'Eight rooms. He can keep up to eight victims here at once?'

Hunter nodded. 'It seems that way.'

'Fuck. This guy is sick.'

Hunter paused and turned around. He had noticed something hanging from the wall before, but he didn't pick up on it. A large metal key ring with several skeleton keys.

'I bet these open the rooms.'

Garcia nodded. 'Let's go give them a try.'

They stepped out of the drawing room and, as quickly and quietly as they could, moved onto the transversal hallway at the end of the corridor they were in. They came out exactly at the center of the hallway. In total, this corridor stretched for sixty or seventy feet. Just like the previous one, a single dim light bulb behind a metal mesh on the wall kept it from total darkness.

'So, what would you like to do?' Garcia asked. 'Split up or go together?'

'Let's give ourselves a better chance and move together. That way we can cover each other.'

Garcia nodded. 'Good call. Which way?'

Hunter pointed right.

Once again they moved in almost complete silence. They quickly got to the first room towards the end of the corridor. A very sturdy and thick timber door. At the bottom of it there was a food hatch. Hunter fumbled through the keys in the large key ring, trying each one. He found the correct key on his third attempt.

Hunter gave Garcia a quick nod, who responded in the same way. They were as ready as they'd ever be.

Both detectives held their breath as Hunter stood with his back against the wall to the right of the door and pushed it open in one fast movement. Immediately, Garcia stepped inside, both of his arms stretched out, his weapon held by a double-hand grip. He was followed a fraction of a second later by Hunter.

The room was in complete darkness, but the tiny amount of light that seeped through from the corridor outside allowed them to understand its setup. It was small, maybe only ten feet in depth by seven wide. There was a metal bed pushed up against one of the walls and a bucket on the floor to the right of the bed; nothing else. The walls were made of red bricks and the floor was concrete. It looked like a medieval dungeon, and if fear had a smell, that room was drenched in it. There was no one in there.

Garcia breathed out and cringed. 'Damn, look at this place, man. Stephen King couldn't have imagined this hellhole.'

Hunter closed the door silently and he and Garcia moved on. The corridor swung left. Hunter went through the same process, trying each key as he reached the first door in this new hallway. The room was identical to the first one and again in total darkness. There was no one in there either.

Garcia started fidgeting.

They reached the next door and the process started again. As Hunter pushed the door open and they stepped inside with their weapons at the ready, they heard a faint and frightened cry.

One Hundred and Ten

Hunter and Garcia paused by the door. Both of their guns aiming at whoever or whatever had made that noise, but neither of them fired. Due to the darkness, it took Hunter a couple of seconds to spot her. She was pressed against one of the corners of the room, curled up into a tiny ball. Her knees were tight against her chest. Her arms hugging her legs so hard the blood seemed to have drained from them. Her eyes were wide open, staring at the door and the two new arrivals. One word could describe her whole being – fear.

Hunter recognized her straight away – Katia Kudrov.

He holstered his gun and quickly lifted his hands up in a surrender gesture.

'We're Los Angeles police officers,' he announced in the calmest voice he could muster. 'We've been looking for you for a while, Katia.'

Katia burst into tears, her body convulsing with emotion. Hunter stepped into the room and approached her very slowly.

'You're gonna be OK, we're here now.'

Her eyes were still wide, staring at Hunter as if he was an illusion. Her breathing was coming to her in bursts. Hunter feared she was too shocked to speak.

'Can you talk?' he asked. 'Are you hurt?'

Katia sucked in a deep breath through her nose and nodded.

'Ye— yes, I can talk. No— no, I'm not hurt.'

Hunter kneeled down before her and took her in his arms. She hugged him tight and broke down in a barrage of desperate tears and high-pitched yelps. Hunter felt as though he was absorbing her fear through his skin.

Garcia stood by the door, both hands wrapped firmly around his gun, his gaze incessantly moving up and down the corridor outside.

Katia's eyes met Hunter's. 'Than— thank you.'

'Are there others here?'

She nodded. 'I think so. I never saw anyone. I'm never let out of this room. The lights are always off. But I'm sure I heard something one day. I mean, I heard some*one*. Another woman.'

Hunter nodded. 'You are the first one we found, we've gotta look for others.'

Katia's arms tightened further around Hunter. 'No . . . don't leave me.'

'We're not leaving you. You're coming with us. Can you walk?'

Katia breathed out and nodded.

Hunter helped her stand up. She looked much skinnier than the pictures he'd seen of her.

'When was the last time you ate?'

She gave him a tiny shrug. 'I don't know. The food and the water are drugged.'

'Do you feel dizzy?'

A succession of quick nods. 'A little, but I can walk.'

Hunter's questioning gaze moved to Garcia.

'We're good here, let's move.'

Hunter moved Katia in between him and Garcia and drew his weapon again. They stepped towards the door cautiously, ready to brave the corridors again.

All of a sudden all the lights went off.

They were left in absolute darkness.

For an instant all three of them were frozen to the spot. Katia let out another cry, but the fear in her voice this time almost chilled the air.

'Oh my God, he's here.'

Hunter reached for her again. 'It's all right, Katia. It's gonna be OK. We're still here with you.' As his hand touched her arm, he felt her shivering.

'No yo— you don't understand. It won't be OK.'

'What do you mean?' Garcia whispered.

'He's like a ghost. He moves like a ghost. You can't hear him when he comes for you.' She started crying and her voice faltered. 'And . . . he . . . he can see you but you can't see him.' Her breathing accelerated. 'He can see in the dark.'

One Hundred and Eleven

Hunter pulled Katia into his arms again.

'Katia, it'll be OK. We'll get out of here.'

'No . . .' Desperation took over her voice. 'You're not listening. We can't hide from him. There's nowhere we can go where he won't find us. We won't get out of here alive. He could be standing behind you right now and you wouldn't know. Unless he wanted you to.'

That statement sent a shiver up Garcia's spine and he mechanically extended his left arm like a blind man, feeling the space around him – nothing but air.

'I could never see him,' Katia continued, 'but I sensed him many times, right here, in the room with me. He wouldn't say a word. He wouldn't make a sound, but I knew he was there, watching me, just observing. I never heard him come in or go out. He moves like a ghost.'

'OK,' Hunter said. 'The three of us moving blind isn't a great idea. We won't be able to cover each other.'

'What do you wanna do?' Garcia whispered.

'Katia, stay in here. Stay in the room.'

'What?'

'I've been checking every inch of this place. He's got no surveillance. There are no cameras, no microphones, nothing. He might know that we're here, but there's no way he can be sure that we've gotten to you or to anyone else. If you stay in the room just like you've been doing since the day you were captured, he's got no reason to be angry with you.'

'No . . . no. I'd rather die than stay here alone for another second. You don't know what I've been through. I can't stay here. Please don't leave me here to face him again. You can't leave me here alone.'

'Katia, listen, if the three of us move out of this room together right now, and if this guy can see in the dark and move as silently as you said he can, we've got no chance.'

'No . . . I can't stay here alone. Please don't make me stay here alone. I'd rather die.'

'I'll stay with you.' Garcia said. 'Robert is right. We won't be able to cover each other if we move out of here together. He could easily pick us out one by one and we wouldn't even know. I'll stay here with you. As Robert said, he doesn't know which room we're in. For all he knows you're here, alone, just like you were minutes ago. I'll stay. There's no way he can know I'm with you. If this door opens without the person identifying himself, I'll smoke the bastard.' He cocked his gun and Katia jumped.

'It's a good idea,' Hunter agreed.

'Why don't you stay too,' Katia pleaded. 'Why can't we all just wait for him in here and fight him together? We've got a better chance that way.'

'Because he might not come directly here,' Hunter explained. 'We know for sure that he's got at least one more victim held hostage. Our captain. He might go straight for her just to punish us. I have to try and find her before he gets to her. I can't just sit here and wait. Her life depends on it.'

'He's right, Katia,' Garcia said.

'We can't waste any more time,' Hunter took over again. 'Trust me, Katia. I'll be back for you.'

Garcia put his arm around Katia and slowly brought her back into the room.

'Good luck,' he said as Hunter closed the door behind him and took a deep breath.

This already looks like a bad idea, he thought. *Walking around in pitch-dark corridors, fighting a killer blind. What the hell am I thinking?*

Hunter knew that there were about twenty feet between him and the end of the corridor. No more doors on this stretch. He moved cautiously, but he moved fast. The hallway swung left again. He stood still, listening as hard as he could.

Nothing except absolute silence.

Hunter had always been good at identifying sounds. Sneaking up on him would be a tough task. Though Katia had told him that Andrew could see in the dark and move like a ghost, he couldn't believe anyone could be that quiet.

He was wrong.

One Hundred and Twelve

Andrew stood just a few meters from Hunter, observing, his breathing so quiet and smooth that even a person standing inches from him wouldn't have noticed him. He'd heard the entire conversation just moments earlier. He knew Garcia had stayed in the room with Katia. But he'd deal with them later. A satisfied smile parted his lips. He could see the anxiety on Hunter's face. He could sense the tension in his movements. Hunter had guts, Andrew had to give him that. He'd knowingly walked into a fight he couldn't win.

Hunter started moving forward again. His left hand in constant contact with the corridor's internal wall as he searched for the next door.

Five steps were all he managed.

The first blow came to his gun hand, so powerful and precise it almost snapped his wrist in two. Hunter never heard a thing. He never sensed another presence. Katia was right. Andrew could see in the dark. There was no other way he could have delivered such an accurate strike.

Hunter's gun left his hand like a rocket propelled into the air. He heard it hit the ground somewhere in front of him and to his right. Instinctively, he pulled back and assumed a fighting position, but how do you fight when you can't see or hear your opponent?

Somehow Andrew had moved around Hunter, because the next blow came from behind him, straight to the lower back. Hunter was catapulted forward and he felt an agonizing pain creep up his spine.

'I guess you decided not to take my advice,' Andrew said, his voice firm and confident – familiar to Hunter. 'Bad move, Detective.'

Hunter turned in the direction of the voice and blindly delivered a punch around chest height. He hit nothing but air.

'Wrong again.' This time the voice came from Hunter's left, just inches away.

How could he move so fast and so quietly?

Hunter twisted his body and swung his elbow around as fast and as hard as he could, but Andrew had moved again. And again, Hunter hit nothing.

The next punch hit Hunter in the stomach. It was so well placed and powerful he doubled over and tasted acrid bile in his mouth. No time to react. A quick follow-up punch hit him on the left side of his face. Hunter felt his lip split and the bitter taste in his mouth was quickly substituted by a metallic and sharp one – blood.

Hunter swung his arm around again. A desperate attempt from someone who knew this war was lost. He couldn't even defend himself. The only thing he could do was wait for the next blow. And it came in the form of a low kick to the knee. A jolt of pain ran up Hunter's leg and gravity sent him plunging to the floor. His back and head slammed against the wall behind him hard. Andrew wasn't only invisible and soundless; he knew how to fight too.

'The question is,' Andrew said, 'should I keep on beating you up until you're dead . . . or should I use your gun and end this with a bullet to your head?'

'Andrew, you don't have to do this.' Hunter's voice was heavy, defeated, and gurgling in blood.

'I told you not to call me Andrew.'

'OK,' Hunter accepted it. 'Do you want me to call you Bryan? Bryan Coleman?' Hunter had finally recognized his voice.

Silence, and for the first time Hunter sensed Andrew's hesitation.

'That's the new identity you chose for yourself, right? Bryan Coleman? Director of Production at the A & E TV network. We sat face to face just a couple of days ago.'

'Wow,' Andrew said, clapping his hands. 'Your reputation is well deserved. You figured out something no one else could.'

'Your identity isn't a secret any more,' Hunter carried on. 'Whatever happens here tonight, the LAPD know who you are now. You can't stay in the dark forever.' Hunter paused, took a deep breath and felt his lungs burn with pain. 'You need help, Bryan. Somehow, alone, for twenty years, you managed to cope with something that no one could handle on their own.'

'You don't know anything, Detective. You have no idea what I've been through.'

Andrew had moved again. His voice was now coming from Hunter's right.

'I spent three days in that attic, hiding, scared, trying to decide what to do.' He paused. 'I decided I didn't wanna stay in Healdsburg. I didn't wanna be taken away to some orphanage somewhere. I didn't wanna be the kid everyone had pity on. So I waited into night-time and then I ran. It was quite easy to hide in the back of a truck at the interstate gas station.'

Hunter remembered that the Harpers' old family house was less than half a mile from Interstate 101.

'You'd be surprised how easy it is for a kid to survive on the streets of a big city like LA. But being away from Healdsburg didn't help. For twenty years I've had the same images playing in my head every time I close my eyes.'

Hunter coughed a red mist of blood. 'What happened in your house twenty years ago wasn't your fault, Bryan. You can't blame yourself for what your father did.'

'My father loved my mother. He gave his life for her.'

'He didn't give his life *for* her. He took his life as well as hers in a moment of rage.'

'BECAUSE SHE BETRAYED HIM.' The shout came from directly in front of Hunter, but too far away for him to react. 'He loved her with every beat of his heart. It took me years to understand what had really happened. But now I know that he took her life and his for love . . . pure love.'

Hunter had been right, Andrew's vision of what true love meant was completely distorted, but arguing it right now was pointless. Hunter needed to try and calm him down, not irritate him further.

'It's still not your fault,' he said.

'SHUT UP. You don't know what happened. You don't know what caused my father to lose his mind. But I'll tell you . . . *I* did. I told him. It was *all my fault*.'

One Hundred and Thirteen

Hunter sensed the anguish and pain in Andrew's voice. Pain that came from deep inside. Something he had been carrying with him for all these years.

'How do you think my father found out about Mr. Gardner and my mother?' Andrew asked.

Hunter hadn't thought of that, but he didn't need to reflect for long to know the answer.

'I saw them together one day. I saw them in my parents' room, in my parents' bed. I knew what they were doing was wrong . . . really wrong.' A desperate quiver had found its way into Andrew's voice, the memory still way too vivid in his mind. 'I didn't know what to do. Somehow I knew that what my mom was doing would destroy her marriage to my father. I didn't want that to happen. I wanted them to be happy again . . . together.' He hesitated for an instant.

'So you told your father,' Hunter whispered.

'A week before it all happened. I told him that I saw Nathan Gardner coming into our house one day. That was all I told him, nothing else.' The hurt in his voice grew stronger. 'I didn't know that my father would be capable of . . .' He trailed off.

'Still not your fault,' Hunter said again. 'As you've said,

you didn't know your father would react the way he did. Your intention was to save your parents' marriage, to keep them together. His reaction wasn't your fault.'

Silence took over for a moment.

'Do you know what I remember the most about my mother?' Andrew had moved yet again. 'She told me that when I was her age I'd find someone just like her – beautiful . . . talented . . . Someone I could fall in love with.' He paused for a second. 'I've waited for that birthday for twenty years. For the day that I could finally start choosing my perfect partner.'

Suddenly everything started to make sense to Hunter. They'd been right. The women Andrew Harper kidnapped symbolized a combination of maternal and romantic love. He wanted to fall in love with them, but he also wanted – needed – them to look like his mother. She had told him that when he was thirty, her exact age when she died, he'd find his perfect match, someone just like her. Hunter had checked Andrew's birth certificate. His birthday was on February 22 – two days before Kelly Jensen, his first kidnap victim, had been taken. Andrew had been searching for his victims for a while, but his subconscious prohibited him from taking any action until his thirtieth birthday. In his fragile mind, his mother's words were a rule that couldn't be broken. He had been waiting for that birthday for a very long time. And he'd lost no time when that day arrived. Andrew's mind had distorted what his mother had said in a way only a severely traumatized mind could.

'So you found them,' Hunter said. 'Women who looked just like your mother. Who were as talented as she was—'

'No one could ever be as talented as my mother.' Anger returned to Andrew's voice.

'I'm sorry,' Hunter corrected himself. 'You found candidates for your love . . . and took them from their homes . . . studios . . . cars . . . But you couldn't fall in love with them, could you?'

Silence.

'You took them and you held them captive. You watched them in silence every day, just like you did with your mother. But the longer you watched them, the more they reminded you of her, didn't they? That's why you couldn't touch them in a sexual way, or in any other way. You couldn't hurt them either. But unfortunately the memory of your mother brought back something else.'

Hunter wiped his mouth of the blood.

'It reminded you of her betrayal to your father's love,' he continued. 'Her betrayal to *your* love. Her betrayal to your family. And in the end, instead of falling in love, you hated them. You hated them for that betrayal. You hated them for the exact same reason you took them in the first place. For reminding you of your mother.'

Andrew didn't reply.

'So just like your father, you allowed rage to take over, and when it did, it took you right back to that day and what you saw him do to your mother.'

Again, no reply, but Hunter sensed anxiety in the air.

'We found the interviews, Andrew. We found the questions you put to them about true love.'

'I gave them what they always wanted.'

'No, you didn't. You distorted their words. Just like you distorted your mother's words. Your mother *did* want you to find love, but not this way. You need help, Andrew.'

'STOP CALLING ME ANDREW.' The yell reverberated all around the underground floor. 'You think you know me?

You think you know about my life, my pain? You don't know SHIT. But if you like pain, I'll give you pain.'

The fresh blow hit Hunter on the right side of his face, filling his mouth with blood again, and sending him back to the floor. It took him several seconds to regain composure.

'And now, I have a surprise for you, Detective . . .'

There was an uneasy silence, followed by the sound of something heavy, like a sack of potatoes, being dragged across the floor.

'Wake up, bitch.'

Hunter heard faint slapping sounds, as if Andrew was tapping someone's cheeks, trying to revive them.

'Wake up,' he said again.

'Umm,' a female voice whispered and Hunter held his breath.

'C'mon now,' Andrew said. 'Wakey, wakey.'

'Umm,' she said again.

From the sound she made Hunter could tell that she was gagged, and in a lot of pain.

'Captain . . . ?' he called, jerking his body forward.

Andrew laughed. 'Where do you think you're going?' He rammed the heel of his boot onto Hunter's chest, sending him crashing against the wall behind him again.

'Umm . . . umm . . .' She sounded frantic, but the gag around her mouth had been tied too tight.

'Captain . . . ?' Hunter called again in a desperate breath.

'I guess it's time we all said goodbye to each other,' Andrew said. 'I'm sick of this shit.'

'Ummmmmm!' This time her tone was full of fear.

'Andrew, don't do this.' Hunter tried moving forward one more time, but again he was kicked back to the wall. He coughed a few times before regaining his breath.

'She's got nothing to do with this. *I* broke your rules, Andrew, not her. If you gotta punish anyone, punish me.'

'Ohhh, how noble, Detective,' Andrew said with disdain. 'You cops are all the same. You all want to be the hero. You never know when to quit, when to give up. Even when it's so obvious you just can't win. And that makes you predictable. So guess what, Detective?'

The pause that followed filled the air with dread.

'This time you don't get to save the day.'

'PLEASE, ANDREW, NO.' Hunter sensed the determination and rage in Andrew's voice and knew he'd run out of time. He lunged himself forward with all the strength he had left, but they had moved again. Hunter reached nothing. 'Captain . . . ?' But all he heard was her dying gurgling cry; a split second later he felt a gush of warm blood hit him across the face and chest.

'NO . . . NO . . . CAPTAIN . . . ?'

Silence.

'Captain . . . ?'

'Sorry, Detective,' Andrew said, sucking in a deep, fulfilling breath. 'I don't think she's listening any more.'

The smell of blood intoxicated the air.

'Why, Andrew? Why did you have to do this?' Hunter shivered with anger.

'Don't be sad, Detective. There's no reason to miss her so much . . . because you're about to join her.' Andrew laughed again. 'Isn't it some sort of dishonor for a cop to be killed with his own gun?'

Hunter heard the sound of a semi-automatic gun being chambered.

In the dark, Andrew lifted Hunter's gun and aimed it directly at his head. Hunter knew it was over. There was nothing more he could do. There was nothing more he could say.

Hunter took a deep breath, and despite the darkness, he kept his eyes open, defiantly staring straight ahead.

The deafening blast that came a fraction of a second later filled the corridor with a sick burning smell.

One Hundred and Fourteen

Bright, burning light exploded in the corridor like a flash grenade. Suddenly, everything was illuminated. Andrew let out such a painful roar it was like he'd been stabbed through the heart, but the pain came from his eyes, as he was almost blinded by the intensity of the brilliance, amplified thousands of times by his night-vision goggles.

Andrew instinctively reached for the device and lifted it from his eyes, but the damage was already done. His eyes were struggling to cope with the light blast they'd received directly to the retina, and he felt dizzy and confused.

It took Hunter just a split second to realize what had happened. From the corner of his eye he could see Garcia standing at one of the turns of the corridor. On the floor in front of him was a flare, burning intensely – one of the trial flares he'd seen just minutes earlier in Andrew's 'factory'.

Garcia had soon realized that the only way anyone could see in the dark was by using a light-enhancing device, like night-vision goggles. And he knew exactly how they worked. From Katia's cell, he had heard Hunter and Andrew fighting. He couldn't just sit there and wait. He knew Hunter was great in hand-to-hand combat, but he wouldn't stand a chance against an opponent he couldn't see. Garcia remembered the 'factory' and the flares. Even in the darkness, he knew he wouldn't get lost in corridors structured to go around in a squared pattern. All he needed was a second of bright light, but to Andrew it would feel like a bomb had gone off inside his eyes.

That was exactly the chance Hunter needed. Without thinking, and in a fraction of a second, he threw his body forward towards Andrew. Garcia did exactly the same. Both of them collided with Andrew at the same time, sending him thundering against the wall. He slammed head first into it with incredible force. The roles had completely reversed. Andrew was totally blinded by the explosion of light, and entirely disoriented by the heavy knock to his head. Just like Hunter moments earlier, Andrew swung his arm around in a desperate attempt to defend himself. But how do you defend yourself from opponents you can't see?

Garcia immediately delivered a well-placed and powerful punch to Andrew's solar plexus. Hunter followed it up with one to his jaw. Andrew's head jolted backwards and hit the wall again with a dull crack.

He passed out immediately.

The last thing Hunter and Garcia saw just before the flare extinguished was Whitney Myers' lifeless body lying on a pool of her own blood on the floor. Her throat slit the entire length of her neck.

One Hundred and Fifteen

Thirty-six hours later – USC University Hospital – Los Angeles.

Hunter knocked twice and pushed the door open. Captain Blake was sitting up in her adjustable bed. Its backrest inclined about forty-five degrees. Her face had been cleaned of all the dried blood, but it still looked black and blue and very battered. Her left eye, lips and nose were still swollen. She looked exhausted, but she certainly didn't sound that way. Her good eye moved towards the door and widened in surprise at the sight of what Hunter and Garcia had brought with them.

'Flowers and chocolate?' she asked skeptically. 'Are you guys getting soft on me? 'Cause two soft detectives is the last thing I need in my department.'

Hunter stepped into the room, and placed the flowers on the small table next to her bed. Garcia did the same with the chocolates.

'You're welcome, Captain,' Hunter said. His bottom lip was also cut and swollen. His eyes carried only half of the sparkle they usually did.

'I'm sorry about Whitney Myers,' the captain said after an uneasy silence.

Hunter said nothing, but the sadness in his eyes intensified.

He knew that Myers' dedication and determination had led her to the killer's clutches, and he could do little to save her. He felt guilty for not answering her call when he was in Healdsburg, and for not calling her back.

'How did Andrew Harper get to her?'

'She was at the airport the day I came back from Healdsburg,' Hunter said. 'And so was Andrew. He spotted her after making the call to me, followed her, and took her as she climbed into her car.'

'How did he know who she was?'

'He probably started following me after Carlos and I talked to him in his office. That same night Whitney and I met in a restaurant in Baldwin Hills. It wouldn't have taken him long to connect the dots.'

'And why was she at the airport?'

'Because she knew I wasn't telling her everything. She had contacts everywhere, even inside Parker Center.'

Captain Blake didn't look surprised.

'Through them she found out I was onto something. She guessed I knew about the kidnapper. And if I wasn't prepared to share information, then she'd find out for herself. She was a very good detective.' He looked away. 'And a very kind person.'

'So she decided to tail you?'

'According to her partner, that was the initial idea, yes.'

The silence returned to the room for a moment longer.

'The other woman?' the captain eventually asked. 'The kidnap victim.'

Hunter nodded. 'Katia Kudrov. She's the violinist concert-mistress for the LA Philharmonic. She was the woman who Whitney was hired to find.'

The captain nodded. 'How is she?'

'Terrified, a little dehydrated and malnourished, but Andrew Harper never touched her. Physically she hasn't been hurt.' He paused for an instant. 'Psychologically . . . she'll need help.'

'Is he talking?'

Hunter tilted his head to one side. 'The psychiatrists are making progress little by little. But this will be a long process. Understandably, Andrew's mind is in a complete mess. We were right. He was kidnapping women who reminded him of his mother, but we were wrong in the assumption that sooner or later they did something to break his projection spell – and made him realize that they weren't who he wanted them to be.'

'On the contrary,' Garcia took over. 'They reminded him of her too much. That remembrance awoke a 20-year-old suppressed feeling that he probably didn't even know it was there . . . and it wasn't *love*.'

'Hate,' Captain Blake guessed.

'Anger,' Hunter corrected her. 'Violent anger. Subconsciously he blamed her for betraying his father . . . destroying his family. He used the knowledge he gained through his interviews and the questions about *true love* to mimic what happened that day in his house. To punish his mother time and time again.'

'How come he wasn't killed by his father?' the captain asked.

Hunter explained that Andrew's father never intended to kill him in the first place. 'Andrew saw everything that happened that day from the attic, and then hid there for three days. When he escaped the house, he hid in the back of a truck at the interstate gas station. By chance, the truck was destined for Los Angeles.'

'He's been here all this time?'

Garcia nodded and took over. 'He slept in the ghettos in South Central and shined shoes in West Hollywood for money. At the age of fourteen he managed to get a job in a clockmaker's and locksmith shop in South Gate. The shop was a family-owned business, run by a childless couple in their sixties – Ted and Louise Coleman. That was where he learned about time triggers, precision mechanisms, building complicated devices, and to pick locks. In fact, he became an expert. It was also where he adopted his new name and identity.'

'Sonofabitch,' the captain said, reaching for the glass of water on the side table.

'He joined *Contemporary Painters* magazine as a runaround boy at the age of nineteen.' Garcia carried on. 'The magazine belongs to the DTP Corporation. They also own *Art Today* magazine and several others, together with the A & E TV network. He was very intelligent, and moved up the ranks fast.'

'A great place to keep an eye out for any female painter or musician who reminded him of his mother,' Hunter added.

'And here's the surprise fact,' Garcia again. 'The St Michael's Hospice building . . . he owns it.'

'*Owns* it?' The captain's stare jumped from detective to detective.

Garcia nodded. 'Bought it a year ago, eight years after a fire destroyed it.' He shrugged. 'What was left of the building was just rotting away. Nobody wanted it, least of all the old owners. He got the whole thing for two thousand bucks. The building was way too far out of town to be crawling with teenagers, drug addicts and drifters. A perfect isolated location. Nobody ever went up there. Few people even knew it existed.'

'What I don't get,' the captain said, 'is why he didn't kill his victims at the hospice? Why take them somewhere else?'

'Because no matter what, they still reminded him of his mother,' Hunter said. 'Despite his anger for what he considered her betrayal, his love for her was undeniable.'

'And that's why he created those trigger mechanisms,' Garcia added. 'So he didn't have to be there when they died. A sort of detachment.'

'Exactly,' Hunter agreed.

'He still could've done that at the hospice,' Captain Blake pushed. 'He could've locked them in a room and left them to their fate.'

'If he did, he'd still have to deal with their dead bodies,' Hunter explained. 'Re-enter the room, dispose of them . . . His brain couldn't cope with the emotion of seeing someone who reminded him so much of his mother dead.'

'The easiest way to avoid all that,' Garcia concluded, 'leave them to their fate somewhere else.'

Captain Blake gently brought her fingers to her swollen lips. 'So the psychiatrists will have a field day with him.'

'More like a summer camp,' Garcia came back. 'The kind of traumatized mind he's got is the stuff of dreams for criminal behavior psychologists.'

The captain's eyes searched for Hunter's. He nodded.

'So after killing six people, this monster will probably end up in a psychiatric institution instead of getting the death penalty,' Captain Blake said, shaking her head. 'As always, we bust our asses to catch the crazy psychos out there, and the goddamn lawyers and the state let them loose.'

'He ain't going loose, Captain,' Hunter said.

'You know what I mean, Robert.' The captain paused and looked at the flowers Hunter had brought her. Her lips almost broke into a smile, but she held it back.

'How did you know?' Hunter asked. 'How did you know where you were?'

Captain Blake explained about how she was abducted, how she pretended to have breathed in large amounts of ether, and her attempt to break away when they got to the hospice.

'When I started running towards the road, I saw the hospice's old sign. I guess I was lucky he decided to make that video. I was afraid I hadn't moved my lips enough for you to be able to read them. I thought he'd see me doing it, so I pretended to be disoriented and moved my lips incoherently, throwing the words in as I did it.'

'Great thinking,' Hunter admitted.

'It saved my life.'

Garcia smiled.

'What are you smiling at?' Captain Blake said, glaring at him.

'I just realized that this is the first time that at the end of a big case I'm not the one with my face all smashed in.'

'Well, that can be easily arranged,' she replied, giving him the evil eye.

'Nope, I like my face like this,' Garcia said. The smile didn't go away.

Everyone went quiet for a moment.

'Thank you,' the captain finally said, looking at Hunter.

Hunter tilted his head in his partner's direction. 'Carlos saved us all when he came up with the flare idea.'

'Well, somebody had to think of something,' Garcia said.

There was a knock at the door and a nurse popped her head through the door.

'OK now, that's enough for today. You must all leave Miss Blake to rest,' she said, her gaze settling on Hunter.

'Rest?' Captain Blake shot back almost laughing. 'Honey, if you think that I'm gonna spend another night in here, you're the one who needs a doctor.'

'The doctor said you should spend at least another twenty-four hours in here under observation,' the nurse replied.

'Do I look like a woman who needs to be observed?'

Hunter lifted both hands in the air and looked at Garcia. 'We've gotta go anyway. We'll leave you two to sort this out.'

'There's nothing to sort out,' the captain blurted. 'I ain't spending another night in here. And that's final.' She could have killed the nurse with her look.

Hunter paused by the door and whispered in the nurse's ear. 'I suggest you sedate her.'

'Oh don't worry, sugar-lips, I was already warned about her.' She tapped her right breast pocket and winked at Hunter. 'I have a needle with her name on it.' She studied Hunter's face for a moment. 'Would you like me to have a look at those cuts and bruises, sweet pie? It looks like you might need a stitching job.'

Hunter and Garcia exchanged a quick look.

'I'll be fine.' Hunter shook his head.

'Are you sure? I'm very good with needle and thread.'

'Positive,' they both said in unison.

Chris Carter

The Executioner

Inside a Los Angeles church, on the altar steps, lies the blood-soaked, decapitated body of a priest. Carefully positioned, legs stretched out, arms crossed over the chest, the most horrifying thing of all is that the priest's head has been replaced by that of a dog. Later, the forensic team discover that, on the victim's chest, the figure 3 has been scrawled in blood.

At first, Detective Robert Hunter believes that this is a ritualistic killing. But as more bodies surface, he is forced to reassess. All the victims died in the way they feared the most. Their worst nightmares have literally come true. But how could the killer have known? And what links these apparently random victims?

Hunter finds himself on the trail of an elusive and sadistic killer, somone who apparently has the power to read his victims' minds. Someone who can sense what scares his victims the most. Someone who will stop at nothing to achieve his twisted aim.

ISBN 978-1-84983-125-3

CHRIS
BRADFORD

PUFFIN

Warning: Do not attempt any of the techniques described within the book without the supervision of a qualified martial arts instructor. These can be highly dangerous moves and result in fatal injuries. The author and publisher take no responsibility for any injuries resulting from attempting these techniques.

PUFFIN BOOKS

UK | USA | Canada | Ireland | Australia
India | New Zealand | South Africa

Puffin Books is part of the Penguin Random House group of companies whose addresses can be found at global.penguinrandomhouse.com.

www.penguin.co.uk
www.puffin.co.uk
www.ladybird.co.uk

First published 2016
001

Set in Sabon LT Std 10.5/15.5 pt by
Palimpsest Book Production Limited, Falkirk, Stirlingshire
Printed in Great Britain by Clays Ltd, St Ives plc

A CIP catalogue record for this book is available from the British Library

ISBN: 978-0-141-35949-6

All correspondence to:
Puffin Books, Penguin Random House Children's
80 Strand, London WC2R 0RL

www.greenpenguin.co.uk

To my goddaughter, Lucinda –
Always there for you

'The best bodyguard is the one nobody notices.'

With the rise of teen stars, the intense media focus on celebrity families and a new wave of millionaires and billionaires, adults are no longer the only target for hostage-taking, blackmail and assassination – kids are too.

That's why they need specialized protection . . .

BUDDYGUARD

BUDDYGUARD is a secret close-protection organization that differs from all other security outfits by training and supplying only young bodyguards.

Known as 'buddyguards', these highly skilled teenagers are more effective than the typical adult bodyguard, who can easily draw unwanted attention. Operating invisibly as a child's constant companion, a buddyguard provides the greatest possible protection for any high-profile or vulnerable young person.

In a life-threatening situation, a buddyguard is the **final** ring of defence.

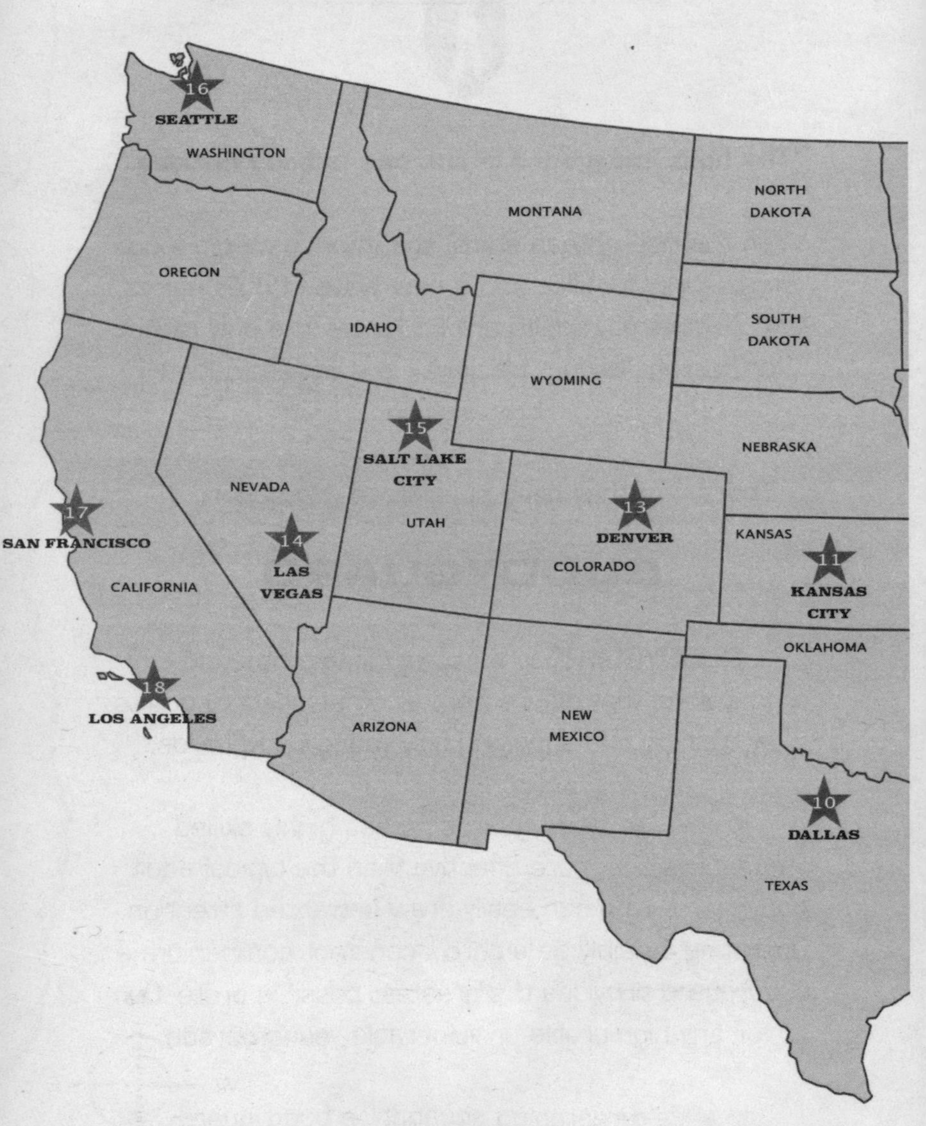
16
SEATTLE
WASHINGTON
MONTANA
NORTH
DAKOTA
OREGON
IDAHO
SOUTH
DAKOTA
WYOMING
15
SALT LAKE
CITY
NEBRASKA
NEVADA
UTAH
13
DENVER
COLORADO
KANSAS
11
KANSAS
CITY
17
SAN FRANCISCO
14
LAS
VEGAS
CALIFORNIA
OKLAHOMA
18
LOS ANGELES
ARIZONA
NEW
MEXICO
10
DALLAS
TEXAS

ASH WILD'S U.S. TOUR

TARGET
PROLOGUE

The hot Californian sun glinted off the SUV's hubcaps as it cruised the quiet suburban street. The man behind the wheel spotted a schoolgirl skipping along the sidewalk, his attention caught by her ponytail of golden-blonde hair flicking from side to side. Judging from the carefree bounce in her step, she was no more than ten years old.

With a quick glance in his rear-view mirror, the driver slowed down. He was almost alongside the girl when a voice cried out, 'Charlotte!'

She stopped and turned. Another girl, petite with almond-shaped eyes, emerged from the porch of a large house. Her pink backpack rode high on her shoulders as she ran across the sun-baked lawn.

'*Nǐ hǎo*, Kerry!' Charlotte called back.

Her friend smiled warmly, revealing a set of braces. 'Hey, your Chinese is getting good.'

'I've been practising,' said Charlotte as the SUV continued past, unnoticed.

'You want to learn some more?' Kerry asked.

'Yeah,' Charlotte replied eagerly. 'We could use it as a secret code at school.'

Kerry moved closer and whispered, 'A best-friend language.' She held up her little finger. 'Friends forever?'

Charlotte entwined her own little finger round Kerry's. 'Friends forever.'

Then, hand in hand, they set off down the road. At the junction the silver SUV with tinted windows pulled up in front of them, and the passenger door swung open.

'Excuse me, girls,' said the driver with a forlorn look. 'Can you help me? I'm a bit lost.'

They both stared at the man, taking in his bald head, reddened cheeks and beginnings of a double chin. Intrigued by his accent, Charlotte asked, 'Are you from England?'

The man nodded. 'On holiday. I'm supposed to meet my daughter at Disneyland, but I missed the junction off the highway.'

'You really are lost,' said Kerry. 'Disneyland's in Anaheim. You're in North Tustin.'

The man sighed and shook his head at the map on the passenger seat. 'American roads! They're almost as wide as they are long. Can you show me exactly where I am?'

'Sure,' said Kerry, leaning in to look at the map.

The man's eyes lingered briefly on Charlotte. Then he turned his full attention to Kerry.

Charlotte noticed an illuminated screen on the dashboard. 'Why not use your satnav?' she suggested.

The man responded with a tight smile. 'Can't work it for the life of me. Rental car.'

Charlotte's eyes narrowed. His explanation was unconvincing; even her dad could work a satnav. 'Kerry, I think we should be go–'

Before Kerry could move, the man rammed a stun gun against her neck. Kerry shrieked, her body juddering with a million volts. Her eyes rolled back and she fell limp. The man seized Kerry's backpack straps and, with a vicious tug, wrenched her body into the footwell.

Shocked by the speed of the attack, Charlotte stood rooted to the spot. She didn't try to grab Kerry, or even call for help. She just watched as the door slammed shut on her best friend. Then the SUV shot off, sped round a corner and disappeared.

TARGET
CHAPTER 1

Four years later . . .

Charley gazed at the thin line of horizon separating sea and sky. In the sun's warm summer glow, she waited for the telltale ripple that would swell into the perfect wave to ride. Yet, as the ocean lapped gently against her surfboard, a shudder of uneasiness swept through her.

On instinct she glanced around but saw only other surfers bobbing on the water, each biding their time for the next decent wave. Charley shook the dark feeling away and focused on the horizon. She was determined not to let old memories surface and cloud the rest of her day.

She surfed to forget.

Out on the water, the rest of the world disappeared. It was just her, the board and the waves.

In the distance a ripple grew into a promising swell. Charley splashed saltwater in her face and ran her hands through her damp sun-bleached hair to clear her mind. Then she heard a name she thought she'd left behind for good.

'Hey, Charlotte!' called a voice. 'Charlotte Hunter?'

Charley turned to see a young, tanned surfer paddle up beside her. No one had called her Charlotte since she'd moved down from North Tustin to San Clemente on the coast.

'It *is* you,' he declared, sitting up on his board. A mop of tousled sandy hair half-covered his eyes but stopped short of concealing the easy smile that greeted her gaze. A couple of years older than Charley, he wore a tight black vest that emphasized his impressive physique.

Good-looking as he was, Charley didn't recognize him. 'Sorry, you've got me confused with someone else,' she said.

The young surfer studied her a moment longer. 'No, it *is* you,' he insisted. 'I saw you a couple of summers back at the Quiksilver surf championships. You were truly awesome! Totally deserved to win. Takes some serious skills to pull off those turns. And that final kickflip was sick!'

Blindsided by his praise, Charley mumbled thanks, then returned her attention to the approaching swell.

'So, where have you been hiding?' he asked, not taking the hint. 'After you won, you kinda dropped off the radar.'

Charley's gaze didn't waver from the horizon and she kept the grief from her voice. 'My parents died in a plane crash.'

The surfer opened then closed his mouth, the lapping of the sea and the breaking of waves on the shoreline filling the awkward silence.

It took all Charley's willpower to suppress the despair that threatened to engulf her. If losing her best friend wasn't enough, her parents had been killed during a terrorist hijacking of a passenger jet only two years after Kerry's kidnapping. The double tragedy had almost broken her.

Charley desperately willed her wave closer. She needed to be in its pocket, surfing at the edge of her ability, where thoughts of her parents – and of Kerry – were drowned out by the sheer power of the ocean.

'No offence, but I like to surf alone,' she said, circling her board round in readiness to catch the oncoming wave.

'Sure . . . I understand,' said the young surfer breezily. 'But if you want to hang out some time we're having a beach party tomorrow night. My name's Bud –' The urgent honking of car horns from the coastal road interrupted his pick-up attempt. 'What's got them so freaked?'

Then they both spotted a huge grey dorsal fin cutting through the waves.

A lifeguard's cry of 'SHARK!' sent a spike of fear through every surfer in the water.

'Let's bail!' said Bud, paddling furiously for the shoreline with every other sane surfer.

But Charley remained where she was. Shark or no shark, she intended to wait for *her* wave. It was a beauty – powerful, glassy and promising a perfect A-frame break. And if she was going to be shark bait, then so be it. In her experience of life so far, she'd learnt that fate had already dealt the cards. She couldn't change the outcome. That fact didn't make her any less scared of the shark. Just realistic.

She watched the ominous fin slice through the water,

then disappear beneath the surface. The presence of the predator at least explained her earlier unease.

With the swell rolling in behind her, Charley began to paddle. She felt the rise of the ocean and the intense energy of the wave building. A familiar thrill pulsed through her veins as her board rapidly picked up speed . . . then, just as she was popping to her feet, the shark broke the surface. It was a great white, some four metres long.

Charley almost wiped out. Only now did she regret letting her stubborn need to surf override her survival instinct. But the shark wasn't interested in her. Its target was a young lad on a long board much closer to shore. Charley watched in mute horror as the great white bore down on its prey, opening its formidable jaws and sinking its teeth into both boy and board, before dragging them under.

Recovering her balance, Charley took the drop down the wave. It was a clean break, offering a safe run all the way to the beach . . . but she made a snap decision to change her line when the boy popped up again. Screaming for help, he was still caught in the jaws of the great white, only his long board preventing him from being torn apart.

She carved her way towards him. She figured she had a slim chance of saving the boy if she could time her descent to collide directly into the shark's head.

Charley had just a second to realize how crazy her stunt was before the tip of her board struck the shark with such force that she flipped over the top. Somersaulting through the air, she plunged head first into the sea. The wave broke hard, barrelling everything along in its path. Charley was spun over and over. Water roared in her ears. For one horrifying moment she believed she might never surface again. Then the mighty wave passed and her head bobbed up in the foaming water.

Gasping for breath, she searched around for the boy. By some miracle her insane plan had worked. The great white had released its death grip, and the boy was floundering a few metres away, blood pouring from his wounds. Retrieving her board on its leash, Charley paddled hard towards him. She could see the great white circling for another attack.

'Take my hand!' she cried.

The boy weakly reached out and Charley pulled him to her just as the enraged shark exploded out of the water. The great white missed the boy by a fraction, its jaws clamping down on to his long board instead. Still attached by the leash, the boy was almost torn from her grip. Charley snatched the small dive knife strapped to her ankle and cut the plastic line.

With blood swirling in the sea, the great white whipped into a feeding frenzy. Within seconds the creature had shredded the long board to pieces, then its cold black eyes turned to Charley. Suppressing a stab of panic, she grabbed the flailing boy and hauled him on to her own board.

'Hold tight,' she told him as the next wave rolled in.

Kicking hard, Charley body-surfed towards the beach. The wave bore them all the way, mercifully dumping them both in the shallows. Four surfers ran in and dragged them the last few metres to the safety of the shore. Once on the beach, the lifeguard began emergency medical treatment on the boy.

'Call an ambulance!' he ordered one of the surfers.

'Will he live?' asked Charley, getting shakily to her feet. She was breathless and her heart pounded. Bystanders were asking if she was all right, but she waved them away.

'I should think so,' the lifeguard replied as he stemmed the boy's blood loss. 'Thanks to you.'

Charley nodded, then retrieved her board and quietly disappeared into the gathering crowd.

TARGET
CHAPTER 2

Having washed the blood off herself and her board, Charley sat down on a secluded sand dune to inspect the damage. Not to her own body, which had escaped with only a few scrapes and bruises, but to her precious surfboard. Remarkably, the board had survived the encounter with the great white. Only the nose had suffered a bad ding. *That'll cost quite a few bucks to get repaired*, she thought. But money was not the problem, as long as her foster-parents allowed her access to the trust-fund account.

For the time being Charley sealed the damage with some epoxy resin from her board bag. As she squeezed the tube's contents over the ding, she noticed her hands were trembling and realized her fixation on the board must be the result of deep shock. She had no idea what had possessed her to tackle a great white head on. It had been insane!

Yet, despite the terrifying encounter, she also felt strangely elated. For the first time in her life she'd confronted death . . . and won.

How Charley wished she'd possessed some of that courage during Kerry's abduction. There wasn't a day that she didn't think of her friend. Despite the state-wide search by police and all the publicity, Kerry had never been found. Nor had her abductor.

For the past four years Charley had played the nightmare scene over and over in her head. How the situation could have been different if only she'd acted on her instinct sooner. If only she'd offered to look at the map. If only she'd reached out and grabbed her friend. If only she'd screamed for help. If only she'd taken the vehicle's licence plate. *If only . . .*

Tears welling in her sky-blue eyes, Charley forced herself to take several deep breaths. She swallowed the sharp pain of her grief that never seemed to dull with time. Gradually the trembling subsided and she regained control.

While she waited for the resin to dry, Charley sat in the dunes, knees hugged to her chest, and stared out at the limitless expanse of the Pacific Ocean. Gulls flew overhead in a cloudless blue sky. Bright sunshine glinted off emerald-green waters. And glassy waves, now abandoned and free of surfers, peeled along the coast in perfect white lines. The sight was breathtaking.

There was no indication that a deadly predator swam just beneath the surface.

Just like it is in life, thought Charley bitterly.

'Thinking of going back out?' enquired a deep gravelly voice.

Charley snapped her head round to see a man cresting

the dune. She raised a hand to shield her eyes from the sun. The stranger was tall and broad with close-cut silver-grey hair. Despite wearing a faded O'Neill T-shirt and board shorts, he was no surfer. A jagged white scar cut across his neck. But it was the man's English accent that put her most on guard.

'Maybe,' she replied tersely.

The man raised a questioning eyebrow. 'You have a death wish?'

Charley shrugged. 'At least I'd get the waves to myself.'

The stranger grunted a laugh, then glanced at the beach where the injured boy was being transferred into an ambulance, its lights flashing. A TV news camera crew was now filming the scene.

'That was a remarkable act of courage,' he said. 'Everyone else fled, but you surfed right into the danger zone. Did you know the boy?'

Charley shook her head.

'So why risk your life saving a stranger?' he pressed.

Charley was uncomfortable with this personal line of questioning. 'I don't know,' she replied honestly, then narrowed her eyes. 'I suppose I don't like the strong taking advantage of the weak.'

The man seemed to smile at this. 'And why walk away? You could be basking in the limelight, rather than sheltering alone in this dune.'

'I don't like attention,' Charley replied.

'That's good,' said the stranger, taking a step closer. 'Nor do I.'

Charley tensed, growing ever more fearful of the man's intentions.

'What's your name?' he asked.

'What's it to you?' Charley shot back.

'I'm not a reporter, if that's what you're thinking.'

'That's *not* what I'm thinking.'

The man studied her intently, his flint-grey eyes finally coming to rest on her damaged board. 'I can see you want to be left alone.'

With that, he tipped his finger to his brow by way of goodbye, then strolled off. As he disappeared over the dune, Charley relaxed her grip on the dive knife she'd kept concealed beneath the board. Only when she was convinced he had gone did she slide its blade back into its sheath.

TARGET

CHAPTER 3

'*Don't* lie to us!' snapped Jenny, Charley's foster-mother. 'We know you weren't at school. We've just spoken to your form tutor.'

Charley stared sullenly at the bare wooden floor of her foster-parents' house. It was bound to come out. The shark attack had been all over the local news when she'd got home the previous evening and speculation was rife about the mystery surfer girl. During a TV news report, Bud had been interviewed and Charley's heart had stopped in her mouth. The last thing she'd wanted was her foster-parents to know that she'd skipped school to surf. And although Bud had kept her identity to himself – for which Charley was grateful – her foster-parents had still guessed, resulting in yet another argument in their 'happy' home.

'You could have been killed,' stated Pete, glaring at her from beneath his bushy eyebrows.

'But I wasn't,' Charley mumbled, wondering how two puritanical churchgoers could only focus on her lies and not the fact she'd saved someone's life.

Jenny folded her arms. 'You're not going surfing ever again.'

Charley looked up in horror. 'You can't take that from me,' she begged.

'Yes, we can. You know how we feel about *surfing*.' She said the word like it was a vulgar term. 'It leads to immoral and sinful behaviour – as your persistent truancy and dishonesty proves.'

'Your board's going to the dump,' Pete agreed with finality.

Charley's mouth fell open. Surfing was the lifeline that kept her going. Overcome with fury, she screamed, 'I wish *you* were dead and *not* my parents!'

Storming out of the hallway, she slammed the front door on them, then stood, fists clenched and body shuddering, on the porch. From the other side of the door, she heard Jenny cry, 'The Lord Almighty give me strength! Why do we even bother? She's a lost cause.'

'We must remind ourselves Charley's been through a lot,' said Pete. 'We need to make allowances.'

'We're *always* making allowances while *she* puts us through hell! I've lost count of the times she's lied, skipped school and been in trouble with the police. What I'd give to see the back of her.'

Pete sighed. 'If that's how you feel, my love, then perhaps it's time we spoke with the social worker about rehoming her . . .'

Charley blinked away the sting of tears. She knew she'd never made it easy for them. The fact was they simply couldn't understand her. They weren't her parents, never would be. But to be treated like some dog to be 'rehomed' cut deep and her heart hardened against her foster-parents.

Charley strode down the driveway, kicking over one of Jenny's prized potted plants. As she reached the road, she noticed a white SUV with tinted windows parked a little way from her foster-parents' house. Charley couldn't be certain, but she thought she'd seen the same vehicle the night before. White SUVs were commonplace in her neighbourhood, but this particular one had cruised up and down as if the driver had been looking for someone. At the time Charley had thought it might be a freelance reporter scouting for the mystery surf girl. But its continued presence this morning raised alarm bells.

As she crossed the street in the direction of school, Charley casually glanced over her shoulder and made a mental note of the SUV's licence plate – 6GDG468. She wasn't taking any chances. After Kerry's abduction, her parents had become understandably overprotective. For the first few months they hadn't let her out of their sight, but eventually they realized she needed more freedom to have a normal life. So the compromise had been for Charley to take up self-defence classes and a street-awareness course. One of the key lessons had been to stay alert for unusual behaviour or repeated sightings of people and vehicles.

As she reached the next junction, Charley looked up and down the road for traffic. But she was only interested in spotting one vehicle: the white SUV.

There was no sign of it and Charley relaxed. Evidently her gut reaction had been wrong. Heading across the road and down the hill, she wondered how to persuade her foster-parents to let her out that evening for Bud's beach party. She wanted to thank him for keeping her name out of the news. But there was no way they'd give permission. Not at her age and especially after their last argument. She could say she'd been invited to a friend's sleepover, but she was probably grounded for life – if she wasn't already rehomed, that was! She'd just have to sneak out when they went to bed.

Charley waited at a set of traffic lights for the pedestrian signal to turn green. Several vehicles pulled up. The fifth in line was a white SUV. Charley clocked the licence plate – 6GDG468 – and felt her pulse quicken. Could it be a coincidence? The road did lead to the highway, after all. But, to rule out any possibility of being followed, Charley took a left instead of going straight on and cut across a small park to a residential road that ran parallel to the highway.

The route was clear, but then she spotted the SUV turning into *her* road. Charley quickened her pace, her heart thumping. The advice from her street-awareness course on being followed was to head for a populated area and find a safe location – a friend's house, a police station, a restaurant or a library. Charley hurried into downtown San Clemente, a wide tree-lined boulevard with mom-and-pop stores on either side. They were just opening so only a handful of early-morning shoppers could be seen.

Charley stopped outside a beauty parlour. She needed a good look at the driver to confirm her suspicions, without him knowing. So she pretended to study the beauty treatments on offer. In the reflection of the shop window, she watched as the white SUV rolled down the street and parked in one of the bays opposite. No one got out.

Charley felt eyes upon her and a shiver ran down her spine. The driver's face was obscured by a tinted windscreen, but she could make out a bald head. Her throat tightened as an old fear gripped her heart: the man who'd taken Kerry had finally come back for *her*!

Seized by a panic attack, Charley half-walked, half-ran down the street. Her foster-mother worked in the community centre near the pier. If she could just reach there, she'd feel safer. Charley risked a glance back. The driver was getting out. He was stocky with a short goatee and pale skin, the lack of suntan confirming he was no local. Dark sunglasses concealed his features and Charley's memory of the kidnapper's face was hazy after so many years. But one thing was certain – this man was following her.

With her attention distracted, Charley ran headlong into the arms of another man.

'Whoa, slow down!' he said, grabbing hold of her wrist as she stumbled back from the impact.

Charley stared into the flinty eyes of the stranger she'd met on the dunes.

'We just want to talk, Charley,' he said, jutting his jaw at the bald man approaching from behind. Now Charley was even more spooked. *He knows my name!*

'Get off me!' she cried, spinning her wrist to break his grip and kicking him hard in the shins, just as she'd been taught in self-defence class.

The man grunted in pain and let go. Charley sprinted past him and across the street, only to collide into someone leaving a coffee shop. A fresh cappuccino and sugared doughnut went flying.

'*What the heck!*' cried Deputy Sheriff Jay Valdez as he shook hot coffee from his hands and inspected his stained uniform.

'Thank God,' said Charley, grabbing hold of the officer. 'I'm being followed!'

The deputy looked beyond her and across the street, a dubious frown on his face. 'By who exactly?'

Charley spun round. There was no sign of the SUV. The stranger and his accomplice had seemingly vanished into thin air.

TARGET
CHAPTER 4

'We've talked about this before, Charley,' said Deputy Valdez as he sat opposite her in one of the coffee shop's red leather booths. 'You can't keep skipping school.'

'But I was being followed,' Charley insisted, a warm latte cupped between her hands.

'So *that's* your excuse this time?' The deputy sighed and put down the napkin he'd been using to mop up his uniform. With a kindly smile, he continued, 'I know you've had a troubled past and it can't be easy for you, but you need to shape up, Charley. You've got your whole life ahead of you. Don't throw it all away just because you've had a rough start.'

'A rough start!' Charley gripped her cup so tightly she thought it might crack. 'My best friend abducted and my parents killed in a plane hijacking. How much rougher can it get? I'm sorry if I'm not exactly looking forward to the rest of my life!'

Valdez propped his elbows on the table and leant forward. 'Listen to me, Charley. We cannot change the cards we are dealt, just how we play the hand.'

Charley stared into the froth of her latte. 'What's that supposed to mean?'

'That it's not life's challenges or setbacks that define who we are. It's how we *react* to them that defines us,' he explained. 'You have a choice. You can give up and let life defeat you – or you can rise up and become stronger.'

'That's easy enough for you to say,' she mumbled.

'Yes, it is. Because I know all about rough starts.' Valdez tugged back the sleeve of his uniform to reveal a small faded tattoo of a five-pointed crown on his inner wrist. 'When I was your age, I was in a street gang.'

Charley glanced up in surprise.

'Drugs, drink, violence, guns. That was my world as a boy. My brother got killed in a fight during a turf war. Then my life spiralled out of control . . . until a police officer arrested me. But he didn't take me to the station; instead he took me back home and told me exactly what I've just said to you.' He fixed her with his brown-flecked eyes. 'His advice changed my life. I can only hope it changes yours too.'

Uncertain how to respond, Charley continued staring at the froth in her cup. The deputy's words had struck a nerve deep inside her. But she had no idea where to begin, or even if she had the strength to fight back against life's challenges.

'You have real potential, Charley, if only you'd apply it,' Valdez encouraged. 'I know Pete and Jenny are at their wits' end with you. Don't you want to make them proud of you?'

'What do they care? They're not my parents.'

'No, but they're good people, trying to do right by you. And you're not making their lives any easier with your truancy and storytelling.'

'I *wasn't* making it up!'

'OK, I believe you,' replied the deputy, holding up his hands. He tapped a finger to the notepad in his pocket. 'I'll look into the licence plate you've given me. Just promise to think about what I've said.'

'Sure,' agreed Charley, relieved that he was at last taking some action.

Deputy Valdez reclined in his seat and gazed out of the window. 'You wouldn't happen to know who rescued that boy from the shark attack yesterday, would you?'

'No . . . I don't know what you're talking about,' said Charley, taken off-guard by the sudden change in topic.

Valdez looked sideways at her, a knowing smile on his lips. 'See what I mean? Potential. Don't waste it.'

The door to the coffee shop opened. A customer walked in and seated himself in a booth by the front window. Charley almost spilt her drink. She leant across the table and hissed under her breath to Valdez. '*That's one of the men I was telling you about.*'

The deputy glanced over at the silver-haired man by the window. Sat ramrod straight, the stranger gave the appearance of someone not to be messed with. He looked in his mid-forties, but had the physique of a much younger man. And, while he was dressed smartly in a suit, his craggy face and visible scar around the neckline told of a more violent past.

'OK, let me speak to him,' said Valdez, rising from his seat. 'You stay here.'

The deputy strode across to the stranger and stood over him, his hand resting lightly upon the gun on his hip. Charley was too far away to hear their conversation, but she saw the stranger hand over his ID. Valdez inspected it, then raised an enquiring eyebrow. The stranger passed Valdez a file. The deputy flicked through it. They talked for several minutes, Charley growing more concerned with each passing second. Then Valdez handed back the documents and, to Charley's astonishment, saluted the man.

Valdez returned to Charley's booth, the expression on his face unreadable. 'I think you should hear what he has to say.'

TARGET
CHAPTER 5

Charley nervously settled herself in the seat opposite the stranger. Deputy Sheriff Valdez remained at the coffee bar, a discreet distance away but within earshot. His continued presence reassured Charley, but her heart still raced. What did this scarred man want?

'What I'm about to discuss with you is highly classified,' said the stranger, his hands folded over a mysterious brown folder on the table. 'In the interests of national security, you're not to discuss this with *anyone*. Understood?'

Charley swallowed uneasily and a shiver ran down her spine. Whatever this man wanted with her, it was serious. She gave a hesitant nod.

'My name is Colonel Black. I head up a close-protection organization known as Buddyguard – a covert independent agency with ties to the British government's security and intelligence service –'

'Am I in danger?' Charley interrupted, her chest tightening.

'Far from it,' he replied with a steely smile. 'In fact,

you're the sort of person we're looking for to protect others from danger.'

Charley frowned, her anxiety now replaced by confusion. '*Me?* What are you talking about?'

'I'm here to recruit you as a bodyguard.'

Charley burst into laughter. She half-expected a cameraman to pop up, with a zany presenter announcing she was on a prank TV show. 'You can't be serious!'

'Deadly serious,' he replied, his gaze unwavering.

From the severe expression on his face, Charley got the sense this colonel wasn't the sort of man who made jokes often, if at all. She glanced over at Valdez for confirmation. The deputy sheriff nodded; evidently he'd been convinced by the man's credentials.

'You do realize I'm only fourteen,' she told the colonel.

'The best bodyguard is the one nobody notices,' he replied. 'That's why young people like yourself make exceptional bodyguards.'

'But I thought all bodyguards were muscle-bound guys. I'm a girl, in case you hadn't noticed.'

'That gives you a distinct advantage,' stated the colonel. 'A female bodyguard can blend into any crowd and is often mistaken for a girlfriend or an assistant of the Principal – the person you've been assigned to protect. But she can drop you with an elbow or a roundhouse punch faster than you could shake somebody's hand. As I said, the best bodyguard is one nobody notices – which makes girls among the very best.'

Charley's head was spinning. This was beyond anything

she'd expected. If not a potential stalker, she'd assumed the stranger might be a truancy officer or an official from child-welfare services. But the head of a secret bodyguard agency!

'Why *me*?' she eventually asked.

'You've proved you have the skills and talent.'

Charley blinked. 'I have?'

'Rescuing that boy from the shark was evidence of your courage,' he explained. 'Willingness to risk your own life for another is a crucial factor in being a bodyguard.'

'But that was stupid of me . . . I wasn't even thinking.'

'No, you were acting on your natural instinct.'

'But I'm *not* bodyguard material,' insisted Charley.

'Really?' challenged the colonel, his flint-grey eyes narrowing. 'What's the registration of the white SUV?'

'Ermm . . . 6GDG468,' Charley answered, thrown by the sudden switch in topic.

'When did you first notice the vehicle?'

'On my foster-parents' street.'

'And when did you realize it was following you?'

'At the traffic lights.'

'What did the driver look like?'

'Bald, slightly fat with a goatee. Why all these questions?'

'That follow was set up to test your observation skills. And it's clear you've passed with flying colours –'

'You're saying that was a *test*?' Charley cut in, her earlier panic now turning to anger.

'Yes, the man who tailed you is called Bugsy,' the colonel revealed, pointing through the window to her 'stalker' leaning against the bonnet of the re-parked SUV. He gave Charley a little wave. 'Bugsy is the surveillance tutor for our recruits. But don't ever tell him he's fat. He won't forgive you for that.'

'I won't forgive him for scaring the hell out of me!' Charley muttered, her anger replaced by relief that she didn't have a crazed bald man pursuing her after all.

'You also employed some excellent anti-surveillance techniques, especially the use of reflections in the shop window. That's another core set of skills a bodyguard needs,' the colonel explained. 'And it's evident you know martial arts from the damage you inflicted on my shin!'

Charley offered a wry smile. The shin kick was her one small victory in the whole set-up. 'Sorry about that,' she said with blatant lack of sympathy.

'No need to apologize,' he replied drily. 'Your reaction was reassuringly quick and effective. Are you still training?'

Charley shook her head. 'No, I quit the self-defence classes when I moved here.'

The colonel frowned. 'Why didn't you join another martial arts club? There's a jujitsu dojo just down the street.'

'My foster-parents aren't keen on girls fighting,' she explained with a sigh. 'In fact they're not keen on *anything* I like doing. They're quite . . . traditional in their ways.'

'Would you like to start training again?'

Charley shrugged. 'Sure. My dad always hoped I'd become a black belt.'

'Well, you can wear any colour belt you like,' replied the

colonel. 'The style of martial arts you'd be taught isn't based on grades in the dojo; it's based on its effectiveness in the street.'

He flipped open the brown folder on the table and Charley saw a ream of papers with her name on, along with a pile of photographs. Several were recent, including some long-distance shots of her rescuing the boy from the great white. The colonel flicked through to a section headed 'EDUCATION'.

'I see from your school reports that you were an A-grade student until recently,' he said. 'Why the sudden drop-off?'

'I couldn't see the point,' Charley replied with sharp honesty, shocked that the colonel had so much information on her.

Colonel Black considered this. 'Loss of focus? That's understandable considering what you've been through in your life.' He flipped past police reports on Kerry's abduction, news clippings of her parents' hijacked flight and confidential files regarding her fostering. 'But the way you're –'

Charley slammed her hand down on the file. 'How did you get all this personal stuff on me?' she demanded.

'Online research and a few connections,' he replied. 'But, as I was saying, the way you're going you're headed on a self-destructive course. Charley, you need to –'

'Listen, General –'

'Colonel,' he corrected her sharply.

'Sorry, *Colonel*. I really think you've got the wrong person. I'm no bodyguard. When my best friend was kidnapped, I . . .' Charley suddenly felt herself choking up. 'I did nothing. I froze. I . . . failed Kerry.'

'You were ten years old, Charley,' said the colonel matter-of-factly. 'You can't blame yourself for what happened. But you *can* stop those things happening to others.'

Fighting back tears at the painful memory of her friend's abduction, Charley quietly asked, 'How?'

'By becoming a bodyguard for other young at-risk individuals.'

Charley stared through the window at the passing traffic, her mind a whirl of conflicting thoughts and emotions. She felt both thrilled and deeply uneasy at the proposal, flattered but puzzled that he'd selected her. How had this so-called colonel found her in the first place? Was he taking advantage of her vulnerable background? Was the whole thing a set-up or a real opportunity?

The colonel closed the file and laid a black business card on the table. Charley glanced at the silver embossed logo of a shield with guardian wings.

'What's this?' she asked.

'Your future.'

Charley eyed the single phone number running along the bottom edge.

'It's entirely up to you whether you call,' said the colonel, rising to his feet. 'But ask yourself this: do you want to run scared all your life? Or do you want to take a stand and fight back?'

TARGET
CHAPTER 6

Charley felt the warm night breeze caress her as she sat on the golden sand, listening to the waves roll in. Further down the beach a campfire flickered orange, illuminating the pack of young surfers gathered to party and surf the night away. Someone was playing an acoustic guitar and singing, '*We all need a shelter to keep us from the rain. Without love, we're just laying on the tracks waiting for a train . . .*'

The song's lyrics hit home hard for Charley. They seemed to sum up her situation. Without her parents, or her best friend, life felt desperately empty and without purpose. She was struggling on a daily basis to fight off depression. Only her surfing gave her a brief respite from the constant storm raging in her mind. No wonder her foster-parents despaired at her! But was she now being offered a shelter from that storm – a chance to give her life real purpose?

The other surfers joined in the chorus and Charley recognized the song as Ash Wild's 'Only Raining'. There was barely a radio station that wasn't playing the track at the moment. The teenage rock star from Britain had taken the Billboard charts by storm.

'*It's only raining on you, only raining. It's only raining on you right now, but the sun will soon shine through . . .*'

Charley prayed that it would. She'd been caught in the rain for so long now that she'd forgotten what it was like for life to shine upon her. But should she take the extreme decision of joining a secret security agency? The whole concept of young bodyguards seemed not only insane but illegal. And could she trust the colonel? His recruitment methods seemed wildly unorthodox. Yet Deputy Sheriff Valdez had checked the organization's credentials and they'd proved to be solid.

The song came to an end and the surfers' applause and laughter carried to her on the breeze. It sounded distant and faint as if from another dimension, and at that moment Charley did feel caught between two worlds – the dead-end one she was familiar with, and a new one that offered a whole host of possibilities. Perhaps it even offered redemption – a unique chance to atone for her failure to save her friend Kerry.

How she wished she had someone she could talk to.

Charley stared up at the heavens, awash with gleaming stars. 'What should I do?' she whispered in a prayer to her parents. How she missed them – her mother's kindness and the loving way she used to brush Charley's hair before bed; her father's strength and the warm secure embrace of his arms. She searched the constellations, wondering if her parents were somewhere up there. 'Should I become a bodyguard?' she asked.

A shooting star traced a line across the sky.

Charley had her answer . . . but did it mean yes or no?

'There you are!' said a delighted voice as Bud materialized out of the darkness and plonked himself down beside her. 'I was beginning to think you'd sneaked away again. What are you doing over here all alone?'

Charley offered him an apologetic shrug. 'I needed some space to think.'

'About what?' he asked, shifting closer.

Charley sighed and hesitated. She hardly knew Bud, but who else could she talk to? Besides, he seemed a genuinely nice guy and had proven trustworthy by not revealing her name to the press. 'Have you ever been faced with an impossible decision? One that could change your life forever?'

Bud furrowed his brow thoughtfully. 'No,' he admitted. 'But I suppose it'd be like confronting that epic wave, the one that promises to break *so sweetly*.' He pointed to the ocean, his hand rising and falling to indicate the immense size of the swell. 'A legendary wave! You may never have surfed anything so huge in your life. The chances are you'll wipe out big time. But – and this is the killer – you *might* conquer it and ride all the way in.'

He turned to Charley, his eyes gleaming with an irresistible zeal. 'That wave might come only once in a lifetime, Charley. So I say, go for it!' He slipped an arm round her waist. 'Now, what is this impossible decision?'

Charley was momentarily stunned by the clarity of his answer. On an impulse, she kissed Bud full on the lips, then stood up and brushed the sand from her shorts.

'W-where are you going?' Bud asked breathlessly, a baffled and forlorn expression on his face as she strode off up the beach.

Charley called back from the darkness, 'To catch that once-in-a-lifetime wave!'

TARGET
CHAPTER 7

'*I saw you stroll across the market place. I caught your walk but not your face*,' sang Ash Wild with gutsy energy into the studio mic. '*Yet what I saw in that one short glimpse is all my mind has thought of since . . .*'

Ash strummed hard on his electric guitar, a bluesy rock riff that harked back to Jimi Hendrix's 'Voodoo Child'. The drummer and bassist were grooving behind him, their rhythms locked in tight. The keyboard player, his head bobbing to the beat, stabbed at his Hammond organ, counterpointing Ash's driving guitar line. When the chorus kicked in, the four of them belted out in harmony, '*Beautiful from afar, but far from beautiful!*'

At its climax, Ash launched into a blistering guitar solo, his fingers ripping up the fretboard. Eyes shut tight and lower lip clamped between his teeth, he pulled every last drop of emotion from the notes he struck. Then, at the solo's peak, a string snapped.

'*Damn it!*' Ash swore as the guitar detuned and he hit a bum note. He threw it to the floor in frustration where it clanged and screamed in protest. 'I was finally about to nail that solo!'

With a furious kick, he punted his drinks bottle, spraying soda over everyone's gear. The drummer rolled his eyes at the bass player, who reached over and pulled the plug to the guitar amp, cutting the ear-splitting feedback.

'Let's take a break,' came the producer's weary voice over the studio monitors.

Ash stormed out of the studio and into the control room. The producer, a long-haired legend known as 'Don Sonic', was stationed at a colossal mixing desk like Sulu from *Star Trek*. He leant back in his chair and interlocked his fingers behind his head.

'I reckon we can patch together a complete solo from the other fifty or so takes,' he suggested.

'That's not good enough!' Ash muttered with a sullen shake of his head. 'It'll sound false.'

'To you maybe, but not your fans. I can make it appear seamless for the record.'

Ash stomped up the basement studio's stairs. 'Never. We'll try it again later.'

Don called after him, 'You're a perfectionist, Ash. That's your gift . . . and your problem!'

'Yeah, yeah, whatever,' mumbled Ash, but he knew his producer was right. And that's what frustrated the hell out of him. He could record a song a million times, yet it never matched the ideal version in his head.

At the top of the stairs, he turned right into a sleek open-plan kitchen. An ageing hulk of a man in a faded black T-shirt, its seams stretched by his bulging tattooed arms, leant against the breakfast bar. He was idly flipping through a tabloid newspaper and sipping from a mug of black coffee.

'Hi, Big T,' said Ash, acknowledging his bodyguard.

'Ash,' he grunted with a nod of his bald domed head. Closing the paper, he took up position by the patio doors, where he casually scanned the garden beyond, taking in its designer wooden decking, oval swimming pool and hot tub.

Ash appreciated Big T. The man knew when to talk and when to give him space. Opening the refrigerator door, Ash took out a fresh soda and twisted off the cap. There was a sharp hiss as the contents foamed up. Quickly putting his lips to the top, he took a long slug and closed his eyes. Ash tried to calm himself down. Just like the fizz in a soda bottle, if he got shaken up, his emotions exploded uncontrollably – often with regrettable consequences. Yet it was this same deep well of emotion that compelled him to write his songs – both a blessing and a curse, he supposed.

Wandering through to the dining room, Ash was greeted by a table overflowing with letters, parcels, teddy bears and bouquets of flowers. On the far side of this mountain of mail sat a young brunette woman in a pearl-white silk blouse and pencil skirt. Her delicate chin was cupped in the palm of one hand as she skim-read a letter.

'Is this *all* for me, Zoe?' he asked, picking up an envelope with his name scrawled in red ink and dotted with glittery hearts and kisses.

'No, darling, not all of it,' the publicity executive murmured, her accent polished by a private-school education. Ash frowned in mild disappointment. Then Zoe pointed a manicured finger towards the hallway. 'There're another six mail bags out there. Whoever leaked your home address on the internet has a lot to answer for!'

Sighing, Zoe returned to sorting the piles of fan mail. Ash picked up a random letter from one of the stacks:

Dear Ash,

I'm utterly WILD for you! Ever since I was introduced to you and your music by a friend, I've followed you online, bought all your records and supported you every step of the way. Your music has inspired me to stay true to myself and never give up on my dreams. One of my dreams is to meet you in person. It would be amazing if I could come backstage at one of your concerts. Would that be possible? Please write back.

All my love, Paige Anderson xxx.

PS. I enclose a photo so you know who I am.

Ash glanced at the picture of a madly grinning girl with braces on her teeth. 'Is every fan letter like this?' he asked.

Tilting her head to one side, Zoe replied, 'No, not all; others are *much* more obsessive than that. Certain fans write to you literally every day!'

'Like my ex-girlfriend?' suggested Ash.

'Ha ha,' said Zoe drily. 'I thought you said Hanna wanted nothing to do with you.'

'Yeah, but she might have changed her mind and forgiven me.' He eyed a huge stack of letters on a separate table. 'What's that pile?'

'Your Wildling fan club from America. Jessie Dawson, the girl who runs it, has forwarded just a *small* selection so far.'

As Zoe continued to sift through the various piles, Ash came across a larger package in a brown padded bag. 'Who's this from?' he asked, inspecting the packaging. 'There's no postmark.'

Zoe glanced up and shrugged. 'I haven't got to that one yet.'

'Feels heavy,' he said, weighing the packet in his hands. His fingers came away slightly oily. 'Smells of marzipan. I think someone's sent me a cake –'

Without warning, Big T burst into the room. 'Don't open that!' he yelled, grabbing the parcel from him. 'It might be a bomb!'

CHAPTER 8

The explosion was ear-splitting. Charley sprinted round the corner of the building to be confronted by utter carnage. Shattered glass and debris were strewn across the charred ground. Her eyes stung from the acrid smoke billowing in the air. And somewhere amid the bomb-blasted wreckage a person was screaming in agony.

Charley started to dash forward but was grabbed by her arm and yanked back.

'Secondary devices!' warned Jason, glaring at her. Jason was a heavyset, breezeblock of a boy from Sydney and a Buddyguard recruit like herself.

'Of course,' Charley replied. She could have kicked herself for forgetting the first rule of attending an incident: *Do not become a casualty yourself*.

In an attack of this nature, the terrorists often planted a second bomb, its purpose to kill and maim those who rushed to help the first victims. And there were numerous other hazards following an explosion: fuel leaks, chemical spillages, fires, loose masonry and exposed power lines. All risks had to be assessed before approaching a casualty.

Charley scanned the first five metres ahead of her: no obvious danger. Then, together with Jason and two other buddyguards – David, a tall loose-limbed Ugandan boy, and José, a street-wise Mexican kid with oil-black hair – Charley performed a wider sweep of the area. They covered a twenty-metre perimeter. All this time the screaming continued, a desperate plea for help that was impossible to ignore.

'Clear!' called David as he finished the initial inspection of the bomb site.

The smoke was beginning to disperse and Charley spotted the casualty – a teenage boy. Propped against a wall, his face was caked in dust and streaked with blood.

'Over here!' she cried, racing across to him. But she stopped in her tracks when she saw the severity of the boy's injuries. Aside from the bleeding gash across his forehead, his upper left leg had suffered a major fracture. A sharp white splinter of thigh bone was sticking out at an odd angle, tissue, muscle and white tendons all exposed. Blood was pumping from the open wound, pooling in a sticky mess on the concrete. The gruesome sight turned Charley's stomach.

'What are you waiting for?' cried Jason, pushing past her with the medical kit.

Snapped out of her daze, Charley knelt down beside the boy.

'It's OK,' she told him, resting a hand gently on his shoulder. 'We're going to look after you.'

The boy's unfocused eyes found Charley and he stopped screaming. 'C-can't hear you!' he gasped.

Charley repeated her words, louder this time, realizing the bomb's blast had deafened him.

Jason glared at her. 'Are you going to talk or act?' he muttered, opening the med-kit and tossing her a pair of latex barrier gloves.

'I'm trying to reassure him, that's all,' she shot back.

'Then do something useful,' said Jason irritably.

Gloves on, Charley pressed her hands to the gaping wound. The casualty cried out in pain. 'Sorry,' she said with a strained smile. 'I have to stem the blood loss. I'm Charley, by the way. What's your name?'

'Blake,' groaned the boy. '*My leg hurts!*'

'Get a tourniquet on him fast,' instructed Jason.

David whipped off his belt and wrapped it round the boy's upper leg. He pulled it tight and Charley removed her blood-soaked hands as Jason applied a dressing. With an antiseptic wipe, Charley cleaned the grime from the boy's face and inspected the gash to his forehead.

'Cut looks superficial,' she told the others.

'But bruising around the area indicates a violent impact. Possibility of concussion,' corrected José, attaching a blood pressure monitor to the casualty's arm.

Charley nodded, disappointed at not assessing the injury correctly. Then she noticed the boy's eyes losing focus and his eyelids closing.

'Blake, stay with me!' He looked at her weakly. 'Tell me, where are you from?'

'M-Manchester,' he gasped between pained breaths.

'I've heard of Manchester. It's in the north of England,

isn't it? I'm from California so this country is still new to m–'

'Blood pressure dropping,' interjected José, studying the monitor's readout. He placed two fingers against the boy's neck. 'Pulse weakening.'

The situation was deteriorating too fast for Charley to compute. Her brain suffered a logjam of information as all her first-aid training spewed out in one garbled mess: *Resuscitation . . . Anaphylactic shock . . . Dr ABC . . . Hypoxia . . . Myocardial infarction . . .*

Dr ABC was the only thing that got through the jumble.

Danger. Response. Airway. Breathing. Circulation.

They'd already checked for danger. The casualty was responsive. And the boy's airway was clear since he could talk. He was also breathing, if a little rapidly. So it was his circulation that was the critical issue now.

'The tourniquet's on. What else is there we can do?' Charley asked, trying to keep the desperation out of her voice.

'He needs fluids,' said José. 'To replace the blood loss.'

Searching through the med-kit, he pulled out a pouch of saline solution and handed Charley a cannula. 'Get this in him,' he said.

Charley tore off the wrapper round the sterile needle and tube. Pulling up the boy's sleeve, she hunted for a suitable vein. Her hands trembled as she held the needle over his bare skin. She'd only ever practised inserting a cannula on a false limb during their first-aid training. In a real-life situation – under pressure – it was far more difficult.

'Let me do it!' Jason snapped.

Charley bit back on her tongue as he snatched the needle from her grasp. Jason always lost patience with her and his attitude made her feel inadequate.

While Jason inserted the cannula, José kept an eye on the boy's blood pressure and David rechecked the tourniquet. This left Charley feeling like a spare wheel on the team. Not sure what else to do, she continued talking to the casualty.

'Don't worry, Blake, an ambulance is on its way,' she told him. 'We'll get you to a hospital in no time. You'll be fine. So tell me about Manchester – is it a nice place to visit? I've heard that . . .' Charley knew she was babbling, but the boy seemed reassured. That is, until his breathing started to accelerate abnormally. His face screwed up in agony as he fought for every breath. 'What's wrong?' she asked.

'Check his chest,' David suggested, his calm manner poles apart from the panic she was experiencing.

Charley lifted the boy's shirt. The whole right-hand side of his chest was bruised purple.

'Looks like a possible tension pneumothorax,' said José.

'A tension *what*?' cried Charley, vaguely recalling the term but not the condition. With every passing second, she felt even more out of her depth.

'Air in his chest cavity!' exclaimed Jason as he grabbed the oxygen cylinder strapped to the side of the medical kit. 'It's crushing his lungs.'

He fitted a mask to the patient and began the oxygen

flow to reduce the risk of hypoxia, a dangerous condition that could lead to permanent brain damage and even death.

'We'll need to perform an emergency needle decompression,' said José, handing Charley a large-bore needle with a one-way valve.

Jason and David repositioned the casualty so he was lying flat. Charley stared at the disturbingly long needle. Determined not to hesitate this time, she located the second intercostal space on the boy's chest and prepared for insertion.

'NO!' cried José, grabbing her wrist. 'It must go in at a ninety-degree angle or you could stab his heart.'

Charley's confidence drained away. She'd almost made a fatal error. Suddenly the boy's body fell limp and his eyes rolled back.

'He's stopped breathing!' Jason exclaimed.

David checked the boy's carotid artery on his neck. 'No pulse either.'

'He's gone into cardiac arrest!' said José, taking the needle from Charley. 'Assume decompression procedure complete. Begin CPR.'

Jason screwed up his face at the idea. 'Well, I'm not going mouth-to-mouth with him!'

'Nor me,' said David.

All eyes turned to Charley.

'Fine, I'll do it,' she said, shifting into position and tilting Blake's head to deliver the initial rescue breaths.

Jason looked at José and whispered under his breath, 'She's eager.'

Charley glanced up and narrowed her eyes at Jason. 'What did you say?'

'Nothing,' he replied. 'I'll do the chest compressions.'

Between them they worked at CPR, delivering thirty chest compressions to every two rescue breaths. As he pressed down on the boy's chest, Jason sang to himself, '*Ah, ah, ah, ah, staying alive! Stayin' alive!*'

'This is no time for singing,' snapped Charley, irritated by his constant sniping.

'It's to keep . . . the correct . . . rhythm,' Jason explained, pumping hard. 'Saw the actor . . . Vinnie Jones . . . do this in a heart advert.'

After two minutes of constant CPR, a dark-haired woman strode through the haze of smoke towards them.

'Ambulance is here!' she announced. 'Well done, your casualty has survived . . . Unfortunately, the other one didn't.'

TARGET
CHAPTER 9

Charley exchanged confused looks with the rest of the team before turning to their Buddyguard close-protection instructor. 'What other one?' she asked.

Jody's olive eyes turned to the area behind them and she pointed. Seeing the bewilderment on their faces, she leapt into a ditch piled with rusting tools, where a body lay partly concealed beneath a sheet of corrugated roofing. 'It's the casualty who makes the least noise that should be checked first,' she stated.

Charley wondered how the team had missed the full-size training mannequin during their surveillance sweep. This was their first real test since arriving at Buddyguard Headquarters in Wales four weeks ago – and they had made a 'fatal' error.

'But Blake was in need of immediate medical attention,' José argued. 'He was bleeding out.'

'You have to resist the impulse to treat the first casualty you encounter. If someone's screaming, you know they're alive at least,' Jody explained as she climbed out of the ditch. 'In an incident with multiple victims, it's crucial to perform *triage*. Assess all casualties and sort them according to the severity of their condition, using the principle of Dr ABC as a guide: airway, breathing and circulation – in that order. Your aim should be to *do the most for the most*.'

Jody paused to allow the significance of this to sink in before continuing, 'That means prioritizing the most life-threatening conditions first. In this training scenario, the victim in the ditch had a blocked airway. If you'd spotted them, taken a moment to remove the obstruction, then put them in the recovery position, that person would still be alive now.'

Jason scowled at Charley and she knew she was to blame. The mannequin had been in *her* area during the initial sweep. 'I suppose that means we've failed,' said Jason.

Jody studied the notes on her clipboard. 'Not necessarily. It's a team assessment. José, you demonstrated excellent medical knowledge and diagnosis. David, a calm and level-headed approach to an emergency. Jason, you were proactive as team leader and performed a clean insertion of the cannula. And, Charley . . .'

Charley braced herself for the worst. She knew she'd suffered a 'brain freeze' and that she'd messed up the needle compression.

'Despite a rash entry into the danger zone and a potentially serious medical error, you showed good communication with the casualty and a willingness to do what was necessary. The rest of the team should take note –' she directed her gaze at Jason and David – 'because one can't be self-conscious or inhibited during an emergency. If the situation demands

CPR, then get on with it. Failure to act fast enough could mean the difference between life and death.'

'And what about me?' asked Blake. He sat up, his fake wound still seeping blood. 'I deserve an award for that acting!'

Jody arched a slim eyebrow. 'Well, you certainly made more fuss than Rescue Annie over there.'

'Yeah, you screamed like a girl,' said Jason.

Blake shrugged it off. 'Wouldn't you, with a bunch of clowns about to jab your arm and pound your chest?' He removed the cannula with José's help and pressed a plaster to the resulting pinprick of blood, then glanced over at Charley. 'At one point I thought you really were going to stab me with that needle!'

Charley responded with an awkward smile, embarrassed by her relative medical incompetence.

José laughed. 'That certainly would have given you something to scream about.'

'What? Isn't this enough?' said Blake, pointing to the gory fake wound attached to his thigh.

Jody cleared her throat to regain everyone's attention. 'Taking into account everyone's marks and considering one of the casualties died, I'm afraid the team didn't make the grade on this first-aid test. I'm recommending a reassessment in a week's time.'

She ignored the team's collective groan. 'You need to practise these skills until they become second nature. Remember, first aid is important in any walk of life but fundamental to being a bodyguard.'

'I'd have thought our martial art skills would be more important,' mumbled Jason.

Jody glared at him. 'Not necessarily. During your assignments, it's unlikely you'll ever need that high kick or spinning backfist you've practised over and over, but you *will* need knowledge of first aid. Your Principal is far more likely to die choking on a pretzel than be shot. In my opinion, if you're not trained in first aid, then you're *not* a real bodyguard.'

TARGET
CHAPTER 10

'Martial arts are essential for a bodyguard!' stated Steve, their unarmed-combat instructor, later that afternoon. At six foot two, the ex-SAS soldier was a walking mountain of black muscle and no one dared argue with him. Nor did anyone risk mentioning that Jody held a different opinion. 'But, as you've discovered over the past four weeks, it isn't necessary to be the next Jet Li or to be able to scratch your ears with your own feet!'

The class of ten recruits chuckled at this, their laughter echoing round the spacious sports hall. They were the first batch of trainees to be drafted into the Buddyguard organization and the facilities, located in an old Victorian-era school in a remote valley of the Brecon Beacons, were a mix of run-down decay and high-tech modern. The newly equipped computerized gymnasium stood in stark contrast to the cold and draughty changing rooms. But Colonel Black had promised that renovation was in progress.

The handful of recruits lined up in two rows to form a corridor down which their instructor slowly paced. Charley was at the far end opposite Blake. A cocky Mancunian with spiked black hair and a permanent grin, he was relatively friendly to her, unlike Jason. The other recruits were pleasant enough, but none had made any special effort to get to know her. Being the only girl seemed to set her apart.

'All you need is an understanding of body mechanics and a few simple techniques to pre-empt or disarm an attacker,' Steve explained. 'With these skills at your disposal, you can control people of all shapes and sizes with very little effort.'

He stopped in front of Jason. Broad-chested with bulging biceps and an anvil jaw, Jason was the largest of the recruits.

'The principle is simple,' said Steve, indicating for Jason to grab his T-shirt as if to assault him. 'For instance, a wrist will rotate only so far. So, by manipulating it and using the attacker's own momentum to force it beyond normal movement, you can control and disable that person. Jason, take a swing at me.'

Still holding his instructor's shirt, Jason chambered his right fist to let loose a roundhouse punch. As the strike arced towards him, Steve gripped Jason's left hand between his thumb and forefinger, twisting it back the other way. As he spiralled the wrist to breaking point, Jason instantly abandoned his punch and doubled over in pain. Steve followed up by firmly pushing the back of Jason's knuckles towards his elbow. With his arm locked out, Jason had no option but to drop to the floor where he lay writhing like a speared snake.

Charley decided that was a technique she needed to learn – if only to put Jason in his place.

'If I applied a touch more pressure, his wrist would snap like a twig,' Steve explained matter-of-factly. 'But to the casual onlooker it would appear I've done relatively little. So it maintains the principle of minimum force, which keeps me within the law. And if the attacker has a broken wrist it's attributed to their own force when resisting, not through any brutality on my part.'

He released Jason, who shook the ache from his wrist and stood back in line.

'For me, this is what makes martial arts so essential for a bodyguard: the ability to control people with the illusion of minimum force.'

'But what if someone has a knife?' asked Blake. 'Surely we have to do more than a basic wrist lock.'

'Absolutely,' said Steve. 'But the principle of NRP always applies. Any self-defence must be *necessary*, *reasonable* and *proportional* to the attack. So, if someone has a knife, you have every right to break that attacker's arm. However, if the potential threat is simply an over-enthusiastic fan, you can't go around decking them.'

'That's a shame!' Jason remarked.

Steve shot him a hard stare. 'Maybe so, but we don't want any of you appearing on a tabloid front page with your fist slamming into a fan's face while your Principal looks on in horror. Remember, you're protecting the Principal's image as well as their safety . . . *and* our organization's covert status.'

He beckoned Blake to step forward.

'That's why I'm going to show you how to take down an opponent with just your fingertips.'

Charley edged forward in anticipation with the rest of the recruits.

'The jugular takedown is an excellent self-defence technique,' explained their instructor, 'especially if the aggressor is trying to strangle you from in front.'

Steve nodded to Blake to reach up and put his hands round his muscled neck in an imitation attack.

'First, locate the notch at the base of the throat, just above the collarbone,' he instructed, spearing the tips of his right hand and resting his middle finger on Blake's soft depression of skin. 'At the same time, slip your other hand behind the attacker's neck to gain control of their body. Finally, push in and down, *hard*, aiming towards the ground behind your attacker's feet.'

Steve's move was so quick and Blake's reaction so sudden and extreme that Charley barely had time to blink before Blake was on the ground, choking and gagging. It was as if their instructor had cut the strings of a puppet.

'If necessary, you can follow up with some disabling strikes before making your escape,' Steve went on, mimicking a punch to the kidneys and groin. 'I guarantee this jugular takedown will drop any individual, however big or ugly they are.'

'And Blake sure is ugly!' teased Jason.

'Take a look in the mirror, dingo head,' Blake rasped as Steve helped him back to his feet.

'I did but you'd already cracked it,' replied Jason, much to the amusement of the class.

'Cut the banter!' barked Steve. 'Now pair up and practise.'

Charley felt like a lame duck, standing alone as the other recruits buddied up. Being the only girl, it seemed she was the last choice, the weakest player on the team. Furthermore, all the other recruits had arrived with some combat training, whether it was David's military experience, José's street-fighting skills or Jason's junior championship boxing title. All she could claim were a few months of women's self-defence classes.

Blake looked at her. 'Want to partner up?'

'Sure,' said Charley, relieved to be asked. She noticed he was still rubbing his throat. 'Are you all right?'

Blake nodded, then snaked a hand behind her neck to perform the technique on her. 'I warn you – it's a shock when it happens.'

'Fine, I'm read–' Blake's fingers thrust into her jugular notch and shut off her windpipe. An awful gagging sensation caused her body to fold in on itself to escape the crippling discomfort. One moment she was standing. The next she was sprawled on the floor.

'Effective, isn't it?' said Blake, offering his hand to help her up.

Charley could only nod as she fought back the desire to vomit. Now it was her turn to inflict the technique on Blake. Clasping his neck with one hand, she placed the tips of her fingers in the notch above his collarbone and pushed.

Blake grimaced and gagged slightly but didn't drop to the floor. His knees didn't even buckle.

Charley frowned. What had she done wrong? Their instructor made the technique look so easy.

'In and down,' Blake reminded her.

Charley nodded and tried again. This time Blake flinched violently and crumpled under her thrusting fingertips. With surprisingly little strength, she forced him all the way to the ground.

'*That's . . . it!*' Blake gasped, his eyes bulging in pain.

Charley smiled and let him go. The jugular takedown *was* that simple after all.

TARGET
CHAPTER 11

'Ready yourselves for the Gauntlet!' announced Steve.

With nervous reluctance, Charley joined the others at the edge of the hall as they suited themselves up in sparring gear – gloves, shin pads, gumshields and headguards. This was the part of the lesson that she least looked forward to. While the other recruits seemed to relish the challenge of the Gauntlet, for Charley the gruelling experience just emphasized how far out of her league she was. Surrounded by bigger and stronger opponents, she was like a lamb among lions.

'Ladies first,' said Steve, indicating for Charley to take up position at the head of the two rows.

Charley braced herself for the walk of pain that was the Gauntlet. Its purpose was to test their developing martial arts skills in preparation for an assault in the real world. She simply had to get from one end of the sports hall to the other . . . in one piece.

The first time Charley had faced the Gauntlet she'd almost fled the hall. The prospect of fighting nine adrenalin-fuelled boys each in turn had been daunting to say the least.

But Steve had talked her through it, offering instruction at each attack. After a month's training, though, he evidently thought it was time she walked the Gauntlet alone.

Heart thumping, Charley took her first step. The hall seemed to stretch on forever while her opponents multiplied like gremlins. Almost at once Blake grabbed the sleeve of her T-shirt. He raised a fist and Charley hesitated, her mind racing through the techniques they'd been taught.

'Thumb compression,' whispered Blake, fist hovering in mid-air.

Grateful for his suggestion, Charley grasped his hand on her T-shirt. Catching hold of his thumb, she squeezed it as if she was gripping a pair of pliers. Blake winced as his thumb joints were compressed. He dropped to his knees in submission.

'Nice choice of technique,' remarked Steve. 'Subtle yet effective. But, gentlemen, don't hold back just because it's Charley. The enemy won't.'

The next recruit took their instructor at his word and launched a left hook that caught her across the jaw. Although the gloves and headguard took the sting out of it, the punch still hit hard and her head rang like a temple bell, stars sparking before her eyes. As she staggered backwards, a second blow struck her in the ribs, winding her. Charley instinctively curled up, shielding herself with her arms and elbows. More punches rained down.

'Come on, fight back!' urged the recruit.

Charley reeled from his attack. Her brain jarred by the first punch, she couldn't think straight.

Seeing her struggle under the onslaught, Steve called out, 'Stun then run!'

A technique from a previous lesson flashed in her mind. Charley flung out her hand in a wild arc, aiming a ridge-hand strike towards the boy's neck. Steve had told them this was one of the best targets to temporarily disable or drop an opponent. A single sharp blow could cause involuntary muscle spasms and intense pain, while a powerful one focused just below the ear could result in unconsciousness through shock to the carotid artery, jugular vein or vagus nerve. It was the ideal target for a 'stun then run' counter-attack.

The edge of her hand impacted against the boy's nerve and he lurched sideways, the blow disorientating him enough for her to get away.

But Charley had barely recovered from that attack when David rushed at her with a rubber knife. She instinctively blocked the weapon with her forearm. It was a messy defence, and if it had been a real knife her arm would have been cut to shreds. He went for another attack. Charley lashed out and punched him in the face. He backed off. But Charley knew that in real life she'd be the loser.

'Don't punch – palm!' Steve instructed her. 'Remember, palm strikes are just as effective as closed fists, without the risk of damaging your hand. Also the strike looks less violent in the eyes of the public. Never forget someone is always watching or filming your Principal and consequently your every move too.'

Charley had just enough time to absorb this advice

when she was grabbed round the throat by José. In this instance, with the jugular takedown still fresh in her mind from earlier in the lesson, Charley jabbed her fingers into José's windpipe. A sharp thrust towards his feet and he dropped to the floor like a stone.

'Excellent!' praised Steve. 'That's the sort of response I'm looking for.'

Charley felt a rush of accomplishment. Finally a technique that worked for her! With four down and only five to go, her confidence began to rise. But she wasn't allowed to relish the moment for long. Jason came up behind and seized her in a reverse chokehold.

'Let's see you escape this,' he hissed.

Charley struggled in his grip. She knew the first thing she had to do was to twist her head in the direction of the attacker's elbow to relieve the pressure on her windpipe. But Jason was too strong. Charley couldn't breathe . . . at all! His bicep pressing on her carotid artery, her head began buzzing. She clawed at his arm, trying to loosen his grip. She elbowed him in the stomach, but to no avail. Within seconds, all the fight went out of her and darkness seeped into her vision . . .

TARGET
CHAPTER 12

'Did you *have* to strangle Charley till she blacked out?' cried Blake.

'Steve said don't hold back,' Jason replied, his tone defensive. 'Anyway, it was for her own good.'

'How's that?'

'If she can't fight me off, what chance does she have against a real attacker? We're not playing games here, Blake. There are no second chances. If you get it wrong on an assignment, you'll be coming home in a body bag. I mean, what was the colonel thinking when he recruited a *girl*?'

'Don't let Jody hear you say that,' warned José.

'Jody's different. She's an instructor. She knows what she's doing. Charley doesn't seem to have a clue. Don't forget it was her fault we didn't spot that second casualty during the first-aid assessment. If it weren't for Charley, we'd be passing all our assessments.'

'That's unfair,' said Blake. 'Charley did her best.'

'Come on, she virtually talked you to death!' said Jason. The others laughed.

'It's important to reassure the patient,' Blake replied evenly.

'Yeah, I bet you'd like Charley to *reassure* you,' teased David.

'Leave it out!' said Blake, obviously embarrassed.

'Well, she certainly didn't hesitate to give you mouth-to-mouth!' sniggered José.

Charley had heard more than enough. Grateful as she was for Blake's defence of her dignity, she now knew the team's true opinion of her. As the boys continued with their banter in the adjacent changing room, she quietly closed her locker and headed for the door. She'd been in two minds whether to join the team for dinner anyway. Now she'd lost her appetite entirely.

Escaping the old Victorian school building that housed their training facility, Charley tramped across the gravel forecourt and wandered the grounds aimlessly. She discovered an old well and perched herself on the lip, her slender legs dangling over the fathomless black hole. Tossing a stone in, she watched it tumble then disappear. A few seconds later she heard it plop into the unseen water below.

Charley contemplated the void beneath her feet. If she'd been in this dark mood back home in America, she'd simply have gone surfing. But there were no waves within a hundred kilometres of Buddyguard's remote headquarters. Here it was all sheep, craggy hills and bleak rain. She wasn't even sure if Wales had sun! The place was a far cry from the warm beaches and glistening waters of California.

Charley had hoped that Buddyguard would be a fresh start for her. So had her foster-parents, who'd readily agreed to the colonel's proposal – sold to them as an extension of the peace corps. Jenny had declared that volunteer work was the best thing for a wayward teenager like Charley and had even helped pack her bags.

But after four weeks of intensive training Charley was still struggling to clear the start line. Aside from martial arts and advanced first aid, she was required to learn about foot formations, body-cover drills, Cooper's Colour Code, threat assessments, operational planning, world affairs, hostage survival and a whole raft of other security topics that left her head spinning. Then there were early-morning runs up the Welsh mountains, followed by gruelling gym sessions and daily combat classes. On top of all this, she was expected to complete her normal school studies. The learning curve wasn't so much steep as vertical!

Charley realized she may have caught the once-in-a-lifetime wave, but she was already on the verge of wiping out. Jason was right: what had Colonel Black been thinking when recruiting her? And why hadn't he told her that she'd be the only girl recruit?!

Hearing the crunch of gravel, Charley glanced over her shoulder to see Jody heading her way.

'Hey, Charley,' her instructor called cheerily. 'Bugsy said he'd spotted you by the well. Are you OK?'

Charley shrugged. 'Yeah, fine.'

Jody wiped the dirt from one of the well's granite stones and sat down next to her. 'You don't look fine.'

Charley stared into the black abyss of the well and said nothing.

'I heard you passed out in Steve's class. You're not suffering any ill effects, are you?'

Charley shook her head.

'Then what is it? You can talk to me, you know.' Her instructor's tone was soft and sympathetic. 'Us girls need to stick together.'

After almost a minute's silence, Charley thought she might as well come out with it. There was no one else she could talk to. 'I'm not cut out to be a bodyguard.'

Jody blinked. 'What on earth makes you say that?'

'*I'm* not saying it. The rest of the team are.'

Jody frowned. 'Those boys are simply intimidated by you.'

Charley let out a humourless laugh. 'Yeah, right. I don't see them making so many mistakes.'

'Well, I do. All the time. You're barely a month into training. It's bound to feel tough.'

'But everything seems to come more naturally for the boys.'

'Don't you believe that!' scoffed Jody. 'They're struggling just as much as you are. They simply won't admit it.'

'But I don't have their advantage of size or strength. Jason's right. If I can't beat him, what chance do I have?'

'That's why you need to be in good shape and in the gym every day.'

Charley made a face. 'I don't want to become some butch bodyguard.'

'You don't have to. Look at me.' Jody spread her slim, well-toned arms and displayed her slender yet strong physique. 'You can be a rose yet still have thorns. Did you know that Wing Chun – the martial arts style Steve is teaching – was developed by a woman?'

Charley shook her head.

'Well, remember that when you're training against the boys. Bodyguarding is far more about brains than brawn.' She tapped a finger to her temple. 'So next time fight smarter, not harder.'

Jody leant in close to ensure she had Charley's full attention. 'You see, the skills required to be an effective bodyguard aren't based on gender. Whether you're a guy or a girl, you need common sense, good communication skills, awareness, self-discipline and confidence. And we girls do have advantages over the boys.'

'Like what?' asked Charley.

Jody shared a conspiratorial grin. 'For a start, women think differently from men. We can multi-task more effectively. We're able to see and hear many separate events at once, processing them simultaneously. This means we can spot a suspect or early signs of an attack before our male counterparts do. And, if an attack does occur, your opponent certainly won't expect *you* to be a weapon!'

Charley felt a spark of hope. 'So you're saying we're better at this than the boys?'

'I'd like to think so.' Jody smiled. 'Female intuition and the element of surprise give us the upper hand. However, we can sometimes talk too much. And that's where there can be conflict between male and female bodyguards. If I've learnt one thing in my career, it's that action speaks louder than words.'

Charley nodded, recalling Jason's criticism of her during the first-aid test.

'Remember, we're both girls in a man's world,' said Jody. 'This role isn't for the faint-hearted. You need guts. You have to stand your ground with the boys. It's a matter of pride for them, so they'll do whatever's necessary to stop a girl showing them up. But prove yourself and you'll earn their respect.'

TARGET
CHAPTER 13

The scissors cut round Ash's head with absolute precision, each snip shearing away another piece to free the idol's photograph from the magazine article. The blades sliced between the gaps of his perfectly coiffured brown hair, round the diamond-studded left ear and along the sleek curve of his jawline to the dimpled chin. His dark hazel eyes smouldered and his up-turned mouth revealed flawless teeth that gleamed like a toothpaste commercial, while the surrounding skin appeared tanned, smooth and blemish-free.

Photoshopped or not, Ash was blessed with the face of a Greek god – the perfect teen heartthrob. No wonder his posters graced the walls of a billion girls' bedrooms around the world.

With a final snip, the blades cut across the rock star's throat and the magazine dropped away.

The scissors were set aside and the cut-out carefully laid on the table, making sure not to crease it. Then some glue was applied to the back and Ash's disembodied head pasted on to a large sheet of pink paper. More glue was dabbed randomly across the collage before glitter dust and stars were sprinkled liberally over the young icon.

In the dim light of the bedside lamp – the curtains of the room still drawn despite being mid-afternoon – the image now sparkled and glistened like a diamond. The love letter to the famous rock star was beginning to take shape. It just needed one final embellishment.

Putting away the glue and glitter, a small bowl and paintbrush were now placed on the table. The contents of the bowl were slowly stirred with the narrow tip of the brush until the red viscous liquid evened out. It had been a grim and sticky job to collect the blood. The piglet had squealed so loudly when the butcher's knife had sliced its carotid artery. Then its life's blood had spurted out in bursts with each beat of its dying heart, making it difficult to direct the stream into the bowl. And there'd been so much blood for such a small creature. It had overflowed the bowl's rim and spilled on to the floor. The resulting mess had been a nightmare to clean up.

But the piglet hadn't died in vain.

Wiping the excess blood from the brush tip against the bowl's edge, a latex-gloved hand held the letter down. With childlike concentration, three words were scrawled across Ash's perfect face:

NO MORE ENCORES!

TARGET
CHAPTER 14

'A crowd is one of the most risky environments you and your Principal will face on a regular basis,' Colonel Black said, his weathered hands gripping the lectern in Buddyguard's state-of-the-art briefing room that doubled as a classroom. On the main wall hung a giant widescreen display on to which the colonel wirelessly cast a video of a throng of people pushing against a barrier. 'In these situations you'll need to constantly scan the area and assess any possible threats.'

Charley listened intently as she sat in one of the sleek high-backed lecture chairs, the furniture so new that the protective plastic film had yet to be removed from the chrome fittings. Although the outer shell remained a nineteenth-century school building, internally Buddyguard HQ was being revamped with the most advanced electronic hardware and equipment available. Charley and the rest of the team were also equipped with the latest tablet computers on which to take class notes and do their homework.

'So, when vetting a crowd, first try to establish brief eye contact with any suspects.' The colonel thumbed the remote in his hand and the bullet points to his lecture flashed up one by one on the overhead display. 'What are their eyes saying? Are they appearing shifty? Nervous? Upset? Are they fixated on your Principal or perhaps another target?'

Charley rapidly keyed the main points on her tablet, aware she was the only one taking detailed notes. But that didn't bother her. Since her chat with Jody a fortnight ago, Charley had committed herself to becoming the best bodyguard in the team. She'd spent night after night rereading the first-aid manual before her team's reassessment. And this time she hadn't suffered a logjam of information. In fact Jody had passed her with flying colours.

Charley also exercised longer in the gym than the others, her efforts already paying off as she began to overtake the boys on their early-morning runs, her long legs and light build allowing her to bound over the rugged landscape, leaving the more hefty recruits behind. And, taking Jody's advice to fight smarter, not harder, she'd persuaded Steve to give her extra martial arts training during the lunch periods, concentrating on techniques suited to her build and abilities so her combat skills would match the boys'.

This wasn't done to earn the boys' respect but to prove that a girl could do the job just as well – and that *this* girl could do it better. She owed it to her parents to be the best. And she owed it to Kerry not to give up.

'Next, look at people's hands,' said Colonel Black, raising his own and revealing the remote. 'What are they holding? Is one of their hands clasped around something? Or are their hands in their pockets? Or behind their back?'

He pointed to David's rucksack at his feet. 'Ask yourself: what's in the bag they're carrying? What about the contents of their pockets? And, finally, their clothes: are they wearing anything unusual? A bulky coat on a hot day? A hat or dark glasses to conceal their identity? All these questions should go through your head subconsciously as you assess each individual in the crowd. With practice, the process should take a matter of seconds per person.'

Blake leant across to Charley and whispered, 'Can I borrow your notes after the lesson?'

Charley could tell from his roguish grin he was turning on the charm, but she didn't really mind. Blake was the only member of the team willing to fight her corner and she had no intention of isolating herself further. 'Sure,' she said.

'Thanks, you're a lifesaver,' he replied with a wink.

'Pay attention, you two!' said the colonel, snapping his fingers. 'You mustn't forget a crowd is a dynamic situation. Once you've decided an individual isn't a threat, *don't* dismiss them entirely. The attacker could be a professional assassin or simply very good at hiding their intentions.'

Triggering the remote, he launched an old grainy video clip of a group of men leaving a hotel and crossing the pavement to a waiting limo.

'The attempted assassination of the former US President Ronald Reagan demonstrates this clearly.' Colonel Black pointed to a suited man walking towards the camera. 'See here! This secret service agent looks directly at the attacker who's off-screen. The agent doesn't consider him a threat, so ignores him and turns inwards to where Ronald Reagan is about to enter his vehicle. He now has his back to the attacker.'

On the video footage several gunshots went off and people dived to the ground in panic. President Reagan was bundled into the limo as one brave secret service agent spread his arms and shielded him from the deadly hail of bullets. A round caught the agent in the gut and sent him tumbling to the tarmac, but by then Reagan was speeding safely away and the attacker neutralized.

When the video clip finished, silence filled the room. For the first time the young bodyguards were confronted with the brutal reality of what it meant to stand in the line of fire to protect another.

Charley raised a tentative hand. 'Did the agent who was shot *die*?'

Colonel Black shook his head. 'No, he made a full recovery. But no one need have been hurt if that first agent had done his job properly and not turned his back on the crowd. Don't make that mistake yourself.'

He switched off the overhead display. 'Now let's put these skills into practice. José, you're a famous film star.'

'Naturally,' he replied, getting to his feet with a swagger.

'Yeah, a stand-in for Speedy Gonzalez!' quipped Jason.

'Ha ha, that's very funny for someone who looks like Skippy the Kangaroo!' José shot back.

Colonel Black silenced the pair with a sharp look before

continuing his briefing. 'Unfortunately, José, your last film offended a few people and you're the target for a potential attack. Jason, you'll be his bodyguard. Blake, David and Charley, you'll form the Personal Escort Section.' He opened a door leading through to an adjacent classroom. 'Now go and meet your fans!'

Leaping from their seats, the PES team hurriedly positioned themselves into a protective arrowhead formation round their Principal, as taught by the colonel in a previous lesson. Then they entered the room to be greeted by a small crowd of the other five recruits and instructors impersonating excited fans.

'Hey, José, can I have your autograph?' asked one lad.

'Absolutely, my friend,' grinned José, play-acting his superstar role to the max. 'Any more takers?'

The mini-crowd surged forward and surrounded him. Charley and the rest of the team struggled to keep them at a safe distance as José signed more autographs and posed for selfies. All the while Charley's eyes darted from each person's face to their hands to their clothes. She hunted for signs of a would-be attacker.

Of course, there might not be one. During their training, they'd enacted numerous different scenarios. Sometimes there was an attack. Other times nothing happened. Just as in real life.

But on this occasion Charley noticed their surveillance tutor Bugsy hanging at the back of the crowd. He was making no effort to meet José the film star, and this unnatural behaviour set him apart from the others.

Suddenly they heard wild shouting. Jason and the rest of the PES team spun towards the disruption. The room's widescreen display had been switched on and was blaring out a newsreel of a riot. With the buddyguard recruits distracted, Bugsy pushed through the crowd and swung a bottle at José's head.

No one on the team reacted to the attack . . . apart from Charley.

Having kept one eye on her suspect, she was ready for the surprise assault. She leapt to José's defence, shoving him aside and shielding him with her body, only for the bottle to strike her instead. It smashed to pieces over her head and she staggered under the impact.

Everyone in the room froze.

'Was that a *real* bottle?' asked Jason, more in awe at the idea than any concern for Charley.

'No. It's just sugar glass,' replied Bugsy in a matter-of-fact tone.

'Well, it hurt like one!' cried Charley. She took her hands away. There was no blood, but she could feel a mighty bruise forming. 'Couldn't you have used a plastic one?'

'Wouldn't be realistic enough,' Bugsy explained. 'You have to be able to take a hit as a bodyguard – and still function.' He eyed the other members of the team. 'Which is the reason I'm wondering why the rest of you haven't evacuated your Principal yet!'

Snapped from their daze, Jason and the others grabbed José and rushed him out. Charley, still reeling from the blow, stumbled after them back into the briefing room.

With the exercise over, José stopped acting the film star as Blake helped Charley to a chair. 'Thanks for taking the hit for me,' said José.

'My pleasure,' Charley groaned, cradling her head in her hands.

'That looked like it really hurt!' remarked Blake as he knelt down beside her.

Charley gave another groan in reply.

Jason grinned. 'She should have blocked it properly.'

'Well, I didn't see *you* react,' the colonel pointed out. 'And you were José's bodyguard!'

The smug grin fell from Jason's face as he was shamed into silence.

The colonel nodded at Charley. 'At least someone was paying attention in my class. You might be hurting, Charley, but you've learnt a valuable lesson – always expect the unexpected.'

TARGET

CHAPTER 15

'Colonel, have you got a minute?' asked Charley, racing after him as he headed for his Range Rover. She'd tried to pin the colonel down on numerous occasions, but, apart from his specialist classes, he was rarely around, always rushing off on urgent business-related matters.

The colonel stopped, his highly polished boots scrunching on the gravel of the school forecourt. 'Of course, Charley. How's your head?'

'OK, I guess,' she replied, tenderly testing the growing bruise with a finger.

'It's a hard lesson. But one you won't forget.'

Charley nodded and winced as her skull gave a throb. 'Colonel, you said to expect the unexpected, but I didn't expect to be the only girl at Buddyguard. If you believe girls make good bodyguards, why haven't you recruited more?'

The colonel's expression remained impassive. 'You were the first I've found up to the task . . . and the only one since to say yes.'

Charley was taken aback to discover this. 'But why didn't you tell me?'

'Would it have made a difference to your decision?'

Charley shrugged. 'Probably not. But it'd be nice to have the company. I feel a bit outnumbered by the boys.'

'Don't worry, I'm working on it,' he said with a wry smile. 'Just takes time to find suitable recruits.'

'So, how *do* you find recruits?' she asked. The question had been bugging her for a while.

'They usually make themselves known to us – through their actions.'

'Like when I saved that boy from the shark?'

The colonel nodded. 'I was actually on holiday,' he admitted. 'But your heroics caught my eye. And after our little chat in the dunes and subsequent research I saw real potential in you.' He placed a hand on her shoulder and looked her in the eye. 'Listen, I know from Jody you've been questioning your abilities. *Don't.* You're doing well. Just keep your chin up.'

He gave her shoulder a squeeze, then pulled out his car keys. The Range Rover beeped, its indicators flashing. He opened the driver's door and got in. 'And my advice for handling the boys: give as good as you get.'

Gunning the engine, Colonel Black saluted a goodbye, then sped off down the long driveway, the Range Rover's heavy-duty tyres kicking up gravel as they went.

Charley stood in the forecourt, mulling over his words, until the car had crested the hill. Colonel Black clearly believed in her. Her efforts *were* being recognized – if not by the team, then at least by those who counted.

With a more confident spring in her step, Charley headed

back inside the school building. She found Blake sitting at the bottom of the staircase in the entrance hall.

'What are you doing?' she asked.

'Waiting for you,' he replied with a warm smile.

Charley blinked in shock. Then she remembered. 'Ah, yes. You wanted my class notes,' she said, pulling out her tablet from her bag. 'I could've just emailed them to you.'

'I know,' he said, his eyes lingering on her. 'But it's nicer to do things personally.'

Charley felt a warmth in her cheeks. Before Blake could notice the effect his gaze was having on her, she busied herself transferring the notes to his tablet. 'There you go,' she said.

Blake smiled again. 'Thanks. I really appreciate it. I tend to miss things – I'm not as fast as you at typing.'

'No problem. Any time,' she replied breezily, returning the tablet to her bag.

Blake stood up, closer to her than she expected, and was about to say something else when they were interrupted.

'Hey, Blake!' called David, appearing in the hallway. 'Are you coming to play football or not?'

'Yeah,' he replied, then turned back to Charley. 'Catch you later?'

Charley nodded and watched him run off to join the others. Perhaps there were advantages to being the only girl.

TARGET
CHAPTER 16

'What's this?' said Bugsy, pointing to a blue Tupperware box on the desk.

Charley and the rest of the team exchanged bemused glances. The answer seemed obvious. 'A lunch box,' said Blake.

'No. It's a bomb.'

Everyone instinctively flinched away, the briefing room suddenly feeling too small.

'A real one?' José queried.

Their surveillance tutor gave a nod of his bald head and grinned as deviously as the Cheshire cat from *Alice in Wonderland*. 'This one happens to be a smoke bomb,' he revealed, removing the lid and exposing the small package of wires and components inside. 'But it'd be a simple matter to upgrade this to a fire bomb or a high-explosive device capable of destroying this entire building.'

He held up a red block of what appeared to be plasticine.

'PBX,' said Bugsy. 'Plastic-bonded explosive.'

He tossed it to Jason, who caught it, freaked out and almost dropped the innocuous-looking block on the floor.

'Relax, Jason, PBX requires a considerable shock to set it off.'

'Better not look at it then,' warned Charley. 'You might trigger an explosion.'

The class burst into laughter and Jason scowled. José raised a hand to high-five her. 'Harsh but fair, girl!'

Claiming the high-five, Charley realized, for the first time, she was making ground with the team. As the colonel said, she just had to give as good as she got.

'Eat PBX!' Jason growled, lobbing the explosive at her.

She caught it in one hand, much to his annoyance. The PBX was surprisingly light, pliable and slightly greasy to the touch.

'You still have to pay it respect, though,' said Bugsy as Charley tested the material with a squeeze. 'What you're holding in your hand would be enough to kill everyone in this room.'

Charley stared in horror at the deadly block, then hurriedly passed it back to her tutor.

'Pound for pound, PBX packs a pretty big punch. So what's the main advantage of a bomb over other weapons?' he asked the class.

Jason opened his mouth to reply, but Charley cut in, 'The bomber doesn't have to be there.'

'Exactly,' said Bugsy as Jason glowered at her and slumped back in his seat. 'They could be thousands of miles away and detonate it remotely with a mobile or by fitting a timer. Compare that to using a knife or a gun, where the perpetrator has to be present and their chances of being captured or killed increase dramatically. And acquiring a gun in countries like the UK can be a serious challenge. However, with a few easily obtainable household items, any schoolboy can make a bomb.'

'Cool!' said José, sitting up in his chair with interest. 'Are you going to show us how?'

'No, but I'll teach you what to do if you spot one,' replied Bugsy as the first slide of his presentation appeared on the widescreen display. 'The rule of the Four Cs: *confirm*, *clear*, *cordon*, *control*.'

Charley picked up her tablet and began to input the meaning of the Four Cs into her class notes. Blake smiled at her and winked, confident he could rely on her notes. Charley smiled back.

'A bomb can be hidden in a suspect car or truck, dropped in a waste bin or left at the roadside. It can be disguised as a rucksack, a rubbish bag or even a mobile phone. Whatever it is that arouses your suspicions, first you must *confirm* those suspicions.'

'Isn't that going to be dangerous?' asked David, his question more a statement of fact than a matter of concern. To Charley, David appeared a strong silent type. She knew little of his past, but he always acted in the same calm and unhurried manner, whether chilling out in the common room or under fire during a training scenario. It was as if he'd seen it all before, or had seen a great deal worse in his life and was numb to it.

'Well, it certainly doesn't mean giving the suspect bag a kick, let alone opening it!' Bugsy replied. 'Any suspect items must be considered booby-trapped. So, for starters, switch off any mobiles.'

'But that would prevent us calling the authorities,' Blake pointed out.

'True, but radio waves are often used to trigger remote-control bombs. You don't want to accidentally set it off yourself!' Bugsy explained. 'Next, establish who the item belongs to. If you can't find the owner, then the item is a threat. Whether your Principal is the intended target or not makes no difference. Bombs are indiscriminate killers.'

'So if we believe it's a bomb we *clear* the area?' asked Charley, looking up from her notes.

'Absolutely.' Bugsy nodded. 'Trust your gut instinct and clear to a safe distance, quickly and without panic. In Hollywood movies, you see the hero outrunning an explosion. In reality no one can outrun an explosion. One second everything is normal and the next second everything is destroyed. The biggest killer can be the blast wave and what's contained in it, shards of glass and debris, so you need to reach a sheltered location.'

'What about the other two Cs?' asked David.

'Once clear, you can call the emergency services and hand over responsibility for them to *cordon* off the area and *control* the situation. Even if the suspect item turns out to be harmless, it's better to make sure your Principal is safe than risk being blown to bits!'

Bugsy picked up a brown padded envelope from the desk and waved it in the air.

'Don't forget your friendly mailman or courier,' he said

with a grim expression. 'Letter and parcel bombs are a favoured device for terrorists, criminals and those with a grudge. Traditionally explosive or incendiary, nowadays they can be chemical, biological or even radiological.'

'A nuclear letter!' José grimaced. 'I'm not handling anyone's mail.'

'Wise decision,' agreed Bugsy. 'Any attempt to open one might set it off. But as a bodyguard you're responsible for all aspects of your Principal's safety. There are a number of telltale signs to look out for – the Seven Ss, to be exact.'

On the display, the presentation bullet-pointed *Size*, *Shape*, *Sender*, *Stamp*, *Seal*, *Stain* and *Smell*.

'*Size*,' began Bugsy. 'The letter needs to be big enough to house the components, so will be at least five millimetres thick, weigh over fifty grams and may feel unusually heavy for its size. *Shape* – the package could be lopsided or lumpy, indicating possible batteries or switching systems. *Sender* – check the postmark. Where did it come from? Is the origin unusual? Is there a return address and can it be verified? *Stamp* – is there one? Or was it hand-delivered? There may even be extra postage since the last thing the perpetrator wants is his letter bomb to be returned to sender!'

The class chuckled at their tutor's black humour. Meanwhile Charley's fingers flew across her tablet screen as she raced to take down the details. Swamped by so much information, the rest of the team had given up taking notes altogether. Charley was aware that Blake shared her notes with the others and the boys had started relying on her to write up their lessons for future revision. Though this irritated her, she hoped it might raise her value within the team, so she let it ride. Besides, she enjoyed her regular meetings with Blake after class and they were becoming close friends.

'*Seal* – one end may have been purposefully secured to force entry at the other end,' continued Bugsy. 'Also look out for a pin-sized hole indicating the use of an external arming device. *Stain* – some explosives can weep an oily residue that will produce marks on the outside of the envelope. Finally, *smell* – if there's a strange aroma of almonds or marzipan, this could indicate nitroglycerin. Then again –' Bugsy switched the presentation to a picture of a chocolate sponge lit by candles – 'it could just be a cake!'

TARGET
CHAPTER 17

The screaming never ceased. A constant white noise of high-pitched delirium, it assaulted Ash's hotel room day and night. He unthinkingly wandered too close to a window and the screaming intensified as his name was chanted to the skies. *ASH WILD! ASH WILD!* It was so loud at one point that the glass actually vibrated in its frame.

Glancing down at the hordes of fans on the street below, Ash gave a dutiful wave. This whipped the fans into an even greater frenzy and the street turned into a seething mass of hysterical girls. Some had been camped there for days, desperate for a glimpse of their idol following the online leak of his hotel location in London. During his initial rush of fame Ash had found their presence flattering, even reassuring. Now the permanent border guard of fans wherever he went had become claustrophobic. He felt like a goldfish trapped in a bowl, a thousand eyes watching his every movement.

Ash went back to pacing the room. The lounge area was exactly twenty-five strides long and fourteen wide. The dimensions hadn't changed during his entire time holed up in his luxury suite and he knew they never would. Slumping on to a plush velvet sofa, Ash picked up his acoustic guitar and began to strum.

'*You lift me up*,' he sang softly to himself, '*because . . .*'

The lyric hung in the air, unfinished. He sought inspiration, but none came. Sighing, he tried again, repeating the phrase over and over, each time hoping to find the elusive line that would lead to the next part of the melody.

But after countless attempts he gave up. His creativity was stifled in this hotel room. He'd been cooped up far too long – at least he hoped that was the reason. Deep down he feared his muse had abandoned him altogether following the shock of the letter bomb.

How could anyone send him a lethal parcel like that? What had he done for anyone to hate him so much? His worst crime in his life so far had been to cheat on Hanna. But ex-girlfriends don't send letter bombs simply for kissing another girl . . . not unless they're totally mental!

Letting the guitar slide to the floor, Ash reached for the remote and surrendered himself to daytime TV. Halfway through a repeat episode of *The Big Bang Theory*, there was a knock at the door. Ash switched the TV off. The door opened and Big T's face with its heavy jowls and wide boxer nose appeared.

'Ms Gibson's 'ere,' he grunted in his hard Cockney accent. He stepped aside to allow Ash's manager into the room. Then, nodding politely to them both, he closed the door and resumed his guard duty outside in the hallway.

Kay Gibson greeted Ash with her arms wide. 'How's my superstar?'

She strode over to him, the high heels of her Jimmy Choos leaving deep impressions in the carpet. At almost six foot with chopped dyed-red hair, ruby lips and a cosmetically youthful face, Kay Gibson was a daunting bombshell of a woman. Record company executives admired her striking looks as much as they feared her brutal negotiation tactics and sharp business acumen. Within the music industry, she was known as the Red Devil or the Ruby Angel, depending on which side of the table one sat, for Kay was deeply loyal and protective of her artists and always struck the best deal for them.

'Glad to see you're not wasting your free time,' she remarked, eyeing the TV remote in his hand.

Ash sighed. 'I need to get out of here.'

'Soon.'

'That's what you always say. I've been living in this hotel room for almost two months!'

Kay gazed round at the fine furnishings, four-poster bed and original artwork lining the walls. 'You don't have any complaints about the room, do you?'

'No, it's just that I'd like to be in my own place again,' he explained, pulling himself into a sitting position. 'I can't write here.'

Kay raised a manicured eyebrow in alarm. 'That's not good. But I've told you – it isn't easy acquiring new property in London. Especially one that's exclusive and secure enough to meet your needs, but . . .' Her green eyes twinkled with promise. 'I'm pleased to say I've found you one at last.'

Ash stared at her in disbelief. 'Really? So when do I move in?'

'With any luck, by the weekend.'

Ash leapt off the sofa, whooping with delight.

'But we need to tighten your security arrangements,' she warned. 'We don't want your new address being revealed. Just because that letter bomb turned out to be a fake doesn't mean we shouldn't take any threat seriously.'

The mention of the bomb punctured Ash's buoyant mood. 'Have the police found out who sent it yet?' he asked.

Kay shook her head. 'They've still no leads. The only fingerprints on the packaging were yours and Big T's. The police conclude it was a well-planned hoax.'

'Is their investigation over then?'

Kay nodded. 'I'm afraid so. With no postmark or any other clues, they say there's nothing they can do.'

'But it wasn't exactly standard hate mail, was it?'

Kay put a motherly arm round him. 'It's a one-off. Think of it as a status symbol. It means you're officially famous now.'

'Wow, that's reassuring,' muttered Ash.

'Don't get down about it. All the great artists receive death threats and acquire their own stalkers. Madonna. Lennon. Beyoncé –'

'But wasn't John Lennon killed by his stalker?' interrupted Ash.

Kay looked pained. 'Bad example. But you don't have to worry – you've got Big T as your bodyguard. And considering what's happened I've employed him full-time now. He's worth his weight in gold. Not literally, of course; that would cost us a small fortune.' She laughed at her own joke, then became serious again. 'But if that had been a real bomb Big T would have saved your life.'

Ash fell silent, his brush with death a chilling thought.

'I've something that'll put a smile back on your face,' said his manager, fishing into the pocket of her tailored suit. 'The master of your new single!'

She produced a memory stick. Grinning, Ash took it from her and plugged it into the portable recording studio set up in the corner of the room. He'd been waiting for his producer to put the final touches to the recording. Switching on the monitors, he loaded the file labelled *Indestructible* into his computer's media player. A driving beat in the vein of Michael Jackson's 'Billie Jean' pulsed from the speakers. A throbbing bass line amplified the groove, then a guitar riff kicked in as Ash launched into the opening verse.

'This song is going to make you a megastar like no other!' declared Kay, tapping her foot to the beat.

As the song hit the chorus, Ash's mobile phone beeped. He glanced at the screen and frowned.

'What's the matter?' asked Kay.

Ash showed her the text he'd received:

Play it backwards.

'Who's it from?' she asked, equally perplexed.

'Don't know,' he replied. 'No Caller ID.'

Curiosity getting the better of him, Ash reversed the media file and hit play. The song sounded warped and alien, the words as distorted and unsettling as a satanic chant. But the message was clear enough: '*Asssshhhhh willlll dieeeee . . . Asssshhhhh willlll dieeeee . . . Asssshhhhh willlll dieeeee . . .*'

TARGET
CHAPTER 18

Clouds streaked across the grey-blue sky, their shadows chasing them over the peaks and troughs of the mountainous terrain that surrounded Buddyguard HQ. Shafts of sunlight speared the summits before sweeping across valleys of lush green fields speckled white with sheep. The blustery air was crisp, cool and clean to breathe – unlike the smog-tainted atmosphere of the Californian coast.

After almost three months, Charley was starting to appreciate the stark beauty of the Brecon Beacons. From her bench in the old school's summer house, she could see the sweeping expanse of craggy mountains and even glimpse the impressive wedge of Pen y Fan in the far distance. However, awe-inspiring as the view was, she could never call it home. The place was just too darn cold, even with summer approaching.

Pulling her jumper round her shoulders, Charley settled back to studying her notes. The wooden summer house with its roof overrun by creeper vines was her secret haven – a retreat from the hectic hothouse of bodyguard training. As she read up on Bugsy's anti-surveillance tactics, she was vaguely aware of the fervent yells and cries of the other recruits playing soccer. There was a loud cheer and she guessed one of the boys had scored a goal.

A ball rolled past the summer house, followed a moment later by the lithe figure of Blake jogging after it. He kicked the ball back to his teammates before noticing Charley.

'Hey,' said Blake, poking his head in.

'Hey yourself,' she replied, glancing up as if she hadn't seen him until then. Although they'd been spending more and more time together, she was keen not to appear needy or desperate for his company.

'What are you doing in here?' he asked.

'Reading.'

Blake spied the tablet in her hands. 'Charley, it's Sunday! Our *only* day off.'

Charley shrugged. 'What else do you suggest I do? Everyone else is playing soccer.'

A twinge of guilt flashed across Blake's face. 'Sorry, but I didn't think football would interest you.'

'It doesn't,' she replied. *But it would have been nice to be asked*, she thought.

Blake hesitated at the door, clearly questioning whether to stay or not. Then he called to the others, 'Play on without me. I'm taking a break.'

He sat next to her on the bench. 'So, what does interest you?' he asked.

Charley stared resolutely at her notes. 'Surfing.'

'I didn't know you surfed,' said Blake, surprised.

Charley looked sideways at him. 'There're a lot of things you don't know about me.'

Blake flinched at the harshness in her tone. Charley didn't know why she was being so rough on him. After all, he was the one who took her side and was pretty much her only friend among the recruits.

'I'm sorry,' she mumbled. 'I'm a bit fed up, that's all.'

'About what?'

Charley sighed. 'We've completed three months of training. I'm working as hard as everyone else, if not harder, yet I still don't feel like a full member of the team.'

'Of course you are,' said Blake.

Charley raised a dubious eyebrow. 'You all treat me as some sort of secretary rather than a serious recruit.'

'I certainly don't,' Blake replied, his tone earnest. He slid closer, his leg now touching hers. 'I mean, I appreciate you sharing your notes and all, but I respect you and your abilities.'

'Thanks. I'm not sure the others do.'

'Listen,' said Blake. 'It isn't easy being the only girl among a bunch of meatheads, but don't let them get to you.' He glanced towards the open door, then back at her. 'I like you,' he admitted with a disarming smile. 'A lot. And I hate to see you upset and lonely. Not when there's no need to be.'

He leant nearer. Charley could see the intention in his eyes. Briefly she considered resisting. But Blake being nice to her meant a lot in the circumstances. And as he put an arm round her shoulders she could feel her defences weakening. She wanted to be accepted, to be liked.

Charley closed her eyes and parted her lips . . . but pulled away at the last second.

'What's the matter?' Blake asked.

Charley looked at the door. 'Didn't you hear something?'

Blake listened. Everything was quiet outside. He shook his head. Smiling, he went back in for the kiss.

This time Charley didn't pull away.

Just as their lips touched, an object clattered on to the wooden floor at their feet. It exploded and the summer house billowed with smoke. Within seconds the two of them were enveloped in an impenetrable cloud. Coughing and spluttering, they staggered out into the fresh air.

Jason and the other recruits stood outside, killing themselves with laughter.

'What the hell was *that*?' Blake exclaimed, tears streaming from his red eyes.

Jason laughed. 'Bugsy's smoke bomb!'

'It looked like things were getting a little hot in there,' sniggered David.

'*What is it with you?*' Charley cried, striding up to Jason, her pent-up fury with him spilling over.

'Calm down, Charley. It was just a joke,' he replied, holding up his hands and backing away. 'The Four Cs!'

Charley glared at him, frowning in confusion.

'We *confirmed* the threat: Blake.' Jason grinned at his spluttering friend. 'We *cleared* the danger zone. Now I'm afraid we'll have to *cordon* off this summer house and *control* you two in future!'

Charley's face reddened. With the boys' laughter ringing in her ears and smoke still billowing from the summer house, she stormed off to her room.

CHAPTER 19

Charley grabbed her duffel bag from under her bed and began shoving her clothes into it. Her cheeks were still burning with shame and her eyes tearful from the acrid smoke. She not only felt humiliated by the boys' prank but was angry with herself for her moment of weakness. Labelled as Blake's *girlfriend*, she'd never be accepted as a serious member of the team now.

While she'd made some headway in gaining their respect, she knew they still considered her the token female. Charley was equally frustrated with being the only girl on the team. Where were the others the colonel had promised to recruit? After months of persistent ribbing, sexist comments and snide remarks about her abilities as a bodyguard, she'd hit her limit.

Emptying the contents of her drawers into the bag, she then picked up the picture of her parents from the bedside cabinet. The photo had been taken the day she'd won her first surfing trophy and the memory was still precious. It had been a perfect day, the sky cloudless, the sun glinting off the glassy waters, the waves curling like massive scoops of ice cream. She'd surfed her heart out and blown the rest of the competition out of the water. She could recall her parents' sheer joy at her achievement. They'd seen it as a milestone in her recovery from Kerry's abduction. And looking now at the proud smiles on their faces Charley sat down and questioned what she was doing. *Am I really going to give up that easily? Let those boys get to me that much? Let them win?*

She remembered her mother once saying, 'When you doubt your power, you give power to your doubt.' And that was exactly what she was doing now.

There was a knock at her door. She glanced up to see Blake standing in the doorway.

'You're not leaving, are you?' he asked, his gaze flicking to her half-packed duffel bag.

'It had crossed my mind,' she replied.

'Come on – it was just a stupid prank,' he said, sitting next to her on the bed.

'I know that,' said Charley. 'But I've had enough of being the butt of all the team's jokes.'

Blake sighed. 'They don't mean it personally.'

'Well, it feels personal to me,' she replied. 'Jason, especially.'

'He's just jealous,' said Blake, taking her hand.

'Of us?'

Blake laughed. 'No, of your abilities. I know it riles him every time you outshine him in class. He simply can't accept a girl can be better than him.'

'Well, he'd better get used to it,' said Charley, returning

her parents' picture to the bedside cabinet. 'Because I'm here to stay.'

'That's the spirit,' said Blake, squeezing her hand affectionately. 'Now, look, the team all know we like one another. So why hide it? Why not just make it official?'

Charley looked at him. It would be so easy to say yes . . . but she wanted to be accepted by the team on her own merits. Not as the *girlfriend*.

'I'll think about it,' she replied. *But first I have a point to prove.*

TARGET

CHAPTER 20

'No sparring gear!' declared Steve to everyone's astonishment. 'This final Gauntlet will be a real-life scenario.'

A rush of adrenalin coursed through Charley's veins and her pulse raced. The recruits had been preparing themselves for this unarmed combat assessment for the past week, but none had expected to fight without protection.

Steve chortled at the shocked expressions on his students' faces. 'On an assignment, you won't have the luxury of pads and headgear, nor will your attacker be wearing boxing gloves. They'll hit hard and without mercy. So get used to it. You've completed basic training – now let's see which of you makes the grade.'

Steve approached Charley. 'First or last?'

Holding her nerves in check, Charley replied without hesitation, 'First.'

She'd trained hard in the gym every day and was at the peak of physical fitness. The weeks of extra combat classes had honed her martial arts skills. So if there was ever a time to prove herself as a bodyguard, once and for all, this was it.

'Remember, in a conflict you only get out what you put in,' Steve advised. 'Speed and aggression will always win, even if your technique is less than perfect. But perfect technique delivered with speed and aggression is *unbeatable*.'

Charley took her place at the head of the Gauntlet. The other recruits were limbering up and Jason stood at the far end, cracking his knuckles in anticipation, his eyes narrowed in an obvious challenge. Ignoring him, Charley bounced lightly on the balls of her feet and shook the tension from her arms. It was time to teach these boys a lesson.

Yet Charley was keenly aware the odds of surviving nine consecutive attacks were slim to say the least.

'Begin!' barked Steve.

With a last deep breath, Charley headed into the Gauntlet.

The first recruit seized her wrist as if to drag her away. Charley spun her arm in a high arc, spiralling her attacker's own arm until the joints locked and pain forced him to let go. Gripping the boy's hand, she then compressed the wrist joint and forced her attacker to the ground. To ensure he didn't get up again, Charley delivered a swift kick to his gut, leaving the boy winded and wheezing on the floor.

Blake was up next. He swung a roundhouse punch at her, telegraphing it early to give her a chance to react. As much as she liked him, how she wished he *wouldn't* keep making allowances for her. In the beginning, his gestures were appreciated, but now they felt belittling, as if Blake believed she wasn't capable of defending herself against a real attack. She blocked it hard, striking at an inner nerve in his bicep muscle so that his arm became temporarily paralysed. As the pain registered, she delivered a one-inch push to his chest. Steve had yet to teach this technique to the other recruits, so it came as a complete surprise to Blake. Like a coiled-up spring, Charley drove her palm into his solar plexus and shoved him backwards. The super-powered push sent Blake flying. He landed in a heap on the floor, utterly incapacitated and fighting for breath.

The other boys immediately upped their game. The next recruit produced a rubber knife and thrust the blade at her stomach. With the speed of a panther, Charley shifted off line and knuckle-punched the back of the boy's hand – her target a *kyusho* nerve point that sent a crippling stab of pain through the boy's hand, forcing him to drop the knife. Then Charley reached for his face, clawed her fingers into his eye sockets and wrenched his head back. At the same time, she side-kicked the back of his knee. The boy slammed into the wooden floor.

'Stay down!' hissed Charley. Terrified by her wild-cat glare, the boy did exactly as he was told.

A moment later Charley was charged by Sean, an ox of a recruit. She stumbled backwards under his assault. Overpowering her through sheer brute strength, he pinned her against the wall and clasped his hands round her throat. Charley spluttered for breath. But she didn't panic. Instead she swung an arm across and down on to his elbow joints. Sean collapsed forward under his own weight. Sliding aside at the last second, Charley drove him head first into the wall. Sean staggered away in a daze.

David now approached at speed. Charley flicked her fingers in his eyes. Half-blinded, David was unable to defend himself as she followed up with a kick to the groin. Although not delivered at full force, the kick was more than enough to drop her team member.

'*That's* for the smoke bomb,' she whispered before moving down the line.

Having just witnessed David's excruciating takeout, José hesitated in his attack. Charley took full advantage of this: she slammed an open palm into his chin. The impact compressed his jaw and caused José to black out momentarily. He slumped to the floor like a rag doll – a perfect stun-then-run manoeuvre.

With six recruits down and three remaining, Charley felt both elated and exhausted. Her breath was ragged and her heart pumping hard. But her merciless onslaught of the others had knocked the remaining boys' confidence and she dispatched the next two with surprising ease.

Charley couldn't believe it. She was almost at the end of the Gauntlet.

Only Jason barred her path and he didn't look at all daunted. He threw a lightning-fast punch to her head. Charley ducked beneath it, only to discover it had been a feint. With his other fist, Jason caught her in the stomach and all the breath was driven out of her. Doubling over in pain, Charley was helpless as Jason seized her neck. Once again she found herself in a lethal chokehold.

'Night-night, Charley,' Jason taunted as he squeezed and blocked off her windpipe.

Charley knew there was little point in struggling – she couldn't match Jason's strength. With no oxygen in her lungs, she had less than ten seconds before she blacked out.

Fight smarter, not harder.

Following Jody's advice, Charley reached across and took hold of Jason's little finger. Hoping he'd forgive her one day, Charley wrenched it back until she heard a snap. Jason bawled in agony and instantly let her go.

'It's for your own good,' she said, delivering his own line back at him, before striding the last few metres of the Gauntlet unchallenged.

Behind her, the sports hall was littered with groaning and injured boys.

Charley couldn't help but smile at the sight. All her hard work and extra training had paid off.

'*She broke my finger!*' Jason cried in disbelief as he stared at his misshapen joint.

'Stop whingeing, Jason,' said Steve, inspecting the damaged hand. 'It's only dislocated.'

Without warning, he tugged on the little finger and realigned the bones. Jason let out a whimper and went white with pain and shock.

'Man up!' said Steve, giving Jason a pat on the shoulder. Then he headed down the sports hall to Charley. 'Congratulations, that was a remarkable performance. Speed, aggression and technique – an unbeatable combination.'

He extended a meaty hand to her. As Charley went to

shake it, she noticed her instructor had kept his other hand behind his back.

Always expect the unexpected.

Letting her instincts take control, Charley swiftly ducked under her instructor's arm. At the same time, she kept a firm grip on his hand, rotating his whole arm until it locked out. Driving it upward, she forced him to flip over to prevent his elbow breaking. Steve landed with a heavy crash on his back. He stared up at her with a combination of pain and pride.

'You made . . . the grade,' he wheezed as the bottle he'd been concealing rolled from his grip and across the floor.

From the doorway came the sound of slow but appreciative clapping.

'Charley, you've surpassed even my expectations,' Colonel Black declared with a rare smile. 'I believe you're ready for your first assignment.'

TARGET

CHAPTER 21

Charley almost went into shock. It was only the second day of her assignment, but she couldn't believe what she'd just witnessed. It wasn't an attack, a kidnapping attempt or even a shooting. Her Principal, fifteen-year-old Salma bin Saud, had just bought a leather Chanel purse for more than a thousand pounds!

Charley knew that Harrods was one of the most desirable and expensive places to shop in the world, but she was truly stunned at the price tag – and even more taken aback by Salma's blasé attitude to it. Then Salma spotted a matching handbag – a snip at just under two thousand pounds – and added this to her growing pile of luxury goods. This girl was spending money like water, not even batting an eyelid when the sales clerk rang up a final bill of several thousand pounds.

For the first time Charley realized just how different this world was. Having been assigned as personal buddyguard to a Saudi Arabian princess on holiday in London, Charley was getting a rare glimpse into how the super-rich lived. It was surreal.

As the sales clerk bagged the stack of purchases, Charley recovered from her initial shock and returned to her close-protection duties. While no specific threat had been identified for the princess, her status and sheer wealth made her an obvious target for criminals and kidnappers alike. Charley's eyes swept the department store for suspicious individuals and any possible danger. This being Harrods, there was ample security in place. Besides the discreet surveillance cameras and peak-capped security guards at the doors, Charley had spotted a number of plain-clothes officers wandering the aisles, impersonating regular shoppers. Harrods was as safe a place as any in London. Still Charley remained in Code Yellow, the relaxed yet alert state she'd been taught to maintain as a bodyguard.

'Take those,' Salma ordered.

Charley looked at the two neatly packed Harrods shopping bags, but made no move to pick them up. 'I'm sorry, Salma, but that's not what I'm here for.'

Salma glared at her. 'You don't expect *me* to carry them, do you?'

Charley blanched. 'I need to keep my hands free in case there's a problem,' she explained.

'Then carry them in one hand,' said Salma, her tone indignant.

Charley didn't know how far to push this. Her duty was to protect her Principal, not the shopping. Yet she didn't want to upset the princess and receive a bad report. As Charley considered her next response, Salma retrieved the Chanel purse from one of the bags.

'Fine, I'll carry this.' She sighed, as if she was doing Charley a massive favour.

Charley bit back on her tongue. Her bodyguard training may have prepared her for physical assaults, terrorist bombs and bullet wounds, but it hadn't prepared her to deal with spoilt rich kids. Picking up the two bags, she followed Salma down the aisle and towards the escalator.

Charley whispered into her discreet lapel mic. 'Bravo One to Delta One. We're coming out. North exit.'

'*Roger that*,' came the driver's reply in her earpiece.

As they approached the exit, a concierge gave a polite goodbye and opened the door. The two of them stepped out on to Brompton Road.

'Where's my limo?' demanded Salma.

Charley checked in with the driver. 'He's stuck in heavy traffic,' she explained.

'Well, how long will he be?'

'He's not sure. There's an accident blocking the road. I suggest we go for a coffee while we wait. There's an excellent Italian cafe nearby.' Charley had already researched the Knightsbridge area in case Salma wanted lunch. And sitting in a cafe was less exposed than standing in the street.

'We have to *walk*?' asked Salma. She looked horrified.

'It's not far. Just round the corner.'

Salma shrugged. 'I suppose it will be an adventure.'

Charley informed the driver of the new pick-up point, then set off. Walking a step behind the princess, Charley kept a careful eye on all the pedestrians. Her nerves were tense. She had no intention of making a mistake on her first assignment.

They turned into a quieter side street that led to the cafe.

'Excuse me! Is this yours?'

Salma stopped as a roughly shaven man in a jumper and jeans approached. He held a silver ring. 'I think you dropped it,' he said with a smile.

Salma looked at it. 'No, it's not mine.'

'My mistake,' said the man. His smile vanished as he produced a knife from under his jumper. 'That purse isn't yours either. Hand it over.'

Salma stood frozen to the spot as the mugger snatched the purse from her grasp. 'Pay day,' he growled, then waved the knife at Charley. 'And the bags.'

'Sure,' she said, calmly holding them out to him. If she hadn't been carrying the princess's shopping, she could have reacted faster. But now she had the bags she intended using them to her advantage. As the mugger reached out, Charley let go and the bags dropped to the ground. The man's eyes followed them and Charley lunged forward. She struck him in the throat with the edge of her hand. At the same time, she seized his wrist, twisting his arm to force him to drop the knife. But, despite choking from the blow to his neck, the mugger managed to wrench free.

'Bitch!' he snarled.

In his pain and anger, he lashed out at Charley and she leapt away from the lethal blade. As he came in for a second attack, Charley pulled a small canister from her pocket. Bugsy had supplied her with several pieces of high-tech equipment, including a legal pepper spray. Depressing the nozzle, she sprayed red gel into the man's eyes. Blinded, he cried out and tried to wipe his face. This only spread the dye, making it worse. Charley side-kicked the man in the knee and he dropped to the pavement, bawling in agony. Without mercy, she stamped on his hand and kicked the knife away. Once sure he was no longer a threat, Charley gathered the purse and bags and guided the shocked Salma quickly away from the few amazed onlookers.

The limo pulled up at the kerbside.

'Are you all right?' asked their driver.

'Fine,' Charley lied, her heart pounding. Opening the passenger door, she ushered Salma into the back seat. Then, picking up the bags, she hurried round to the other side and jumped in. The limo drove off, leaving the mugger still writhing on the ground.

Thc two of them sat in silence.

Charley scolded herself for letting the mugger even get near the princess. She should have been aware of him much earlier. The ring had been a ploy to distract them and put them off-guard. It had almost worked as well!

Charley noticed the princess's hands were trembling. 'Are you OK?'

Salma nodded. 'Is London always like this?' she asked, her voice almost a whisper.

Charley shook her head. 'No, not as far as I'm aware. We were just unlucky.'

'Shame,' she said, turning to Charley with a timid smile.

'That's the most exciting thing that's ever happened to me. I was hoping we could do it again.'

Charley stared at the princess, dumbfounded.

Then the two of them burst out laughing, releasing the tension. Charley's heart was still thumping and her nerves buzzed with adrenalin. But she had to admit the act of protection felt almost as thrilling as catching a wave.

Only now, after taking out an attacker in real life, did Charley realize she was no longer a victim – no longer the vulnerable girl she'd been when her friend Kerry was abducted.

Now she was a force to be reckoned with.

TARGET
CHAPTER 22

'Was this hidden message your idea of a joke?' Kay demanded, her green eyes blazing at the producer. 'Because it *wasn't* funny!'

'Of course not,' replied Don, visibly wilting under her ferocious glare.

The other record company personnel sat rigid and mute round the conference table in Dauntless Records' headquarters, watching the producer's mauling with a combination of fearful fascination and evident relief that it wasn't them.

'Then exactly how did it get on to Ash's song?' enquired Kay.

Don swallowed nervously. 'I've no idea –'

'You're the producer, goddammit! You oversaw the recording process.'

Running a hand through his greasy locks, he replied, 'Play anything backwards and you'll likely find something. People thought Led Zeppelin had inserted *Here's to my sweet Satan* into "Stairway To Heaven", but they hadn't.

The message in Ash's song is just a coincidence – a phonetic reversal.'

'That's hard to believe,' said Kay.

'If you're suggesting the message was backmasked on to the track, then I certainly didn't do it.'

'Could anyone else have tampered with the recording?' asked Harvey, the vice president of Dauntless Records, a slick-suited man with a preened moustache and tight-knit hair.

Don shrugged. 'It's possible but unlikely. They'd need access to the studio, and advanced knowledge of the recording process.'

'Some zealous fan could have hacked into the system for a joke,' suggested Joel, Ash's sharp A&R manager.

'The media believe it's a publicity stunt,' said Zoe, the PR executive, immediately regretting she'd spoken at all as Kay turned on her.

'Is it?' she demanded.

'No, of course not,' Zoe replied. 'But it has rocketed pre-orders for the album. Whoever did this has done us a massive favour.'

'*Favour?* This is a serious death threat to my client.'

'Kay, might you be overreacting just a little?' interjected Harvey. 'It seems an extravagant way to send that sort of threat.'

'Well, explain the text message . . . and *this*.' Kay laid a sheet of pink paper on the table. Glued to it was Ash's face sparkling with stars and glitter, the words NO MORE ENCORES! scrawled in red across his features. 'You think

I'm overreacting, Harvey? This was written in blood. *Pig's blood* according to the police report.'

'Aww, that's creepy.' Zoe grimaced.

Joel leant forward to inspect the letter. 'What sort of sicko slaughters a pig for ink?'

'Possibly the same one that sends hoax letter bombs and subliminal song messages,' stated Kay.

'Has Ash seen this?' asked Harvey, jutting his chin at the letter but not making any move to touch it.

Kay shook her head. 'No. I'm having all his mail intercepted. He's got trouble enough focusing as it is.'

'Do you think he's actually in danger then?' asked Zoe.

Kay nodded. 'The threat against him is very real.'

Joel coughed hesitantly. 'You're not thinking of cancelling Ash's US tour, are you?'

'Certainly not,' replied Kay. 'Pulling Ash out of the limelight at this point would kill his career. And I will not be dictated to by some maniac.'

'Good,' Harvey chimed in. 'Besides, there's far too much money at stake to cancel.'

'The tour security needs to be airtight,' Kay declared, producing a document from a leather-bound folder and passing it to the vice president. 'Here are Ash's protection requirements.'

Harvey scanned the document. He looked shocked. 'You don't expect us to foot the bill for this, do you? He's not royalty, you know.'

Kay resolutely held his gaze. 'Considering how much money Ash makes for your record company, he's royalty to you. And, as per the contract I negotiated, it's part of tour support.'

Frowning, Harvey studied the document again, then pointed to a particular line. 'What's this extra cost here for?'

'It's for a company that deals in specialized close protection,' explained Kay. 'They come highly recommended by my inside source on the military security circuit.'

TARGET

CHAPTER 23

'Look who's back!' said Jason, ditching his dumbbells and towelling the perspiration from his face.

The rest of the team stopped their fitness training and turned to see Charley standing in the gym doorway. She was dressed in a running top and jogging pants, her hair bunched behind in a ponytail, face drawn and eyes ringed with tiredness.

'How was Colombia?' asked Blake, leaving the treadmill to greet her with a sweaty hug.

'Tough.' Charley sighed. She was exhausted after the long flight but glad to be back among the team again. It seemed as if she'd been away on missions forever. Each time she'd returned, Colonel Black had another lined up. Having completed five assignments in as many months, Charley was looking forward to a break – especially after the trouble she'd encountered in Colombia.

Jason eyeballed her. 'Dislocate anyone else's fingers while you've been away?' he growled.

Charley held his gaze. While the rest of the team's respect for her had grown with each successive assignment – as

Jody had predicted, *Prove yourself and you'll earn their respect* – Jason still hadn't forgiven her for the Gauntlet incident. 'No, but I did break a man's kneecap,' she replied.

José laughed. 'You're one kick-ass bodyguard!' he said, fist-bumping her.

Charley appreciated José's support, but it had been no laughing matter at the time. She and her Principal Sofia, the daughter of the Colombian Minister for Justice, had been in her father's car when it was attacked by hit-men from a notorious drug cartel. Charley had barely escaped with her own life. Sofia hadn't been so fortunate – as they'd fled, a stray bullet had hit her in the abdomen and she was now in hospital in a critical condition.

Blake noticed the mournful look in Charley's eyes. 'Are you all right?'

'Yeah,' she lied. 'I'm just a bit jet-lagged.'

'I bet you're hungry after the long journey too,' he said, putting a comforting arm round her shoulder. 'Let's go for lunch. That'll make you feel better.'

After freshening up, the whole team headed to the dining hall only to discover a queue.

'Who are all these people?' asked Charley, gaping at the unexpected line of kids.

'New recruits,' David explained. 'Buddyguard is expanding to meet demand.'

'Yeah, fresh meat!' sniggered Jason.

One of the new recruits, a petite Asian girl with a bob of jet-black hair and a silver piercing through her left nostril, glared over her shoulder at him. 'At least we don't smell like rotten meat,' she said, wafting a hand in front of her nose.

Jason bristled at the insult. 'Hey, pipsqueak, we just showered.'

'With soap or manure?' retorted the girl, and everyone laughed. Charley took an instant liking to her.

Jason clenched his fist. 'Zip it, newbie, unless you want a fat lip.'

The girl turned on him. 'And how are you going to do that with your broken arm?'

Jason furrowed his brow in confusion. 'I haven't got a broken arm.'

'Not yet, you haven't.' She squared up to him, even though she was half his height.

Jason puffed out his chest.

'OK, let's chill,' said Charley, stepping between them and smiling at the girl. 'What's your name?'

'Ling,' she replied, her dark half-moon eyes still blazing at Jason.

'Well, I'm Charley, and I can't tell you how glad I am not to be the only girl here any more.'

'Of course you're not,' said Ling, pointing to a small group of girls at a table beneath the hall's main window. 'You should join us, instead of hanging with this loser.'

Charley was amazed at the sudden influx of female buddyguards at the school. Colonel Black had been true to his word after all. 'Thanks, I'd love to. I just need to catch up with my team first.'

'Sure,' said Ling, flashing Charley a smile before

narrowing her eyes once more at Jason. 'Meathead here probably needs your help to eat.'

Jason scoffed. 'Can I borrow your bib and high chair then?'

Ling flipped him the finger. 'Eat this,' she said.

As Ling strolled away to join the other girls, José and David exchanged astonished looks at the girl's brazen attitude.

'She's a fiery one,' remarked Blake.

Jason surprised them all by grinning and saying, 'Yeah, I like her.'

'Careful what you wish for,' said José. 'She might end up in your team.'

'*Jason's* team?' exclaimed Charley as she chose her lunch. 'What's happened to our team?'

'Given the number of new recruits, the colonel plans to split us into different squads – Alpha, Bravo, Charlie and Delta,' explained José.

Charley frowned. 'That's the first I've heard about it.'

'He wants us experienced buddyguards to babysit the newbies,' said David.

'Yeah, and by the looks of it they're gonna *need* babysitting,' remarked Jason, nodding in the direction of a skinny Indian boy. 'Where did the colonel find that beanpole?'

'Bodyguarding's not all about muscle,' Charley told him.

'Well, let's hope his brains are bigger than his biceps, for his *and* his Principal's sake,' muttered Jason, filling his plate with a mountain of pasta and sauce.

After lunch, Charley chatted with the girls before jet lag finally caught up with her. Yawning, she left the dining hall and headed up to her room. But she was stopped at her door by Blake.

'So, are you really OK?' he asked. 'I heard from the colonel it was a pretty rough assignment.'

Charley responded with a tired smile. 'Yeah, it didn't exactly go according to plan.'

'But you did your job and that's what counts,' he said, trying to reassure her. When she didn't reply, he took both her hands in his. 'I was really worried about you, Charley,' he admitted.

'That's sweet of you, Blake. But I'm fine. It was my Principal who got shot.' Charley felt a tightening in her throat. 'I-I tried to give her body cover, but there were just too many bullets flying . . .'

Blake wrapped his arms round her and drew her to him. Charley closed her eyes and hugged him back.

After the smoke-bomb incident, their relationship had stalled for a while. But Blake had been persistent and, against her better judgement, the two of them had become an item. Charley had made it clear, though, that they needed to keep it low key. She had no intention of being judged by their relationship rather than her ability as a bodyguard. Yet at moments like these she was deeply glad of Blake. Assignments took their toll and it was comforting to have someone she could talk to and rely on, even if they did barely see each other between missions.

Blake lifted her chin with his finger and stared into her

eyes. 'I missed you,' he said. Gently brushing aside a lock of her hair, he went to kiss her.

'There you are, Charley!' called Jody. Their instructor bounded up the stairs. 'The colonel wants to see you right now.'

TARGET

CHAPTER 24

The colonel's office was a large wooden-panelled affair furnished with high-back red leather chairs and a heavy mahogany desk. The faint aroma of polished wood and rich leather gave the room an aristocratic air. Yet the antique design and old-world atmosphere contrasted sharply with the state-of-the-art LED displays on the walls and the ultra-slim glass monitor on the desk's integrated computer system.

Charley stood to attention in the middle of the room. It took all her willpower not to just collapse on to the carpet. Her body was weary and stiff from the long flight; her thoughts were chaotic and strained from exhaustion, concern for Sofia and dread at what the colonel had to say about the mission.

Colonel Black leant forward across his desk. 'It's good news,' he announced. 'Your Principal Sofia's on course to make a full recovery.'

Surprised and relieved by the news, Charley felt a huge weight lift from her shoulders. 'I thought she was as good as dead.'

'Not at all – your quick thinking and first-aid skills actually saved her life,' he explained. 'Minister Valdez is deeply grateful for your bravery.'

Charley forced a smile. 'That's wonderful to hear, but I shouldn't have let his daughter get shot in the first place. I tried to give her full body cover, but there was simply too much crossfire –'

'Don't be so hard on yourself,' scolded the colonel. 'Without you, Sofia would most certainly have been kidnapped or killed.'

He pointed to the monitor where images of the crime scene in question scrolled past.

'I've the complete report here,' Colonel Black explained. 'The bullet ricocheted off the minister's armoured car. You couldn't have done anything about it. We just have to be thankful it was a ricochet and not a direct hit. That slowed the bullet's velocity and stopped it reaching her spinal cord. If you hadn't carried out emergency first aid at the scene, she'd have bled out. You acted like a true professional.'

'It should have been *me* that took the bullet,' she insisted, still feeling guilty.

'*Never* say that!' snapped the colonel. 'A bodyguard with a death wish is a danger to everyone. Yes, we need to be willing to stand in the line of fire – but *only* if absolutely necessary to protect the life of a Principal. Charley, you need to value your own life as much as theirs. Remember, a dead bodyguard is no protection to anyone.'

Colonel Black rose from his seat, stepped round his

desk and laid a paternal hand on her shoulder. 'I realize you're trying to compensate for not being able to save your friend, but you owe it to Kerry's memory to forgive yourself.'

Swallowing back the long-held grief for her friend, Charley blinked away a tear. 'I know how crazy it sounds, but I felt that by saving others I could somehow bring Kerry back.'

The colonel shook his head. 'You don't need to save everyone, Charley. Nobody could do that. You've honoured Kerry a hundredfold with your commitment to bodyguard training and your heroic actions in the field.'

The colonel pinned a silver shield with guardian wings to her T-shirt.

'What's this?' she asked, staring at the badge in puzzlement.

'For courage and outstanding performance in the line of duty,' replied Colonel Black. 'I consider you our top-ranking buddyguard, and you should be officially recognized for that.'

Charley studied the shield, feeling a small flush of pride. This acknowledgement was proof that she was indeed the best of the best. She could almost picture her parents' proud smiles, if they'd still been around.

'Which brings me to your next assignment,' announced the colonel, returning to his desk.

Charley blinked, her moment of glory swept aside by the prospect of yet another mission. 'My next? But I've only just got back.'

'Don't worry. You'll have ten days to prepare. But I thought you'd like to know who you'll be protecting . . .'

'Who?' Charley prompted when the colonel seemed to be purposefully holding back on her.

'Ash Wild.'

TARGET
CHAPTER 25

'The rock star?' questioned Blake next day, his jaw dropping in astonishment.

Charley nodded with enthusiasm. 'Yeah, I can't believe it either. He must be Buddyguard's most high-profile client yet.'

'But he's a guy.'

'Good observation skills,' said Charley sarcastically. 'Your point being?'

'Well . . . you've always been assigned to protect girls before,' replied Blake.

'And? You've protected boys *and* girls on your missions.'

'Yeah, but that's different.'

Charley narrowed her eyes at him. 'Why's it different?'

'Because . . .' Blake averted his gaze, clearly stuck for a suitable answer.

'Because he's jealous, that's why.' Jason smirked as he strode into the briefing room with the others and took his seat.

'No, I'm not,' Blake shot back a little too quickly.

'Of course you are. Ash Wild is every girl's fantasy,'

Jason declared. 'A super-rich famous rock star. You're no match for him.'

'Nor are you, dingo breath!'

Jason held up his hands in defence. 'Hey, I'm not competing for the same girl's affections.'

His jaw tensing in anger, Blake started to rise from his chair.

Charley placed a hand on Blake's arm, urging him to sit. *So much for keeping our relationship low profile*, she thought. 'For the record, I'm not interested in Ash Wild.'

Jason gave her a look. 'Yeah, right.'

'I don't even like his music,' she stated. 'Besides, that's a line we're not allowed to cross. Rule number one: never get involved with your Principal.'

'Oops! I must have missed that one in the manual,' Jason remarked with a roguish grin.

Charley stared at him. 'Are you serious?'

Jason gave a non-committal shrug. 'It was only a kiss and she made the first mo–'

'Oi, Casanova!' José interrupted. 'Colonel Black's coming.'

Everyone stood to attention as the colonel took his place at the head of the briefing room. He indicated for them to sit.

'Operation Starstruck,' announced Colonel Black, wirelessly connecting his tablet to the overhead display and launching straight into the briefing. On the screen appeared a picture of a handsome teenage boy with brown hair and hazel eyes. 'Our Principal is Ash Wild. British-born music prodigy, talented in guitar, piano, singing and songwriting.'

'Well, that's a matter of opinion,' mumbled Blake, slouching in his chair.

Ignoring his sullen remark, Charley powered up her tablet to take notes. She really couldn't deal with a jealous boyfriend, especially during a briefing. This was one of the reasons why she hadn't wanted to get involved with someone on her team. It just complicated matters.

'Not according to his chart success, Blake,' Colonel Black countered. 'At fourteen, Ash was the youngest artist ever to achieve a number-one album in the UK. He's topped the charts in sixteen other countries, including America where he became the first British solo artist to enter the Billboard 200 at number one with a debut album. Now fifteen, he's about to embark on one of the most eagerly anticipated US tours ever.' Colonel Black paused and swept his gaze round the room. 'Our job is to keep him alive on this tour.'

'What's the primary threat?' asked David.

'An unidentified stalker, responsible for a hoax letter bomb and two death threats so far,' the colonel explained as he presented the evidence on screen. 'A nasty piece of hate mail written in pig's blood and a message hidden within Ash's latest single release.'

'Yeah, I heard about that on the radio,' said José. 'Everyone thinks it's a PR stunt.'

'Well, they're letting that story run, but it's not the case,' replied the colonel. 'I was contacted direct by Ash's manager, Kay Gibson.' The display switched to a photograph of a striking red-headed woman in a black tailored dress. 'Ms Gibson, who happens to be Ash's aunt, is taking these threats *very* seriously. She's already upped Ash's normal security arrangements, including making his personal bodyguard full-time.'

The overhead screen filled with the image of a hulking twenty-one stone man with a head like a wrinkled bowling ball and tattooed arms that could put a gorilla to shame.

José let out a whistle through his teeth. 'He's one mean-looking BG! Any stalker's got to be crazy to take him on.'

'What's his background?' asked Charley, suddenly feeling out of her depth in comparison to the colossal bodyguard.

'His name is Tony Burnett, known better as Big T,' said the colonel. 'He's old school. Started out in security when he was a teenager, just like you lot. But he got his training at the school of hard knocks, working the pub doors in the East End of London where he grew up. Later he moved on to concert security at the Hammersmith Apollo. From there, he toured with the likes of Iron Maiden, Black Sabbath, Slipknot and the Foo Fighters. Now approaching sixty, he's somewhat of a legend among music security professionals. That's how he acquired his position as Ash's personal bodyguard.'

David raised a hand. 'Why does Ash need Charley, or any other bodyguard for that matter, when he's already got Big T to protect him?'

'Big T will act as high-profile security, warding off the

obvious threats,' Colonel Black explained. 'But Charley is needed for low-profile, discreet protection – to counter the unseen and unexpected dangers.'

'But why choose Charley? Especially after her last mission,' said Jason, glancing across at her. 'Wouldn't it be better if I went? I could pretend to be one of the band.'

He thinks he's One Direction, thought Charley, bristling at Jason's never-ending doubts about her ability.

'No,' replied the colonel. 'Charley has a distinct advantage over you. The fact she's a girl will allow her to blend in better. Officially she will be on the tour as a trainee PR girl, but to any casual observer she'll appear as just another Ash Wild fan.'

'So does Big T know I'll be Ash's buddyguard?' asked Charley.

José laughed. 'Yeah, better not step on the big man's toes!'

Colonel Black nodded. 'Ms Gibson's informed him. As I understand it, he'll be the only other person in the entourage, aside from Ash and the tour manager, to know your true role.'

Charley made a note of this as the colonel turned to the others in the team. 'Blake, you'll be the prime point of contact for Charley here at headquarters.'

Having sat silent throughout the briefing, Blake glanced up from his sulk and nodded.

'Jason, investigate Ash's background and run a threat assessment on him.' A long series of dates flashed up on the screen. 'José and David, this is the planned tour itinerary.

Research each venue, hotel and location, so that Charley has instant access to maps and all other essential information.'

'Yes, Colonel,' replied José and David in unison, both opening up the tour file on their tablets.

The colonel turned back to Charley. 'We've a meeting with Ash and his manager at the end of next week. Ensure you're fully prepped. Bugsy's updating your Go-bag, so remember to stop by the logistic supply room. Other than that, you know the drill.'

TARGET
CHAPTER 26

'Meet Amir,' said Bugsy, introducing the skinny boy Jason had spotted in the dining hall the week before. 'He's assisting me with mission logistics.'

Amir stared wide-eyed at Charley from behind the work counter of the supply room, giving the impression he was a little in awe of her.

'Hi, I'm Charley,' she said, leaning against the counter.

'I know,' he replied with a timid but endearing smile. 'Everyone knows who *you* are.'

Charley raised an eyebrow. 'They do?'

'You're quite a celebrity now, Charley,' said Bugsy, dumping a light green rucksack on top of the counter and unpacking its contents. He laid out the items in two rows, then stepped back.

'You explain what's in her Go-bag, Amir,' Bugsy encouraged, popping a stick of chewing gum into his mouth. 'It'll be good experience for you.'

Clearing his throat, Amir picked up the first item. 'Well . . . this is a phone,' he began.

'I can see that.' Charley smiled.

'A smartphone actually . . . it has all the usual features,' he continued, his voice quivering slightly. 'High-res camera, video capability, GPS, internet . . . but it's also a weapon.'

Now Charley was interested. 'What sort of weapon?'

Amir pointed to two small metal studs at the top of the device. 'A stun gun. Slide the volume button up a notch and simply press to deliver over three million volts of electricity . . .'

The ghost image of Kerry's tortured face and shuddering body flashed before Charley's eyes. She blinked and the vision was gone, but the chill of grief and guilt lingered. Amir was too involved in his description of the phone's workings to notice her brief pained expression.

'The shock will effectively short-circuit the attacker's nervous system, causing loss of balance and muscle control, confusion and disorientation. It's like being shocked by a cattle fence, only fifty thousand times stronger. Even through clothing, it can take out a fully grown adult.'

He pressed the button; there was a fearsome crackle and a blue bolt of electricity arced between the two studs. The boy grinned. 'I like to call this device the iStun.'

But Charley didn't laugh. Instead she quietly replied, 'I know from experience what it can do.'

'You do?' he said, stifling his own laugh when he saw her expression. 'What happened?'

'I'd rather not talk about it, if that's all right.'

'Sure, I understand,' he replied with an earnest nod. 'Client confidentiality and all that.'

Amir put the stun phone aside and picked up a small

aerosol can. 'This looks like a standard deodorant. But in fact it's –'

'A legal pepper spray,' Charley finished for him. 'I've used it on a previous assignment. Fires out a red gel that disorientates an attacker and stains their skin.'

Slightly crestfallen at missing an opportunity to explain this himself, Amir held up a tiny white box no bigger than a sugar cube instead. 'OK . . . how about the Intruder?'

'Go on,' encouraged Charley. She felt bad after realizing Amir was trying desperately to impress their instructor. So she leant forward and made a show of interest.

'This is a mini portable surveillance device,' he explained eagerly. 'Instant set-up. Just fix it to a wall using the reusable adhesive on the back. If someone crosses the sensor's beam, the device instantly alerts your phone with a text message. Bugsy thought these would be ideal for detecting intruders while you're on tour.'

Charley examined the box. 'It's certainly compact.'

Heartened by her approval, Amir moved on to the next set of items in line. 'Now these are really cool! Bugsy got them custom-made.'

'What's so special about a T-shirt?' asked Charley as he unfolded the first black garment and laid it out on the counter.

'It's woven from a high-tech super-fabric,' he explained. 'This T-shirt is not only fireproof, it's stab-proof too.'

'Stab-proof!' exclaimed Charley, feeling the thick cotton-like fabric between her fingers and doubting its capabilities. 'Are you sure?'

'Well, I haven't tested it *personally*,' Amir admitted. 'But Bugsy assures me it is.'

Charley glanced at her instructor, who gave a single nod of his bald head. 'Do you want to test it out?' he asked.

'No, it's fine. I believe you,' Charley replied quickly as he began to unsheathe the knife on his utility belt. She returned the T-shirt to Amir.

'There's all your standard gear too,' said Amir, sorting through her remaining equipment and repacking the items carefully into her Go-bag. 'First-aid kit, comms unit, torch –'

'What's this? A secret poison dart?' asked Charley, picking up a biro from the counter.

'No,' Amir replied, looking at her as if she had a screw loose. 'It's just a pen. But I thought I'd include it in case your Principal is asked to sign autographs. You don't want to be hanging around, exposed any longer than necessary, while a fan searches for their own pen.'

On hearing this, Charley reappraised the potential of the raw-boned boy. He might not have the muscles, but he certainly had the brains to be a bodyguard. 'Good thinking, Amir.'

Amir beamed at the praise.

'Actually, this *isn't* just any old pen,' said Bugsy, stepping in and taking it from Charley. 'The casing is made from high-impact hardened polycarbonate. This means it functions as a very effective self-defence weapon too.'

Amir frowned. 'How can a pen be used as a weapon?'

'Allow me to demonstrate.'

Holding the pen in an ice-pick grip, Bugsy said, 'Like a

Japanese *kubotan*, you can use this to strike at pressure points on the human body. The neck is the best place to target.'

Without warning, he drove the tip of the pen into the clump of nerves just above Amir's collarbone. Amir let out an anguished cry and crumpled to the floor where he lay gasping in pain.

'Highly effective, as you can see,' said Bugsy, returning the pen to Charley.

Collecting her Go-bag, she slowly shook her head at Bugsy. 'No wonder no one ever wants to be your assistant!'

TARGET

CHAPTER 27

'New York, Dallas, Las Vegas, Miami, LA . . . Talk about one awesome assignment!' said Blake, loading Charley's travel case into the boot of the Range Rover. 'Wish I was going with you.'

'You forget, all that travelling's a hard slog,' replied Charley as she crunched across the gravel driveway with her Go-bag.

'Yeah, right. Free concerts, celebrity-filled parties, exotic locations. I'd kill to go on a mission like that.'

'Well, if you recall, I'm on this mission because someone wants to *kill* Ash.'

'As if that's going to happen with all the security his manager's put in place.'

'Don't underestimate the lengths celebrity stalkers will go to,' said Jason, coming up behind them. 'I've read some pretty disturbing stuff during my research into possible threats against Ash. Breaking-and-entering to lie in wait for the celebrity. Fantasies of torture and mutilation. Killing of family pets. Voodoo dolls sent in the post –'

Charley rolled her eyes. 'You're not going to scare me, Jason.'

'You should be scared. Celebrity stalkers may seem like over-obsessed fans, but they're often deluded, mentally ill and can be violent – even deadly.'

'Well, that's a cheery note to say goodbye on!' said Blake, closing the Range Rover's boot.

'Have neither of you read my threat report?' asked Jason, indignant.

'Not yet,' Charley admitted.

'Well, I wouldn't recommend reading it before bedtime. It'll give you nightmares.' Jason offered Charley a half-hearted wave and strolled back inside.

'Man, he can be an idiot at times!' said Blake. Once certain Jason was gone, Blake reached tentatively for Charley's hand. 'Listen, I'm sorry for being a little . . . grumpy with you lately. It's just that . . . I worry about you.'

'I can handle myself,' Charley replied, thinking, *Why did he wait until now to make his apology?*

'I know you can,' he agreed. 'And I admit it: I'm jealous. Ash is going to spend all that time with you and I'm not.'

Charley squeezed his hand in response. 'We always knew this would be difficult,' she said. 'We only get to see each other between missions. That's why we should try to make the most of it when I am here.'

'You're right, of course.' He moved closer, his expression hopeful. 'Are we good now?'

Blake's sullen attitude since discovering she'd be protecting Ash Wild had been tiresome. It was hard enough preparing for a mission, let alone managing a moody boyfriend at the same time. But he *had* apologized . . . and he was cute. And it was reassuring to know she had someone back at base who truly cared for her.

'We're good,' she said.

Smiling, Blake wrapped his arms round her waist and drew her close. But, as he moved in to kiss her goodbye, there was a crunch of gravel behind and they both turned to see Colonel Black making his way towards the Range Rover. They broke their embrace a second or two before he spotted them.

'Ready to go?' Colonel Black asked.

Charley nodded. The colonel clambered into the Range Rover and gunned the engine. As she jumped in beside him, she secretly blew Blake a goodbye kiss. 'Save that for my return.'

Blake caught it and mouthed in reply, *Stay safe*.

TARGET
CHAPTER 28

'The media has become so intrusive that celebrities have little privacy any more,' cxplained Kay, reclining in a designer chair, her long legs crossed beneath the oval glass table that she'd invited Colonel Black and Charley to sit round. 'That's why we need exclusive residences like this.'

She waved a hand at the stylish decor and plush furnishings. White leather sofas, black walls, the largest flatscreen TV Charley had ever laid eyes on and, most impressive of all, a teardrop swimming pool that started in the living room and finished outside in a landscaped garden enclosed by high walls topped with razor wire.

'Of course, it all costs money,' Kay admitted, 'but it's worth it to keep Ash safe.'

'The security here is most reassuring,' confirmed the colonel. They'd entered the West London estate through a manned gate, then had their IDs verified again by Big T at the door. Along with the razor wire on the walls, Charley had noted discreet CCTV and infrared cameras strategically located around the residence. There were even panic buttons installed in every room. The villa was a literal fortress.

'Has Ash received any more death threats?' the colonel asked.

'Nothing in the post since moving here,' Kay replied. 'So far we've managed to keep Ash's new address a secret and we're monitoring all the mail that does come in.'

'That's good news,' said Charley.

'It would be if that was the only source of threats.' With an icy fury in her eyes, the music manager opened a super-slim laptop and turned the screen towards them. 'Like any celebrity, Ash is a target for online abuse. He receives a constant stream of insults and threats from haters eager to criticize, belittle, character-assassinate or worse. These sort of people make me sick!'

Colonel Black and Charley studied the sample of online posts on the screen. They varied from childish name-calling and scornful posts to harmful rumours and threats of physical violence. The messages became more and more extreme the further down the page Charley read:

> #AshWild music's torture, someone should torture him!
>
> What an utter $%&*!
>
> I'd stab his eyes out if I could #AshWild
>
> Burn in hell @therealAshWild

'Of course, all this abuse is accessible to Ash,' Kay said with a sigh. 'I can't shield him from it.'

'But *we* can shield him,' stated Colonel Black. 'It'll be a tricky task to sift the genuine threats from the trolls. But I'll have my team run a search of these users through the police database to establish if any of them have a criminal record or a history of violence. That should help identify potential suspects.'

'Do you know anyone who might have a grudge against Ash?' asked Charley.

Kay tapped a polished nail on the glass table while she considered this. 'There is one: a songwriter who's convinced Ash stole his hit song, "Only Raining".'

'Did he?' asked Colonel Black.

'*No*,' Kay replied emphatically, then threw up her hands. 'However, where there's a hit, there's a writ. The guy was furious when he lost the court case, along with all his money paying the legal costs. His name is Brandon Mills. The police interviewed him over the letter bomb, but they found nothing that linked him to it.'

Charley ran a quick search on the internet and pulled up an image on her tablet screen. 'This him?' she asked, pointing to a middle-aged man with dark blond hair, designer stubble and steel-blue eyes. He looked like a wannabe George Michael.

Kay winced, then nodded.

'You knew this man?' asked the colonel sharply.

The music manager's eyes narrowed. 'We lived together. Briefly.'

'And?'

'It didn't work out. Nothing to do with Ash.'

Charley downloaded the image and associated links to the threat folder in her operation file, making a note of Kay's involvement with him.

'Anyone else?' asked the colonel. 'One of Ash's ex-girlfriend, perhaps?'

Kay pursed her lips. 'Ash has had a few girlfriends. Hanna Price was the latest, but she's busy with her own modelling career now. And she doesn't strike me as the revenge ty–'

'Sorry I'm late,' said Ash, strolling into the room. 'Got stuck songwriting and lost track of the time.'

He pulled out a chair and plonked himself down next to his manager. His smouldering eyes were enough to melt any girl's heart and he used them to full effect on Charley along with a dazzling smile. But, having seen the exact same look in one of his publicity photos, Charley had no difficulty resisting his charm. She had to admit, however, that Ash had a certain star quality. When he'd entered the room, there was an instant frisson in the air, like a build-up of static electricity.

'So, you must be my new bodyguard,' said Ash, addressing Colonel Black with a salute.

The colonel stared straight back at him. 'No, Charley is.'

Ash did a double-take. '*Seriously?*' He laughed out loud and, when no one else joined in, it quickly petered out. 'You *are* serious.'

'Yes,' said Charley.

'No offence,' said Ash, 'but you're, like, my age and a *girl.*'

'That's the point,' replied Charley, trying hard not to take offence. 'The best bodyguard is the one nobody notices, and I can blend in as one of your friends or as a fan.'

Ash responded with a strained smile. He leant over to his manager. 'When you said Charley, I thought you meant a guy,' he hissed.

'Does that make a difference?' said Kay.

'Of course it does! How's *she* going to protect me?'

'*She* is a trained bodyguard,' responded his manager.

Ash glanced doubtfully over at Charley. 'But I already have Big T. Why do I need her?'

Kay replied, 'Your protection is my highest priority. I want all bases covered. And Charley will be your final *invisible* ring of defence.'

'Invisible? It's non-existent! If some maniac can get past Big T, they'll be able to take out a girl. I don't think you're taking my death threats seriously! This has to be a joke.'

'I'm deadly serious,' replied Kay.

'Then hire a *real* bodyguard.'

'I have,' stated Kay, her tone hardening. 'Do you question whether I'm up to the job as your manager just because I'm a woman?'

Ash shook his head. 'Of course not.'

'Then *don't* question her ability as a bodyguard.'

Charley sat awkwardly with Colonel Black as this heated discussion took place in front of them. While Ash's initial reaction hadn't come as a complete surprise to Charley, it was a disappointment and not the best way to start an assignment. Still she was heartened by the manager's stated confidence in her.

'I can assure you, Ash,' said the colonel, 'that Charley is very much up to the job.'

'Well, I'll believe it when I see it,' replied Ash with a strained smile. He looked at Charley. 'Sorry for any confusion on my part. But an easy mistake to make, eh? Big military guy. Blonde sexy girl. Who'd have thought *you* were the bodyguard? Anyway, I've a band rehearsal now, so I've got to run. I expect I'll bump into you on the tour then?'

'You can guarantee it,' replied Charley.

As Ash excused himself and headed out of the living room, Kay turned to Charley. 'Ash is worth a fortune to a lot of people. He must be protected at all costs. Now I've backed you up, you'd better not let me down, Charley.'

'Don't worry,' Charley replied, sounding as self-assured as possible despite the huge weight of expectation on her shoulders. 'I'll accompany him like a second heartbeat.'

TARGET

CHAPTER 29

Colour posters swamped the four walls of the cramped little bedroom. Glossy calendars – some official, some not – were pinned alongside, while cut-out magazine articles filled the remaining spaces. Not a single square centimetre of the original wallpaper was visible beneath the massive unbroken montage. Even the ceiling was blanketed in pictures, postcards and concert memorabilia.

Every photo, every image was of Ash Wild.

His face grinned out in perfect heart-throb style – performing at a concert, appearing on television, posing on the beach. Tabloid shots showed him going for a jog, having dinner, shopping for food, walking in the street, his whole life – professional and private – exposed by the lens of a million cameras.

A full-size cut-out of the rock star stood in one corner of the room. Creepily lifelike, the guardian watched over the most precious items of the collection: an Ash Wild baseball cap, a signed tour programme, a limited-edition vinyl copy of Ash's first single, a guitar plectrum thrown by the star during a gig. And, at the heart of this treasure trove of souvenirs, a photo signed by none other than Ash Wild himself.

The bedroom was a virtual shrine to the rock star.

And, to leave no one in doubt, on the bedroom door hung a sign saying I'M A WILDLING!

The computer on the desk displayed a Wildling fansite – *Wild: For the fans by the fans* – updated seconds before with a new post enthusing about the forthcoming tour. From the desktop speakers, on endless repeat, Ash's voice sang 'It's only raining on you, only raining . . . '

The single bed, the only other piece of furniture in the room, was covered with an Ash Wild duvet and pillow case. On top lay an open suitcase. Inside, clothes were folded neatly and packed in individual clear plastic travel pouches. A washbag, containing shower gel, face cream, hairbrush, deodorant, a blister pack of tablets and a tube of toothpaste, was carefully stowed. And tucked inside a money belt was a slim stack of highly sought-after concert tickets, plus the necessary travel documents and a crisp new passport.

From downstairs came the sound of a doorbell ringing.

'Hey, sweetie, your car's here!' called up a shrill voice.

With a final check of the contents, the Wildling fan closed the suitcase, slipped on the money belt and rushed down to the waiting taxi.

TARGET
CHAPTER 30

'Sandy Higgs, ABC News,' said the reporter, introducing herself. 'Ash, your rise to fame has been meteoric. When was the first time you realized you were famous?'

'When I got my first death threat!' Ash replied.

A ripple of laughter filled the conference room in New York's Soho Grand Hotel. Ash sat relaxed in front of a microphone; behind him a huge backdrop of his face announced the start of his Indestructible tour.

'But, seriously, I'm not in this for the fame,' Ash went on. 'I'm in it for the music. And for my fans.'

Charley stood just offstage, out of the limelight. She stifled a yawn, fighting the remnants of jet lag after the long flight from London Heathrow. It was the first official day of the assignment and she was determined to be on the ball. She'd had little time to settle in or get her bearings, aside from checking into the hotel and catching a glimpse of the Statue of Liberty as her taxi had crossed the Brooklyn Bridge into Manhattan.

Beside her towered the monstrous frame of Big T. She'd been briefly introduced to the veteran bodyguard on her arrival, but received no more than a grunt of acknowledgement before the press conference had begun. She hadn't tried to strike up a conversation with him, since experience had taught her when to talk and when not to talk on an assignment.

'Harvey Lewis, *TeenMusic Mag*,' called out another reporter. 'Your face and album are everywhere. Your songs dominate the charts and airwaves. Are you worried about overexposure?'

'I think it's too late for that!' Ash joked, indicating the massive publicity image behind him.

Another round of laughter greeted his response. Charley saw that Ash was in his element. With all the attention focused on him, he shone like a true superstar.

'It's better to burn out than fade away, right?' continued Ash. 'No, I'm not worried about overexposure. I love touring, travelling the world, seeing new places and meeting new people. That's the joy of being a musician. And I've just released an album of new songs that'll keep my fans happy, for a while at least.'

'Sara Jones, Heaven Radio. You're known for your close interaction with your fans. But surely that's an issue given the recent threats made against you?'

'Not really. Anyone has to get past Big T first!' Ash gestured towards his colossal bodyguard at the edge of the stage. Big T put on a suitably hostile scowl, playing up his role for the cameras. The photographers seized the opportunity and snapped away.

A man in a blue shirt and jeans stood up from among

the reporters. 'Stephen Hicks, freelance. Ash, is it true you received a death threat written in pig's blood?'

A hushed silence descended on the room. This was clearly news to the other reporters as well as Ash.

Ash frowned. 'No . . . not as far as I'm aware.'

'Well, I've a reliable source that says you did.' Sensing a story, the reporter pressed on. 'How do you feel about your team hiding this letter from you?'

'W-what letter?' demanded Ash, his previous cool demeanour fracturing. He glanced sideways at Zoe for guidance. The Dauntless Records' PR exec shook her head in reply.

'Doesn't that make you question who you can trust?' asked the reporter.

Ash didn't respond, his eyes now darting nervously round the room.

'Don't you fear for your life on this tour? Are you going to cancel if you get another death threat?'

Ash gripped the microphone firmly in both hands. 'Listen, there's always going to be haters, no matter what,' he answered, a tremor entering his voice. 'But *nothing's* going to stop me from this upcoming tour!'

'Not even a maniac promising "no more encores"?'

Realizing the reporter was out for blood and seeing Ash's troubled expression, Zoe stepped on to the stage and took over the mic.

'Thank you, everyone, for your time,' she said, smiling brightly. 'Press conference is now over. The tour commences this Friday at Madison Square Garden.'

Ash left the stage. Donning a pair of sunglasses, Big T immediately flanked the rock star and led him out of the room. Charley joined them, blending in as part of Ash's official entourage – a work-experience PR girl, if anyone asked.

They crossed the almost-deserted reception area in silence.

A flustered Zoe caught up. 'Sorry about that,' she said to Ash. 'That reporter won't ever have access again.'

'Why wasn't I told about the letter?' Ash demanded angrily.

'Kay didn't want you worrying.'

'Sounds like I should be!'

'Don't be,' said Big T, striding alongside. 'You're safe as houses with me.'

And me, thought Charley, keeping guard on Ash's other side.

'Thanks, Big T,' said Ash, beginning to smile again.

Approaching the exit, one of Big T's security team took point and opened the hotel doors. Emerging on to the street, they were hit by a tidal wave of people – paparazzi with cameras blazing like strobe lights, teenage girls screaming like banshees, young lads fist-pumping the air and chanting, 'ASH! ASH! ASH!' Tourists and bystanders flocked to the scene to witness the commotion. Overwhelmed by sheer numbers, the police were swamped by the ocean of fans who'd broken through the barriers.

Big T carved a path through the seething mass, a protective arm round his charge. Charley trailed behind. She shielded her eyes against multiple camera flashes and tried to scan the crowd for threats. But it was pandemonium. Never before had she tried to protect somebody in chaos like this. Disorientated, deafened and half-blinded, she could barely guard herself, let alone Ash, as the mass of fans swarmed round to get a piece of him.

A paparazzi guy with a buzz cut and two days' worth of stubble barged Charley aside. She stumbled and almost fell to the pavement, where she would likely have been trampled in the crush. 'Watch it!' she cried.

He turned on her. 'You watch it!' he said in a nasal tone and flashgunned her with his camera.

Blinking away stars, Charley soon lost track of Ash. In fact, she lost track of everyone. Jostled all over the place, she could barely stay on her feet. The only still centre amid the storm was Big T. She spotted him, towering above the gaggle of girls, groupies and photographers. Immovable as an oak tree, he barely swayed as the crowd pitched and rolled around him.

Ash, smiling and laughing, had paused to sign autographs and pose for photos, giving Charley the chance to catch up.

'You all right?' asked Big T, barely glancing at her.

'Yeah,' Charley replied breathlessly. 'Had a run-in with a photographer.'

'Careful,' he warned. 'Don't get on the wrong side of the pap. They'll make your life hell.'

A girl squealed in delight as Ash signed her poster. Another began crying when he hugged her. Charley thought one fan was actually going to faint when he signed her arm with a heart.

'And what's your name?' Ash asked a lad with dark blond hair whose starry-eyed look suggested he might explode at being so close to his idol.

'P-P-Pete,' he managed to reply, grinning broadly as Ash signed his autograph book.

Then Ash held up the boy's camera phone and took an impromptu selfie with him. Glancing at the result, he noted the similarity in their features and said, 'Hey, you could be my twin brother!'

'Really?' said the awestruck boy.

'Well, apart from your blond hair and blue eyes, we could be identical.'

The fan gaped at him, wide-eyed. 'Perhaps we're related.'

'In another life, my friend!' Ash laughed good-naturedly and patted him on the shoulder.

Then Big T was steering Ash towards the waiting limo. Charley fought hard to keep by their side but, a few metres from the vehicle, she was caught in a riptide of fans and dragged in the opposite direction. Digging an elbow into the girl in front, she forced the fan aside. But it was no use. Another simply filled her place. Meanwhile Ash was edging further and further away.

Then a meaty hand grabbed her wrist. Yanked through the pressing crowd, Charley was back beside Big T. 'Keep up!' he grunted, his other arm shielding Ash.

Charley now stayed determinedly in his wake. As Ash disappeared inside the blacked-out limo, there was a surge of fans behind. At the same time Big T let Charley through. Her foot caught on the door frame and she landed in a heap in the footwell of the limo. The bodyguard slammed the door behind her, the driver automatically locking them in for safety.

As Big T waded round the vehicle to the front passenger seat, the fans pounded on the roof, the thunderous sound like an army of jackhammers. Humiliated by her unceremonious entry into the limo, Charley quickly pulled herself into the soft leather of the rear seat, straightened out her top and combed a hand through her dishevelled hair.

Meanwhile Ash sat cool, calm and collected beside her. He gave her a smug look. 'Welcome to my life, babe!'

CHAPTER 31

'You're not on the list,' said the gruff security guard, barring entry through the artists' entrance to Madison Square Garden, the iconic circular arena topping Pennsylvania Station in the heart of Manhattan.

'But I'm a personal guest of Ash,' Charley insisted.

The security guard, a large man with a beer belly, let out a snort of laughter. 'So is every other Wildling fan.'

He turned to the other two guards manning the entrance with him and rolled his eyes at Charley's pitiful attempt to gain entry.

'Listen – if you call through to his manager, she'll explain –'

'Don't push your luck, girly. No pass, no entry!' he snapped.

Charley sighed. This was all she needed. First day of the tour and she couldn't even access the venue. Having got the security guard to check the guest list three times, she began to wonder if she'd been left off the list on purpose. Following her failure in even the most basic close protection of Ash during the press conference the previous day, perhaps his manager had decided she wasn't up to the job and cancelled Buddyguard's services. But, if that was the case, surely she'd have heard from Colonel Black by now?

Charley checked her phone. No messages. She tried calling Kay Gibson direct, but her phone went to voicemail. Charley approached the security gate again.

The guard squared up to her, his fists planted on his ample hips. 'I told you to leave.'

'Can you just radio Big T? He'll vouch for me.'

'Oh, you're a friend of Big T's!' said the guard, suddenly all smiles. 'Why didn't you say so?'

He shifted aside and waved her through the gate. But she hadn't taken two steps when the guard seized her by the wrist.

'Don't be so dumb!' he growled, pushing his pudgy face into hers. 'As if Big T knows *you*.'

'Ouch!' Charley exclaimed as he wrenched her into an armlock.

'I've had enough of you and your stories, little lady,' hissed the guard in her ear, forcing her arm further behind her back and clearly enjoying his moment of dominance.

But Charley wasn't going to be strong-armed off the premises. What would Ash and Big T think when they heard about it?

Goaded by the man's bullying tactics, Charley threw her head back. The guard cried out as his nose crumpled under the impact. She then scraped the heel of her shoe down his shin, before stamping on his foot. Spinning out of the armlock, she promptly twisted the man's arm and drove him to the ground. As blood poured from his nose on to the concrete, the other two guards rushed to his defence, one pulling out an extendable baton.

Charley released the man and stepped away, her hands held up in surrender. 'Just call Big T.'

'We'll be calling the police,' said the other guard, closing in.

'No, you won't,' grunted a voice. 'She's with me.'

The three men spun to see Big T standing at the gate. They stood open-mouthed as he waved Charley through the barrier.

'Here's your security pass,' said Big T, handing her a plastic ID card on a lanyard. 'Don't lose it.'

Charley slipped it over her head. 'Thanks . . . I wasn't on the guest list,' she tried to explain.

'That's cos you're part of the crew, not a guest.' He glanced at the guard with blood splattered down his shirt. 'Well, you certainly know how to make an entrance.'

'Sorry. He was a bit heavy-handed.'

Big T strode off down the corridor with Charley following.

'They weren't going to let me in,' she explained, wondering how much trouble she'd got herself into. 'But at least it proves security is tight.'

'Not really,' said Big T. 'Most of these venue guards are inexperienced jacket fillers who haven't a clue how to do their job properly. Back in my day, the security industry was for the elite. Now muppets, like that idiot you decked, pass two-week bodyguard courses and think they're Jason Bourne!'

Charley looked hesitantly up at the bodyguard. 'Do you think I'm a "jacket filler"?'

Big T stopped, eyed her intently, then laughed a deep throaty growl. 'That press conference exit was some baptism of fire, eh? Listen, Charley, we've all gotta learn from experience. Anyone would be knocked for six when confronted by a mass of crazed Ash Wild fans for the first time. Mind you, if you can take down an eighteen-stone guard like that, then I'd say you're up to the job.'

He grinned at her, revealing a gold-capped tooth.

Charley smiled back, deeply relieved at his apparent approval.

'Here, these are for you.' Big T handed her a pair of designer sunglasses. 'Essential kit for celebrity protection. Stop you getting blinded by paparazzi cameras. They're also good for hiding your line of sight,' he added as she tried them on for size. 'If an attacker can't see where you're looking, they don't know when to make their move. This gives you the edge over them.'

They walked on, turned a corner and entered the main arena. Thousands of empty seats encircled a stage in the shape of a massive guitar. Suspended above like a futuristic battleship was a rig of spotlights, speakers and plasma screens. Swarming over the stage, a team of roadies and sound technicians were making their final checks for that evening's performance. The sheer scale of the operation took Charley's breath away.

'Twenty thousand screaming fans will be packed into this venue tonight,' remarked Big T. 'Any one of them could be a nutter and it's our job to spot 'em and stop 'em.'

TARGET
CHAPTER 32

'Check . . . one . . . two . . . three. *It's only raining on you, only raining*,' sang Ash into his microphone.

'That's good, Ash,' responded the sound engineer over the monitors. 'Now your guitar.'

A tattooed roadie, his face swamped by a caveman-like beard, ran on stage with Ash's signature Fender.

'Thanks, Geoff,' acknowledged the sound engineer as the roadie checked the leads were all plugged in.

Slinging the leather guitar strap over one shoulder, Ash let rip along the fretboard. A gut-shredding riff blasted out from two stacks of speakers towering either side of the stage. The sound engineer tweaked the levels, then gave a thumbs up.

'OK, let's go through the "Indestructible" routine one more time,' announced the tour's choreographer.

A group of dancers joined Ash on stage. The drummer thumped out the distinctive beat that started the song and the dancers launched into a tightly synced routine.

'*In-des-tructible!*' belted out Ash as he simultaneously busted moves with the dancers.

‘Isn’t he amazing?’ came a sigh.

Charley, who’d been watching the rehearsal from the stage’s wings, turned to see a slightly plump girl gazing in awe at Ash. Though her brown eyes were over-mascaraed, her round face was pretty in a girl-next-door kind of way and she’d clearly made an effort with her appearance. Her auburn hair was brushed into a fine sheen, she wore a flattering summer dress and her hands were manicured with dark red false nails.

She smiled at Charley, revealing a set of braces that slightly spoiled the effect. ‘Hi, I’m Jessie! I don’t think we’ve met.’

Charley returned her smile. ‘Jessie? You run Ash’s fan club here, don’t you?’

The girl beamed. ‘Why, yes! How did you know?’

Charley didn’t want to reveal that she recognized the girl’s face from a file in the operations folder that listed all the key people associated with Ash Wild. Nor that she knew Jessie was seventeen years old, lived alone with her mother in Columbus, Ohio, and that she had a cat called Ash . . . Charley pointed to the lanyard hanging around the girl’s neck instead. ‘Your guest pass told me.’

Jessie glanced down at herself, then back at Charley. ‘Of course. So who are you?’ she asked, squinting to read Charley’s pass.

‘I’m Charley.’

With an admiring look at her athletic physique, blonde hair and sky-blue eyes, Jessie said, ‘You’re very beautiful. Are you Ash’s . . . ?’

Charley shook her head. 'No, I'm a PR trainee.'

Jessie smiled with what looked like relief, then her gaze returned to the performers on stage. 'I've been following Ash since day one. I was like the first American to truly recognize his talent – set up his fan website here, spread the word, did everything I could to build up his following. And now look at him. His first US tour! I can't believe he's really here.'

The song came to an end and the choreographer dismissed the dancers. Swigging from a bottle of water, Ash strolled over to where the two girls stood chatting.

'I see you've met my number-one fan,' said Ash, wrapping an arm round Jessie's shoulders and giving her a hug. 'This girl made me in America!'

Jessie blushed at the praise. 'Not at all. It was your songs . . . your voice . . . your talent . . .'

'Yeah, but without fans like you I'm nothing,' admitted Ash. He turned to Charley. 'That's why Jessie's joining us for the tour – the least I can do after all she's done for me.'

Ash perched on a guitar amp. 'So, Jessie, let's do that interview you wanted for the website.'

Jessie looked startled. 'What, now?'

'Why not?' he said. 'It'll get more crazy later on.'

Jessie fumbled for her smartphone and a list of questions from her bag. Ash smiled for the camera and Jessie began recording. Charley could tell the girl was nervous as her hands were shaking while she held the camera.

'Let me do the recording,' offered Charley.

'Thanks,' said Jessie, passing over her smartphone. 'So, Ash, you're finally here in the USA. How's it feel?'

'It's *wild*,' he replied with a smile. 'I never thought I'd be playing my first gig in the States at Madison Square Garden. It's a real kick.'

Jessie glanced at her question sheet. 'Have you managed to visit any of New York yet?'

'Not much. It's all go when on tour, but I did get up the Empire State Building. Awesome view! I saw all the way to the Statue of Liberty.'

'So, what are your first impressions of us Americans? Like, when you got off the plane and saw everyone there, what did you think?'

Ash ran a hand through his hair. 'I was blown away. I couldn't believe there were so many waiting for me. I only wish I could have got to meet them all.'

'Would you say your American fans are any different from your fans back home?'

'Well . . . if the fans at the press conference were anything to go by, they sure know how to scream! My ears are still ringing.'

Jessie checked her prompt sheet. 'Now you're so famous, if you want to see a movie with a friend, can you go out and do that?'

'It's a lot harder than it used to be,' admitted Ash. 'But I suppose I could, as long as I have my security with me.' He shot a wink in Charley's direction.

'And who would you invite as your date?' asked Jessie.

Ash pursed his lips and tapped a finger to his chin. 'Well, I'm single so I'm open to suggestions!'

Jessie stared wide-eyed at him and for a moment Charley thought that she was about to volunteer herself. But the girl buried her nose back in her list of questions, asking a few more before ending with, 'So . . . do you ever get stage nerves?'

'Not at all,' replied Ash, his eyes gleaming. 'It's like I was born to perform.'

CHAPTER 33

Ash danced and sang his way along the fretboard of the guitar-shaped stage. As he shimmied further and further out over the arena's sell-out crowd, the screams of the fans intensified and Charley wondered if any of them could even hear Ash singing. Big T had given her earplugs as well as a comms unit for the concert, but she could barely make out the security chatter above the noise of the band and the fans' insane shrieking.

Reaching the end of the headstock, Ash pirouetted on the spot, then sprinted back down the oversized fretboard. As he hit the main stage, he slid on his knees, snatched up his guitar and launched into a searing solo. His high-octane performance whipped the crowd into an even greater frenzy.

Witnessing Ash live in concert for the first time, Charley began to understand the mania surrounding this rock star she'd been assigned to protect. Ash lived up to his boast: he was a born performer – a rare superstar with the elusive 'X Factor' that legends like Prince, Michael Jackson and Justin Timberlake had all possessed. No wonder Ash attracted so much attention . . . both the good and the bad kind.

Leaping back to his feet, Ash strode towards Charley's side of the stage. She stood in the wings with Jessie and the rest of the tour guests, all of them watching awestruck as Ash brought the song to its climax. His voice soared into the chorus: '*You light up my life. You light up my heart. You light up the moon and the stars and the dark . . .*'

As he sang this line, he locked eyes with her.

'He's singing to you!' cried Jessie excitedly.

Charley felt an inexplicable thrill race through her body. Then instantly quashed it, firmly reminding herself that she wasn't supposed to be watching Ash perform. Her duty was to keep an eye out for threats – not easy when captivated by his stunning showmanship.

Charley broke away from his gaze to refocus on the crowd. Scanning the front rows for potential 'nutters', as Big T had put it, she thought the screaming fans *all* looked a little crazy. Of course, she'd experienced her own crushes on pop idols and movie stars in her time. But, seeing it from the performer's perspective, only now did she appreciate just how hysterical teenage girls could get. Some were crying with joy, their mascara running in black streaks down their faces. Others were frozen in open-mouthed shrieks, like multiple copies of Edvard Munch's *The Scream*. Many were jumping up and down as if electrified, while the remainder simply stared in simpering devotion.

With a crowd so demented, Charley was glad for the security guards posted at regular intervals round the arena.

Given half a chance, the over-enthusiastic hormone-fuelled fans would likely mob the stage and smother their idol to death.

Beyond the first few rows, the crowd turned into a sea of diminishing faces in the dark. There was no hope of Charley spotting a threat out there. That was the responsibility of the other members of the security team.

Before the concert, Big T had taken Charley on a tour of the arena as part of his security sweep. 'Large venues with lots of people should always come with a health warning,' he had explained as they'd walked the corridors and service tunnels of the building. 'Any hint of a fire or an emergency and big crowds can turn dangerous very quickly. That's why you should always familiarize yourself with a venue. Know where your exits are. The best evacuation routes. And the designated locations for transporting the VIP. Some venues are like rabbit warrens and, trust me, you don't want to get lost in a crisis.'

Charley had followed his lead, observing as the veteran bodyguard spot-checked emergency exits, identified potential security weak points and allocated postings for his team of guards. So she knew that the crowd was covered throughout the rest of the venue as best it could be. Backstage was even more secure since an official photo pass was required to gain access. Big T had made it Charley's responsibility, along with another bodyguard stationed in the opposite wing, to stop anyone who mounted the stage from reaching Ash.

The fans cheered, whooped and clapped as the song 'You

Light Up My Life' came to an end. The backing band immediately struck up the next number – 'Indestructible' – and Ash leapt into the choreographed routine with several dancers. The beat was infectious and Charley couldn't help glancing at Ash's impressive moves. That's when she noticed a red bead of light in the middle of his chest.

A moment later it was gone. Had she imagined it?

Ash danced across the stage, whirling round with one of the girls. Then, as he stopped on the beat, the red dot appeared again. Charley didn't remember seeing the light during the rehearsal earlier that afternoon and she was certain it wasn't part of the show. To her, the small red dot looked like the laser sighting of a rifle.

Caught in the haze hanging over the stage, Charley followed the beam's path up into the darkness. The laser didn't originate from the lighting rig. It came from one of the private corporate boxes, a box she knew from their security sweep was closed for refurbishment.

Charley stepped away from the other guests and thumbed her comms unit. 'Charley to Big T, code red. I think someone has a gun.'

There was a crackle in her earpiece. 'Big . . . *crzzzr* . . . say aga . . . *crzzzr*.'

Charley repeated her warning, but interference was breaking up the signal. She tried shouting to one of the security guards near the stage, but the noise of the concert drowned out her voice. And the bodyguard in the opposite wing was too distracted by one of the pretty dancers to notice her madly waving for his attention.

As Ash danced, the laser beam tracked him across the stage. It leapt and spun, working hard to stay on target. The music stopped and Ash froze in a dramatic pose, one fist raised to the sky.

'*In-des-tructible!*' he cried.

The red dot came to rest in the middle of his chest once more. Ash was oblivious to the threat as he basked in his fans' applause.

No more encores, thought Charley, recalling the ominous death threat.

With perhaps milliseconds before the shooter pulled the trigger, she dashed on to the stage.

TARGET
CHAPTER 34

Charley was first blasted by the noise of the crowd, then hit by the heat of the spotlights as she raced past the dancers. The stage suddenly seemed to stretch before her and she prayed she'd reach Ash in time. The red laser dot remained fixed on its superstar target.

'*What the hell?*' cried Ash as Charley leapt on him, breaking the beam.

Shielding Ash with her body, she bundled him offstage to the shocked screams of his fans. Ash was too stunned to resist at first, but quickly regained his senses.

'Let me go!' he shouted, struggling in her grip.

Only when she reached the safety of the opposite wing did she release him.

Ash glared at her. 'Have you gone completely insane?'

'You were about to get *shot*!' replied Charley.

This news shocked Ash into silence. He reached out to a nearby speaker for support.

'*What in God's name is going on?*' demanded a squat black guy with a trimmed moustache and shaved head. Terry was the tour manager, a hard-nosed, flinty-eyed man with a reputation for running a tight ship on tour. He hated any disruption to the schedule.

'A red laser sight was targeted on Ash. Someone was about to shoot him,' explained Charley.

Terry frowned. 'Did anyone else see this laser?'

The group of road crew, dancers and musicians who'd gathered round Ash and Charley all shook their heads.

'Did you see it?' Terry demanded of the other bodyguard, as Big T came hurrying along the gangway to join them. He was a little out of breath and perspiration shone on his bald dome.

The bodyguard, a blond-haired Adonis with a chisel jaw, crossed his bulging arms and grunted a definitive 'No'.

Realizing her credibility with Big T was at stake, Charley said, 'Of course you didn't. You were too busy eyeing up that dancer.'

The bodyguard shot her a dirty look. 'Who is this girl?' he sneered.

'A PR assistant,' cut in Big T. 'Now, let's establish if Ash is in danger or not. Charley, did you actually see someone with a gun?'

Charley shook her head. 'I spotted the laser sight, that's all.'

There was a groan of irritation from the band and road crew.

'Did *no one* else see it?' she asked, her tone almost pleading. 'It was following Ash round the stage!' She was met by blank and hostile looks.

'It was probably one of the stage lights,' said the bassist.

'Yes, most probably a stage light,' agreed the tour manager, his eye twitching as he barely kept his anger in check.

'No. It wasn't,' said Charley. 'The beam came from a corporate box. The one closed for renovation.'

Big T radioed up to one of his team to check out the box. The group stood in tense silence as they waited for a response. In the main arena, the bewildered crowd started chanting Ash's name, at first with enthusiasm, then with growing impatience.

'The box is empty. No one there,' came the reply eventually.

Everyone stared accusingly at Charley. As a flush of humiliation reddened her cheeks, she wished the ground would just swallow her up.

'False alarm,' Big T confirmed.

'On with the show!' ordered the tour manager, shooing people away with his hands.

Ash shook his head angrily at Charley, then strode back on to the stage.

'Hey, you fans are crazy!' he called out to the whistles and cheers that greeted his return. 'Next time one of you wants a hug, just ask!'

This offer sent the crowd into hormonal meltdown and almost lifted the roof with shrieks of delight. With a nod to the band, Ash kicked off the next song and the set resumed.

The stage wing quickly emptied as the crew returned to their duties. Charley remained where she was, her head hung in shame. She'd screwed up again! How could her judgement be so off? She was acting like a rookie on her first assignment. But she *knew* what she'd seen: a laser sight tracking Ash's every move. Her gut instinct had told her to act – if she hadn't, Ash might now be lying on stage in a pool of his own blood!

On the other hand, perhaps it had just been a harmless trick of the light, a reflected beam from the show or some other stage effect. Whatever, the threat had come to nothing.

'We all make mistakes,' said Big T, his tone surprisingly sympathetic.

'Not this big,' she replied, unable to meet his eye.

As the dancers congregated in the wing for another routine, Big T took Charley to one side.

'I don't doubt you saw a laser, but it's most likely to have been one of these,' he said, pulling a small silver pen-sized pointer from his pocket. He pressed a button and a red dot appeared on the floor. 'These things are banned from concerts, but people still smuggle them in.'

'I'm a complete idiot!' said Charley, holding her head in her hands. 'How could I have thought that was a laser gunsight?'

'Don't be so hard on yourself. To the untrained eye, there's virtually no difference between the two,' he said, pocketing the laser pen.

Charley wondered why the old bodyguard was being so understanding about her monumental mistake. She'd disrupted Ash's first night of the tour, potentially blown her cover as his secret bodyguard and made enemies of virtually everyone on the crew.

'Did you know I was once Stevie Wonder's personal bodyguard?' revealed Big T. 'Didn't last long, though. On my second night, I was guiding him up a podium, didn't spot a loose cable and he tripped. Fell flat on his face. Even in my early days as a bouncer I never managed to put someone down so quickly.'

Charley looked up into his heavily worn features. 'That must have been awkward.'

'Yeah, it was a real bummer,' Big T admitted. 'After that, I was guarding the toilets for the rest of the tour!'

Charley let out a heavy sigh. 'I suppose that's what I'll be doing then?'

'No, Jon will be,' he said with a fierce glare in the direction of the blond-haired bodyguard. 'He should have been keeping his eye on Ash, not that redhead.'

'So you're not throwing me off my assignment?' asked Charley, astonished.

By way of an answer, Big T showed her the tattoo on his inner forearm: *Only the paranoid survive*.

'As a bodyguard, this is a useful code to live by. I'd rather you overreact than not react at all,' he explained. 'When I started out, there was no training. Just thinking on your feet and learning from your mistakes. And, believe me, I made a truckload. But each mistake taught me something. You see, good judgement only comes from experience – and much of that experience comes from bad judgement. Live and learn, Charley, live and learn!'

TARGET

CHAPTER 35

'It's all across the internet,' said Blake, speaking to Charley on her smartphone the next day.

Charley groaned. The nightmare wasn't over for her yet. Backstage the road crew were preparing for Ash's second night at the arena, everyone giving her odd looks and a wide berth as they went about their business.

'Don't worry,' Blake continued. 'The only footage of the incident shows a flash of blonde hair, then you and Ash were gone. It was a textbook-perfect extraction of a Principal.'

'So my cover's not blown?' she asked.

'Not by the looks of it. All any photographer got was the back of your head. The story is that a Wildling fan jumped Ash in a fit of starstruck excitement. What spooked you anyway?'

'A laser dot. Thought it was a gunsight,' she admitted. 'But I was wrong. In fact, everything seems to be going wrong on this assignment. First the press conference, then the security guard and now this –'

'Whoa, hang on! What guard?' interrupted Blake.

Sighing, Charley explained the incident that had occurred when she'd tried to gain access to the venue.

'You headbutted a security guard!' laughed Blake. 'You're out of control!'

'Thanks,' she replied flatly. 'That's what everyone here thinks too. And after last night I've ruined any chance of gaining Ash's confidence. He now thinks I'm highly strung. A liability. He hasn't let me anywhere near him all day. How am I supposed to protect him? The only person showing any faith in me is Big T.'

'Best person to have on your side.'

'I suppose so,' said Charley, pacing the corridor outside Ash's dressing room. 'I've been learning a lot from him about celebrity protection. He really knows his stuff.'

'He should do,' said Blake. 'He's been in the game long enough. And that's what you have to remember. This may be your sixth assignment – more than any other Buddyguard recruit – but that's nothing compared to his experience. Hang on in there, Charley. I'm sure as the tour goes on, things will calm down. Just keep your head and do the best you can. I've faith in you too.'

'Thanks, Blake,' she replied, feeling better with his support.

'I'm missing you, by the way.'

'Yeah, I'm miss–'

'Charley!' called out a gruff voice.

Covering her mobile with a hand, she turned to see Big T's bulky frame heading down the corridor towards her. 'You need to hear this,' he said.

Blake's muffled voice sounded from the mobile's speaker. 'Charley, are you still there?'

She took her hand away and put the speaker to her ear. 'I'll call you back.'

Ending the call, she slipped the phone into her pocket. Her mouth had gone dry and her chest tightened at Big T's approach. She feared that he'd reassessed her actions in the cold light of day – and the conclusion wasn't good.

'What's up?' she asked.

Big T scratched at the stubble on his chin. 'I've just heard from the venue manager that the corporate box being renovated was broken into last night. Also, the fire exit nearby had been jammed open.'

Charley's jaw went slack. 'You mean . . . I was right, after all?'

Big T gave a non-committal shrug. 'We've no proof of a shooter, but there was certainly an intruder. Whatever, I'm taking no chances tonight. There'll be guards patrolling the boxes. Terry's been updated and it's gone a long way to easing his concerns about you. I've informed Ms Gibson too.'

'Thanks. What about Ash?'

'I'll tell him after tonight's show. Best let him focus on his performance rather than worry about getting shot or not.' As Big T strode off, he patted her on the back with one of his meaty hands. 'Good work, Charley.'

Charley allowed herself a smile. Her gut reaction hadn't failed her. There *had* been a threat to Ash's life. While it wasn't good news for Ash, it did mean her actions on stage were justified. The tension she'd felt in her chest subsided.

Pulling her phone from her pocket, she went to dial Blake's number when the door to Ash's dressing room burst open and his bassist rushed out. His eyes were wide with panic.

'Charley, come quick!' he cried, seizing her by the arm.

They ran into the dressing room. The other members of the band were crowded round Ash, who lay on the floor not moving.

'What's happened?' Charley demanded, hurrying to his side.

'I don't know,' replied the bassist. 'He simply collapsed.'

The drummer knelt beside Ash's prone body. 'He's not breathing!'

'Move back, everyone,' instructed Charley, trying to get a grip on the situation. *Dr ABC* flashed through her head. There was no apparent danger. The floor was clear and Ash wasn't touching anything electrical.

She knelt down next to his head. 'Ash? Are you all right?'

No response.

She gently shook his shoulder. Still no response.

Airway was next. After checking nothing was blocking his mouth, she tilted his head back and lifted his chin to open his airway. Then she placed her cheek close to his mouth and nose and looked down his body for any signs of breathing. She waited ten seconds but felt and saw nothing. A spike of alarm shot through her.

'Call 911,' she ordered. 'We need an ambulance *fast*.'

While the bassist fumbled for his phone, Charley assessed Ash's circulation. There was no obvious sign of bleeding. She checked his pulse. A little fast but strong. That was a good sign. But he still wasn't breathing. She had to begin CPR immediately.

Pinching Ash's nose, Charley took a deep breath and placed her lips around his mouth. Before she could breathe out, an arm wrapped round her waist and a tongue caressed her own. Ash's eyes opened and met her startled gaze as he began to kiss her in earnest.

Charley leapt away in shock.

'Now that's what I call mouth-to-mouth resuscitation!' cracked the bassist, having taken a video of the intimate moment with his phone.

The other band members were all apparently in on the joke. They laughed heartily.

'I thought you were dying,' Charley exclaimed, wiping the back of her hand across her lips in disgust.

Ash sat up and grinned mischievously. 'One false alarm deserves another!'

Charley was too stunned to reply.

'Go on, admit it. You liked it,' he said, getting to his feet. 'Most girls would give their right arm to kiss me.'

Now over the initial shock, Charley felt a surge of anger at being duped. She was even more outraged at Ash's arrogance that he imagined she'd liked it!

Charley responded with a tight smile. 'How lucky I am.' Then she drew closer and whispered in his ear, 'You *ever* try to kiss me again, I'll break your arm.'

Ash laughed it off. 'Worth the risk!'

He waltzed out of the door with the rest of his band, their laughter echoing down the corridor as they headed for the stage.

TARGET

CHAPTER 36

Big T checked his watch and yawned. 'The older I get, the more I hate these after-show parties,' he grumbled.

Charley stood beside him as he guarded the entrance to the private club that had been reserved for the sole use of Ash and his entourage. Even Charley was fading at three in the morning. She'd been invited to join the party, but after Ash's ridiculing of her she was keeping a professional distance – far enough away to be unnoticed, but close enough to react if there was any trouble. Meanwhile, Ash and his band were still grooving on the dance floor with a group of VIP guests: local celebrities, TV personalities and the prettiest female fans picked out from the audience by the security team. The band were so pumped up on adrenalin from the concert that they needed to let off steam before heading back to the hotel to sleep.

'I heard about Ash's prank,' remarked Big T over the heavy drum and bass of the DJ's music.

Charley grimaced with embarrassment. 'Yeah, I'm sure everyone did,' she said bitterly.

'Don't take it personally,' he said. 'Tour pranks are something of a tradition. When I was working security for Black Sabbath, Ozzy once poured Tabasco sauce into my mouth while I was sleeping! I sure woke up fast. I thought my tongue had been set on fire. He helpfully handed me a glass of water to wash the taste away. Turned out to be vodka! I vomited all over the bed.'

'Well, Ash was lucky I didn't vomit over him,' replied Charley, glaring at the rock star who was encircled by a gaggle of gyrating girls, any of whom would probably give their right arm *and* right leg to kiss the rock star.

'Don't worry – I'm sure you'll get your chance for payback later in the tour. I certainly did with Black Sabbath.'

'You did? How?'

Big T grinned. 'I replaced the contents of a stick-on air freshener with raw chicken and hung it in their tour bus. After a few days, the rotting meat began to smell. Really badly. But nobody on the bus could figure out where the stink was coming from. The air freshener was the perfect disguise. The band spent the rest of the tour reeking of rotten chicken!' He let out a gutsy laugh at the memory.

Hearing this tale from the old bodyguard, she realized Ash's prank was just part of band touring and began to feel better. However humiliated she'd been at the time, she had to take it on the chin. Besides, from her training, she knew she had to give as good as she got – and she vowed she would when the opportunity arose.

Charley glanced out through the tinted glass of the

club's doors. A crowd was still gathered outside. 'Don't they have homes to go to?' she remarked.

Big T eyed the crowd. 'Paparazzi never sleep.'

Charley spotted a face she recognized. Unshaven with a hook nose, close-set mud-brown eyes and a buzz cut of black hair, it was the photographer who'd flashgunned her outside the press conference.

'Do you know who that guy is?' asked Charley, pointing to the man through the glass.

Big T snorted his disgust. 'Yeah, that's Gonzo.'

'Gonzo?' queried Charley.

'His real name's Sancho Gomez, but he looks more like the Muppet Gonzo to me. He's one of the paps that follow Ash around the world. In fact he's the worst of them – a piece of scum, a former gang member turned freelance photographer. Guys like him should be called the stalkerazzi!'

'Can't you get rid of him?'

Big T shook his head. 'Nothing we can do. Those guys justify their presence by citing the rights of freedom of the press. But ultimately it's all about the money.'

'What money?' asked Charley.

'Paparazzi can earn tens of thousands of dollars for a single photo, sometimes even more. That's why they're so determined and desperate, Gonzo in particular. I hear he owes a large gambling debt to the mob. But, lucky for him, some tabloids are willing to pay six-figure sums for a unique shot.'

'What do you mean by unique?'

'Anything that's a scoop, like an affair or a new relationship,' explained Big T. 'Or a picture that makes the celebrity look bad, like a car accident, appearing drunk, unattractive or angry. And, if they can't get their shot naturally, they'll try to goad the celebrity into losing their cool.'

Charley reappraised the group of paparazzi hanging outside the club. They were beginning to look more like a pack of sharks awaiting their prey. 'So what can we do to stop them getting that shot?'

'Not much. Just have the patience of angels,' Big T replied. 'No matter how rude they are, how much they push and shove or shout and scream at you, always keep your cool and a smile on your face. Remember, the key rule is to keep moving. Never stop among a pack of pap. Otherwise they'll eat you alive. If you do need to block a photo for any reason, simply put your body in the way. *Never* put your hand up to the lens.'

Charley frowned. 'Why not?'

'It'll give them a dramatic picture of your hand looking very large and very menacing in the lens. And then they'll have the story they were seeking: *Violent bodyguard attacks innocent photographer*.'

Ash strode up to them with two girls on his arm. 'I'm beat,' he said with a sigh.

'Sorry, Ash, no room for guests in the vehicle,' said Big T in a polite yet firm tone.

Ash grinned and shrugged. 'Guess the party's over, girls,' he said, kissing both on the cheek and letting them go. They giggled and swooned. Charley rolled her eyes.

The rest of Ash's band and entourage joined them at the door.

Big T raised an eyebrow at Charley. 'Time to meet the great unwashed!'

The cool night air hit them as they emerged on to the street. Immediately the paparazzi pounced. They swarmed round Ash, some even fighting one another to get in position for the best shot. Flashes burst like fireworks in the night. But Charley was more prepared for the craziness this time. Even though it was dark, she wore her sunglasses against the blinding flare of multiple cameras on full auto. And she kept her footing despite the mayhem of pushing and shoving.

'Make way, please,' called out Big T, cutting a path through the throng.

'Ash, over here!' shouted a photographer.

'Look this way, Ash!' cried another.

But Ash kept his head down and followed in Big T's wake.

'Ash, have you been drinking?' accused one guy. 'That's illegal at your age, you know.'

'Excuse me,' insisted Big T, positioning his ample frame to shield Ash from the onslaught of photographers. However, the paparazzi proved experts at walking backwards while taking their shots.

'Looks like you're on drugs, Ash!' taunted a pap. 'What did you take?'

Ash shook his head. 'I *never* take drugs,' he snapped, obviously annoyed at the line of questioning.

With the paparazzi becoming more antagonistic, Charley moved closer to Ash, protecting him from behind while appearing like a tagger-on of his entourage.

'Got a thing for blondes now, have you?' taunted Gonzo, his ratty eyes fixing on Charley. There was a brief flicker of recognition. '*Hola*, blondie. Are you his latest girlfriend?'

'No, just PR,' she replied with a smile.

'Yeah, I believe you, *chica*. How about a picture of you two lovebirds together?'

Charley kept moving. Gonzo shoved a camera in her face and reeled off several shots. He was invading her body space, but she held her smile and didn't slow her pace.

More taunts and insults were hurled at Ash in a bid to spark a reaction, but Big T swiftly escorted the rock star into the awaiting minivan. Charley clambered in with the rest of the entourage and Big T slammed the door shut. The paparazzi flocked round the vehicle, pressing their lenses against the tinted windows and assaulting the van with camera flashes.

As Charley took her seat, she heard Big T's voice in her earpiece.

'See what I mean? Those guys will do anything to get their shot.'

TARGET

CHAPTER 37

It hadn't taken long. All the instructions were there on the internet – even a helpful video.

The ingredients had been bought readily and without suspicion. Sugar and a frying pan from the supermarket. Saltpetre from the fertilizer section of a garden centre. A small torch bulb, a nine-volt battery, a relay switch and some electrical wire from a hardware store. Finally, a large can of Hyper energy drink and a cheap digital watch from a gas station.

The sugar and saltpetre had been mixed in a bowl at the exact ratio specified on the web. Then the white powder tipped into the frying pan and 'cooked' under a low heat. Constantly stirring the mixture with a wooden spoon, the grains of sugar had started to melt and caramelize. Gradually the white powder liquefied into a light brown paste with the consistency of peanut butter.

The resulting gooey liquid had been poured into the now-empty soda can. As this mixture was left to cool and harden, the back of the digital watch had been prised open, its alarm buzzer disconnected and electrical wires attached.

A circuit had then been made with the battery, relay switch and bulb.

With great care, the glass of the torch bulb had been broken to expose the filament. This was buried in a small wrapper of uncooked sugar and saltpetre and inserted into the opening of the soda can. The watch and battery were taped to the outside of the can.

All the key components were now in place: a timer, a battery, an igniter and an incendiary mix – small enough to conceal in a backpack.

The bomb was complete.

TARGET

CHAPTER 38

Charley reclined in the upper-front lounge of the double-decker bus as it headed west towards Pittsburgh and Ash's next stop on the tour. She'd never been in a vehicle like it before. The tour bus was a Tardis. There were sixteen curtained-off bunk beds, three separate lounges, a fully equipped kitchen and a designer-tiled bathroom complete with its own shower unit. The lounges were upholstered in sumptuous black leather and boasted high-definition televisions, games consoles and top-of-the-range sound systems. Charley would have believed she was in a high-class hotel if it wasn't for the subtle sensation of movement and the suppressed noise of traffic outside.

Ash was downstairs in one of the air-conditioned bunk beds, sleeping off the night before. When she'd passed him earlier, Charley had contemplated pouring Tabasco sauce into his mouth. But fortunately for him there wasn't any in the kitchen. Leaving the superstar to get his beauty sleep, she'd made her way upstairs where she found the drummer and bassist absorbed in a two-player shooter game. A coffee in hand, she'd settled herself in the sofa by the front window.

Gazing out at the traffic, service stations and fast-food joints that whizzed by, Charley's thoughts turned to the tour that lay ahead. There were still some twenty dates and a whole continent to cross. This bus would be their home for much of it and the one place that Charley could relax from her duties protecting Ash. That's if he let her protect him. At the moment he still seemed to consider her some sort of joke. But the threat against him wasn't a joke. His stalker could strike at any point on the tour. And she'd have to be ready, whether Ash took her seriously or not.

'How was the party last night?' asked Jessie, coming up the stairs and plonking herself down beside Charley.

'All right,' she replied. 'Where were you? I didn't see you at the club.'

'Oh, I had to update the website. Lots of photos to add and a blog to write about the opening shows,' she explained. Then, leaning closer, she lowered her voice in a conspiratorial tone. 'Don't worry, though. I didn't reveal it was *you* who ran on to the stage the first night!'

Charley cringed with embarrassment. Despite her instincts having been right about the potential threat, she was still regarded as the 'guest' who'd freaked out over Ash's performance and stopped the concert.

'I don't blame you for doing it,' whispered Jessie. 'I know how hard it is. Any time I see Ash, I just want to grab hold of him and never let go.' Her eyes took on a faraway glaze.

'Still can't believe I'm on his tour bus. It's like a dream come true. So, how did you get invited?'

'My guardian knows Ash's manager,' Charley replied, hoping the half-truth would be convincing enough. 'Which reminds me, I totally forgot to call him back. Will you excuse me?'

'Sure,' said Jessie. 'I should really phone my mom before she thinks Ash has abducted me!' She giggled at the idea. 'It took a lot to persuade her to let me come on this tour. I had to promise that I wouldn't do anything stupid, like drink or take drugs. But I explained Ash wasn't that sort of rock star.'

'Yeah, my guardian warned me to be careful too,' said Charley with a rueful smile.

She rose from her seat and headed down the stairs. Seeking some privacy, she found the toilet cubicle and locked the door. She dialled Blake's number rather than Buddyguard HQ. It rang for several moments before being picked up.

'Hey!' she said brightly.

There was a slight pause, then a 'Hey yourself', followed by silence.

At first Charley thought it was a delay on the line, but the silence became more drawn out. 'Are you OK?' she asked.

'You didn't call me back,' said Blake.

'Yeah, sorry about that. There was an emergency.'

'I guessed as much. That's why I've been worrying all this time.'

'Nothing to worry about,' said Charley. 'Ash had pretended to pass out and tricked me into doing CPR. Turned out to be a tour prank.'

Blake snorted. 'Sounds like a dumb joke to me. So, how is the almighty Ash? Is he all he's cracked up to be?'

'Truth be told, he's pretty amazing. Having seen him live, I can understand why his fans are so crazy about him.'

'Can you now?'

'Don't get jealous!' she cautioned with a laugh. 'Ash is way too arrogant for my liking. Besides, he isn't half as cute as you.'

'That's good to hear,' said Blake, his voice still flat. 'I was beginning to think the radio silence meant you'd forgotten me.'

'Of course not,' she insisted. 'Listen, my hunch was right about the laser. There *was* an intruder in the b–'

A knock at the door interrupted her.

'Charley?' called Big T's voice. 'We'll soon be coming into Pittsburgh.'

'OK,' she replied. Then in a quieter voice: 'Listen, Blake, I've got to go. Missing you.'

'Yeah, you too,' he said, and cut the call.

Charley stared at her mobile, half-wishing she hadn't phoned him. Blake was clearly annoyed she hadn't rung back the other day. But what could she do? She was on an assignment. Aside from the routine report-ins, she rarely had time to make social calls. He of all people should understand that. With a sigh, she pocketed her phone. *Long-distance relationships are a nightmare*, she thought.

Charley made her way down the corridor and joined Big T at the front of the coach.

'I hope you're well rested,' he said to her. 'It's about to get crazy again. I've heard from the security advance party that Ash's hotel is mobbed with fans.'

'I'm getting used to that now,' replied Charley, gazing through the windscreen at the city skyline ahead.

The bus mounted a ramp and approached a monumental golden bridge. Spanning the breadth of the Monongahela River, the bowstring arch structure was an impressive gateway to their next stop on the tour.

'Welcome to Pittsburgh, the City of Bridges!' announced their driver, a grizzled man with a beer belly the size of a space hopper.

As they crossed the bridge, following the signs towards the Consol Center, Charley glanced up at the lattice of golden steel girders whizzing over their heads.

'Ford Pitt Bridge,' said the driver, noting her interest. 'Just one of four hundred and forty-six bridges in the city. I bet you're wondering why it's painted gold?' He didn't wait for her to answer. 'It's to match the city's official colours – black and gold.'

Charley nodded and smiled at the talkative driver.

'A very iconic bridge, this one,' he said, continuing with his monologue. 'Been featured in many films. *Striking Distance*, *Abduction*, *The Perks of Being A Wallflower*, as well as the documentary *The Song Remains The Same* about Led Zeppelin's legendary 1973 tour. This bridge is constructed from over eight thousand tonnes of steel and –'

A muffled bang rocked the coach.

Charley grabbed hold of a handrail as the tour bus suddenly veered across the road. The driver fought to control the wheel. There was another bang and the whole coach shuddered.

Cars honked and swerved at the last second to avoid a collision. Charley clung on for dear life as the bus headed straight for the barrier and the dizzying drop into the river below.

TARGET

CHAPTER 39

Bracing herself for the impact, Charley wished she'd been strapped in by a seat belt. Her only thought was how ironic it would be if, after all the danger she'd faced on assignments, she died in a coach crash.

The barrier came rushing towards them. At the last second, the driver wrenched the wheel hard and steered the bus away from its fatal course. Glancing off the barrier with a screech of metal on metal, the bus swung the other way and careered across four lanes of traffic towards the opposite barrier.

Wrestling with the wheel and working the accelerator and brake, the driver fought to regain control. Despite his efforts, the edge drew ever nearer.

Behind her, Charley heard the other tour members screaming. A passing car was knocked spinning across the lanes. The jolt of the impact was felt through the entire bus, sending people to the floor like skittles. Yet still the coach headed towards the drop.

No longer was the Ford Pitt Bridge a welcoming sight. With a crunching of gears, a squeal of brakes and a grating of metal, the bus rocked to an unsteady halt, teetering next to the edge. Below, Charley could see the cold grey waters that would have been their grave.

By some miracle the driver had managed to stop the bus just in time. Sweat patches staining his white shirt, he let out a shuddering breath and switched off the engine.

'Everyone OK?' asked Big T, hauling himself to his feet.

Charley nodded. She was shaken up but otherwise unhurt. The bassist came staggering down the stairs with Jessie and the drummer, while the others picked themselves up from the floor.

Ash emerged bleary-eyed from his bunk and yawned. 'Are we here already?'

Oblivious to their almost-fatal accident, his question prompted a burst of nervous laughter from everyone on board. 'Not quite,' replied his drummer. 'Looks like we might have a bit of a walk ahead.'

'Walk?' said Ash. Then he noticed the slight tilt to the tour bus and saw the waters of the Monongahela River outside the window. 'Hey, did we crash?'

'No, of course not,' said the bassist, his tone sarcastic. 'The driver just thought he'd do an emergency stop on the edge of a bridge!'

Clambering off the bus, Charley joined Big T and the driver to inspect the damage. Her legs were a little shaky. She couldn't believe they'd all escaped the crash with their lives. A few more metres and they would have plunged over the side. The coach's front grille was heavily dented from the collision with the car and the right-hand side was scraped down to the metal.

'Looks like we had a blowout,' said the driver, pointing to the nearside front tyre. All that was left was a shredded mess of rubber.

'One of your rear tyres blew as well,' noted Big T. 'Surely that's not normal?'

'Can happen. Once one tyre goes, the others have to bear the load,' the driver replied, hunkering down to examine the wheel rims. 'We'll have to call a tow truck. This bus ain't going nowhere.'

The flash of a camera caught Charley's attention. Gonzo was at the roadside, capturing the accident scene as Ash stepped off the wrecked bus. His lens then focused on the shunted car as the dazed passengers climbed out.

'Hope you've got insurance, Ash!' called Gonzo, snapping away. 'Think you might have a personal injury lawsuit on your hands.'

'How the hell did Gonzo get here so fast?' exclaimed Charley.

Big T narrowed his eyes at the shutterbug. 'Must've been following us.'

In the distance the sound of police sirens could be heard.

'Let's get Ash out of here,' said Big T, 'before this accident scene turns into a publicity nightmare.'

TARGET
CHAPTER 40

Expecting a large tour bus, the horde of Ash Wild fans barely gave the yellow taxi a second glance as it pulled up outside the Pittsburgh Hilton Hotel. Then their idol stepped from the vehicle and all hell broke loose. Fans swooped on him with deafening and delighted screams. Instantly he was surrounded and being barraged with requests for photos, autographs and kisses.

Ash dutifully signed and posed as Big T tried to keep the crowd at bay and steer him towards the hotel's reception. Charley remained close to Ash, blending in as one of the fans. She was still tense from the coach crash, but this served to heighten her senses, helping her to stay sharp for danger.

She scanned the faces surrounding them, looking for any person who appeared unusually nervous, shifty or out of place. But the fans were so hysterical that it was impossible to tell if anyone posed an actual threat – they *all* looked dangerous.

One girl had her hand deep inside a bag, her eyes glued to Ash. Since most of the crowd were reaching out to the rock star, this girl's behaviour seemed odd to Charley. Wondering what she was concealing, Charley positioned herself beside the blonde-haired girl. She couldn't see into the bag and tensed in readiness to react at the slightest threat.

As Ash approached, the suspect pulled out . . . a stuffed teddy bear, with a red heart clasped between its paws.

'Ash! This is for you!' she cried, thrusting the toy at her idol.

Accustomed to being showered with gifts by his fans, Ash accepted the bear with good grace and thanked the girl. Charley resumed her surveillance of the crowd. With the teddy bear tucked under his arm, Ash moved on to the next fan. Taking a souvenir concert programme from a brown-haired lad, he scribbled his signature across the front.

'What's your name?' Ash asked, to personalize the cover.

'Don't you remember me?' said the fan with a mild look of disappointment.

Ash glanced up and did a double-take. So did Charley. There was a distinct familiarity *and* similarity. Charley's alert level shot up.

'It's me, Pete!' said the boy, smiling. 'Your "twin"?'

'You look different . . . or should I say the *same*,' remarked Ash.

'Yeah! After what you said, I dyed my hair the same colour as yours,' he explained, running a hand through his matching hairstyle. 'I also got my ear pierced and contact lenses to match your eyes.'

He stared unblinking at Ash so he could show off his dark hazel lenses. The effect was disturbing – like a reflection in a mirror taking on a life of its own. The two boys were practically identical.

Charley instinctively moved in to shield Ash from his self-styled doppelgänger. Other fans noticed the similarity too and began taking photos.

'I'm flattered,' said Ash as he handed back the signed programme. Then he indicated his left forearm. 'You only need my phoenix tattoo now to complete the look.'

Big T moved Ash on and through the revolving doors into the hotel.

'Didn't you find that lad a bit creepy?' Charley asked Ash as they entered the relative calm of the hotel's lobby.

Ash shrugged. 'That's fan devotion for you.'

'But he's followed you from New York. Surely that's odd?'

'Not really,' he replied. 'On any tour I see loads of the same faces.'

'But your *own*?' questioned Charley.

'Ash, darling! Are you OK?' cried Zoe, rushing across the lobby towards them. 'I heard about the crash. Sounds awful.'

'To be honest, I slept through it,' he replied.

'Well, let me take that for you.' She indicated the teddy bear under his arm. 'I'll put it with the rest of the gifts in your room. Now I've a full schedule of interviews lined up. They'll probably ask about the crash, so I'd better brief you . . .'

As Zoe led Ash away, Charley went to follow, but Big T called her back, indicating for Rick and Vince, two other members of his security team, to keep guard.

'My orders are to stick with Ash,' objected Charley.

'He'll be fine for the moment. First, we need to security-check his room.'

Crossing the hotel lobby, they entered the lift and the old bodyguard thumbed the button for the fourth floor. As the lift slowly ascended, Big T explained, 'Hotels throw up a whole host of security issues. First and foremost, we don't have exclusive use. Which means anyone can enter. The hotel doormen will keep the majority of fans out. But with so many entrances and exits, any determined individual can find their way in. And some fans will even book themselves into the hotel. So stay alert for possible intruders.'

'Like that copycat fan?' said Charley. 'Should we be worried about him?'

Big T raised an eyebrow. 'Granted he's a bit weird, but I wouldn't lose sleep over it. I've witnessed far more obsessive fan behaviour in my time. Once a girl turned up to a concert in a wedding dress, hoping Ash would marry her!' He shook his head in wonder. 'However, I agree we should keep an eye on the boy. There's a fine line between devotion and stalking.'

The doors to the lift pinged open and they stepped out. 'Good. Ash's room is at the end of the corridor.'

'Why's that good?' asked Charley.

'Because anyone approaching his suite needs to have a

reason to do so,' he explained. 'If there are rooms beyond, then guests can walk past and this undermines our security.'

As they made their way along the corridor, Big T pointed out a red fire-exit sign. 'In every hotel we stay in, always locate the two nearest fire exits,' he instructed. 'Count the doorways, note corridors and any furniture in between, and commit the route to memory. If there's a fire and the corridor's choked with smoke, you'll thank me for it.'

Inserting a key card, Big T opened the door to Ash's suite. A luxurious cream-carpeted room spread out before them. There was a walnut desk, coffee table and L-shaped sofa. Through a second doorway lay a king-size bed, widescreen TV and en suite bathroom. Big T went into the bathroom, checked the shower cubicle, then opened all the wardrobes.

'What are you looking for?' asked Charley.

'Groupies,' he said, getting on his knees and peering under the bed.

'Seriously?' asked Charley.

'Along with hidden bugs, cameras and any other sort of surveillance device.' Big T took out a small black box from his jacket pocket. The palm-sized unit had two antennae and an LED indicator. Switching it on, he held the device over the telephone on the bedside table.

'Bug detector,' he explained. 'Know how to use one?'

Charley nodded. 'Our surveillance tutor Bugsy showed us a whole bunch of them.'

'Good.' He tossed her the unit. 'Scan the rest of the room while I finish off the physical search.'

'Is this necessary every time?' she asked as she slowly swept the device over the pictures, the plug sockets, the lights and every other fixture and fitting in the room.

Big T nodded. 'Remember, we're not only protecting Ash's physical safety – we're protecting his privacy too. In my time as a bodyguard, I've come across bugged pens, phone chargers, you name it. I've found fans hiding in closets, paparazzi impersonating cleaning staff, pranksters doing dares. Believe me, I've seen it all!'

TARGET
CHAPTER 41

'*Please* tell me that was my last interview,' said Ash, slumping back in his chair as Big T closed the door on the departing reporter.

Zoe smiled. 'Yes, that was your last interview . . . for today at least.'

'Thank goodness.' Ash rubbed his eyes with the palms of his hands. 'My brain's fried.'

Charley wasn't surprised. Ash had slogged through ten interviews back-to-back, each reporter asking a variation of the same questions and Ash having to respond to each as if for the first time. A few brought up the 'Only Raining' court case with the songwriter Brandon Mills, but most grilled him about the coach crash earlier that morning. Ash's responses were carefully prepared and guided by Zoe to avoid any statements that could be misinterpreted or taken out of context. Charley was now seeing the reality of a superstar's life. There was a lot of hard graft behind the success and a lot of media traps to avoid.

Getting up from his chair, Ash went over to the window. 'I need to get out. Go for a run or something.'

'The hotel has excellent gym facilities,' said Zoe helpfully.

'No, I need fresh air. I've been cooped up far too long.'

Big T coughed. 'Ash, have you seen the crowd outside?'

Ash slid the balcony door open and stepped out. Instantly an ear-blasting chorus of screams erupted from the street below. Ash gave a quick wave to his fans, causing another torrent of delighted shrieks, before coming back inside.

'Yep,' he said with a smirk. 'Looks like we'll have to sneak out the back.'

Big T regretfully shook his head. 'There are fans camped there too. Why not use the gym as Zoe suggested?'

'But I *have* to get out of here!' cried Ash in a surprisingly childish tantrum. He strode through to his bedroom, opened his suitcase and rummaged around for his trainers and sports kit.

'I'm not employed to tell you what you can and can't do,' said Big T calmly. 'But I'd advise against it.'

Ash kicked off his shoes. 'I can't be a prisoner of my own fans.'

Big T let out a heavy sigh like a steam train coming to a stop. 'If you must go for a run, keep a low profile. Otherwise your jog will end up looking like the London marathon!'

'We could leave through the loading bay,' suggested Charley, recalling the hotel's layout from the operation folder that José and David had compiled. 'It leads on to a side street – unlikely any fans would be there.'

'And I'll wear my hoodie and sunglasses,' said Ash, heading into the bathroom to change.

'Fine,' relented Big T. 'But Rick and Vince will accompany you.' He radioed for the two security guards.

'Aren't you coming?' asked Ash in a teasing tone.

'I'm a tank, not a sports car,' Big T replied with good humour. 'I'll leave the jogging to the younger pups.'

'I'll go too,' volunteered Charley.

'As long as you can keep up,' called Ash.

Charley held her tongue, reminding herself that action would speak louder than words. She hurried to her room, almost as eager as Ash to escape the confines of the hotel. Touring wasn't exactly a healthy lifestyle and she missed her daily runs in the Welsh mountains. She quickly slipped into her running gear and was already waiting outside Ash's door when he emerged.

'Right, let's go,' said Ash as Rick and Vince joined them in the corridor.

To avoid detection, the four of them headed down the stairwell to ground level, then worked their way through the kitchens to the loading bay. They got a few stares from the hotel staff but were otherwise unopposed.

'You were right!' said Ash as they walked down the ramp and on to the side street. 'No fans at all.'

But no sooner had he said this than a figure leapt out from behind a dumpster. He was armed with a rapid-fire SLR camera and began to reel off shot after shot.

'Trying to sneak out unseen, are we?' said Gonzo, his ratty face triumphant at another exclusive photo. 'Running from an accident? That's a criminal act.'

Ash kept his hoodie up and his head down. Rick

stepped between the camera lens and Ash. 'Give it a rest, Gonzo.'

'We've all got to make a living,' snapped Gonzo. Scuttling ahead to secure a clear shot, he noticed Charley. 'So, are you two lovebirds eloping or what?'

'Beat it, Gonzo,' said Vince, breaking into a jog with Ash up the street.

'Hey, my name's Gomez!' he spat irritably.

Vince waved him off. 'Whatever, Gonzo.'

Gonzo now targeted his camera on Charley. 'What's your name, *chica*?'

Charley kept a fixed smile on her face and didn't reply, at the same time wondering, *How the hell did he know when and where we'd be coming out?* It was like he had a homing beacon on Ash.

'Not letting your new boyfriend out of your sight, eh?' he continued. 'I wouldn't trust him either. Not after how he treated Hanna.'

Charley knew the pap guy was trying to bait her, but she had to quash any rumours before they got out of hand and drew too much attention to her. 'For the record, I'm *not* his girlfriend.'

'Then . . . what are you?' panted Gonzo, struggling to keep up with the group.

'PR,' replied Charley, and she raced on.

'And I'm Santa Claus!' he called after her.

Leaving the creep behind, the four runners reached the main road and headed away from the hotel. Charley looked back over her shoulder and saw the horde of fans gathered outside the entrance, still believing their idol was inside. Gonzo emerged from the side street a moment later, puffing and panting. He took a few last photos as they jogged on. Then, leaning against a wall, he lit a cigarette.

'So, where are we going?' Vince asked, running a little ahead of Ash.

'Wherever,' he replied. 'Just as long as I get some headspace.'

Charley glanced at the map on her smartphone, strapped to her upper arm. 'Schenley Park is four blocks up, if you like trail running.'

'Sounds good.' Ash flicked back his hoodie and picked up the pace.

They pounded along the pavement, four anonymous runners. But to the trained eye there was a definite formation – Vince a little ahead on Ash's left, Charley on his right and Rick a few paces behind to his left. The subtle positioning provided all-round protection while still remaining low profile.

Ash jogged steadily, only slowing at intersections. No one took much notice of them and they were almost at the park entrance when Vince glanced back to check on Ash, then went down suddenly, hitting the pavement hard.

TARGET

CHAPTER 42

Charley saw Vince drop and instinctively shoved Ash sideways into a nearby bus shelter. Believing the bodyguard to have been shot, she kept Ash pinned behind the cover of an advertising sign, while her eyes darted around for the shooter.

'Are you all right?' asked Rick, running up to Vince and offering his hand.

'Yes,' Vince groaned. 'Twisted my ankle, that's all.'

'Chill out, Charley!' said Ash, shrugging her off.

Charley relaxed her grip on him. 'Sorry,' she replied, annoyed at her overreaction.

Ash grinned at her. 'Can't keep your hands off me, can you?'

Charley responded with a tight smile. 'Remind me to wash them later!'

Rick helped Vince over to the bus shelter's bench. 'You carry on into the park,' said Vince, examining his grazed leg and swollen ankle. 'I'll wait here until you're done.'

'Are you sure?' asked Rick.

'Yeah, just make sure you don't run into any trouble.'

Entering through a main gate, the three of them passed an information board. A quick glance at the large map told Charley that the park was a sprawling woodland of hills, valleys and open grass areas. There was a lake to the west and running trails criss-crossed the park like the roots of a tree. Ash followed the top path that looped across the park's north end, then dropped downslope into a wooded area. Almost immediately the noise of the city was muffled by trees and it felt as if they were deep in the countryside.

'So, you like keeping fit?' asked Ash.

'Sure,' replied Charley.

In response Ash increased his pace. Charley sped up to stay by his side. Rick maintained his position several steps behind. The path wound through the woods, across a grassy knoll and past a pond into another woodland. Taking a trail that cut left, they crossed a bridge over a stream and followed a gully through the middle of the park. The pace was fast but easily within Charley's capabilities. They ran steadily, covering three miles in little under half an hour. The fresh air and exercise did wonders for Charley, reinvigorating her and clearing her mind. In hindsight, she didn't regret overreacting to Vince's fall. After all, only the paranoid survive! The question was, why hadn't Rick responded? Was he simply more experienced? Or was he less on the ball?

Passing a sign indicating one mile to the lake, Ash glanced at Charley. 'Race you to the lake?'

Charley nodded, up for the challenge. As Ash pulled away, Charley got the sense he wanted to prove something.

But she was used to this macho behaviour from her bodyguard-training buddies. She lengthened her stride and drew level with him as they followed a trail upslope. The pace was now seriously challenging and Rick showed signs of flagging, with rapid breathing, a sweat-soaked T-shirt and heavy footfalls.

'Hey!' he panted. 'Hold up, you two!'

But Ash and Charley were in the zone and left Rick behind. After a few twists and turns of the path, they completely lost him in the woods. As Ash ran faster, Charley pulled out all the stops to keep up. She was impressed by his fitness, but she shouldn't have been surprised considering the energy he expended on stage each night – he must run at least half a marathon every performance! As they sprinted along the path, her heart thrummed in her chest, her pulse raced and her breathing quickened. They emerged from the woods with the lake only a few hundred metres ahead. Ash went flat out. Charley pushed herself to her limit. Matching Ash stride for stride, the finish line drew nearer and nearer. Ash was unable to shake her off. They hit the lakeside path together, a result too close to call.

'Well . . . you're certainly fit . . . I'll give you that,' Ash panted, bent over double to regain his breath.

'Want to . . . keep going?' asked Charley, hoping he didn't, but aiming to make her point.

Ash glanced up at her, then laughed. 'No . . . I need to save *some* energy for tonight.' He nodded at a sign pointing to the park cafe. 'Besides, I could do with a drink.'

Charley looked behind for Rick. He was nowhere to be seen.

'He'll catch us up,' said Ash, dismissing the security guard with an exhausted wave of his hand and striding off in the direction of the cafe.

Charley knew Rick would probably be having a fit that he'd lost his Principal. But at least she was still there to guard Ash.

Following the signs to the cafe, they found an empty table outside and sat down. A waitress brought over a menu and they ordered a Coke and a bottle of water.

Ash took a deep draught of his drink, then said, 'So, Charley, are you *really* a bodyguard?'

Charley held his gaze. 'Are you really a rock star?'

Ash laughed. 'OK, why be a bodyguard then? Seems an odd decision, especially at our age.'

'Being a world-famous rock star seems equally odd to me,' replied Charley, sipping her water.

Ash nodded. 'Fair point. I must admit, it's been a crazy couple of years. Who'd have believed posting a video online would have led to all this? While I wanted to be a musician, I didn't decide to be famous. That just happened. But at some point *you* had to decide to become a bodyguard. Why?'

Charley stared out across the lake. 'It's complicated. I'm not sure I even had a decision to make. Certain events in my life took me to this point . . .' She thought back to that fateful day in the coffee shop. '*We cannot change the cards we are dealt, just how we play the hand.*'

'What did you say?'

Charley looked at him. 'We cannot change the cards we are dealt, just how we play the hand.'

'That's a great lyric!' said Ash, grabbing a napkin and trying to get the waitress's attention for a pen. 'So, what do your parents think of you being a bodyguard?'

Charley's face clouded. 'They're dead . . . but I hope they'd be proud.'

'Oh, I'm sorry,' said Ash, instantly forgetting his need for a pen. A similar dark cloud settled over Ash's expression. 'I understand how you must feel. I'm sure you know, it was in all the papers, but my mum died last year from cancer. And I don't speak to my father. He left me and my mum when I was a baby – so he's pretty much dead to me. Of course, now I'm rich and famous, he wants to know me! It's Aunt Kay who's been my rock in this whirlwind of fame. She looks out for me now.'

'Well, she certainly has your safety as her top priority. Otherwise she wouldn't have contacted Buddyguard.'

Ash nodded, then a frown creased his brow. 'Charley, is my aunt telling me *everything*? It's just that after finding out about the pig's blood letter, I question if I'm being told the whole truth. I mean, have I received more death threats that I don't know about? When Vince tripped up on the street, you literally leapt on me like my life depended on it.'

'Only the paranoid survive,' replied Charley.

'That's Big T's tattoo!' laughed Ash, but his laughter quickly died away and his expression grew dark once more. 'He mentioned there might have been an intruder that first night. Am I really in danger on this tour?'

For the first time, Charley saw the scared boy behind the facade of a self-assured, ever-smiling rock star. She thought carefully before answering. 'You've got Big T, me and the rest of the security team watching out for you. And, as far as I'm aware, no further threats have been made. But that doesn't mean the threat has gone away. That's why I react the way I do. There are no half measures in this –'

'Excuse me . . . are you Ash Wild?'

Ash looked up into the bright eager face of a young girl and her friend. He smiled.

'You are, aren't you?' she squealed. 'Can I have your autograph?' She held out a paper napkin.

'Sure,' said Ash. 'Do you have a pen?'

The girl shook her head and there was a moment of panicked dismay. Charley wished she'd brought the pen Amir had supplied, but it wasn't exactly running gear. The girl's friend darted off and grabbed the waitress, who helpfully provided hers, then requested an autograph for herself. As word spread and the excitement grew among the cafe's customers, the two young fans took selfies with Ash on their smartphones. Then they skipped off, thrilled at the chance meeting and instantly sharing their experience online.

'You like the attention, don't you?' said Charley.

'Who wouldn't?' replied Ash, finishing off his drink. 'Besides, my fans make me who I am. If I don't give them the time, why should they give me theirs?'

Charley spotted a group of excited girls hurrying along the path towards them. 'Well, by the looks of it, a lot more are about to give you their time.'

CHAPTER 43

'We need to go, Ash,' said Charley as more and more fans descended on the cafe.

Wildlings seemed to be materializing from the woods in their thousands. As word spread, girls of all ages swarmed into the park. But that was the power of social media: instant communication, instant crowds.

Ash seemed oblivious to the growing numbers. He finished signing a girl's T-shirt, then posed for a photo. Before Charley could pull him away, another girl leapt beside him with a camera and he dutifully smiled.

'Come on!' insisted Charley, taking hold of his arm.

'Hey, I'm next,' said a disgruntled fan, shoving Charley aside with an elbow to the ribs.

Briefly, Charley considered dropping the girl with a ridge-hand strike to her neck. But she remembered her unarmed combat instructor's advice: *Any self-defence must be* necessary, reasonable *and* proportional *to the attack*. So Charley waited for the fan to have her photo with Ash before stepping sharply on the girl's toes. A little twist of the heel ensured maximum impact.

'Sorry,' said Charley with an apologetic smile as the girl's eyes widened and she gasped in pain.

'Is she all right?' asked a concerned Ash.

'Yes,' Charley replied breezily. 'Just a little overcome at meeting you.'

Leaving the injured fan to limp over to the nearest chair, Charley escorted Ash away from the cafe.

'Gotta go!' called Ash, waving goodbye to his fans.

But that didn't stop them following him. Like the Pied Piper, Ash led his ever-expanding flock through the park. All the time people snapped away with their cameras, filmed with their phones and demanded autographs. Even as he walked, Ash kept his trademark smile and turned his head towards each and every lens he could: the consummate professional.

'Excuse me! Make way,' Charley requested as several fans stood directly in his path.

'Who do you think you are?' challenged one of the girls, squaring up to her.

'Let him through!' ordered Charley, her gaze taking on a steely quality that convinced the girl to step aside.

With ever more fans demanding his attention, Charley had to be Ash's eyes and ears as she shepherded him in the direction of the main gate. But it soon became apparent they'd never reach it. As the woods opened out on to a grass area, she spied a mass of people heading their way. The fans waiting at his hotel must have got word and rushed the four blocks down to find him. *Where the hell was Rick?* Without him or Vince to back her up, Charley was way out of her depth. She simply didn't have the physical presence or authority to protect Ash among so many people. To those surrounding the rock star she was just another fan.

Charley reassessed their options. If she could get him to the main road, then perhaps they could dive into a taxi and get back to the hotel. 'I hope you've got the energy for a final sprint,' she whispered to Ash, pointing to a nearby side gate.

She rushed Ash towards the exit. But this only excited the fans more. Like a herd of wildebeest they stampeded across the park, chasing their idol down. Reaching the gate only a few paces ahead of everyone else, Charley burst on to the street with Ash and looked up and down for a taxi . . . but there were none in sight.

As countless fans spilled out of the park and clogged the road, the traffic came to a standstill.

'We love you, Ash!' cried a group of ecstatic girls wearing Wildling Tour T-shirts.

A teenager, waving a banner pronouncing KIM & ASH 4EVER, screamed 'Marry me!'

'Sign this for my daughter,' panted a red-faced middle-aged man, thrusting a notebook into Ash's face.

The barrage of requests and declarations of love were overwhelming and the crush of the crowd quickly turned frightening. Although Ash was used to his fans' hysterical response, without the rock of Big T, he was being tugged and torn like a kite in a storm.

Charley tried to keep hold of him, but she was equally

drowning in the sea of people. Her phone vibrated on her arm. A few moments later it rang again, but there was no way she could answer it in the mayhem of the heaving crowd. Paparazzi now jostled shoulder-to-shoulder with the fans, cameras flashing like strobe lights.

'Hey, Ash! Have a good run?' called out Gonzo, his rat-face grinning from among the pack.

Suddenly the crowd lurched sideways. Ash stumbled and fell to the pavement. Charley fought to pull him to his feet. His fans, she realized, could be the death of him – trampled and crushed by love.

'Back away!' Charley shouted, dragging Ash to standing and forcing a path through the horde. But mob mentality had taken over. People pushed, shoved, kicked and elbowed to get a glimpse of their idol. No one took any notice of Charley's requests. She now understood why celebrity bodyguards had to be so huge and intimidating. In a crowd like this nothing but a battering ram would get them through.

'*Where's Big T?*' cried Ash over the hysterical screaming. His voice was taut with panic as countless hands reached out and pulled at his clothes and hair, everyone trying to get a bit of him.

Charley felt herself losing him to the crowd. She had to find a safe haven. Fast. She spied a bank on the other side of the road and grabbed Ash's hand, hauling him across the street with her. Every step was a battle, like fighting the current of a massive flood. She could feel Ash's hand slipping from her grip.

Then somehow she reached the bank. In a last-ditch effort she shoved Ash through the door, following in behind. A perplexed security guard rushed up to them.

'Lock the doors!' shouted Charley.

Confronted by a mass of screaming hysterical girls, the guard slammed the doors shut and barricaded them in. The fans clamoured at the windows, hundreds of faces pressed up against the glass, peering in at their idol.

Ash collapsed into a chair. 'That was beyond crazy!'

'You can say that again,' gasped Charley, amazed they'd escaped in one piece. Glancing up at the fan-plastered windows, she was glad the glass was reinforced. Then amid the mayhem she spotted a familiar face. Staring at Ash, his gaze unwavering, Pete raised a bandaged arm and smiled. The smile sent a small shiver through Charley – it was like a ghost copy of Ash's trademark grin.

'So, where do we go from here?' asked Ash, oblivious to his stalker clone.

'Well, there's always the vault!' Charley half-joked, as she took out her mobile and saw the multiple missed calls from Big T. Guessing he was worried about Ash's whereabouts, she immediately rang him back for an emergency pick-up.

TARGET

CHAPTER 44

'You two clowns are about as useful as a chocolate fire-guard!' bellowed Big T, the tendons in his thick neck bulging so much that he looked like he might burst a blood vessel.

Charley stood motionless as the veteran bodyguard vented his fury.

'I put you in charge of the *single most important person* on this tour and you balls it up!' he barked, wagging a gnarled finger at Vince and Rick. 'One of you princesses sprains an ankle, while the other can't run a mile without having a heart attack! The very least I expect from my security team is to be fit, effective and competent. Qualities neither of you seem to possess.'

The two security guards stared shamefaced at the carpet as their boss laid into them.

Big T pointed his finger at Charley. 'If it wasn't for this young lady here, Ash would likely be in hospital now or worse. You two excuses for bodyguards are on night shift for the next week! Now get out of my sight!'

Vince and Rick scurried out of Big T's hotel room, their

tails between their legs, simply grateful not to have been sacked on the spot.

'And what are you looking so smug about?' snapped Big T, turning on Charley.

She stiffened and swallowed nervously.

'I called you *five* times! Why the hell didn't you answer?'

'I-I was busy protecting Ash,' she explained, stumbling over her words. 'I didn't see the missed calls . . . until I got to the bank.'

'You stopped at a bloody cafe for a drink! You had more than enough opportunity to report in before the situation got out of hand. Next time you're solo, call in *immediately*. You're not some Katniss Everdeen. You may be trained as a bodyguard but you're still just a girl! And an inexperienced one at that.'

Chastened by his stern words, Charley bowed her head and fell silent. She had hoped for some praise for her actions, but deep down she knew that Big T was right. She'd ignored one of the basic principles of close protection: constant communication. She should have reported their location and status.

Big T continued to glare at her, the vein above his left temple throbbing. Then his fierce expression eased a little and he let out a heavy sigh. 'That said, you made the best of a bad situation. Holing up in a bank was smart thinking. And at the end of it all Ash is unharmed, if a little shaken.'

Charley allowed herself to breathe again.

'The press, though, are going to have a field day that Ash was out in public without apparent security.' Big T ran a hand over his wrinkled dome. 'And Ms Gibson will have my guts for garters over it!'

'I'm sorry, Big T. I just didn't expect so many fans to turn up so quickly.'

'Always expect the unexpected,' stated Big T, echoing Colonel Black's own words of advice during her training. 'In future, heed the patron saint of bodyguards: Murphy's Law.'

Charley frowned. She noticed the same words tattooed on his neck. 'Murphy's Law?'

'Anything that can go wrong, will go wrong,' Big T explained. 'Now get some rest before tonight's concert. I've a nasty feeling that Murphy might make another appearance.'

Charley headed to her room, then stopped at the door. 'Talking of Murphy's Law, there's one thing bothering me still.'

'What's that?' asked Big T.

'How did Gonzo know Ash would exit through the loading bay?'

Big T shrugged. 'Luck, probably. He hangs out in all the sewers.'

Charley shook her head. 'No. He was lying in wait. He knew.'

Big T furrowed his brow. 'How, Sherlock? We swept Ash's room, remember, and it was all clear.'

Charley thought for a moment. 'Either someone told him or . . . I missed a bug during the surveillance sweep.'

Going over to the large desk in his room, Big T picked up the bug detector. 'Only one way to find out.'

Ash was down in the hotel lobby, chilling with the rest of the band in the VIP lounge, so his suite was empty. Big T let himself in with a spare key card. Charley closed the door behind them and they began a second security sweep of the room.

Big T ran the detector over the TV, phone, plug sockets, pictures, lights and every nook and crevice of the suite. But the LED indicator stayed resolutely green.

He glanced up at the ceiling. 'Did you check the smoke detector?'

'No,' Charley admitted. 'I don't think so.'

He held the device up to the white plastic casing. The LED indicator didn't even flicker.

Big T looked at Charley. 'Maybe we do have a snitch among the team.'

Then Charley's eyes were drawn to the pile of flowers and gifts on the central table. 'These weren't here when we did the security sweep the first time.'

Big T handed her the detector. She swept the device over the various bouquets, boxes of chocolates and cuddly toys. As the sensor passed a teddy bear clutching a heart, it buzzed in her hand and the indicator shot into the red. Big T picked up the suspect bear and examined it. He tugged on the black bead of its left eye. The eyeball popped from its socket to expose a camera lens attached to a transmitter. In its ear he discovered the tiny bud of a microphone.

'You sneaky son of a bitch, Gonzo!' exclaimed Big T, before ripping the bear's ear off.

TARGET

CHAPTER 45

The glass-fronted Pittsburgh Consol Center, usually the host venue for ice-hockey matches and basketball games, had been transformed into a fifteen-thousand-seater concert hall. Ash's unique guitar-shaped stage had been installed the day before and the immense speaker stacks and complex lighting rig rapidly constructed overnight. Fans who'd arrived early were already filtering into the arena and there was a buzz of anticipation in the air.

Charley hung backstage. Ash was secure in his dressing room, preparing himself for the gig. Big T had instructed Charley not to tell him about the teddy-bear spycam they'd found. 'It doesn't represent a threat, merely an irritation,' he'd explained. After her conversation with Ash at the cafe, though, Charley wondered if it was right to withhold that information from the target himself. She found Big T by the coffee machine in the artists' lounge and questioned this decision.

'There's no point worrying Ash unnecessarily,' said Big T, pouring himself a double espresso. 'He needs to focus on performing. It's *our* job to worry on his behalf.'

'But I've only just started building his trust. I don't want to break it.'

Big T took a sip of coffee and grimaced at its bitter taste. 'Hey, imagine if the President of the United States was told about every threat to his life. The poor guy would be a gibbering wreck by the end of the week. Ash is on a need-to-know basis. For his own good.'

'What if our assumption is wrong?' pressed Charley. 'What if the teddy bear wasn't planted by Gonzo?'

'Who else could it be? Motive and circumstance point to Gonzo. Granted, the girl who gave Ash the bear might be an infatuated fan wanting to spy on her idol, but those devices cost a fair whack. We're not talking pocket money here.'

'How about the maniac who's been sending Ash the death threats?' suggested Charley. 'He could have bribed, persuaded or even *threatened* the girl to do it.'

'You assume the maniac's a guy,' said Big T, raising a world-weary eyebrow. 'Unless we see that girl again, we won't know one way or the other. Whoever's to blame, our response is the same. We tighten security around Ash. Which reminds me, I need to check in with the venue manager about the corporate boxes. Murphy's Law and all that.'

He drained his espresso and headed out of the lounge. Charley followed Big T into the corridor. One of the security team was stationed outside Ash's dressing-room door. With her Principal secure, Charley took a walk backstage to familiarize herself with the new venue. She noted the fire exits and quickest routes to each. Passing various road crew and sound technicians, her eyes flicked to their photo passes, checking everyone had one. As she approached the main stage, Charley's attention was caught by a shadowy figure dropping down from one of the lighting rig's wire-rope ladders next to the backstage curtains. This behaviour seemed odd and out of place compared to the rest of the crew and she immediately went on the alert. Heading over to where the person had disappeared, she pulled back the drape to discover Jessie crouching in the darkness behind the drum riser.

Jessie flinched and looked shocked. 'You startled me!' she exclaimed, resting a hand on her heart.

'What are you doing?' asked Charley.

She responded with a guilty smile. 'I can't resist peeking out on the stage before a concert. It's fabulous! This is exactly what Ash sees each night.' Jessie stepped aside and invited her to climb the ladder. 'Go on, take a look yourself.'

Clambering up a few rungs, Charley peered over the top of the riser. The stage rolled out before her, its catwalk guitar neck protruding deep into the audience. With the venue lights on, she could see thousands upon thousands of fans gathering in the stalls, their excited chatter echoing round the vast arena. She glanced up at the mega-video screens running pre-concert footage, then at the lighting rig high above where she spied the tiny figure of a spotlight operator moving among the struts.

'Cool, isn't it?' said Jessie.

Charley nodded and dropped back down. 'I don't know

how Ash has the courage to step out and perform in front of a huge crowd like that.'

'It's because he's a god,' replied Jessie reverentially. She crept through the curtain. 'I'll catch you later. The concert's going to start soon.'

'Don't forget your bag,' said Charley, noticing a small backpack on the floor, partly hidden by the curtain's black fabric.

'That's not mine. But thanks anyway.'

Jessie disappeared round the corner.

Charley bent down to pick it up. Then stopped herself. Something about it made her think twice.

She spotted a guitar technician nearby. 'Is this yours?' she asked, pointing to the suspect bag. The long-haired technician shook his head and went back to fine-tuning the row of electric guitars. Charley asked another crew member, but it wasn't his either.

Charley reminded herself of the rule of the Four Cs: *confirm*, *clear*, *cordon*, *control*.

She had to confirm her suspicions first.

A bearded roadie, whom Charley vaguely recognized from rehearsals, came down the ladder. She asked if he knew who the backpack belonged to. He grunted a no and carried on. Charley asked several more people, but no one laid claim.

If you can't find the owner, then the item must be considered a threat, Bugsy had said.

Charley bent down and gave the bag a sniff. There was the faintest aroma of almonds. Charley decided it was time to alert Big T. She was about to call him on her radio, when Bugsy's voice sounded in her head again: *Radio waves are often used to trigger remote-control bombs!*

Charley immediately switched off her mobile and comms unit, then dashed away to find Big T.

TARGET
CHAPTER 46

'We should clear the area, at the very least,' Charley insisted as she stood with Big T and the tour manager at a wary distance from the suspect backpack.

'How can you be certain it's a bomb?' asked Terry, peering at it in the dim light of backstage.

'I can't,' replied Charley. 'But so far no one's claimed it and I smelt almonds which could mean plastic explosives.'

Terry spoke into his radio. 'Attention, all crew. Has anyone lost a backpack?'

Charley instinctively flinched. But the bag didn't explode. *Well, at least that's been cleared up*, she thought. *The bomb isn't triggered by radio waves.*

Big T turned to the tour manager. 'Anyone respond?'

Terry shook his head. 'What do we do now?'

'As Charley said, clear the area,' replied Big T. 'Get Ash off the premises.'

'But the concert!' Terry exclaimed. 'It's due to start any minute now.'

'Not with Ash, it isn't,' said Big T, directing two security guards to immediately move people out of the vicinity.

Shocked at the news of a bomb, the technicians and road crew dropped what they were doing and headed to the exit on the direction of the guards.

'But we can't just cancel the gig over a lost backpack!' Terry argued, as Big T sent word to evacuate Ash at once.

'With the death threats made against Ash,' argued the bodyguard, 'we must assume the worst-case scenario.'

'Why can't we just look inside the darn bag?' said Terry, walking over to it.

'NO!' said Charley, grabbing his arm. 'It could be booby-trapped.'

Terry held up his hands in frustration. 'It's just a bag!'

'A bag that *could* be a bomb,' said Big T. 'We need to call the authorities.'

'And how long's that going to take?' Terry shrugged off Charley's hand and marched over to the backpack.

'Don't!' warned Big T, moving rapidly away from the suspect bomb.

Terry bent down to open the bag. Big T pushed Charley behind a transport crate, then dived for cover himself. There was a long deafening silence.

Then Terry appeared, holding a can of soda, an open packet of mixed nuts and a sandwich box in his hand. 'Some bomb,' he said, glaring at Charley and Big T crouched on the ground. 'For heaven's sake, Big T, keep that girl of yours on a leash! She's going to be the death of this tour.'

The manager strode off in a fury and started barking orders to get the concert back on schedule.

'Sorry,' said Charley, feeling like she'd let Big T down again.

'Nothing to be sorry about,' he replied, lumbering back to his feet. 'You alerted me. I take responsibility thereafter. Besides, it's better to be safe than blown to bits! Even if the bomb does turn out to be a mouldy cheese sandwich.' He grunted a laugh.

Charley was grateful for Big T's good humour, but she knew she'd screwed up *again*. 'You were right to call me inexperienced. On this assignment, I feel like I'm always calling wolf.'

'And one day there might be a wolf,' said Big T. 'As a bodyguard, you have to suspect everything and everyone. *Guilty until proven innocent* is my motto.'

'I thought it was: *Only the paranoid survive*.'

'Depends on which arm I look at,' replied Big T, showing her the opposite forearm with a tattoo of a pair of weighted scales and the words GUILTY UNTIL PROVEN INNOCENT inscribed beneath it. 'Now, don't lose faith in yourself. Ash has a gig to do and you need to be on the ball.'

With the emergency over, the crew and technicians hurriedly returned to their duties. Everyone was under pressure to make up for lost time.

'Don't forget,' said Big T as he headed to Ash's dressing room. 'Murphy's Law applies at all times.'

Charley nodded. She was now a full convert to Murphy and his Law. Anything that could go wrong for her on this assignment seemed to be doing exactly that! She took up her position at the side of the stage as instructed by Big T, only too happy to comply since it allowed her to keep a low profile. Her name had to be dirt among the crew after a second false alert.

Jessie ran up to her. 'Did you hear there was a suspected bomb threat?' she gasped.

Charley nodded and said nothing.

'I never imagined a tour could be so *dangerous*,' remarked Jessie, her tone suggesting excitement rather than fear at the idea.

The house lights suddenly went dark and the video screens began a countdown. Fifteen thousand fans yelled along with it: '*FIVE . . . FOUR . . . THREE . . . TWO . . . ONE!*'

A huge explosion shuddered through the arena . . .

But Charley didn't flinch. She knew this explosion was all part of the show. Fireworks lit up the stage in a waterfall of red and gold sparks and a pounding heartbeat throbbed from the speakers at a gut-thumping volume. Images of a winged boy flashed across the video screens, his silhouette leaping from frame to frame as a blazing fire took hold and raced after him. The fierce crackle of burning grew louder and louder as the winged boy was surrounded, then consumed by flames.

Out of the heart of the raging fire, a single word pulsed in time to the dying beat of the music.

INDESTRUCTIBLE.

The word shone like a beacon, then morphed into: *IMPOSSIBLE?*

Before transforming one final time . . . *I'M POSSIBLE!*

A thunderclap burst from the speakers and Ash shot up from a toaster lift in the floor. He landed with the grace of an eagle on the stage. Behind him on the video screens, a flaming phoenix burned bright.

Ash pumped a fist in the air. 'What's up, Pittsburgh!'

The arena erupted with screams and cheers. Picking up his guitar, he struck a chord that started the blistering riff of his first hit, 'Easier'.

Out of the darkness, a large missile-like object plummeted from above. Charley glimpsed it only at the very last second as it flashed past the central screen. There was no time to react.

The spotlight dropped from the lighting rig like a meteor. It smashed into the stage right where Ash was standing. Knocked off his feet by the impact, he crumpled to the floor. The audience fell deathly silent as their idol lay motionless among the debris of shattered glass, splintered wood and twisted metal.

CHAPTER 47

'Tell me what happened,' demanded Kay. Her green eyes blazed with emotion on the computer screen. Despite it being two in the morning in the UK, she still managed to look glamorous. Yet the news about Ash had visibly shocked her and her face was porcelain white.

'It was an accident,' explained Terry, seated beside Big T in his hotel room. 'The clamp securing the spotlight failed.'

'What about the safety cable?' said Kay. 'Shouldn't that have stopped the light from falling?'

Terry swallowed uneasily. 'For some reason, it wasn't attached.'

'*Not attached!*' Kay exclaimed, her familiar tiger spirit returning. 'That doesn't sound like an accident to me.'

In the context of Ash's death threats, Charley was compelled to agree. But she kept her opinion to herself as she sat quietly with Zoe on the edge of the bed.

'There's no evidence that the light was tampered with,' replied Big T.

'Then how could it happen?'

Terry wiped a hand over his dry mouth. 'We were in a

rush to set everything up. The safety cable was likely overlooked.'

Even across a divide of four thousand miles, everyone felt the ferocity of Kay's glare.

'As you know, the crew are always under pressure to set up for each gig,' Terry hurriedly explained. 'But even more so when a false bomb alert delays the already tight schedule.'

Kay's smooth brow wrinkled slightly. 'What bomb alert?'

Terry directed an accusing stare at Charley. 'That's down to your *guest* here.'

With open-mouthed dismay, Charley realized the tour manager was trying to shift the blame for the incident on to her. 'I don't see how that's got anything to do with it,' she protested.

'It's got *everything* to do with it,' he insisted.

'Hang on, what about that man I spotted in the lighting rig prior to the concert? Perhaps he's responsible? Maybe it wasn't an accident at all.'

'Enough of your paranoid assertions!' said Terry. 'That could only have been Geoff, one of my most reliable roadies. And he'd have been able to complete his checks properly if you hadn't raised the alarm over a lunch box!'

'The backpack *could* have been a bomb,' argued Charley.

'But it wasn't, was it?' countered Terry, glowering at her.

Charley knew she was being made a scapegoat for his road crew's mistakes and this time Big T wasn't stepping to her defence. But she realized he could only put his neck on the line so many times.

Then Big T broke his silence. 'Pointing the finger doesn't change what happened. The most important thing at the moment is Ash.'

'Quite true,' said Kay from the computer screen. 'How is he doing?'

Zoe leant towards the webcam with a reassuring smile. 'He's recovering fast. Like the song goes, he's indestructible!'

'Ash got away with only a few cuts and bruises,' explained Big T. 'If he'd landed on stage from the toaster lift even one step further back, though, the spotlight would have crushed him.'

'That doesn't bear thinking about.' Kay sighed. 'Where is he now?'

'In his room, sleeping,' said Big T.

Terry pinched the bridge of his nose and rubbed his weary eyes. 'We had to cancel the concert, of course.'

'What about the rest of the tour?' asked Kay. 'Is Ash able to continue?'

Terry gave a nod. 'The doctor says he's physically fine. So I don't foresee any problem.'

'Yes, but the question is, does he *want* to?'

CHAPTER 48

The atmosphere on the repaired tour bus the following day was subdued. Ash had holed himself up in the back lounge, making it clear he didn't want to be disturbed. The next stop on the tour was Columbus, Ohio, and as far as everyone knew the concert was going ahead. But there was deep concern among the band and crew whether Ash was in the right state of mind to perform.

'So, apart from being withdrawn, is he otherwise OK?' José asked Charley during the conference call to Buddyguard HQ. José was the go-to for any medical-related issues during Operation Starstruck.

'I think so. I haven't had much chance to chat with him,' said Charley. She was in the toilet cubicle as had become her custom to ensure some privacy when reporting in. 'As I understand it, Ash is more upset for his fans that the concert was cancelled. But he does seem a lot quieter than usual.'

'I guess it's pretty traumatic if a forty-kilogram spotlight almost crushes you to death!' snorted Jason.

'It was certainly a close call,' replied Charley coolly.

'Jody says he's probably in mental shock, like after a car crash,' continued José. 'Hang on, she's just handed me a list of symptoms . . . OK, it says here that he may swing between bouts of depression, anxiety, anger, despair, hyperactivity and withdrawal. But the symptoms usually resolve themselves in a few days or so.'

'Thanks, José, that's good to know. I'll keep an eye out for them.'

'You worried about him?' asked Blake. These were the first words he'd spoken since she'd reported in.

'Of course I am,' she replied. 'That's my job.'

'I know,' he shot back a little too quickly. 'I meant whether you thought he was becoming unstable. I hear rock stars can be a little unhinged.'

No, you didn't, she thought, guessing exactly what he was pushing at. Charley was growing tired of Blake's jealousy and snippy remarks every time she reported in. Either he was short with her, mistrusting or simply in a mood. She understood that it was hard them being apart for so long. And difficult to find the time to resolve any issues. But if he couldn't trust her with Ash, then what was the point in them going steady?

'So, Charley, have you faced any more crowds single-handedly?' asked David when she went quiet.

'We all saw the news footage of Ash being mobbed by his fans, supposedly without protection,' remarked José. 'Can't believe you got him out of that situation alive!'

'Nor me –' Through the wall of the toilet cubicle she heard an anguished cry, then a loud bang. 'Gotta go!'

Ending the call, Charley rushed out into the corridor. Her first thought was that it was another tyre blowout. Then she heard a crash and splintering of wood from the back lounge. She burst through the door to find Ash furiously smashing his acoustic guitar on the floor. The body cracked. The strings twanged. And the neck snapped.

'Ash! What are you doing?' cried Charley, stunned to see him destroying one of his most prized guitars.

Ash tossed the shattered instrument to the ground, then stamped on the broken remains.

'You useless piece of junk!' he cried as his foot went through the guitar's body. His fit of fury eventually ebbed away and he slumped back into the sofa, sobbing with his head in hands.

Cautiously Charley approached, sat down next to him and put an arm round his heaving shoulders.

'I-I . . . can't write any more,' he cried, hitching in a ragged breath. 'I've . . . lost the songs. I-I can't hear them any more . . .'

Charley patiently listened to his distress, realizing this was the mental shock Jody had diagnosed. He trembled uncontrollably and she gently held him in her arms. Jessie popped her head round the door, a concerned look on her face. Charley held up a hand to say all was OK and to give them some space. With a small nod, Jessie quietly retreated from the room.

As Charley waited for Ash's sobs to subside, she spotted his laptop open on the table. A mostly blank page had the beginnings of a song that was stalled on the first line: *You lift me up because . . .*

In an open smaller browser window was a feed from Ash's social media site. A stream of well-wishers were posting messages of support following the previous night's cancelled concert. Interspersed between these, like poisonous thorns on a berry bush, were acid comments from haters either joking about the near tragedy or wishing the spotlight *had* hit him. Charley disregarded these.

'Judging by your fans' response, they love your songs and you,' she told him. 'I'm sure you haven't lost your touch. You're just in shock and a little stressed out at the moment, that's all.'

Ash looked up at her with reddened eyes. 'B-but writing songs is all I know. It's who I am. It's *why* my fans like me. I'm terrified my muse won't come back.'

'Of course it will,' assured Charley. 'If you can write a song like "Only Raining", you're born with the gift.'

This only made Ash sob again.

He eventually regained control of his emotions. 'But w-what if it doesn't come back? I've tried everything I know. Nothing seems to break the block. Ever since that letter bomb, I've been struggling. I can't sleep. I have nightmares about it. I just don't understand why anyone would hate me that much. What have I done to them?'

Charley thought about the man who'd snatched Kerry all those years ago. And of the terrorists who'd hijacked the plane her parents had been on. Tears now threatened to come to her eyes. 'There are people out there who hurt and hate for no reason but their own. It's not your fault. You've done nothing wrong.'

'Then why is someone trying to kill me?'

'Last night was just an accident, like the coach crash,' assured Charley. She pointed to his computer screen. 'You have to ignore the haters and focus on those who love you. Besides your band, crew, Big T and your aunt, you have a whole legion of fans supporting you. They'll inspire you. You just need to give it time.'

Ash nodded. 'You're right,' he said, wiping his nose with the sleeve of his sweatshirt. 'Not much of a rock star, am I? You must think I'm a right idiot for crying like a baby.'

'We all have to cry sometimes,' replied Charley.

Ash managed a weak smile. 'You should be a lyricist.'

His laptop pinged as a new message came in. A photo appeared in the browser window of Ash on stage, the blur of a falling spotlight just behind his head.

The caption beneath read:

Accidents don't just happen.

TARGET

CHAPTER 49

'Cancel the gig,' insisted the bassist. 'In fact, the whole damn tour!'

'No. There's too much at stake,' said Terry. 'We risk losing millions.'

'We risk losing our lives!' the bassist shot back.

The band, tour manager, Big T and Charley were all crammed into Ash's dressing room backstage at the Nationwide Arena in Columbus. Word had leaked out about the message on Ash's computer and the band had been spooked.

'I tell you, it was an accident,' insisted Terry. 'Just because some anonymous hater posted a message online claiming he was responsible doesn't mean it's true. There's absolutely no evidence of foul play. This is simply an opportunist taking advantage of a news story. Now get yourselves ready for the concert.'

Charley kept her mouth shut. She no longer knew what to think. Big T had launched an investigation into the source of the message, but it had so far come up blank. This was suspicious in itself. Yet an examination of the spotlight had pointed to basic mechanical failure of its clamp as the reason for the accident. The fact that the safety chain hadn't been attached was put down to human error, rather than a premeditated murder attempt. Nor had there been any reason to suspect the coach crash was anything more than an accident. However, following the ominous message, Charley began to wonder if that was really the case.

'Hey, it's not just Ash out there on stage,' reminded the bassist, crossing his arms defiantly. 'Any one of us could be hurt or killed. So we've a right to say whether we go on or not.'

'Fine,' said Terry. 'If you don't want the gig, we'll get another bassist in.'

'Well, I hope he wears a crash helmet!' he sneered.

'Terry, you're missing the point,' the drummer piped up. 'We all know about the death threats. Someone has it in for Ash.' He directed his drumstick at Ash, who sat mute in his chair, staring blankly at himself in the mirror as the stylist made the finishing touches to his hair. 'Are you willing to gamble his life, and ours, like this?'

'There is no gamble,' said Terry. 'I've discussed this with his manager. Someone is playing a cruel game, that's all. They're trying to scare Ash, intimidate him – sabotage his career. And we won't let that happen. Apart from the threats before the tour, it's all been false alarms. The crew has double-checked everything at this venue. I can assure you, there'll be no more accidents on this tour.'

'That's comforting to know,' replied the bassist. 'But what about actual attacks on us?'

Terry jabbed a thumb in the direction of the veteran bodyguard. 'That's the job of Big T and his security team to prevent – and I've complete faith that they'll keep Ash safe.'

The bassist snorted. 'That's all well and good for Ash. But what about *us*?'

'My security team covers you as well,' said Big T.

Terry glanced impatiently at his watch. 'Now the gig's going ahead with or without you. What's it going to be?'

'Surely, it's *my* decision!' interrupted Ash. 'Whether the show happens or not?'

Everyone in the room turned to him. Dressed in his glittering stage gear, his hair perfectly coiffured, Ash looked more than ready to go on stage. But, having seen him with his defences down, Charley knew the paralysing fear that haunted Ash's every waking moment. In her opinion he was in no fit state to perform.

While the others in the band had a right to be concerned for their safety, Ash was the real target.

CHAPTER 50

Pete was as jittery as any one of the twenty thousand Wildling fans packed into Columbus' Nationwide Arena. Perhaps even more so because he knew what was coming.

This time he'd managed to get a standing ticket and, after a fair bit of pushing and shoving, was in prime position right beside the neck of the guitar stage. The atmosphere in the arena was highly charged. After the tragic curtailment of the Pittsburgh show, Ash's fans were even more desperate to see him. Rumours had been flying that the concert would be cancelled at the last minute and a barely suppressed panic spread among the audience. Some fans had even resorted to praying in groups for Ash's delivery on to the stage.

Thirty minutes later than scheduled, the house lights dimmed and the countdown began.

The audience screamed in delight. Pete enthusiastically joined in with the countdown, barely able to hear himself above the noise. His gut tightened as the opening explosion rumbled from the speakers and he had to shield his eyes from the blinding cascade of red and gold sparks. His own heart seemed to beat in unison with the intro's heartbeat. Then he felt a rush of exhilaration as the winged silhouette flitted from screen to screen before being consumed by flames.

INDESTRUCTIBLE . . . IMPOSSIBLE? . . . I'M POSSIBLE!

Ash shot up from the toaster lift and landed on the stage. *Not as perfectly as in New York*, thought Pete, *but still an impressive entrance.*

Immediately Ash took two strides forward before thrusting a fist into the air. 'What's up, Columbus!'

The audience roared their approval, relieved and overjoyed to see their idol. After a swift, almost unconscious glance upward, Ash struck the opening chord to 'Easier' and the band kicked in.

Pete sang along to every word. He watched Ash dance across the stage, his eyes never wavering from his idol. Even after a couple of shows, Pete was beginning to recognize some of his routines. But he could tell Ash wasn't as self-assured as in previous gigs. His performance seemed a little 'tight' and every so often the rock star would look nervously up at the lighting rig. That was to be expected, though, considering Pittsburgh.

Pete's arm started itching. He tried not to scratch the scabbing skin underneath the bandage, otherwise he'd damage his new tattoo.

Midway through the gig a dark-haired girl with freckles stood on his foot. She was fifteen, maybe sixteen, and chewing gum voraciously. She shot him an apologetic smile, then did a double-take. The girl opened her mouth and said something. But Pete couldn't hear her over the noise of the band and screaming fans. He leant closer and she shouted in his ear, 'I said, you look just like Ash. Has anyone told you that before?'

'No,' he replied, shaking his head.

'Well, you do!'

Pete grinned. He'd made an extra-special effort to resemble his hero. He'd even managed to find some clothes that matched the ones Ash wore. And it pleased him every time some fan mentioned the similarity.

All through the next set of songs, Pete was aware that the girl kept sneaking peeks at him. She'd 'bump' against him, her bare arms touching his. With so many people crowded round, it was impossible not to be in contact with one another, but the girl seemed to be doing it on purpose. He caught her eye and responded with the Ash Wild trademark smile he'd been practising every night in the mirror. She coyly looked away, but remained close, their bodies touching.

Halfway through Ash's lush ballad 'Kiss & Tell', the girl spoke in his ear again. 'I love this song. I know you're not Ash, but –' She put her hand on his neck and ran her fingers through his hair. Standing on tiptoes, she drew his lips to hers and kissed him. Pete could taste the minty freshness of her chewing gum.

Ash's voice sang in his ears: '*If you kiss me, I won't tell, cos your lips are a wishing well . . .*'

As the girl continued to neck him passionately, Pete thought to himself that he would like Ash's life. He'd like it very much.

TARGET

CHAPTER 51

The Columbus gig proceeded without a hitch. Although the band knew that Ash's performance wasn't as slick as usual and a couple of times he missed his cues, his fans were too delirious to notice. Over the course of the following Louisville, Nashville and Charlotte dates, Ash's confidence gradually returned and by the time the tour reached Atlanta, he was fully back on form – the spotlight incident little more than a bad memory.

But Charley hadn't forgotten. Nor had Big T. Security had been quietly stepped up and everyone on the team was in a permanent state of Code Yellow. The tour schedule was punishing: early starts, late finishes and periods of mind-numbing inactivity followed by sudden bursts of chaos; long journeys, multiple locations and different hotel rooms every night. After only a week, Charley was shattered with the effects of tour fatigue. She became worried that in her exhausted state she might make another error of judgement, overlook a threat or simply not react in time to an attack. Thankfully, there had been no further incidents or threats made since Pittsburgh. But whether that was due to the security team's diligence or the fact that the maniac fan was biding his or her time, they'd never know. They simply had to stay alert, day and night, hour upon hour, minute by minute.

On arrival at the five-star Mandarin Oriental Hotel in Miami, Big T gave Charley her key card and a spare key card for Ash's suite. 'Security-check his room, then get some rest,' he ordered. 'You look knackered.'

Leaving Big T to guard Ash, Charley headed up in the lift and found his room. This time it wasn't ideally positioned at the end of the corridor. But they'd block-booked all the rooms surrounding Ash's to make the floor as secure as possible. Her room was opposite. She dumped her bags, then let herself into Ash's suite. The VIP room was as luxurious as ever, if not more so, with its dramatic views over the turquoise-blue waters of the Biscayne Bay.

She'd always wanted to visit Miami and it certainly didn't disappoint: the colourful art deco buildings lining the sun-kissed streets, the pure white sand of the glorious beaches and the trendy surfside hotels packed with celebrities and wannabes. Sets of waves peeled along the coast, beckoning to her, as surfers rode the white water into the shore. Charley was itching to go out on a board herself but doubted she'd get the time on tour. Perhaps, she thought, she'd ditch the planned rest and go surfing instead. But first she had to security-sweep Ash's room.

Charley checked the bathroom, a spacious marbled affair with a roll-top tub and walk-in shower. Then she returned to the adjoining bedroom and opened the mirrored wardrobes.

'Lost something?'

Charley spun round to find Ash at the door. 'No, just checking for groupies,' she replied, echoing Big T's answer.

Ash laughed. 'Now that *would* be room service!'

He strolled in, glanced at the king-size bed swathed in soft linens and coral-coloured throw cushions, then went to the window and peered out at the idyllic view.

'I haven't finished my security sweep,' explained Charley. 'It might be best if you wait in the lobby with Big T.'

'Don't let me stop you,' replied Ash. 'I just needed to escape the madness downstairs.'

'Does Big T know where you are?'

'No. But I'm with you, so I'm safe, aren't I?'

Charley thought about insisting that he leave. She knew the room wasn't technically safe yet. But, like Big T, she wasn't employed to tell Ash what he could or couldn't do. Besides, she was too tired to argue and resumed her search.

'So, do you always have a key to my room?' he asked, watching her as she looked under the bed, then opened the drawers to the bedside cabinets.

Charley nodded. 'So does Big T. In case of an emergency.'

As she passed Ash on her way into the lounge area, he treated her to a roguish grin. 'I can think of a few emergencies.'

'So can I,' replied Charley, and pointed to the hotel map on the back of the door. 'In case of fire, your nearest exit is to the right, five doors down.'

In recent days, she'd noticed Ash had returned to his usual flirtatious and slightly arrogant self. In fact, having bounced back from his low point, he was acting even a little hyper. She suspected he was still suffering from shock.

'Boy, you must be a fun date!' said Ash, collapsing on the bed and scattering the carefully arranged cushions. 'Don't you ever relax? Let your hair down?'

'Sure,' Charley called from the lounge, 'but not when I'm on an assignment.'

'How many assignments have you done?'

'This is my sixth.'

'Six! Who were the five before me?' he asked.

Switching on Big T's bug detector, Charley began a scan of the lounge's furnishings and fittings. 'Sorry, that's confidential information.'

'Well, have you protected anyone as famous as me?'

Charley rolled her eyes. 'No, of course not,' she replied, holding the detector over the phone. 'But they were no less important.'

There was a moment's silence, then Ash asked, 'Did you keep them all safe?'

Charley thought about Sofia, the daughter of the Colombian minister. 'They're all still alive, if that's what you're asking.'

Having established the lounge was clear of surveillance devices, Charley slid open the door to the balcony and stepped out. The late-afternoon sun was warm on her skin and the light sea breeze refreshing. The ocean was calling to her. She glanced down at the line-up of surfers bobbing on the water and longed to join them. A quick inspection of the balcony confirmed that it wasn't overlooked or easily accessible from another room.

Ash jumped from the bed and joined her. 'Worried that ninjas are going to attack me? We're four floors up!'

Charley leant over the rail and gazed down at the large oval swimming pool beneath, its waters glinting in the sunlight. 'Just checking alternative escape routes,' she half-joked. 'You could jump into the pool as a last resort.'

Ash looked over the balcony. 'Well, there's only one way to find out.'

Before Charley could stop him, Ash vaulted over the side.

CHAPTER 52

'NO!' cried Charley, her heart stopping in her chest as Ash plunged to almost certain death. Gripping the rail so tightly that her knuckles went white, she stared after the diminishing body of the rock star. Images of newspaper headlines flashed before her eyes . . . *Rock Star Commits Suicide . . . Wild Leap Ends In Tragedy* . . . accompanied by paparazzi photos of a broken body beneath a bloodied white sheet.

A second later, there was a distant splash and a fountain of white water. Ash surfaced and whooped with delight. He waved up to Charley. 'What a rush! Your turn!'

Charley shook her head. 'No way,' she shouted back.

'Come on! Live a little!'

Charley was sorely tempted by the challenge. But she knew it was utterly crazy. Four floors up and several metres of patio to clear, there was a huge risk of missing the pool. You had to have a serious death wish to attempt it. Nonetheless she found herself emptying her pockets, clambering over the rail and perching on the edge.

'Take a leap of faith,' cried Ash.

Summoning up the courage, Charley launched herself from the balcony. The wind whistled past her ears, her clothes flapping madly like a flock of starlings. For a moment the azure waters of the bay filled her entire vision. It was beautiful. Then she glanced down and saw the patio rushing up towards her.

She wasn't going to make it.

Arms and legs flailing, she braced for a bone-crushing impact . . . then, by some miracle, her forward momentum carried her over the pool. She hit the water hard. All the breath was knocked from her lungs. Her feet touched the bottom and she kicked herself back up to the surface.

'*Whoa!*' she cried, the tension and tiredness of the past week obliterated in a single mad leap.

'Awesome, Charley!' said Ash, swimming up and hugging her. 'Don't you feel *alive*?'

Charley nodded, the adrenalin coursing through her veins. For the first time in a long while, she felt exhilarated and unburdened by life. 'You're one crazy rock star!'

'And you're one crazy bodyguard,' he shot back.

In that instant their eyes locked and there was an undeniable spark. Charley had no idea whether the attraction was a result of their shared thrill-seeking experience or something deeper, but she reminded herself that was a line not to be crossed. A bodyguard should *never* get involved with a Principal. Besides, she had Blake to think about, didn't she?

'Hey, you two idiots! What do you think you're playing at?'

They broke away from their gaze. A furious pool attendant stood at the edge of the pool pointing to a sign that read: NO DIVING!

'Sorry,' Ash replied. 'Must have missed the sign on the way down.'

The two of them swam to the side and clambered out. Dripping wet, they hurried back into the hotel and through the lobby. There was a burst of excitement as a group of fans behind a roped barrier spotted Ash.

Big T came thundering over. 'I've been looking everywhere for you, Ash! Don't sneak off like th–' Then he noticed their soaking clothes. 'What the hell have you two been up to?'

'We took a dip in the pool,' replied Ash with a grin.

Big T gave Charley a hard stare, his eyes almost bulging from their sockets.

'Don't worry, I was with him the whole time,' she replied, edging past the mountainous bodyguard to avoid any questions about how they'd ended up fully clothed in the pool.

Taking the lift back to the fourth floor, they caught themselves in the mirror and burst into laughter at their bedraggled appearance.

'I still can't believe you jumped!' said Charley. 'And that I followed. You scared the hell out of me. That was a really insane stunt, you know.'

Ash shrugged. 'Live fast, die young, eh?'

'Not too young, I hope,' she said. 'At least not while I'm protecting you.'

Ash looked Charley up and down. 'Seriously, could you *really* protect me?'

Charley's eyes hardened and her nostrils flared. Just as she was beginning to like him, he had to put his big foot in his mouth and question her ability as his bodyguard – simply because she was a girl.

'Don't take offence,' said Ash, holding up his hands. 'It's just by comparison to Big T, weight for weight, you don't look like you could pack the same punch.'

Charley squared up to Ash in the lift. 'Take a swing at me.'

'What?'

'Come on! Punch me,' she said. 'Or don't you fancy your chances?'

Ash became visibly flustered. 'No . . . it's just . . . I . . . don't hit girls.'

Charley laughed. 'Well, that's my first advantage in a fight,' she replied. 'Believe me, I pack a punch and I know where to hit.' She lowered her gaze slightly.

Ash instinctively drew back. 'OK, I believe you!'

The lift pinged and the doors parted. Ash was only too eager to step out. Charley laughed at his swift retreat. As they turned down the corridor, a hotel employee in a maroon uniform was exiting Ash's room. He walked off in the opposite direction.

'Hey!' called Charley. 'Can we help you?'

'Porter,' explained the guy, not looking back. 'Just brought up your bags.'

The employee disappeared through a service door and down the stairs.

Surprised the man hadn't bothered to wait for a tip, Charley followed Ash into his suite. While he headed to the bathroom for a towel, she collected her phone and belongings from the balcony table, along with Big T's bug detector. She noticed she had a text from Blake asking her to call. The message was from his personal mobile so she knew it wasn't urgent or mission sensitive. But the two of them hadn't chatted properly in a while – the hectic tour schedule and the time difference making it hard for them to hook up. When she was back in her room, she'd make sure to phone him.

'Sorry for my remark in the lift,' Ash called out as she pocketed her mobile. 'I didn't mean –'

'Forget it,' replied Charley, catching a glimpse through the open bathroom door of him taking off his shirt. She found herself staring, admiring his toned body . . . *What's going on?* she thought. Ash wasn't even her type. She tried to get a grip on herself. 'Listen . . . I'm just going to my room to find some dry clothes. I'll radio Big T to send up security.'

There was a knock at the door.

Charley opened it. A man in a maroon uniform greeted her with a tip of his cap. 'Sorry to disturb you. I'm Christian, the hotel porter. Does Mr Wild have his bags?'

'Yes,' she replied, indicating the two suitcases embossed with his initials on the luggage rack.

'Ah, good,' said the porter, evidently relieved. 'I was concerned they'd been misplaced. But it appears your team has done my job for me. Have a nice day.'

TARGET
CHAPTER 53

'Did you get a look at his face?' asked Big T, sitting down opposite Ash and Charley in the suite's lounge area, his ample bulk filling the armchair.

Charley shook her head, her hair still damp and her wet clothes clinging to her body. 'The first porter, or whoever he was, disappeared down the back stairs before we even got close.'

'Rick, examine the hotel's CCTV,' ordered Big T. The security guard nodded and headed for the lift. 'Have you noticed anything out of place in the room since you got back?'

Charley glanced round. 'No, nothing obvious.'

'Ash, has your luggage been tampered with?'

'Not as far as I can tell,' he replied, sitting on the sofa, wrapped in a hotel robe.

'Well, until I give the OK, leave them be,' instructed Big T, his tone firm. 'Charley, did you complete the surveillance sweep before your unscheduled dip?'

Charley shifted uncomfortably under the bodyguard's hard gaze. She sensed the big man held her partly responsible for this breach of security. 'Pretty much. The room was clean.'

'Sweep it again. Top to bottom,' he ordered.

'Can I get changed first?' she asked, the air-con in the room chilling her to the bone.

'No,' said Big T emphatically. 'This takes priority.'

Rising from the sofa, Charley picked up the bug detector and began a second inspection without argument. At the same time, Big T carried out a full physical search of the suite. He started with the two suitcases, checking the locks for damage and any signs of tampering before sifting carefully through the contents. Once satisfied with the cases, he looked and felt under the sofa and chairs, behind the cabinets, inside the wardrobes and every other item of furniture in the room.

With nothing better to do, Ash headed into the bedroom, threw himself on the king-size bed, grabbed the remote and switched on the TV. He flipped through the channels to a classic rock show and turned up the volume.

'Good idea,' Big T remarked to Charley as 'Sweet Child O'Mine' by Guns N' Roses blared from the speakers. 'Anyone listening in won't hear a thing over this!'

Halfway through their rigorous search, Rick radioed up to Big T. Charley heard the conversation over her earpiece. '*The security manager re-ran the CCTV feed for the last hour. A uniformed man is seen heading down the staff stairwell at 16:07 hours, but his face is obscured by a porter's cap. Then we lose him. Sorry, Big T, not much help.*'

'Roger that,' replied Big T. 'Ask the hotel staff if they saw anyone suspicious or a new face on the team. You never know, we might get lucky.'

Charley moved through to the bedroom. Guns N' Roses had given way to Nirvana's 'Smells Like Teen Spirit'.

'Find anything?' asked Ash, slumped against the pillows, his hands clasped behind his head.

'Not yet,' Charley answered, waving the detector over a picture frame.

'I reckon it'll turn out to be nothing,' said Ash. 'Reception probably told another staff member to bring up my bags and the head porter is peeved he missed out on a fat tip.'

'Let's hope that's the case,' said Big T, entering the bedroom to the fading guitar distortion of Nirvana.

'We Built This City' by Starship began playing on the TV and Ash made a face in disgust. 'Oh, this has got to be the worst rock song ever!'

Looking through the drawers, Big T pulled out a TV remote. 'Have you scanned this?' he asked Charley.

She nodded. He was about to return the unit to the drawer when Ash switched channels.

Big T frowned. 'Hand over *that* remote,' he demanded.

'Sorry, I didn't take you for a Starship fan,' replied Ash, switching back channels.

'I'm not,' stated Big T, taking the suspect unit from Ash and examining it. As soon as Charley passed the bug detector over it, the detector vibrated and the indicator shot into the red.

'Bingo!' said Big T. He prised open the plastic casing to expose a SIM card, microphone and transmitter.

Ash stared in disbelief at the covert bugging device. 'You can't be serious! That's James Bond stuff.'

'Who do you think planted it? Gonzo?' suggested Charley.

'Him or another pap guy,' Big T replied. 'Whatever, someone is going to great lengths to keep tabs on Ash.'

'Surely it's *illegal* to bug someone?' exclaimed Ash, his tone turning angry. 'Gonzo needs to be arrested for this!'

'There's no hard proof it's him,' said Big T. 'Besides, while unauthorized telephone tapping is illegal, bugs and covert cameras fall into a grey area of the law.' He snapped the SIM card in half, then crushed the fake remote in his beefy fist. 'That's one less bug to worry about. Just a damn shame we can't do the same to the shutterbugs outside.'

Completing their surveillance sweep, they confirmed the suite was now clean.

'Are you absolutely certain?' asked Ash, still freaked out by the discovery. 'I don't want strangers listening to my every word.'

Big T nodded, then glanced at his watch. 'You'd better freshen yourself up, superstar. We leave for the venue in an hour. Don't worry, your privacy is secure and I'll post someone outside your door.'

Charley returned to her own room, shed her damp clothes and jumped into a hot shower. As the water ran down her back and warmed her, she thought about the mysterious porter. Had Gonzo been responsible? Or was someone more sinister involved? It had been a bold tactic to impersonate a hotel employee and enter Ash's room. Why were they so determined to spy on Ash? Was it purely to listen in and get a news scoop, or had they a more dangerous motive in mind? There were too many questions and Charley had no answers. But she did have one idea.

Charley dried herself, then clambered into bed and managed to snatch half an hour's rest before they left. On waking, she hunted through her Go-bag for what she needed, then joined Vince outside Ash's suite. As the two of them waited for Ash to make his appearance, she casually leant against the door frame and fitted one of the Intruder devices Amir had given her. Positioned at knee height, the pill-sized white sensor was barely visible against the white paint.

If anyone tried to enter Ash's room while they were away, she'd be the first to know about it.

CHAPTER 54

'Awesome gig!' Jessie gushed as Ash came offstage following his second encore at the Miami arena. 'I especially liked the moment when you pulled that girl from the audience. She almost *fainted* in your arms.'

Jessie gazed longingly at her idol, clearly wishing she'd been that girl. Charley didn't blame her. Almost every girl in the arena must have wanted to be serenaded in Ash's arms like that.

'Thanks,' said Ash, swigging from a water bottle. 'What did you think, Charley?'

'Probably your best gig yet,' she agreed, though she knew from the sudden burst of radio chatter on her earpiece that the unplanned invitation of the fan on to the stage had thrown the security team into a minor panic.

As the road crew set to work packing away the instruments and dismantling the stage, Big T escorted Ash to his dressing room. Charley followed close behind and stationed herself outside his door. Once Ash had showered and changed, they prepared to leave the venue.

'OK, scrum time!' Big T announced, then opened the stage doors.

Outside, hundreds upon hundreds of fans were packed like cattle behind metal barriers. They shrieked in ecstasy when Ash emerged, the noise louder than a dozen funfairs. Charley stayed close with Big T, her eyes scanning the crowd as Ash worked his way along the line signing the fans' programmes and smiling for countless selfies.

By now Charley was accustomed to the deafening screams and crazed antics of Wildling fans. But the task of protecting Ash in that ear-splitting chaos had not become any easier with so many new faces. And everyone had the potential to be the maniac who'd promised Ash *no more encores*.

A pack of photographers, including Gonzo, vaulted the barriers and rushed towards them. They scuttled round the rock star with their cameras clicking and flashing, a constant strobe of white lightning. As the pack pushed and shoved for prime position, a telephoto lens hit Ash in the head.

'Ow! Watch it,' he cried as his baseball cap went flying.

'Keep back!' Big T growled, using his bulk to shift the cameramen out of their way.

A loud metallic *clang* caused Charley to turn on her heel. A barrier had toppled over and the fans spilled on to the walkway, all madly trying to get their hands on Ash's lost cap. And when the rest of the barriers collapsed hordes more fans surged forward.

'Time to make like a shepherd and get the flock outta

here!' said Big T, his voice harsh in the security team's earpieces.

The PES team closed ranks and spearheaded Ash through the crowd towards the waiting SUV. But with every step the crush of fans grew greater and the determination of the paparazzi intensified.

'Ash, look this way!' called a photographer, half-blinding him with a blaze of flash shots.

Ash shielded his eyes and kept his head down.

'Running scared of your fans?' taunted another pap.

Gonzo bobbed up, his finger pressed on auto-shoot. 'Any more *accidents*?'

Ash glared at the rat-faced photographer. 'Stop bugging me!' he cried, flinging his water bottle at the man. The bottle struck the telephoto lens, spraying water everywhere. Paparazzi cameras flashed, capturing the moment.

'Hey! That's assault!' snarled Gonzo, unable to suppress his triumph at antagonizing the rock star. 'That's assault with a weapon!'

'You're having a laugh, Gonzo,' said Big T. 'Ash was being nice. Thought you could do with a drink.'

'I'll sue you for damages, Ash!' Gonzo shouted, ignoring the bodyguard.

Big T blocked the pap's path, then bent down to his ear level. 'And I'll have you arrested for trespassing and illegal bugging,' he hissed.

'Don't know what you're talking about,' snapped Gonzo, waving his camera in Big T's face. 'Look at this. It's ruined. Are you gonna pay for it?'

The bodyguard laughed. 'Hope you've got insurance!'

Big T and his team fended off Gonzo and the rest of the paparazzi, insults flying thick and fast, while Charley continued to escort Ash towards the SUV. But more and more fans pressed in, slowing their progress to a crawl.

Charley's mobile pinged and vibrated. Her first thought was the Intruder. Had it caught someone sneaking into Ash's suite? Despite the crush she managed to slip the phone from her pocket and glance at the screen.

But it was just a text message from Blake.

Too busy with Ash to call?

Charley swore under her breath. She'd forgotten to phone him back! And no kiss. That didn't bode well. But she was in no position to reply to him now.

When Charley looked up, a tall Hispanic lad had blocked Ash's path. With a cut-off T-shirt and gold chain, a buzz haircut and shadow of a moustache, the boy didn't look the typical Ash Wild fan.

'You were eyeing up my girl,' he accused.

Ash looked perplexed. 'Sorry, was I?'

The lad nodded. 'Pulled her on stage. No one touches *my* girl, you pumped-up little popster!'

Without warning, the jealous boyfriend launched a fist at Ash's face. Ash stared at the approaching knuckles, frozen like a rabbit in headlights. A millisecond before the fist struck its target, Charley shoved Ash aside and deflected the punch with her forearm.

The lad glared at her. 'Out of my way!'

As he tussled with her, he attempted to throw another wild punch at Ash. Left with no choice, Charley palm-struck him in the face. There was a crunch of bone and a spurt of blood as his nose broke under the impact. The boy staggered backwards to the horrified squeals of the fans and the inevitable flash of the paps' cameras.

Stun then run, thought Charley.

'Come on!' she said, hustling a shocked Ash into the SUV before speeding away.

TARGET

CHAPTER 55

WILD CAT!
FAN LASHES OUT
TO SAVE ROCK STAR

Many pop idols inspire devotion from their fans, but the followers of teen sensation Ash Wild take their duties to the max. When the English rock star was allegedly attacked by Miami resident Carlos Sanchez, 16, following a sell-out gig, a mystery blonde stepped to his defence.

Emma Hills, 15, saw the whole incident. 'The girl came out of nowhere. She was like a ninja. Before you knew it, the boy was on the ground, crying about his nose being broken.'

Carlos Sanchez insists, 'I was the victim of a misunderstanding. The girl just lashed out at me.'

But several eyewitnesses state that Carlos threw the first punch. According to Kelly Jackson, 14, 'He was jealous that his girlfriend had been on stage with Ash and the idiot thought he was making a move on her. He went to punch Ash, but this girl stopped him. Never mess with a Wildling, that's what I say!'

The blonde who'd come to Ash's rescue was seen disappearing into a vehicle with the grateful rock star. CelebrityStarz.net has attempted to contact Ash Wild's management about the incident, but they've so far declined to comment.

Who is the mysterious Wild Cat? And will she make another appearance?

A picture of Charley in mid-strike accompanied the feature. It didn't show her face completely, her hair getting in the way, but it did illustrate the devastating impact of her palm strike. The boy's head was rocked back like a PEZ sweet dispenser, with blood flying from his nose. The surrounding witnesses all wore stunned expressions, in particular Ash, who was staring at her in open-mouthed astonishment.

More pictures and amateur video clips capturing the moment followed the article posted on the celebrity news site. The internet was literally exploding with the story and #WildCat was topping the social media trends. Charley couldn't have drawn any more attention to herself if she'd tried.

As she sat alone in the rear lounge of the tour bus on its way towards their next destination, her phone rang.

'Charley, it's Colonel Black,' spoke the terse voice.

She closed her eyes and braced herself for the reprimand. 'You've seen the coverage then?'

'Hard not to miss,' said the colonel. 'You've done exactly what Steve warned you *not* to – get your face splashed all across the tabloid news! Need I remind you that any self-defence must be necessary, reasonable and proportional? That boy could have you arrested for assault.'

'But he attacked first,' protested Charley.

'That may be the case. But there's a fine line between acting in self-defence and breaking the law. What is deemed "reasonable" in the eyes of the law is a matter of opinion. You must be seen to use the *minimum* force necessary. Busting a guy's nose with a palm strike is not the most subtle response.'

'At least I didn't *punch* him,' she responded tartly.

'I appreciate that you did what you considered necessary to protect Ash, but your actions have not only reflected badly on his public image, they've threatened to expose the whole Buddyguard organization. In future, I expect your responses to be *low* profile.'

'Yes, Colonel,' she muttered before signing off.

Charley put down the phone and held her head in her hands. She couldn't believe the colonel's reaction. What was she supposed to have done – sweet-talk the guy?

'Hey, Charley, don't sweat it,' said Big T, lumbering into the lounge. 'The colonel wasn't in your shoes at the time. He didn't have to make the snap decision that you did. Besides, the boy isn't pressing charges. Too many witnesses saw him strike first. And he's too ashamed to admit a girl decked him!'

Charley sighed. 'But I've blown my cover.'

'No, you haven't. Everyone thinks you're just a fan. But you did step up to the plate. And that's what counts. I despise people who talk the talk, then bottle out when the time comes. You learn who's who in your own journey of life. And you're the real deal.'

Charley was surprised and heartened by his support. 'But the colonel's right,' she admitted. 'I should have put him in an armlock, stunned him, anything but hit him in the face in front of the press.'

'You reacted on instinct. There wasn't time to think. If you had, Ash would have suffered a painful and embarrassing attack – one that could have damaged his rock-star looks permanently. That would have been a lot worse for his public image.'

Big T pulled back the sleeve of his T-shirt and flexed the massive bicep of his right arm. A tattoo of a cruise missile bulged on his weathered skin. The words DANGER: WEAPON OF MASS DESTRUCTION were etched inside the body of the missile.

'In my days as a bouncer, my right hook ended many arguments,' he explained. 'At one stage, this arm was so legendary people called it TNT. I only ever needed to land one punch in a fight.'

He unflexed his arm and rolled down the sleeve.

'But, over the years of facing violence, I've learnt that size means nothing and that your voice is the greatest weapon. It can control a situation, it can calm a person down or it can incite a riot. You can throw an opponent off-guard by speaking softly. Your voice can charm and persuade, threaten or placate. It's the solution to most problems we face as bodyguards. Only bring out the big guns as a last resort –' he cracked a smile – 'like you did.'

TARGET
CHAPTER 56

'They're still following us!' said Charley as their blacked-out SUV raced through the streets of downtown New Orleans. They'd barely made it to their vehicle following the packed-out concert at the Superdome. Some eighty-five thousand fans had crammed in to see Ash perform and seemingly almost as many had waited to catch a glimpse of him leaving with the now-infamous 'Wild Cat'.

'Can't you go any faster?' asked Ash, peering through the rear window at the eleven cars, three scooters and two motorbikes that pursued them.

'I have to obey the speed limit,' replied Shane, their driver, gritting his teeth in concentration.

'*They're* not!'

From the front passenger seat, Big T eyed their pursuers in the wing mirror. 'Paparazzi pay no regard to road rules.'

As if to confirm this, a rented SUV sped up the wrong side of the street as the cameraman jockeyed with the other pap vehicles for the best position. A car coming the opposite way blared its horn and the cameraman swerved at the last second to avoid a head-on collision.

'Isn't this how Princess Diana died?' exclaimed Ash, clinging to his seat as their SUV rounded a corner at speed.

'Buckle up and you'll be fine,' Big T told him.

Behind, the paparazzi motorcade scrambled to follow them – overtaking and undertaking, speeding and blocking one another, taking whatever steps would keep them close.

Coming to a stop at a junction, their SUV was swamped by vehicles and was almost boxed in. Photographers leant out of their windows and filmed and photographed whatever they could. The lights changed. Shane forced his way through the blockade and the chase resumed.

Ash sighed. 'Don't they ever give up?'

'They're like vampires,' grunted Big T. 'Whatever they get is never enough.'

Their SUV passed through a junction just as the traffic lights turned red. Behind them car horns blared and there was a screeching of tyres. As the convoy of paparazzi ran the red light, two vehicles collided, blocking the junction.

Charley had never experienced anything like it. The chase was straight out of a Hollywood movie, except that real lives were at stake. And all for a sordid celebrity photo!

Turning on to the freeway, Shane was able to put his foot down on the accelerator at last. He weaved in between the traffic, trying to put some distance between them and the relentless shutterbugs. But it was futile. Without breaking the speed limit and risking the lives of his passengers, Shane was limited in what he could do to shake off their pursuers.

At the last possible moment, he took the off-ramp to

their hotel. Three vehicles on the outside lane were too late to make the exit, but the remainder of the unwanted motorcade funnelled down the ramp and back into the city.

As they neared their hotel, a motorbike came up alongside, the rider brandishing a camera. Hardly looking where he was going, he pressed the lens to the front windscreen and ran it on full auto. The multiple flashes lit up the darkened interior of the car like a magnesium flare.

The driver instinctively held up his arm to shield his eyes, but he was already blinded by the glare. He swerved, hit the kerb, bounced back into the road, then veered off.

Big T had just enough time to shout, 'Brace yours–', before the SUV hit a lamp post. Ash and Charley were flung forward, their seat belts jerking them to a violent stop. The airbags in the front saved the driver and Big T.

For a moment just the hiss of the SUV's radiator could be heard. Then Big T broke the silence: 'Everyone all right?'

Charley's heart was pounding hard, her hands trembling. She felt bruising where the belt had dug into her ribs and it hurt to breathe, but she didn't think anything was broken. She gave Big T a thumbs up, then looked over at Ash. He appeared dazed and blood was running from a cut above his left eye.

'You OK?' she asked.

Ash met her gaze and nodded. She quickly inspected the cut. It was superficial, caused by a glancing blow to the side window. She noticed some bruising, indicating a chance of concussion, but Ash's eyes were focused and he seemed only to be in shock.

Through the windscreen, Charley spotted the helmeted motorcyclist responsible for their crash. To her disgust, he took several photos of their disabled SUV before racing away from the scene. Around them, the other paparazzi discarded their vehicles on the roadway and swooped like vultures on the accident.

'Shane, you stick with the car until the cops turn up,' ordered Big T. 'Charley and I will get Ash to the hotel.'

As the three of them emerged from the wrecked SUV, they were assaulted by a hailstorm of camera flashes.

'Ash, you're hurt!' cried one photographer, not with concern but glee at the chance to get a dramatic shot. He shoved the camera in Ash's face to snap away at the blood seeping from his cut.

'Who was driving?' another shutterbug asked. 'Are you responsible, Big T? Or Wild Cat here?'

Big T pushed through the ring of cameramen, brushing them firmly aside. He kept an arm round Ash, ensuring his charge remained steady on his feet.

'Ash, I thought Wild Cat was your bodyguard now?' teased a pap.

Big T scowled at the man and pushed him from their path.

'Ooh, touchy!' taunted the pap. 'Worried you'll be out of a job? You're pretty old for this game, aren't you?'

Big T turned sharply on the man. 'Want to meet my *old* fist?'

Surprised to see her mentor losing his cool, Charley urged the veteran bodyguard on. 'Ignore the idiot,' she hissed. Taking Ash's arm, she helped escort the dazed rock star towards the hotel entrance.

Gonzo suddenly appeared amid the pack, eyes gleaming. 'Does she hold your hand at night too, Ash?' he goaded with a lewd grin.

Charley had wondered where the despicable rat had been all this time. The taunts wouldn't have been the same without him. Ignoring the loaded question, she headed for the sanctuary of the hotel with Ash and Big T. Cameras continued to hose them down with flashes as they were heckled every step of the way. Charley found it hard not to respond to the offensive and suggestive comments, but she knew that any answer she gave would only stir them up more.

Bundling Ash through the hotel doors, they left the hungry shutterbugs in the street. Cameras flashed through the glass and their taunts, though muffled, could still be heard.

Charley glanced back at the mob of photographers. How was she expected to keep a low profile now?

CHAPTER 57

'So there you have it, folks,' said the presenter, flashing her crystal-white smile at the camera. 'Ash's guardian angel wasn't just a fan after all. The Wild Cat, as we've all come to know her, was a trainee PR girl on his team. It seems that protecting a rock star's image nowadays takes more than the ability to type up a press release. You have to be a ninja!'

A picture of a black-hooded assassin flashed up on the studio monitors and the sound of clashing swords and the shouts of *kiai* were overdubbed.

Charley stood off-camera with Big T and Zoe, watching Ash's interview from the darkened wings of the recording studio in Dallas, Texas. Kay had agreed with Zoe's suggestion that their best PR strategy was a straight exposure of Charley by Ash on national TV. This, they all hoped, would bury the story and the news agencies would move on to the next celebrity scoop.

Charley felt her phone vibrate in her pocket. She glanced at the glowing screen. Following the porter incident in Miami, she now routinely fitted an Intruder device outside

Ash's hotel room. But it wasn't an Intruder alert. It was a text from Blake:

Can you talk?

Outside the official report-ins, it was always difficult to find time to chat and Charley sensed something was on his mind. She thumbed a reply:

Can't speak now. In TV studio. Will call later. Promise x

The presenter swung her beaming smile back towards Ash and concluded her interview. 'Thank you for coming into the studio, Ash. I'm glad the paparazzi didn't run you off the road like they did in New Orleans. And good luck with the concert tomorrow. I hear it's a sell-out!'

'It sure is!' Ash replied with enthusiasm, the cut above his left eye now healing and hidden by make-up. 'I can't wait to see all my Dallas fans go WILD!'

'Well, judging by the crowd outside our studios, they can't wait to see you either. Now, I believe you're going to play us out with your biggest hit, "Only Raining".'

Ash nodded, then joined his band on the opposite side of the studio. The cameras moved in for a close-up as he began the opening riff to his worldwide smash.

Charley found herself bobbing her head in time to the music. As Ash sang, '*We all need a shelter to keep us from the rain . . .*' her thoughts drifted back to the moment on the beach in California when she'd decided to catch that once-in-a-lifetime wave and become a bodyguard. How her life had changed – from being a surfing beach bum to protecting one of the most famous teenagers on the planet! And, though being a bodyguard wasn't easy, her life no longer felt empty or without purpose. Yes, Kerry was still a huge hole in her heart, but the memory only stung . . . it didn't burn any more. For that she was thankful. She just wished her parents could've been around to witness this. But if they were, of course, she'd never have become a bodyguard in the first place.

Charley became aware of someone at her side. Glancing over, she did a double-take: same quiff of honey-brown hair, identical hazel eyes, dimpled chin, a matching smile. Standing next to her was a carbon copy of Ash.

'How did you get in here?' hissed Charley, suddenly realizing who it was.

'The receptionist thought I was Ash!' The clone laughed quietly. 'Look, I've even got the same tattoo now.'

Pete pulled back the sleeve of his shirt to reveal an identical phoenix design on his right forearm.

'You really shouldn't be here,' insisted Charley.

'I know,' he said with a charming smile he'd stolen straight from Ash, 'but I wanted to see what a TV studio was like.'

The band brought the song to an end and, after thanking Ash, the presenter made her closing remarks. As the studio's red recording light switched off, the producer announced, 'OK, everyone, we're off the air.'

'Excellent interview, Ash, and even better performance,'

praised Zoe, handing him a bottle of water as she led him from the set.

'Thanks,' said Ash, lifting the bottle to his lips. But he didn't get any further with his drink, literally stopped in his tracks by the sight of his double.

'Hi, Ash! Check out my tattoo,' said Pete eagerly.

Ash glanced at it. 'Nice tat,' he mumbled, then studied his apparently identical twin. 'You're . . . *me*!'

Big T came striding over and, after a momentary blink of disbelief, immediately took charge. 'I'm going to have to ask you to leave,' he said firmly to Pete.

The doppelgänger held up his hands. 'Hey, Big T, I'm no threat to Ash. I *idolize* him.'

'That's more than apparent,' said the veteran bodyguard, stony-faced. 'But you'll still have to go. This is a restricted area.'

'I understand,' said Pete, shrugging his shoulders as two studio security guards appeared. 'See you at the gig tomorrow night, Ash.'

'Yeah,' said Ash, still staggered at his fan's devotion. As the guards escorted Pete away, he leant over to Charley. 'Don't tell him, but he's got the tattoo on the wrong arm!'

Charley stifled a giggle – the poor lad, after the lengths he'd gone to in mimicking his hero.

'Sorry about that,' said the producer, running over. 'I'll be having a word with our security manager later. But first let's get you on your way.'

The producer guided Ash and his entourage out of the studio and down the corridor. Turning a corner towards the reception, they caught a glimpse through a window of the heaving throng of photographers and fans packing the studio's plaza entrance.

'This is ridiculous,' said Zoe. 'We can't even get out to the car!'

Following the assault in Miami and the crash in New Orleans, the paparazzi had intensified their pursuit of Ash and his Wild Cat. It seemed every shutterbug in the United States had descended on the tour and it was now a challenge just to reach the venues, let alone keep Ash safe.

'We could try the emergency exit,' the producer suggested.

A squeal of excitement in the lobby caught their attention. An intern had spotted Pete being escorted away and rushed over for his autograph. Pete signed the girl's notepad with a flourish, the two security guards barely able to contain their amusement at the case of mistaken identity.

'I have a better idea,' said Ash.

TARGET
CHAPTER 58

Shades on, Ash emerged from the TV studio into the teeming plaza. The crowd erupted with screams and surged forward. A strobe of camera flashes lit up his exit as the paparazzi swarmed round their target. With his arm protectively over the shoulders of the young rock star, Big T forged a path through the ocean of hysterical fans and in-your-face photographers. The rest of Ash's entourage followed in his slipstream.

It took almost ten minutes to reach the car, even though it was parked only fifty metres away. Unwilling to disappoint his fans, Ash spent time signing autographs and posing for numerous selfies. Eventually Big T bundled him into the back of the car and they drove away from the studio. The paparazzi immediately piled into their vehicles and set off in hot pursuit.

Their idol gone, the fans dispersed and the plaza emptied.

'That worked like a dream!' said Ash, emerging from behind the reception desk with Charley.

'Pete certainly lived up to his role,' agreed Charley. The plan had been that Pete would go straight to the car with

Big T, but the boy had obviously been swept up in the thrill of adulation and exploited his sudden stardom to the max.

'I'll have to employ him full-time as my decoy,' continued Ash. 'I'll get Big T to give him a backstage pass.'

Charley frowned. 'Are you sure that's wise? You hardly know him.'

Ash laughed. 'Of course I know him. He's me!'

Charley gave him a hard look. 'Seriously, Ash, what normal fan goes so far they get the same tattoo as their idol?'

Ash waved away her concerns. 'Thousands of people copy their heroes. Girls are always imitating their favourite pop stars. Why should it be any different for a guy? Pete is just super-dedicated. And if he can fool the paparazzi, then I'm all for it.'

'We should at least run a background check on him,' insisted Charley.

'Fine, whatever. But look outside.' He pointed to the deserted plaza. '*No paparazzi!*'

He grabbed Charley and did a little jig in the lobby. Charley couldn't help smiling. His joy was infectious and she too felt a weight lift from her. The constant surveillance and taunts had made her more tense than she'd realized. It would be a welcome change to walk outside without cameras being thrust in her face.

'Your car's here,' announced the receptionist.

Ash danced his way through the revolving doors as a second vehicle drove up to the studio entrance. Charley followed him out and jumped in the back with him.

'Time to celebrate my newfound freedom.' Ash tapped the driver on the shoulder. 'Take us to the best restaurant in Dallas.'

'Big T said we should go straight to the hotel,' reminded Charley.

'Come on, Charley, live a little! Besides, what could possibly go wrong? I've got the Wild Cat to protect me!'

TARGET

CHAPTER 59

'I'm sorry, sir, we're fully booked for dinner,' informed the bow-tied, strait-laced maître d' at the door of the ultra-chic restaurant in downtown Dallas. His hair was a splash of oil slicked to his scalp, his hands manicured to a high sheen and his shoes polished to within an inch of their lives.

'But I can see a free table in the window,' said Ash.

'That's reserved for special guests,' the maître d' replied haughtily. 'Perhaps I can recommend the burger bar down the street?'

Ash ignored the man's snub. 'How special do you need to be? I'm Ash Wild.'

The maître d' looked down his thin nose at him. 'And who's he?'

'*Who's Ash Wild?*' exclaimed a gruff voice from behind a velvet curtain that separated the restaurant's entrance from the dining area. 'Only the greatest songwriter since McCartney!'

Pushing through the curtain, the head chef, with flushed cheeks and a reassuring ample belly, bowled over to greet Ash with a warm handshake. 'My word, it *is* you! My daughters adore your music. And I must admit I'm a real fan too. Just adore "Only Raining"! I was so disappointed when I couldn't get tickets for your concert. But you've come to *my* restaurant and it'd be an honour to cook for talent like yours.'

'Why, thank you,' said Ash, startled by the gushing praise. 'I'm sure that my publicist can arrange tickets for you and your daughters.'

The chef's face lit up. He turned to his maître d'. 'Show Ash to the best table in the house,' he ordered.

'My apologies, Mr Wild,' said the maître d', a bald patch gleaming in the spotlight as he bowed his head. 'I don't keep up with modern music.'

'No, I'm sure you don't,' said Ash politely.

The maître d' led them through the curtain and over to the table by the window. He drew back the chair for Charley.

'We can't sit here,' Charley said to Ash, still standing.

'Why not?' he asked with a puzzled frown. 'This is the very best seat in the house.'

'The very best seat is often the worst from a security point of view.'

Ash looked out of the window. 'But we've got a great view over the park.'

'That's the problem,' said Charley, lowering her voice. 'It makes you vulnerable. Anyone could spot you or –' she thought back to the laser at the first gig – 'attack you.'

Ash stared at her. 'Wow, you make for a romantic dinner date!'

Charley tilted her head. 'I didn't know this was a *date*.'

Ash glanced at the red rose decorating the table, then met her eye and smiled. 'Neither did I.'

'Mr Wild, is this table not suitable?' enquired the maître d', raising a needle-thin eyebrow.

'It's perfect,' replied Ash, and sat down. 'Listen, Charley, no one knows we're here, so let's just enjoy this moment of rare freedom.'

Charley reluctantly took her seat, but positioned it so that she at least had a view of the other restaurant guests. Besides, it wasn't quite true that no one knew where they were. She'd texted Big T an update of their location while Ash had been speaking with the head chef. She certainly wasn't going to make the same mistake twice with the veteran bodyguard.

The waiter came over with a bread basket, poured them some chilled water and presented the menus. There was a ripple of excitement among the other diners and staff as word spread of their special guest.

'So what other security advice should we be following?' asked Ash as he browsed the menu.

'Well, we should have our backs to a wall,' replied Charley. 'Then we only have to worry about threats from the front. Also, it'd be better if I had a direct line of sight to the restaurant entrance and any other doors. That way I can keep an eye on who comes in and who goes out.'

Ash set aside his menu. 'They taught you all this in bodyguard school?'

Charley nodded. 'Among other things.'

'Like how to deck a guy with a single punch!'

'It wasn't technically a punch,' replied Charley, sipping her water. 'It was a palm strike.'

'Whatever, you laid that idiot out good time,' said Ash, grinning at the memory. He leant forward, elbows on the table, his fingers interlaced as if in a confession. 'I haven't thanked you properly for protecting me. The guy blindsided me. I just never expected it.'

'No one ever does.'

'But you did. You reacted.'

'I've been trained to,' said Charley. 'It's all part of the job.'

'Some job!' remarked Ash, shaking his head in amazement.

A waiter approached and took their orders.

'To be honest, I thought having you around was going to be a real drag,' Ash admitted once the waiter had gone. 'And, after that first gig, I had serious doubts about you. But . . . you're one amazing girl, Charley.'

He gazed at her across the candlelit table, his smouldering hazel eyes both sincere and irresistible. Charley felt that spark again and her pulse raced. Trying to keep her runaway emotions in check, she selected a bread roll from the basket and began to butter it. 'Don't get slushy on me,' she said. 'I'm your bodyguard. Not your girlfriend.'

'I know, but it's really nice having you around,' Ash admitted. 'If I haven't said it before, I'm sorry for the tour prank we played on you. It was the bassist's idea. I didn't think you'd –'

'Forget about it. I have,' said Charley, glancing up with a smile.

'Well, I haven't.' Ash held her gaze as he took a sip of water. 'Being a rock star isn't all it's cracked up to be,' he confessed. 'Everyone just sees the riches, the fans, the celebrity lifestyle. But life on the road can be so lonely.'

'You've got the band around you,' Charley pointed out.

'The band and crew are all mates, of course. But it's different – they're older. They're not going through what I am as the frontman. They don't have to contend with the pressure of fame . . . the haters . . . or the death threats. You see all that. You understand it. I can talk to you about it.'

'Of course you can,' said Charley.

Ash pulled out his phone, thumbed an app and showed her his social media feed on the screen. 'This is what I have to put up with every day, every minute of my life.'

He pointed to a post that read: *Drop dead, you talentless waster!*

Another below it declared: *Your music is an insult to God and anyone with ears.*

There were several other messages of abuse and threats to knife, maim and harm the rock star. But, as Charley had noted before, the majority of the posts were from loyal and loving fans:

I adore u @therealAshWild
So Xcited, #AshWild Dallas gig tm night!
Hoping for an *electrifying* performance! #AshWild
@therealAshWild has the voice of an angel.

Charley drew Ash's attention to these. 'This is what you should be reading. Not those other insults. Ignore the haters. If you don't, they win.'

Ash sighed. 'I know, but that's easier said than done, especially when one of them could be the maniac who's trying to kill me.'

Their conversation was interrupted by the arrival of their first course. Ash was presented with a plate of roasted maple-leaf buffalo wings, while Charley had chosen king prawns in a coconut mayonnaise. With a flourish, the waiter laid the napkins on their laps, then departed.

'Anyway, enough about my problems,' said Ash, tucking into his starter. 'You still haven't told me why you became a bodyguard.'

Since Ash had opened up to her, Charley felt she could do the same. As they ate, she told him about Kerry, about the bald-headed abductor and how she'd failed to react and save her friend, then how her parents had died in a plane hijacking and her life had lost all meaning.

'They say time heals all wounds,' mused Charley. 'But, if that's true, the memories still leave a scar.'

Suddenly she realized Ash was texting on his phone under the table. 'Sorry, am I boring you?' she asked, her tone sharp.

'No, absolutely not. You're inspiring me!' he replied, rapidly typing away. After a minute or so, he put his phone down and sighed with deep relief. He gazed at her in awe. 'Charley, I know you'll think this is just a chat-up line, but you're my missing muse. I've been stuck for lyrics for weeks. Now I can hear the songs again – thanks to you.'

Leaning closer, he sang softly to her, a beautiful heart-aching melody: '*Time will heal yet memories scar, when the hurt's so deep, a bridge too far . . .*'

Charley felt her eyes moisten and her throat constrict.

'*In times of trouble, I need a helping hand. I look for you, breathe for you, have a need for you . . .*'

The words and tune combined to squeeze at her heart, the song seeming to be a distillation of her enduring grief. A tear escaped and rolled down her cheek. Still singing, Ash reached out with his own hand, gently caressed her face and wiped away the tear.

A sudden flash lit up the scene. Ash jerked his hand back. Charley blinked in half-blinded surprise.

Outside the window, grinning like a peeping Tom, was Gonzo.

TARGET
CHAPTER 60

'It's not what it looks like,' protested Charley over the phone the next morning.

But Gonzo's photo was compromising in every way – the candlelit restaurant, a red rose on the table, Ash with his hand cupping her face and her mouth slightly parted.

From the angle the photo had been taken, it appeared the famous rock star was about to kiss her. And the camera never lies.

Charley stared in dismay at the image now making the front page of every tabloid and celebrity newsfeed in the world. 'Wild Boy Tames Wild Cat' and other puns accompanied the picture that had been published within hours of their dinner.

'Yeah, you're just doing your job,' said Blake flatly. 'It's good to see you're so committed.'

'For heaven's sake, nothing happened. Please don't get jealous.'

'How can you expect me *not* to be jealous?'

'I expect you to trust me,' pleaded Charley.

'Well, that's a little hard considering the evidence,' he

replied frostily. 'And you rarely return my calls. You're obviously too busy with Ash. I think we should end it, don't you?'

Charley couldn't speak; Blake had been her friend since joining Buddyguard. He'd been the one to stand by her when all the others had doubted her abilities. She didn't want to lose him, not like this.

But before Charley could manage a reply he dropped another bombshell.

'Anyway, I've started seeing someone else, so it's probably for the best,' he said. 'That's what I've been wanting to tell you.'

'What?' exclaimed Charley, but he'd already ended the call. For a moment she sat staring at the mobile still in her hand. Then she picked up the newspaper with the offending photo and flung it across her hotel room. It hit the opposite wall, its pages scattering like autumn leaves.

'I warned you the paparazzi could make your life hell,' said Big T, leaning his great bulk against the door frame to her room.

Her vision swimming with tears, Charley sobbed, 'Blake's dumped me because of it!'

Stepping into the room, Big T wrapped a heavy, tattooed arm round her shoulders to comfort her. 'Then the boy's an idiot. He's no idea what he's lost.'

'H-he says he's seeing someone else!' said Charley, her voice hitching.

Big T scowled. 'Then he's a *double* idiot! But maybe it was just a cheap shot to have the last word?'

'Why would he do that?' asked Charley.

'He's a boy. His pride's been hurt.'

'But I didn't cheat on him!'

'I know,' said Big T with a sympathetic smile. 'But bodyguarding and boyfriends don't mix, I'm afraid. There's little room for relationships in this line of work. I should know. I've two ex-wives!' He gave a hollow laugh.

'None of this would have happened if it wasn't for that photo!' Charley ground her teeth, her sorrow now replaced by anger. 'How did Gonzo find us?'

Big T shrugged. 'Most likely an informant in the restaurant itself. Pap agencies spend literally tens of thousands of dollars a year on their snitch network. It's hard to keep any celebrity's movements secret these days.'

'But wasn't he fooled by Pete?'

'Yes, hook, line and sinker,' said Big T. 'Gonzo followed us all the way back to the hotel. He staked out the entrance with everyone else. The only way he could have known you were at that restaurant was a tip-off. And whatever he paid the snitch it's nothing compared to the small fortune he's raked in selling that single photo of you two.'

Charley clenched her fists in frustrated fury; while she suffered the consequences of the lie, that leech had profited. 'Well, he'd better leave us alone now.'

'Fat chance. They're vampires, remember?'

Charley's phone rang. It was Colonel Black. She braced herself for another reprimand.

'Charley, this *isn't* what I meant by keeping a low profile,' he began, his tone surprisingly even and restrained.

'But I suppose it was inevitable. You can't protect one of the most famous pop stars in the world without attracting attention yourself. I just need to know, has a line been crossed here?'

'No, of course not,' she replied.

'Good. If that's the case, then stay on the assignment, for now at least.'

'Thank you, Colonel,' she said, relieved simply to have escaped a shameful dismissal. Besides, after her messy break-up with Blake, she didn't want to go back to headquarters any time soon. 'I assure you it won't happen again.'

'No, I'm sure it will,' Colonel Black corrected her, much to her astonishment. 'Kay and I are both in agreement. Considering the circumstances, being Ash's girlfriend is the perfect cover.'

TARGET

CHAPTER 61

'There are literally millions of girls who'd kill to be in your position . . . me included,' said Jessie, giving Charley a brief congratulatory hug when they met at the side of the stage for Ash's Dallas concert. 'Ash always had eyes for you, so I'm not really surprised. You two are a match made in heaven.'

'Well, it was certainly a surprise to me,' Charley replied with an awkward smile. She was still reeling from Blake's betrayal. *How could he be so heartless?* She'd tried calling him on his mobile, but he refused to answer – his determined silence as hurtful as his sudden dumping of her. However, becoming Ash's official girlfriend overnight was an even greater shock to the system. Suddenly everyone wanted to know her – fans and paparazzi alike.

There'd been a huge explosion of online chatter and gossip about the blossoming romance. More of Gonzo's pictures had been released: early shots of the two of them leaving the after-show party in New York; the time they'd sneaked out of the hotel in Pittsburgh to go running; the now-infamous moment she'd leapt to Ash's defence; the anxious seconds after the car crash in New Orleans and other random shots from the rest of the tour. Ignoring any timelines or contexts, the press had created a whole fiction around the photos – a celebrity story of young love through the tabloid lens of the paparazzi.

Guardian Angel Turns Love Angel . . .

Ash Runs Wild With New Girl . . .

PR Blonde Captures Rock Star's Heart . . .

Investigative reporters had tried to dig up dirt on Charley, some even resorting to fabricating lies about her past, but Charley knew the press wouldn't find anything on her. Besides her surname being changed for the assignment, the personal records of all Buddyguard recruits were meticulously doctored to conceal their double lives as young bodyguards. This was for the security of the Principals as well as the recruits.

But the past wasn't as interesting as the present for the celebrity-hungry masses. Besides the big question of whether it was true love or not, Charley's looks were a huge subject of debate among girl fans – her blonde hair, her sky-blue eyes, her slim neck, her athletic figure, her teeth, her nails, her taste in clothes. There was no part of her body or image not dissected and commented upon.

The internet was teeming with these posts and, against her better judgement, Charley had read some. She couldn't stop herself. Skimming the comments, she was relieved to discover many opinions were flattering and supportive. But there were also a lot of spiteful remarks and cruel barbs. Some had been deeply personal and truly hurtful. Even though Charley realized they were written by trolls – bullies who only wanted to offend and humiliate – she couldn't help feeling upset at the unjust and unwarranted abuse. Many fans wrote that they hated her and she didn't deserve to be Ash's girlfriend. Some wished her dead. A few even threatened to kill her if she hurt Ash or broke his heart.

After a miserable hour of internet surfing, Charley forced herself to stop. Like poison ivy, the hate infected all the fan forums and dominated her thoughts, sending any nice remarks into oblivion. Charley's sense of self-worth was becoming seriously undermined. She was having a taste of Ash's celebrity life and she didn't like it one bit.

Pete, on the other hand, was relishing his role as Ash's decoy.

He'd once again fooled the fans and diverted the paparazzi before the real Ash left his hotel for the gig at the Dallas arena. A few photographers had lingered behind, hoping for an exclusive shot of the rock star's new girlfriend. But Charley, along with Ash in a hoodie and dark glasses, had managed to evade detection, departing from a side entrance thirty minutes later. The two Ash Wilds had eventually been reunited in the venue's dressing room.

Now disguised in a baseball cap and horn-rimmed glasses, Pete stood beside Charley and Jessie, his backstage pass worn like a medal of honour on his chest. He had the biggest grin on his face and his eyes never left Ash as his idol entertained the Dallas crowd.

'How are you enjoying the show from backstage?' Charley asked him.

'It's amazing,' he replied, his gaze not wavering from his rock-star hero. 'I feel this affinity with Ash. It's like we're one.'

Charley just nodded. The background check had revealed Pete lived in Norwich, England, with his grandmother. He was actually eighteen years old, but looked and behaved much younger. He worked for a delivery company as a packer, had six GCSEs and a Diploma in Computing to his name, and held no criminal convictions. The boy was totally unexceptional. He simply seemed to live his life through Ash, as confirmed by the photo he'd posted on a Wildling fansite of his bedroom plastered with Ash Wild posters and memorabilia. For that reason alone, Charley thought the boy a little weird and intended to keep a close eye on him.

When the band kicked off with the track 'Been There, Done That', Pete started busting moves, playing air guitar and belting out the words to the song. Charley and Jessie exchanged glances, trying not to laugh. Pete may have looked like Ash and been able to replicate his dance routine, but he certainly couldn't sing like him.

'Hey, Pete! Do you want your own mic?' suggested Jessie, grabbing a microphone from a nearby stand.

Pete glared at her, his eyes flashing like a wild animal's and his lips curling into a snarl. Any resemblance to Ash vanished and for a moment Charley thought he might pounce on Jessie.

Then the bearded roadie Geoff intervened and snatched the mic back from her. 'I told you before – *don't* touch the gear!' he hissed.

The joke having fallen flat, Jessie meekly apologized and backed away. Pete returned to staring at his idol, the mocking apparently forgotten.

On stage Ash proved why he was the superstar he was, dazzling the audience with a guitar solo that would have made Jimi Hendrix proud. In response the Dallas crowd almost lifted the roof with their screams. Charley spotted the chef in the front row with his two daughters. He looked to be having the time of his life.

When the song came to an end, the stage lights faded and the roadie hurried past Charley to set up the stage for Ash's final acoustic set. This was the part of the show Charley enjoyed best. Stripped of all the high-end production, video effects, dancers and backing band, this was Ash at his most pure and honest.

A boy, his guitar and a voice.

It was hard for anyone not to fall in love with him when he performed like this.

The arena darkened until a single spot illuminated Ash in a halo of golden light at the tip of the guitar-shaped stage. He adjusted his stool, checked the tuning on his acoustic guitar, then put his lips to the mic. At once his whole body went rigid and he keeled sideways, crashing to the floor.

CHAPTER 62

Charley raced out on to the stage. She had no idea what had happened. Had a fan thrown something at Ash? Was it a heart attack? Had he been shot? Had the maniac promising 'no more encores' struck? Whatever the cause, her overriding instinct was to protect him from further harm – if he was still alive.

The whole arena had fallen into stunned and horrified silence as Ash lay motionless in a heap at the far end of the stage. For Charley, the guitar-shaped runway seemed to extend forever as she sprinted towards his inert body.

A technician reached Ash first. He took hold of Ash's shoulder, then shuddered, jerked his hand away and fell backwards. In that instant Charley knew what was wrong. Ash had been electrocuted.

Picking up the fallen wooden stool, Charley shoved the lethal microphone away from Ash's body. She checked for any other dangers, then knelt down beside Ash, praying he wasn't dead. An electric shock with a strong enough current could stop the heart.

'ASH!' she called, but there was no response.

Confirming his airway was clear, she checked his breathing and circulation. His pulse was a little weak, though the fact he had a pulse was reassuring. The problem was . . . he *wasn't* breathing.

This time Charley knew Ash wasn't faking it.

Pinching his nose, she leant over him, covered his mouth with her lips and began CPR. She was vaguely aware of anxious tour crew and security gathering round her. The offending microphone was isolated and disconnected. A stretcher was brought down by two medics. The audience were softly whispering and weeping as they watched the scene play out. Still Charley kept up her rescue breaths, focusing on the task in hand and not letting panic control her emotions.

'Charley, it's Big T,' said a voice in her ear. 'The medics can take over.'

Charley shook her head and persisted with CPR. Ash was her responsibility. She would not let him die in her arms. She lost all track of time. It could have been seconds, minutes or hours that passed, but halfway through a set of rescue breaths Ash regained consciousness. His eyes flickered open and he took several breaths on his own.

'Hey, Charley . . .' he said, smiling. 'Hope you're not going to break my arm for this.'

'No,' she replied with a relieved smile, recalling her previous threat about if he ever tried kissing her again. 'As you said, it's worth the risk.'

One of the medics helped Ash sit up. Seeing their idol rise from the dead, the whole audience applauded and whooped.

'OK, let's get you to the hospital,' said the medic.

'Later,' said Ash, waving off his help. 'I've a gig to finish.'

'But we need to do a thorough medical examination,' insisted the medic.

'I feel fine,' declared Ash, standing up on his own. 'If Dave Grohl can finish a tour with a broken leg, I can certainly perform after a little shock to the system.'

'Little?' queried the medic. 'You were knocked unconscious and stopped breathing.'

'That's rock 'n' roll for you!' Ash laughed. 'Besides, can't you hear that?'

His legion of fans stamped their feet and chanted, 'ASH! ASH! ASH!'

'The show must go on,' he said, grabbing a wireless mic.

Charley thought Ash was a little high on adrenalin, but otherwise he seemed unharmed. It was nothing short of a miracle. Ash took hold of Charley's hand and raised it to the sky.

'Talk about the kiss of life,' he announced to loud wolf whistles and rapturous applause. 'My guardian angel!'

CHAPTER 63

Charley closed the door to her hotel room and collapsed on the bed. It was gone midnight and she was exhausted. But she had to report in to Buddyguard. They'd want an update on the situation.

Her finger paused over the dial button. She still hadn't spoken with Blake. Since she was using the official Buddyguard line, though, he'd have to answer her call now. Both dreading and needing to talk to him, Charley took a deep breath and dialled.

The phone rang three times before it was picked up and a voice answered. 'Report in.'

She hesitated. 'W-where's Blake?'

'He's been reassigned,' Jason explained. 'I'm now your official contact.'

'Oh . . .' said Charley, disappointed yet somewhat relieved that she wouldn't have to speak to Blake.

'Don't sound so pleased to hear my voice,' said Jason. 'I'm equally happy to be working with you. Now, are you going to update me on your Principal or not?'

'Sorry,' Charley replied, a little thrown by the change in

contact. She felt awkward talking with Jason when they didn't exactly get on. 'Well . . . according to the doctor, Ash is fighting fit. After finally being convinced to take a ten-minute break for a medical check-up, he finished the gig to a standing ovation.' She half-smiled at the thought, still in awe of Ash's dedication to his fans. 'But he was extremely lucky to survive – that direct shock to the head could have fried his brain.'

'I've seen some of the fan footage online,' said Jason. 'Looks like he was shot by a stun gun. Any idea what went wrong?'

'Faulty microphone,' Charley replied. 'The sound technician says the wiring wasn't earthed properly. Terry – the tour manager – is furious. He's got the whole tech team retesting all the electrics before the next concert. He says these things *shouldn't* happen.'

'Well, it did,' said Jason. 'Kay just called the colonel to praise your fast response. She credits you with saving Ash's life.'

Charley felt a flush of pride.

'Kay's also reviewing all security measures with Big T,' Jason went on, 'so don't be surprised if there's a bit of a shake-up in the ranks. She wasn't happy with the rest of his team's response to the situation, so she's flying out to join the tour to keep a closer eye on things.'

'Big T did mention Kay was concerned.'

'Well, Ash does seem prone to accidents on this tour,' remarked Jason.

'Accidents don't just happen,' said Charley, repeating

the sinister message that had popped up on Ash's computer.

'What? You think this was another attempt on Ash's life?'

'Yes.'

'But isn't using a microphone to kill someone rather hit-and-miss?' Jason wondered. 'Anyone could have used that mic before Ash. A roadie during the sound check or one of the band in the show.'

'True. But the night before the concert Ash showed me his social media feed. There was a whole bunch of posts from haters, but one, apparently from a fan, read, "Hoping for an electrifying performance!" That's too much of a coincidence for me. Someone wants Ash dead and they're going to great lengths to make it look like an accident.'

Jason went quiet for a moment. 'Then the question is, who is this fan?'

'Exactly. If we could trace the two online messages, and any others sent by the same accounts, then we might identify the user. I know Big T didn't get anywhere with the first message, but perhaps Bugsy has access to higher-level resources?'

'Bugsy's away on an assignment for the colonel,' informed Jason, 'but I'll ask that newbie Amir if he can help. I hear he's something of a whizz with computers.'

'Thanks,' said Charley, surprised at how willing Jason was to help. Perhaps it wouldn't be so hard to work with him after all. 'I'll email you the links now.'

She pulled up Ash's social media page on her phone and

searched for the two suspect messages. With a couple of taps, she forwarded them to Jason.

'Got 'em,' said Jason. 'Anything else before we sign off?'

Charley hesitated. 'Jason . . . can I ask you something?'

'Sure.'

She swallowed hard, her mouth going dry. Jason was the last person she wanted to discuss this with, but she had to know. 'Is Blake seeing someone else?'

There was a long pause. 'Forget about Blake, Charley. You're better off without him,' he replied. 'You need to focus on the mission.'

Charley felt her eyes prickle with tears. It was obvious Blake had cheated on her. Stifling a sob, she went into the bathroom and grabbed a tissue from the box next to the washbasin.

'Besides, you're the girlfriend of a famous rock star now!' Jason went on. 'Not a bad swap for you. I mean, how much better could it get?'

Dabbing at her eyes, Charley looked up from the basin and let out a small cry.

'You all right?' he asked, finally aware she was upset.

'Yeah, everything's fine,' replied Charley in a voice as calm as she could manage. She hadn't cried out because of Blake. On the bathroom mirror, scrawled in her own red lipstick, were the words:

TO BE AN ANGEL
U NEED 2 DIE FIRST!

TARGET

CHAPTER 64

Ash Wild must have the nine lives of a cat! How else could that snivelling, screeching pop prince defy death twice? *It's beyond belief. That boy deserves to die. Has to die. Must die.*

I should have shot him that first night. Why the hell didn't I pull the trigger?

I might have missed, that's why . . . Don't be stupid, you had him in your laser sight. The man at the gun store said it was just a matter of point and shoot . . . Wherever the red dot was, the bullet would go. So why didn't I pull the trigger?

Just admit it! You didn't have the guts, did you?

No.

The gun was too personal, too hands-on. And too risky. The police would easily have traced the bullets and gun. Besides, that blonde bitch Charley interfered. Ran Ash off the stage before I could change my mind and fire. It's her fault.

That's why an accidental death is a far better idea. No *one can foresee it. No one can stop it.*

The spotlight took a lot of planning, though – the exact positioning of the light, the removal of the safety chain, the sabotaging of the clamp, the precise timing of the fall – every detail had to be accounted for. Then the little ego-fuelled superstar lands in the wrong bloody place!

How unfair is that? Only a few centimetres between life and death.

Ash certainly had a guardian angel watching over him then.

At least the microphone was easier to tamper with. I don't know why I didn't think of that in the first place. The only tricky part was ensuring Ash would be the victim.

But the plan worked – like a dream.

Oh, the thrill! The sheer joy when Ash dropped dead!

Then that blonde bitch again, the Wild Cat. She brought him back to life.

It was her fault, his guardian angel. Yeah, all her *fault!*

Next time . . . I'll guarantee she can't save her precious rock star.

Next time . . . he won't rise from the ashes. Nor will she.

TARGET
CHAPTER 65

'If you're my girlfriend, you should really be holding my hand,' said Ash as the two of them arrived in a stretch limo outside the Bellagio Hotel in Las Vegas.

Since Dallas, the tour had taken them to Kansas City, then through Minneapolis and Denver to the entertainment capital of the world. With a day off between gigs, his manager had acquired VIP invites for Ash to attend an exclusive star-studded fashion show before his concert the next night at the Mandalay Bay Events Center – and it would be Ash and Charley's first official appearance as a couple.

Ash offered his hand. He seemed totally at ease with the arrangement made by his manager and Colonel Black – in fact he looked proud to have her on his arm. Considering Ash could have almost any girl he wanted, Charley felt flattered by this. She took his hand, telling herself it was purely to keep up appearances. But after the messy break-up with Blake and the deluge of hate messages online she couldn't deny it was a much-needed boost to her battered self-esteem.

He smiled, gave her hand a reassuring squeeze, then stepped out into a blaze of camera flashes.

The press were out in full force. The fashion show was a focal point for all the celebrities in Las Vegas and a long red carpet had been laid for their arrival. Ash was requested by an event marshal to stop halfway along for the official photo op. Dressed in a black silk shirt, jacket and coal-black designer jeans, he looked the epitome of the teen rock star. Charley, in a sleek satin gown and high heels that Ash's stylist had picked out for her, caught everyone's eye, more than fulfilling her role as the chic glamorous girlfriend. The cameras simply couldn't get enough of the hip young couple.

As they posed for photos, Charley kept her designer sunglasses on. She couldn't risk getting dazzled by all the flashes. She may have become Ash's 'girlfriend', but she was still his bodyguard. Her eyes scanned the huddle of photographers and, to her dismay, spotted Gonzo's rat-face among the pack. How on earth had the lowlife got an official press pass?

Still smiling for the cameras, Charley surveyed the crush of tourists and fans behind the metal barriers, checking for signs of a potential threat – those directed not only at Ash but also at herself.

For she was now a target too.

That had been made abundantly clear by the sinister threat left on her bathroom mirror. After taking a picture for evidence, she'd wiped away the lipstick-smeared message and hadn't mentioned it to anyone for fear of being pulled off the assignment. If she couldn't protect herself, then how could she be considered fit to protect Ash?

As more celebrities spilled out of limos to make their way up the red carpet, Big T came up alongside and indicated they should enter the hotel. Accompanying them, he kept at a respectful but responsive distance, his massive bulk a high-profile deterrent to any troublemakers. They entered the famous Bellagio lobby, its ceiling adorned with two thousand handblown glass flowers, the display suspended over their heads like a glistening rainbow. Ushered through to the ballroom, Charley found herself among a menagerie of movie stars, musicians, TV personalities and supermodels – many of them drawn to Ash and keen to meet his new girlfriend.

'Hey, Ash, how ya doing?' drawled an impossibly handsome and instantly recognizable figure.

'Hi, Kyle, good to see you again,' said Ash, embracing the movie icon like an old friend.

'And this must be Charley, your guardian angel.' Kyle lifted the back of her hand to his lips. '*Definitely* an angel.'

For a moment Charley was speechless. She was glad of the drink offered to her by a bow-tied waiter – it gave her a chance to compose herself. 'Thank you . . . I'm sure everyone says this, but I love your films. No one does action movies like you.'

'Hey, I only act the hero,' he said humbly. 'You're the *real* action hero.'

He did a couple of karate punches. 'I saw those photos

from Miami. You were like Bruce Lee with that palm strike! Ash, I'm surprised you even need Big T any more,' he said, glancing at the bald-headed veteran behind. 'You should just hire Charley to be your bodyguard.'

Ash laughed. 'It had crossed my mind.'

Charley gave a small smile, but Big T's jaw clenched and he clearly didn't appreciate the joke.

They circulated among the other guests, Ash introducing Charley to more A-list celebrities than she ever dreamt possible. The glamorous side of his superstar life was intoxicating and she had to keep reminding herself that she wasn't there for her own enjoyment but for Ash's protection.

At last the guests were called for the start of the show. With reserved seats in the front row, she and Ash were in prime position next to the catwalk. But no place was reserved for Big T and he was relegated to the ballroom entrance. The house lights dimmed and a thumping dance track blasted out of the speakers. Spotlights lit up the runway stage and a long-legged model glided out from the wings. Wearing only a gossamer-thin dress that shimmered like moonlight, she was greeted by collective gasps of delight and wonder. Another model appeared and strutted down the catwalk in an equally breathtaking design, her off-the-shoulder kimono-inspired gown seeming to have been spun from spider silk.

The ballroom was abuzz as ever more cutting-edge fashions were paraded in front of the celebrity audience. But Charley paid little attention to the clothes and the models. Her mind was too distracted. It kept returning to the ominous message on the mirror.

TO BE AN ANGEL
U NEED 2 DIE FIRST!

The key question was: who had written it?

A jealous fan? With a hurricane of abuse online for being Ash's girlfriend, that was a strong possibility. She'd have to keep tabs on any repeat haters to see if there was a link. But how had the fan accessed her locked hotel room?

This made her think it could be one of the band. If it was, perhaps the death threat was just a tour prank? She'd witnessed the guys playing some pretty cruel jokes on one another. Everything from cling film on the toilet and duct-taping their belongings to the hotel ceiling, to swapping shampoo for hair-removal cream.

But this message didn't feel like a joke, not with the threats made against Ash. Could the maniac trying to kill Ash now want her dead by association? That was a distinct possibility.

Charley figured whoever had written the message wanted to frighten her. Why else give a warning first?

'I don't believe it,' said Ash, his jaw dropping open in shock.

'What?' said Charley, suddenly on high alert.

'It's Hanna.'

A gorgeous teenage girl with dark brown locks was

parading in a show-stopping bejewelled silver dress. As she approached the end of the catwalk, she spied Ash. There was a momentary flare of recognition in her eyes, then she pirouetted away and strode back down the stage.

Ash spent the rest of the show squirming in his seat every time his ex-girlfriend appeared. The model seemed to be purposefully strutting in front of him as if to show him exactly what he'd lost.

After the show, the guests mingled and chatted, the stunning designs a focus of most conversations. As Ash and Charley did the rounds, Hanna made her appearance. She now wore hipster jeans and a cropped white bodice-top that accentuated her toned body, her glossy hair was pulled into a tight ponytail and with only the lightest touch of make-up her natural beauty was stunningly apparent. Charley instantly felt out of her league.

But Hanna's attitude certainly didn't match her looks. 'So, you're into blondes now? I thought it was redheads,' the model said cuttingly to her ex-boyfriend.

Ash gave a pained look. 'Hanna, I've said I'm sorry. Many times.'

Hanna looked down her nose at Charley. 'I'd be careful if I were you. You're playing with fire.'

Charley responded with a civil smile. 'I'm used to getting my fingers burnt,' she replied.

'Well, as long as you've got your eyes wide open. This boy is a player and he'll break your heart.'

'Hey, I'm still here,' said Ash, mortified by her scathing comments.

'More's the pity,' said Hanna, turning on her heel and sashaying away.

Ash stared after her, a wounded look on his face.

'She doesn't like you very much, does she?' remarked Charley.

He shook his head. 'I don't blame her. I made a stupid mistake. Let's go. This party's lost its appeal.'

Charley followed Ash back into the lobby, Big T falling in behind. As they exited the hotel, the line of cameramen beckoned for a photo, but Ash wasn't in the mood to play the gracious rock star. He headed straight for the limo.

Then Gonzo heckled. 'Hasn't Hanna forgiven you?'

Ash shot him a ferocious glare.

'I've still got the picture I took of you and that redhead,' goaded Gonzo, snapping away at Ash's scowl. 'That was a real money shot. Care to repeat your performance?'

Charley saw Ash flush with anger and turn on Gonzo. Before he could launch himself at the lowlife, Charley pulled Ash back and bundled him into the limo.

CHAPTER 66

'What about this one?' asked Ash, pointing to a solid gold Rolex in the jewellery store's display case.

'Very nice,' said Charley. But she barely gave the watch a second glance. Her senses were on full alert. She was convinced someone was following them.

They were browsing in the Grand Canal Shoppes mall inside the Palazzo Hotel. A mini-indoor Venice, it boasted high-end designer shops, upscale boutiques and even water-filled canals complete with gondolas to take people around the mall.

Pete had once again led the paparazzi on a wild goose chase, allowing Ash and Charley to slip away unseen. Ash had admitted he was feeling a little low and Kay had recommended some retail therapy before his gig that evening. At first Charley had thought Ash's mood was to do with bumping into his ex-girlfriend, then she recalled the day's date from the operation folder. It was the anniversary of his mother's death.

As Ash continued to browse the rows of designer watches, Charley studied the reflection in the plate glass of the store window. Applying her anti-surveillance training, she was looking for multiple sightings and any sign of unnatural behaviour among the passing shoppers: people peeping round corners, fidgeting or acting shifty, showing a vacant expression, talking to themselves or fixated on their target.

A steady stream of tourists and shoppers ambled by. Some loitered, others browsed, a few took holiday snaps by the mock canals. But there weren't any faces Charley recognized and no individual stood out from the crowd.

Yet her gut told her someone was out there, watching, waiting, preying on them.

'Have you seen these bracelets, Charley?' said Ash, beckoning her into the adjacent store.

The shop assistant welcomed them and laid out a selection of silver and gold designs. Ash ran his gaze over them, then turned to Charley. 'Which one do you like the best?' he asked.

Charley took a moment from her surveillance to have a quick glance. Her eyes were instantly drawn to a simple bracelet woven from three bands of white gold. 'That one's beautiful,' she said.

'I'll get it for you,' said Ash, pulling out his wallet.

'But it's five thousand dollars!' protested Charley.

He smiled at her. 'So? You're worth it.'

Charley put her hand over his wallet. 'Listen, it's very sweet of you, Ash. But I can't accept it.'

Ash ignored her, handed the shop assistant his debit card and looped the white-gold bracelet around Charley's wrist. 'A thank-you gift,' he said. 'For saving my life.'

As she admired the exquisite piece of jewellery, wondering how she could refuse now, Charley heard the faintest click of a camera.

'It'll be an engagement ring next,' said a snide voice.

At once she knew who'd been following them. Charley couldn't believe it. Was there no place Gonzo couldn't find them? Hounded at every turn, tormented at every moment, she was truly experiencing the claustrophobic nightmare of being a celebrity in the twenty-first century – no privacy, no boundaries, no escape.

Gonzo was their very own stalker.

'Go crawl back into whatever sewer you came from!' Ash snapped.

'That's no way to treat a friend,' replied the pap.

'Friend? Even my worst enemy is more of a friend than you.'

'Harsh, but you've got a lot of enemies from what I hear.'

Fuming, Ash stormed out of the store.

'Just leave us alone, Gonzo,' said Charley, struggling to keep the anger out of her voice.

But Gonzo stalked them through the shopping mall, snapping and filming away non-stop. Each time they entered a store, he'd wait outside, his lens tracking their every movement.

'I'll have you arrested,' Charley threatened as they came out of a boutique.

'I know my rights. I'm on public property – nothing you can do about it.'

Charley felt her fury rising with the man. Even while they had lunch, his camera recorded their every mouthful. They visited a designer clothes store. When they came out, they passed a florist and Gonzo goaded Ash once again. 'How about a bouquet for your girlfriend? And don't forget . . . one for your mother! Lilies are a good choice.'

Charley noticed Ash's eyes redden and his fists clench. Gonzo had taken it too far, even for a paparazzi. Charley felt something snap inside her too. What right did this piece of scum have to stalk and harass them? What right did he have to bring up Ash's dead mother? What right did he have to bait people purely for the purposes of a 'unique' photo he could sell for thousands?

Charley reached into her bag and pulled out a small canister. Before Gonzo knew what was happening, she sprayed his camera lens and face with red gel. Spluttering and swearing, Gonzo furiously tried to wipe the gunk from his eyes.

'Sorry about that,' said Charley. 'It just went off in my hand by accident.'

As Charley sauntered away with Ash, who was staring at her in stunned admiration, Gonzo yelled after them, 'You'll live to regret that, *chica*!'

TARGET
CHAPTER 67

Charley woke to the insistent blare of her alarm clock. Surely it couldn't be morning already? Often on this tour she was so exhausted that she lost track of time, with no idea what day it was, let alone which hotel she was sleeping in. After a while the bedrooms all looked the same. She vaguely recalled they'd reached San Francisco. The gig in Las Vegas had gone without a hitch, as had the ones in Salt Lake City and Seattle, and they were now entering the final phase of the tour. She only had to keep Ash safe a few more days, then the threat of 'No more encores' would be just that – an empty threat.

Groggily, she reached over to switch off the clock. But the alarm continued to ring in her ears. Shrugging off sleep, she smelt the acrid tinge of smoke in the air. At once she sat bolt upright in bed.

FIRE!

Barefoot and in only her T-shirt and shorts, Charley grabbed Ash's spare key card from the bedside table and sprinted for the door. Bugsy's emergency fire training had drilled into her that every second counted in a fire. She tested the temperature of the door handle, then pressed the back of her hand to the door itself. Both were cool to the touch. Confident she wouldn't stumble straight into a blaze, she opened the door and peered out.

A noxious grey haze immediately enveloped her and she started coughing. The corridor was filled with smoke. Guests in all states of dress and undress were fleeing in panic, many with no idea where the nearest fire escapes were and running the wrong way. Jessie and Zoe flew past, along with other members of the road crew.

'Have you seen Ash?' Charley called out.

'No!' cried Zoe, not stopping as she disappeared into the haze of smoke.

Pulling her T-shirt up to her mouth, Charley hammered on Ash's door. No answer.

She guessed that Big T had already evacuated him. But she couldn't take that chance. Slotting the key card into the lock, she accessed his suite.

'ASH?' she called, hurrying through the lounge to the bedroom.

A figure lay sprawled underneath the covers. Charley wondered how on earth Ash could sleep through the klaxon of the fire alarm. Then she spotted the in-ear noise-cancellation headphones.

Charley shook Ash awake. 'GET UP!' she shouted.

Ash blearily opened his eyes. 'What! W-what's going on?'

'Fire!' explained Charley as she dashed into the en suite bathroom and soaked a couple of hand towels. When she came back, Ash was busy gathering up his songbook, laptop and acoustic guitar. 'Leave them! We don't have time.'

'My life ain't worth living without my guitar,' said Ash as he stuffed his songbook into his shorts.

'If we don't get out *now*, you won't have a life, never mind a guitar!' She grabbed his arm and hauled him to the door. She opened it a crack and smoke surged into the room. She slammed it shut.

Ash looked to the balcony. 'Why don't we jump?' he suggested.

Charley gave a strained smile. 'We could. But the pool's on the other side.'

She handed him a dripping wet towel. 'Put this over your mouth and stay close.'

Crouching low to the floor to avoid the worst of the smoke, she eased the door open and led Ash out. The corridor was now a darkening tunnel of grey-white fog. It was impossible to see more than a few feet. She could hear a few straggling guests coughing and spluttering, and in the far distance the howl of fire engines. From her security checks on arrival at the hotel, she knew the nearest fire exit was eight doors and one corridor down. Keeping a hand to the wall, she counted them off as they scurried like frightened mice along the carpet. Her eyes stung from the toxic smoke and she now appreciated how easily disorientated a person could get in a fire. There was no sense of distance or direction; everywhere was a murky grey cloud, furniture and figures appearing and disappearing like ghosts.

After what seemed an age, they reached the fire door. She pushed against the locking bar, but it wouldn't budge. Charley shoved harder. To no avail. Now she knew why the hotel guests had been fleeing in the other direction.

'Let me . . . have a go,' Ash coughed, taking the damp towel from his mouth.

He kicked at the bar. Nothing. So he barged his shoulder against the door. This time it screeched open a fraction. A lick of flames shot out. Ash leapt back, yelling as the sleeve of his top caught alight. The flames rapidly spread across his back.

On impulse Charley dragged him to the floor and rolled him on the carpet. At the same time, she smothered him with her body. She knew her T-shirt was fireproof and prayed she could put out the flames before Ash was seriously burnt.

'I'm . . . all right,' gasped Ash, his top singed black.

But they were now in even more immediate danger. The corridor was on fire. Despite the door being open only a crack, it was enough for the blaze on the other side to finger its way in. Cursing herself for not checking the door first, she pulled Ash to his knees and headed back the other way. Having lost their wet towels, their lungs now filled with suffocating smoke. Coughing and choking, they crawled along the corridor. But in their hurry to escape the advancing flames Charley lost count of the doors. With no clue in which direction or how far the next fire exit was, the two of them stumbled on blindly.

Ash was coughing uncontrollably and Charley's head

pounded and she felt sick. The flames would be the last of their worries. She knew from Bugsy that the majority of deaths in a fire were caused by smoke inhalation rather than burns. They had to escape the corridor and find clear air.

Blinking away acrid tears, Charley reached out desperately in front of her. In the gloom, she discovered a door to a guest room had been left ajar. Pulling Ash inside, she kicked the door shut behind them. Smoke hung around the ceiling in a thick cloud and still seeped in round the frame. But it was a far better situation than the corridor. Leaving Ash hacking on the floor, she threw any towels that she could find into the bath and ran the taps. As soon as the towels were wet, she stuffed them against the edges of the door.

'Charley! Look at this!' croaked Ash, leaning out of the balcony window for fresh air.

Six floors down, a huge crowd had gathered in the darkness. Fire engines, their lights flashing and reflecting off the other buildings, jammed the streets. The beam of a searchlight swept the hotel and illuminated the two of them in the window.

Ash looked at Charley, his face streaked black with soot, and said, 'Take a leap of faith?'

With a final glance back at the smouldering door, Charley nodded and climbed over the balcony. Hand in hand, they jumped.

CHAPTER 68

'I hate to admit it,' said Kay, shaking her head wearily as they breakfasted in the diner opposite the fire-damaged hotel, 'but that makes a great picture!'

She tapped the newspaper with a manicured fingernail. Below the headline – 'Love Birds Flee Nest Fire' – was a photo of Ash and Charley caught mid-plunge over the hotel pool, still clasping one another's hands, the flaming building behind making a dramatic backdrop to their death-defying escape. Of course, Gonzo had been there to catch the moment in all its glory, along with a handful of other shutterbugs in the city. But *he* had been the one to nab the front-page shot.

'The headline's predictably trashy, though,' Kay went on, sipping from her coffee. Despite having been up most of the night, as had everyone else, she somehow managed to retain her elegant looks even in a hotel robe and slippers. Charley and Ash were wrapped in blankets, Big T in a white T-shirt and grey jogging bottoms and, much to the road crew's amusement, Terry had fled the hotel in a pair of blue pyjamas embroidered with yellow teddy bears.

Only Jessie had managed to escape the fire in any reasonable state of dress. She sat with Zoe at the next table in jeans, T-shirt and sneakers.

'But, in all seriousness, either this tour is cursed with the worst bad luck or someone is seriously committed to killing Ash if they're willing to burn down an entire hotel.' Kay put a protective arm round her nephew and smiled at Charley. 'If it wasn't for you, Charley, my Ash wouldn't be sitting here with us now having breakfast. You're certainly proving your worth, young lady.'

'Yeah, well done, Charley,' said Big T, cupping a mug of coffee between his huge hands. 'But next time . . . take the stairs.' He forced a tired smile.

Kay turned to Big T. 'Might I ask where *you* were during all this? Because you certainly weren't at Ash's side.'

Big T dropped his grin and responded with a defensive frown. 'I'm not sure what you're getting at, Ms Gibson. When the fire alarm woke me, I discovered Ash already gone from his room. So, after ensuring everyone else was out, I made my escape. I was the *last* of the crew to leave our floor.'

A frosty look entered Kay's green eyes. 'Not quite the last, as it turned out. Ash was still up there!'

'With Charley,' he pointed out. 'I knew she'd carried out the fire security check so was confident she'd get Ash to safety.'

'Yes, and thank God she did!' said Kay, turning her back on Big T.

Charley saw the wounded look on the old bodyguard's

lined face. She wanted to say something in his defence, but Zoe cut in from the next table. 'Hey, listen to this! Latest update on CNN . . . the fire was no accident!' she exclaimed, reading from a news app on her smartphone. 'The police report states it was arson . . . They've found what appears to be the remnants of a home-made incendiary bomb.' She showed them a picture of a charred can of Hyper energy drink and the remains of a cheap digital watch. 'The fire was started in a housekeeping store cupboard . . . and someone had disabled the hotel's sprinkler system!'

Big T leant forward in his seat. 'Any suspects?'

Zoe read a little further down, then shook her head. 'The police have no leads whatsoever . . . and no one has claimed responsibility so far.'

Charley put down her orange juice. 'The fire *had* to be targeted at Ash.'

Ash glanced up from his omelette, his fork hanging halfway between the plate and his open mouth.

'Fire is a very indiscriminate method of murder,' Big T noted. 'Ash may have escaped unharmed, but other guests didn't. It's a miracle so few were actually hurt in the blaze.'

'But if some maniac is willing to go to those lengths,' Charley pointed out, 'it shows how determined they are.'

Kay narrowed her eyes. 'Aside from the death threats we know about, what makes you think Ash was targeted?'

'Our closest fire exit was blocked,' Charley explained.

Zoe gasped and looked at Jessie. 'Thank heaven you made me run the other way.'

Jessie nodded. 'Yeah, we'd have been trapped too!'

'Good thing you did,' said Ash, setting down his fork. 'The fire was on the other side of the door. Without Charley smothering me, I'd have been burnt to a crisp.'

He took Charley's hand in his. She smiled warmly in response. Their near-death experience had definitely brought them closer.

Big T rubbed his chin thoughtfully. 'It might not have been blocked on purpose. Many fire doors have smoke seals that expand under heat to close the gap between the door and its frame. The fact they worked in this case probably saved your lives.'

'That does seem more likely than a direct attack on Ash,' admitted Kay.

The diner's entrance swung open and Vince approached their table. 'I've been informed that it's safe to return to the hotel and collect our belongings,' said their security guard.

'Well, thank God for the San Francisco fire service,' said Kay. 'I just hope they managed to save my dresses.' She raised an eyebrow in response to Terry's shocked expression. 'That's a joke, Terry, in case you're wondering.'

They rose from the table and headed back to the hotel. From the outside there appeared to be little damage, just a few shattered windows and black smears of soot staining the outer walls. Entering the lobby, the reception area was in organized chaos, but a VIP representative from the hotel swiftly escorted their group past security and up the stairs.

The benefits of being a celebrity, thought Charley.

On the sixth floor, she and the others were confronted by the full devastation wreaked by the blaze. The corridor was scorched and the walls blackened. The harsh acrid tang of smoke still hung in the air and the carpet was soaked with water from the fire hoses. As they each peeled off to gather their belongings, Charley was amazed to discover her and Ash's rooms were untouched by the fire, their closed doors having held back the flames. There was still the reek of smoke, but that appeared to be the only serious damage.

Next door she heard Ash exclaim his delight at finding his guitar in one piece. She looked in and smiled to herself when she saw him caressing the instrument like a long-lost lover. But she noticed the Intruder device that she'd attached to Ash's door frame had melted beyond repair.

Returning to her room, Charley checked and repacked the contents of her Go-bag: spare Intruders, half-empty pepper spray, high-impact pen, first-aid kit, comms unit, torch. As expected, her phone registered several missed calls from Buddyguard HQ – Jason's concern growing with each voicemail message – and a bunch of warning texts from the Intruder device catching her entering and leaving Ash's room during the fire. She deleted these, then called HQ.

The phone was picked up on the first ring. 'Charley! Is Ash OK?' asked Jason.

'Yes, he's fine,' she replied. 'I am too. Thanks for asking.'

'That's a relief,' he said, though Charley wasn't sure if he was referring to her or Ash or both of them. 'We saw the fire on the news and pictures of your dramatic escape, but we were worried that we hadn't had any contact from you.'

'I'd left my phone in the room. For obvious reasons, I was in a bit of a rush to get out,' she explained. 'But I've got your messages now.'

'Yeah, the colonel insisted that I kept calling.'

'And I was beginning to think you cared.'

'Not a chance,' Jason replied. 'Report in later.' Then, before signing off, he added, 'Stay safe, Charley.'

'Will do,' she replied, unable to suppress a smile at his note of concern.

Putting the phone back in her bag, she hunted through her suitcase for some clean clothes that didn't stink too much of smoke. She was now grateful for Bugsy's foresight in supplying fireproof clothing. As she pulled on a pair of jeans, she noticed a white hotel envelope on the carpet behind the door. She picked it up, frowned at the blank front and peeled open the seal. Inside was a clipping from a tabloid magazine: Gonzo's photo of her with Ash at the restaurant in Dallas. Pasted beneath it in letters cut out from a newspaper were the words:

ASHES 2 ASHES, DUST 2 DUST

SO WILL U BE

TARGET
CHAPTER 69

Ash was certainly a trouper. Despite a sore throat from smoke inhalation and surviving yet another attempt on his life, he was resolved to perform for his San Franciscan fans at the Oakland Oracle Arena that night. He burst on to the stage with a kamikaze-like energy, his gravelly voice more than suiting his style of rock music. As Charley watched him literally rip one of his guitars apart during a solo, then set it on fire, she wondered if Ash's third brush with death had tipped him over the edge. He was acting as if this might be his last ever concert on earth.

Then again, she thought, his extreme performance might be his way of letting off steam. Whatever, this gig was jaw-dropping and his fans, sensing Ash's desperation, were going wild for him.

Behind the scenes, Kay had taken up the reins alongside Terry as tour manager, her presence an iron rod to band and crew alike. Nothing was being overlooked in terms of stage management or venue security. Everything had been triple-checked. The gigs were being run like a military operation.

But Charley knew someone had slipped the net.

The newspaper threat she'd received couldn't be any more clear. The fire had been a premeditated attack on her and Ash. And if she needed any more proof she'd subsequently read in a news report that the arson investigators had found the burnt-out remains of a cleaning trolley wedged behind the fire door on their floor of the hotel.

Charley had harboured a tiny hope that the message on the mirror had been a prank, a hoax, or at the most a knee-jerk reaction by a jealous fan at the Dallas concert. But she could no longer delude herself.

The homicidal maniac was on the tour with them.

How else did that person know the hotels they were staying at, discover which rooms she and Ash were in, and pass unquestioned through their security checks?

In order to carry out the crimes, the culprit had to have access backstage, to the hotels and to the tour bus. Only somebody with an official pass could move unseen and undetected. The idea of it chilled her blood and made her more paranoid than ever.

The enemy was definitely within!

Charley had her suspicions who the perpetrator might be, but no direct proof. The envelope with its newspaper clipping was now in the pocket of her jeans. She hadn't yet told Big T or Buddyguard about it. She knew that Colonel Black would instantly pull her off the assignment and she didn't trust anyone else, not even Big T, to keep Ash safe. She had to see this assignment through to the end. It was her duty.

Besides, if the maniac was who she thought it was, then she could handle them easily enough when they showed their hand. But when would that be? And would she be in the right place at the right time to stop them?

Any mistake, delay or miscalculation in her reactions could result in Ash's death.

Charley remembered the tattoo on Big T's inner forearm. A pair of weighted scales and the words: *Guilty until proven innocent*.

She couldn't afford to wait. She couldn't risk Ash's life any longer.

Pete was standing beside Jessie, bobbing and weaving in time to the music, mouthing the words in sync with Ash, as he did every night. Jessie was gazing in reverential awe at her hero on the stage, her hands clasped to her chest in deep devotion. Both had an unnatural obsession with Ash, but only one had a motive to kill him.

Convinced who it was, Charley made up her mind to act. She radioed for back-up, then confronted Ash's stalker.

CHAPTER 70

'What's all this about?' demanded Jessie, as she was shoved into a chair in an empty dressing room.

Vince stood by the door, while Rick kept a hand on Jessie's shoulder and ensured she stayed seated.

'Don't play innocent with me,' said Charley. 'You know exactly why you're here.'

Jessie's eyes flicked from Vince's impassive face to Rick's stony expression and back to the furious glare Charley was giving her. The startled girl looked like she might burst into tears at any moment. Charley thought Jessie was putting on a convincing act. But of course she'd have to be a good actress in order to con her way into everyone's trust.

'Charley, what have I done?' she pleaded.

'Aside from set fire to the hotel? Try to kill Ash.'

'What?' exclaimed Jessie. 'Why would I want to hurt Ash? I love him.'

'That's exactly why. That's your motive. You're obsessed with Ash to the point of madness.'

'No, *this* is madness. I haven't done anything but support

him,' said Jessie angrily. She tried to rise, but Rick firmly pushed her back down.

The door to the dressing room opened and Big T stormed in. 'What's going on?' he demanded.

'This is who's behind all the threats and attacks on Ash,' stated Charley, stepping aside.

Big T stared at the frightened girl in the chair. 'What, Jessie?' he said, his thick brow creasing in scepticism. 'But she runs Ash's US fan club. She's his biggest fan.'

'Gives her the perfect cover,' argued Charley. 'In order to stage these so-called accidents she needed to have complete access to all locations. Her tour pass is the ticket to her crimes.'

'You're insane!' spat Jessie. 'You're making accusations without any shred of proof!'

Big T cocked his head at Charley. 'She's got a point. Where's your evidence?'

'Well . . . there isn't anything that directly incriminates her,' admitted Charley, 'but there's a lot of circumstantial evidence that points to Jessie.'

'Go on,' said Big T, leaning against the wall and crossing his arms.

Charley took a deep breath. She'd been thinking hard since the discovery of the envelope that morning. 'I can't say whether any of this links back to the original letter bomb or the "No more encores" death threat. But I do know that I found Jessie sneaking around backstage the night of the spotlight accident. She was hiding behind the drum riser, right next to one of the wire-rope ladders that led up to the lighting rig.'

Jessie rolled her eyes. 'I told you at the time I wanted to see the stage setting like Ash does.'

'I believe she'd just come down the ladder after rigging the spotlight and was checking that it was aligned with the toaster lift,' Charley continued, ignoring the girl's incredulous laugh. 'Next, a little before Ash was electrocuted, Jessie took his microphone for the acoustic set. I think she may have switched it for the faulty one.'

Jessie snorted in disbelief. 'Oh, come on! Really? You were there with me. How was I supposed to do that? I'm not a magician.'

'But you were the only one to handle it, apart from the crew. Geoff also complained that you had touched the gear before. That in itself is suspicious,' responded Charley. 'Then there's the fire last night. A few things have struck me as odd. First, it's funny how you knew not to go to the closest fire exit, the one that was blocked.'

'I didn't know *which* way I was running,' argued Jessie. 'I don't think anyone did. It was chaos.'

'But at breakfast Zoe said you made her run your way. Why?'

'I-I . . . don't know. I thought that way was the closest exit.'

'But you just said you didn't know which way you were running. You're lying!'

Jessie began to cry, her mascara running down her plump cheeks in black lines.

Charley wasn't going to let herself be swayed by crocodile tears. 'Second, I found it strange that you were fully dressed in the middle of the night. That indicates you were ready for the fire.'

'I-I don't go to bed until late,' sobbed Jessie. 'I was updating Ash's fan website . . . Honest . . . You can look at my posts. You'll see the times I uploaded them.'

'Posts can be scheduled in advance.'

'Oh, you have an answer for everything, don't you?' snapped Jessie, glaring at Charley through tear-filled eyes. 'You just want to get rid of me. You're the one who's paranoid. You've got your claws into Ash and now you want to make sure no one else has him.'

Charley laughed. 'That's exactly what *you're* trying to do. You've admitted you love him many times. You even stated that you'd kill to be in my position. You're jealous. And because you can't have him you've decided no one will.'

Leaping up from her chair, Jessie swiped her false red nails at Charley's face. 'You liar!'

Charley barely managed to evade the razor-sharp points. Instinctively defending herself, she aimed a knife-hand strike to the girl's neck.

'Enough!' barked Big T, grabbing hold of her wrist mid-strike. Rick seized Jessie in his arms and pulled the two girls apart. 'Charley, this is all very thin. Pure speculation. Don't you have any firm proof?'

Charley took out her mobile phone. 'The day after Ash and I were photographed in the restaurant, I too started receiving death threats. Most were online, but this one was written on my bathroom mirror.'

Charley brought up the photo she'd taken of the lipstick threat:

TO BE AN ANGEL
U NEED 2 DIE FIRST!

'Recognize your handwriting, Jessie?' she asked, tilting the screen in her direction. Jessie's eyes widened and she shook her head vigorously in denial.

'Why the hell didn't you bring this to my attention sooner?' said Big T, his jaw tensing.

'I thought it was a tour prank,' Charley replied. 'But then I got this.'

She pulled out the magazine clipping and showed it to him.

ASHES 2 ASHES, DUST 2 DUST
SO WILL U BE

'I'm sure this'll be familiar to you too, Jessie,' said Charley.

Jessie stared at the picture in horror. 'I didn't do *that*,' she replied, her voice small and quiet.

Big T grabbed the clipping from Charley's hand. 'This is no tour prank! When did you get this?'

'I-I only just came across it . . . earlier this morning,' explained Charley, stumbling over her words.

'*This morning!*' Big T threw his hands up in disbelief, then he waved the clipping in her face. 'This changes everything. This confirms the fire was a direct attack on

Ash! The police need to be told. If I'd known you were under threat too, I'd –'

Charley's phone rang. She turned away from Big T and answered it. 'Hello?'

The voice on the other end of the line declared, 'I've done it.'

TARGET
CHAPTER 71

'Done what?' asked Charley, pressing her mobile to her ear.

'I've traced the accident messages,' repeated Amir, the excitement in the new recruit's voice matched only by the speed at which he tried to explain his findings. 'I'm sorry it took me so long, but you didn't give me much to go on. A couple of internet posts with different accounts. But I managed to hack into them both easily enough and dig up more messages. Of course, they were dummy accounts, created with false email addresses that led to fake personal information. Pretty much a dead end for your average hacker. But I reverse-tracked *how* the messages were posted.'

He paused, clearly expecting Charley to be impressed at this flash of hacking insight.

'OK . . . and?' prompted Charley, holding up a hand to stop Big T interrupting the call.

'All of them were posted using the *same* phone,' he revealed. 'Obviously, the IP addresses were dynamic so I couldn't discover it that way. And the suspect kept changing the SIM card so the phone number wasn't fixed or traceable. They're being very careful to cover their tracks. But the IMEI number of the phone itself is constant.'

'IMEI number?' asked Charley, bewildered by Amir's technical lingo.

'IMEI stands for International Mobile-station Equipment Identity number. You can easily find out your own phone's IMEI by typing *#06# into your keypad. The number is used to identify any device that uses terrestrial cellular networks. By that, I mean non-satellite communication. Each number is unique to its device and coded into the hardware, making it virtually impossible to change.'

'That's all very informative, Amir, but how does any of that help me?'

'It means the device can be tracked!' said Amir, a broad smile evident in the tone of his voice.

Charley smiled too. She eyed Jessie. She had her now!

'Since the suspect is using prepaid SIM cards, we obviously don't know who the phone belongs to,' continued Amir. 'But I managed to hack the network carrier and source the current mobile phone number associated with our suspect's IMEI number. I'm texting you both of them now.'

Charley's phone beeped with a received message.

'I'm also updating your phone remotely with a tracker device,' Amir explained. 'It's a program I've designed. It'll take a minute or so to upload, but then you'll be able to pinpoint the suspect's phone to within two or three metres –'

'Charley!' cut in Big T, his wrinkled face hard and unforgiving as granite. 'We need to talk about this threat *now*. And I think we can let Jessie go, don't you? There's nothing credible linking her to the accidents, apart from your rather tenuous speculation.'

'Guilty until proven innocent,' Charley reminded him, pointing to the tattoo on his arm. She waved her mobile in the air. 'I've got the proof we need right here.'

Turning to Jessie, she ordered, 'Give me your phone.'

'Why?'

'Just do it.' Charley snatched the mobile from Jessie's hand and typed in *#06# to reveal its unique IMEI number. She compared it with the one on her screen, confident of exactly what she'd find.

It didn't match.

Charley checked it again and an awful sick feeling weighed heavily in the pit of her stomach.

Wishing the ground would swallow her up, she handed back Jessie's mobile. 'I'm sorry . . . I've made a mistake.'

'You most certainly have!' snapped Jessie, shooting her evils, before stomping out of the dressing room.

Big T let out a heavy sigh and shook his head in disappointment. 'Charley, we've some serious talking to do.'

In her despondent daze, Charley heard Amir's voice drifting up from her phone. 'Hey, Charley, are you still there? The tracker app should be working now. The green dot is you. The red dot is your suspect.'

Charley studied the screen. A map of the venue was displayed. The app correctly located her in the dressing room.

A red dot appeared right next to the stage.

TARGET

CHAPTER 72

How could she have been so stupid! She'd made the wrong assumption. Jessie wasn't Ash's stalker. Barging past Big T, Charley ran for the door.

'Where are you going?' shouted Big T.

'It's Pete!' Charley cried, dodging Vince's attempt to grab her and sprinting down the corridor.

At this very moment the killer had been left all alone and unguarded. Charley wasn't there. Nor were Vince, Rick or Big T. Ash was completely vulnerable to an attack . . . and she was responsible.

Shouldering a roadie aside, she rounded a corner at speed and dashed down the hallway that led to the stage. The sound of twenty thousand fans screaming echoed off the walls. Her heart was pounding in her chest almost as loud as the heavy bass thud blasting from the venue's speakers.

She'd always suspected Pete. Why hadn't she listened to her gut instincts? Yes, Jessie was the obvious and logical candidate for the infatuated stalker. But Pete was the deluded and dangerous one. His copycat behaviour was a clear sign of his mental instability. What sane person would imitate their idol to the point of changing their appearance entirely and getting the exact same tattoo on their arm?

It only struck Charley now that her death threats had started right after Pete had joined the tour in his semi-official capacity as a decoy. With his ability to pass off as Ash, he could have easily accessed her room without question from security, especially since she and Ash were perceived to be an item. Similarly, Pete had the golden opportunity to wander around backstage without anyone so much as batting an eyelid. He was Ash the rock star! He could go anywhere he wanted. Not only could he have swapped the mics, but Pete was likely the one who'd started the fire at the hotel.

And at any moment Pete could strike again.

Charley ran up the steps to the wings of the stage. In the dimly lit recesses, a couple of sound technicians were prepping gear and a small group of VIP guests huddled to one side watching the show. But where was Pete?

Charley hunted around for him. He was nowhere to be found. Perhaps he'd moved over to the opposite wing? She checked Amir's tracker app. Her green dot was now situated beside the stage; the red dot was *on* the stage.

She was too late!

Elbowing her way through a knot of VIPs, she ran on to the main stage. The music was thunderous. The spotlights were blinding and she had to shield her eyes as she looked for Pete. Was he among the dancers? The band? The front row? Or already attacking Ash?

The dancers were moving at such a frenetic pace it was hard to keep track of everyone. Ash was strutting down the stage's guitar neck, singing for all he was worth to the audience, lost in the zone. But Pete wasn't anywhere to be seen. She rechecked the tracker app. The red dot definitely located him on the stage, less than fifteen metres from where she stood. Maybe Amir's app didn't work after all.

'*Get off the stage!*' hissed a beer-bellied roadie, yanking Charley by the arm.

As she was dragged back into the wings, she happened to glance up and notice the lighting rig. Of course, the app only displayed a two-dimensional map. Pete could be right above her. Squinting her eyes, she searched the rig. It was difficult to make out much against the multiple banks of flashing lights, but she could see the spotlight operators in their suspended chairs, tracking Ash with their focus beams. If Pete was up there, they'd surely know about it and have radioed security by now. All the wire-rope ladders had been hauled up before the start of the concert, so how would Pete have climbed there mid-show?

The song 'Every Day Like The Sun' came to an end and the drummer began pounding out a distinctive backbeat. The crowd went into a frenzy as Ash launched into his 'Indestructible' routine. Above the noise, Charley heard Big T's furious voice in her earpiece.

'*Charley! What's going on? Where are you? Report in right now!*'

Charley couldn't think straight with all his shouting in her ear. She tugged out the wireless earpiece, pocketed it and studied the tracker app again. She racked her brains as to where Pete could be hiding. If he wasn't on the stage . . . or above it . . . he had to be *under* it!

Bounding down the steps two at a time, she reached the bottom, then dashed round to the walkway that led beneath the stage to the toaster lift. The passage was poorly lit by a scant run of bulbs, the criss-cross of scaffolding to either side looking like a steel forest in a horror movie. It wasn't the sort of placc to explore alone. Nevertheless she entered the passage and crept along, her eyes darting from side to side. From above, the muffled beat of 'Indestructible' thumped away, sending vibrations down the steel struts.

Her face lit by the soft glow of her phone screen, she advanced deeper under the stage, watching her green dot slowly converge with the red one. Up ahead in the gloom, she spied someone moving. A figure was hunched over the hydraulic controls to the lift. He had a wrench and was uncoupling a pressure valve. Charley allowed herself a triumphant smile. She'd caught Pete in the act of sabotaging the toaster lift. She had all the proof she needed.

'Stop *right now*!' she warned, coming up behind him.

The figure spun round in shock and Charley was confronted by the roadie with the caveman-like beard. 'You're not Pete,' she gasped.

'No, I'm not,' grunted Geoff. 'What are you doing under here? It's restricted access.'

'What are *you* doing?' she replied, eyeing the open hydraulic unit.

He held up the wrench. 'Safety inspection of the lift. We

have to triple-check everything now. It's a flipping nightmare,' he grumbled.

'Sorry, I was looking for someone else,' she said, turning and heading back the way she'd come. Charley glanced again at her phone. On the screen her green dot sat almost right on top of the red. She peered into the dark recesses beneath the stage. Pete had to be hiding somewhere in the shadows.

Somehow she had to flush him out.

Bringing up Amir's text, she selected the mobile number linked to the IMEI and pressed *call*. In the darkness, a phone buzzed and a screen lit up.

TARGET

CHAPTER 73

If Charley hadn't turned towards the sound of the vibrating phone, her brains would have been splattered all over the floor. But she caught sight of the wrench a millisecond before it struck and managed to dodge the fatal blow. The heavy metal tool glanced off her shoulder, sending a rivet of pain through her arm.

Crying out, she dropped her phone and staggered backwards.

Geoff swung the wrench again. Charley ducked and the tool clanged loudly against a metal strut. She tried to defend herself, but her arm was dead. The wrench came down and Charley dived between the scaffolding. She landed hard against a cross-beam, all the breath knocked out of her.

The roadie stepped through the gap as she tried to crawl away.

'Where you going, Wild Cat?' he taunted. '*Ashes to ashes, dust to dust, so shall you be!*'

Charley's eyes widened in horror. The roadie had made the death threats! He was behind everything: the letter bomb, the spotlight, the mic, the fire . . .

The killer roadie raised the wrench above his head, a maniacal grin cutting through his thick bush of a beard like a sliver of bone. 'Time for Ash's guardian angel to become a real angel!'

Charley held up her hands in a vain attempt to protect herself as Geoff brought down his wrench with the force of a sledgehammer. But an overhead strut stopped the tool dead. He glanced up in stunned annoyance. Seizing her chance, Charley kicked out hard and connected with the roadie's kneecap. Geoff bellowed in agony and crumpled to the floor.

Charley scrambled to her feet. As she tried to get away, he made a wild swing with the wrench and struck her across the shins. Screaming from the bone-numbing pain, she fell forward and caught her chin on a steel strut. Stars burst before her eyes. Through the ringing in her ears, Charley could still hear Ash singing, oblivious to her plight just a couple of metres beneath him, the music on stage drowning out the noise of their brutal fight below.

Geoff began pulling himself upright. 'For that I'm going to break every bone in your body, Wild Cat. Ash won't even recognize you when I'm finished!'

Dazed and hurting, Charley dragged herself through the maze of scaffolding. She needed help. Glancing around, she spotted her smartphone on the floor. The roadie limped after her. Charley scrambled forward and snatched up her phone. Flicking the volume button, she turned to face her attacker.

Geoff laughed. 'Too late to call for help,' he said, winding up to beat her senseless.

Before he could whip the wrench round, Charley darted forward and thrust the arcing stun phone into the roadie's chest. Geoff's whole body convulsed and he let out a guttural shriek. His muscles locked up and the wrench clattered to the floor. Totally incapacitated, he toppled backwards and would have fallen if not for the scaffolding behind. Instead he hung like a limp rag doll from the bars.

'How's that for a stunning performance?' said Charley, her head still reeling from chinning the steel strut.

She leant against the toaster lift for support. Her shins were on fire, her ribs ached, her shoulder throbbed and she tasted blood in her mouth from a split lip. Yet she knew she was lucky to be alive.

She also knew she needed back-up. Charley fumbled in her pocket for her wireless earpiece.

But the iStun hadn't stayed in contact long enough to knock the roadie completely out. All of a sudden he lunged at her. Charley tried to stun him again, but he batted her arm aside and the phone went flying. Geoff threw himself on top of her and his heavy bulk sent them both crashing to the ground. In their struggle, his hands found her neck. Charley gasped for air as he began to squeeze mercilessly.

With only seconds on her side, Charley drove the tips of her fingers into the notch above his collarbone. Geoff gagged and jerked away. Charley tried to kick him off, but he was too big and strong.

Fight smarter, not harder, Jody had said.

Charley now targeted a knife-hand strike at his neck. Though she couldn't put her full force behind it, the single sharp blow to the man's jugular vein caused an involuntary muscle spasm and a burst of intense pain. Eyes bulging, he rolled away in agonized shock.

Charley found her feet. But the roadie, recovering fast, had the wrench in his hand again. As he swung wildly at her, she tried to block his attack, but her arm was still dead and her reaction too slow. The wrench hit her in the stomach. She doubled over in agony. Taking full advantage of her weakened state, Geoff shoved her against the toaster lift and forced the edge of the wrench against her throat. Charley choked as she felt her windpipe being crushed.

'Where's *your* guardian angel when you need one, Wild Cat?' he hissed, digging the wrench harder into her throat.

TARGET

CHAPTER 74

Charley couldn't breathe. Her feet barely touched the ground as the roadie pinned her to the side of the lift. She clawed at his face in an attempt to blind him, but her efforts to stop him killing her were becoming weaker with every second. Her eyes rolled in their sockets and what little light there was below the stage began to fade from her vision. Her own frantic heartbeat pounded louder in her ears than the muffled thud of the bass drum above. In the swirl of sound and fury, she'd heard the roadie hiss, '*Where's* your *guardian angel when you need one, Wild Cat?*'

His savage face leered at her like a bearded devil, the bloodlust in his eyes horrifying. Then out of the darkness another face appeared, ghost-white and hairless.

'Right behind you,' said the angel, swinging a massive right hook into the man's jaw that almost knocked his head clean off.

The pressure on her throat instantly ceased and Charley dropped to the floor. Spluttering and gasping for air, she looked up into the wrinkled face of her guardian angel.

'The legend strikes again!' Big T grinned, flexing the enormous bicep of his right arm and enlarging the words DANGER: WEAPON OF MASS DESTRUCTION inside his cruise-missile tattoo. 'You OK?' he asked.

Rubbing at her tender throat, Charley nodded. She found it painful to swallow; otherwise she was in one piece. She glanced at the roadie now lying flat out cold on the floor. 'Is he dead?' she croaked.

'He deserves to be,' said Big T, kneeling down to check. 'But he's not. So what's Geoff's grudge with you? I thought you were looking for Pete.'

'I was,' rasped Charley. 'But Geoff's the one responsible for all the attacks on Ash.'

Big T raised a dubious eyebrow. 'Are you *certain* this time?'

Charley nodded and pointed to the hydraulic unit. 'I caught him sabotaging the toaster lift. Amir's tracking app brought me to this exact location. If you look at the roadie's phone, I guarantee you'll find the IMEI number matches the mobile used to post the accident messages. And I think the fact he tried to kill me confirms it all!'

'Good enough for me,' said Big T. 'Vince! Rick! Pick up the garbage, will you?'

Big T helped Charley to her feet. 'You look like you've gone ten rounds with Tyson.'

'I feel it too,' Charley told him, limping over to retrieve her phone.

'You're lucky Jessie spotted you going beneath the stage. I never would've found you otherwise,' said Big T as he picked up the roadie's mobile from the hydraulic unit. 'Next time respond to my calls.'

'Sorry,' said Charley with a weak smile. 'My earpiece fell out.'

Big T narrowed his eyes, but let the matter drop.

Above, the concert was still going on, the audience screaming in delight. Charley followed Big T out from under the stage, wincing at every step. The unconscious Geoff was dragged to an empty dressing room by Vince and Rick, and dumped in a chair.

Big T chucked a glass of water in the man's face. 'Let's see what this scumbag has to say for himself.'

Geoff groaned. His eyes flickered open and darted nervously between the faces of the bodyguards. 'Whasss . . . what's going on?' he slurred, holding his fractured jaw.

Big T bent down to eye level with the roadie. 'You're being held under suspicion of attempted murder of both Ash Wild and Charley here.'

'I don't know what you're talking about. I was just doing my job and this wild cat jumped me.' He pointed an accusing finger at Charley.

Before Charley could protest, the door opened and Terry strode in. He stared at the broken-jawed roadie. 'What the hell's happened to Geoff?'

'He had a run-in with my fist,' explained Big T. 'You see, Geoff's the maniac trying to kill Ash.'

'*Geoff?*' exclaimed Terry. 'But he's been with the tour from the start. One of the hardest-working roadies – first to arrive and last to leave.'

'Charley caught him sabotaging the toaster lift,' Big T told him. 'We suspect he was trying to rig another accident.'

'That's not true!' Geoff turned to Terry with pleading eyes. 'I was following your instructions. You asked for everything to be triple-checked.'

Terry nodded. 'That's right, I did.'

Big T held up the roadie's mobile. 'Charley has hard proof your phone was used to post the accident death threats against Ash.'

'That's not my phone,' stated Geoff.

Charley gasped. 'That phone was right next to him. He's lying!'

Big T frowned and Charley saw his belief in her claims beginning to waver. 'So why were you trying to kill Charley then?' he demanded.

Geoff put on a wounded look. 'What? *She* attacked me! I was trying to restrain her.'

'That's a lie too!' cried Charley. 'He repeated the "ashes to ashes" threat, then attacked me with a wrench! He's a maniac. He wants to kill Ash *and* me. Big T, you *saw* him choking me!'

Terry held up a hand. 'Enough! Big T, I told you to keep this girl on a leash. First it was the laser, then the backpack bomb and now this. Attacking one of my own road crew! She's gone too far this time. I want her out and off this tour right now!'

'But –'

'No buts, Big T. You're already on thin ice with Kay.

Don't give me an excuse to have you fired too!' Terry put his arm round Geoff and helped him to his feet.

'Thank you, Terry,' slurred Geoff. 'If she goes, I might not press charges.'

'That's more than they deserve,' said Terry, leading the injured man towards the door.

Charley watched speechless as the killer roadie walked free.

TARGET

CHAPTER 75

Charley knew if Geoff stepped out of that door they'd never see him again and Ash would forever be in danger.

So would she.

As the roadie limped past, the malice in his steel-blue eyes was terrifying. Compelled to act, Charley ran to block the doorway but stopped as Kay marched into the room.

'What's this about Ash's attacker being caught?' she demanded.

'Afraid not, Kay,' said Terry, still supporting Geoff, who had his head bowed and a hand to his fractured jaw. 'It's yet another false alarm from your pet bodyguard.'

Kay glanced at Charley, raising an eyebrow at her split lip and bruised throat. She turned to Big T. 'What's going on here? And what's happened to Charley?'

Big T glared at the roadie in Terry's arms. 'I just managed to stop that man strangling Charley with a wrench.'

'My God!' gasped Kay. 'Why would he do that?'

'Charley didn't realize he was carrying out a safety inspection of the toaster lift,' explained Big T. 'It seems a case of mistaken identity. Things got out of hand and –'

'NO!' shouted Charley. 'That man was sabotaging the lift to kill Ash. Why won't anyone believe me?'

Big T laid a hand on her shoulder. 'Charley, enough's enough. You've already accused one innocent person today.'

'And you're always crying wolf,' Terry added. 'Kay, I can vouch for Geoff's innocence. In my opinion, Charley is the paranoid lunatic that should be locked up.'

'Well, *I* don't trust any man who beats up a girl.' Kay's eyes blazed. 'Vince, radio a technician to check the lift.'

Vince nodded, thumbed his mic and made the call.

'I was in the middle of fixing it,' protested Geoff, his hand still pressed to his bearded jaw.

'He's lying again!' cried Charley. 'Look at him! He's got guilt written all over his face.'

For the first time Kay properly looked at the roadie's face. Her eyes widened. 'I know you! Your name's not Geoff!'

Dropping his hand from his face, the roadie snarled, 'Screw you, Kay!'

Shrugging off Terry, he pounced on the music manager. His fingers dug into her throat as he slammed her against the wall. Big T and Rick were on him in seconds. But the roadie refused to let go. Charley stepped in and side-kicked his kneecap, targeting the same one as before. There was a sickening crunch and the roadie shrieked as he dropped to the floor.

'Good kick, Charley,' grunted Big T as he and Rick pinned the man down.

Running a trembling hand through her red hair and flattening her creased blouse, Kay looked scornfully at the squirming roadie. 'You can tell that to the police when they arrive . . . *Brandon*.'

'Brandon?' said Charley, staring hard at the roadie. Now that Kay had said his name Charley vaguely recognized the man. She'd downloaded his picture into the operation folder. He'd been slimmer, blond-haired and with stubble, unlike the dark-haired bearded man now writhing on the floor at their feet. But his steel-blue eyes were unmistakable. This was Brandon Mills, the songwriter who'd accused Ash of copying the hit 'Only Raining'.

Brandon squirmed in the bodyguards' grip, spitting at Kay. 'Ash stole my song! My life!'

Kay regarded him with contempt. 'And you broke my heart, among other things.'

As she strode out of the room, her sharp stiletto just happened to stamp on his hand.

CHAPTER 76

'I blame myself,' admitted Kay, standing with Charley and Big T at the side of the stage as Ash prepared for his encore at the Oakland Oracle Arena. They'd all been unnerved to discover Terry's trusted roadie was Brandon Mills. However, since his arrest by the San Franciscan police, it looked as if Ash would be safe from any further murder attempts. 'If I'd joined the tour earlier I might have recognized that psycho songwriter!'

'None of us did,' said Big T, 'and he was right under our noses.'

Kay rounded on the veteran bodyguard. 'Perhaps you should get your eyes tested?'

Big T's jaw tightened and his nostrils flared.

'Brandon was well disguised,' said Charley, coming to Big T's defence. 'He fooled us all.'

Charley cast her mind back. She remembered the bearded roadie descending the wire-rope ladder just before the bomb scare and spotlight accident. And he was the one who'd yelled at Jessie for handling the microphone before he set it up himself on stage. After seeing the 'ashes to ashes' death threat, the police were going to review the hotel CCTV footage for any sign of Brandon before the fire. Charley had no doubt they'd find that evidence, just as they'd be able to link him to the 'No more encores' letter and the backmasking threat on Ash's last single. Nor would she be surprised if the tyre blowout that caused the coach crash had been another of his deliberate accidents. Brandon was a nasty piece of work.

A technician had inspected the toaster lift's hydraulic unit and discovered that it was primed to go off like a cannon. On its next use, the central piston would have shot straight through the platform and speared Ash like a harpooned whale. It would have been a gruesome and very painful death.

Charley wondered how anyone could become so deranged over an Ash Wild song that he wanted to kill not only Ash but anyone else who got in the way.

A single glance at the hysterical audience clamouring for an encore answered that question. There didn't appear to be a sane person in the whole venue. With mad eyes, wild hair and mouths fixed in permanent screams, everyone was going crazy for the rock star as he walked out on stage and began playing his worldwide hit 'Only Raining'.

The familiar chimes of the song's opening riff filled the massive arena and as the crowd roared their approval Charley thought her eardrums might burst.

'Ash is on fire tonight!' remarked Kay, tapping her thigh in time to the beat of the music.

She was right. This had to be one of the best concerts of

the whole tour. And, though she'd missed most of it, Charley could finally enjoy Ash's performance without worrying that some tragedy was about to hit him.

Ash was safe now, his stalker destined for a lifetime in jail.

The threat of 'no more encores' was no more.

Leaning close, Kay spoke above the music into Charley's ear. 'You certainly lived up to your word and protected Ash. In fact, I intend to speak with Colonel Black at the end of the tour about extending your –'

From the opposite wing, they both saw Ash dash on to the stage.

But that was impossible since Ash was already performing.

Before Charley or anyone else could react, the new Ash shoved his other self violently off the stage. The assaulted Ash flew through the air and disappeared into the security pit. It happened so fast that many fans wondered if they'd seen it at all – especially since the band played on and their idol still stood on the stage, haloed in a spotlight, no break in his performance. But when the new Ash began singing it was obvious to everyone that he was a fraud.

Sprinting over, Charley leapt down from the stage, reaching the real Ash at the same time as the other security guards. He lay in a heap, having fallen head first more than two metres on to the concrete floor.

'I think I've broken my neck!' Ash gasped.

Charley knelt down beside him.

'Keep still,' she whispered. 'We'll call an ambulance.' Tears clouded her vision and her throat choked with a sob.

After all she'd been through that night, she'd failed to protect him from the forgotten threat – Pete.

'I don't need an ambulance,' explained Ash. 'I need a new guitar.'

He held up his busted instrument, its neck cocked at a severe angle, only held on by the steel strings. 'I had to let it go to break my fall.'

Charley burst into relieved laughter and hugged him. 'I thought you were really hurt.'

'Nah, I'm fine,' said Ash, sitting up.

She helped the dazed rock star back to his feet. On stage Big T had seized Pete in a headlock and the band finally stopped playing.

'I *am* Ash!' declared the boy, struggling in Big T's crushing grip. '*He's* the impostor!' He pointed an accusing finger at Ash in the pit with Charley.

'Save it, Pete. We all heard your lame attempt to sing,' said Big T.

'But . . . I've got a sore throat from the fire,' Pete pleaded as he was dragged away.

Ash clambered back on stage to the rapturous applause of his fans. Shouldering a new guitar, he joked to them, 'Fame must have gone to his head!'

As the audience laughed, Charley called up from the pit, 'You sure you're OK to go back on?'

Ash nodded and grinned. 'You'd have to *kill* me to stop me doing an encore.'

TARGET
CHAPTER 77

As the tour bus headed south on Route 101 to Los Angeles the following day, Kay called a meeting in the upper-front lounge. Ash, Charley, Big T and Terry settled themselves into the leather sofas while Vince and Rick stood with the band to hear the update on Ash's demented double.

'The doctor says Pete is suffering from grandiose delusions,' Kay explained. 'The boy is convinced he's Ash Wild. No one can persuade him otherwise.'

'What if he is? And we've got the wrong one?' The bassist scrutinized the Ash sitting beside Charley on the sofa.

Ash's lip curled. 'Ha ha! We'd soon know if *you* were replaced. The bass playing would be better!'

'Dissed!' The drummer laughed, punching the bassist's arm at Ash's joke.

Kay silenced them with a glare. 'According to the doctor, Pete has a history of mental health issues, usually kept in check with medication. But it appears he's been forgetting to take his.'

'Where's Pete now?' asked Charley.

'He's being held in a secure psychiatric clinic,' Kay replied. She turned to Ash. 'The question is, do you want to press charges?'

Ash gazed through the window at the passing traffic. 'Pete did me a favour. As my decoy, he gave me the space that I needed.' Ash glanced fondly at Charley, who felt an unexpected flush rise in her cheeks. She still wore the white-gold bracelet he'd bought her in Las Vegas. 'Besides, I wasn't hurt badly. Let's call it quits.'

Kay looked surprised. 'That's your final decision?'

Ash shrugged a yes. 'He's a super-fan, and they can all get a little crazy sometimes.'

'Fine. I'll let the clinic know, so he can be sent back to the UK.' Her tone hardened. 'But what *I* want to know is how a mentally disturbed fan was allowed backstage in the first place?'

Her eyes raked across Vince, Rick and Charley before settling on Big T. Just as she was about to rip into the veteran bodyguard, Ash cut in. 'That was my idea,' he admitted. 'As I said, Pete made a great decoy.'

'Still,' said Kay, her glare returning to its original target, 'it was Big T's responsibility to security-check *everyone* on the tour.'

'I did do a background check on Pete. It came up with nothing,' said Big T.

'Well, you obviously didn't do it thoroughly enough,' said Kay. 'How could you miss –'

'I got the same result when I ran a separate check,'

Charley interrupted, trying to take the heat off Big T as he'd so often done for her. 'There'd been a huge database crash and Pete's medical records were corrupted. From what was available, he appeared normal, aside from his obvious fixation on Ash.' She held up a picture on her phone of a room wreathed from floor to ceiling in Ash Wild memorabilia. 'Pete posted this online. As you can see, his bedroom's a virtual shrine to Ash.'

'Jeez, that guy is beyond a super-fan! It's creepy,' remarked the bassist. 'He's even got Ash Wild duvet covers! Now that *is* terrifying.'

Kay stabbed a gold-ringed finger at the photo. 'Shouldn't *that* have rung alarm bells?'

Charley winced at the sharpness of her tongue. 'Like Big T, I was always suspicious of Pete, but his room isn't any different from countless other fans' bedrooms around the world.'

'That may be so –' Kay turned on Big T again – 'but Pete was the *second* danger to slip through your fat fingers last night.'

The bodyguard puffed up his chest. 'Kay, we *all* missed Brandon. Terry hired him! Even defended him, for heaven's sake!' The tour manager said nothing, but shrank into the sofa, hoping not to attract Kay's wrath. 'Brandon was a devious psychopath. He altered his appearance, faked his ID and credentials, and even fooled *you* for a while.'

'It still amounts to a major oversight in security,' snapped Kay. 'You and I will revisit this issue at the end of the tour.

In the meantime, please reassure me that it's within your capability to keep Ash alive for the final two dates in LA.'

Big T bristled, but he kept his cool. 'Yes,' he said through clenched teeth. 'Ash is safe as houses.'

CHAPTER 78

'Ash, five minutes to show time!' called Terry, knocking on his dressing-room door at the Staples Center in downtown Los Angeles.

Charley stood with Big T either side of the door, ready to escort Ash to the stage.

Security was super-tight. No one was allowed in or out without a pass and faces were being checked against computer records. The entire security team was on duty and in a state of heightened alert. Only an hour before Ash was due to perform, Kay had received a disturbing call from the San Franciscan police. Brandon Mills had escaped earlier that morning after the vehicle taking him to the courthouse was involved in an accident. An official manhunt was now under way.

On hearing the news, a heated argument broke out among the team whether to go ahead with the gig. But Ash had been adamant that he wouldn't be terrorized into cancelling. These were the final two dates of his sell-out tour, his fans were waiting and he *wouldn't* disappoint them. Terry had backed this decision, pointing out that

Brandon's pass had been confiscated. And, after repeated reassurances from Big T that his security could handle the threat, Kay had reluctantly agreed.

Terry glanced at his watch impatiently. 'Ash?' he called. He was about to knock again when the door opened and Ash emerged, shades on and stage ready.

'You all right?' asked Terry.

'Yeah,' replied Ash, his voice still hoarse from the fire. 'Just a little nervous, that's all.'

'No need to be,' said Charley, offering him an encouraging smile even though she was as tense as a wire. 'You're safe as houses.'

Big T shot her a sideways look. 'Now you're stealing all my lines!'

Surrounded by his entourage, Ash made his way along the corridor towards the stage like a prize fighter about to enter the arena. No one could have got near the rock star. Any attacker would have to battle through a first ring of bodyguards, then tackle Big T and his legendary right hook, after which they'd still face Charley, the final invisible ring of defence.

Of course, Brandon Mills knew from experience that Charley was someone to be reckoned with and he might even suspect she was Ash's personal bodyguard. But now the whole team knew who Brandon was, every eye in the place would be on the lookout for him.

As they approached the auditorium, the entourage split. Ash headed beneath the stage with Big T to the toaster lift, while Charley and the other bodyguards peeled off to take up strategic posts around the venue. Stationed in the wings, Charley peered out at the stage to be confronted by an endless sea of faces. Once more the task ahead seemed insurmountable.

How am I supposed to spot a killer in a crowd of fifty thousand screaming fans?

Her eyes scanned the front rows of frenzied teenage girls, embarrassingly excited mums, pockets of rocker boys and a handful of reluctant fathers dragged along yet secretly thrilled by a live rock concert. The lack of adults, Charley realized, should make it easier to spot a lone man in the crowd. But she couldn't take anyone for granted. Brandon had already shown a cunning talent for disguise.

As her gaze swept the audience, Charley spied a familiar ratty face in the press pit.

Gonzo.

How the hell has he, of all paps, blagged a press pass for the final shows? she wondered.

Then the house lights went down and the video screens began their countdown. The crowd shouted along, cheering as the number one flashed up on the monitors and a huge explosion rumbled through the arena. The cascade of red and gold sparks lit up the stage like a supernova and the gut-thumping throb of a heartbeat blasted out of the speakers.

At that moment Charley was blind and deaf to any threats.

The sound of a blazing fire grew and the silhouette of a winged boy flitted from screen to screen until consumed by the flames.

INDESTRUCTIBLE . . . IMPOSSIBLE . . . I'M POSSIBLE!

Charley felt her stomach clench as a thunderclap heralded Ash's dramatic entrance. From now on until the end of the concert, Ash would be exposed and unguarded on the stage.

Charley could only watch, hope . . . and react.

Shooting up from the toaster lift, Ash flew through the air and landed to the sound of euphoric screaming. He stood, legs astride, relishing the adulation.

Then Ash pumped a fist in the air and cried, 'What's up, Los Ang–'

But he didn't finish the sentence. On the massive screens overhead, in full glorious definition, every fan watched in horror as a spurt of blood burst from Ash's chest.

TARGET

CHAPTER 79

Charley was running before Ash even hit the ground. At first she thought she was experiencing déjà vu, a flashback to when the spotlight had almost crushed Ash. But then reality struck. She'd seen the red laser dot – a second too late.

Charley was first at Ash's side, shielding his body from whatever attack might come next. He lay in a pool of his own blood, spluttering and writhing in pain. His shades dislodged, hazel eyes bulging, he caught sight of Charley and desperately tried to focus on her face.

'H-h-help!' he gasped, clasping her wrist.

'Don't try to speak,' said Charley as she rapidly assessed his condition. His shirt was soaked with blood, his breathing wet and rapid, and his pulse erratic.

Ripping off his top to examine the damage, Charley discovered a small round puncture wound in his upper-right chest.

A bullet hole.

Big T, now at her side, barked into his mic. '*Gunshot confirmed. Secure all exits. Suspect armed and dangerous.*'

In her earpiece, Charley heard a burst of security chatter. More and more people crowded round the bleeding body. Kay, Terry, Zoe, Jessie, band members, roadies . . . even Gonzo, who'd broken through the security line determined to capture the money shot that would become the defining image for the world's media. In the background, Charley was dimly aware of chaos in the arena, fans screaming and panicked parents fleeing with their children in their arms.

The venue's medic appeared with a first-aid kit and dropped down opposite Charley.

Ash was now panting rapidly, each breath more strained. His chest barely moved and there was a blue tinge to his lips.

'Oh my!' exclaimed the medic, turning pale at the profusion of blood.

When he failed to act, and simply stared at the dying rock star, Charley took the situation into her own hands. 'Give me your med-kit,' she ordered.

In his shocked state, he handed it over. Rummaging through the bag, Charley found a large-bore needle with a one-way valve and tore off the sterilized wrapper.

'What are you doing?' the medic cried, suddenly alert that a teenage girl was about to perform a serious medical procedure.

'He's suffering a tension pneumothorax,' explained Charley, locating the second intercostal space on Ash's chest. 'His injured lung will collapse and he'll die if we don't release the pressure.'

Placing the sharp point against his skin, Charley prayed

her diagnosis was correct and that she didn't puncture any vital organs. But there was no time to hesitate. Ash's life was on a knife's edge. She drove the needle in at ninety degrees. Ash was in too much pain to notice it slide between his ribs and penetrate deep into his chest cavity. Opening the valve, a sharp hiss of air was heard and Ash's breathing immediately eased.

But the medical emergency wasn't over yet. In her head Charley ran through *Dr ABC* again. Big T was dealing with the danger. Ash was still responsive. His airway and breathing were stabilized, at least for the time being. But, judging by the ever-expanding pool of blood on the stage, Ash's circulation was the critical issue now.

Kay was on the phone to the emergency services. '*Of course he has insurance! Just send a bloody helicopter!*'

'He needs fluids,' said Charley urgently.

The medic nodded and took out a pouch of saline solution, a sterile tube and a cannula. With practised efficiency, he inserted the cannula into Ash's forearm, while Charley set to work bandaging and sealing the open chest wound.

Yet, despite all their efforts, Ash's condition continued to deteriorate. His breathing was shallow, his heart rate more erratic than ever. Then suddenly his eyes rolled back in their sockets and his head flopped to the side.

'Ash! Stay with us!' cried Charley, shaking his shoulder. 'The ambulance is on its way.'

But Ash no longer responded. Charley looked to the medic for help.

'Possible internal bleeding,' he said, noticing the saline solution already three-quarters empty. 'Little we can do until we get him to a hospital.'

He took out the other saline pouch in the med-kit, but as he was attaching it to the drip Charley noticed Ash had stopped breathing altogether. The medic checked his pulse. 'His heart's stopped!'

The two of them immediately commenced CPR, the medic administering chest compressions while Charley delivered the rescue breaths. They were still going when two paramedics arrived on the scene.

Exhausted and emotionally drained, Charley didn't put up any resistance as the paramedics took over.

Not long after their initial assessment and attempts at resuscitation, the older of the two spoke to his colleague: 'Record time of death as 20:16 hours. Cause of death: gunshot trauma.'

The words hit Charley like a punch to the guts. For a moment, she simply stared at the paramedic, imagining . . . hoping . . . praying she'd heard wrong. Ash *couldn't* be dead.

'I'm sorry for your loss,' said the paramedic, as he ran through the routine death-declaration procedure.

Stifling a sob, Kay's knees went weak and Terry had to support her. Big T stood motionless and silent as a rock. Charley clutched Ash's lifeless hand in her own and wept.

Gradually she became aware of a heartless photographer snapping away right next to her, capturing her grief from every angle.

Charley could take no more.

'*You vulture!*' she spat at him. 'Have you no respect?'

Zooming his lens in on her tear-stained face, Gonzo answered with another flash of his camera.

CHAPTER 80

Big T wrapped Charley in one of his massive arms and led her away from the frenzy of photographers that had now descended on the stage.

'Charley, you did all that you could for Ash,' he said, his voice on the point of cracking. 'But we still have a job to do.'

Stunned with grief, Charley barely heard him. Ash was unique among all the boys she'd ever met. And only now did she realize how much he'd worked his way into her heart. She felt another hole of grief open up next to those for her parents and Kerry.

'Brandon's somewhere in this building and we have to hunt him down,' said Big T fiercely. 'We owe it to Ash to find his killer.'

Charley gazed at the white-gold bracelet on her wrist, now glittering against the blood from Ash's wound. Her sorrow turned to anger: Brandon would pay. He *couldn't* be allowed to escape. Leaving the stage, she took a last glance back at her rock star. The paparazzi buzzed like flies over his dead body as the paramedic removed the cannula from Ash's tattooed arm.

Then it hit her. 'That's not Ash!'

'Charley, don't fool yourself,' said Big T softly. 'Denial is a natural stage of the grie–'

'Ash's phoenix tattoo is on his *left* arm, not his right!' she cut in.

Big T's bald head swivelled round like an owl's and he stared at the body lying on the stage. '*Sweet Mother of Mercy!*'

'That's got to be Pete,' said Charley, at once saddened and elated at her discovery. 'Which means . . . Ash must be at the psychiatric clinic.'

Big T's thick brow creased into a frown as he tried to get his head round this. 'Keep it quiet until I've got confirmation from the clinic. We don't want to raise anyone's hopes . . . or alert Brandon to his mistake.'

As Big T stepped away to tell Kay, Charley spotted Gonzo heading backstage. She wondered what the little creep was sticking his nose into now. Then a thought struck her. On his camera he probably had photos of the moments running up to Ash's – or Pete's – murder. This might give vital clues about where the gunshot had come from and Brandon's location, even his possible escape route.

Maybe Gonzo could prove useful for once.

'Hey, Gonzo!' called Charley, hurrying after him.

But he didn't seem to hear. Pushing through the blackout curtains, she saw his wiry figure disappear down a corridor. *Why is he in such a rush?* she wondered.

She chased him through the warren of backstage

tunnels, always several steps behind. He rounded a corner and when she reached it Gonzo was nowhere in sight.

Then she heard a door click shut at the far end of the hallway. Dashing down to the door marked BAY D: AUTHORIZED PERSONNEL ONLY, she barged her way through into a darkened loading bay. Gonzo was scurrying across the concrete towards an as-yet unsecured exit.

'Hey, Gonzo, hold up!' she shouted.

Startled, the pap guy froze and turned, as if caught in the beam of a searchlight, but immediately relaxed when he saw Charley. 'If it isn't Ash's guardian angel,' he sneered. 'Not much left to guard now, have you?'

Charley ignored the cruel taunt. 'Where do you think you're going?' she demanded, running over to him.

'None of your business.'

'I think it is. The venue's in lock-down.'

'I've got to take these photos to my agency *right now*,' he snapped. 'If I don't, I'll miss the scoop of a lifetime.'

'Can I have a look first?' Charley asked.

Gonzo blinked. 'Not on your life.'

'I'm not going to delete them,' she said, reaching out to the camera dangling round his neck. 'They could hold clues to identify the gunman.'

Gonzo clasped the camera to his chest as if she was asking him to hand over his own baby.

'I only want to look,' insisted Charley. 'Surely you owe me that?'

'I owe you nothing!' he spat, turning to leave.

Big T's voice sounded in her earpiece. '*Charley, where are you?*'

'In loading bay D,' she responded into her mic.

'*Security upda . . .*' Interference broke up the signal. '*Caught . . . in San Jose . . . killer is . . .*'

'Say again,' said Charley, clasping a hand to her ear.

'*. . . the killer isn't Brandon.*'

TARGET

CHAPTER 81

'Stop!' Charley cried as Gonzo reached the emergency exit. 'You're not going anywhere.'

Gonzo swivelled round to face her.

'How about a last shot?' he said, pointing his camera at Charley. 'The grieving girlfriend.'

'Gonzo, I don't have time to play games,' said Charley. 'You might have evidence of the killer. Hand it over.'

Gonzo adjusted the flashgun on his camera. 'Smile for the birdy!'

Charley noticed the little red laser dot on her chest a moment too late. *The flashgun was a real gun!*

Gonzo's finger depressed the shutter button. Charley braced herself for the impact . . . There was a click but no flash.

With a blast of expletives, Gonzo furiously tapped away at the button.

'Run out of film?' asked Charley, diving forward to tackle him before he could clear the jam.

Gonzo tried to bat her away with his camera. The flash caught her a glancing blow on the cheek, but she managed to pin him against the wall. As she tried to wrestle the lethal camera off him, Gonzo grabbed her hair and yanked her head backwards. She gave a shriek as he tugged mercilessly. Before she could tear herself free of his grip, he whipped her head to the side and she collided, bone to brick, against the wall. Stars burst across her vision, her skull rang like a bell and she was forced to let him go.

Taking advantage of her dazed state, Gonzo swept her legs from under her. Charley fell to the floor where he roundly kicked her in the stomach. Winded and retching up bile, Charley lay gagging for breath, pain racking her body. She heard the scrape of metal and saw Gonzo picking up a crowbar from the top of a crate.

'I said you'd live to regret your actions, *chica*.'

As Gonzo raised the crowbar to deliver a killing blow, Charley gasped, 'Ash isn't dead!'

'What?'

'You shot his decoy.'

'You're lying.'

But the hesitation in his attack was all she needed.

Fight smarter, not harder.

Charley drove her fist into his groin – always the smartest move in female self-defence.

Gonzo yelped like a wounded puppy and dropped to the floor, the crowbar clattering to the concrete. As he knelt with his hands clasped between his legs, she slammed her palm into the bridge of his crooked nose. There was a satisfying crunch and blood streamed from his nostrils. Stunned and in obvious pain, Gonzo hissed and bared his teeth like a cornered rat. He lashed out at her with a fist, but she caught his hand and spiralled it into a wrist lock. Applying pressure, Charley forced him to the concrete, where he lay squirming like a pinned beetle.

Though restrained, Gonzo still struggled and spat at her. Charley took hold of his index finger. Any further injury, she reasoned, could be blamed on his own force in resisting.

'I assume this is the trigger finger you use to take your vile photos?' she said coolly. 'So I suggest you keep still.'

She applied an extra-hard twist to his wrist to drive home her warning.

Wincing, Gonzo glared up at her and snarled, 'Shove it, Wild Cat!'

Charley smiled, then wrenched the finger all the way back. A sickening crack resounded through the loading bay, swiftly followed by Gonzo's agonized scream, just as Big T and two other security guards burst through the door.

'I *told* you to keep still,' she said, confident her action was *necessary*, *reasonable* and *proportional* to the pain and suffering he'd inflicted on her and Ash.

Big T came running over, stared at the deformed finger, then smirked at Gonzo. 'Well, you won't be taking any shots for a very long time!'

TARGET

CHAPTER 82

'It's an impressive piece of kit,' remarked the officer in charge, inspecting the flashgun weapon before it was bagged for evidence. 'Criminals are becoming more inventive every day.'

He sipped from a takeaway coffee cup and grimaced at the taste. 'Man, that's gross! Don't they have any decent coffee in this venue?'

Tossing the cup into a nearby bin, he turned to Charley and Big T in the loading bay. They'd given their statements and were just waiting to be dismissed. 'I think we're done here. That was pretty brave of you, young lady, to tackle the suspect alone. But next time leave it to the professionals, like your bodyguard friend here. Without proper training, you could easily have been killed.'

Charley said nothing. Big T suppressed a knowing grin.

'She's a psycho! A wild cat! *She broke my finger!*' bawled Gonzo as he was bundled into a police car. 'You should be arresting her, not me!'

The officer in charge snorted. 'Why is it that killers always think they're the victims?'

He shrugged and strode away to his car.

Charley glanced up at Big T. 'Leave it to the *professionals*? What am I then?'

'You're the real thing,' Big T replied. 'Just a pity you didn't break *all* his fingers.'

Charley responded with a strained smile.

'Hey, I certainly would have!' admitted the veteran bodyguard. 'Now, come on – we should update the others.'

Charley followed Big T back through the maze of corridors to the artists' lounge. The atmosphere among the band and road crew was subdued, though there was a buzz as Charley entered the room. She heard whispers of '*Did she really catch the killer?*'

Kay, Terry and Zoe were embroiled in a heated discussion in the tour manager's office.

'It could so easily have been Ash!' said Kay fiercely.

'Just be thankful Brandon's been recaptured,' replied Terry. 'At least he's no longer a threat.'

'But we were looking for the wrong guy! And now Ash is locked up in a mental ward! How did we ever make that mis–' She broke off as Big T knocked at the door and entered.

'Charley! Are you all right?' Kay asked with genuine concern as Big T closed the door behind them.

'Just about,' Charley replied, still feeling the throb in her gut where Gonzo had kicked her. 'That rat Gonzo tried to shoot me with his camera, *literally*.'

'Gonzo's a murdering scumbag,' declared Big T. 'But he's now where he belongs. Behind bars.'

'What I don't understand is why Gonzo would want to kill Ash in the first place?' said Zoe incredulously.

'He needed the money,' Big T replied.

'What money?' said Terry.

'The fees he'd earn from his photos,' explained Big T, 'to pay off his gambling debt to the mob.'

'If that's the case, why wasn't Gonzo identified as a threat before?' demanded Kay.

'He was,' said Big T. 'None of us ever imagined, though, he'd go to *these* lengths to engineer a "unique" photo. He'd bugged Ash's hotel room, tried to incite him to violence, even caused our car crash in New Orleans – I traced the registration plate of the motorbike back to him. But these tactics are typical of the paparazzi. And, after photographing the fire in San Francisco, it seems he was inspired to murder by Brandon.'

'Brandon?' exclaimed Kay.

'Yes,' said Charley, joining in the discussion. 'It bothered me that Gonzo was always in the wrong place at the wrong time. It was as if he knew about the accidents in advance. We suspect he and Brandon made a deal. Brandon set up the accidents and Gonzo captured them on film.'

'So, when Brandon was caught, Gonzo took things into his own hands,' continued Big T. 'You see, to kill Ash would be the ultimate pay-off in terms of a money shot. It would be like catching the moment John Lennon was murdered.'

'But he'd be killing the golden goose,' remarked Terry.

Big T nodded. 'Yeah, but he'd have made his fortune.

Photos of Ash dying would have been sold around the world and earned him millions.'

'And how is Ash?' asked Charley. In all the craziness, she'd yet to ask about him. 'I need to see him.'

'I gave the clinic a call, but it's out of office hours,' replied Kay. 'The night-duty nurse had an emergency number for the doctor in charge, so I'm waiting for a call back.'

At that moment her mobile rang. She snatched it up and listened. 'You're absolutely certain?' she asked, before listening some more. 'Thank you, Doctor.'

Frowning, Kay put her phone down. 'The doctor says the client was escorted to the airport, checked in and taken through to the departure lounge. But it appears he never got on the flight to England. What's really odd, though, is the doctor insists the tattoo was on his right arm. They definitely had Pete, *not* Ash, in their care.'

Charley stared at Big T. 'So where's Ash?'

TARGET
CHAPTER 83

'No more encores? You've got to be kidding. This is my third!' yelled the teen rock star, running back on stage to ear-splitting screams and thunderous applause on the final night of the Indestructible tour.

And what a perfect name for the tour it is, thought Charley. For someone who'd been threatened with death, almost crushed by a spotlight, electrocuted by a mic, trapped by a hotel fire, thrown off the stage, and finally tied up and blindfolded by his doppelgänger, Ash had an amazing resilience – fuelled, it seemed, by the undying devotion of his fans.

After a frantic search of the Staples Center, they'd found Ash bound and gagged inside a locked wardrobe in his dressing room. He'd been in the venue the whole time. According to Ash, Pete had caught a flight down to LA and then taken a taxi to the Staples Center. After conning his way into the venue as 'Ash', he'd waited for Ash in his dressing room. Ash had been taken by surprise, tied up and shoved in the wardrobe by Pete.

On his release, Ash had been furious. But when he

discovered Pete's fate he was first shocked and then thankful that his decoy had saved him from that fatal shot. After hearing about Charley's encounter with Gonzo, his concern focused on her, but Charley assured him she was fine. She was his bodyguard and it was all part of the job.

Kay had launched a demonic investigation into how Pete slipped past security, but gradually calmed down once she knew that Ash was alive and well. With Brandon back in custody, Gonzo behind bars and Pete lying in a morgue, Ash was no longer the target of any known death threats. All the same, everyone on the security team remained alert and on edge for his final concert.

Miraculously, the gig went well – with just one small hitch at the end.

'I've got no more songs!' Ash admitted, spreading his arms wide in apology to his insatiable fans.

There was an arena-sized groan.

He smiled. 'Perhaps . . . I do have *one* more.'

A huge cheer rocked the venue.

'It's brand new. Not even my band has heard it,' said Ash, perching on a stool and taking an acoustic guitar from a roadie. After a strum to check it was tuned, he reached out to adjust the mic stand . . . and stopped himself. He glanced offstage at a small group of sound technicians. 'This one's earthed, isn't it, guys?'

Like a group of dutiful meerkats, they all nodded their heads, then laughed at Ash's joke.

'This song is inspired by a very special girl in my life,' Ash announced. 'It's called "Angel Without Wings".'

The audience hushed into near silence as Ash plucked a bittersweet melody from his guitar. With a soulful voice that belied his young age, he began to sing. '*Time will heal yet memories scar, when the hurt's so deep, a bridge too far . . .*'

Once more Charley felt her eyes well up with tears and her throat constrict.

'*In times of trouble, I need a helping hand. I look for you, breathe for you, have a need for you . . .*'

Ash looked in Charley's direction. His eyes met hers as he sang the chorus.

'*You lift me up, lift me up. Make all my troubles fade away . . .*'

For Charley, the whole arena faded to nothing. It was as if Ash was singing only to her. And only she mattered.

'*There stands my angel without wings. Who needs wings . . . to be an angel?*'

TARGET

CHAPTER 84

'That's a number-one hit!' declared Kay, hugging Ash as he joined them in the artists' lounge for the after-show party. She was beside herself with excitement. 'We must get you in the studio as soon as we're back. It's all about the moment – and you've captured it!'

Charley was equally overcome with emotion. Still reeling from being serenaded to with her very own song, she walked alongside Ash as if floating on air. For the first time in years, her heart felt full – untroubled, complete, at peace.

But she wouldn't get a moment alone with Ash to thank him for quite a while yet. Band members, road crew, invited guests and media were all lined up to congratulate and compliment him. Ash beamed and nodded his thanks, basking in the praise. After all the storms he'd weathered, Charley felt he deserved his time in the sun.

Stepping away from the throng of well-wishers, Charley spotted Jessie standing alone and apart from the others. The fan-club organizer had been quiet and withdrawn ever since Charley had accused her of trying to kill Ash. The two of them had not spoken a word to each other since. Realizing there'd never be a good time to apologize with the tour ending, this seemed like the best opportunity. Steeling herself, Charley went over to the buffet table, picked up a plate and pretended to browse the food on offer. Oriental spring rolls, gourmet pizza slices, fancy sandwiches, chicken-satay skewers and other delicacies all surrounded a massive tiered cake decorated with candles and the word INDESTRUCTIBLE in icing.

'Hi, Jessie,' she said, as lightly as she could.

Jessie ignored her.

'Listen . . . I'm sorry for what I said.'

Jessie shot her a hostile stare. 'Oh, you're sorry, are you? A little late for that.'

'Please understand –'

'No, I understand all right,' Jessie snapped, rounding on her. 'It's not enough for you to steal Ash's heart. You have to break mine too.'

'That wasn't my intention.'

'Wasn't it? You accused me, of all people, of trying to kill Ash!' she said, her mouth twisted into a furious snarl. 'Ever since we met, you've wanted me off this tour. When Ash was upset, you pushed me away. You hogged him to yourself.' Charley saw Jessie pick up a large knife from the buffet table. 'You're always following him around, never letting him out of your sight. Wherever he goes, you go! You're like his shadow. The poor guy can't even breathe without you at his back. I don't know how he stands it.'

Charley took a step away. 'I said, I'm sorry. I was just doing my job.'

'*Job?* Being Ash's girlfriend isn't a job!' exclaimed Jessie in outrage, waving the blade in Charley's face. 'And from what I've seen you haven't a clue what PR is either. What I do for Ash is a proper publicity job. I've slaved on his fan website night and day, built up his following in this country from *nothing*. I've never asked for thanks. Never asked for anything. I do this because of the love I carry in my heart for him. But still he loves you more. He even writes a song for you!'

She thrust the tip of the knife accusingly at her. Charley didn't like where this was going and reached for her mobile phone.

'It doesn't surprise me you've had death threats,' Jessie went on, still waving the gleaming blade around. 'You deserve all the hate you get online. I just wish I'd written some of it. Cos that's how I feel about you!'

As Jessie raised the knife, Charley thrust her iStun into the girl's gut. Jessie's whole body convulsed and jerked as three million volts of electricity coursed through her system. The shock was too much for her and she passed out, dropping to the carpet in a heap.

People were quick to notice and Ash came dashing over with everyone else. 'What's happened to Jessie?' he asked.

Not wanting to make any more of a scene, Charley quietly pocketed her phone and shrugged. 'Jessie must have been . . . overcome by your performance. She just fainted.'

'Poor Jessie,' said Ash, as Big T knelt down beside the unconscious girl and tried to revive her. 'She was so looking forward to cutting the end-of-tour cake with me.'

TARGET

CHAPTER 85

'You stunned her for trying to cut a cake!' Jason exclaimed during her video call to Buddyguard HQ the next morning from her hotel room on Sunset Boulevard. He laughed. 'I got away lightly with a dislocated finger then.'

'You won't ever forgive me for that, will you?' said Charley, her cheeks reddening with shame at her over-reaction in using the iStun – the fangirl might have been angry with her but not to the point of murder.

'Hey, I deserved that,' said Jason. Charley saw him glance round the briefing room, then lean closer to the webcam. In a lowered voice, he said, 'Listen, I know we got off on the wrong foot, Charley, and we haven't exactly been best of friends, but I think it's time I gave you an apology.'

'For what?' asked Charley.

'For being an arse!'

Charley was rendered speechless by his stark self-assessment.

'I was . . .' Jason seemed to struggle for the right words, '*wrong* to assume just cos you're a girl you'd be no good as a bodyguard. After seeing you in action on this operation – palm-striking guys, resuscitating Principals and taking down not just one but *two* maniacs – it's obvious you're more capable than any of us boys.' He smiled. 'Can we start over?'

Charley realized how much Jason must have swallowed his pride to admit this. And, despite their history, she found it easy to forgive and forget. 'Of course,' she said. 'And I'm sorry for dislocating your finger.'

'No worries, they still all work.' Jason wiggled his fingers in front of the camera. 'Besides, it was my fault. I shouldn't have been so tough on you during training.'

'Yes, you should,' Charley said, to his surprise. 'It was your fight-or-fail attitude that pushed me to go beyond my limits. I've a lot to thank you for. The fact you didn't make any allowances for me during training prepared me for the real world – a world that makes no allowances whatsoever.'

'Well, if I'd have known that,' said Jason, grinning, 'I'd have been an even bigger arse!'

Charley laughed. 'No, you're big enough as it is.'

'Thanks! And you're one kick-ass bodyguard,' he replied warmly. 'I'm proud to be on your team. Well . . . until I get my own team!'

'Is that still happening?' she asked. Having bonded with Jason at long last, the thought of splitting up the original team saddened her.

Jason nodded. 'As soon as you return from this assignment.' He glanced off-camera, then back at her. 'Hey, the colonel wants to speak to you.'

Jason left his seat and Colonel Black's craggy face appeared on her screen.

'Outstanding work, Charley. It seems your suspicions were right about Brandon and Gonzo,' he said. 'The police have found evidence of coded text messages on the pap's phone. They contain times and locations that match the accidents and attacks on Ash.'

'I knew it!' said Charley.

'It certainly explains how Gonzo popped up at every disaster on this tour,' Colonel Black continued. 'And you've done well to keep Ash alive through it all. Operation Starstruck has been an unexpectedly tough assignment. But, as you've discovered, fame is a killer.'

TARGET
CHAPTER 86

Once known as the Riot House, the hotel on Sunset Boulevard was a legend among rock stars. In the 1960s and 1970s, it held the likes of The Doors, The Who and The Rolling Stones. Led Zeppelin would rent as many as six floors and stage motorcycle races in the hallways. The Who's Keith Moon threw a TV out of the window, setting a trend that John Bonham, Keith Richards and countless other rock gods followed. Lemmy of Hawkwind wrote the classic track 'Motorhead' in the middle of the night on one of the hotel balconies. Jim Morrison even hung from a window once by his fingertips, causing a traffic jam in the street below. The Riot House was *the* place to hang out and party.

Tonight it hosted the official Indestructible end-of-tour party. The rooftop pool and bar were buzzing with celebrities, models, musicians and movie stars. Roadies wandered around wearing T-shirts saying I SURVIVED A WILD TOUR! And security was so tight that even the most famous faces had to produce ID and guest invitations.

Charley, in a strapless white top and black leather jeans, stood with Ash by the pool when suddenly there was a scream from the men's toilets. The bassist came dashing out, his trousers round his ankles. He shuffled to the bar, grabbed a handful of ice and shoved it down the back of his pants. Everyone stared in stunned silence at the musician's bizarre behaviour as his pained face melted with relief, then turned to anger.

'Who laced the toilet paper with chilli powder?' he demanded.

A ripple of laughter spread among the guests.

Ash turned to Charley. 'It wasn't me, but I wish I'd thought of that.'

Charley, fighting to keep her expression straight, replied, 'He should probably put yogurt on it.'

Ash narrowed his eyes and studied her. 'I think I'd better watch my back from now on.'

Charley laughed. It had been a long time coming, but she'd finally got her revenge for their prank on her at the start of the tour. She couldn't bring herself to set up Ash, but the band members were still fair game.

The party soon lost interest in the bassist and his burning backside, conversation resumed and the DJ upped the music volume. A group of girls – super-fans who'd won a competition to meet their idol – approached Ash.

'Can we have your autograph please?' asked one of the girls, presenting their party invites for signing.

'Sure,' said Ash. 'Do you have a pen?'

When the girl began searching in her bag, Charley produced her own pen from her back pocket – she'd come prepared this time. Ash autographed the invites with a flourish, then handed them back.

'Yours too, Charley,' insisted the girl with a hopeful smile.

'Me?' questioned Charley, blinking in surprise.

The girl nodded. 'You're a real inspiration. We all want to be Wild Cats like you!'

Taking the pen back from Ash, Charley signed her name next to his. Then the girls huddled close for a round of selfies with her.

'Looks like you're becoming a star yourself,' Ash remarked as the girls trotted away, delighted with their collection of autographs and photos. 'Before you become too famous, there's something I need to say.'

Taking her hand, Ash led her to a gazebo in the far corner of the rooftop garden. With the guests clustered round the bar and pool, the gazebo was unoccupied and the surrounding potted plants gave them some privacy. He stopped by the rail, where the sun was setting pink-orange over the haze of LA.

'I see you're still wearing the bracelet,' he said, the woven bands of white-gold gleaming on her wrist in the dying light.

'Of course,' she replied, feeling his arms wrap round her waist.

Ash gazed intently into her eyes. Once more it seemed only she mattered.

'I wouldn't have survived this tour without you,' he said. 'And, while I wouldn't want to go through that hell again, I really don't want this tour to end.'

'Why?' she asked, a little breathless.

'Because it means you'll no longer be with me. At my side.'

'Surely that'll be a relief?' she said, trying to make light of their parting. 'The fact you don't need constant protection any more.'

Ash shook his head. 'Charley, you're my inspiration, my muse. I'll be lost without you.'

He cupped the back of her neck in one hand and drew her close.

'I told you I'd break your arm if you ever tried to kiss me again,' she warned, but her tone was gentle and inviting.

Ash smiled. 'Worth the risk.'

Charley felt her resistance crumbling. 'I'm not one of your groupies,' she said.

'No, you're my guardian angel.'

He leant in to kiss her and Charley knew she was about to break the cardinal rule of bodyguarding. *Never get involved with your Principal.*

The battle with her conscience didn't last long.

She gave into him, her heart ruling her head. Their lips were no more than a breath apart when she heard a whirring sound like an angry mosquito. She pulled back from the kiss. Hovering in the air, only a few metres from them, was a drone with a camera attached.

'For heaven's sake!' exclaimed Ash, glaring at the flying

intrusion. 'I can't even escape the paparazzi fourteen floors up!'

Charley calmly picked up a stone from one of the potted plants, judged the distance and flung it at the drone. The stone struck it dead centre, cracking its casing, then rebounded and shattered one of its plastic propellers. The drone lurched sideways and plunged out of view.

Slipping her arms round Ash's waist, Charley now drew him to her. 'So where were we?'

'I think about *here*,' said Ash, pressing his lips against hers.

Closing her eyes, Charley lost herself in his exquisite kiss.

'Ash?' called Kay, her high heels clicking across the stone paving towards the pagoda. Charley quickly broke away from their embrace. 'Ah, there you are! There's someone I need you to meet.'

Ash squeezed Charley's hand. 'Wait here for me. I won't be long,' he whispered, then went off with his manager.

Leaning against the rail, Charley gazed out over the West Hollywood skyline, the city lights twinkling like stars. Realizing she'd crossed a romantic line with Ash, she felt overwhelmed by a kaleidoscope of emotions. Was there a chance of a real relationship or was that a farewell kiss? Could she remain his bodyguard and be his girlfriend too? Would she have to quit Buddyguard?

Whatever the answer, she had to face facts. Ash was a world-famous rock star with countless beautiful girls at his feet. She shouldn't read too much into a single kiss, however intense.

Her phone buzzed in her pocket. She pulled it out and glanced at the text – an Intruder alert.

TARGET
CHAPTER 87

The hotel corridor was deserted, with everyone on the roof for the party. Charley had spotted Ash and Kay talking with a famous film producer so decided not to disturb them. No one could access the penthouse floor without an authorized key card – so more than likely a security guard or a hotel employee had entered Ash's suite, despite instructions not to service the room without advance notice.

Charley stood outside Ash's suite. The door was closed and there were no signs of forced entry. The Intruder device was in place and undamaged. Taking out her spare key card, she slipped it into the lock and cautiously entered.

Subdued lighting illuminated the spacious lounge area with its deep leather sofa and private bar. The air conditioner hummed and the distant thrum of passing traffic drifted up through the open patio doors leading to the balcony. Outside dusk had settled and LA glowed like the embers of a dying fire.

On initial inspection the suite appeared unoccupied.

Her steps muted by the thick carpet, Charley crossed the empty lounge towards the bedroom. She peered inside.

Nothing seemed to be disturbed. Ash's suitcases were on the rack and his king-size bed untouched.

Then she noticed a light on in the en suite bathroom – and a twitch of a shadow.

With ninja-like stealth, Charley approached the door and eased it open.

Big T stood with his back to her, a black marker in his hand.

On the mirror, scrawled in disturbingly familiar handwriting, were the words:

YOUR GUARDIAN
ANGEL
WILL BE
YOUR ANGEL OF DEA

'What the hell are you doing?' exclaimed Charley, shocked and confused by what she was witnessing.

Big T spun round, the black marker now clenched in his fist like a knife. On seeing Charley, he lowered his guard. 'I . . . just discovered this death threat,' he explained.

'But I saw *you* writing it.'

Big T's weathered face hardened to stone. Then he gave her a sorrowful look. 'I wish you hadn't.'

He made a step towards her. Charley instinctively backed away. That's when she spotted a red block, with a mobile phone taped and wired to it, perched on the basin's vanity unit. She instantly recognized the putty-like block to be PBX.

'What the hell, Big T!' she cried, her eyes widening in alarm. 'I thought you were Ash's bodyguard!'

'And I always will be.'

'But that –' she indicated the bomb – 'looks like you're trying to *kill* him.'

Big T responded with a single shake of his head. 'I'm not one to kill the golden goose like Gonzo. My job is to protect Ash. In fact it's the only job I know.'

As the veteran bodyguard moved steadily towards her, Charley retreated through the bedroom into the lounge. 'Then why the mirror threat and bomb?'

'Because I must remain essential to Ash's survival.'

'What makes you think you aren't?'

'Kay Gibson.' He scowled at the manager's name. 'Charley, I'll let you into a secret. I sent the original hoax letter bomb.'

Charley almost stumbled over the sofa in shock at his confession.

'That red she-devil wanted to fire me before the tour even started!' he revealed, still advancing on her. 'Thought I was too old for a bodyguard. But I proved I wasn't by "saving" Ash's life. It worked. My contract was renewed. She even gave me a pay rise!' He laughed. 'Then that Brandon began sending Ash *real* death threats. That's when Kay decided to hire you.' His eyes narrowed. 'In fact she *insulted* me by hiring a teenage girl!'

'But you've helped me, backed me up when things went wrong!'

Big T nodded, the smile on his lips both tender and

regretful. 'I like you, Charley. You impressed me from the start. I've seen many wannabe bodyguards come and go in my time. Until a person's tested, you don't know them. And very few have the right stuff. But *you* do.'

Charley found herself backed up against the bar. 'Then why are you doing this?'

'Because you're *too* good. After defending Ash in Miami, then resuscitating him in Dallas, you started to eclipse me. And, when the student becomes greater than the teacher, the teacher must crush the student.' The marker pen in Big T's fist snapped in his furious grasp. 'I tried to get shot of you! Give you a way out with the first threat on your mirror. If you'd told your colonel, you'd have been reassigned. But you kept quiet. That's why I need *you* to be seen as a security risk to Ash – to fail in your duty while *I'm* the bodyguard that saves the day.'

'But my assignment's over. I'm no threat to you.'

'Yes, you are,' he contradicted, sorrow entering his old watery eyes. 'Kay's sacking me. You're to be my replacement.'

Charley's mouth fell open. 'What?'

'She spoke to your Colonel Black this very evening about extending your contract.'

Charley held up her hands. 'Believe me, I had no idea about this.'

'Well, you do now,' growled Big T, closing in on her. 'Tonight I was going to be the hero and discover the bomb. Change of plan, Charley – *you're* going to discover the bomb.'

'Me?'

Big T nodded, his expression grim. 'Unfortunately, you'll set it off "by accident" – a tragic end to a promising career. But at least you'll have the consolation of dying in the line of duty.'

TARGET
CHAPTER 88

Charley bolted for the door. Big T lunged forward and seized her by the arm. 'Sorry, Charley, can't have you blabbing.'

'Let me go!' screamed Charley as he dragged her towards the bedroom.

'Everyone thinks you and Ash are an item. So it won't be suspicious if you're found in his room,' said Big T more to himself than her.

Unable to break his iron grip, Charley pulled out her phone and depressed the volume button. Intent on shocking the traitorous bodyguard senseless, she thrust the arcing metal studs into his large gut.

'No, you don't!' said Big T, grabbing her wrist before she could make contact. 'I saw what you did to Jessie.'

He slammed her hand against the edge of the bar, forcing her to drop the iStun. He kicked the phone under the sofa. Despite having both hands pinned, Charley booted him hard in the shins. His eyes flared with pain, but he didn't let her go. With the practised brutality of a bouncer, he lassoed a muscled arm round her neck and trapped her in a crushing headlock.

'Please don't struggle!' he said, his tone more imploring than angry. 'You'll only make it worse for yourself.'

Fighting for breath, her neck was crushed in his grip. Charley reached across to Big T's hand, found his little finger and wrenched it backwards. There was a sharp snap and a pained grunt. But the pressure on her throat didn't ease.

'Nice try,' he hissed through clenched teeth. 'But I've broken too many bones in my lifetime to worry about a little finger.'

He began hauling her across the room like a giant with a doll. Charley clawed at his arm, but it was pointless. His muscles were as unyielding as steel.

'Why did you have to find me?' he muttered. 'I had it all planned. No one was supposed to get hurt, especially not you. But you've forced me into this . . .'

Darkness began to seep into Charley's vision. Then she remembered the *kubotan* pen in her pocket. Seizing it like an ice pick, she drove its reinforced point into a cluster of nerves in Big T's forearm. The sudden unexpected jolt of concentrated pain ripped through him. Charley felt the headlock loosen and she stabbed the tip into his upper thigh. A second excruciating burst of pain caused Big T to crumple and he dropped Charley to the floor.

'*You really are a wild cat!*' he raged as he hobbled to the wall for support.

Gasping for air, Charley used the bar to pull herself up. Out of the corner of her eye, she caught a flicker of movement and ducked. Big T's legendary right hook whistled a hair's breadth from her head. Knowing she wouldn't survive one of those punches, Charley grabbed a glass bottle from the bar, spun round and smashed it on Big T's bald head. Vodka and fragments of glass showered over him, but he barely flinched.

'Now the gloves are off!' he snarled, and brought a bottle hammering down towards her head. But her earlier strike had obviously had some impact for he wasn't quite on target. The bottle caught Charley a glancing blow – enough to briefly stun and drop her, but not to knock her out. With her skull throbbing and her vision doubled, she collapsed beside the sofa.

'Now stay down!' Big T slurred, propping himself against the bar.

In her daze, Charley spotted the gleam of two metal studs beneath the sofa. Reaching out, her fingers found the edge of her phone. Desperately she tried to get a grip. Behind she heard a tinkle of glass and knew Big T was heading for her. He grasped the back of her top and pulled her away from the sofa.

With a hand clamped round her throat, Big T lifted her off the ground. Charley spluttered and gagged.

'You were like a daughter to me,' he said, looking at her with bloodshot eyes. 'Believe me, I didn't want it to end like this.'

'Nor me!' she gasped, thrusting the iStun into his chest. The points contacted straight over his heart.

Big T convulsed, choked and staggered back through the open patio door.

But one jolt wasn't enough. The bodyguard was as strong as a grizzly bear. He still had her by the throat. Charley hit him again. Big T's body went into spasm. He fell backwards and hit the balcony rail. It cracked under his weight. Losing his balance, Big T began to topple over the side.

He made no effort to save himself.

'I'm so sorry, Charley,' he gasped, regret in his eyes as he tumbled into the darkness.

But his muscles were still locked out by the iStun – and Charley was caught in his death grip. Screaming, she was dragged over with him.

TARGET

CHAPTER 89

'The doctor tells me people who fall more than ten storeys rarely survive,' said Colonel Black, standing stiff and awkward beside Charley's bed in the intensive-care unit of Children's Hospital Los Angeles. 'Big T died on impact, but his body broke your fall. You were extremely lucky.'

Charley stared down at herself, her eyes unfocused, yet seeing all too much.

Lucky? she thought bitterly.

Her paralysed legs were sprawled on the bed, lifeless and bizarrely misshapen. She felt sick. They looked like a scarecrow's in a horror movie, feet bent at unnatural angles. She couldn't feel them. It was as if they weren't *her* legs at all.

'Mostly it's positive news,' the colonel went on, a leaden smile on his haggard face, but Charley was barely listening. 'Your broken arm and cracked ribs will heal with no long-term effects. You haven't got any pelvic injuries, which is a miracle – that can be problematic, even fatal. The only serious damage from the fall is to the base of your spine, but the doctors are doing more tests.'

Charley had little memory of the fall. She recalled the bright joy of the rooftop party, the thrill of her kiss with Ash and her wide-open hopes for the future. And she remembered the scrawled threat on the mirror, her deep shock and sadness at Big T's treachery and the crushing grip of his fingers round her throat. Then she had been falling . . . plunging into a deep well of blackness. Drowning in darkness, she almost never came back up. Perhaps that would have been a blessing? For when she did surface again, she knew that not all of her had returned.

'And I guarantee you'll get the best care possible. No expense spared.' The colonel paused and fished something out of his pocket. He tried to make eye contact with her and failed. 'Charley, I realize this isn't much after all you've lost but . . .' He held up a small gold shield with guardian wings. 'For outstanding bravery and sacrifice in the line of duty.'

When she didn't react, he swallowed uncomfortably and placed it on her bedside table.

Charley ignored the gold badge . . . and Colonel Black.

'Right. I'll return tomorrow,' said the colonel, a crack in his voice. 'Is there anything you want?'

YES! A pair of legs that WORK! Charley screamed in her head.

When she remained silent, Colonel Black nodded goodbye and walked out.

Charley stared at the two lumps of meat that had been her legs, now propped on the bed. In her head a single maddening question repeated over and over . . .

Will I ever walk again?

TARGET
CHAPTER 90

At first Charley grieved the loss of her legs, crying herself to sleep each pain-racked night.

In her dreams she was whole again, surfing endless oceans or running over mountains, faster and faster, her feet barely touching the ground. Then she'd wake believing she could walk, her heart light and her head happy until she tried to move. Her legs would refuse all commands. Sweat would pour from her brow as she mentally screamed at them to respond.

This denial of her crippled state didn't last long. Soon Charley grew to hate the sight of her legs. *What use were they if they didn't work?* They were like two logs of rotten wood. She could saw them off and wouldn't feel or notice a damn difference!

At the end of her first week in hospital, she was moved from the intensive-care unit to the high-dependency unit. *Progress*, the nurse told her with a cheery smile.

It didn't feel like progress to Charley – just a different room with the same antiseptic smell and the same routine as before.

Then, in the second week, while a nurse was washing what used to be her legs, Charley felt a slight sensation of pins and needles. She still couldn't tell which leg the nurse was touching, but there was a definite feeling. She'd enthusiastically told the nurse and a doctor had been called. But when he performed a series of sensory tests her legs didn't react to any other stimuli. The doctor was encouraging, but Charley's spark of hope faded.

Yet a couple of days later some sensation returned to her bowel. This time the doctor was noticeably animated. *A vital neurological sign for future leg function*, he'd said. It still seemed like the thinnest of threads reconnecting her to her lower half. But it was enough to reignite Charley's hope and carry her through the long dark hours, alone and scared of what the future might hold.

The changes were small, but towards the end of the first month Charley was convinced some feeling had returned to the soles of her feet. It was as if her legs were waking up from a decade-long hibernation. Some days she could even sense their position on the bed. At night the nerves inside buzzed, like a broken hard drive trying to reboot itself.

One glorious morning Charley discovered she could wiggle her toes. Only a fraction – but it was movement. Then, just as she was celebrating this progress, her whole body went into spasm. It started in her legs, rushed up like a tsunami through her body, arched her spine backwards and turned her hands into claws, crushing the paper cup in her grasp and sending water flying.

There was no pain. But Charley was terrified.

The spasm lasted a minute or so, yet felt like eons to Charley. When it subsided, she discovered the doctor at her side. Soothing her, he explained that spasms were a side effect of her spinal injury. Her body's normal reflex system was being short-circuited. The explanation brought Charley little relief.

One afternoon, after a particularly violent spasm, there was a knock at her door. Ash popped his head in.

'How you doing today?' he asked.

'All right,' she lied, wiping perspiration from her forehead with the back of her hand.

'I've brought some more grapes and a couple of new books.'

'Thanks,' she replied as he put the gifts on her bedside table and pulled up a chair. He'd visited her almost every day and this afternoon he seemed more lively than usual, his knee jittering up and down with repressed excitement.

Ash took her hand. She let him, her fingers lying in his palm as lifeless as her legs. 'I know I've said this before, but I'm so sorry about all this.' He glanced down the length of the bed.

Charley forced a smile. 'Pool had to be on the roof, didn't it?'

Ash's laugh was as hollow as her smile. 'Hey, I'm not doing that crazy stunt ever again. Where's your phone, by the way?'

Charley nodded to the desk drawer. Pulling it open, Ash paired his own phone with hers and transferred a file. As he waited for it to download, he explained enthusiastically,

'I finished recording your song last night. Finally nailed it. The producer and Kay both think the track's a classic. It's going to be the lead single off my new album –'

'Why do you keep visiting me?' Charley interrupted.

Ash blinked in surprise. 'Because I want to.'

'No, *really*?'

'To support you, of course. Like you looked after me. That's why I've stayed on in LA to record my album.'

'Not because you feel obliged to . . . or guilty?'

Ash averted his eyes. 'Of course I feel guilty. You were hurt protecting me.'

Charley withdrew her hand. She no longer wore his bracelet and she was sure that he'd noticed – not that she cared. During her enforced stay in hospital, she'd had a lot of time to think and one doubt had been plaguing her. 'How come so many people were out to get you?'

Ash shrugged. 'I've wondered that myself. I suppose, fame makes for an easy target.'

'OK. Then tell me one other thing. Did you honestly write "Only Raining"?'

Charley saw the answer in his eyes before Ash even replied.

'Yes . . .' he began, before looking away from her withering glare and admitting, 'Most of it.'

He sighed heavily. 'I had a verse but no chorus. Brandon Mills wrote the chorus. And he would've been credited if he hadn't cheated on Kay. He knocked her about too. Brandon wasn't a nice guy. So Kay literally wrote him out of the song. Her revenge. She swore me to secrecy. You see, Kay was building a story around me as this genius singer-songwriter. We had to protect the legend.'

Charley nodded, accepting it without judgement.

'I wrote *all* of "Angel Without Wings", though,' Ash was quick to point out. 'And it's better than any song I've ever recorded.'

He reached out to take her hand again, but this time she refused to take it.

'Charley,' he said, 'I'm donating all the royalties from this song into a recovery fund for you.'

Charley was briefly lost for words. Then she snapped, 'I'm not a charity case! Don't pity me!'

'I'm not,' he replied, his tone wounded. 'I just want to help you.'

'Then leave me alone.' Charley turned her head away and stared resolutely out of the window.

'No, you're my muse, remember? My inspiration. I have to take care of y–'

'I said, *LEAVE ME ALONE!*'

Stunned by her hostile reaction, Ash sat motionless for a full minute, then stood up. 'If that's what you really want, Charley. But I won't abandon you. The song is yours. The money too. And if one day it can help you walk, then it'll be the greatest song ever written.'

With a longing last look at her, Ash left the room.

When he was gone, Charley sobbed her heart out. Why was she pushing away the only person she'd truly fallen in love with?

But she already knew the answer. Ash reminded her too much of all that she'd lost.

Through tear-filled eyes, she saw an update blink on her phone: FILE DOWNLOADED.

Slipping on her headphones and pressing *play*, Charley listened to the song – *her* song – and wept . . .

TARGET
CHAPTER 91

'Why here in particular?' asked Jason, pushing her wheelchair down the boardwalk of San Clemente pier. 'There are other beaches far closer.'

'I used to surf here,' replied Charley sadly. 'Used to.'

Foaming white breakers rolled in like familiar friends along the sandy strip of coast. But they passed her by on the pier, like they'd forgotten who she was, no longer recognizing her.

And who'd blame them. She was a cripple in a chair.

Charley watched a young girl with blonde hair catch a wave and ride it all the way in. It could so easily have been her. But surfing was just a pipe dream now. Like everything else in her broken life, nothing was simple or easy any more. Just taking this trip down to the beach had been a mission. Climbing out of bed, going to the toilet, putting on clothes, getting in and out of the car, negotiating the path, even making it up the shallow incline to the pier. It had been one major challenge after another. On this, her first excursion into the outside world, Charley was confronted by all the things she used to do effortlessly.

Instead of celebrating her day out of hospital, she just felt an aching sense of loss.

The sight of the surfer girl was the final straw.

She began to cry.

Jason stopped pushing her. 'Hey, Charley, what's the matter?'

'I-I'm not meant to be trapped in a chair!' she sobbed. 'I can't dress or wash myself or even go to the toilet on my own. And I can't walk, can't surf – can't do anything! I can't stand another day of this. I simply don't have the strength!'

Jason knelt down beside her, placing a hand on her knee. She could feel it now – just.

'Charley,' he said softly. 'You've more strength and courage in your little finger than all of us boys together. What was it that philosopher said . . .? *Whatever doesn't kill you makes you stronger*.'

'If that's true,' she retorted through clenched teeth, 'I should be stronger than reinforced steel!'

But she certainly didn't feel that way. Inside she felt as brittle and fragile as Styrofoam.

'You are,' said Jason, his gaze unwavering. 'You overcame everyone to be the best in bodyguard training. You overcame every threat in every assignment. And you will overcome this setback. Nothing has stopped you before. Why should this?'

Charley didn't answer him. Jason couldn't possibly understand what she was going through. Only those suddenly paralysed could.

The two of them fell silent and Jason continued pushing her along the pier, the wheels of her chair rattling over the wooden boards. Charley felt every bump and jerk as she sat immobilized, a prisoner in her chair. She was surprised and touched that Jason had made the effort to visit her. But she was also cut up that Blake hadn't come – he'd sent her a get-well card, but that was it. Jason had been right. She was better off without him . . . better off without anyone.

'I hear once you're fit, Colonel Black's asked you to return and head up Alpha team,' he said casually as they reached the end of the pier. 'I think that would be good for you. Give you a focus. Have you thought about it?'

Charley gave a barely perceptible shrug.

'For what it's worth, I've asked to be part of Alpha team if you take up the offer.'

'What? So you can be my legs for me?' she said, more harshly than she intended.

'No,' said Jason, brushing off the sting in her words. 'Because I think you'd do a great job, with all your experience.'

Charley glanced up at him. 'I thought the colonel was going to put you in charge of your own squad.'

'He was, but I want to be in the *best* team. Led by you.'

'Listen, Jason, that's very flattering of you. And I appreciate you flying over to see me. But . . . can I have some time alone?'

'Sure,' said Jason, flicking on the chair's brake. 'I'll get us a drink.'

As he headed back down the pier, Charley gazed out at the shimmering blue ocean. She studied the thin line of horizon that separated sea and sky and waited for the telltale ripple that would swell into the perfect wave to ride.

It wasn't long before a glistening ridge of sea rose up in the distance. Subtle at first but approaching with ever more promise. As the wave rolled towards the shoreline, Charley desperately wanted to throw herself off the pier and surf her way in. But that was impossible.

IMPOSSIBLE . . . I'M POSSIBLE.

The opening to Ash's show flashed before her eyes and a small voice in her head spoke up. *Who's to say you'll never surf again? It's only yourself putting up barriers.*

Charley pushed away the false seeds of hope. As the wave drew nearer, she took out the badge from her bag and clasped it in her palm: the gold winged shield of a guardian angel.

Who needs wings . . . to be an angel?

She'd come full circle. This was where her journey had begun – and where it would end.

She'd lost her best friend and her parents, and now the use of her legs. What more could life take from her?

Charley drew back her arm to toss the badge into the sea, but stopped in mid-throw. She stared once more at the gleaming gold badge, then pinned it to her shirt. Fiercely, she flicked off the wheelchair brake and used the strength of her own arms to turn and roll herself back down the pier. One thought in her head . . .

We cannot change the cards we are dealt, just how we play the hand.

INDESTRUCTIBLE
NORTH AMERICAN TOUR

NEW YORK, NY
PITTSBURGH, PA
COLUMBUS, OH
LOUISVILLE, TN
CHARLOTTE, NC
ATLANTA, GA
MIAMI, FL
NEW ORLEANS, LA

DALLAS, TX
KANSAS CITY, KS
MINNEAPOLIS, MN
DENVER, CO
LAS VEGAS, NV
SALT LAKE CITY, UT
SEATTLE, WA
SAN FRANSISCO, CA
LOS ANGELES, CA

New Album *Indestructible* Out Now

bodyguard-books.co.uk/ashwild #AshWild

WILD: For the fans by the fans

An interview with Ash Wild

by Jessie Dawson

J: Your fans seem to always know where you are, and you've got so much power over them – can that be scary?

A: Yes, it's crazy that fans start crying when they hear a song like 'Kiss & Tell', but at the same time I've written the song for them to react to emotionally. Do I sometimes fear the fans? There are situations that are overwhelming, but you get used to it and my bodyguard is always there to handle the situation if things get out of control.

J: Are there ever any moments when you're on your own?

A: Yes, usually when I go to my hotel room at night and shut the door behind me. Then I'm all by myself. I usually don't do much. Unless I'm inspired to pick up my guitar and write a new song.

J: Who are your musical influences?

A: I listened to a lot of Prince growing up. He is such a musical genius. In the future, people will remember him as the Mozart of our time. But I've always been one for classic rock music. You know, Guns N' Roses, Foo Fighters, the Rolling Stones, Black Sabbath, Nirvana. Bands with big guitars but also an ear for great songs.

J: What was your inspiration for the song 'Only Raining'?

A: I was in a pretty low place after my mum died. But I remember sitting in the garden just after a thunderstorm had passed and the sun came out and shone down on me. The whole garden sparkled with life. It was at that moment I realized that, however bad the storm, the rain will eventually pass and the sun shine through.

J: Who do you most admire in the world?

A: My aunt. She picked me up when I was at my lowest. Gave me a focus. Kay protects me as fiercely as a tiger. And in this business, believe me, you need protection.

J: Do you ever get stage nerves?'

A: Not at all. It's like I was born to perform.

ASH WILD

INDESTRUCTIBLE TOUR
SET LIST

Intro ← VT 1

1. Easier
2. Beautiful From Afar

Welcome from Ash Wild

3. Something's Got to Give
4. Born to Love You
5. Crushed
6. You Make Me Feel
7. Been There, Done That

Fan section A / Instagram Videos

8. Enough
9. Summer Sun
10. Sweet, Sweet Love ← VT2
11. Indestructible
12. Stop the World

Acoustic set

13. Every Day Like the Sun
14. Wrapped Around Me
15. Roses

Interlude and Fan Section B

16. Give It Up
17. You Knocked Me Off My Feet

Encore ← VT3

18. Only Raining
19. So Good Now ← PYRO/LASERS

Only Raining

We all need a shelter to keep us the rain
Without love we're just laying on the tracks
Waiting for a train
When I miss you so much I can't explain
I pray for the sun to come and chase the rain
Don't you know that . . .

It's only raining on you (only raining)
It's only raining on you (only raining)
It's only raining on you right now
But the sun will shine on through

You've begged for forgiveness
You long for the day
The brightest light to come shining through your door
And chase those clouds away
And I miss you so much I can't explain
And I long for your touch to come and take the pain
Don't you know that . . .

Chorus

You're all I need
And all I see
Come set the sun in me, baby
You need time to breathe or maybe
Life owes me a thing or two

Chorus

WILD CAT!

FAN LASHES OUT TO SAVE ROCK STAR

I adore u @therealAshWild!

3 1 View media

So Xcited, #AshWild Dallas gig tm night!

16 View summary

Guardian Angel Turns Love Angel

#AshWild music's torture, someone should torture him!

PR Blonde Captures Rock Star's Heart

Hoping for an *electrifying* performance! #AshWild

16 22

www.bodyguard-books.co.uk/AshWild

ACKNOWLEDGEMENTS

My books have always included strong yet feminine heroines: Akiko and Miyuki in the Young Samurai series, Cho in my Ninja series, and of course Charley and Ling in my Bodyguard series. But *Target* is my first opportunity to write entirely from the perspective of a female lead character . . . and what a heroine Charley proved to be! I hope you enjoyed reading her adventure as much as I did writing for her.

So, with Charley in mind, I'd like to thank all the ladies who have had a major influence in my life. First and foremost, my mum – thanks for all your support, love and sacrifice. I am blessed to have you as my mother. Next and equally as important, my beautiful wife, Sarah, and the mother of my two whirlwind sons, Zach and Leo – I truly appreciate all the patience, love and tenderness you show me and the boys. And of course my dear departed Nan – you gave me a head start, steered me in the right direction and left me with words of wisdom that will last a lifetime. Your light forever shines in my heart.

Karen, as you know, I consider you a sister – thank you for being there for me through thick and thin, joy and sadness, and being a constant friend in my life.

Sam Mole, my awesome sister-in-law! And Sue Mole, a dream of a mother-in-law!

This book is dedicated to my gorgeous goddaughter, Lucinda Dyson. May you grow up strong, confident and happy. I'll always be there for you.

I'd also like to thank my friends Emma Gibbins, Hayley Drew, Katharine Ravetz, Alessia Sardella, Abbie Moore, Georgie Farmer, Fiona Findlater, Lisa Martin, Barbara Horsfield and Clare Hatfield – each of you have had a significant and positive influence on my life.

Then there's my Bodyguard squad at Puffin: Jessica Farrugia Sharples, Hannah Malaco, Wendy Shakespeare and Helen Gray. And, finally, one person I must thank and who is an exception to the female rule: Tig Wallace, my brand-new shiny editor – I couldn't ask for a more enthusiastic, hard-working and dedicated editor. Keep up the good fight!

Stay safe,
Chris

Any fans can keep in touch with me and the progress of the Bodyguard series on my Facebook page, or via the website at *www.bodyguard-books.com*